David Lockwood

Annie Matthews

My Remarkable
Grandmother

First published in 2011,
by Dr Wilhelmina Lockwood
Copyright © Dr. Wilhelmina Lockwood
All rights reserved

Set in Classical Garamond by
Graficas Design, Glasbury-on-Wye, HR3 5LU

Design © Graficas Design

ISBN
978-0-9572458-0-8

This book is sold subject to the condition that it shall not, by way of trade or otherwise, be lent, re-sold, hired out, or otherwise circulated without the publisher's prior consent in any form of binding or cover other than that in which it is published, and without a similar condition, including this condition, being imposed on the subsequent purchaser.

Annie Matthews

My Remarkable
Grandmother

Dedication

To Laura Hermione Bolton Lockwood,
whose gaiety enriched us all
1963 - 2009

Continuum

The resin in the plank bubbles,
A sullen volcano sobs, spits,
Old sap, once green blood
Spurring on a tree
Flames and becomes
Once more energie,
The continuum, the wonderful continuum

David Lockwood 2004

CONTENTS

Part One: Marianne Taylor

Chapter 1 - Armitage Bridge	1
Chapter 2 - Berrow Brow	31
Chapter 3 - Benton's Illness	58
Chapter 4 - Wakefield	70
Chapter 5 - Stanley Royd	82
Chapter 6 - Wakefield Model Prison	104
Chapter 7 - Pupil Teacher	109
Chapter 8 - The Yorkshire School	113
Chapter 9 - Party Dress	131
Chapter 10 - William is Home	147
Chapter 11 - Leaving Party	172
Chapter 12 - Swale Hall	186
Chapter 13 - Leiden	191
Chapter 14 - Marianne's Illness	209
Chapter 15 - Sinterklaas	223
Chapter 16 - Schiedam	231
Chapter 17 - Skating	238
Chapter 18 - Bulbs & Sea	249
Chapter 19 - Yorkshire, Grandma and Edith	255
Chapter 20 - The Ball	264
Chapter 21 - The Theatre Visit	302
Chapter 22 - Perzik Hof	317

Chapter 23 - Cologne	336
Chapter 24 - Holland	373
Chapter 25 - Prestayn	380
Chapter 26 - Noordeinde	387
Chapter 27 - Doorn	446

Part Two: Annie Matthews

Chapter 28 - Scarborough 1893	456
Chapter 29 - 12 The Cliff	483
Chapter 30 - Bicycles and the Theatre	500
Chapter 31 - Town Councillor	543
Chapter 32 - The Great War	554
Chapter 33 - Post War	581
Chapter 34 - Double Marriage	597
Chapter 35 - Married Daughters	611
Chapter 36 - The Mayor	628
Chapter 37 - Cancer	641
Chapter 38 - 7 Cliff Bridge Terrace	646
Chapter 39 - Winchester	661
Postcript	685

Annie Matthews 1862 - 1948

Chapter 1

Armitage Bridge

Bang, bang, bang, slam, slam. Mrs Somerset drew back from the carriage on to the platform as the guard hurried along closing the doors with a practised swing. Inside, the leather strap of the window catch leapt out of its button and fell inert and the window descended a few more inches.

She leant out and clasped the sad woman who had come forward again. Marianne wanted to say so much, but all she managed was "I am very grateful. Don't worry about me."

The older woman seemed moved beyond words and she put up her gloved hand to the young girl's cheek and gazed for what seemed a minute.

"I know, I know, my dear. Remember, remember, if you need help, write. Do write."

They kissed. There was a billow of smoke and steam, a whistle blew, a shudder and the train began to move. They waved but very quickly they were out of sight of each other.

She pulled at the leather strap and nothing happened. The man in the carriage rose and grasped it with a little jerk, released some catch and gently drew the window up. Marianne watched and wondered why she had not been able to do it, it seemed easy.

She very slowly began to unbutton and draw off her gloves finger by finger. Black gloves, black mantle of merino, a black bonnet with a white ostrich plume, but the skirt of her dress was a pale French grey.

She was in half mourning. It was December 1861 and the Prince Consort had been dead for only a week. Everyone wore black, or at least something black, even a bride like Marianne. But it was not of the Prince she thought at all, she was thinking of the doors.

There had been such a shutting of them recently, one after another, her beautiful little room in Hampstead, the door of the house, the careful shut of the carriage door that took her to the station and now all those rapid slams.

Yet she also knew that a new vast door was opening, a new life.

It both lured and alarmed. She was sad to leave Mrs Somerset. She had been more than kind to her, for her home had these past three years been Marianne's home and a sort of fiction had arisen that Marianne was her daughter.

Then a year ago, Benton Taylor, a theological student, but much more a poet, had entered into Mrs Somerset's circle. Marianne had fallen in love and Benton adored her. She was 18 years old and so determined that Mrs Somerset had to give way and Marianne was to be married in exactly a week's time on Christmas Day.

Since his proposal he had been ill. He had given up his studies and returned to teaching at the Grammar School in Huddersfield. Mrs Somerset, who was that frequent amalgam of undoubted and sincere piety mixed with great awareness of social distinctions, was very, very disappointed. She had had much greater hopes for her protégée.

Marianne with her smooth round face smiled to herself as she thought of this. She felt the diamond and ruby ring on her finger beneath her glove. She loved that ring but she also knew it was the cause of the shutting of so many doors.

She looked at the fields flying by and something akin to panic suddenly fluttered in her breast. But it was quickly subdued for her disposition was calm and linked with youthful optimism and the inexperience that co-exists with it.

Yet the thought flashed, "What if Benton does not meet me?" The thought was ludicrous and she answered herself, "Spend a night in the station hotel and return to London in the morning."

The smiles and preoccupations of Marianne amused the other lady in the carriage. She mused on the unchaperoned girl. She, herself, was middle-aged and returning to Yorkshire to her husband. She kept looking at the dark young girl with her smooth olive complexion, dark, but definitely English, she thought.

In fact, Marianne was half Welsh and her darkness came from her father's Celtic blood, together with the smallness of her stature. But what interested the older woman was that a girl so small in stature could have such narrow and long fingered hands. They were the most beautiful hands she had ever seen.

The train relaxed into a familiar speedy rhythm, clicketty-clack, clicketty-clack. Books were taken out by passengers, but Marianne was too excited to read. She thought of Yorkshire, her new home, what would it be like? Mostly, though, she thought of Benton.

It had been a most precipitate love affair. He had come with one of the lecturers at King's to the Mission where Mrs Somerset helped and where Marianne had naturally joined her.

It had been their task to write letters for the illiterate and to teach some simple sewing. Marianne had been busy listening, rephrasing and writing for a young woman who was not only illiterate but inarticulate as well. The poignancy of the occasion had affected her and she had been looking at the unhappy creature who was fumbling and lying, too, in her dictation.

"Wouldn't it be better if we told the truth?" asked Marianne.

"No, it would only worry my Mother." So Marianne continued the epistle about bright prospects and a happy situation.

It was her expression as she regarded the girl that quickened Benton. It was a look he was to come to know well, a ready compassion for the unfortunate, which was very soon hurried into practical action.

It was also sympathy rarely deceived. This encounter has been followed by Benton's visit with a professor to Sunday dinner at Hampstead, where profound curiosity, always the beginning of love, had burgeoned. It was then that all Mrs Somerset's schemes had foundered.

The lady in the corner coughed gently into a small lace handkerchief, smiled and said: "We shall be travelling a long way together. It would seem a pity to remain silent."

So began a long conversation in which the woman found out much about Marianne and her marriage. Of the woman Marianne found out little, she did not enquire. But she learnt much of Yorkshire, for the woman had married a Yorkshire man. Marianne received a summing up she was often to remember.

"They are much slower to accept you than we southerners. But, I think, in the end they are more to be depended upon. They will never flatter you, but, though rough, they are not unkind. The women are not often catty.

"The men can, especially in business, be very hard. And, oh! They are generally so stubborn." She laughed at her forthrightness and excused it by saying, "I must be becoming Yorkshire myself."

The conversation dwindled, as they do. Each felt that a little too much had been divulged to a stranger.

Time, like the countryside was passing quickly. The hills had become quite suddenly more mountainous and there were stonewalls, dry stonewalls such as Marianne had loved in Cardiganshire.

Marianne wanted the journey over, but, at the same time, she wanted the train to go more slowly. Something of her was being left behind and the future was unknown. Another wave of fear overcame her. It calmed as she remembered that Mrs Somerset had made minute enquiries through her network of clergy.

The Vicar of Huddersfield had been corresponded with and, to Mrs Somerset's relief, he actually knew Benton. There was still a large blank space in Marianne's imaginings and she was not quite old enough to realise the vast difference between imagination and reality.

She found herself speculating upon his home, she even began rearranging it to her ideas of home, and then she saw the futility. These were all idle dreams. It grew dark, they stopped at the next station. The porters came in to light the lamps and Marianne hired another rug.

The woman looked as she read Marianne's thought, "Yes, the North is colder than the South – but, you know, not so very much. And if you feel far away in the North, then say to yourself, 'There is more land North to John o' Groats than there is to Cornwall'. Southerners always forget that. I should know, I've lived in Scotland too".

"That's true", said Marianne approvingly. The idea appealed to her. The idea of living nearer Scotland did as well. She wondered if they would be able to visit Edinburgh. Like most of her generation she had been brought up on Sir Walter Scott.

Again she found herself wondering about her future life. Poverty did not dismay her. She had lived in its proximity ever since her father had died when his ship went down off Africa. She, her mother and her brother had lived through great periods of stringency, life had taught them to be ingenious and hopeful.

When her mother, that happy, pretty woman, had died so suddenly, then, Marianne's world had darkened. She had been alone, too, for her brother had gone to Sunderland. The thought of being closer to him did not bring a smile to her face. She had, in spite of the sharing of suffering, never been close to him and his wife she disliked. But she thrust such thoughts away, and concentrated on Benton. As she was thinking so vividly of him, her fellow passenger broke through her dreams, saying, "You will be soon be arriving."

Marianne started up and groped for her luggage in the net rack overhead. Once again, the sudden fear surged, "What if Benton is not there!" And again a calmer voice said, stay at the hotel and return to London.

The weather on Huddersfield Station was bitter. An east wind blew, whistling round the iron pillars of the platform. Benton paced up and down, up and down. He clapped his hands to keep them warm, he flung out his arms and flung them around himself.

He disappeared into the waiting room where a huge coal fire burnt, but he was too restless to stay, and out he would go again. Other travellers were annoyed for each time he left, or re-entered he let in an icy blast of air. He was aware of their irritation, even apologised, but seemed unable to keep still.

He watched the patterns of the signal lamps. He noticed scraps of conversation, he was acutely aware of everything. He heard the brusque matter-of-fact speech of the guard and the driver; one cockney, one Derbyshire and he felt their contempt for the station-bound porters and officials. Still he stamped up and down.

At last, and on time, in came the London train. The carriage doors opened and there was a flood of people and luggage on the platform. It was like a wounded snake, slit up its side disgorging all its undigested victims.

Benton for an odd moment wondered what Marianne looked like, she whom he had been thinking of hourly for months. Would he recognise her? He need not have feared, she was obvious, standing out from the black crowd, minute but with her ostrich plume of white in her bonnet and her pale grey skirt.

For a fraction he just beheld her face happy, but with a certain stillness, which was accentuated by the violent tugging by the wind of her satin ribbons from beneath her chin. Benton's love rose like a flock of birds from a lake and he rushed forward and clasped her.

Just holding one another, not kissing, they stood, their hearts beating with a thud they thought could be heard.

Some looked on them with disapproval, but some smiled, especially one woman who had been in the waiting room, and she understood why he had been so impatient.

He called a porter. Her two trunks and various boxes were placed on a trolley and trundled over to another platform. They followed. A great peace seemed to settle upon them, they were together. She looked at him earnestly to see how well, or ill, he was. He looked just the same.

They boarded another train, a much smaller one, even more dimly lit. The other passengers looked tired, some from work, others from the exertions of a shopping expedition, the evidence of which was on their laps.

From a number Benton received a rather gruff 'Good Evening'. When, after what seemed to Marianne an interminable delay, the whistle blew and they were off. Marianne peered, but the darkness was great. She saw nothing beyond a reflection of herself, which grew steamed on the window glass.

Benton grinned and held her hand tight. He was happy, happier than he had ever been. He had won the girl of his choice. The train stopped not many minutes later at Berry Brow Station, a small station, and very dark. After claiming the luggage, Benton led her down a steep flight of steps which seemed endless. At the foot there was a cab ordered by Benton. The trunks were heaved on top, the boxes on the seat before them.

"Not long now, my dear".

"Oh, I am glad". She was seized with exhaustion, but knew that she must be alert for the next important hours.

The cab stopped. She wished it could have gone on a little further so that she could gain confidence. Benton handed her out. She made out in the dark a row of houses. In the one immediately before her she saw a curtain lift, light flashed, and then a bright oblong of light beamed out as the door was opened, falling across a neat garden.

A yellow globe like a moon moved down the path and slowly advanced. Marianne saw an old man with a bright halo of white hair encircling his head and his face. He was holding the lamp with his right hand, but with his left he seized her hand, looked closely, searchingly into her face.

She could see nothing, but strength and benevolence in his countenance. He, seeking above all honesty, saw it and more.

He spoke, "Tha's welcome… tha's reet welcome."

This was her future father-in-law, Benjamin Woodhouse. Inside the cottage, his wife rose from an old-fashioned mahogany armchair at the head of a table spread for high tea. For a second the two women made a sharp appraisal of one another. It was more critical than Ben's. Each made a swift discernment of character, then the older woman, with a quick movement and a rustle of silk that reminded her of Mrs Somerset, came and took the girl in her arms.

At tea Marianne looked at Benton and compared him with his mother. In features there was a similarity, the same oval face, the same pink and white skin, like a child's, but Mrs Woodhouse had a deep line running from the corner of her nostril to the corner of her mouth.

That line was not yet on Benton. The spirit was altogether different. She seemed to lack Benton's dreamy quality, the pensive look, yet with bright eyes that he managed to combine. Mrs Woodhouse had a face to be trusted, admired, but not, she thought, loved. Respected, yes... but at the moment no more.

The quantity and the quality of the food amazed her, as a child she had been used to plain fare. This was superior to much on Mrs Somerset's table. She thought that it must be due to the exceptional circumstances of her arrival in the family. She soon learnt otherwise. Yorkshire food was good food and very important. Mrs Woodhouse asked Marianne if she cooked.

"Very little, Ma'am, that is beyond the simplest things."

The reaction to this was disapproval, unexpressed, then Mrs Woodhouse rallied and said:

"Then, I shall have to find you a girl that can cook. Benton is very fond of his food."

"Yes, I have noticed that."

The answer pleased the older woman.

Later, as they sat by the heat of the fire, Marianne muddled the conversation.

There were snatches about the Prince's funeral and her luggage, a bright copper kettle and a brass fender. They wavered and wove before her, until abruptly they were dispelled by two dangling lace lappets. She started and the face between the lace smiled.

"My dear, you are terribly tired, you must come to bed".

Meekly she rose. Benton pressed her hand but did not kiss her. She managed to pat the knee of the white-haired old man as she trailed out of the room and up the stairs, which, to her surprise were not of wood, but stone.

She was too weary to protest when Mrs Woodhouse untied some tapes at her back.

At last her head touched the pillow and the nape of her neck was encircled with down. She was so tired and so relieved that she burst into tears.

The lace lappets dangled again and she was kissed on her forehead. The light left the room and she was in a surging swinging world of dreams, arrivals, departures, greetings, farewells and more than anything else doors closing, some softly, others with a clash of finality.

Her wedding lay ahead and that meant a duty, an urgent duty, something unknown to be performed, a duty she neither understood, but feared. Even this fear was dismissed by sleep.

Christmas Day chimed loudly in to Marianne from the bells of St Paul's Church across the road. She woke unwillingly for she had spent a wakeful and apprehensive night. As the noise dinned into her ears she snuggled deeper into the feather bed.

Before long she heard the sound of people going to communion and the hollow clunking clip-clop of their feet crossing the narrow plank bridge. Then there were sounds from below, the sound she equated with 'a well ordered household' for so she had seen it described so in a children's book. Again the fears rose up, she feared the new way of her life, it seemed full of threats and menaces. She feared Yorkshire and its people. She felt intensely lonely, she wanted her mother, and she wanted Mrs Somerset. She wanted a woman to ask about the unknown intimacies of marriage, things nameless to herself.

It was at that moment Mrs Woodhouse entered. She wore an apron round her waist and Marianne in her misery thought, 'She looks like a housekeeper'. She wondered why she had not heeded Mrs Somerset and married someone of her choosing, not Benton. These thoughts tumbled like quick dreams and were dispelled when Mrs Woodhouse sat on the bed.

She did not say, "You do not look as if you had slept very well'. She said: "I expect you were too excited to sleep very much."

She seemed on the verge of saying more, but instead just took Marianne's hand. She did not like to intrude on this small girl whom she took to be so composed. Instead she remarked: "Benton had a sister, as I expect he told you. If she had lived she would have been your age – no – a little older. Strange, I keep thinking of her. This could have been her wedding."

She patted the hand lying on the coverlet. "Well, it's going to be a grand morning. The sun is going to shine on you."

When Marianne was up, the people were returning from communion. Many glanced at the house and lowered their heads and spoke. Marianne drew back from the window. Yet from a pace back she still watched. So many of them were poor people, it was marked on the faces and their gait. She wondered if she would ever understand them.

She was always a slow dresser but today she began even more slowly. Every tape, every button had to be adjusted meticulously. Mrs Woodhouse entered at the precise moment she needed help with her stays and when she stood before the dressing table her heart rose and she looked quite different. Her dress she knew was a success. It was so simple, a finely striped grey and white silk over a crinoline. The sleeves were as large as a bishop's and gathered in to a small wristband.

She fixed her mother's large gold brooch like a targe at her throat and the black silk belt round her waist. The clasp was of silver gilt and had belonged to her father's dress uniform. By these little belongings she felt their kinship. But she was also very loyal, she looked at her bridal array, the bonnet still on the bed and she suddenly thought of the dead Prince, whom she had once seen at the Crystal Palace, a tired looking man.

She un-looped the long gold chain of her watch and from a box took a very long silk cord of shiny black which she tied around her neck, putting the knot behind her brooch. The rest fell down and ended holding the watch in the little pocket above her waist line. She looked in the mirror and she was pleased. Mrs Woodhouse entered and said with faint surprise: "Why, my dear, you look beautiful."

"You think I will do for your son?"

"But, of course, I trust his judgment entirely."

As they talked, a vehicle drew up at the gate. A tall man, very upright, got out and then very gently lifted his wife from the seat and carried her up the path. As soon as Mrs Woodhouse had seen their arrival she had hurried downstairs, but not before she had said: "That is Mr And Mrs Hirst."

Marianne looked again, first at the frail thin woman, then at her husband. He was to give her away. She did not like the thought of being 'given away'. It made her into a parcel. But she thought no more of it because, at that moment, Benton and John Nash, his best man came down the road.

They both looked so handsome in their black coats and tall hats. Benton looked across at the house, and Marianne again drew back. She saw them disappear into the trees and heard their footsteps on the bridge. Marianne turned to the bed and picked up her bonnet. It was the latest fashion, another of Mrs Somerset's presents, spoon-shaped and trimmed inside the brim, on top of her head with snowdrops. It was made of plaited horsehair.

Again, Mrs. Woodhouse entered, again she stopped. "Oh that is beautiful. But you must come and meet my sister" and taking Marianne's hand, escorted her down the stairs.

Mrs Hirst lay on the sofa and looked up. She had that air of remove that comes to many invalid people. She looked, then giving herself a firm push with her arm, rose from the sofa. Such movement was unusual. She held out thin arms, took Marianne's hands and said: "Welcome, you are very welcome to our family."

It was touching for it was all obviously an effort to the sick woman. But more was to come. As Mrs Hirst surveyed the bride she made a defiant and totally unexpected decision.

"I am coming to the church – and I'll sit on your side, my dear."

It was all beyond belief. She rarely left her room, let alone her house. Her husband demurred but there was nothing for it but to comply. So Marianne was left alone while Mr Hirst carried his wife to the church accompanied by Mrs Woodhouse.

Marianne ran up to her room and looked at the veil on the bed. They had all gone and left her with the most difficult task of all. She took off her bonnet and pinned the veil. She went downstairs and Mr Hirst entered.

"Is my veil quite straight?" she asked.

""No", he said, and with fingers neither clumsy or fumbling, he took out one pin, made the veil straight in front of her, pinned it and saw that it hung properly at the back.

"My, lass, if I'd known what I agreed to give away this morning,

I wouldn't have done it. I'd have kept you to mysen".

Outside there was a little knot of women and children. Her dress drew a sigh of admiration as in the frosty sunshine its orange flashed beneath the silvery grey and white stripes. They crossed the bridge, paused in the porch where Mr Hirst again surveyed the bride, making certain everything was as he said 'shipshape'.

The small church was nearly full. Even Marianne's side had people, Benton had seen to that. The service began, the vows, the taking of hands, the exchange of the ring, all duly and significantly took place. She looked at Benton, but not as frequently, or as long, as he looked at her. She felt encompassed by love, not just him but all these people.

At last the service was over, the signing of the registers done. At the bridge they faltered. They could not walk across together. It seemed to Marianne that the sun went behind a cloud for a second, a sudden, strange chill.

The crowds on the other side had increased and they had rice which they threw and it stung their cheeks. A woman called out: "Give us a smile for luck, missus."

In the house, Benton kissed her and held her tightly. Then came many relatives and friends and the Vicar congratulated them, yet again. He asked Marianne with a wry smile if she always took this book to church with her. Instantly she recognised it. It was not her prayer book... it was her copy of Milton.

The happiness, which soon became jollity, rang around them. But gradually, the party thinned until only the family and intimate friends remained. It was still Christmas Day and Christmas dinners awaited them all, but none so great as the one prepared by Mrs Woodhouse.

As they sat around the table, Marianne began to identify them. First of all, there was Mr Woodhouse. He looked so benign, yet with his white beard and hair looked more like King Lear than anyone she had ever seen.

Mr Hirst, Uncle Alan now, was brisk, neat and humorous. He was considered one of the best judges of worsted in the West Riding. "Ah", thought Marianne, that was why he showed no embarrassment when he pinned her veil. He was used to handling material.

She found it difficult to realise that his wife, Elizabeth, was the sister of Benton's vigorous, comely mother. There was a whole pride of cousins and it was with pride Benton pointed them out. It was interesting, for they were all leaving the woollen trade of their fathers' callings. One was becoming a solicitor, two were schoolmasters and there were three girls, all to be school mistresses.

The girl that interested her most was Cousin Lydia. She had the pallor that goes with red hair. At one moment she looked plain and then she would smile. Marianne had never seen a face more transformed, almost beautiful.

Her survey was interrupted when Uncle Alan rose to make a speech. This was the moment she feared. They were not like Mrs Somerset's friends, not learned, even, she thought, well educated. She feared improprieties and surreptitiously and superstitiously crossed her fingers and prayed that he would not be coarse.

Benton leant his head towards her and said: "Listen to uncle, he's bound to be funny". Marianne thought that her worst fears would be justified.

He began a little haltingly, but not as much as Marianne expected. When launched, he was in full sail of anecdote and on a sea of quotation from Robbie Burns. With the first quotation came a roar of welcoming recognition. Glasses were raised. Marianne found herself happy and at ease, but it was time for her to change.

As she edged her way round the tables placed together, she put her hand on Lydia's shoulder, and asked her to help her.

The girl rose with alacrity, Uncle Alan turned and grasped Marianne's arm. "Am I displaced? I was a very good bridesmaid, this morning."

Marianne only blushed and smiled. In the room above she said: "If I had known you, Lydia, I would have chosen you to be my bridesmaid properly."

"But I am, Mrs Taylor, and to be chosen at the feast is even better. Friends go up higher."

The wedding dress was placed on the bed. Marianne looked at it with a pang – its duty done. It had shrouded her last day of maidenhood, the last of her old self – it was discarded. As she sat re-arranging her hair, old fears arose. She was very afraid of the night. She did not know what was to happen. She looked at Lydia and knew that to ask her would never do.

"Could you get Mrs Woodhouse for me and leave us alone."

Mrs Woodhouse came in. She was not an imaginative woman and so she was not made anxious at the prospect of horrible revelations.

"Mrs Woodhouse, I am frightened. I do not know what will happen tonight."

"Has no one told you?" Marianne shook her head.

Fortunately, the older woman was born in a less squeamish age. Even she halted for words, but managed to convey a basic message. She was glad to leave the details and tell her that marriage was very enjoyable. Her smiles, her touch, her confidence reassured Marianne.

Downstairs Uncle Alan had a present. He produced from behind a chair a large very soft cloak with dolman sleeves of the finest dove grey wool.

"I hope it fits. I hadn't reckoned on Benton choosing someone so small."

It was warm, it was enclosing. She looked at the faces around her and felt wrapped in understanding. She had made the right choice.

At the gate a high gig stood, many hands helped the couple up. Their trunk was placed behind. There was another squall of stinging rice and they were off. Down the village, down the road that followed the beck, then by turns they zigzagged up and out of the valley. They were climbing to the moor.

For more than three quarters of an hour, the pony climbed all the way up and up through the silent villages, all families gathered round their fires. Up, at last, to the moor, first fields enclosed with stonewalls and the occasional farmhouse. Here a light powdering of snow lay and the wind was keen. Marianne rejoiced in her new mantle that kept out every breath of wind.

It was at the crest of the road that Marianne gasped. She seemed never to have seen so immense a view, rolling moor upon rolling moor as far as the eye could see. It surprised her and it elated Benton, it seemed endless and amazed their souls.

Only at points did they see lights and know that there was habitation. At a glance it seemed, what it was not, an empty land. They dropped down from this plateau, to a lane bordered with outcrops of rock and huge boulders.

Quite suddenly before them was the house. It was sheltered by the hill on one side and a plantation of fir trees on another; a garden sloped at the front exposing a vast view.

"What a wonderful place!" exclaimed Marianne?

"You like it? That's good. I've always loved it." He smiled. "Another, yes, another aunt, a great aunt lives here. I vowed long ago that I would spend my honeymoon here. And here we are."

The sound of the hooves clattering on the frosty road had brought lights to the windows. The door was thrown open, a boy unstrapped their trunk, and a man led the pony towards a stable.

Inside was a narrow wainscoted passage. A door opened from this to a large room paved with stone and where there was a great fire burning. Marianne looked about in surprise. This was a room of the past, a tall settle stood gauntly by the fire, a great dresser with pewter plates against a wall.

All the furniture was old. Marianne could tell by the legs, they were all straight. She really preferred curves, what she called Queen Anne, but she still loved all this for it all fitted.

"What a peculiar old place... time has stood still here".

"Wait until you see the bedroom."

Marianne glanced at Benton wonderingly and reprovingly. She thought him indelicate. She looked at him, there was no smile, no smirk, so she brushed it aside and continued her exploration. There was a spinning wheel in use and several implements she had never seen before lying around.

Benton watched her with amusement. She reminded him of a puppy sniffing out new surroundings. She became aware of his pleasure.

"But, Benton, you know this place. It's all very strange and new to me! But where is your aunt?"

"You will see her when she sees fit, perhaps in a day or two. In the meantime the house is ours."

"That is very kind and, if I may say so, very strange,"

"There is a simple answer. She is kind and she is strange."

A girl came in, evidently a servant. She laid one end of the massive table. There was cold goose, a pie, potatoes, pickles, a jar of ale and the largest apple pie Marianne had ever seen. The tea tray, which was what they both really wanted, was placed on a small table by the fire. A kettle hung on the hook and what most amused Marianne was the long white satin ribbon tied to the key of the tea caddy.

They put the potatoes and the pie on the hearth to keep warm and made tea. They watched the fire and the sparks when Benton pushed a log. Then they went to the table and Benton stood to carve the goose.

"Our first meal Benton, alone. It's rather like playing houses, isn't it?"

"I don't think so, I've never carved before. Mother always does it."

To their great surprise they were hungry and they began to eat with relish. Then back to the fire. They talked of the day, the relations, their clothes and Marianne found herself in the wafts of heat from the fire, falling asleep on Benton's shoulder.

Benton was becoming restless. His hands moved around her, as they had never moved before… she felt a fire possessing her too. She saw a glint in his eyes that fascinated and frightened her.

"It's time for bed."

"Yes, I'll go first – you must give me a full quarter of an hour."

She left the room, only to return a few seconds later saying there was no light.

"Shall I light you to bed?" Benton asked. At the same time, he rang a brass bell on the dresser and the little girl came.

"May I have a candle, please?"

The girl already carried one and going on before Marianne, she lighted the way.

They went up the wide square staircase. The candle's light threw great shadows, so vast for so small a flame. The girl opened a door and the warm glow of a fire shone out.

"Stay a minute please. I shall need you to undo the buttons at the back of my dress."

The girl willingly stayed. Marianne was tempted to keep her there, but she took command of herself and bade her goodnight. Quickly she undressed in front of the fire, where her nightclothes were already warming on a chair.

She let loose her hair and then looked at the bed. It had heavy red curtains. She rushed to it, untied the loops, drew the curtains and then dived beneath the sheets. She lay very still and quiet, listening to the flurry of the fire and the ash as it fell.

She then heard Benton's foot fall on the stone staircase and her heart beat a little faster. She heard him enter, he hummed as he undressed, and she shivered a little although she was warm. He seemed very slow. Through a crack in the curtains she realised he had turned down the lamp and then there was a strange silence. She then heard his breathing... he was saying his prayers. Then he lifted aside the curtain. He was in nightshirt and not frightening at all.

He climbed in he leaned across and kissed her. She lay absolutely still, her heart beating hard. For minutes they lay there. Then Benton edged downwards and put his arm beneath her neck and the other over her waist.

Her fear began to ebb with the flow of love and her body took on an entity of its own. Slowly his hand pulled up her nightdress and one hand caressed her breasts. Silently she gasped to herself, "It's true, as Benton's mother had said, it is enjoyable."

Suddenly, like herself, he was possessed, she felt it in his movements, he kissed her again and again, she clung to him uncertainly, vaguely trying to control him, yet her hands instinctively sought him and then the movement she dreaded began.

For a moment the vision of a clumsy attempt at love in a hayfield, seen long, long ago, in Wales on holiday, flashed in her memory. But it was swept away as deeper and deeper she felt love. She was falling, falling, falling into a well of rapture.

Dreams rose up around her, beauty such as she had seen and dreamt of, great houses, colour upon colour. Colour became sensation, velvets, silks and every tactile luxury. Rhythmically, she sank deeper and deeper into this phantasmagoria of loveliness.

Then she rose higher and higher and Benton, with a quivering throughout his frame, lay in her arms inert. She stroked his head, some of the dreams departed, but the reality remained and that had the quality of a dream.

Relief then flooded upon her, this was the unknown, this was the solemn duty she had dreaded. Again she heard the sigh of the ash falling in the grate. With a sigh, she too, fell fast asleep.

In the morning, they looked at one another. It was as if they sought a change in one another's features. There was no change.

"Were you afraid, Marianne?"

"Yes, very much, at first".

"So was I."

"But you seemed so sure."

He only smiled. Light crept in at the windows, even in to their curtained bed. They realised that it must be late.

When Marianne began to dress, she found blood on her nightdress. She continued dressing, then went to the bed and gave a gasp of horror… there was a blackish-red pool. Benton too looked aghast.

They turned back the bedclothes, removed the sheet and Marianne washed it in the basin. They then hung it over a chair before the fire and went down for breakfast. This discovery cast a shadow over their first breakfast and Marianne kept listening for sounds of someone in their room. Marianne was unaware of the second staircase and the solidity of the house.

The meal over, Marianne went up to conceal all the evidence. She found the bed made and a white counterpane over it all. The damp sheet on the chair had gone, the chair was back in its place. She lifted the counterpane… the sheets were clean and new.

"Oh well, this must have happened before to a young woman", she philosophically said to herself.

They went out. It was cold and they left the yard and went down the grassy lane bordered by the dry stonewalls. Looking down the valley they saw rising up, as if from nowhere, tall chimneys that marked the small mill town of Meltham.

The sun lit up the stone. Grey and green were the predominant tones, backed by the blackish moors. They left the lane and went through a stile such as Marianne had never seen before. It was one of three large flat stones set upright through which an average sized human being could squeeze, but not an animal.

She felt a certain kinship with Wales in these surroundings, yet it was different. She could not analyse the difference, it seemed to her to be in the atmosphere. Yorkshire seemed to belong to a modern age, it was harnessed to industry, and the tall chimneys kept reminding her that this was no idle landscape.

The Wales she knew was not of the south, where the mines and terraces might have reminded her more forcibly of their links with the West Riding. She contented herself with looking at Benton and saying to herself, "You don't see many men as tall as him in Cardigan."

They crossed several fields, going down into the valley, where they came to a small wood of sycamores. Benton led the way down the bank, and then he stopped.

"Listen, was it the wind in the trees?" she asked herself.

It was a continuous drumming sound... a waterfall. He stretched out his hand and, taking hers, led her to a promontory of slimy rock. He held her firmly. Away and below them ran and fell a steady rush of water.

Benton's face was alight with pride. "This is my 'sounding cataract'."

On he led her, scrambling, sometimes lifting her. He was boyish and excited, showing off his treasure and when they reached the foot, some 30 feet down, Marianne shared his enthusiasm as she looked up at the water spraying in veils, heavy in curtains and flat masses of sheets, pouring over the rocks and fissures.

It was small, but it was very beautiful. The trees above them arched, leafless boughs, etchings against a sky. With the ferns, the brilliant green moss, the old stained stone and the white-laced water, it all made an indelible picture on her mind.

"I give you all this, Marianne, it's been mine since I was a small boy."

"Really yours?" she asked.

"No, not really. It belongs to Aunt Christiana - but mentally it's mine."

"It is beautiful and so secret. Does no one ever come here?"

"Sometimes on Bank holidays a family or two will picnic here. But most of the year it is left unvisited."

They climbed back, happier than ever. He had found someone who loved the same things as himself, it was so comforting, so enriching. He was sharing something, but strangely, someone who was also a part of himself.

When the house came back into view, Marianne said: "Am I never to see your aunt?" It is so funny living in the same house and never seeing her."

Benton was quite matter–of-fact about it, totally unconcerned.

"Oh yes, you'll see her, in her own good time, not before. She is the oddity of the family. She can, though, be extremely tactful."

Meals were brought in, cleared away and all Marianne did in the great room was brush the hearth and play with the bellows. In the evening, Benton began reading to her while she embroidered. They ended with arms entwined, staring into the fire and plotting the future. Still Marianne had not seen the house they were to rent.

It was closer to Huddersfield, in a district poorer than Armitage Bridge.

Marianne wished to know more and Benton drew maps of the district and plans of the house. Marianne, knowing nothing of the area, imagined it all wrong. She knew too, that she did, but that did not stop her dreaming.

At last it was time for bed. Desire and modesty resumed their fight and Marianne decreed that, again, she would be first and taking her candle, she went upstairs. Only on her way up did she remember the sheets. She compressed her lips with a shamed embarrassment as she thought of the aunt and the maid knowing this secret.

In the room the fire burnt. She undressed and put on her nightgown in the glow of the fire and then leapt into bed. She did not let all the curtains down around her this time. Benton came in and he too undressed by the fire. They talked and Marianne told him about the clean sheets. Again he was unperturbed and replied:

"I am not at all surprised. Aunt Christiana is a most methodical and particular woman."

Marianne was alarmed. She could think of no one more efficient than her mother-in-law, and here was a woman even more talented in household affairs. But all these ideas were dismissed when she saw Benton pull his shirt over his head.

He had hair on his chest, she had not realised that. The joys of the previous night were repeated but with a deeper happiness for all fear had been removed.

At breakfast next morning the silent maid spoke. "The missus would like to see you at 12."

They went out climbing up to the moor behind, but the bitter wind made them turn back and it began to rain. Both felt that they were glad that they would be returning to a more ordinary life next day.

Benton's mind kept considering his syllabus for the next term and Marianne found herself arranging and rearranging a house she had not yet seen. This annoyed her for it was useless. At noon, they were called to 'the house', as the kitchen was called.

Having seen most of Benton's relations, Marianne prepared for someone tall, but Aunt Christiana towered. She was nearly six feet and appeared taller, for she was clad entirely in black, even her apron was of black satin and her cap of black lace. She stood gaunt and forbidding and Marianne found herself bobbing a curtsey. This evidently pleased the old lady who relaxed her severe face and, to Benton's surprise, pecked a kiss on Marianne's cheek.

They seated themselves on oak chairs with high backs by the fire with its ovens and spit. The aunt asked Benton to pour out Madeira wine from a squat square decanter which Marianne thought the ugliest she had ever seen.

She listened and discovered that this angular woman, who seemed so hard, had much in common with her nephew. She thought it akin to the landscape, hard even harsh, eschewing the pretty and achieving grandeur, even beauty, all half hidden, like the waterfall. Suddenly the manner changed, and her eyes narrowed and glinted;

"So, Benton, you have chosen to work with the enemy?"

Benton evidently knew what she meant. He smiled.

"I suppose, to you, it looks like it. But I don't see it that way. I shall help as many lads to escape the valley as stay in it you know?"

"I am glad to hear that. But, beware, don't let them trap you. You think that you're safe". Then, turning to Marianne, she spat out: "Trust nobody in the valleys. Mammon is their God and the valley the world. But we, on the moors, know differently."

As she spoke she glanced at the sledgehammer that hung on the wall by the side of the fireplace.

"Aye, I wonder what Enoch would say if he could speak. He'd be none too pleased."

"Who is Enoch?" Asked Marianne rather puzzled.

"Hark at the girl! She's a southerner. That's Enoch." The black figure sprang up and proudly pointed to the hammer.

"He smashed many a loom in the past. He was kept in this house and lent out to men of spirit, Luddites they were called. No one suspected this house, no magistrate looked here."

Marianne felt almost fear; there was such love for ancient hostility. This strange woman exulted in it all. Benton now spoke.

"Aunt, that is old, old history. Progress cannot be stopped. That great hammer lost in the end."

"Yes, we lost, but I haven't forgiven."

"But, aunt, why?"

"Because my family was fighting the mill owners, who sucked us dry, luring men away from the land and leaving us helpless. I hate their noise, their filth, the children labouring and the women - that's why."

"You know that I hate all those things too. But your family failed with the hammer. I will teach peace. We're winning. The children only work half time now. We want love, not hate. I'm on your side, but I shall fight in a very different way."

"I am an old woman. I hope you are right. But, both of you never trust a mill owner, never. But this is no talk for a wedding journey."

She rose and led the way back to the great room that Marianne and Benton now called their own. Marianne felt little like food, she was frightened. It was as if the earth had moved beneath her feet. The talk had reminded her of *Wuthering Heights* and *Shirley*. She thought the old malice had come to an end, but felt that this old woman was continuing it, even Benton to an extent.

She asked herself if she had come to a land of ill will and brooding discontent. Benton smiled at her and her fears vanished.

As they ate, the aunt looked out of the window and smiled. She looked so different when she smiled.

"I am glad you started your marriage here. This is Yorkshire – a farm fighting the moorland on a hill. The old Yorkshire is slipping into the valleys. Here men slaved against the elements. Down there they bend and twist their bodies over looms and vats. I always know a valley man by his crooked body. Yes, I am glad you started your marriage here."

Marianne was no longer quite sure. However, politeness bade her say: "As soon as we have a home of our own, I hope you will visit us?"

"No, my dear, I never go to the towns."

"Not even to visit us?"

"Aunt" interposed Benton, "You treat us like enemies, at least in speech. But if I had not loved the true Yorkshire, I would not have brought Marianne here, would I?"

"Forgive me. I'm a crabbed old woman. It's just, I hate the new life. We seem to have lost the battle. Don't ask me to look at the conquerors, or their slaves. And, Benton, whatever happens, don't become their slave."

"Oh, he won't", laughed Marianne. "I shall see to that."

Next day, the gig descended into the valley again. As Marianne looked at the limestone houses, streaked with soot perched and nudging one another on the hillside, she saw it all rather differently. There was something to fear. She held Benton's sleeve to reassure herself. No, it was not a dream, he was real, and as long as he was there it would never be a nightmare.

As they slowly clip-clopped down the steep streets to Armitage Bridge, Marianne steeled herself to meet Benton's family. She felt so sure that they would see that she was no longer the girl who had left a few days before, but someone quiet different. It amazed her that nobody seemed to notice the difference.

Benton was immediately busy preparing lessons for the term that was shortly to begin. The day came when she saw him off and although she was busy, one dared not be idle in the presence of his mother, yet the day seemed so long.

She tidied and arranged the little living room downstairs which had been handed over to them. It was a severely and sparsely furnished room. Here Marianne unpacked some of her belongings. She hung up a few pictures and over the mantelpiece her most prized possession, her Queen Anne mirror with its walnut frame and gilded bird on the fretted pediment.

Beneath it she arranged the miniatures and on the shelf a number of pieces of china. She was pleased with her fiddling, as her mother-in-law called it, and in the afternoon she lit the fire. She looked at the miniatures, the happy smiling face of her mother beneath her lace cap and unconsciously Marianne smiled back, moved with many memories. She thought that if her mother could see her now she would smile even more.

From time to time, she glanced out of the window at the church and the hill climbing up to Berry Brow. It was a tranquil scene and she wondered why Aunt Christiana disliked it so intensely. As she watched, she saw Benton hurrying down the hill. Snatching up a bonnet and shawl, she went out to meet him.

He was delighted to be met. It was something he had not anticipated.

Next day, a little earlier, Marianne set out to meet him again. She had more time, so she dressed with more care, wearing her new mantle and her white horse hair bonnet. She was too early for the train so she walked down another street.

Berry Brow seemed very black, but the carefully whitened stone steps shone and in many instances the windowsills were whitened, too. She noticed the glimmering ghostly whiteness of lace curtains within.

She was aware that these people were waging a constant battle with grime. She saw some children released from school. They did not run, or laugh, they walked in sullen groups, like shoals of fish. They stared at her, some were barefoot, their eyes were large, their mouths huge.

She recognised the symptoms of poverty; she had seen it in London. But there was an addition here, the cockney was usually lively, these children were pale, like plants confined to darkness, they lacked substance and she had to remind herself that they were living beings.

Then she saw the women, she had never seen such before. They stared at her. They were gaunt with hair pulled starkly back into a bun, which threw their cheekbones into greater prominence beneath their dark shadowed eyes.

They seemed to wear a uniform, a black or grey dotted bodice, possibly a skirt of the same material, but this was not seen for they were hidden by stiffly starched white aprons. The women from the doorways watched her. She was almost afraid.

She felt very alien, an animal that had strayed into another pack. She was aware of her new bonnet, her mantle. Then one of them smiled and said something that Marianne did not comprehend. She returned a "good evening." She relaxed and encountered more smiles.

But within herself she was horrified. Sooty dirt lay over everything. She climbed up another hill towards the station and, looking down, she saw twinkling lights. She could make out the tall brick chimneys, she could not see smoke, but she could smell it.

She understood what Aunt Christiana hated, and was inclined to agree. It was evil, it was cruel, and it was ugly. Below her were the mills. She heard the thunder from the engine house and the staccato clatter of the looms. Suddenly from beneath her a great plume of smoke and sparks flew up and for a second she panicked. It was horrible, but she merely said, "Don't be silly."

She moved out of the smoke and there was Benton hurrying down. He was instantly concerned, for she looked pale, even frightened. He asked her what it was, thinking that she might have had a row with his mother, something he was waiting for. Only later, as arm-in-arm they were beneath the familiar sycamore of Armitage Bridge did she say, "I didn't think Yorkshire would be like this."

"It takes some getting used to, my dear, but this is not all Yorkshire, you know."

Back at home having their high tea before a blazing fire, the mean streets seemed far away. Marianne watched Mrs Woodhouse with a new understanding that her preoccupation with cleanliness was her way of rebelling against this hideous situation.

When they had nearly finished, old Mr Woodhouse came in. She watched him closely. He looked tired, but also very satisfied. It was the secret happiness of a craftsman. The gaslight fell on his silver hair and again she thought of *King Lear*.

When Benton was busy marking, she told him of her walk and the dirt.

"Aye, it's mucky, but it's not that bad, lass."

"But it is." She expostulated, "the children. Why doesn't someone do something?"

"I'm too old now, Marianne. But I've done my part. I helped Richard Castler and we won, the children no longer work so long. Then there's your Benton doing his best with the next generation. Things, I know, aren't right. But they were a lot worse."

"Yes, charity begins at home," chimed in Mrs Woodhouse.

"What on earth has that got to do with it?" demanded Marianne.

They all laughed, her dramatics had misfired, but they still laughed. "Oh you'll learn. You'll learn."

In the little room she showed off her improvements. They all admired them.

It was the miniature of her mother that aroused most interest. They sought features of Marianne in the jolly woman. There was a constraint, the trifles that had seemed so important in the morning, did, now, seem indeed to be trifles. She loved the elegance of the mirror, but it did not cancel out the memory of Berry Brow.

"I wish you had not returned here, Benton."

"My dear, there's a lot you'll find wrong here, still more that is ugly. But it must improve – we must improve it.

Do you remember Mr Maurice, when I first saw you?"

"That little man from King's?"

"Yes, that's the one. He said that the church must be society's conscience. We are the church - we must look after our brothers. Whenever I heard him speak I thought of Huddersfield. We have work here Marianne."

Marianne listened in silence. She felt contrite, selfish and condemned not just by his ideals, but by a word. When he had said society, she had thought of it as Mrs Somerset used it, a minute section of people at the top of an entire structure. She realised that she had much to learn.

When they went to bed they fell asleep instantly. Marianne woke early, about six and heard a clatter that she had missed before. She rose and looked out of the window. At the mill entrance she saw children beneath the lamps waiting to enter for their morning shift.

Her revulsion returned and she tried to find comfort in Benton's arms, but deeply asleep, he turned away. When, an hour later, he did awake, he saw two large and troubled eyes gazing into his. Her eyes, so perplexed, worried him and it was as if her eyes had invaded his, for on the train he saw Lockwood in a new harsher, more real light.

He had grown used to the soot, the railway bridge, the pawnshop and the thin children. He felt ashamed that he had moved her from the rural gentility of Hampstead to this. In Huddersfield, he was joined by some of the grammar school boys. The younger ones chattered unceasingly and he only gave them half an ear. He realised they were questioning him about the Queen and whether it was true that she was mad with grief? No, he did not think she was mad, just very unhappy.

The question interested him no more. He thought of the mill children, the half-timers. He had taught them, worn-out creatures, old before their time and too tired to learn. They had barely known that there was a queen, let alone married or widowed.

Once in school, its momentum carried him along and he forgot these anxieties. Marianne, more naturally, was constantly aware of the change in her life and every difficulty she embraced, slightly magnifying it as though to prove her love. The little parlour was, by now, a place entirely of her own and there she read, she sewed, she thought. She also had to escape from the indefatigable industry of her mother-in-law. She watched her and learnt a great deal. She compared her with Anne Owen, her old nurse in Pontrhydfendigiad... they had much in common, but Mrs. Woodhouse's resources were greater, so she did more baking, preserving, brewing.

Ironing and washing and bread-making, each item had to reach perfection and if it was not achieved, then a post-mortem was conducted that frightened and bored Marianne still more.

In fact, Marianne had to learn quickly because Mrs Woodhouse was so often away. She had many relatives and acquaintances, and her skill as a nurse and organiser was widely known, so that whenever sickness struck, she was called upon.

Marianne alone took up the cooking and the cleaning. In this time she formed a true friendship with Benjamin Woodhouse. He loved to talk of the old days, days before the mills had come, when it had been a land for farms and sheep and individual weavers.

She listened to her *King Lear* as he talked by the fire and learnt a very great deal of the story of the development of the valleys. It was a story of growth, of ambition, greed, and charity, everything that made her heart cry. But he was sensitive and would shorten her sorrow by telling an anecdote of compassion or humour.

She used to relate it to Benton. He was surprised at how much information she had gleaned from him. He corroborated all she had been told and one evening, he stared into the fire and said: "This is why it grieves me so much that I can never be a clergyman to help them."

"But you do help them. You teach them."

"I teach the brighter ones and the better off. Not the really poor."

But their delight was still in one another and his resentment was quelled when he saw the movement of her hands as she sewed. He had never in real life seen such beautiful long-fingered hands – they were like those seen in Elizabethan portraits.

Saturday was the day they both longed for. After dinner, they would climb up to the moors. Here the clouds seemed always to sweep from the west and the stunted trees pointed its direction. They would join hands and run, they felt free, they were alone... they were in love.

On Sundays they went to church. It was usually full and

Marianne, on her first Sunday here, had been surprised at the smart appearance of the congregation. The women wore fine mantles and shawls, the men good cloth coats.

It was obvious that they all knew good material when they saw it. She grew to love the new church with its stone pillars, still bright with their fresh cut stone. She particularly liked the sanctuary with its painted angels and figures.

Strangely she felt here another surge of freedom, the prayers, the singing. The order of it all brought the feeling, the realisation that although her life mattered, yet also it was only one of many.

It was here, after church, that she met the mill owner. She had come from the porch and saw her father-in-law talking to another silver-haired man.

"Come and meet Mr Brooke, Marianne."

She had conjured up in her head a picture of a tyrant. Mr. Brooke was disposed to be courteous and friendly, he was not condescending. She noticed that neither Mr. Woodhouse, nor Benton seemed in any way awed by him. He welcomed her to Yorkshire and told her not to mind their blunt ways. Such an easy familiarity would not have been possible, she thought, in London, where the delineation of class was more marked.

She did not think of these things long. Soon they were among friends, some recognisable from the wedding, but only a few known, except Cousin Lydia. From all sides she heard, "See you at Uncle Alan's tonight."

"What is this about Uncle Alan?" she asked.

"Oh that, we go there every first Sunday night of the month." It was the first Marianne had heard of it.

After the evening service, where Benton read the lesson, they set out for the Hirsts. They toiled up some steep streets and steps and came to a path overlooking the valley. A lamp hung in the window. They entered a large stone-flagged kitchen. A huge fire burnt in the range, the light flickering on the plates on the dresser. It was warm, cosy and homely. They were the first and a circle of empty chairs stood round the room. Marianne asked if she might see Aunt Elizabeth. Uncle Alan immediately led the way through a small parlour.

Half way up the stairs he called: "I'm bringing a visitor, luv."

He opened the door and there in the light of a lamp was the

frail little lady in a lace cap and shawl. She stretched out her arms in an almost childish manner.

"I'm so glad you've come. I thought you might."

Marianne glanced about her. This was not just a room; it was a whole world. There were plants, books, sewing and ornaments all casually but with care disposed about. It had something in kinship with her own room.

"Well, how do you find Yorkshire?"

Marianne was beginning to resent this question. It was asked as if Yorkshire was a land apart from England. She, of course, recognised the great pride behind the remark, which very nearly made her answer, "Very nice, thank you."

But stifled it and honestly said: "It is dirty, but very cheerful. It's also a mixture of good and bad, kindness and cruelty. I don't know whether I like it or not, yet.

"The people are like their county, many sided. People come to be like their landscape. The hills are bleak, rough, but the dales are gentler. The people are like both and many harsh exteriors have quite soft hearts. But industry is breeding its own kind of people, I must admit."

"Yes, it is the mills that frighten me. They seem to menace. But what I really hate is seeing the children go to work. I wonder, then, if anyone has any heart. But I suddenly see those same children laugh and it does not seem quite so bad after all. Oh, I don't know."

"Of course you don't know, you have only been here a few weeks. Things will improve. I have seen many changes in my lifetime. You will see more".

Marianne found it difficult to believe that this invalid was the sister of busy Mary Woodhouse. They were very different. This encounter began a relationship that was to last until death. Elizabeth Hirst had learnt to live within her capabilities. She had time to think and ponder, and this had made her wise.

She read widely, not the romantic novels of the Brontes - she did not take those seriously. She preferred Dickens, Thackeray and Disraeli. With Marianne she would discuss the London Society, whom she had never known. She gave her opinion that Thackeray spoke very truly of ambition and cynicism - Marianne always thought Mrs. Somerset was a character of Thackeray.

All this Marianne took in greedily and the interflow of

understanding between them both surged as they found here a common ground. While they talked a steady burble of talk, it seemed argument rose from the room beneath them. Marianne cocked her head to listen. She caught the tone of Benton's voice but she could not quite hear.

"Yes, that it what is so tedious. You cannot quite hear what they say. But it must be good or they wouldn't have come", said Elizabeth.

There was a gust of laughter. Its infection reached them and they smiled.

"You had better go down, my dear, they will want to see you. But come again soon."

Outside the door, Marianne was attacked by shyness. But she turned the doorknob and went in. Every chair was occupied, equal numbers of men and women.

"Ah, here's Marianne. Come and sit thee down here." He indicated a chair. She sat down, no longer shy, but very surprised. Not one of the men had stood up for her. Benton had made a faltering gesture. She was angry and condemned them as rude and uncouth.

She looked at the people. They were not so well-groomed as Mrs Somerset's friends, but they were in no way differently featured. They varied, just as all faces varied. She looked at the furniture. Here there was a difference. It lacked elegance and as she regarded the range, she remembered Mrs Somerset's great marble fireplace in the drawing room. She was unhappy, but roused by another gust of laughter, she began to listen.

A religious discussion was in progress and Benton very wittily was defending the church and condemning dissenters. She listened and her prejudices began to crumble. Here was aspiration and a seriousness that rarely appeared in the drawing rooms she knew. They were seeking truth and earnestly and she admired it. It was, though, becoming intense and Uncle Alan by the fire thought a change was needed.

"Have you heard of the brethren at Slaithwaite?" They shook their heads. "Well, it seems they rent a warehouse for meetings once a week. But last week, a party of musicians and minstrels needed somewhere to sleep, so the owner's wife let them have the loft.

"Up they went and fell asleep. The brethren came and with them a softheaded lad. They had their prayers and a good few hallelujahs. Now and then, a strange hallelujah broke out. They took no notice at first, but they began to be afraid.

"The leader read the scriptures and as he said, 'And the trumpet shall sound', it did, and looking down at them was a smiling nigger minstrel with his trumpet and they all ran out. All, so it is said, but the new convert who fell on his knees thinking it was the Devil himself and he blabbed out 'Ah never been here afore, Sir, and ah promise as ah won't agin'."

Everyone laughed. So did Marianne, but she couldn't but think it cruel. After tea and beer, they sang and Uncle Alan recited Burns.

Going home beneath the stars, neither Benton nor Marianne felt the cold. They were warm through and through by the warmth of the room and even more the warmth of the people. Everything for Marianne seemed to be falling into place.

She was not alone. His arm in hers felt almost a part of her. She knew that she must stop comparing, banish thought of alien classes, alien people and just accept.

That night as Benton took her in his arms and visions pulsed through her dazed and drowsy mind, she saw beauty upon beauty. There were banked splendours of colour, treasures in one gallery after another. It seemed she was in some palace... it all swept before her as Benton gently but forcefully pounded upon her.

She saw Venice, light sparkling on the water. She saw a barge, oars rising and dipping, like stiffened beating wings. The water splashing from them fell like jewels. A company feasted on board. Such were Marianne's dreams in a small house in an industrial village as she lay in the arms of the man she loved.

Chapter 2

Berrow Brow

Spring was felt rather than seen. It was slow coming to the valley, but the snowdrops did come making their chaste announcement of the season. Marianne was finding the first weeds among the flowerbeds when she heard Benton whistling. He was at the gate and waving a large iron key. He threw it to her and it fell at her feet in the grass with a thud.

She retrieved it. She looked at him eagerly.

"Is it for our house?"

She began to ask a hundred questions. Benton said nothing, only telling her to hurry with the tea, and then they could explore it for themselves.

They climbed up over the ridge and looked down into the vale of Milnsbridge. Along its sides ran terraces of houses. It was by no means as pretty as Armitage Bridge and the light of the evening seemed to throw into relief its meanness rather than veil it and soften it.

Marianne held Benton's arm tighter. Suddenly from the other side of a stone wall, a plover flew up. It mewed, as though startled, and reassured her that nature was not so far away.

They descended. The way seemed narrow and confined, the crossroads were hemmed in and Marianne disliked it. They crossed a road and went down a still steeper bank and then up a small road. Here there were a jumble of stone houses, all older than the canal and the railway, the one at the foot of the slope and the other built up on shelf and a viaduct on the other side.

They stood before a flight of steps, which climbed up through an unkempt garden to a large front door. They walked up, they were more anxious than joyful. Benton put in the key and left it for Marianne to turn. They pushed open the door and went into a hall. It was larger than she expected. There were two rooms on either side of the hallway, a drawing room, and a study. Behind lay a dining room with a kitchen beyond that a scullery with a pump.

She whisked through them all and back to the windows at the

front. The outlook was what worried her. They looked right over the houses, over the mills, to the railway and the houses parallel with the line. It had a certain beauty, something especial, and she felt relieved and happy and Benton felt it all.

They went more slowly up the stairs to find four bedrooms. Marianne's eyes shone with anticipation. She liked it... there was much she could do with this house.

Back in the parlour, Benton stood by the window and looked out. A shadow crossed his face. He was wishing that it had been a vicarage, but he said: "We shall be happy here. I know we will. We shall make this house shine like a beacon, 'a city that cannot be hid'.

"I cannot be a clergyman, but I shall teach and here, here we can never lose sight of the poor. There is much to be done. But most of all I want you to be happy."

"But I am happy. And if you are happy, then I am happy too. This is my home and that is as far as I look at the moment."

Within three weeks they had moved in. Mrs Woodhouse had supervised the scrubbing and cleaning, taking two women over from Armitage Bridge. Ceilings and pantries were whitewashed by them while Marianne attended to the equipping.

She made more purchases in a fortnight than she had made all her life. For the parlour she bought a suite of rosewood, upholstered in red velvet. She bought carpets and chairs, chests and one of the new brass bedsteads. They thought it very grand indeed.

It was over Easter that they began to feel that the house belonged to them. In the great quietness that hung over the valley, usually incessantly active, Marianne rejoiced. Benton started working in the garden. Here he found an old nest, still perfectly shaped of green moss with tufts of sheep's wool woven in neatly and firmly.

He gave it to his wife who immediately pricked it with primroses and carried it into the parlour. There she laid it on a table. Cordelia, the maid, viewed it with unconcealed distaste and pronounced that nests were always full of moth grubs. Marianne did not mind, to her it was a symbol of home, her one abiding joy of the moment.

It was Mrs. Woodhouse who had insisted on a maid. Marianne had objected, but Benton and his mother convinced her of the necessity, particularly if she should have a baby. Often Marianne thought how extremely odd it was that her first impression of her father-in-law had been a very benevolent King Lear, and, now, she had a maid called Cordelia. She lived up to her name - she was loyal and loving and stubborn.

On Easter Day, church services over, Benton led Marianne to the parlour where on table stood a large box. She began to unwrap it. When she lifted the lid she cooed with delight, for there was an alabaster urn on a pedestal with doves, some alighting, some drinking.

It was the very one she had seen in Bradford, loved instantly and rejected as too frivolous as she purchased carpets and fenders. Benton watched her with delight as she carefully lifted it in her long narrow hands and sought the right place for its disposal.

The room did look elegant and the 18th century wainscoting of oak did not jar with the curved and curled modern furniture.

"Benton, I think this room is every bit as beautiful as the drawing room in Hampstead, don't you?"

"Do you know, I don't really remember the details of that room, only the icy reception I got from Mrs Somerset."

"Oh yes, she had much grander designs for me, but they would never have worked. After all, who was I?"

"But you must admit life here is different."

"Yes, but not so different. My only regret was when I saw the children early in the morning waiting to go to the mill. I shall remember that always. I sometimes thought that if I had married a politician I could have persuaded my husband to do something about it.

"Then, I thought, if I had done that, I would not have known anything about them. You and can I do much more here."

That night, as they sat by the fire, preparing for a quiet evening, there was a knock at the door. Answering it, Marianne found a crowd of relations and friends. One glance, and she called back over her shoulder:

"Benton, come quick!"

They surged in like a tide, discarding hats, bonnets and shawls on the way. They billowed round the piano like a wave and suddenly sang. It was like an episode in an opera and left the couple looking on bashfully. Quickly, Marianne made the excuse of making tea and busied herself in the kitchen where Lydia joined her.

She was full of admiration for everything and ruefully said:
"I wonder if anyone will ever marry me?"
"Of course they will", answered Marianne a little too quickly.
"Well, nobody has yet."

Marianne cast a look at Lydia. She was not pretty, until she smiled. There was, though, character in her face and more than that, the gentleness of love.

"Oh, my dear, you will marry, I know. Don't worry."

When they returned to the parlour they found the table for their tray covered with presents, a table cloth, a rag mat for the hearth, a canary in a small wooden cage, a nutmeg grater, a pound of tea and presiding over all, in a tall glass dome was a white statuette of the Queen.

Benton had seen them gradually accrue on the table. They suddenly confronted Marianne, and she could hardly speak. She felt that there were more and more bands of love around her. It was only as they left that she discovered from whom they were.

It was Uncle Alan who surprised her most of all, by saying: "The queen is from Benton's Aunt Elizabeth and me. We thought she might make you feel more at home. Remind you of your people in London. I bought it at the Great Exhibition and it's been in our parlour ever since. Since Elizabeth has been ill, no one goes there. So we thought she ought to have a new home."

When the last of them had been seen through the gate they walked up the path extraordinarily happy, the silence folded around them. It was Benton who scoffed a little as he surveyed the presents: "What an odd collection. I hope you like birds?"

"I've never had one. We shall have to get another cage immediately." The poor confined creature hopped an inch from one perch to another.

"Whatever shall we do with the Queen? It's been uncle's pride for a long time."

Marianne looked at it, it was, most certainly the Queen, the imperious small profile, but much slimmer and prettier than when she had seen her. Some tears came into her eyes, it was not loyalty, but love. It was a sacrificial gift and was given a place in the parlour, but it did not displace the urn and the doves.

"Well, that's the end of our first Easter here."
"There'll be many more."

The gathering of the friends became a monthly ritual. The house resounded with music, especially Handel, so much so that Marianne could bear his *Messiah* no longer.

When the spring arrives in the valley it comes with drama. Plain banks show faces golden with daffodils and time slips by more quickly. As Marianne watched the birds feeding their young so she became aware that she was pregnant. At first she was incredulous at her condition.

Having babies was something other women did, she had never thought of having them herself. She was ignorant of tiny children, she had not considered a family, but she soon found that Benton had. When she was certain, she hurried over to confer with her mother-in-law. Mrs Woodhouse's casual approval and pronouncement further disconcerted her.

"I'm not at all surprised. Your face has been sharpening these past weeks."

It was a matter entirely after Mrs Woodhouse's heart and within minutes Marianne was viewing the oaken cradle that had rocked Benton and many before, which would, in time, house her baby. It was the sight of this old well-polished piece of furniture, so solidly constructed, that brought to her the realisation that being a mother might be very pleasant.

She put out her foot and touched the rocker. It rolled gently back and forth very easily and she had a vision of the baby falling asleep.

It had pleased her to see Benton so delighted. To him, a child seemed the seal of their life together. It made Marianne his, whereas she had been content with Benton and the dreams that came to her in their closest union.

In the summer the valley, unshaded by trees, often became oppressive. Still the chimneys billowed out their smoke and the sun peered through a heavy pall of soot. Marianne longed for fresher air... she wanted Wales and the sea.

She kept silent for she had discovered that many of her acquaintance rarely went away. However, Benton read her thoughts, and one evening as she put down her sewing and gazed out of the window and sighed, he was moved by her beauty and her strange unspoken sadness.

He decided to give her a change so he hired a gig for a week and each day they drove out. They went back to Helme and even went down to the waterfall. They drove up to Aunt Christina who welcomed them with a pleasure she tried to conceal.

Tea was soon on the table. Marianne and Beth the maid exchanged glances and friendly smiles. Aunt Christina from behind the tea-pot looked keenly at Marianne and said with no hesitation whatsoever: "So you're expecting. When?"

Marianne was very surprised, even shocked.

"How do you know?"

"Your face is sharpening."

"The baby is due in December."

"Bad time for childbirth. The weather is bad for all that washing. Pity it isn't the spring."

"Oh, I am sure we shall manage, shan't we Benton?"

With a big smile Benton said: "And we have my mother you know."

This made the aunt smile too.

"Yes, that of course, but if you feel you want more room, you can always come here. Benton knows that."

Marianne looked at the intimidating woman and saw revealingly the warmth within her. She had never encountered anyone quite like her, nor would she ever. She replied with a touch of pride: "Yes, that would be very nice. I should be glad of it, but, you know. We have quite a sizeable house of our own, now."

The rap was laden with eggs, butter, bacon and jam before they went down the valley.

"I wonder what made your aunt so shy, for that is what she is. She's not hard really, it's a front."

"There was a man involved. Ask my mother she'll know more. He left the farm and he never came back, as far as I know."

"So her heart was broken. Thank goodness not all of it."

Their own future seemed endless and serene.

The moon began to rise.

October was mild and the autumn late, a soft winter was foretold. In November, the fogs climbed down the hills and then froze. Though close to the town, few people ventured up their steep bank. At the beginning of December snow came floating down. After the darkness, it was enchanting. For a few days everything seemed wonderfully clean and lighter than ever before.

The light reflected from the snow on to the ceilings and for a reason Marianne could not analyse, she did not try. It gladdened her through and through. The snow fell more heavily, again they became isolated and they realised that they must move down to Armitage Bridge for the birth.

The fly was hired and all the clothes and the cradle so carefully carried to Whiteley were now taken back. Benton was never to forget the day he carefully led Marianne down the path. He was watchful at every footfall lest she slip.

The icy snow was treacherous. The horse's breath hung like a balloon about its head, as its hocks shivered. Benton watched Marianne constantly in the cab. He feared the horse might fall and jolt her too roughly.

The whole episode was etched by anxiety on the plate of his memory. It was a great relief when they slowly crept over the bridge and he was able to hand her over to his mother.

Mrs Woodhouse saw that they had not come too soon. Marianne was placid, resigned and moving into that strange animal world where only feeling, not thought, mattered. She was very cold and the whistling of the wind in the chimney made her feel still colder.

Hot bricks were put in her bed, hot drinks were dispensed and Benjamin kept going to the window to report on the snow. Suddenly, without, any warning, Marianne who sat so silently, gave a slight cry, leapt to her feet and clutched the mantelpiece.

Instantly, her mother-in-law was vigilant and totally prepared. Marianne was ushered up the stairs and helped to bed.

Benton waited below. He heard uncanny moans and he could not think why his mother delayed in sending him to fetch the doctor. At last the command came and, seizing his scarf, coat and hat, he ran doggedly through the snow. He knew that partly he was running away from the horror of it all, but he also ran for Marianne's life, or what he believed to be her life.

The doctor was slow. Benton thought him callously indifferent and marvelled at the calm with which he packed a small bag with instruments. Together they drove back and the doctor talked to Benton of wool prices, the poverty in Lancashire caused by the Civil War in America and other matters, entirely inconsequential that he almost cried out.

At St Paul's Terrace, Benton stayed with the horse, walking him up and down, as the cold was intense. At intervals he went inside, stood by the fire, drank tea and then returned to the horse. At last the door opened and the muffled doctor came out:

"Well Taylor, congratulations. You have a fine fat daughter. She objects to the cold as strongly as I do. Goodnight."

Almost before Benton could thank him he had taken the reins and was away.

Inside the house his mother was in complete command.

"Come and see your daughter." Benton peered into the cradle before the fire. She lay like a chrysalis in a cocoon of blankets. He saw a tiny red head, making ineffectual fumbling movements. He thought of monkeys, he thought of caterpillars, and all these thoughts he kept wisely to himself. He bounded up the stairs to his wife.

He stopped in the doorway. She looked so different. Her pale complexion had under the strain turned olive. She looked foreign. She smiled and lifted her hand wearily.

"Oh Benton, it's all over, isn't that good. They say she's lovely baby. Have you seen her?"

He nodded.

"But Benton, they won't give me what I ask for."

"What's that?"

"I want a drink of your mother's beer. I'm so thirsty."

Benton rushed downstairs, grabbed a mug from the dresser and filled it from the barrel in the scullery. Going back through the room he heard his mother say reprovingly, "Oh Benton." He took no heed.

Marianne struggled up, took the mug and drank. She did not drink much, Benton smiled, and raising the mug, said: "To your health, and to . . .." There was a pause. "We haven't a name for her."

"We'll think of one very soon," said Marianne very quietly. She was fast asleep. He stayed holding her hand until it grew cold, then slipped it beneath the bedclothes and crept down the stairs.

For days the snow fell. It came up to the windows and had to be cleared away to let in the light. They dug a way to the road. The snow they could remove, but not the cold.

The cradle never left the hearth and on one side it became

scorched, but the nappies over the fire were stiff with frost.

Marianne was supposed to stay in bed but the cold drove her to her feet and she wanted to move. The doctor, who had seen many of his poorer patients rise swiftly from childbed, did not reprimand her. Benton watching the mother and child no longer saw the baby as a monkey, but a part of mankind and it was then they decided to call her Annie Elizabeth.

A second Christmas was spent in Armitage Bridge. They had looked forward to celebrating it in their own house. It was not until mid-January that they climbed into the fly again and journeyed up and then down to Whitley Bottom to their house and the excited and eager young Cordelia.

The bank, the gate, the house with its white windows seemed to rush towards them as they hurried towards it. Benton thought it as pleased to see them as they it. Cordelia stood beaming at the door and then ran, and with outstretched arms, took the baby.

Inside, the joy of being on their own seized them. While tea was made, Benton took Annie in his arms and showed her every corner of the house. He even declared that she took an interest. He was amazed at his own delight in the baby. It was not the strange phenomenon he had expected, but a new extension of himself.

Marianne was calmer. After all, it was her lot to feed and wash and tend the baby. Benton just looked on marvelling at these ministrations. Yet she found motherhood an almost unmixed joy and even at this stage found companionship in Annie.

The weather remained cold and hour after hour was spent in the parlour reading and sewing and gently rocking the cradle with her foot. At least twice a week she had a visitor, her father-in-law. He had retired and he loved the baby.

One dark afternoon, he discovered a way to make her coo and wave her arms in delight just by raising and lowering the flame in the gas bracket. He never tired of standing up doing this. It enchanted her and she enchanted him.

Years later, she would be told jokingly: "You don't need loving. You had more than your share from your grandfather while you were a baby."

Another year slipped by and then, with less drama, William Henry was born. Marianne found herself sewing still more, Cordelia ran the house, and her reading was confined to children's stories for Annie. In the evenings, Benton read aloud, often it was Dickens. His days were busy, the school took most of his time and he was now a churchwarden, which meant a lot of duties. In these, Marianne was involved and to her fell the task of visiting the poor.

So much so that Annie's first memories were of poverty-stricken homes. Before she went to school she had seen many strange and macabre sights. Men and women disfigured with facial cancer, children horribly crippled, her small face often crumpled in sympathy. She felt no horror, only compassion. Life was continuing on a chosen path and they all felt fulfilment.

Then a blow fell. Benjamin Woodhouse died after a short bronchial illness. Benton and Marianne were grieved for he had been so lovable. His face had written upon it the contentment often found on a craftsman.

It was the confident knowledge that he knew his task, that of master dyer. Marianne missed the dignified face with the 'Lear'-like silver hair sitting opposite her at teatime. Her grief was shared with dread. Mrs Woodhouse had now to leave St Paul's Row and make her home with them.

She thought that all her joy was over on the day she saw the van stop and men begin to unload furniture into their house. Her home, she thought, would no longer be her own. She had forgotten that her mother-in-law was equally regretful to leave her home.

Mrs Woodhouse was wise, she furnished her own room, other belongings spread into the house and Marianne was quick to appreciate them... the grandfather clock, the rocking chair, the mahogany bureau.

Mrs Woodhouse, too, was an asset to the place. She busied herself in the kitchen and the washhouse, baking, brewing and doing all the things she loved. Cordelia liked the old lady, so life continued much as before.

The children accepted her immediately, they loved her even though she was often sharp and tart with them, but they soon learnt that this was a façade. Annie and William never tired of playing hide-and-seek and one of the favourite hiding places was beneath the cage of her crinoline.

There they learnt to differentiate the difference between the fabric texture of the stiff starched petticoats and the warmth of the soft flannel ones.

A grandmother in the house gave Benton and Marianne greater freedom and they used it to walk. One summer day, as they returned wearily and thirstily through Crosland Moor, they decided to call on Cousin Polly.

Polly's father managed a mill. He spent his money wisely and he had enough vision to see that a good education was as beneficial to a woman as a man. He had sent his only daughter, Polly, to the Moravian school at nearby Fullneck, where she had boarded.

Here she had blossomed and risen above some of the narrow provincialism of her life at home and when, on the death of her much loved mother, she had become the mistress of her father's house, then it took on her own character. It was here that Benton was happiest, and here with Marianne they could talk of books and religion without narrow confines.

So often at Milnsbridge books were ignored and religion meant fierce partisanship of some particular sect. Lydia, with her gentle but lively eyes, created an atmosphere of speech and vision. Their arrival caused a slight flutter for they found her not alone but with a very small, very dark and very plain little woman. She was Dutch. She had taught Polly at Fullneck. When she spoke her features became charged with enthusiasm and she became inwardly illuminated.

Benton questioned her, about Holland and about education there. He was impressed by Miss Van Zuyl and so, too, was Marianne. In this household, Miss Van Zuyl fitted well. She was above the dead hand of money, neither the want of it, nor the pride of it. Here in Polly and now in her friend, they found beliefs and hopes far greater than purses.

Marianne, like most women, sat and appraised these two women. She saw clearly the primness of Polly, but she acknowledged that it was allied with softness. The foreigner Marianne found was totally unlike her vague impression of what a Dutchwoman would look like.

She had imagined them to be fair and of middle height and plump. This little woman was bird-like, and though keeping to the point, her mind flashed and darted. What neither Benton nor Marianne realised was that they too were making a vital impression.

Both of them glowed with health, their cheeks freshened by the wind, their skins tanned slightly. They both looked far younger than their years. Though these were not great, Marianne was not yet 23.

Going home Marianne expressed her surprise at Miss Van Zuyl's dark looks.

"But darling, don't you realise that she is a Jewess?"

Marianne had not. She now understood why there was tragedy in the full black eyes. It was not her own, it was hers by inheritance, generations of ghettoes had cast their shadow.

Milnsbridge lay beneath them. It was clearer to view than usual, Saturday was a day of rest for the chimneys. It was their home, their duties lay there, but neither loved it. Benton had meant to make it his escape, but it had failed. He resolved to make certain his children were freed.

"You know, Marianne, I would like Annie to go to Holland to have such an education. We must manage it somehow. I am sure we can if we are determined."

"I would hate her to go so far away. Why she's only five in December."

"I don't mean at this moment, silly goose, but later. Think of the advantages she would have. The world would be before her."

The following week, Cousin Polly and Miss Van Zuyl came to Whiteley. Annie was fascinated by the ruched satin collar that sat around Polly's neck and over her shoulders. She had not seen such trimmings before.

Polly liked the attention. Miss Van Zuyl was interested and amused that Annie, after listening to her speak, suddenly imitated her precisely, offering her some 'boter and bread'. William was much more shy and turned to his mother. Annie snuggled closer to the Dutchwoman and when tea was over, slipped her hand into hers. This tiny gesture plotted something of her future.

Life was busy in the house in Whiteley Bottom. Marianne organised her household. She was so fortunate in having such good lieutenants in Mrs Woodhouse and the very intelligent Cordelia.

The house inside was beautiful, the garden also neat and tidy. The children were always well dressed and so, too, were the adults.

But it was what went on in that house that was interesting. From it Benton went to his teaching each day of term, Mrs Woodhouse made her sudden forays into places of sickness and distress. Marianne kept her eye on the poor around her and cared for her three children, for there was now another sister, Edith.

There was a definite rhythm and tempo to their lives, as had most middle-class families of their day. It swung gently around the church and every six days were punctuated by the quiet of Sunday when the church bells rang out. Benton and Marianne were unfailing in the attendance, but Mrs Woodhouse belonged to an older and more cynical generation. Her attendances were erratic and largely depended on whether her bonnet was new, or freshly trimmed. Church to her was a kind of entertainment. To her son and daughter in law it was much, much more.

The Choral Society in Huddersfield also took up much of Benton's evenings and when summer came they needed a rest. So they all went to Southport.

The children had their first view of the sea, they paddled, they bathed, and they built sandcastles. Annie, though, begged to be taken to the shops, so Marianne and Grandma took her on one of their expeditions.

Annie remembered this. The splendours made a very great impression upon her, the dresses, the colour, the arrangements of the windows and all the souvenirs, which are offered, to visitors. At the end of the week Grandma and Cordelia went home, leaving the parents behind.

Alone they felt younger and freer than they had ever done since their marriage. The lack of responsibility, the air, the exercise brought a sparkle to their eyes and every day they walked for miles on the long, long shoreline.

One day they came to a deserted place and there Benton decided to swim. Marianne was afraid he might be seen, but that did not make her cease in her admiration of him as he ran white and shapely to the sea.

In the water he seemed in his element, laughing and splashing and rising like Neptune with brine in his beard. She would run down to him with a towel. They repeated this several days. Then they would wander back to their lodgings overlooking the sea.

Each hour seemed filled with happiness and they did not worry about the children, Grandma or Cordelia. They lived those days for themselves alone. But they did talk of the future as they paced the sand. They discussed the education of William and Annie.

William must go away to school and Annie, well, Benton still wanted her to go to Holland. Edith did not really claim their plans for education as she was too small. They planned also for themselves, they wanted to move... Marianne still did not love Milnsbridge.

In winter she found it bearable because she was busy, there was always so much to do. The poor were in constant need then. She loved Christmas and hailed it each year as something new. When spring came, then her heart would sink for she saw it through a shroud.

Every spring was besmirched with soot, even the primroses and the house looked northwards at the front and the sun always seemed to be shining more on the house of Longwood and Lindley. Marianne wanted to live up in the Marsh district. There were houses she coveted in Luck Lane. But when summer came she knew that even up there she would feel oppressed by the lack of clarity in the sunshine.

For much longer than usual the memory of the holiday was etched in Marianne's mind. She was thinking of it as she took Annie to her new school. It was a sandstone building and to Marianne looked forbidding, to Annie it was foreboding.

Annie was handed over to the teacher who seemed kind but in a manner purely professional. Marianne watched the fair reddish curls go down the corridor... they went very steadily, not one bobbed.

Annie did not look round and Marianne thought this to mean resentment. It was a fear allied to curiosity, Annie was anxious to know what everything would be like. Marianne was supposed to go home, but instead she climbed the hill, she wanted to be alone.

She was aware, almost desperately, of her intense love for her child. It was a fierce love and as she climbed the street, she acknowledged to herself that it was fiercer than the love she had for her other children.

This partiality worried her, she strove to suppress it. It seemed that her love for her first-born was more related to her love for Benton... she was their first creation.

At the brow she crossed the road, where the horses sweating and heaving pulled the great bales of wool.

She wanted to sit in the new church, to be quiet, the heavy iron gates were locked and the church, not yet blackened, seemed aloof and disdainful looking down upon the grubby houses.

It was in an angry mood that she prayed for her children, and particularly Annie. She prayed that they would soar up and away from Huddersfield. She did not ask for escape for herself, for the busy life with Benton was all that she wanted. To be with him was heaven and for that she thanked God, but for her children she wanted more beauty, she wanted a wider world for them.

The winter was foggier than usual, the dank mists swirled slowly – so that the house seemed to stand still – and a strange world moved outside. It was warm, the red curtains hung before the doors and windows and the fires were banked. It was an orderly contented household. Her humour rose and she adjusted herself to the musical evenings, the continual *Messiah* and her poor visiting.

Politically, Marianne was not awake. Poverty distressed her, its by-products worried her. She disliked the acceptance of it, by those with and those without money.

Sometimes, the ecstatic gratitude for a worn blanket made her ashamed. She had seen more and more squalor, the sick dying on filthy mattresses, sometimes covered with sacks. She was horrified that anyone could live like that in the mid-19th century. Sometimes she returned home from these errands with a taut white face.

One such day she came in… and found a reproachful mother-in-law boiling a kettle.

"What is wrong? Is it Annie?"

"No, it's Benton. He has a very bad sore throat and a fever. I think you should be looking after him, not dirty, idle people."

"That's not fair Grandma, and you know it."

Marianne ran to the parlour.

"He's not there. I've put him to bed."

Marianne flew up the stairs. Benton smiled but looked very pale and was extremely hoarse. But the look of him was in such marked contrast to the child she had left that she sighed with relief.

She stroked his hair, which was beginning to recede. "What you need is sleep."

Mrs Woodhouse was soon bustling around with beef tea and a hot brick wrapped in flannel.

The evening seemed long and dull. Mrs Woodhouse darned socks and Marianne made a dress for Annie from her wedding dress. It, now, seemed so very old-fashioned.

As she stitched the striped material she pondered on time. It seemed only yesterday that she had worn it with such pride and fear, but she felt also that she had been married a lifetime. She could not imagine a life without Benton. She worried a little about his hoarseness, but dismissed apprehensions. In fact, next day he was very much better, but the hoarseness persisted and he became irritable and most especially with Annie, always his favourite.

She was so delighting in school that overnight she had become an independent little person, a tease and imperious. This was received by her brother and sister sometimes as comic, others as annoying and tempers flared.

One Sunday, after Christmas, Marianne felt unwell, so Benton took the children to church by himself. It was his custom to read the lessons during the service. The second lesson was very long and Annie and William shut into their seat, shielded from the sight of the congregation by the high backs of the pews, began to play.

They assembled all the prayer and hymn books into a train. It puffed its way sedately along the shelf. Then William saw the larger Bible with its silver clasps. This became a most superior engine and its puffs, at first inaudible, grew louder as confidence was gained and their imaginations swelled.

They were so lost in the wonder of their creation that the silence that fell upon the church mid-way through the reading went unnoticed. Chuff, chuff, puff, puff, echoed in the nave, a sound joined by the resolute tread of their father.

Benton left the lectern, strode down the aisle, flung open the pew door and seizing two hands marched driver and guard out to the porch. There, the great door all shiny with varnish and black with hinge work closed upon them and a voice, seemingly not their father's said: "Wait there."

They waited bored, yet fearing the end of boredom. They dreaded seeing their father again. He claimed them and walked home wordless, they remembered the greyness of the streets, the shuttered looks of the shops, which extended to their father himself. He usually told them a story on the way home. As home came in sight again there was a mix of longing and dread. They began to wonder just how great their crime was. Their mother was informed, she looked grieved, but the secret smile to Benton, was not lost by Annie.

The culprits in the glow of pardon bustled with fiendish activity by helping in every way to blot out their misdemeanour. Annie trotted back and forth with knives and forks, in and out she went, over the stone flagged floors.

They were to have custard and the little glass cups with handles were used. She carried them in one by one, marvelling at the facets of light glinting. With the last cup she ran, tripped, fell, lifted up her beautiful burden to save it... and then the glass, the stone, her head all met. Tears, blood, glass and custard made a most horrible amalgam.

Without waiting Benton ran out of the house, hatless into the prim Sabbath air. He ran as he had not run since Annie was born. He repented of his stern behaviour of the morning, he prayed to Heaven with more fervour than he ever adopted in church that her sight might not be impaired.

The young doctor ran back too, the young men flew up the road, up the path, lace curtains of neighbours were drawn aside, and murmurs were made about the age of Mrs Woodhouse. Inside the doctor was full of unspoken admiration for the preparations, the child lay on the sofa, but the kitchen was ready, the table had been pulled to the window, towels were before the fire and a bowl of hot water was ready.

Benton picked up Annie and carried her in. Her brow was cut right through to the bone above her left eye, the skin turned back, the bone gleamed glassily.

"Now Annie, we are going to put you right. It won't take too long, we just have to sew you up a little bit."

She lay very still, she saw the flash of the silver needle, she saw the thread. She lay patient and still. But what followed she could not believe, they were attacking her forehead again. She screamed and kicked, but she was powerless.

Grandma and her mother held her shoulders and head and her father clamped down her legs, and Cordelia held her arms. As the second incision was made she fainted. Noisier screams arose, angry shouts and kicks... it was William lunging against the kitchen door, shouting, shouting: "Leave Annie alone, leave my sister. Leave her!"

Within comparatively few minutes, she was still, on her mother's knee, shocked into silence, totally exhausted. A very gentle, loving and subdued Annie with a bandaged head remained at home and her brother regarded her with awe.

She enjoyed the solicitude and the first one to perceive her exploitation of the occurrence was Grandma. The doctor was interested in the family, and particularly in the little girl as he peered into the one-and-a-half eyes emerging from the bandage. He thanked God that such eyes had been spared. But he worried about the scar on her brow.

Such minor accidents broke the calm of life at Whitley Bottom. The children grew, the new baby was born, Benton lost a little more hair, but his whiskers thickened and Marianne was no longer mistaken for a sister when she collected her children from school.

The new quality of her face was serenity and it was enhanced by the thick chignon of hair that she wore. It imparted a new dignity as well as elegance. She was happy, she was fulfilled, her husband, her children, her home filled most of her life and Mrs Woodhouse and the loyal Cordelia completed the picture.

Benton was not so happy for he felt threatened. On many mornings during term time, he would wake with a hoarse throat and often in the evening he had a slight fever. He ignored it as much as he could and he shielded Marianne from the knowledge, but he was still aware of the portents.

He worried whether his voice would last through the day. The oral lesson of the day was the one he dreaded, but he usually managed to given them work to do to spare his voice. One evening, off his guard, he stared into the fire and Marianne asked him what he was thinking. His dreads were in the caverns of the burning coals, he dragged himself back to reality.

"I do not know how much longer I can continue teaching. My voice is troubling me again."

Her hand sought his. "But, Benton, you never wanted to teach. You can do something else."

He smiled wanly at her optimism and asked, "What?"

Surely there could be something in the church?"

"I doubt that very much, my dear, the church nearly always involves speaking."

A fear she had never contemplated came like a spectre into the room, which, until that moment, had seemed so secure.

"We still have my annuity. Let's go into the country and you can write."

Her apparent unconcern supported him. But the thought of living on her minute annuity amused him.

From that day, the realisation dogged Benton that he could not go on forever. He began to live for each day. Sometimes, he regained his strength and they thought the evil was behind them. Then he fancied that the headmaster was scrutinising him.

He thought he was being pitied and that riled him. Therefore, he spoke to Mr Cholmondley. To his surprise the headmaster had suspected nothing and he made light of Benton's fears. But he did say.

"Taylor, what will you do if you do not teach?"

"I do not know."

"Then we will consider this conversation unspoken. Do not be hasty." Remember that your first duty is to your family. You've told your wife, I take it?"

The West Riding was noted for its hard matter-of-fact approach to life, often 'The Devil take the hindermost' was quoted, but it was more rarely acted upon.

Summer came and Benton seemed better. Mr Cholmondley, however did not forget. So that when Sir George Armytage, chairman of the governors, spoke of needing a really competent manager of the works offices, Mr Cholmondley instantly said that he possibly knew the man he wanted, but withheld his name.

When he put the project to Benton the young man's soul felt iron. The mills, cloth, industry… the cause of so much misery, something which he had always wished to escape. On his way home, he glowered at the mills in the pale sunshine. He saw the blackness everywhere and it seemed to be claiming him, just as Aunt Christiana said it claimed everyone.

After supper that night, Benton told Marianne and his mother of the plans mooted. Had he placed this before them when he was ill they would have accepted it more easily, with greater adaptability. But he looked so well with a high colour. So he encountered cold disapproval. Marianne's pride was hurt, she despised business.

Mrs Woodhouse was disappointed. Her hopes for her son were foundering. On him she had set all her ambition.

The meal was eaten in silence and Benton thought that his wife looked like a Holbein drawing, a woman deeply mistrustful of all around her.

Suddenly he exploded with anger and threw down his knife and fork. "You are hurt, both of you. Have you thought that I am hurt as well?"

He marched out of the house without grabbing his hat, and striding, he mounted the hill. He strode on and on until he came to the vast landscape. He felt a certain release from the fierce resentment in himself. He felt at one with the freedom of the view, yet the contrast between this immensity of moor and sky and the confines of his own life were not lost to him.

He trudged into the heather and then flung himself on to it. As he lay there his horizon contracted to the springing wiry stems of the heather and the peaty soil beneath. He became prey to all the 'ifs' of his life.

If he had been ordained. If he had better health. He seemed to see promise after promise being broken, he was the sport of Fate. Then he thought of Marianne, that was a promise more than fulfilled. He thought too, of Annie, there was another great hope for the future.

And as the mood of despondency began to recede he remembered reading Thomas Carlyle. He even smiled as he recalled his tutor warning him against him, an anti-Christ he named him. But Benton had been spun into a new realm of thought by his words.

He thought of his deliberations on the fate of Robert Burns. It was about reconciling with necessity. The very thought of having a small intellectual task in looking it up made him rise to his feet and go homewards.

As the houses began singly, then in groups and then in solid terraces to line the road back, he felt himself walk into his unhappiness. He saw the chapels, the children playing about the steps, women grey and weary.

He saw men already staggering with too much drink. It became even more real and closer. He saw one man from the choir catch sight of him and with a great effort, control his wilful legs and then bid him a slurred 'good-evening'.

He was heartened, for it reminded him that he was still needed here. As he made this realisation, he saw Marianne in her blue summer coat walking along the street, Annie trotting along in her wake, holding an empty basket. He called to them, they turned and waited. Annie looked self-conscious beneath her father's oncoming gaze. Marianne smiled too, and he saw that she was becoming reconciled.

When he reached home he looked up his copy of *Carlyle*'s *Essays* and finding Burns copied it into his commonplace book.

"Manhood begins when we have in any way made a truce with Necessity; begins even when we have surrendered to Necessity, as the most part only do; but begins joyfully and hopefully only when we have reconciled ourselves to Necessity; and thus, in reality, triumphed over it, and felt that in Necessity we are free."

Marianne watching asked him what he was doing and he read it out. With great gravity, she said, "That's true."

Within a few days, Benton was called to Sir George Armytage. On sight they liked one another and Sir George found himself being almost indiscreetly frank about the management of the office. The senior clerk, Enoch Woods, known to Benton, was old, but once he had been capable of running the accounts of the mill with two assistants.

The firm had expanded; the bookkeeping had become more complicated. He often misunderstood foreign currencies and in the last months there had been the loss of large sums of money. The thought of having a schoolmaster in charge appealed to Sir George. He was even more eager when he discovered that Benton had a good knowledge of French.

They went down to the offices, down wooden stairs and across several yards to a brick building. It enclosed one large airy room where everything seemed built on a monumental scale, heavy desks, heavy ledgers bound in leather, heavy pewter inkstands.

The clerks all stood leaning at their slopes. In their midst, at a large table, sat Mr Woods. He shuffled littered paper. His growing incapability for the task was evident. Benton pitied him - he had been overtaken by time, his very coat tails proclaimed another age. Benton looked into the tired face and expected to see jealous resentment but saw only relief.

As they left, Benton looked again at the high room with its tall columns, the long pipes of the two stoves. He saw coming down from the ceiling the thin pipes of the gas brackets, which branched in to green and white glass shades. In a strange way the place seemed sympathetic to him.

Back in Sir George's room, he was offered the post and at a salary that surprised him, though he managed to conceal it. It was two thirds more than he received as the school. He accepted and walked home more easy in his mind that he had been for some months. He had made his truce with Necessity.

It was only after a week had passed that Benton helped his mother one evening to wash up the supper things. During that week, Benton had been to Helme and told Aunt Christiana what he was about to do. He told his mother of the occasion and the old woman's wrath, which had soon waned. His mother listened intently, her conscience stirred.

"I am sorry that I was so harsh when you told us. I simply must learn that "Beggars can't be choosers." But, oh Benton, I had hoped for better things for all of us. We seem to be pulled down and down into the valley. I admire Christiana that she keeps her head so high."

"Do you think she really does, mother? I think she is a frightened old woman. She never moves from the farm - that is the only place she feels safe. She is remote from the changes of life. And don't forget, mother, we have one another and that is more important than what we have or what we do."

As he talked, he realised that he had forgotten to speak so intimately to her since his marriage. He remembered many occasions like this when he had been on vacation from King's. Then they had talked and talked and spun dreams of the future. It had made Mrs Woodhouse feel young and loved. She had missed it.

"Yes, we've got a grand little family and I'll always be proud of you all, whatever happens."

"Aye, and you'll have reason". This job won't be forever, you know. "No, not forever." Her heart lifted, her old ambitions glowed again and Benton left her happily shelling young peas for the next day.

In the parlour, Marianne sat at the piano. The candle sticks stood on the little ledge for them on the raised flap of the keyboard, the light from the candles wavered over the pleated silk behind them and over the music.

Her hands moved up and down like small friendly ghosts dancing. Benton sat and listened. Her music always made him think of London, it was Mozart which was rarely played here. He sat down by the fireplace, he looked at the waterfall of wood shavings silvered and gilded as they flowed stiffly and convolutedly in the grate.

All this was Marianne's world, it announced her everywhere he looked, the dried trembling grasses in the ruby vases, the roses in the cornucopia held in a hand, the Queen Anne mirror over the mantelpiece. It was all light and pleasant, far removed from the mills, even from his mother shelling peas.

She played some Handel for him and he began to hum and then to sing. They moved closer together and he leant over her shoulder. Then he lifted the music and chose some Mozart again. It was the *Marriage of Figaro* and soon it was Marianne who was singing, 'Fling aside all your airs your graces'. She laughed and said: "That is very, very right for me. Isn't it?" and she laughed adding, "It's taking me a long time to come down to earth."

"Don't ever come down too far, or I shan't have the same woman to love".

"And what would you do then?"

"Oh, very simple. Look for another."

She threw a cushion at him, he returned it and the bric-a-brac began to shiver in the room and they stopped. But they continued to play, collapsed like exhausted puppies on the sofa and, like all lovers holding hands, entered another world of dreams. They realised that their love was going to carry them though all disappointments.

When the day came for Benton to go to the Mill, he found the reality far from as oppressive as he had imagined. He even found it engrossing and the task of bringing order into a system that had depended entirely on Enoch Woods' memory was a fascinating challenge.

He spent weeks devising a new method of bookkeeping. He split the office so that the correspondence was no longer a minor branch of the accounting department. He was viewed at first with some uncooperative stubbornness and prophecies that this and that would not work.

But the system did work after a few initial spasms. The clerks found their work clearer, easier and much more defined. They had their own areas in which they could take a pride. They came to admire Benton and even more because he never aroused the hostility of old Enoch who was retiring only very gradually.

Benton's day had yet to come, however. He was looking at a copy of the *London Illustrated News* and his eye was caught by the pictures of New York. He saw typewriters and his own stubbornness resented these, but he saw that the bookkeeping was being done by men sitting at their work.

Since the first mills had been built, clerks had stood at their high desks. Benton began his hardest struggle, to convince the directors that men sitting would not be idle, but more efficient, because less tired.

After months, the carpenters were called in and the desks lowered and stools introduced. Once again, the simplest stool was made in the workshop with four legs all parallel. Benton decreed it useless immediately as it would fall over too easily.

Even Sir George thought Benton was being over-fastidious. So Benton agreed for two of them to be allowed in for a trial. As Benton remembered from his schooldays in the laboratory, a tall stool pushed only slightly topples and falls. Benton had the two stools put close to Sir George's inner office. Within a week he stormed out, "Can't you cease this clatter?"

"Yes, Sir George, easily if we had a stool with splayed legs."

"Then for God's sake go the carpentry shop and show them what you want."

The clerks were the first ones in the West Riding to sit at their work,

It not only made their work easier, but it enhanced their social status. They were grateful and Benton became, in a strange way, venerated.

At dinner time when the great bell clanged and the hands ran home, the clerks often gathered round the fire and ate sandwiches.

Here Benton enjoyed their company. In many ways it reminded him of student days at Kings. They talked of many things, football matches, boxing, religion and politics, and though less ably argued, he saw them in the same profundities and the same ignorance which had surprised him when he first went to London.

He had expected the student world to be one apart and almost omniscient. Sometimes, as he listened he thought that their ideas were lively and sparkling for the very reason that they had not been channelled into conventional means of expression.

There were often great roars of laughter as they scraped their stools on the stone floor and formed a circle around the stove. Often he would return home with a new bit of gossip, a new piece of slang. From them he heard for the first time that the Queen was referred to as Mrs Brown. He had been both amused and shocked.

Her fondness for John Brown, her attendant was well known. When he told Marianne, she was equally shocked and amused. She thought of the plump ill-dressed little woman, seen, it seemed now, an aeon ago. She thought the new title did not sit too uneasily on her dowdy shoulders.

Autumn became winter and Marianne became pregnant. She described it as 'with child'. There were already three Annie, William and Edith. They were all high-spirited and the girls were quicker and brighter than William.

The thought of a fourth did not alarm Marianne unduly. They were far less anxious than they had been, for Benton was so much better now that he did not have to strain his voice so much teaching. He had even done some singing again in the Choir. If Mrs Woodhouse was worried, then it was all transmuted into the constant search for fresh rich and sustaining food for them all.

As the weather clammed in and the steps were coated with rime and then the boughs of the trees, still more when the moss on the wall was hard and spiky, so they all watched, as the entire valley did for sore throats and a cough.

There was a certain restrained terror among all mothers for a hard, dry cough and a fever. February became March and no illness had struck and when the crocus bloomed they all began to look forward to the new baby.

In April, Sarah was born. She was the prettiest of all the babies and was, at once, the delight of them all. She seemed to have Annie's charm - her eyes were as big and blue, but even as a babe, her features seemed more regular, less blunt. She was put out in her cradle beneath the tree in the sunshine and Marianne smiled a little ruefully to herself when she recalled that she had not really wanted her. But now she was the best baby of them all.

In June, John Nash, Benton's oldest friend and best man came to stay. They went tramping on the moors and they talked, John talked most. He spoke unendingly of his church, his plans, his work. At first Benton had felt resentful, he thought it insensitive for had things transpired differently, he, too, might be talking like this.

His reorganisation of the office seemed paltry in contrast. With an effort, Benton became sympathetic, but as every topic led back to the same suburb of Leeds, he grew tired. He wished to listen to the larks that John apparently never heard.

He wished to point out the Lancastrian Hills from a high point, but the whereabouts of Leeds proved a much greater interest to him. He seemed unable to escape from his parish.

Benton began, for the first time, to be glad that he was not ordained if this was what happened to a man. He knew, however, that every clergyman is a world unto himself. But in Lamb's phrase he discovered an 'Imperfect Sympathy' and he kept his thoughts and plans of writing to himself.

One Sunday night, John preached at the Milsnbridge Church and both Benton and Marianne found another side to their friend - he had become a most powerful preacher. The congregation was rapt and Marianne was aware that Benton was proud of his friend, but she found it theatrical, there was an inner emptiness.

She looked at the successful man and knew that she loved Benton far more. She felt that a man so sure, so confident must have too simple a philosophy... it was too easy, too glib. Later in her parlour the friends began to sing and Marianne accompanied them.

Nash leant against the piano. Once again she felt his power, his bass voice made the ornaments tinkle and rattle. She discovered his dominance, he would not wait, he just would not wait, he continually forestalled her. She knew that she played well, her timing was accurate, but his desire for mastery was greater than his fidelity to the music. He saw the Mozart, *Don Giovanni*... "Play this for me", he said.

"No, I do not know it well enough, I am afraid."

Benton noted this. He had heard her play it perfectly the previous week.

Marianne distrusted him, beneath his humour, and even that had an edge, there was something not just strong but harsh. His voice boomed on in conversation and she felt distrust become dislike, razor width only, but razor sharp.

Next morning, Nash's last day, as the men joked and laughed at breakfast, Marianne thought that her feelings had been unworthy and as like boys they clattered out in walking boots with sticks, she regarded them fondly. "Men often never grow up", she said to Mrs

Woodhouse, who agreed profoundly.

The June sun climbed higher and higher, and the scent of growth was all around them. They found patches of thyme, pennyroyal. The vigour of the day charged them. At times they lay basking in the sun, then on again.

After a long climb they came to a tarn, a heron was startled and then flapped languidly away. For a moment Benton sat, then he tore off his tie, undid his shirt, pulled down his trousers and stood for a moment completely naked and, then, rushed to the water.

He dived in and rose with a gasp, it was icy, but he shouted an invitation. More cautiously, John joined him. The chill stung but refreshed and they swam and played like seals, then they lay on the grass to dry.

Benton watched little rivulets run down his chest, become a small river and run towards his navel. He felt very free and unexpectedly began to tell John of his book. He explained that his present life was only temporary, that he really wished to be a writer.

John referred to this calling as 'book-writing'. It indicated, Benton thought, clearly his unfavourable regard for the plan. Benton regretted his momentary confiding, for John missed entirely his friend's enthusiasm. Their interests were so different, the friendship unbalanced.

They still preserved an air of conviviality as they returned home. Benton knew that Nash no longer needed friends, or so he thought, he was only interested in disciples.

At supper they both looked sunburnt and Marianne thought how much brighter more open a face her husband had. Nash was handsome, vigorous, but there was much hidden, secret.

The holiday ended and Benton returned to the Mill and John walked to the station. Marianne saw them disappearing down the path. At the gate, Nash went through first, and again she felt dislike.

It lasted but a moment, for when she picked up Sarah and preceded to give the pink squirming babe her bath, her delights were in the present and her thoughts in the future.

Chapter 3

Benton's Illness

A few days after Nash's departure, Benton developed a sore throat. He became hoarse, it persisted and he became feverish. The sweating at night kept recurring, but gradually it eased off and Marianne and Mrs. Woodhouse were beginning to be relieved when they noticed his hard dry little cough.

They exchanged glances that Annie, now seven years old remembered well. She knew that something was wrong, but not what was wrong. Consumption was well known in these valleys, hardly a day passed without a victim being mentioned. It was a fear that they all lived with as the antelope lives with the lion. The hope is that another, not yourself, is pounced upon.

Benton too, was well aware and he hid his anxiety. Only on his lonely walks, which he made with increasing breathlessness, did he give way to his anger. One evening, Annie returned from Crosland Moor down a grove of sycamores, she saw a man approach, then she saw it was her father. He was pounding his right fist into his left palm and talking to himself.

He seemed more furious than she had ever seen him. At first she pretended not to be there, but then instinct warned her to call out to him. The fury dispersed like a mist, and a smile replaced it. It was the father she had always known and going along with him happily she almost forgot what she had seen.

There was so much Benton wished to do, there was, he said to himself, even more that he must do and already he knew that it was too late. He felt scourged by Fortune. At first and for many months he kept his illness secret.

It became a game of deceit, playing the fit man, and in so doing he often deceived himself. His mother was never fooled. She turned from her recipes to potions and made many nauseous mixtures, which he very obediently swallowed.

The hardest time of all was in the evening when he sat alone with Marianne in the parlour. Once it had been such a haven, peaceful, but it was no longer so secure. Illness had invaded and with it another spectre of Victorian life, poverty.

August, September, October passed fairly easily, November brought thick fog and he caught a cold. It aggravated his cough and for the first time there were specks of pink in his phlegm. His brow, always clear, seemed transparent, his cheeks were often flushed. In the morning he invariably had another bout of coughing.

As Marianne saw the disease encroach she slowly relinquished some of her outside tasks. Reading to the sewing class was the first to go. She found it much harder to give up her visiting and Christmas was coming and her visits were anticipated.

Annie and Willy had got out the box of Christmas decorations for the tree. They were squabbling over the baubles and the glass chains. They only united when Edith wished to join them. As they quarrelled, their father entered and he testily told them to keep quiet. He dropped his hat and gloves and then himself into a chair.

The children stood and stared. He was so pale with a wild harassed look in his eyes. He had been worried for a fortnight and felt unable to cope any longer. He had an overwhelming desire for rest and quiet.

His mother, without speaking, pushed the kettle on its hook over the fire. Benton saw and a wan smile of gratitude crossed his mouth. After some tea he revived, climbed the stairs and undressed as if in a dream, too ill to be quick, yet not tarrying for fear of fainting.

At last the mattress greeted him. He felt the warmth of the hard brick, but it was softness of the featherbed that enfolded him. He was buoyed up by comfort and he wondered if this was how a ship would feel, if it could feel, when water is let into the dry dock and it floats once more.

Such contentment swept over him that he was soon fast asleep. Then Marianne saw him. She had been putting Sarah to bed, and saw him at peace. The terror had gone, the near helplessness, only his mother had seen the truth and she kept her counsel.

Benton soon responded. His coughing lessened and on Christmas Day he was bright and happy and waved them all goodbye as they went to church telling them that he and Cordelia would have everything ready for dinner when they returned.

Annie and Willy walked together. They were like twins, the same height, the same build, they skipped together. Edith held tight to her mother's hand - she was a thinner, plainer child, lacking the confidence the other two had in such abundance.

During the service, Marianne prayed hard that soon Benton would be restored to health, but it seemed a forlorn hope, yet she was not depressed, more disquieted.

At the door afterwards she was heartened by the many enquiries about Benton and they all returned cheered by good wishes and the children by silver sixpences. In the house, Marianne recounted the good wishes of, the Entwhistles, Sir George and Lady Armytage, little Miss Brown, the vicar, of course, everyone.

The children watched as their mother, her bonnet strings undone, put her arms around Benton. She looked young and charming, but to Annie not adequate.

"Mother hasn't told you that Lady Armytage wore a new dress, a new black silk one with seven flounces."

"How do you know there were seven?"

Annie raised her head haughtily, "I counted them."

"Oh, so we have a modiste in our midst."

"What's a modiste?"

"Another name for a dressmaker, my dear."

"Why don't you wear black?'

"I will when I am old, not yet".

"I shall wear nothing else but black once I am 30."

"Do you think I ought to wear black and be respectable, Benton?"

"Well, it would suit you... you'd look more Spanish than ever. Very mysterious!"

Benton joined them all at dinner. They noticed how thin his hands were as he carved the goose, then they saw that his starched collar was too large. Yet his face remained the same.

When darkness came, the church choir arrived. They grouped themselves by the door of the parlour and Benton, a rug across his knees, sat by the fire. They sang carols, they all joined in and a look of great happiness crossed his face.

Annie nestled against his feet on the hearthrug. But he grew tired. Marianne saw it, the shadows about his eyes darkened. She gave them beer and cake, but they were slow to depart, another joke, another story. Caped, capped and hatted they still lingered, but at last they went and Marianne strode back anxious.

"I thought they would never go. You must be tired."

"Kind, dear people" was all that he said.

"Well they may be, but they should know when to go. Now, it really is time for bed."

"I will know when it is time for me to go and it won't be until I have heard some Mozart."

The Magic Flute filled the room. It lifted them to a world of order and happiness and they both clutched at it more than ever before.

When she had finished she came over to Benton. The 18th century sprightliness lingered on. It had been a happy day, happier than she had dared to hope. She glowed not because of the music, but because of the affection shown to Benton.

"Soon, very soon, I shall be better and a new life will begin."

"Yes, yes, but bed first."

The early part of 1870 was not cold but rainy and gloomy. Benton was often able to get out and spend a day at the office, and as he felt so comparatively well, he had work sent up to him on other days.

Annie and William were used to seeing Sir George's carriage waiting by the bridge when they came home from school on Fridays. This pleased them for he always had sixpences for them.

In February there was a bitter east wind. It was furious and it was persistent, it cut, it found the cracks and holes in buildings and the weaknesses of men... it blew with a killing monotony. Annie and her brother were well wrapped each morning before being sent out to school and William had two baked potatoes in his pockets to warm his hands and Annie one in her gloves. In spite of a good breakfast of porridge followed by bacon, the potato was always eaten before they reached school. The house was ablaze with fires, which Cordelia stoked all day.

The baby so bonny and thriving one day laboured for breath and, to their astonishment, strove no more. They could not believe it. Benton blamed himself and his illness and Marianne was overthrown with grief.

She, too, wondered whether she had neglected her. Benton insisted on attending the funeral and he would not heed Marianne's pleas, nor his mother's, so the doctor and Sir George Armitage were called in to control him.

It was a tiny ceremony. Uncle Alan supported Marianne and her much-loved new cousins Lydia and Polly. The wind still blew and the earliest of the snowdrops were blasted by the wind. Marianne likened them to her small child. She felt that even in this funeral not enough attention was given her. She had spent a life when they all had been preoccupied by Benton's illness.

When Benton was in bed the grieving mothers sat by the fire alone. Still she seemed to hear Sarah whimper, or cry, and in the night, she often found herself sitting on the edge of the bed ready to go to her. Then the agonising truth would dawn again. Too late, too late.

It was while sitting alone she had her first great intimation of fear. She was afraid, desperately afraid of the future. She felt inadequate; she was sure that in her years of marriage she had become dependent and less mature. She was certain that this little death, which to her was not small, was only a presage. She began to panic; her thoughts fluttered like bats in a cave.

She jumped up and was determined to cast her thoughts in another direction. She went to the piano and very softly began to play some of the *Marriage of Figaro*. She saw the photos of Benton and herself on the little table and she asked herself, "Why, oh why, did you never have Sarah's photo taken? She answered herself that there had never been time....

Anyway, she did not have photos of any of the children. It led back to the awful guilt-implying question: "Did I neglect her?"

Spring in the valley always surprised her - it was precipitate and dramatic. Benton was better, his wretched morning cough lessened considerably, they all rejoiced and, it seemed, that a weight had lifted from the household.

Easter did seem a resurrection to them that year and when Marianne hung out the washing she began to laugh at her winter fears. The grey-green tips of the apple tree announcing the assumption of festive pink made a surge in her heart.

She noticed that the birds were nesting and it was then that she recalled Sarah's cradle under that very tree and a sharp pang came to her. But she had seen in Milnsbridge so many children die and she argued within herself better, perhaps, Sarah's death, than Benton's.

Benton not only managed his work, but also began outlining

some stories. He began looking to the future. Sir George saw an improvement and he with the doctor decided that a holiday by the sea would be very beneficial. At first they thought that Scarborough would be a good place for him, but then friends decreed that it was too bracing. So they decided upon Southport.

Though only Benton and Marianne were to go, the family eagerly looked forward to it because it was to make their father better. The children were excited as they saw their parents off to the station in the cab. It was on Huddersfield station that Marianne became frightened. The jolting of the cab, the swirl of smoke from the engine caused him an alarming fit of coughing.

When they were in the carriage, Benton fell fast asleep in the corner. Marianne watched him - she saw that he was thinner, but not emaciated, but she was afraid and prayed that he would live to breathe in the good air at the seaside.

As he slept his colour returned. At Southport some of his vigour seemed to return and he gave instructions to the porter. He proffered and kept the tickets, but in the cab he collapsed again. Within 10 minutes they were at the boarding house. Marianne looked at the flight of steps up to the front door. She lowered the window and called to the cab to drive the length of the front and back again.

"Thank you, Marianne."

She saw a movement at the window and realised that the landlady had seen them, so she called to the cabby again, got out, and while he got down the small trunk, she went into the house. She explained to the landlady that they would return very soon and asked for Benton's bed to be warmed.

Then sitting close together they drove slowly along the promenade. Many of the shops were still winter shuttered, the streets bare and empty like husks, and it seemed only half lived in. The tide was out and as the sun lowered in the sky it was all golden, orange and pink, laced with bright porcelain blue and it was all mirrored in a subtly different shade in the ribbed sandy pools. They both saw it and loved it. Benton pressed Marianne's hand.

"That makes one feel better. Why, life looks better."

Back at the house, Benton paid off the cabby, walked unaided up the steps and greeted the landlady. Marianne felt so such relief, but it was instantly dispelled by the look on Mrs Bury's face.

Beneath professional welcome and imperturbability, Marianne saw the look of shock at the sight of her visitor. The climb up to their rooms exhausted Benton and he accepted Marianne's help.

It was the room they had had before, overlooking the sea. The landlady's explanations bored them, but, at last, she went and hurriedly Benton undressed, put on his nightshirt and thankfully sank into the bed.

He looked at Marianne as she tidied away the clothes. "I am afraid this won't be as happy a holiday as last time."

"Of course it will. It is just the journey that has tired you".

Downstairs in the fussy, yet still impersonal drawing room, Marianne wondered about the future. It was in that alien room that it came to her that Benton would not live very long. A vague fear now became a future fact to be encountered.

She wondered how she would manage financially when Benton had gone. She was alarmed about the children. She wanted the best of educations for both William and Annie. Then there was dear little Edith and Mrs Woodhouse. How would she manage to keep them all?

She heard the rattle of teacups. Mrs Bury came in and put down a tea tray and sat herself by the fire.

"l am very sorry to see Mr. Taylor so poorly", she remarked, "He was so well set up when last I saw him."

"He has been rather unwell this winter. But we hope that your good air in Southport will put him right".

"So do l, Mrs Taylor, so do I". There was a negative knell in each syllable. For a moment, Marianne wondered if they were to be asked to leave. Hotels, like Versailles, she thought, do not like death. Another question followed,

"Have you experienced much of illness and death?"

Marianne was angered at the insensitive impertinence.

"Yes, Mrs Bury. I lost a most beautiful baby, very suddenly this winter. And will you please put two lumps of sugar in that cup and I will take it to my husband."

The hint was taken and when Marianne returned, the landlady made sprightly but aimless conservation.

After supper and a lonely evening, Marianne crept quietly upstairs. It was so still she was almost afraid. In the candlelight she saw his brown eyes open and a great smile greeted her.

Panic consumed her, how could she live without him?

For a minute she forgot her children, everyone, she only wanted him and alive and well. She knew that she loved him more than anyone, anything else.

Outwardly, though she gave him a kiss and he put his arms slowly around her.

Next morning, Marianne woke with the dawn and waited, as she always waited, for the sound of Benton's cough. Every morning it continued for at least a quarter of an hour. It seemed by its duration she could gauge Benton's vitality for the day.

If extended by a few minutes then he was exhausted for a long time. If short, then he was livelier. She awaited it with apprehension. It was short. He had slept well and he looked bright. He dressed, he went down for breakfast, but then he had to rest.

They had planned a walk in the morning. They delayed it until late in the afternoon.

They walked slowly along the promenade and came to the shops. They were both fascinated and had forgotten that such elegant trifles existed. They looked at china, leatherwear and papier-mâché. Some dresses and bonnets entranced Marianne, but she was keeping a tight watch on Benton and when they came to a teashop they went in.

While they sat there, she wondered whether the children were home from school. She hoped that they were not playing up Grandma... they did sometimes, especially Annie and William. Benton asked her what her thoughts were and as he had guessed correctly they talked immediately of them. Benton still wished for William to go away to school, but it was of Annie that he spoke with the special tenderness she long recognised in him.

He adored the lively child, who was, as he put it 'framing' so well at home and at school. Marianne forbade herself any preferences. Soon it was time for them to make their leisurely way back.

When they were inside the house, Benton sat by the fire and recovered his breath. The late post arrived and to their surprise there was a letter from Annie. It was the first letter they received from any of their children.

Benton scrutinised its carefully ruled and spelt lines. He kept turning it over in his hand. To Marianne's horror, he reminded her not of a father but a grandfather. He kept returning to it in the evening forever saying, "It is good, who would ever think it was from a child of seven?" He wished to reply, but was already too wearied.

In the morning he wrote on paper with a thin black edge, mourning for their dead child, Annie's first letter. He wrote it slowly in the most formal of copperplate:

"My darling child,

It is my wish to write to you, for the very beautiful letter I received, one in return that you can read by yourself. I was very much pleased with your letter and if you go on improving, as I trust you will, you will prove a credit to your kind teacher Miss Robinson.

We shall have to tell you of a great many pretty things, which we have seen when we come home. Perhaps, sometime, you and Willy and dear little Edith can all come to the seaside together with Father and Mother and Grandma. Wouldn't there be a lot of us?

I am sorry Willie's holiday was not as long as yours, but hope he enjoyed what he had and know what a good boy he is for going to school.

And now, my dear Annie, I must draw my letter to a close. I am much better today tell Grandma. I am sure this will be good news for you all.

Mother sends her love and kisses for each and all and I do the same.

I am, my dear Annie Elizabeth, ever your loving Father,
Benton Taylor."

He lay down his pen and read the letter. He thought it formal, even dutiful. It was not how he felt at all. He was throbbing with love and devotion and great sorrow. He knew, too, that he was about to leave them. How could he say farewell to such a child, how could he prepare her for the dreaded eventuality? Quickly he sealed the letter and stamped it before he thought better of it and as he saw the sun rising from a low cloud, he walked to the letterbox with it, quite alone.

The following days were warm and bright and they walked further, even with a semblance of vigour, and they looked pityingly on the figures trundled along in the hooded bath chairs.

They both dreaded the journey home, but, it was true, the air had made his lungs easier.

The journey back was tolerated more easily and there were great rejoicings in Whitley Bottom, on their return. Marianne, however, felt the heavy hand of fatality as soon as she put her foot in the house. She reasoned with herself, but the inevitability remained.

She looked out of the window at the steep hills, the steep sloping roofs, she felt hemmed in, crushed. An anger seized her. The place, this awful place, was killing them all. The bedroom seemed stuffy, she wanted to throw open the window, but remembered the doctor's words that nothing was worse for Benton than cold air.

Yet logic told her that he had been better by the sea, but she obeyed the rules even if she did not agree. Immediately, his coughing increased, not with the old force but with a new insistence. The doctor said little. He never spoke of death, he had no need to. He saw it in their eyes. Benton asked for a solicitor to come.

Marianne watched neat, spruce, little Mr Hillyard come up the path, avoiding the puddles with great delicacy. His precision amused her fortunately, for she dreaded his errand. She led him upstairs, she wished to leave but Benton asked her to stay and she sat at the end of the bed.

To her great surprise, Benton drew from beneath his pillow a will. His assets were small, but his chattels numerous. The list of bequests was detailed and to John Nash went all his theological books. There were instructions too, for the education of the children.

Mr Hillyard was gladdened by such precision and the will was witnessed by their neighbour Jonah Cliff and Cordelia.

Benton rested now that this done. His breathlessness was more frequent and he tired much more easily. There was, though, a special time of day for him. It was when Annie brought up his tea tray. She climbed on to the bed beside him and would tell him of her day. Miss Robinson figured largely in these conversations and Benton was always told exactly what she wore.

Her opening mind thrilled him. It was unfolding and seeking and grasping, so easily, so many things. She loved these times with him... sometimes she was very quiet, for she saw him suddenly sleep. She was ever to know what he looked like. She knew the shape of his brow, the set of his eyes and the exact angle of his nose. It was all imprinted on her mind for evermore.

She even knew that he would die, but this seemed natural although she did not entirely grasp its meaning.

Marianne did know, she did understand. One morning after washing his limp body she thought of Christ and Mary Magdalene going to the tomb to anoint the body. Her thought was that she had done this before his death and she gulped back her horror at this realisation.

She finished her task of emptying bowls, straightening bedclothes and bottles. Before going down she bent to kiss him... his beard tickled her where once it had scraped. She went carefully down the stairs, crossed the kitchen wordless, she emptied the pail in the yard, re-entered the scullery, closed the door, then the door to the hall, sank to the settle and lifted her apron to her face and began to weep.

It was a controlled outburst of a defined hysteria, and she heaved with sorrow. Cordelia, peeling potatoes, wept too, but Mrs Woodhouse continued kneading dough. She had seen so many deaths, but none so terrible to her as this, but she knew that nothing adequate could be said.

She knew that emotion must have its play. She let the sobs rise and fall and only as her task was fulfilled and the sobs began to subside did she dust her hands, wash them, dry them, and then sit by this girl, put an arm around her and grieve outwardly with her.

Death has a fascination of its own. There is a Death dream and a Death reality, they are alike, but a strange vale parts them. Perhaps it is true that the true death, the real death we cannot and will not encounter, there is too great a fear. Yet the fear lures.

Marianne walked numbly in the shadow of her husband's death, too tired to be defiant, but not too tired to feel. She had feared the future... this she did no longer, time was only present time, the world this bedroom. This room seemed overtaken by another power, the very impedimenta of illness made it no longer their own.

Only Edith chattered and ran from garden to yard to kitchen, she remained untouched. Annie and Willy felt the strangeness overtaking their lives. Benton was now only exhausted, no longer in pain. This was caused by his illness and the laudanum prescribed. He had, though, strange disturbing dreams, his past rose up, old situations were relived, old enemies, and old friends seemed to re-appear.

It worked through a cycle that seemed always to end with happiness with Marianne in Helme. Then he would awake and gasp with relief that Marianne was there with her Holbein face.

She was always with him. Others watched for short periods, but when he woke he always asked for her. Then, he seemingly got better, sat up in bed, and he washed himself in the basin held before him. He asked for the window to be opened wide and he declared he could smell the moor.

This lasted two days and at night he slept so peacefully no watch was kept and Marianne once more slept by his side. During the second night he called out. She was awake instantly, he smiled, it was dawn.

"I'm better. I can feel it, I really can".

Was it a miracle? Marianne said and felt nothing. She gave him a drink and fell asleep. At seven she rose… he was still. She crept downstairs to make tea. Taking it up to him, she stooped to look. For a moment she failed to recognise his face. She bent closer and then fled with horror to Grandma's room.

"'Mother, mother, he's gone, he's gone".

Mrs Woodhouse flung back the bedclothes and turned Marianne into her warm bed.

"Stay there."

Swiftly the elderly woman crossed the landing, went in to her son, unflinchingly removed the pillows, straightened his limbs, thanked God that his eyes were shut… and went out.

Chapter 4

Wakefield

The black gloves on the hall table supplied by the undertaker were not seen by Marianne, for on the day of the funeral she shut herself up in the bedroom. Sometimes, she tried to pray, but it seemed that her faith had died with Benton.

She felt numb, yet she argued that if she were numb why did she manage to feel such utter despair? She had hardly spoken since her husband's death and the children, for the first time in their lives, feared her, she was a stranger in a black dress.

Their grandmother they recognised more easily. She had always been stiff, her sadness stifled in harder work and more trenchant remarks. She set about the funeral feast with a fearsome determination.

When the mourners, nearly all men, returned to the women in the house, a new atmosphere came with them. They were relieved they had attended… the final duty to a friend was done. The women had experienced no such catharsis.

The hush slowly lifted. They were all surprised at the absence of Marianne, and it showed itself in concern for her, but with some there was a slight resentment. As they ate and drank so the whispered conversation grew in volume and a subdued chuckle became a laugh.

They were experiencing the joy of being alive that follows the burial of those distant, but never to those who are close.

Marianne upstairs heard the gathering sound. At first, she was surprised, then amazed and lastly angered. She pushed herself up from the pillows where she lay face down. In her fury she beat the pillows with her fists saying: "How can they? How can they?"

Then resolute she stood. She smoothed her hair and descended the stairs very tense and pale… there was even some malice in her intent. She wished to make a scene, to reprimand. But when some of the choir friends saw her as they stood in the hall, they fell silent and then Lydia moved forward and put her arm around Marianne's neck.

They were, she had forgotten, all Benton's friends. She was enclosed in a warm circle of sympathy - she just managed not to weep.

When they had all gone, the three women, Marianne, Grandma and Cordelia sat around the kitchen table. At first they were silent, then very gradually they began to talk of the guests, but not as after an ordinary gathering, where criticism of behaviour and dress often is the main topic.

No, they spoke of each person and of their relationship to Benton. The children were playing on the floor, and Marianne watched Annie as she supervised the other two in a game of her devising. Annie leant forward and brushed aside the hair at the nape of the child's neck and so exposed a fair white column of a strange beauty, a well-fashioned neck carrying an appealing but not beautiful face. Marianne saw very clearly the shadow under which the children had lived:

"You know Grandma, I think we all ought to go away. We all need a change."

They went to Blackpool and Sir George Armitage so approved of the trip that he paid for it entirely. On the sands the children, all in deepest black, built their castles. The two women, their chairs close, together talked.

With sad faces they made plans. They envisaged a small cottage in a village not far from Huddersfield, where there was a good school. As they looked to the future they even smiled and forecasting brought some light to their eyes.

In fact, they were so much lighter of heart that seeing a photographer's studio Marianne had the children and Grandma's photo taken. Annie remembered the occasion the rest of her life. She was frightened and her suspicion made her sullen and haughty. Afterwards, they bought more black material for dresses.

Back at Whitely Bottom, they found a pile of letters and bills. The house depressed Marianne and her unhappiness was magnified appallingly when she discovered that they were almost destitute. Her tiny annuity was the sole bulwark against penury.

She was frightened and horror seized when she considered the children. The working children had always appalled her; her own seemed so perilously close. She knew that she must find work, but what work?

She could not be a mill hand and with her family she could not be a governess. It was Uncle Alan who had the answer. They must move to Wakefield. It was a growing city, not far away; it had hospitals, offices as well as industry. There they would find schools and work for Marianne.

Uncle Alan took her there and they looked at a number of houses to let. They found one, a narrow house with the front door right on the street.

Marianne hated it. She hated it so much and considered it so unworthy of her family that she made a strange decision. She had received an offer from John Nash to bring up Annie with his own children.

At first Marianne had dismissed the proposal without thought. As she looked at Plumpton Street its meanness seemed to rear and become a living element. The thought came, perhaps she could spare Annie this, and perhaps life with the Nashes would be better. She even reasoned with herself that if she parted with Annie then William and Edith would have a better chance.

As she tucked Annie up she tentatively put the plan before her. She emphasised the superior house, the children to play with.

"But I have William and Edith here."

"Yes, dear, but things are going to be very difficult, we are terribly poor, now."

"Well, if it will help, I could go for a little while."

"Yes, yes. That is a good idea."

Had Annie been more experienced she might have recognised the panic in the "Yes, yes". As it was, Marianne went downstairs with a heart heavier than since Benton's death. She meant Annie to have a new life, a new start and she would, she thought, grow detached from us all. She tried to write to Mr Nash but the correct words failed her all the while.

Instead, she remembered him singing in this very room and she recalled her memory of his confidence, his dark good looks and something she could not analyse, but she called it vulgarity. It was at that thought that she rose and closed her desk and joined Grandma in the kitchen.

The old lady was ripping up old sheets and then systematically removing each thread. Marianne joined her.

They were making wadding, which they called lint, for the Red

Cross for the wounded in the Franco-Prussian War.

"Have you written to Mr. Nash, my dear?"

"No. I tried, but the words did not come. I asked Annie and she said she would go but rather stay".

"I think you should keep her, she's very much your child."

"That is why I want to give her a chance to grow up to be a lady."

"She will do that anyway. She's got Benton's blood you know".

"But how shall we manage? I just don't know. Don't know".

In silence they went on picking the threads. The siege of Paris seemed a very long way removed. Their own siege took all precedence in their thoughts.

Days of strain followed. The tension broke a little when, at tea time, Marianne told them that they were to move to Wakefield the next week. It was then revealed that Mr. Nash would be coming for Annie on Saturday.

None of them of them wished to leave the house, but the uncertainty of their future had gone and that had tried them all.

When Annie's last evening with them came, Marianne hardly dared tuck her up in case she betrayed herself. She had few special words... she usually lingered with each in turn. She passed a sleepless night and seemed just asleep, when her body felt the seemingly damp cold of Annie's feet. In the half sleep they cuddled one another and also wept,

Early in the afternoon, John Nash arrived alone. This displeased Marianne... she had never met his wife. He went to great lengths to be pleasing but still Marianne felt her old distrust. When he asked to see her alone she was irritated - had he imagined that she would see him off without a private word? She led the way to the parlour, but the fear of doubt, the heavy press of responsibilities and the overwhelming desire to do what was best for all, was vanquishing her spirit. She gave the lead in the interview to him.

"My wife and I have considered everything very carefully in respect to both Annie and our own dear children."

The "dear children" grated ominously on Marianne.

"What, then, is it you require, Mr Nash?"

"We have concluded that if we are to bring up Annie properly as we wish, and, of course, as you also do, then contact must cease between you both".

He saw horror, she was aghast. She was encircled, she was trapped.

"I know that it sounds harsh, but it is the kindest thing. Come now, you know how quickly children forget".

"Annie will not. Annie's affections, like her fathers are very strong".

"Mrs Taylor, I know children".

You may know children, but you do not yet know Annie".

A flush was rising on her pale cheek.

"Perhaps you do not wish us to offer Annie a home?

"I have no choice, Mr Nash, as well you know. I am grateful. But under no circumstances shall I lose contact. I shall write and I shall expect a reply from you. And your wife, and Annie... at least once a quarter.

She felt traitorous and whisked from the room so swiftly that the lustre's jangled. Nash mused on the lack of reason in women. He thought Marianne too emotional and then he remembered her Welsh background that seemed an adequate explanation to his superficial musings.

Annie was in the kitchen. Grandma was telling her what a fine time she would have in Bradford. Annie looked with wide, round eyes that were full of the questions she never uttered. Marianne tied the black be-ribboned hat on... the child was quite wooden, she made no protest, but looked resentful. Marianne's heart was cleaving.

"Now darling, do all that they tell you. Be a credit to Grandma and me. We shall think of you and pray for you all the time." She could say no more and she hugged the stiff little figure. Annie relented a little and all Marianne's love for Benton seemed in her arms, this child was all their first love, the courtship, the wedding, the moors. This child was his warmth, his passion, and his tenderness. But more than that, she was her own small personable self.

They watched her go down the path with Mr Nash. He held her hand very firmly. Only once did she look back. Marianne flew up to her bedroom and wept. For all this seemed another death.

John Nash on the train marvelled at the precise, good child. She sat very quiet and still answering his questions with a 'yes' or 'no'. Her hands were folded neatly on her lap.

It was John Nash's custom to engage his fellow travellers in conversation for there might be souls to be saved. Annie became aware of earnest words flying above her... salvation, redemption and election were some of them. It was a mighty flow, which seemed, only seemed unstoppable. It was, in fact, curtailed by another flow, sickness from Annie.

It was an attack, which had not taken her entirely unawares. It left her jacket and dress untouched but not so Mr Nash's trousers. Nothing had been entirely unpremeditated.

The light fell in through an oblong pane of glass above the door, revealing to disadvantage the narrow confines of the hall. Two doors at right angles, so saving the speculative builder money on door mouldings, led to a small parlour a slightly larger living room behind and the kitchen beyond. It was all Marianne had remembered when she first saw it with Uncle Alan - on a second viewing she disliked it still more.

With a great will she, with her mother-in-law, showed the men where to place the furniture and they began transforming it into a home. There were too many belongings. The children soon tired of the place, there was no real garden, only a yard, and because they were bored, they got in the way of their elders.

Marianne had to find work. She began by doing some nursing, as a companion to an old lady. It was irregular and very poorly paid but it just kept them together with her own small income and the remnants of the savings once the many bills had been paid.

Then, one day, the doctor of one of her patients asked her if she had considered applying to the Stanley Royd Hospital. They needed staff and he would give her a reference. She wondered about this - she had a fear of madness, which she would have to conquer, but a week without any work made her apply. By return of post she was asked to attend an interview.

She dressed most carefully, brushing and brushing her hair to remove the wave. Neat and trim she walked through the town and out to the boundaries. She made her way towards a handsome cupola, which rose elegantly over the trees.

She had expected walls of great height around a lunatic asylum and a great gate, but she found railings and an iron gate open. She was directed to the Matron's office and in a corridor waited with several other women sitting on a bench.

At length 'Taylor' was called and she entered. Immediately she felt a reaction to her presence from the Matron, a doctor and a secretary who sat at a table. Marianne instinctively looked for a chair but there was nowhere to sit. Standing she answered their questions. To both her relief and alarm she was told, somewhat curtly, to apply for duty at 6 a.m. on Monday with the words "Uniform will be provided" closing the encounter.

She walked away swiftly. She did not like the idea of working there. She felt humiliated by the interview, it stung very hard that she had not been asked to sit and had been addressed by her surname alone. Fortunately, the sun shone and a light wind rustled the air.

"It will do. It will do, at least for the time being." But to herself she added that life was very terrible. But she thought of Annie and gave thanks that she was spared this awful privation. She came to some shops and with the knowledge that she was, now, a steady weekly wage earner she allowed herself the indulgence of looking at them.

She did not linger. First of all she was not happy enough to even wish to buy, second there was no money to spare. At the corner, near Plumpton Street, she saw a bakery and in the window there were some Gingerbread Men.

The sight of this gay little band brought a smile to her face and she went in and bought one for each of the children. When she reached home they were just about to sit down for tea. Catching up a plate from the dresser, she placed it on the table and emptied her bag on it. There were squeals of delight.

"One for each."

Then she looked. There were three, and for a moment, she had forgotten that Annie was no longer there.

In Bradford Annie went into the dining room with the two children. They stood behind their chairs awaiting both their elders and grace. Mrs Nash came in first followed by her husband. He offered up a prayer so loud that Annie wondered if the Almighty was in the room above and one had to make sure that he heard. They all sat.

As the bread and butter plate came round Annie, by chance, got the crust. For a moment she hovered, she had just lost her front teeth. Her hesitation was seen.

"Really, child, what bad manners you have," said Mrs. Nash.

"Always take the bread, or cake nearest to you," her nostrils pinched, her voice fluted.

Annie was overcome with confusion. She wished to defend herself... it was unfair, because usually she liked the crust. She remained quiet and opened her round eyes to an even greater innocent circumference.

Mr Nash looked down the table. He was not a harsh man, but he had grown insensitive. He felt, as a Minister of God, that it was imperative, upon him to comment upon any misdemeanour and reprove it. A homily on morals fell easily from his lips. As he talked two tears ran down Annie's cheeks... he was glad that her guilt had been quickened. They were tears not of penitence but of misery. She heard him say,

"One might wonder whether your poor brother and sister are, at this moment, enjoying such good food?"

Until then Annie had never thought that their lot was not infinitely better than her own.

"I am sorry," she murmured, but she knew she was not. She was learning the art of dissembling.

Afterwards in the nursery Harriet asked: "Is your family so very poor?"

Annie looked at the girl and her brother George. They had dull faces. "Poor? Why we have so much food we throw it away, barrels of it."

"But if you are so poor?"

"But we are not. Your father brought me here because I ate too much."

So began for Annie a new role, the storyteller, and her inventive power, she discovered brought with it another power as well.

Marianne wore a black uniform and a chain with a bunch of keys and a whistle at her waist. Her patients filled her quietly with alarm and pity and frequently with frustration. The event she lived for was the day off she spent with the family in the little house, which seemed smaller every time she returned.

When away she wondered about the children, she wondered even more about Mrs. Woodhouse, who began to look worn beneath the outward starch of her countenance. Life was a burden on them all.

When Marianne hugged William she often wished that he were

Annie, for she responded well to loving. William, though the loved one, wanted to be off to play. Edith, she reflected ruefully, was entirely her mother-in-law's child. They were forever together, and though she was only four, she knew the elements of cooking.

Grandma and Edith managed the kitchen and Marianne, when she thought of the meal awaiting her, anticipated it eagerly. At first she had quailed at the thought of the cost, but she had learnt that Grandma was adept at disguising economy.

Since Benton's death there had been a change in the relationship between Marianne and her mother-in-law. Marianne had become a daughter, and though the breadwinner, she was aware that Grandma was the lynchpin of their independence.

On the Sundays when she was free, Marianne walked with the two children to the Parish Church. As they walked past the seemingly blind houses, she was well aware of the prying eyes that deemed that she 'gave herself airs'.

To go to the big church was regarded presumptuous and added to that was the stigma to Marianne's working at the Asylum. Since she had gone there, neighbours had become cool, and the children were shunned.

It did not worry her for she was away, but she grieved for Grandma and for the little ones. She felt that she was being pushed into an ever-narrower world, their dark mean house the only refuge and she did not love that either.

Whenever, she entered the different dimness of the church and saw the pillars sweep up to the roof then she felt her heart grow lighter. She joined very gladly in the hymns, often found strength in the sermons and often some of the old joy would shine in her again.

The Vicar noted the young widow with two children and wondered who they were. Young widows were by no means unique then, however. It was William who began talking of Annie as they walked home and they began to paint a cheerful picture of her return from church.

It was a very long way from the chapel in the town centre to the suburban house where the Nashes lived. It seemed still longer when you were frightened. Annie wished for cover, she longed to be beneath a roof sheltered from the wrath of God.

That morning she had learnt much of Hell and it frightened her. She knew very well that she was often naughty, sometimes she did not know why... what was inevitable was that she would be punished for it.

Dinner on Sundays consisted of cold meat and even cold potatoes - nobody looked forward to it. Even worse was the afternoon, an arid desert of vacant boredom. The children were not allowed in the schoolroom, their toys were there, so they remained in the dining room.

The blind was half drawn and the only books were a large Bible, but not illustrated, together with two pious books, *The Children of Claverly* and *Jessica's First Prayer*. They knew every word of these two books. George and Harriet hated the imprisonment of the Sunday afternoon and Annie, to whom it was new, loathed it even more.

Mrs Nash in the drawing room musingly regarded the leaping bronze horses on the mantelpiece. They were most inadequately reined, plunged and reared, not unlike her flatulence. Her book slipped and she found herself thinking of some vases she had seen which she would prefer to the horses. But she wondered if John, her husband, would agree.

She then thought of the sacrifices she had to make in accordance with his ideals and wishes and thought that his sacrifices on her behalf were very few. This led her to think of Annie. She was not an unkind woman, but she did resent the child.

Often she saw not the child but the dramatic gesture of her husband in offering her a home. These were, she thought, easily made by him, but it was the household, and she in particular, who had to tolerate them.

Annie was not the first 'lame duck'. She, also, feared for her own, for they were not as spirited as Annie and she resented that, in company, it was Annie who was noticed for her looks, not Harriet. She rose up and decided to go to her room and take some medicine. As she crossed the hall she paused at the dining room door. There was hardly a sound; no rustling page, but the steady histrionic reading of a story. Was it from the Testament?

"So there they were on the stricken ship, the captain, two men and a cabin-boy, the boats had all gone. They were doomed. They prayed for a lifeboat, but the people on shore were afraid to put to sea. Suddenly, from the crowd, a girl ran forward.

"I will go", she cried.

"There was a cheer and quickly I ran down the slippery steps, jumped into the boat, seized the oars and tugged with all my might. I turned into the waves and rode over the crest. There was another cheer from the crowd. I almost overturned, but on I went, hearing only the stricken cries of the drowning men."

Mrs Nash threw open the door, her eyes glinted, her anger included them all, but it was chiefly directed at Annie, for she was ashamed that her children should believe this nonsense. Annie was lost in the telling of the tale and she suddenly felt a sharp stinging slap on her bare neck and shoulder which she was never to forget and a voice shouting 'Liar'.

For minutes Annie was lost in a red blaze of anger, a fierce hatred, much tugging, a recollection of stair carpets, banisters and the indignant shimmer of black heavy silk. Silence after the turn of the key in the door. Never had Annie longed for her mother quite so intensely.

When she roused herself from her misery and crying, she became aware of the familiar sounds of the house. She knew by footfalls, creaks and the opening and shutting of doors exactly what everyone was doing. They were getting ready for church. She awaited someone coming up for her, nobody came. She heard the front door bang. She was evidently too wicked to go to church.

Her imagination bounded, what if they never returned? Would she starve to death? Should they not return and she was found, would she be sent to the workhouse?

The silence was intense and when most profound she heard a noise in the hall and again the rustle of silk. It was Mrs Nash. She jumped off the bed and beat on the door and shouted: "You can't come in. You can't come in!"

The key turned and the door opened slowly. Annie stood by the bed... it was Cook, not in her usual print dress but her best Sunday silk. She carried a bowl of porridge.

"Quick, eat this up, luv. I know you like it."

Annie went limp, she began to cry, not anger, not frustration, but at this understanding.

Cook sat by her side on the bed and watched her eat. Then when the child was calm, said: "Now, Annie, no more of those tarry diddles. You stick to the truth. It will be easier for you and everyone. I know you don't mean harm, but it upsets folk."

Annie took it to heart and next morning when Mrs Nash entered, she found Annie dressed, washed and waiting for her hairbrush. Mrs Nash plaited the fair faintly red hair and looked at the pale face, the child looked penitent.

But she could not believe it - she was right.

Chapter 5

Stanley Royd

The strangest summer of Marianne's life began to fade. She watched the change of season as she walked her patients in the exercise area of the gardens. It was a place forever etched in her memory, the neatness, and the exactness of weeding, tending and edging.

The strong straight 'unnatural' precision made it unforgettable, together with her unhappiness. Often she felt that she was living another life, not hers at all.

One afternoon, as she watched the women walk, skip and some trot back and forth over a small track, she was overcome by the terrible aimlessness... individually, there was no co-ordination, as a group there was even less. She was struck by the appalling ludicrousness of their lives. For a moment she was annihilated in spirit, for her own life seemed the sport of gods as well. She shut her eyes.

At the zoo in Leeds, Annie shut her eyes tight and pressed her head closer and closer to the bars of the cage. She was wearing her much-hated black straw hat with its 'fall' of black ribbons at the back. She longed to be rid of it and as she saw the monkeys shred nuts and paper bags, dropping the debris from their perches, she had an idea.

The Nash family were gathered round a cockatoo, she was out of sight, alone. She pushed the ribbon through the bars, quickly, far swifter than she had imagined. A monkey advanced, hand over hand. Before she closed her eyes she saw his brown teeth, then she felt the tug, the scrape of the ribbon beneath her chin.

She was suddenly afraid, screamed, but kept still. The ribbon tugged at her chin, she heard people run towards her. Snap! Her scream was one of triumph. She opened her eyes and there swinging on a trapeze was the monkey.

With one deft pull between hand and teeth a long coil of dingy black straw floated down. Then came down shreds of silk and she jumped with sheer pleasure when the monkey placed the absurd crown on its head. Laughter rippled from the small crowd that had gathered and Mr and Mrs Nash had to join in.

It was an amusing sight, but although Annie assured all the bystanders it had been snatched from her head, they were by no means sure.

To them, it seemed yet another episode in the naughtiness of this unpredictable child. Their more immediate concern was where to purchase another hat, for even at 11 a small girl could not walk through the streets without head covering. A very plain one was bought, but to Annie's delight it did not have the dangling ribbons.

At home Annie was cross-questioned, but she remained firm to her story of the sudden thrust of the monkey's arm through the bars. She did not convince them, but judgement was suspended and no punishment possible.

Grandma, seeing Marianne, only once a week, noticed that the youth, which had, for so long persisted in her face, fade. She was not surprised, she could well imagine the things that her daughter-in-law saw and heard and above all experienced.

When she was in the narrow little house, she had so despised, but no longer, she never spoke of her days at Stanley Royde. She banished the pictures of flapping limbs that betrayed vacant, flapping minds. She never mentioned the strait-jackets.

One evening as she returned she found some very late ox-eye daisies and some yellow flowers she did not know.

She picked them, reminders of summer. She put them in a vase and sank into a chair, too tired to take off her cape, or untie her bonnet. But Edith gladly did both of these things while Grandma bustled in the kitchen.

"Here, now, Marianne, drink this tea. It is just what you need."

"Oh, how dark it is."

"These are the dull dark days before Christmas."

"Don't mention it, I cannot bear the thought, this year."

"Come now, I've already made the puddings and two cakes."

Rather ruefully Marianne smiled, but then asked, why she had made two.

"Can't you guess? One is for Annie."

Marianne's half smile was eclipsed. "Don't, don't mention her. I cannot bear it."

"I know you can't and that is why you never speak of her.

But you think of her all the time. I think she should come home. This is where she belongs."

"But, how could we manage? You know how it is, even better than I do."

"I've been working it all out and, I know that I can manage."

"But Grandma, her chances are better with the Nashes."

"I wonder about that."

"If only we had some news. They write to rarely and so formally."

That same afternoon Annie was alone while the Nashes went out as a family.

As it grew dark, Lizzie, the maid, came to draw the curtains and make up the fire. As she came to the hearth she found Annie curled up on the rug, her back to the sofa.

"Oh, you gave me a fright." She thought Annie was lonely, she was in fact enjoying her solitude, or would have been had she not been thinking of her home. She was bewildered and could not understand why her mother has sent her away.

She kept asking herself, "What, what is to happen?" She thought, as children do, that the present is endless, never changing. She was without hope. Lizzie's cheerful voice broke in,

"Come downstairs, now, we'll have tea and toast with Cook by the fire."

They clattered down the stone steps to the basement. The paintwork was dark, and the adjective used was serviceable. In the kitchen the gas flares lit the great table and shone greenly on the domes of the silver plate covers, more brightly on the copper pans. The large fire glowed in the range.

It was a warm friendly world and more than a few steps seemed to remove it from the rooms above. Annie sat at one end of the table where a rough white cloth was spread. She was given a fine brown boiled egg and bread and butter. It was delicious... it seemed the best food she had eaten for a long time.

Mildred, the cook, watched. She was both curious and pitying and as she regarded Annie. She seemed to see a thaw, the very straight little back relaxed and she leant against the chair back, then she turned her face to the fire and stared into the flames. Lizzie gazed, too, the defiance she had so often seen with the family had gone, though she still stared self-absorbed.

The absorption was withering and some tears trickled down her nose.

"What's up love?"

The blue eyes looked up, the chin quivered, but she remained silent.

Mildred smoothed down her skirt. "Come here love. Tell me what it is?"

Annie slipped from her chair and climbed on the broad lap and laid her head on the firm, large breasts. At the touch, she sobbed and sobbed and sobbed again.

The two women looked distressed, shook their heads, but let her have her cry until she was exhausted. When the gasps of breath become less laboured Mildred said: "You still haven't told us what it is. Come on now."

"I want my mother."

"Shall I write to your mother then?"

The gasps stopped, the stubborn look returned,

"No, I'll write."

"Lizzie. Get me the pen and ink and paper from the drawer."

These were spread out on the table, with difficulty the cork was prised out of the inkbottle. Annie then, with great deliberation wrote the address and the date, 21st November 1870, she then sucked the penholder for a moment, dipped the pen in the ink once more and wrote.

Dear Mother, Please come and take me home. Annie.

Mildred looked. "It's very short, isn't it?"

Annie, with her set look, replied: "It's all I want to say."

The envelope was written and the maid and Annie, like two conspirators, put on their coats, went down the street and slipped the letter into the pillar box.

That night, Mr Nash noticed a new fervour in Annie's prayers. At long, long last, he thought, the grace of humility is coming. But Annie prayed for deliverance as hard as any of the Jews, of whom she had heard so much, in Babylon.

She prayed and she willed that her mother come for her. At times the thought rose to a scream within her mind, "She must, she must, for I know she loves me."

The letter came immediately after Marianne had returned to work. She would not be home for another week. Grandma knew it was from Annie, but she would not open it. Instead, when William and Edith came from school, they found her wearing her bonnet and shawl and after giving them milk, they all walked to the hospital. They had never been there, it seemed very large.

Mrs Woodhouse, tall and erect, enquired for Marianne, regulations were mumbled, but she said that she had urgent news. They were led from block to block and, at, last shown into a waiting room awaited Marianne. The room seemed like a sitting room, it had chairs, pictures, a chenille-covered table and an aspidistra, but it held a taut menace... it was not even as relaxed as a dentist's waiting room.

Marianne entered. The children had never seen her in her uniform, with the silver chain with the whistle and the jangling chain of keys. She instantly turned pale,

What is it? Mother. Is it Annie?"

"Yes, she has written." She handed over the letter.

Marianne, with the scissors, also on the chain, slit the envelope. She did not know what to think, it was more than wonderful to have a note from her, but the heartbreak behind it was all transparent. She clutched it to herself and then pushed it to Grandma who had been longing all day to read it, but she had no spectacles. Marianne read it to them all. There was silence. They were all shocked by its brevity.

"We will write immediately""

"Yes, and you will tell here that we are all expecting her. I said she should come back didn't I?"

Marianne back in the ward planned her letter to the Nashes. She weighed each word with anger. Then when she actually came to write it, it was done without emotion. She thanked them for all that they had done, but with great firmness she explained that she wanted Annie back.

Her firmness in argument need not have been so vehement for the letter was hailed with relief by them all.

When Annie was told she kept very quiet, but when she left the room she darted down to the kitchen to tell Mildred and she threw her arm round the ample waist.

The days that intervened between the receipt of Marianne's letter and her arrival to collect her child were days of revelation to the entire Nash family. Annie ceased to be secretive, she stopped boasting, she was eager to please. As John Nash said to his wife, "She even looks different."

When the day came for Marianne to collect her, the Nashes greeted her with a similar openness and admitted that they had not been able to take her place... the experiment had been a failure. The love between Marianne and her first child was unique, and no one could have succeeded.

It was not, however, until they were alone together in the railway carriage going to Wakefield, that Annie really embraced her mother. Then she kept stroking her arm as if to make certain that her mother was real.

At last she fell asleep and with her face turned upward, Marianne looked at it minutely. It was her own dear, dear child, but it was strangely different. There was a certain blankness and Marianne knew that she had not been sufficiently loved. She did not blame the Nashes, she blamed herself, she had no right to forfeit her child. She knew too, the clerical households she had seen before, where a purpose came before the person.

They were efficient and so busy, but never, thought Marianne with quite the right thing. They grew to overlook the smaller, more sensitive inner world... it became lost in the undergrowth of business. For the first time, she thought that Benton had been spared a great deal. He would not, as he thought so idealistically, have liked it.

She brushed back Annie's hair from her brow. She recognised Benton's high pale brow. She remembered the first time she had brushed his hair back, not the first night, nor the second and when done it had seemed very daring. It had been a strange moment of beauty and so transported was she by its memory, she bent over the child and kissed her.

People boarded and got off the train and Marianne watched them all. It was good for her to see normal people. Sometimes in the Asylum she wondered whether there were any ordinary people. She saw some people obviously poor, she wondered if they were as poor as her little family. It did not matter, they were together and she was determined no one would know how poor they were.

At last they neared Wakefield, she woke Annie who stared unseeingly about her, held her hand very tight and stood dazed on the platform. Marianne called an out-porter, who shouldered the hamper and following him, they swiftly crossed the town towards the new streets and to Plumpton Street.

"Is this where we live, now?" asked Annie.

"Yes, this is our home," and for the first time Marianne felt a pride in it.

In the dining room Edith and William leapt up, Grandma turned and held out her arms. Annie went in shyly, but also taking note of everyone and everything in it. She saw change - her brother and sister were bigger, only Grandma remained the same. Grandma, like her daughter-in-law, sought and found likeness to Benton in the small face before her.

The children could not wait to show Annie the house. Edith ran upstairs to show her big sister where she was to sleep. Willy hung round the door a little and he watched the sisters open and close drawers, peering into the wardrobe. There was a gulf between himself and his sisters.

After supper, it seemed that Annie had never been away, except to Annie, her ecstasy was so poignant it hurt. The dam on her feelings only broke when Marianne tucked her up in bed. Annie stretched up her arms - her fingers linked behind the heavy chignon of hair - then in every fibre of her being she knew that she was home, she wept, she laughed, it was the happiest moment of her life.

She invented subterfuge after subterfuge to keep her mother there. Marianne was not unwilling to be delayed. When finally she came down the stairs she was proud and happy, the family was all beneath one roof, this was worthy of any sacrifice.

On the table Grandma and Marianne opened their purses, got out their cashbooks. Marianne's wage was £15 per annum. That, with her annuity and Grandma's savings, would just keep them.

Marianne's brow puckered and it was the older woman who stretched out a hand and said: "We'll manage easily."

It took Marianne a long time to sleep. At first she was too happy, later her anxieties returned. To manage was going to be a great problem. She saw that everything depended on the health of her mother-in-law. However, at last she fell asleep and soon, far too soon, it was five o'clock.

She rose, hurriedly dressed in her underclothing and went downstairs. It was very cold and dark, the gas mantle popped and then shed its greenish shadowed light over the room. Marianne hated these mornings, her spirits were always at their lowest.

The fire, she discovered, had gone out completely, the wood, put to dry, would not kindle, so she could not make tea. There was, though enough hot water in the tank in the range to fill the brass canister, which she then carried to her room. She finished washing and dressing by the light of a candle - it always irritated her that the contractor in his many economies had not installed gas lighting above the ground floor.

As she brushed her hair the light threw shadows, which she did not think flattering. She thought that she looked old. She heard a sound, the door cautiously opened. It was Annie, pink-faced in a white nightie. She ran across the room.

"Oh Mother, wasn't yesterday the most beautiful day ever?"

Of course it was and Marianne set off into the dark street with a renewed heart. She usually hated these early morning pacing. Only, she thought the humblest of workers were abroad at this hour, it made her despair. But today she strode along almost gaily.

Halfway to Stanley Royde she saw a holly bush, thick with berries, "On my way home I shall pick some." She did and that was her first contribution towards Christmas.

Alone, next day, with Grandma busily occupied in the kitchen, Annie made a survey of the house from top to bottom. It took longer than would imagine, for she was encountering old friends in the furniture all the time.

Every room contained something that she had known all her life. The rocking chair, the dresser with spice cupboards, the grandfather clock, each of these meant something of her past. Starting at the attic she worked down and as she descended the steep stairs, she wondered what had happened to the things she called lovely, that had been in the parlour at Whitely Bottom.

She pushed open the door of the tiny front room. There were all the things she remembered, the lustres, the alabaster font with the doves, the white china figures of the Queen with her little dog Dash. On the wall above the mantelpiece was the mirror that she loved together with the miniatures of her unseen, long dead, grandparents.

She looked at the round happy face of the grandmother and wondered whether she was like her. She felt much older since she had seen it all, she saw it with different eyes. She had never noticed before that the carpet was darned in places. It was all very different to Bradford, not so grand, she said to herself, but much much nicer.

She looked out of the window to the house opposite, all-identical. It was a poor street and she realised that since her father had died, everything had changed. She sat in a chair and thought about it all and she asked herself a question, "How do you stop being poor?" She did not know, but there was a tiny resolve in her that she would help them rise above this. She did not know how, but she would do something.

It was dinner time. This, too, was a great surprise, the table was laid in the kitchen and the meal consisted of bread and cheese and Grandma's home-made beer. The beer she found bitter and Grandma promised that she would make some of ginger for her. She learnt that they had their main meal later in the evening.

The afternoon seemed long. She went into the yard and it saddened her. She went in, found a book, sat by the fire and was lost the immediate world.

At last, she heard the children at the door and in came Edith and William. Tea was already on the table and they sat around, but it was her mother that Annie wanted and after a. while she asked, "When does Mother come home?"

"Not until Saturday night."

She had not foreseen this and two tears ran down the sides of her nose. Being back was not quite as wonderful, desirable as she had thought. The two young ones had accepted the situation, but Grandma understood, reached out her hand and assured her that Saturday night was not far away. When Marianne did come late even Annie in her excitement saw how tired her mother was. She revived, however, and she tucked them up and the asylum receded from the forefront of her mind.

When the children were away the two women again took out their purses ad counted and planned. There was three shillings to spare for Christmas presents. Marianne had set her heart on buying lace for Grandma, a book for Annie, soldiers for Willy and a doll for Edith.

Instead, it would have to be a length of ribbon, at best a three penny hook, a lead soldier and a three penny doll to be dressed. Her heart seemed to clench itself into a fist of pain and misery, but she resolved to spend the money and even more difficult find the time to spend it.

So, she wrote notes that evening, folded them into the little tricorns, such as Mrs Somerset had always used and next morning, as she went through the town, delivered them to the toyshop, the milliner and the stationer. Her greatest sadness was that she would not be with the children - she was on duty, being much a junior member of the staff.

As she approached Stanley Royde a tall woman who had a whining voice, which well accompanied her complaints, a long recital, overtook her. Marianne usually tried to avoid her but this time she could not. Christmas was mellowing both, for Marianne listened with patience and Mrs Paine even questioned and listened to Marianne. She discovered that Marianne dreaded Christmas away from her home and she told Marianne that her dread of Christmas was so great she longed to be away from the home that reminded her of her husband's death. Marianne understood so well that she broke her rule of keeping her work and her home life utterly apart and she invited Mrs Paine to Plumpton Street.

"It won' t be a party, just my mother-in-law and my son and daughters."

The discontented face smiled, "So you have children. That's what we always wanted. You are lucky".

The woman seemed to lapse into her usual state of envy. It was with an effort that Marianne said, "You won' t forget my invitation will you?"

The day was spent like all her days, exercising the more able patients, supervising their attempts at knitting and sewing. Putting a violent woman to bed and always, locking, unlocking and relocking door upon door upon door.

In the evening she was called to the sister's room.

"Taylor, Nurse Paine has offered to do your duties on Christmas Day. It is not regulation practice, but she is very insistent. Does that suit you?" Marianne's joy ballooned within her. Demurely she agreed.

"It is very kind of her indeed. I hope you appreciate her sacrifice."

Marianne was thus dismissed. She felt a momentary rage, then the knife of humiliation. "How long, O Lord, how long?" was her thought. That night she found it difficult to sleep, her anger, her pride seemed to revolve as if on a spit over a fire, the flames renewing the hurt.

Christmas Eve did come and when she hurried away she feared that the shops would be shut. Instead, she found Wakefield busy.

Naphtha flares leapt over the market stalls, globes of light shone in windows. First the milliner, they had the ribbon she had in mind to trim a cap and a bodice, they even had better for the money she could spend.

At the toyshop she was handed a box containing not one soldier but three and the doll had a simple dress and a more extravagant hat.

She reached the stationer just as he was pulling down his blinds - he had put some books aside for her.

One of these was *The Lamplighter*. It was illustrated and had an embossed and stamped green cover. It cost one shilling.

Well-pleased with her purchases, Marianne crept into the house, but was heard. She called out, "No-one one must come into the hall", and put the presents in the front room under a cushion and closed the door.

Clapping her hands she entered the living room. "Guess what, I am to be home tomorrow, after all". Christmas began instantly.

After tea it was bath time. Marianne and Grandma carried the shallow round bath from the scullery to the kitchen, they removed the steel fender and pushed the bath up to the brass tap in the range. Quickly the kitchen filled with steam.

It billowed around the dresser and the two girls undressed in the clouds. Edith was still so round and pink. This was a scene Marianne had missed for months. She was still reminded of the cherubs painted on the ceiling of Derry Ormond where she had stayed with Mrs Somerset.

The girls first, then William, they all squeaked, they were all reluctant to come out and sit on either Grandma's or Marianne's lap to be dried in the warm towels. The glow of the range, the smell of the soap, the innocence of it all removed the world, Marianne had almost forgotten the asylum, and momentarily she thanked Mrs Paine.

All in bed they tied up the presents and Grandma produced her surprise, a Christmas tree. They ferreted out the glass baubles and set it up in the parlour. Their eyes shone as they anticipated the eager eyes of the morrow.

Marianne was feeling quite light-hearted. It came to earth when it collided with Grandma's fatalism and hard-headed Yorkshire realism. She knew long, by now, that she was an irrepressible Celt and that her spirits rose and fell as Grandma's continued on a more even track.

Last thing, everyone in bed she carried stockings to the bedrooms, each one containing an orange and a sugar mouse. As she looked at them asleep she thought Stanley Royde worthwhile for them all. But with glee she added: "But not tomorrow, not tomorrow."

The surprise of the day was a very large parcel from Crosland Moor. All the cousins and aunts had partaken in it; it contained food, clothes, toys, crystallised fruit. It was so generous a gift that it brought tears to Marianne's eyes. A letter from Aunt Hirst promised a visit from Uncle Alan in the New Year. The little family, already happy, just being together, was now even happier, for it realised that it was part of a larger family.

The meal was nearly over, five mouths around the table were greasy "Os" spotted with pudding crumbs. There was a shout from William for he had found the silver threepenny bit. He knew immediately how he would spend it, more soldiers.

They all rose, no orders were given, no pleas to be made, everyone helped. Grandma was sent to the parlour and Marianne washed and dried the children. It had been a wonderful meal and Grandma congratulated herself on its excellence. It had been an achievement and it had meant much saving. She was glad to think her midday meals could now be more varied. She had tired of bread and cheese everyday.

Marianne 'sided up' sending the children to the parlour. She straightened the copper pans on their shelves, the range needed sweeping. It was growing dark and the gas needed lighting, but in the parlour she lit the oil lamp. The yellow flame gleamed in the frosted and engraved globe. It was a warmer light than the gas. She carried it to the small table.

"I know. I'll read you a chapter from Annie's book."

Grandma slept and later snored. The three sat on the mohair rug, but the chapters were long and the story slow, so Edith and

William were soon bored. Annie began to tell them a story. It was of Grace Darling and she remembered when last she had related the tale with some very unsubtle and egotistical variations.

Marianne listened. She had not realised that Annie was a born storyteller. When the mission to the wreck was completed, Marianne lit the candles on the piano and sat down. She played a carol they had sung in church that morning, then, unbidden came Mozart which led by stages to the climax of the *Magic Flute*. The children began beating time with their teaspoons.

When Marianne finished she went to her chair.

"Do you know when I first heard that music?"

They shook their heads.

"It was in the Opera House in Covent Garden. I went with Mrs Somerset, the lady I lived with in London. You will all have to go to Covent Garden one day. Why, you haven't even been to London yet. Well, it was a great occasion and everyone wore their finest clothes and jewellery. The Duchess of Kent, that was the Queen's mother, was there. She sat in the royal box. She looked very majestic."

"But, Mother, what did you wear?" asked Annie.

The answer came out pat, as though long waiting to reveal itself. "I wore green satin trimmed with a great many pink roses."

"That must have looked lovely", sighed Annie.

"I thought it the prettiest dress there and I had real rosebuds in my hair."

She told them of the chandeliers, the footmen and the grand staircase. Annie treasured every word and stored them in her memory. She did not get many glimpses of the past from her mother.

From the past they began to talk of the future. William told them that he wanted to be a sailor, like his grandfather. Marianne helped him paint a dream picture of his ship, a schooner scudding through the sea and far outstripping all rivals.

"And what about you Annie, what will you be?"

"Oh, I shall have a shop. I shall be a milliner and make the most beautiful hats ever seen. I shall have feathers, roses, ribbons and birds. The best hats in the world."

Quite primly, almost reprovingly, Marianne replied: "But you cannot, my dear, no lady is ever a milliner."

Annie felt that she had failed her mother.

"And you, Edie, what will you do?"

"Stay with Grandma for ever and ever."

It was a reply that melted the stiffness of the old lady so that she bent forward and kissed the child's cheek.

When everyone was in bed, Marianne sat by the embers of the fire. She, too, dreamt of the future. The fiery caverns gave her hope. She knew that she would not stay at the asylum forever - it was just too heart-rending, it was also too poorly paid.

She wondered what she could do to keep her children and attain the respectability she craved. Life was indeed, very strange. She had not foreseen Wakefield, when she had been in London, she had hardly heard of it.

She reached up to the mantelpiece and took down Benton's photograph in the black case. She looked at the face that she still loved, the wide brow, the round eyes. He had had such hopes, ambitions and fate had intervened and pushed them all to the crater edge of poverty.

She recalled his long illness and with the wisdom of hindsight she recognised the symptoms, which had appeared long before. The exhaustion, the too-high spirits... and then the irritability when he became frustrated. Thinking still of London, she thought it strange, that Benton, born of Yorkshire people, bred in that county, had, yet, to her eyes, been one of nature's southerners.

For a few moments she wondered what marriage would have been had she followed Mrs Somerset's advice. The answer was that it would have been easier, much easier, but not a whit as happy. She thought of the love and she blushed for it reminded her of bed. The blush faded, for bed meant sleep too, and it would so soon be time to set out into the dark for Stanley Royde.

Wakefield in January and February is a black and shining landscape, the wind clears the smoke and the light falls on the wet slate and reflects in the black tar. It is a whiteness that somehow is not light, it lacks lustre.

Marianne lacked lustre, too, as she hurried through the streets. Tired by her work, wearied by the hopelessness, and undermined by the winter, she again echoed, "How long, o Lord, how long?"

Fortunately there was her home, the narrow house was her refuge, and those in it worth all the struggle. It was a struggle in many ways. Recently, it had been the children's manners, now it was their speech.

They were, in her absence developing Yorkshire accents. This she deplored and ruthlessly tried to expunge any tendencies that way. The girls were fortunate in their schools and Annie, particularly, was soon gaining ground, learning quickly and easily.

William was the worry - he seemed in his element in a rougher set. This also pained his grandmother, who sought, to everyone's unhappiness, including her own, a replica of her son. What both mother and grandmother failed to understand was that schools of the boys and the girls, although adjoining, were very different and the boys subjected to a far harsher discipline.

They saw, and experienced often, beatings, fierce detentions and the brutality that breeds brutality and most of all in the mind.

Marianne worried and she thought constantly of the future lives of her children. Annie would have to work and there was only, virtually, one function permissible to a young woman, she must teach.

William had far more choice; she hoped, like most mothers, far a professional career. The more immediate problems were their education at that moment and she had not forgotten Benton's desires in education either.

As the days perceptibly began to lengthen, the walk home from the hospital was no longer in entire darkness, and so Marianne's hopes and fears increased. The winter like a cat released and then pounced again upon its victim.

Marianne felt utterly within its power. She tried to rejoice in the suspicion of spring, but often even when she saw it clearly the thought came - "whatever the season can I really go on?" She was exhausted and she felt helpless.

One day, scenes in the ward having been particularly painful, she felt unable to gather strength for the walk. She leant against a tree and misery surged up and totally enveloped her. She prayed to a Providence she doubted. The pit of despair seemed very deep. Suddenly, she heard a child laugh. It was far removed from the mirthless laughter she frequently heard... it was pure and simple happiness. It reminded her of Annie and from the pit she began to climb.

She lifted her head, summoned her feet into a firm step and

hurried home, even more she hurried to Annie. Annie was so much her child. William she loved but failed to really understand and Edith had become her grandmother's child. So much together, they formed a unity. She did not resent this.

In early March, Uncle Alan made another visit. Grandma was especially happy to see him for he was from her own land. Wakefield, of which she knew little, was alien country. Hearing of Berry Brow, Armitage Bridge and Crosland Moor brought her own home close and flushed her cheeks. Uncle Alan brought not only news but a great basket of food.

During tea, Annie claimed much of her uncle's attention, as she always did. However, he turned deliberately to William and made much of him and the boy responded.

Seeing them all so light-hearted and happy, Marianne felt a surge of unusual joy. There was colour and movement and glory in life and it would soon include her, too.

A little later, alone with Uncle Alan, she saw him looking at her quizzically when she glanced up from her tea cup. His thoughts were made open by his question, "Are there any nice doctors in the Asylum?"

She parried it with, "As patients?"

"You know very well what I mean. Any likely to marry you?"

"Uncle Alan." She was shocked. The thought of another marriage had never crossed her mind. She laughed and said: "Who would want a widowed woman like me with a brood of children?"

"Any man in his right mind."

She shook her head, "No, I don't think so. We'll just go on from day to day."

"Well, lass, don't put it out of thy mind."

Just as she was beginning to be affronted at his advice, he added: "But there won t be another Benton, as you know. Why he had to die so young, so full of promise, I shall never know?"

"Those whom the Gods love die, young, Uncle. The trouble is that we love them, too."

"Aye. It's hard. I had a mind that Benton would be Yorkshire's Burns, but it was not to be."

"Now, now, I know you mean that as a compliment, but they were as different as chalk and cheese. Benton was a poorer poet, but a better man."

"Then you're a prettier lass than ever Jean Armour was. You find yourself a man."

It angered Marianne that marriage seemed the only answer men could offer to a woman. Life conspired, too, that it should be so. If Marianne had known, it was at that moment Uncle Alan knew that another answer had to be found, for he recognised Marianne's fierce independence.

He pondered on it in the train, something had to be done and he did not know what. He put all cogitation aside for he thought, "must talk it over with Elizabeth."

Aunt Elizabeth up in her room was eager to hear and she had a husband who for many years had made it his practice to relate, often more vividly than the reality, the account of his day.

That evening there was little need for heightening as he described the excitement of the children at his arrival, the buying of the boots and the alpaca cloth. It was not, though, of the doings that his wife wanted to hear, but the people. Especially she wished to know how Marianne was.

"Well, she looks tired, not faded. She's worried and she does not like her work. But, my, she has spirit. I admire her more than I can tell."

"Then we have to do something for her" and she folded her hands carefully on the unruffled counterpane. This Alan knew was always the prelude to a deep consideration of a problem.

It was not until the middle of the night that the solution came. She woke up saying, "Lady Armitage".

Next morning, she wrote a letter to Lady Armitage saying that it was time for her visit and that she was looking forward to it. It jogged the memory and the Armitage carriage was a few days later climbing the hill to Crosland Moor. The visit was not unheralded for Elizabeth Hirst was ready in her best cap and shawl. The two women had been at school together, there was a long intimacy between them. They talked of their families and Elizabeth had no difficulty in coming round to the subject of Marianne.

Lady Armitage knew Benton well. She had been grieved at his death and her sympathy was quick, but it hissed in consternation when she heard that Marianne was working at the County Asylum as a nurse. She also saw that something had to be done.

"My husband seems to think that a husband is the answer."

"All men think that. It is their pride."

"They think that we cannot manage without them."

That evening as Sir George sat with his wife in the great oriel window of their 'mediaeval' home. Marianne's plight was discussed. Sir George instantly felt guilty, though he failed to admit it, even to himself, that he had forgotten Marianne under the pressure of business.

They were still busy with cloth for the Prussian armies for the Franco-Prussian War had boosted trade. He was well aware that he should have done more, he had much to thank Benton for, the system he had inaugurated still stood. Furthermore, he had suggested his replacement, John Donkersley, and he was also proving his worth.

"Yes, I will do something."

"Yes, we must and we must do it before it is too late."

His immediate reaction was to send a cheque. He knew that was only a temporary alleviation. What she needed was work, responsible work and with a house. He muttered, "It's bad, bad."

Life is criss-crossed with encounters, some are never noticed. Challenges are often mutely, even unconsciously thrown down... these are sometimes silently ignored, or else too seized upon.

So character meeting character begets or rejects in its meetings and the opaque and amoebic continuity of life forms. It is strangely vague, some claim a structure and find in it a divinity. Chance seems to play a part which is then modified by belief, philosophy, but most of all the extraordinary sequence of events that have raised our own series of prejudices, some unique, some shared. It is nearly chaos to some. To Marianne it was undoubtedly the hand of God.

That week a distant cousin called upon the Armitages. He was a tall, strong-featured man who had served in the army in both the Crimean War and the Indian Mutiny. He was, at that time, Governor of the Wakefield Prison.

During lunch, Lady Armitage questioned him on the type of woman engaged as wardresses. As she listened, she dismissed it as a post for Marianne. Then Captain Armitage said: "I shall, in fact, be seeking for a superior woman for the post of Deputy Matron. This and the Matron's post are never easy to fill."

I think that I might know the very person for you, a widow, and a gentlewoman with three children. Her husband was a schoolmaster and later George's secretary and manager."

"She is educated, I take it?"

"Certainly."

He asked more questions. When he discovered that she already lived in Wakefield, he decided to see her.

"I need someone naturally absolutely trustworthy and with authority."

So it was with such simplicity Marianne entered the Prison Service and played her own part in the reform of these immense institutions.

All that passed was unknown to Marianne. She knew that Uncle Alan would do what he could. She also knew that people sometimes forget. On her way home, she passed a newsagent and she went in and bought a copy of the local paper to scan the advertisements, something she had vowed that she never would do.

At home, propped on the mantelpiece was a letter in a hand she did not recognise and with a local postmark. It was from Captain Armitage and requested her to come for an interview in a fortnight's time. She read it many times and discussed it with Grandma. The letter spoke of Sir George's recommendation and they suspected the hand of Lady Armitage and Aunt Elizabeth. The prospect of a prison alarmed Marianne, but the thought of a house and a greater margin of safety in their finances overcame most of her fears.

At last the day of the interview came. Marianne awoke with a sudden startled bump and looked at the clock in the half-light. She had overslept. Then she remembered that she had the morning off and did not have to go to the asylum. She luxuriated in the extra hour in bed even though she began to be apprehensive about the interview.

She rose and helped Grandma get the children off. When they had gone, she went once more carefully through her clothes. She had rubbed and brushed the long hem of her black silk dress, there was no more to do. When the fire was burning well and throwing out some heat she once more curled the ostrich feather in her bonnet with a knife before the flames. At half past 10 she left the house.

It seemed strange to be in her best clothes in the morning. But she knew well that her strength of character would weigh far more heavily than just her outward appearance.

She was very apprehensive. So much depended on this interview, but her determination was steely. Like a soldier polished and re-polished, scrubbed and with a spotless uniform ready for a grand parade, so Marianne's clothes boosted her confidence.

She hurried through the town, beneath the railway arch to the prison. At the great gateway she was directed to the Governor's house, which was adjacent. She expected to find others waiting but there was no one in the hall.

She waited. This could not be a proper interview she thought. A door opened and she heard the murmur of cheerful, confident voices - the Board – and the door closed.

At last she was summoned. It was a narrow room with a long baize-covered table. At the head rising was the Governor, the chaplain, two military looking gentlemen and three ladies, one was evidently the Matron, for she was not hatted, but wearing a lace cap.

The men all stood as she entered. It pleased her and she recalled the last interview she had had. She was prepared to stand, but was motioned to a chair. The Governor's hawk-like face, with sunken dark eyes and deep lines running from his nostrils to the edges of his mouth, dominated the room. It was a face frightening in its gravity. It was the facsimile of Justice.

There were many questions, her age, the date of her marriage and widowhood, the number of her children. Then she was asked whether she knew that the prison was not an ordinary one, but a model. It was not merely punitive but endeavouring to fit convicts for a future life. This she knew. This she had studied over the last few days.

The Matron leant forward. She had a smooth, even placid face. "Mrs Taylor, this work is at times frightening, are you nervous at all?"

She was aware of her tightly clasped hands, but smiled, "No ma'am, I am not afraid, I have been alone too long to be afraid. Also, I do not think a prison can be very much more heart-rending than an asylum."

The questions dwindled and an almost conversational spirit took its place, Marianne remained quiet. She was asked to leave the room.

In the hall she thought of everything that could be construed as ignorant, or foolish that she had said. The Matron emerged.

"We thought that it would be valuable for you if I took you round." Marianne agreed.

She stood aside as keys were turned in locks. She was never to escape keys. As soon as she entered, she felt keenly the singular spirit of the place, like nowhere else. She saw the prisoners in their grey coarse dresses and white linen capes. Her thought was, all these women needed care, but they were not irrational. She felt far less afraid than she did at Stanley Royde. She saw kitchens, dining halls, cells and workshops and the hospital. It was a world of its own. The Matron was observing her all the time, but so subtly that Marianne was never conscious of being tested.

Walking home, Marianne went quickly as hope was dying in her. If they had wanted she was sure they would have asked more searching questions. As she came to Plumpton Street her heart sank. She went straight to the dark little room where Grandma was darning socks over the fire.

She put one hand on the shawled shoulder and stretched the other out to the fire. She needed warmth and love. She sank down on the rag mat saying, "I don't think I have any hope there, Grandma."

"No. Well perhaps it would not have been such an improvement on what you are doing. Did they say no definitely?"

"No. I just felt that they considered me unsuitable."

"Oh, what a girl for feelings you are. You must just wait and see."

She did not wait very long. As she was telling the children a story while they finished their supper, there was a knock at the door. Grandma answered it. Marianne heard men's voices, she guessed whose... and next moment the prison chaplain, Mr Alderson and Captain Armitage stood in the room. Marianne rose, putting Edith down, who had been on her knee. The children were admired and spoken to and then at a nod from Marianne they went upstairs.

Captain Armitage sat down and there was a moment of quiet. It was such a sympathetic silence that again Marianne thought that they were breaking bad news as gently as they were able.

"Mrs Taylor. As you know, we are very proud of the unique position our prison holds in England. We try, always, to find the right person to serve it, who will be happy with us. The Board has asked me to offer you the post of Deputy Matron. Will you accept it?"

She felt that she was being lifted, lifted up above the squalor of the last months. She was regaining her own selfhood once more. She felt enclosed with a bright plumage of gratitude and she found herself inclining her head very gracefully, a formal bow and she heard herself say, "How very kind." Then there was silence and she remembered that she had more to say and for the moment her joy forbade her speaking. Then she heard herself say, and she was relieved to hear it. "Of course, of course I accept and I hope that I fulfil my duties well."

It was Mr Alderson who now spoke. "I am quite certain you know what you are undertaking, but there must be much you cannot imagine. Please, please feel always at liberty to come to me if you need any help".

She looked at the extremely well-bred grace beneath the fine white hair. It was austere in an entirely English manner. Whether she could turn to such a face, she did not know, but she thanked him for his kindness.

It was Captain Armitage who said, "I think that you have, of late, been schooled by the hard nurse of Necessity. It will have helped you. At times in India I wondered why I had to live though some of the things that I did. Very oddly, very oddly indeed, I am almost grateful for them now." A time for her to view the house was made and a provisional date for beginning her duties.

She gathered her skirts and flew up the stairs. She rushed in and leapt on the bed that Grandma was carefully tucking in. "I've got the post. We shall all move to a bigger house. Isn't it wonderful?"

The children were full of questions. She described the prison, the neat little houses of the warders. The children wanted to know more of the convicts and were very disappointed when she said that she expected them to be very much like other people.

Only when there was peace upstairs did Marianne and Grandma really talk. They were thrilled by the prospect and for the first time they both admitted to a fierce dislike for the dark and damp house in the dismal street.

At nine o' clock Grandma came into the room with a tray, glasses and a bottle of her homemade wine. Together they drank to their future.

Chapter 6

Wakefield Model Prison

In May the move took place. For days there had been constant rain, which flooded the cellar, an event that alarmed Grandma but delighted William who immediately launched a barrel into the muddied water and punted himself around.

When the day of removal came, the sun shone. Marianne and Grandma supervised the men, the children were sent off to school. It was only Annie who looked at the house with affection as she left. It was the home she had been restored to and it would always mean something to her. But like the others, she looked forward to a room of her own.

When Marianne and her mother-in-law arrived in the street where the prison officers lived, they smiled. There was a broad road and the houses stood in neat gardens. The house allotted to Marianne was semi-detached and when she went in, her nostrils were immediately assailed by the smell of fresh scrubbing.

Everything shone, a part of 'trusties' had prepared her new home for her. When the children returned from school they were surprised to find the house already carpeted, furniture in places where they seemed always to have been.

After tea, there were callers, warders and their wives came with gifts of flowers. The whole house was now scented with wallflowers. When darkness came they had supper. As they remained at the table, Marianne got her Bible and read Psalm 122.

"I was glad when they said unto me, 'Let us go into the House of the Lord!" They said the Lord's Prayer. They all knew that a new phase in their life had begun and they faintly realised that they were in a little world of its own. It was Annie who saw the irony of the psalm.

"Mother, I don't think that this is often said by the convicts when they arrive here!"

Marianne tried to look severe and shocked but William and Grandma laughed and her reproof was defeated.

On the first morning, Marianne was woken by the sound of a

blackbird singing in the apple tree. It reminded here of Whitley Bottom and as she lay in bed she examined the ceiling and its shape, its angles and the manner in which the window cut into it.

She felt, as she had not felt for a very long time, secure. She rejoiced to have the Asylum behind her and she smiled when she recalled giving in her notice to the Sister, and how pleased she had been to inform her that she was to be the Deputy Matron at the Prison.

The surprise on her face had been gratifying, especially as the news had rendered her speechless. They had disliked one another most intensely. Marianne was glad to be 'shot' of her, a phrase she would never have allowed her children to use.

She sighed, though for experience had taught her that there would almost certainly be another like her, there always was.

When she got up, she went to the window. There beyond a high brick wall growing grey beneath the sooty air stood the Prison, her next world to encounter. She was determined to succeed and very rigorously she banished any apprehensions.

As she looked, the blackbird flew from the tree and she gazed down into a bed full of wallflowers, stocks and tulips. She had seen them before, but forgotten them.

She called to the children to dress and eventually they all went out into the small garden. The scent enfolded them and Annie was to remember it for the rest of her life.

She said to herself, 'This is Paradise'. And so it ever remained. It was an anchorage in a strange haven.

The night before her first day of duty was spent in fitful sleep and she was unable to eat much of the breakfast that Grandma had provided. As she left the house and walked towards the main gates, in spite of her apprehension she thought how handsome they were, the huge columns punctuated by four worm stone blocks.

It was immense, but to her not frightening. She admired the round, headed windows with many panes. She pulled the bell set into the stone wall then walked two yards to the small door set in the great panelled doors.

She was let in immediately, the door clanged behind her and before her were gates of steel. The warder smiled and called her by her name, unlocked the barred gate and directed her to the Matron's office. The sun broke through, she looked up at the sky, and almost in surprise she recognised it to be the same sky that covered the outside world.

The sun lit up the red brick and lightened sandstone sills and lintels. The office was scrupulously neat and a fire blazed in a shining steel grate. Marianne was learning of the faultless neatness and exactitude of prison life where there were so many too perform so few tasks.

Matron rose and shook Marianne's hand and welcomed her. She outlined briefly and methodically her duties, picked up a bunch of keys and gave them to her. Unlocking another door they entered the women's block. It was vast and at once both solid and skeletal. It was eerily silent, but there were constant echoes in the bays and grottoes of this enclosed space.

First of all there was a peculiar smell that seized her immediately – a stale foetid scent. It nauseated her, but within minutes she failed to notice it.

A wardress was ushering a prisoner. Marianne looked at her with interest, and she bobbed a curtsey to them. She was a plain creature, thin and sallow, and the grey dress and white apron and cap emphasised her lack of colour. One glance told Marianne that the woman was a whiner. She knew exactly what her voice would be like, though she had not heard it.

They went past cells, down scrubbed stone corridors, their footsteps sometimes clanged on spiral stairs. It was another world within the world, but as they passed the kitchen she heard laughter and instantly she knew that it would be easier for her than the Asylum, for the peal of laughter contained a note of reason that had been absent in the ward she had worked in.

She saw more convicts. They were not as pitiful as the patients, she felt a greater kinship than she had ever experienced at the hospital. There was here a basis for understanding, a real possibility of helping. That morning she supervised the dining hall and did it with amazing ease. She was glad to see the room fill up with the women, it had been so bare. At the end of her day she was very aware that life here would not be beautiful, useful, perhaps, but home it would be. So she began, at once, to practise the balancing of the dichotomy of her life.

She often recalled that first day when she had looked at the women, as though her eyes and mind could probe out their secrets that brought them here. She soon ceased, for she found that they were like the rest of humanity varying in their degrees of goodness and badness... though she saw quite clearly that here there was more stupidity, more weakness and more immaturity – and – almost always poverty. She remembered the phrase she had known long before she had came here... 'prisons are the palaces of the poor.'

Tiles, bars, gates and keys, and echoing and re-echoing footsteps were to be the background of her days. Soon, it seemed, on that first day when the steel gates clanged and then the small door in the outer gate banged behind her, that her first day was over.

She went out with a wardress who was also a widow. Together they talked of their children and the difficulties of settling into a new home. When they parted and Marianne stood at the gate of her garden and her home, she wondered what she should tell the children of her life. She decided to answer their questions, no more.

Indoors they were already at tea. Grandma looked up anxiously and Marianne smiled back such a smile that all the old lady's fears vanished. Marianne awaited the questions. None came... they were far too busy retailing their own adventures at their new schools.

It made her smile as she saw how egotistic each one of them was. Only as she tucked up Annie was she asked what the prison was like. Marianne told her and she promised that they could all go with her to the Chapel on Sunday and see for themselves.

Downstairs, Grandma had far more questions to ask and as she told her, she felt the shame that the old lady's heart experienced so bitterly.

"Grandma, you are upset. Now why? This is good work, you know. I can help people and they need it. Best of all I can keep all of us together."

"It is just so different from all that I had planned, all that Benton had planned. God has been very cruel to me, Marianne, very cruel indeed."

Marianne had long known that the perpetual need of a new bonnet to wear to Church had been an excuse. Long ago, Grandma had renounced all belief in God. She did not try to argue. It would have been useless. Instead she twined her arm around the still slim waist and very upright back and said: "We have one another. Benton would like that. Some people have nobody at all."

Mrs Woodhouse was in retreat from the world. She went out

increasingly rarely. She had to be coaxed into the parlour when visitors called. Twice a year, though, she returned to Crosland Moor staying with her sister and going out a great deal, but Wakefield held no interest for her.

Their lives fell into a strict routine imposed by the Prison and Schools. Marianne's days were made up of inspection, interrogation and ever watchfulness. The life had a momentum of its own, it carried her along, giving her neither the time nor the inclination to brood. She was often tired when she reached home.

There were joys at home nearly always, joys too at the Prison. Quite often it was her duty to interview a prisoner on the eve of her release. Sometimes, she escorted these women herself to the gate.

She saw it always as a day of hope, a dramatic moment when the cage door was opened. More frequently than she liked, the bird clung before taking the plunge. Always Marianne prayed that she would not see the women again - but some she did.

Chapter 7

Pupil Teacher

A year passed by very swiftly and the family became daily more secure. It was something they had not known for two years. The unease had begun when Benton was so ill. Marianne was duly appointed as the Deputy Matron officially and one of the delights was that there was no jealousy, only appreciation from the wardresses.

It brought many more responsibilities, a longer day, but no shift duties. Most nights, the children sat with their mother at the chenille covered table beneath the gas bracket.

They did their homework while Marianne sifted through many dossiers. Her thin, italic hand scratched precisely, even prettily, but not very legibly, on the pages beneath the photographs of the prisoners.

The prison world was one of its own, and like the outer world, was strongly structured by class distinction. To Marianne the greatest benefit of her new position was the one of rank - her place in society was no longer anomalous. The hierarchy around the prison walls was echoed within them and as Britain looked to the sovereign, so the officers looked to the Governor and his wife. There was, though, something unique to the Prison of Wakefield. Adjoining the warder's quarters was a large house in extensive grounds. Here lived Miss Senior, a maiden lady with a small fortune. She was tall, of solid stature, dark-haired and with a rosy, even red complexion. She was a lady of generous and liberal principles. Having been brought up in a village where her father had been the squire she repeated the life of her mother. She took the warders, wardresses and their families beneath her observant care. She was their patroness, self-elected and by them wholly accepted.

Miss Senior and Marianne had not been in one another's company for many minutes before friendship grew and flourished. Marianne was glad to have her confidence and she was glad that her children had access to the house of a lady.

Few who knew Marianne ever plumbed the depths of her pride,

even her children only gradually became aware of it. They saw mainly her passionately-held ambitions for them and they were resigned to it as children are. She watched over their homework and as it was regarded as a matter of the greatest importance, regular hours were allotted to it.

Willy was the first to show signs of rebellion. This surprised Annie who accepted her mother's rule unquestioningly - there was no one she loved so ardently.

In the evening she waited and watched for her return. Often, she waited at the great gate. She claimed later to know every nail around its 14 panels. She would listen for the muffled clang of the inner gate, the footfalls, the turn of the key in the well-oiled lock and the rustle of the heavy silk dress Marianne wore in the summer. The warder would poke his head out through the narrow doorway, remark upon Annie's height, or faithfulness and then Marianne, taking Annie's arm would tuck it beneath her own and they would walk down the road.

Annie stored up these moments, they were an essential in the fabric of the most important relationship in her life. She was proud when not only trusty convicts working on the flowerbeds saluted her and wardresses bobbed a curtsey, but when Captain Armitage swept off his hat.

She noted, too, the gracious incline of the mother's head as she acknowledged these greetings. It implied so much, it was not only an acceptance it was a classified one. It was also a proclamation of her right to receive these deferences.

Annie imbibed this pride and subscribed unconsciously to the ethos behind it. Yet, in a strange way, she was also protective towards her mother, perhaps, she acquired this attitude from her grandmother, who was constantly putting aside small delicacies for her daughter-in-law... a large brown egg, the farmhouse butter.

Edie, too, joined in this adoration. She picked wild flowers, sewed pen-wipers and kettle-holders. But William remained aloof though, so young he led a life of his own, independent of his family. Only Annie was permitted, at times, to enter his sphere.

At the age of four Annie had been able to read, so that, now, nearly 10, she was extraordinarily fluent.

It so happened that one day the headmaster came to Miss Robinson to complain of the slowness of the infant class to pick up this skill, "the slowest ever" he called them.

He felt it as a personal blow for he had great ability at teaching children to read. He was an authority and had invented and published his phonetic system. At that moment, Annie was at Miss Robinson's desk, her sums were being marked.

"You should have Annie Taylor there, she's a great reader." To the surprise of everyone, the headmaster seized upon the idea and marched her to his class. She was seated in the front row and given, like all the rest a limp backed red reader.

The headmaster stood before them and in a gentle voice he talked to the class. "I believe that you think only grown-up people can read. Now, we have Annie Taylor here, she not so much older than you and I will show you how she can read. Will you stand up, Annie, and read from page four."

Annie rose, she turned very pink, fluttered the pages, but found the fourth page. Her confidence rose to something nearing contempt.

"The cat sat on the mat. The dog got the log."

"Page 10, now."

"The mill is on the hill. Give a pill to the miller."

"Page 12."

"The sea is green, or blue. Fish live in the sea. They are grey."

"Thank you very much. Come here, Annie. Will you tell the class how you learnt to read?"

Again she blushed and shifted from foot to foot.

"By looking at papers, notices and shops."

"How old were you?"

"I don't know."

"Was it before you came to school?"

"Yes."

So began a twice weekly visit by Annie to the infants' class where by cajolery and shame they were goaded into reading. Annie enjoyed these visits. She particularly loved it when a child began to read. She was excited for them, life was more exiting.

At the end of the term Annie was called to the headmaster's room. He sat behind a desk. He smiled as she entered - they were very nearly friends by now.

"Do you know, Annie, that you are the youngest pupil-teacher on our staff?" Annie nodded. The large man bent down and opened a drawer. He took from it a cash box, unlocking it, her took out a silver crown piece. Solemnly and wordlessly he handed it to her.

Annie received it with a sense of triumph, she felt incalculably wealthy and she thought of her mother. She was still aware of the account book, the money spread over the table cloth and the sighs.

She looked at the large coin, this would, she thought, end all that.

At long, long last the final prayer of the term was ended, the final bell rang and Annie ran across the playground, down the street, past the pillared Unitarian chapel, under the viaduct.

Home was in sight and the coin sticky in her hand. Suddenly, she tripped and fell, the money, the money she thought as the air burst from her lungs. The glory, the wonder had gone, she limped on. As she went round to the back door, she saw her mother making jam. She put down the spoon and came directly to Annie.

She gathered up the child. Annie's tears flowed as soon as she received comfort. Sobbing, she pressed the money into her mother's hand. When between gasps Marianne learnt where the money came from and how, she had difficulty in restraining her tears as well. Pity and admiration, love and pride swelled within her as she hugged her favourite child and carried her to the sink to wash the cut knee and grazed hands.

She pulled the head of curling hair to her and as she felt the tiny, snub nose snuggling into the cleft of her bosom, she felt a delectable union, almost as she had had with Annie's father.

Next day, Marianne took the crown and Annie to the High Street. They went to Mr Hemingway, the jeweller, and bought a silver case for the coin. It thus became a brooch and Marianne pinned it at Annie's neck.

"Your first wages", said the proud mother.

Annie wore it a great deal, but for weeks it would disappear. The temptation to spend it was insurmountable at times and took so long to put back a replacement.

Chapter 8

The Yorkshire School

Just as the keys turned in the well-oiled locks of the prison, the years slipped by. There were incidents in both prison and home that caused anxiety and distress, but, which like many of our preoccupations of the moment, were suddenly in oblivion.

The family was a tight small unit, each one with his or her individual tasks and division of time. For Grandma, the organiser of the household, the week was composed of washing days, ironing days, baking days.

The seasons were marked in the kitchen by simnel cakes, marmalade making, the salting of bacon and, of course, the gargantuan preparations for Christmas. She was happy in her constant toil and Edith was always by her side watching, helping and learning.

Annie's life was encompassed by school. She loved it and longed for the day when she would be enrolled as a pupil-teacher. She took extra lessons, she worked hard and, at last, the week was appointed for the Inspector to visit. It was a day much anticipated, but fearful when it arrived.

Throughout the morning she expected to be summoned to his presence. She had seen him at the assembly, a tall man in a well-cut black frock coat. When the command came, Miss Beloe, her classmistress accompanied her.

The Inspector sat at a desk swinging his monocle. Annie noticed that it was most elegantly chased. He smiled asked her name and age and then rapped out some questions of mental arithmetic.

Only once did she falter and then righted herself. The he set a spelling test, which she looked forward to until he asked her to spell 'syringe'. She had never heard the word and brought up in the Lancastrian system she spelt it phonetically, s-h-r-i-n-g-e.

He laughed and called her "a true daughter of her school", which she did not understand. She named the Danube as Europe's longest river, but failed to place Rome on the banks of the Tiber. She surprised Miss Beloe by naming correctly the chief ministers in the

Government. Like her mother she was an ardent admirer of Lord Beaconsfield.

She was dismissed. For a brief moment the sun lit Annie's fair skin giving it a lustre and her large blue eyes shone. They shone more brightly because she was eager and she was tense. Her neat hair escaped in tendrils on her forehead and the sun showed that the blue bows catching her hair at the back were exactly the same colour as her eyes.

She looked beseechingly at Miss Beloe for she was sure that she had failed and a good word from her mistress might redress the balance. Miss Beloe's face betrayed nothing... she thought that Annie deserved to fail, but was sure to pass.

"A charmingly mannered child. What are her parents?"

When Miss Beloe informed him of Marianne's position, there was a pause.

"How very interesting. Well I am sure you agree that we can safely take her on."

At the end of the day, Miss Beloe tied on her bonnet, and paused before the mirror. She saw very clearly a face without an inner light. She remembered Annie's glow and sighed.

Annie hurried home. When the road was deserted she skipped, fitting "Pupil-Teacher" to her steps. It was far from easy. She could not wait to tell the family, she could not wait to tell the world.

Then she saw William ahead of her. He was standing in the gutter stubbing his boots against the kerb. Annie pretended not to notice the gloom, but she respected his mood sufficiently to keep her news to herself. At home he sulked... he would not even play his favourite game of gobbling his bread and butter so quickly he never gave his grandmother time to sit down before she had to cut yet more of the loaf.

Late that evening, Marianne returned. First of all she tucked up Edith, then William, and came down to the room with a troubled look. Annie looked up from her books.

"This is the moment to tell my news." Marianne and Grandma listened and they stretched out hands to pat Annie's.

"You are my clever and bonnie girl."

It was, now, Annie's turn to be disappointed, the rapture seemed so limited.

Then, as they talked, she realised that her success had been assumed by them long ago. She found their confidence in her ample repayment.

A little later Marianne said without warning: "Oh I do wish Benton was here. I don't know what to do with Willy, he needs a man so badly. There is something wrong at school and I cannot get to the bottom of it."

"His father was no trouble at school, or at home – ever," asserted Grandma, a remark that brought a rare glint to Marianne's reply.

"No, he had a father – and then Mr Woodhouse to help him. Benton's case was quite different."

Grandma looked up surprised and fell silent.

Next day, William's spirits were high. He returned home happy and it was Annie who was downcast. Grandma kept questioning her and Annie became stubbornly quiet. It was Marianne who said, "Leave her, Grandma, she will tell us in her own time," and eventually Annie confided in them.

"Miss Beloe said before the whole class, "Blue ribbons may hoodwink an inspector, but they do not fool me Miss Annie Taylor."

Then to Annie's utter amazement, her mother laughed and said: "Oh my bonnie lassie. This is the price of your looks. These are poor Miss Beloe's sour grapes, very sour indeed."

That Miss Beloe could be jealous had never entered Annie's mind. The laughter made her realise that the matter was not as grave as she had thought.

As dusk crept up over the street, Marianne came into the parlour where Annie worked. She was wearing a cloak and had a key in her hand.

"Come, leave your homework. We're going for a walk." They went towards the Governor's house and to a door in the high brick wall. Inside was a beautiful but too tidy garden. Fruit trees opened like fans against the walls, or in espaliers, emphasising the straightness of the paths.

Each strawberry plant had its cushion of straw. The bulbs grew in straight and oblique lines. The path seemed not merely raked but combed, there was not a weed to be seen. They walked past the parade ground of vegetables to a lawn were the scent of carnations upset the military precision, softening it, weakening it.

Annie had grown so fast that Marianne found it easy to slip her arm around her daughter's waist as she did now. Every fine evening they came there to walk up and down. Here they plotted and planned the future for the family. It took on an urgency as William became rude and defiant. It forced an admission from her that though she might impose her will on the prisoners, even sway criminals, it was a rule denied her at home and she did not know how to handle her son.

She was surprised, she had thought it would be easy, arguing that most mothers had a bond with their sons, but Marianne's bond was with Annie.

"What are we to do with William?"

"Send him away to school. That is what he wants. He's tired of all of us." The plain statement shocked Marianne. The problem had become so involved in her mind she saw no solution.

"How do you know William wants to go away to school?"

"Oh Mother, surely you know, he's always talking of it."

Marianne looked across the path at the bright delphiniums and the phrase, "he's always talking of it" pricked like a nettle in her mind. He had never spoken of it to her. She felt a failure and the blue flowers held no consolation.

Marianne knew what she would do. She would discuss the matter with the Governor.

The next day, their business meeting concluded, she asked him if he knew much about boys' boarding schools. Beyond Rugby he knew very little, but he warned her against small schools in remote areas and he promised to find out more for her.

Within days, he called Marianne to his office. He placed before her the name of The Yorkshire School in London. It was a college designed for the sons of widows of Yorkshiremen. In a matter of weeks it was decided that he should go there in the autumn.

Because of the expense of his outfit, the family gave up their summer holiday. The packing of the trunk seemed to take its place. They all sewed and handkerchiefs, vests, garters of knitted wool, boots and mufflers all disappeared into the deep tin chest painted to resemble wood. They never seemed to tire of it.

William became tractable overnight. He loved the attention and Marianne wondered if under his love for Annie, he had really been jealous of her success at school and, with some guilt, her own preference for Annie.

Soon it was time for William to go and the family watched him with pride as he marched to the Governor's house to say goodbye wearing his new school uniform.

He looked so handsome, so tall and straight that she thought that perhaps she would take him to see Mrs Somerset in Hampstead. It would prove that her choice had not been such a disaster as had been prophesied. William returned not with a crown, as more or less expected, but with a sovereign. "The Captain said 'Take this, Taylor, you will find the capital is an expensive place.'"

The tin trunk, which indoors had seemed so vast, shrank to pitiful proportions when seen on the roof of the cab. Grandma, Annie and Edith waved Marianne and William off. Marianne was flushed with excitement - it made her appear far less that her 28 years. Her emotions were mixed, she looked forward to her first return to London - she felt pride that she was able, with help, to send her son to a boarding school.

William was the most excited of all and so full of anticipations that Marianne feared that school might prove a disappointment.

In the train he talked more and more. He sat close by her and, as the carriage was empty, even permitted her to put an arm around him, but not for very long. He was restless and moved about and, even more, he was a very independent masculine being. As he stood leaning at the window that he had opened, she looked at him, curly haired, fair, tall but sturdy. She saw clearly that he was no member of her family, but of Benton's. There was the round faced, round-eyed handsome family. She saw in him some of Benton's pride, different to her own, a certain heedlessness of some social graces that she knew was Yorkshire. Yet, still there was something of her family... she had yet to discover what it was. When she did it was to be the strongest element of all in him.

In London, they drove to a small hotel in Russell Square. They dined inadequately in the fly-blown dining room and resolved to go out afterwards. They walked to Piccadilly, to Trafalgar Square and then down to Whitehall to see the Houses of Parliament. It was the river that really brought light to William's eyes and Marianne only dragged him from the bridge by amazing him at her aptitude in hailing a cab to take them back to Russell Square. Marianne felt happier, now that dusk had fallen, and in the cab she found herself less afraid of pick-pockets and rogues. She felt, too, very insignificant amongst the myriads of people. She realised that it was because she had lived so long in the narrow circumspection of life by a prison.

When William was in bed she decided to make a call on Mrs Somerset. At breakfast she decided against it, and instead, they went down to Westminster Abbey.

They paid their entrance fee and went in. It seemed much dirtier and smaller than she remembered. She led him to the South Aisle, then Poets' Corner. She wanted to see Dickens' name. Benton had so loved his novels, she found it poignant that her husband's death was divided by only a month from that of Dickens.

London authors fell away and she was back at Whiteley Bottom, awaiting Edith's birth and Benton was reading *Bleak House* to her as she sat by the fire sewing. She led William away to see the tombs of kings and queens. In the chapel of Henry VII she was filled with joy in the beauty and pride in the associations.

She pointed out the stall of Nelson. Again she thought her son so comely she went out and found a cab and they drove the long pull up to Hampstead.

She had plenty of time to doubt the wisdom of her decision. She did not have her card case with her, she had given no warning, and wondered if she would be welcome at all.

They stopped before the house and Marianne went through the garden and up the steps and rang. A footman, whom she did not recognize, answered and she entered. Everything was the same, strangely the same - she had changed so much she could not imagine other things remained static.

The carpet, the green carpet on the stairs and the curtains were all the same. The butler appeared, an ageing man.

"Why it's Miss Arnold."

"Yes, Mr Saunders, it is, or was. How are you?"

"Very well Ma'am, only older."

"And Mrs Somerset, how is she?"

"Like myself. She will be glad to see you, let me take you up."

"I have my son in the cab, I will fetch him." She made to go to the door.

"No, no, Miss, I will send Henry."

Marianne then remembered that in this world there were so many things one did not do oneself. When William entered

Marianne introduced him and instantly William put out his hand. The butler, after a momentary hesitation, shook it.

They ascended the stairs in the sombre light. The window on the stairs was of stained glass and a crowded scene showed Titania and Bottom awaking from their sleep. William felt uneasy and slipped his hand into his mother's. He found it strange to think that she had lived here.

They passed the boudoir door and Saunders knocked at the drawing room. The voice bidding "Come in" was exactly as she remembered it. At the end of the room was Mrs Somerset, the same bows, the same silks and lace, but they had taken possession, the woman within had crumpled. She rose, peered, extended her hand, the poise of the head was the same... but all aged.

They kissed. Then William was introduced. The usual expostulations on size and appearance ensued. Soon the bell pull was seized and Saunders was bidden to pay and dismiss the cab and two extra places had to be laid for lunch.

Marianne glowed as she saw William take his food proffered by the footman and Saunders as if it was customary and every day the same. Mrs Somerset had many questions to ask and when she discovered that Marianne was the Matron of a prison, not only her eyes opened wide but those of Saunders and Henry as well.

"But, I assure you it is not awful at all. Wakefield Prison is a model for the whole of England. It is good to be able to do something for those unfortunate women. My latest innovation is a schoolmaster. He is teaching them to read."

In her happiness Marianne had harboured resentment against Mrs Somerset, who had obstructed her marriage for a long time. But now she saw her mother's old friend, still brilliant, shrewd and charming, not an ogre at all. She understood, as she had not in her youth and her love, the old lady's disappointment.

When they were alone, the old lady bent towards her and said: "Why didn't you let me know? I could have helped."

"How could I ask you when I upset all your plans?"

"Well, looking at your son, I think, perhaps you were right."

Marianne wanted to ask much more, but felt that the past must be undisturbed. Mrs Somerset looked again at her old protegee, there were questions she, too, wished to ask. She saw a thinner Marianne, more poised and in spite of the chignon, she still had what she had invented, 'the Holbein look'. Yet she still regretted the disruption of her old plan. She thought Marianne wasted on a prison.

When it was time to go, she wished to do something. So she had a large basket filled with jams and cakes for William and then insisted that they used her carriage to go to the school. So it was William arrived at the Yorkshire School in a private carriage and with plentiful tuck. It was a good beginning for him, very propitious, but scarcely in keeping with a semi-charitable institution.

On the way back, Marianne had plenty of time to think. She found it unusual - her days were so full that weeks went by without her ever really dreaming, let alone pondering.

She enjoyed it. First of all, she rejoiced that William was where he wished to be, at a boarding school. Then she was pleased that what she had seen had assuaged any fears and, indeed, had pleased her and she thought that she was qualified to assess institutions.

She wished, however, that it had been a finer school.

She rested in the thought that she had no fears for him and it would equip him for his proper place in a secure profession.

Then, as was inevitable, she thought of Mrs Somerset. She had refused an invitation to go back there for the night. She had various reasons. Partly, she wished to be alone, partly because her life had changed so much, that she did not wish to disturb herself by thinking of what might have been.

It had been so easy, she had found, to slip back to the old standards and old attitudes even for a few hours. Yet she did not find herself hankering for that life again, it was too circumscribing. It imposed too blinkered a view. She was glad, with all its disadvantages, to be able to see all around and not like a carriage horse, only forwards.

It all came down to one basic fact. She had loved Benton so much that he had made everything worthwhile. And above all else, she was returning to her home, to Benton's mother and to her girls. What she failed to realise was that though she spoke of her daughters in the plural, it was the image of Annie that was most clearly in focus and which ultimately dominated.

When she arrived at Wakefield, she was surprised to find both Annie and Edith on the platform. They were beaming and eager and wanted to know exactly what the school was like and what they had done.

With a daughter on each arm they went thought the streets briskly towards Love Lane and Grandma.

In the little house she looked round, the faces, the things. "No, I would change none of this for Hampstead."

The removal of a young boy had the effect of changing the constitution of the little household in Wakefield completely. It became wholly feminine. There was no talk of football and quite another side of school life. There were fewer tantrums, less tension, but much more boredom.

The conversation was usually constricted to persons, their speculations were often of domestic situations in other people's houses. A small boy had strangely brought in another element and been a brake upon their pre-occupation with clothes.

They trimmed their hats continually, forever planning new wardrobes for the following season. Yet this was in many ways only a veneer to cover a real seriousness. Marianne was exact and precise at her work, it absorbed her. Marianne knew, however, that the prison and school were not enough and she encouraged every social activity that took her girls out of the perimeter of the prison.

The society of Wakefield was divided by politics, but even more by religion. It was not a matter of being of the Established Church or Non-Conformist only - it was also a matter of whether one was High, or Low Church. Groups gathered into their respective categories. The family hovered on the border of the tea party givers. The hostesses found it very difficult to place a widow who obviously respectable, well-read and elegant, yet worked for her living. She was accepted both for herself and for her daughter who was bright, well-mannered and almost pretty.

There was, however, something uneasy in their situation. Then Annie made friends with two girls whose father, a solicitor, lived at Horton. The walk out to the village was long, but, there, it was a different world, it was a village where the divisions of creed and politics were not felt so keenly and where the circumstance of a widow was more readily understood because there was less pretension.

Mr Outhwaite was a widower. His girls had led a lonely life, they were wrapped up in each other.

Priscilla, the elder, was a pupil-teacher, like Annie and they found much in common, so that frequently Annie was at their house. Annie well remembered her first encounter with Mr Outhwaite. The girls had been dressing up and Annie, with a long tapestry curtain train, believed herself to be Queen Elizabeth. She met him at the bottom of the stairs and so powerful was her imagination that when she was introduced she expected him to bow.

He did not and with open eyes she glared at him, then suddenly retracted into her own self and bobbed a curtsey. The momentary scene had amused him and he had smiled when the girls ran merrily upstairs. He continued to be amused by her and encouraged the friendship.

Within weeks of meeting Annie, he met her mother. He had gone to the prison to interview a client. He knew that his errand was futile, the woman was cowed, she feared her husband and found prison preferable to the tyranny of her husband.

He was, as usual, shown to the lawyers' visiting room, a place quite familiar to him, and he waited. He heard footsteps, the echo in a corridor as a door was closed and locked, then a rustle and the unlocking of the door to the room. The prisoner, in her grey dress, white apron and white cap was followed by a woman, not in wardress's garb, but in black. She came forward and extended a hand.

"Mr Outhwaite. I am the deputy Matron. Have I your consent to remain?"

He turned to his client. "Is this your wish?"

The cowed woman looked up for a moment and replied, "Yes."

"You are technically at liberty. Please speak freely. You are under no duress."

"No, please let her stay."

Mr Outhwaite was quite startled. He had never known her be so positive in anything. Three chairs scraped on the highly polished oil-cloth and they sat around the table. Questions were asked and, at first, they were answered, being quite simple.

As the lawyer probed more deeply, as there were implications in the answers, so the prisoner became more uneasy, embarrassed and uncommunicative.

Mr Outhwaite was becoming impatient and his manner became brusque. Marianne saw precisely what he would be like in court, a sudden assumption of an entirely new mood and expression. Mrs Rumbold's replies were vital to her freedom, but slowly her head descended upon her arms resting on the table. Mr Outhwaite rapped on the table,

"I am doing my best to help you. I must have your co-operation. Come, now." There was no response at all. He rapped harder on the table and became angry.

Then he was aware that he was being reprimanded and he looked round at Marianne swiftly, fiercely, he would truck no interference. She was sitting bolt upright and smiling at him and waving her finger at him as though he were a naughty child. She whispered so low she nearly only mouthed, "Slow, slow."

Then, to his surprise he saw her bend down towards the huddled figure and place a hand very gently on her shoulder. There was great compassion and understanding and, to his further surprise, Mrs Rumbold lifted her head and looked at him.

The interview, the questioning was resumed, but Mr Outhwaite was not unaware of shakes of the head from Marianne when she thought he pressed too hard in his hunt for the truth.

Quite suddenly, he realised that he had gone far enough for one day and that he must give the poor woman time. With courtesy he closed the encounter. When the door shut behind the poor woman, Marianne smiled at him again and said,

"I am so sorry to intrude so. But that poor woman has become friend, as much as is possible in this place. I can tell you nothing, of course, but if you proceed gently you will discover enough. Poor thing, she is such a coward. She fears her husband far more than being here."

"I find that very difficult to understand."

"You would not, when you have been here. Here they have a room to themselves and no responsibilities and are protected from many fears. But, of course, the mothers suffer terribly not seeing their children."

"So you do not think this too bad a place?" He said it almost playfully.

Marianne bridled, like all the officers at Wakefield did and replied: "Mr Outhwaite, this is a model prison."

He looked at her again and suddenly saw Annie Taylor, his daughters' friend in Marianne's face.

"How stupid of me, you are Annie Taylor's mother. We greatly enjoy her company."

John Outhwaite left the prison a very satisfied man. He had far more of the information he required than he thought possible and he was very interested in Mrs Taylor. He remembered not so much her face, her hair, as the still authority about her tinged with humour and so strangely, in such a place, elegance.

He even momentarily imagined her sitting opposite him at the supper table. As quickly as the vision appeared it was dismissed. John Outhwaite was a man of infinite caution.

The quiet life continued. They were secure, while Marianne was earning, but they were still poor. Holidays were restricted to visits to Crosland Moor or in Annie's case, to her friends. The event they most looked forward to was the return of William from school. His letters had revealed nothing, they were formal, and the first hint of a personal wish came in the last letter written that term.

He requested that none of them should kiss him at the station as other boys would be present. Annie laughed and thought that it was just like a boy, Marianne was hurt. She felt that it was yet another step that William was taking from her side.

When the day came, the train drew in, the doors opened and people flooded out, and there was William. He saw them and walked quickly towards them raising his hat. Marianne remembered the request and put out her hand to his only to suddenly feel his arms around her neck. She wanted to pick him up but knew that was impossible - he had grown several inches.

Only gradually did he slip back into the old life and old ways and it was with Annie that the bonds were first re-established. Together they played and together they excluded Edith. Edith after a show of temper did, what she always did - retreated to Grandma, finding there the comfort and love she desired.

One evening, Marianne called William, as well as Annie, to walk with her in the Governor's garden. Marianne found herself almost unwilling to admit him here. She felt it was private to Annie and herself alone.

They walked down the broad paths, they smelt the roses and carnations. Soon William began hunting for frogs by the pond. He very soon caught a small young green creature and they all watched it swim away perfectly.

"I can do the breast stroke. We go to some baths every fortnight," volunteered William and both of the women found this an interesting and very male phenomenon. They were even more startled when he continued: "I have to learn to swim, for you never know when you are at sea when it may save your life. I cannot imagine a sailor being unable to swim. But there are some, you know."

"Are you going to be a sailor, then, William?" asked his mother.

"Oh yes. Didn't you know?"

"No, but I am not surprised. Your grandfather was a sea captain. That is why I know so little about him. He was always away. Do you really want to go to sea?"

Marianne was chilled, she hated the sea. She had seen the worry and the responsibility age her mother. She even saw, for a moment, the graveyard, which she thought she had forgotten, at St Dogmael's where so often the gravestones mentioned someone "lost at sea", "died in the Canary Isles."

She laughed away her fears and, she hoped, William's juvenile ambitions. "Sail away and leave your poor old mother?"

"But I shall always return."

"No, you stay with me. We'll send you to a medical school, won't we Annie? You'll become a doctor and we will look after you until you are married."

William was not listening. He was off down the path ahead of them. Mother and daughter walked, as they always did, arm-in-arm. The Governor, glancing out of his study window saw the scene.

He smiled. It was, he thought, all as it should be, the boy adventuring ahead and the women walking together behind. He liked the idea of William being free - there were enough imprisoned people.

Edith, supposedly asleep, saw them return. She pretended when her mother came in, but Marianne was not deceived and kissed and cuddled her.

Soon William was back at school again and the cycle of work continued. Edith was at the Lancastrian School, now, and following in Annie's footsteps, she, too, was quick and eager, but lacked Annie's zest and delight in the school for its own self.

Annie was a tall girl. She had shot up and was much taller than her mother. Her face was round and, until she smiled, was almost plain. Her front teeth were too large and she tended to slouch.

One day, returning home on a hot June day, she idled up the path to the back door. Grandma was hovering between the sink and the hob with a tea pot. She was gently swirling the hot water around to warm it. She looked up and the sight she saw made her straighten an already erect back. As the latch of the door scraped she took in a sharp intake of breath.

When Annie entered, she hissed: "Goodness girl, hold yourself up, you languish like a dying bluebell. I saw your nose come round that corner five minutes before the rest of you. Have you a backbone?"

Annie's round eyes flashed with an anger that died like a falling star and, bursting into tears, she flung down her books and ran upstairs. Mrs Woodhouse was taken aback. She tut-tutted and continued to make tea, dismissing the incident as "a girl's foolishness".

Upstairs, Annie, in a fever, rummaged through her chest of drawers. Finding an old petticoat, she tore it up and with fear and horror, removed her clothes gingerly. Sick with apprehension, she tried to stem the fount of blood. She fainted on her bed and recovered only to swoop with vertigo again into blessed forgetfulness.

She came round into the frightening world, panic stricken because she was ignorant. The blood alarmed her and she wondered if she was having a baby, but she assured herself that this was impossible because she had never kissed a man. The very thought caused her to shudder.

Slowly she felt better, pouring water into the basin she carefully washed her face. She dressed carefully and, steadying herself, went downstairs. Grandma gave her a dismissive look but kept silent. She cut bread and poured out tea. Annie forced herself to eat, but, at that moment she hated her grandmother and snapped at Edith who used her knife for the butter.

"None of that Miss High and Mighty" said Grandma, rising to her favourite's defence.

Annie relapsed into stubborn quietness. Then as she ate, she suddenly became aware of blood again and she fainted, slithering to the floor. This time, when she returned to consciousness, she found herself gazing into the tender and concerned eyes of her mother.

Distantly, she heard the adults murmur, far away she felt them support her and propel her up the stairs. There Marianne began to undress her, unbuttoning her dress, untying the tapes of her petticoat and the buttons of her bodice.

Annie submitted, dazed. But when her mother undid the button of her drawers, Annie went rigid and dashed her hands into the cleft of her lap as she sat on the bed. She defied her mother with hysterical rage. Grandma entered at this moment and said: "Slap the bad girl."

But as Marianne saw the white-faced child, she saw that she was becoming a woman. She suddenly knew the cause and blamed herself that she had been so slow to prepare her daughter.

"Go downstairs, Grandma. Annie and I want to be alone."

When the door was closed she sat by Annie.

"My poor lassie. I know just what has happened. It happens to all of us - it still happens to me."

"I am not going to have a baby?"

"Goodness me, no."

Annie's relief was in itself a pain. She wept in her mother's arms and Marianne wished, at that moment, to protect her child from all possible harm, and that included growing up.

She instructed Annie and the rest of the evening was like the calm after a storm. Except that the air became closer and closer, the air strangely still. Every window was opened but still the heat oppressed.

When they were all in bed, sleep came very slowly and as the doors were open on to the landing, they were all aware of the odd little noises personal to each, sounds usually never heard, a groan, a cough, a sigh.

Annie asleep dreamt of a mysterious house. There was thunder and lightning as she approached. She awoke to find the storm was real, but her dream lingered and her heart beat hard as she heard a step on the staircase.

She saw a light, then the familiar swish of her mother's dressing gown as it plop-plopped down each step. She then heard movements in the kitchen and went downstairs.

Marianne was stirring the embers of the fire to boil a kettle, a thunder clap rolled overhead and the house shook.

Annie was afraid and went to her mother.

As she shivered Marianne said: "Think of those poor creatures who are frightened locked in their cells. The thought brought action and she hastily put on a dress and a cape over her dressing gown. Annie opened the umbrella for her and she saw her mother in the deluge disappear down the road towards the great gate. She was filled with admiration and pride and longed to grow up to be like her.

She crept upstairs with a candle, fumbled beneath the mattress and drew out the copy of *Jane Eyre* which Grandma considered immoral. She opened it but in spite of her love for it, she found that the figure of her mother crept always between her and Jane.

Had Annie followed her mother, her admiration might have grown. Marianne was greeted with questioning though the grill and then surprise. When she was let in, she swiftly crossed the yard and let herself into the women's quarters. The unease was immediate, the wardresses moved along the galleries, their chains clanking, betraying their nervousness.

Marianne went from spy hole to spy hole and found an anxious, terrified eye looking at her in more instances that she had bargained for. To them all she spoke words of reassurance. By the time she had made her round, the storm was moving on with a large rumble and crash just to remind that great might still lingered there.

When she got home, she found Annie reading and was greeted not with praise, but the outraged propriety of the young.

"Mother, you never went around the prison like that!"

Her cape had slipped pulling her imperfectly buttoned dress, so that the ruffle at the neck of her nightgown showed. Marianne laughed and said: "No wonder Mr Roberts looked at me so approvingly."

William was growing up too, in the school. Ever since the moment of his arrival with his hamper of provisions in the private carriage, he had been marked out as special. True, the contents of the hamper soon disappeared except for two pots of despised plum jam. But he kept his sovereign.

It was also easier to hide as he saw the rapidity with which his possessions vanished and the so-called friends with them. He became much more cautious.

The aura of wealth lingered and he did not let his associates forget it. In school he was average, he mastered most things easily, too easily, so he was often careless.

He reserved his real energy and thought for athletics. He ran, swam, jumped and became in due course captain of various teams. Prefects' studies welcomed him and early he was initiated into their ethos - with them he drank on rare occasions, more frequently he smoked and behind the closed doors garbled sexual information was exchanged and prowess boasted.

It was one February when the frost lay so thick that no games could be played that the masters, wearied by the noise and mischief of unexercised boys, gave permission for couples to make their own walks.

William and Richard, his friend, gave their names and mentioned Greenwich Park as their destination. Once out, muffled and gloved they counted their money, boarded a bus and then the underground and reached, at last, with great triumph, the docks.

They wandered among the packing cases, the derricks, stepped over ropes and chains. They watched the dockers handling sacks and huge cases... they were impressed by the self-importance of the foremen walking with their sheaves of papers.

They observed the sailors hanging over the ships' sides, lazily regarding the activity, their work in bringing it done. Some were steamboats, more were sail, but whichever it was exercised a powerful fascination on William.

It was a longing, a desire, greater than any he had known before. His imagination was fed and grew rich as he saw names of ports, Amsterdam, Stockholm, Barcelona, Marseilles, Genoa. The sea surged in his thoughts, pounding and swelling. It swelled, heaved, it was rough, it was smooth, it was always in motion and for days it remained with him.

Richard was fascinated too.

He was hard to drag away, but William was well aware that if they stayed too long, they would be found out at school and the adventure could never be repeated.

At five o'clock, the boys stood in their places at the white scrubbed table while Grace was said. They looked at the thick white slices of bread and butter. William gave thanks far more for the glimpse of the world that they had seen than in anticipation of the dull fare.

That night, before he slept, William was again at sea. There was darkness, only lights on the ship and the distant shore could be seen. The whole life of shipboard surrounded him, harsh orders, fierce hazards, caves, depths, shoals, ports, other vessels. He was enraptured, he was enslaved, the salt in his blood had found its affinity.

As he had thought, Richard talked. But William told nobody, and when asked if he would lead a party in a repeat performance, said no more than he might.

William gazed at the globe. He imagined tropical heat, imagined icebergs. He vowed that he would see it all for himself. Alone he made many trips to the docks.

When he was at home he kept his secret. Not even Annie heard. At tea parties when Dr Wood, the prison's medical officer came, or Mr Wilkinson the prison visitor, and they asked him what he wished to do, he remained non-committal.

Only once, in the garden alone as he was practising some knots and the Governor came suddenly upon him and asked him to explain them, did he tell the truth. Captain Armitage approved and when William asked him to keep it secret, he agreed and most honourably complied.

Chapter 9

Party Dress

The sun beat down. It pierced the haze that so often hung over Wakefield. Walking in the shade were Marianne and her two daughters. It was early-closing day and they were in the High Street near the great cross-road at the centre of the town.

The roads were deserted and there were very few pedestrians, only a few cats basking in the sun. Slowly, the three made their way, but their progress was erratic for they wandered from one side of the street to the other.

They darted across whenever something caught their eye. Together they inspected the bootmaker's shop where his wares were neatly placed in rows caught by the heel on slim brass rods.

They spent less time looking at the grilled window of the jeweller, the furniture shop interested them a little more, but then they came to the Yorkshire Emporium. Here were the gowns, dresses, coats, capes, hats and scarves they really wished to see. A window was filled with clothes for weddings and garden parties.

Standing at the rear of the window on a round platform was a dress of thin grey silk. It was the palest ash colour with white spots, it had ruffles of its own material and, at the neck, white lace which was repeated at the wrists and in the bustle.

It was exquisitely feminine. Marianne exclaimed at its charm - it spoke to the repressed frivolous side of her nature, the part which she thought had been dormant for years. She was tired of economy, tired of black and not only did she like it, but Annie and Edith loved it too.

"But when on earth should I wear such a dress?" enquired Marianne. Annie replied very swiftly, "In three weeks' time when the Governor gives his party."

It was wholly suitable and there was an occasion.

"But when should I wear it after that?"

"You will look so nice at the party many people will invite you out just to see the dress again," said Edith.

Marianne was troubled and the rest of the windows were an

anti-climax for she kept thinking of the dress. She knew, only too well, how close was their budget. She knew of a bill unpaid, yet still, the dress remained vivid before her. The girls kept talking of it too. In the evening, after supper, she got out her account book and reached down the coal-merchant's last bill. She carefully added up the figures, counted her past quarter's salary and looked to the next.

The dress still stood there, but reason bade her acknowledge that it was out of the question. For almost the first time since her widowhood she became petulant. She knew that she had faced greater issues than this more calmly and shown far greater resolution, but she was angry at being forced to make so many denials. Even next day in the prison office, even as she interviewed a new prisoner, she fleetingly recalled the ruffles of the dress.

During a sewing lesson Annie also thought again of the dress and she decided to have another look at it on her way home. School over, that evening there was no extra class for the pupil-teachers, she found Edith and together they went to the High Street.

At the Emporium, the dress stood delicately aloof on its little platform. They gazed and imagined their mother wearing it. Together they said, "Let's see how much it costs."

They went in. The front of the shop was lined on each side by counters and they looked at the gloves, the handkerchiefs as they shyly made their way to the stairs leading up to the salon where the dresses were.

They had rarely been in such a shop before, but both of them were determined and bent on their scheme. An assistant came a little too slowly for Annie's liking to them. Annie drew herself up. She was taller than the assistant.

"I wish to see a dress, if you please. The grey silk one in the window."

"Was it for yourself?"

Annie sensed impertinence and with the authority teaching had given her 14 years, she replied, "Of course not. It is far too old for me. I wish to look at it for an older relative."

They were motioned to two chairs and they sank on to them putting their leather satchels on the carpeted floor. Annie looked at her sister.

"Sit up, Edith, don't slouch."

The gown was brought in over the assistant's arm. She held it up before Annie.

"Very pretty, can you just turn it round so that I can see the train. Hmm, it's a little shorter than I thought."

She then asked to feel it. It was the softest of silk and Annie saw that it was beautifully made.

"And what is the price?" She managed to sound casual.

"This is an expensive dress. It costs four guineas. It is hand sewn."

Edith looked alarmed. Annie's face remained expressionless. She loved the dress dearly. She had thought that it would cost more. She had been telling herself so often a prodigious price, that it appeared almost cheap. Her savings amounted to eight pounds and over many years.

"It is for my mother. She finds it very difficult to shop, she is matron of the Prison. Might we be allowed to have it on approval?"

Edith was very impressed by Annie's courage. The assistant went over to an older woman who returned with a look both perplexed and amused.

"We do not usually allow gowns out on approval without a deposit. In fact, we hardly ever let them out at all until purchased."

"I expect many of your customers have accounts?"

"Why, yes."

"Then we will open one in my mother's name." It was said so calmly that the manageress agreed, even more when she took down the name and address. "They must be honest," she said to herself.

"Do you wish to take it with you?"

"No, we have other purchases to make and calls to pay. Would you deliver it please and this evening, if possible. If it does not fit and look right, it will be returned tomorrow at half-past eight."

Annie rose slowly, Edith jumped to her feet. Smilingly Annie led the way out and down the stairs.

Outside Edith gasped, "Oh Annie."

"Wasn't that lovely? I mean everything, not just the dress. Oh, when I am grown up I shall buy dresses and dresses in just such shops. It was wonderful."

Only at home, as they ate their tea and awaited their mothers's return, did Annie's exaltation began to decline. She wished for her mother to be present when the package should arrive, and explaining it all to Grandma, thought Annie, would be difficult.

Marianne returned, tea continued and the knocker on the door thumped. With a heart beating to match it, Annie ran to receive the parcel. She then flew upstairs with it, unpacked it and laid it out gracefully on the bed.

"Who was that?" asked Marianne when Annie came back.

"A package. It is for you upstairs, there's no hurry."

"What is it?"

"You will see."

Edith giggled. Grandma, quick to notice her favourite said: "And what's come over you, Miss?"

Marianne's curiosity was aroused then died down. It was Annie's turn to be impatient. Her feet kept pattering about as though she could not control them. There was the table to be cleared, the washing-up to be done and Annie thought that her mother would never go upstairs.

At last she did. There was a cry from upstairs and Annie, preceded by Edith, bounded up and there was a sight they were never to forget... their mother blushing with tremendous pleasure, holding the dress up before her in front of the long mirror.

"Look what is here. How did it get here?"

Annie ignored the questions and said, "You must put it on properly, Mother."

With two very eager helpers, buttons were undone, tapes untied and the dress lowered over her head. It looked elegant, lovely, and Marianne seemed 10 years younger, and she saw it. She whispered, "It's beautiful. But isn't it too young?"

"Certainly not."

"You look lovely, Mother," pronounced Edith with great feeling.

Marianne looked at herself more severely, more critically. It was the smartest dress she had worn since she became a widow. She wanted it badly.

"Annie, you are behind all this. How much does it cost?"

"Three pounds." Edith again marvelled at her elder sister.

"Then I shall have it."

The girls were so delighted they danced and it was Grandma who opened the door upon three young females all agog with joy. She, too, stopped and looked at her daughter-in-law.

"Well handsome is as handsome does, and you done us all

handsome, my dear. Is that for the garden party?"

As with all such purchases, the one garment demanded others to accompany it. It was Marianne who decided that the grey spotted silk would be improved and made more matronly by the addition of three black silk bows, one on the breast and two on the sleeves. It turned it into an 18th century dress and looked very patrician.

It was Edith who made a pronouncement in the bedroom. "Something very nice and very exciting will happen to you in that dress." Marianne merely laughed.

But as the garden party approached and the sky was searched for the sign of clouds and deliberations on what to wear, Marianne was quite sure... her only prayer was that rain would not spoil everything.

Annie took the three pounds to the Emporium adding on the way 24 shillings. She did it without any hesitation for she loved her mother and she loved clothes.

The Governor's garden party was one of the annual events of Wakefield, awaited by a large proportion of its society. The upper staff of the Prison eagerly anticipated their invitations and watched with even keener interest the selection among their fellows.

The entire staff was never invited. They could not be, for the rule was absolute fairness. Yet sometimes, a name was overlooked, a tick from a previous year had been omitted and so there was supposed favouritism and some jealousy. The inclusion or exclusion of the children was also a point for discussion – and inflammation and balm.

It so happened that it was Marianne's turn to attend. She alternated automatically with the Matron, and when her expected card came, she discovered that both Annie and Edith were included, which gave her a great pleasure indeed.

So once more there was concern, if not consternation, shown over what the girls should wear. As Annie contemplated her wardrobe she regretted, for the first time, her extravagance over her mother's dress. But when some blue voile was bought she forgot the loss of her savings.

A green dress was made for Edith that went well with her red hair. Homework was overlooked until a severe reprimand came from Miss Robinson and conversation between Edith and Annie was so concentrated upon headgear that Grandma placed an embargo on the discussion of clothes at meal-times.

When the day came the sun failed to shine but the rain also forgot to fall. The garden was even more finely brushed, seemingly combed and generally arrayed more than ever. The locked door, by the main gates, was open and through it could be glimpsed the coloured dresses of the ladies and black coats of the men. But what heartened everyone was the sound of the band, The Prison Officers brass ensemble.

They sat in a double semi-circle in their best frogged uniforms, tightly, uprightly blowing into their instruments. Annie, as she passed them, looked at familiar faces in unfamiliar guise and she wondered how it was possible that such stiff stout figures could produce such supple sound. She noticed, too, the swift movement of the eyes of Mr Hodgkin as he saw her mother as she went by looking so pretty in the soft grey with its black spots and ruching that spread right round the hem.

Annie was so proud, for her mother looked not merely lovely, but so very dignified and Annie resolved to emulate her. Their mother shook hands with the Governor and Mrs Armytage and Annie and Edith, in the wake of the small ruched train, curtsied and then descended to the lawn.

What the two daughters never realised was how fast Marianne's heart was beating as she went into the midst of Wakefield's elite. She wondered whom she would know and, more significantly, who would wish to know her. There were smiles and distant nods and inclinations of the head and suddenly a cry. It was neat, pretty and fair Hannah Roberts, a fellow pupil-teacher, and instantly there was girlish chatter.

This brightened up the staid and respectable aura of the occasion and Marianne talking to the Vicar and Canon Alderson looked at the brightly- clad group where all the allure of youth seemed concentrated.

She crossed over to them and, kissing Hannah, saw her father. He came forward taking off his hat.

Immediately, Marianne felt the force of male interest - first of all he recognised her from the encounter in the prison and as she took his hand, she thought that there was a certain pressure on her hand. Annie was aware of it, too, but she failed to see it in Mr Roberts - she saw the sudden mantle of youthfulness that enveloped her mother. It was mysterious.

Later, she became suspicious as Mr Roberts was almost officious in his zeal to find chairs and tea for them all. While they delicately devoured sandwiches it was arranged that they should all go for Sunday dinner to the Roberts'. Annie was delighted, for she wanted to show the home of her friends to her mother. A date was fixed before they parted.

By now Marianne was surprised to find that she had so many acquaintances, she was enjoying herself in a manner that she had not done since her marriage, if the truth be known. Annie and Edith watched closely, half-consciously they knew that this event must be remembered over many months of dullness and mere routine.

Gradually, the more static colour of the garden regained its usual place and pattern as the contending hues of the ladies left. Soon, the Taylor women were at home and in need of another cup of tea. Marianne lay on the sofa in the parlour, she had reverted to an old self, a self older than herself, her mother, possibly Mrs Somerset too.

She let her daughters wait on her and Annie unlaced her boots for her. As she did so, she marvelled at the slenderness and fine line of the foot. It matched the matchless hands and Annie grumbled that hers were not so narrow and her fingers not so long. She had Benton hands.

"Wasn't Hannah's father kind?"

Again the flush of girlhood crossed her mother's face and it was qualified by the colder remark.

"Not really any more than a gentleman should be. But he was very pleasant."

Edith smilingly said: "I told you that something very nice would happen when you wore that dress."

Marianne looked down, she admired the ruffles. "Yes, it is very lovely. I am glad you, naughty girls, made me buy it. I hope that fashions won't change, then I can wear it at your weddings."

Annie looked very shocked. "But, Mother, that won't be for years and there'll be many more dresses and fashions before then."

Soon the party was a memory and the usual sequence of school, exams, filled the days of the girls, and for Annie part of the night. Marianne's days opened and shut, unlocked and locked with a grave regularity. Her main scheme at the time was to engineer the

Prison Board into engaging a teacher for the women prisoners. Marianne was shocked that so many of them were unable to read, or write. Most could sign their names, a trick that covered much ignorance.

Events, small events, had clustered in so fast that it was a great surprise when a letter arrived asking her, and the girls to lunch on the following Sunday. They were all pleased and Marianne's first thought was, "I shall be able to wear my dress again."

They travelled to Horbury by train and were met at the station by Mr Roberts with his trap. They trotted though the little town with its shops all shuttered and, turning up a lane, came to his house embosomed in laurels. The girls knew it well, but it was Marianne's first visit. Hannah, Mr Roberts' daughter, was hostess and she led Marianne upstairs to take off her cape and bonnet.

She was a little surprised that Marianne had not brought a small covered basket with her holding her lace cap for indoors. Marianne had long considered such caps were for old widows and the elderly, not the young and she would add: "I am only 34."

Dinner went off well. There was a sense of freedom in the house, the girls giggled and when reproved mildly by their father they were subdued only for the shortest time. When the good Sunday dinner was finished, the girls supervised the clearing of the dishes to the kitchen and tidying the room, but Mr Roberts took Marianne out into the garden.

The house, Marinanne had thought, was well-appointed but dull. It lacked a wholeness and missed the presence of a woman constantly presiding. The garden was different, it was a paradigm of horticultural precision. There were espaliers with bordering carnations beneath. The vegetables were in drilled rows, the onions seemed to shoot up the left leaf then a right leaf like soldiers at command.

Marianne wondered who the fugleman was and, as it reminded her too vividly of the prison gardens, was not charmed. She was shown the melon house where the fruit hung suspended in nets which allowed them to expand. From the staging in a fernery, Mr Roberts took a maidenhair fern: he was about the give it, but hesitated. Marianne thought that he had changed his mind, and was a little amused, then she heard him say that it would soil her hands, so her carried it.

All the while he had been enchanted by this pretty woman with her dark hair who moved so quietly and with such dignity. Marianne looked at him, he was as neat as his garden, but from both a quality was missing.

As they approached the house, girlish laughter came though the open windows. She realised then, that she had never seen Mr Roberts laugh... smile, but never laugh outright.

It was time to go and they were driven to the station. The horse hitched up to a rail and Mr Roberts saw them on to the little train. Marianne was on the point of making an invitation for the following Sunday, but withheld - she thought it might be indelicate.

Instead, she just smiled over the waving, fluttering fronds of the green fern.

As she lay in bed that night she thought of her day and she wondered why she had not asked him to Sunday dinner. Then, quite clearly, she knew why... she did not like him sufficiently.

A few evenings later, Marianne wearing an apron went into the hall. A male figure was outlined though the glass panelling of the door. She knew who it was and before he knocked, she quickly removed the apron. She opened the door and exclaimed at the unexpectedness of his visit. She led him to the parlour and the small fern on a table stood between them. In the stillness the fronds did not shimmer. Marianne, then, sensed the reason for his visit and his mission. She was alarmed and for a moment was tempted to call in her children and Grandma as a barrier, a defence.

It vanished as she saw his plump hand tremble slightly. She noticed a flush upon his cheek. He saw a woman, still young whose apparent calm was betrayed by the flutter of her eyelids. Twice in succession she had asked him if he would take tea or coffee and on neither occasion had she heeded, even heard, his answer.

The studied demeanour of the solicitor overcame the suitor and very solemnly, and without touching as much as her hand, he asked her to become his wife. Marianne was not only flattered she was touched, but had no answer. She truly did not know and she said so.

Robert Roberts was committed. He could now speak openly, and he said, for the third time, that he would enjoy a cup of coffee. While alone, he looked about the room and gazed at the old fashioned furniture. He was impressed by the miniatures and the mirror - those he knew to be good, though he knew nothing of such things. But he saw the poverty behind the gentility. When she returned with a tray, he launched into his desire to give her a worthier home. He spoke of the assets, foremost among them the friendship that already existed between Hannah and Annie.

Marianne listened. She mentioned Edith and William and then even more seriously, Grandma.

Holly Lodge was, she was informed, large enough for them all. Marianne asked for time to consider it all. As he left, he kissed her on the forehead. She looked into a face that was kindly, but which awoke no response in her. He left.

For a while she sat alone in the parlour, her thoughts were in turmoil. She was excited and perplexed at once. She did not stay still for long but picked up the key of the Governor's garden and went out. She walked down the smooth gravel paths, past lupins, past dark delphiniums, but saw none of them.

She walked beneath the apple trees and a hard green apple fell into the folds of her shawl. She picked it out. It was a miniature apple and she dug her nail into it. No juice came, but it smelt like an apple – yet autumn was three months away.

Would marriage be like that, an almost, looking like marriage, acting like marriage but lacking the feeling? Should she marry him? She thought of the security, the ease from the burden of finding enough money. She would be able to take rest and no longer be so dreadfully tired. Theatres and concerts would be possible and she could awaken her children's minds to these delights. It would no longer be just reminiscent of her London days but the plays of the present.

Up and down the path she went, her face darkening with indecision. What should she do with this opportunity? They could all benefit by it, but the question nagged, would they? Annie was great friends with Hannah, she assured herself, but a step-sister was a very different relationship to a friend. She looked at the prison. She was often wearied by its unchanging routine, and the strain of constantly watching weak and tortuous minds.

But this work gave her freedom, she was her own mistress, she had no domestic tyrant to contend with.

She went out of the garden, locking the gate, quieter in spirit but with no resolutions.

The neatness and the lack of imagination in the warders' gardens tried her, they betokened small minds. Was hers so much greater, she asked herself, as she thought of Holly Lodge and of herself trailing among the flowers in gowns with ruffles.

Once within doors, she went up to see if Edith was asleep. She was. She looked in at Annie's room.

"Can't you sleep, my dear?"

"No, I'm wondering."

"What about?"

"Whether you will marry Mr Roberts?"

"How did you guess?"

"I just knew. I have never seen you look quite as you did look when he had gone."

"What would you think if I did?"

"I don't think I would like it."

She did not know precisely why her memories of her father were mere episodes. They were episodes though, to last her a lifetime. She recalled him carrying her over the canal lock, the waters deep and dark on one side churning and low upon the other.

She had her arms around him and his about her protected her from every vestige of fear. It could never be so with Mr Roberts. She remembered cutting her forehead and even as her father firmly held her down as the doctor sewed the wound, his face so anxious, had also been tender.

"I could never think of Mr Roberts as my father."

"Why, my dear?"

"Because he is so unlike Father. But, of course, I don't really need a father now."

"Well, don't worry. I don't think I shall marry him and whatever I do, you will be the first to know."

Downstairs, "So unlike Father" repeated constantly in her mind. It was true. The phrase led her to the parlour to the daguerreotype in its black hexagonal case on the mantelpiece. She picked it up and looked long at the long rounded face, the clear complexion, just like Annie's, the fringe of dark hair all around it.

He was utterly unlike Mr Roberts and she sat down and thought of Benton as she had not dared for a year and more. He had never disillusioned her and if time were to repeat itself, she would link her life with his again – even to that last and terrible year.

The year that robbed him of his looks, his gaiety… that sank his cheeks and hollowed his chest. She thought of his body so smooth and so firm. She had loved that body that had crept within her, pounding upon her. All the rhythm of their life returned, she experienced again the fluidity of their souls. Mr Roberts was so dry, poor man. She put back the photograph and looked around the room. Even, now, it was not her's alone, it was Benton's too. They had made it together when they chose the furniture.

As she looked she asked another question. "Where would Grandma fit in as a step-mother-in-law at Holly Lodge? The ideal of security did not seem to include the old lady."

The morrow dawned like any other and as Marianne awoke she remembered her task for the day. It was not at the Prison, but at home. Mr Roberts was to call for an answer and her heart sank. Breakfast was eaten, the girls despatched to school.

Marianne appreciated the sunshine as she walked to her office, but when indoors was glad of the warmth, for there was a nip in the air. She sat at her table, felt as well as looked for her pencil, pen and ink before her.

Her feet sought out the black fleecy rug and she then rang her bell. Troubles were reported, three prisoners interviewed, routine duty, routine inspection following.

The morning had almost passed before she had time to remember her problem and the decision she had almost arrived at. At that moment, Father Eyre, the Roman Catholic chaplain, knocked and came in. She was very fond of him. He appeared older than he was for his head was bent and his hair sandy grey. He was no great gentleman like Chaplain Alderson, but thought Marianne, a greater man of God. Yet he had for all that, a very clever face, narrow with a shrewd 'inquisitor's' nose which agreed wholly with his sharp eyes. He never missed an advantage in argument.

Marianne asked after his health, to which he replied,

"I am always well, thank God, for I have no wife to plague me."

"So you are in a teasing mood. Well, Father, though fond of your celibacy you seem to visit us a good deal, why is that?"

"Though one rejects temptation, one may still enjoy being tantalised by it. So I come to see you."

"Oh, I know why you have come. It is not us, it is Mary Docherty."

So they fell to discussing a prisoner. Marianne listened to a very clear and accurate description of Mary's character. The swiftness with which he sped to the core of a person's disposition never ceased to surprise her into admiration. Without thinking she found herself telling Father Eyre of Mr Roberts' proposal and she mentioned the security that it would bring her and possibly the family.

"So it's security you want, is it? It is a strange thing. When we do not have it then it is immensely desirable. When we have it, it is often a stranglehold and often far less secure than it seemed at a distance." Then he wagged his finger and said: "Remember, you have security here and with it, what I like, independence. Don't throw that away for a Will o' the Wisp."

Marianne laughed. "You would never call the man who has proposed a Will o' the Wisp. He's very solid indeed."

Father Eyre was not to be diverted. "Then you have your responsibilities here."

"But, don't you think that my family comes first?"

"I do, but soon, very soon, you will be launching them. Your days of responsibility for them are nearly over."

He rose to his feet, "Anyway, if you loved this man you would not, I think, be asking my advice. You would marry him."

Marianne knew that he was right. Life would continue to have innumerable difficulties, but she knew that she must, not battle, but just go on.

"My daughter, I shall pray for you. You will be shown a path. Leave it in the hands of God." He lifted his hand in blessing, a thing he had never done before and she felt strangely comforted.

At home for lunch, she found two letters awaiting her from London. She broke them open eagerly for one was from William. He said that he had decided to leave school and the headmaster agreed.

When she turned to the headmaster's letter she found the same news given more cautiously. William was given a good character with the qualification that it remained so if he kept in the right company.

He had proved himself very capable in the science laboratory and it was suggested that an opening as a chemist would be a good career for him.

Marianne was delighted. If he could not be a doctor then a

chemist was a good substitution, and it would mean that he could remain at home.

In the afternoon, she kept thinking of the immediate future and she saw that William and Holly Bank would not mix. To bring three children to the Roberts' household would be an imposition that would strain the best of relationships.

Mr Roberts came that evening. Marianne was very used to unpleasant interviews from her work. However, this one caused more unease for it was so personal. She began formally.

"You have done me a great honour and I am very greatly obliged, but I am unable to accept your offer."

At the stilted words she winced. Mr Roberts betrayed no emotion whatsoever, but he reached towards his hat.

"Well, there is no more to be said. I will go."

He was hurt, more than Marianne had expected. She nearly leapt to her feet, but restrained herself... it might undo all she had said.

"There is much more. I must tell you why I am refusing." Involuntarily she glanced up the photograph of Benton.

"I loved my husband very dearly. I cannot quite overcome the idea of infidelity in marrying another. Yet, I could, perhaps, overcome this. But I do feel I might draw unfair comparisons and then I would be unjust."

"I, too, can make all those excuses. Believe me, I do understand. We are older, this would be a different kind of marriage."

"Ah, but there is a still bigger reason, Mr Roberts, one that will surprise you. I have been independent for so long, I do not think I could return easily to a married state again. I have been in sole charge of my home and my work a long time."

She felt that she was not saying half of all that she felt. It seemed rather lame. She knew that often in the past she had grumbled to herself about the burdens, but she knew, now, that she had grown used to them. Her independence was very dear to her.

This did puzzle Mr Roberts. How could a woman refuse his income, his house? He wondered if underneath the charm there was a very commanding woman that he had not perceived. He found that difficult to believe, especially as she now insisted on his taking tea and cake before he left.

When he had gone Marianne wondered if she had been wise.

Then she remembered Father Eyre, she went into the little parlour and instead of taking the tray to the kitchen, she sat down.

Both Edith and Annie came in, Edith sat on the hearth rug and nestled against her legs.

"I am glad you haven't married Mr Roberts. We would not have been happy at Holly Bank. Certainly not Grandma."

Annie seemed very happy. They both looked forward to William's return for good. She saw that they looked forward to being a unity again. Yes, paths were being shown.

Summer suddenly came and with it the usual discontent that arose in the penned up community of the prison.

It was a revolt against monotony. This time the atmosphere seemed more silent, more oppressive. Everyone hoped that it would pass without incident, all were vigilant.

A day was proposed for a picnic to Sandal Castle. The girls cut the sandwiches in the morning ready for Marianne's return from morning duty. They were anxious to be off, at last she returned, they had lunch, and she changed into an old cotton frock.

She felt as young and light as her daughters. They set off down the street and round the corner they were confronted by two warders.

"Come quickly, Mrs Taylor, there's trouble."

Without question Marianne ran with them to the gate, where they were immediately let in. Inside all was as quiet as usual. Then Marianne noticed that it was an ominous silence. She hurried to the women's wing. The prisoners should have been in the exercise yard - they were locked in a workroom and by themselves. The Governor, the Matron and Chaplain Alderson were all gathered together.

"Thank goodness, you have come. They are armed with scissors and needles. They have begun to quarrel among themselves." He made as to hand over a megaphone. Marianne shook her head. "No, I must be among them."

While her courage was at its crest, she ran down the staircase, automatically taking from Mr Alderson's hand a small Bible. She knocked on the door loudly, a hush came from the growing volume of sound and a voice demanded who it was.

Marianne announced herself. There was a long pause, obvious conferring, and then the dragging away from the door of a heavy piece of furniture. She entered, her heart beating furiously. She managed to smile and raised a finger to her lips.

She walked forward, quiet rippled out from her. She came upon two who had been struggling over a chair and pretended that they were bringing it to her. "Thank you, Mrs Danson."

She sat down. She motioned them to sit. "Now, Mary Docherty, you tell me what it is all about." The secret was that although removed from them she remembered their names - that was her power.

They began to talk of their grievances. She learnt how a feud had arisen. It was an old story, a slight favouritism by a wardress, greatly magnified, a slight injustice vastly exaggerated.

It had all been heard before. Half an hour later she rose up. Promises had been made and they knew that they would be kept. Then a voice, an Irish one, said, "Why are you in that dress?" For a moment she faltered, then the truth came, "I was going for a picnic with my daughters. I am afraid it's too late, now. They'll be very disappointed."

There was an instant wave of commiseration that made Marianne bite her lip. "They are children. No more than naughty children," she said to herself.

The girls at home were anxious, then eager to hear and then proud. They were prouder still when Mr Alderson called and then Father Eyre. To Father Eyre Marianne said: "Well, I have been shown my path very clearly, haven't I?"

Chapter 10

William is Home

The little household awaited William's return eagerly. Grandma baked a special cake, Annie gave up her room and moved in with Edith and Marianne counted the money and planned new clothes for him.

Most of all, Marianne longed to have her son beneath her roof once more. Now that he was growing up it seemed like the return of something of Benton. She was on duty when his train arrived so she was unable to meet him.

Annie and Edith brought him from the station with an air of triumph. Marianne looked up, for a moment she hesitated, then ran to him... he towered over her. She was, as they all were, surprised by his extreme good looks, very tall and broad shouldered with thick fair hair.

As they sat down to tea, Annie noticed immediately that he did not move as they did. He was casual, he pulled back his chair so that it scraped on the floor, he dropped into his seat and as he crossed his legs, bumped the table and the teaspoons jumped in their saucers.

An interloper, though long desired, had arrived in a very prim and extremely feminine little world. Marianne had imagined she would find something of her husband in her son, instead she recognised what she thought she had forgotten, her father and he had been distant to her and she feared that William would be as well.

Before he started work William had a fortnight of holiday. It was not successful for the warm weather broke and it rained most of the time. Annie invited Hannah and Mary, her friends to tea, and was annoyed because Mary giggled most of the time and kept looking at William.

She could not understand why everything should be different because William had arrived.

One afternoon, William and Annie decided to walk out to the ruins of Sandal Castle. As they went through the town, Annie found herself pointing features out as though he had never been there before.

Wakefield was home to her and she knew many people to whom she smiled and waved. She was glad that they had seen so many, but William seemed indifferent and shocked her by saying that it was a poor and provincial place.

Then, as they were about to pass a tobacconist's shop, William stopped, thrust his hands into his pocket, looked at his change and went in. Annie halted, she was not going in, it was a masculine lair, to her it looked ugly and alien, she did not like the smell that wafted from the doorway.

She watched with amazement as William, without any embarrassment bought a packet of cigarettes. They continued the walk. Annie said nothing but thought a great deal. Over the bridge with the chapel, out on the road past the cemetery they walked.

As the road became rougher, more countrified, so they forgot their near adulthood and began to run and race. At the castle ruins they hid from one another. The ice was broken, they were children, they were brother and sister again.

William climbed a tree. Higher and higher he went and Annie's pleading that he stop only urged him to greater heights. He hailed her from a high stone wall. She had unpacked the basket and spread out tea… that would bring him down, she thought. It did.

As he munched a sandwich he talked critically of Grandma, Edith and even their mother. Annie was, again, shocked and wished to stop him, but kept silent for there were truths in what he said that she had not seen before. It was good that he spoke of them to her for she could keep, as she knew, her counsel.

It was then that the pulled the packet of cigarettes from his pocket, took one out, put it between his lips and lit it. Annie stared like a bird mesmerised. Lying there so nonchalantly he looked so beautiful, like a satyr in a wood and the smoke gave an air of wickedness as it came in a thin stream from his mouth and then in two puffing little clouds from his nose.

She watched fascinated. William became aware and groping in his pocket pulled out the packet and proffered them to her.

"Annie, do try one."

The thrill faded instantly and startled shock usurped its place.

"Oh, no. I couldn't possibly."

"Go on. Many of the fellows at school told me that their sisters sometimes have a puff."

Annie was now horrified. "No. Definitely not. And I don't think you ought to either. Mother won't like it at all." Her large eyes grew still larger.

"Then Mother will have to grow accustomed to it, won't she?"

Such rebelliousness left Annie speechless. It ended the pleasantness of the day. For a moment, the past seemed to have been regained, but everything was different, everything was changed. William made Annie, his senior, feel very immature and very inexperienced. He was, to her, so worldly and very masculine.

William was perplexed, he felt an oddity in this little community of women, he missed his friends from school. The only one he felt kinship with was Annie and she, too, was very circumspect.

He looked at her as they walked home, she was undeniably very pretty. He wondered what life was going to be like and reassured himself that it would be different when he started work and made friends.

But he hated the idea of working for Mr Homer, the chemist. But he knew that he had agreed and that the premium for his apprenticeship had been paid.

In the evening, Marianne asked Annie to light the stove in the parlour. Annie went to the oil stove and opened the twin doors of the cast iron structure - it was not unlike a font cover. She lifted the lamp glass inside, put the taper to the wick and closed the doors of this quasi-ecclesiastical edifice and gazed bemused.

She loved this stove, it was one of the few new things they had bought. She loved its lace-like form and the flickering cobwebby shadows it cast. It had been bought for her so that she could work alone in that room.

She returned to the table. They were all quiet except William whose appetite was large and the noise he made chewing equal. The four women were all aware of the noise, but Marianne had instructed them all the say nothing for, she said, William had been lectured enough since his return.

This was aimed most particularly at Grandma, who like all elderly ladies, felt every event, small or large, called for her voluble opinion. When the china was washed and put away the three young people accompanied their mother to the parlour. The red light glowed in the darkness making a filigree pattern on the ceiling.

It was Annie who said: "Oh let's sit in the dark just as we did when we were little."

"Don't be daft, you can't just sit in the dark" said William.

"Yes, we will sit in the dark," said Marianne.

She welcomed the idea - it would make her task easier, she hated talking about money. She saw William fumble in his pocket and saw he had cigarettes. Her first thought was, "Benton never smoked." She checked herself and smiled and said, "Are you going to smoke, William, that will be nice. I hope they smell good."

Annie was very surprised, but stored the remark in her memory. Edith and Annie sat on the floor leaning against their mother's legs. William sat rather stiffly on a chair. He dispelled the darkness as his match flared and they saw his face. Marianne was staring at the red and black of the stove.

She began to outline the income of the family, her annuity, the savings of their father, which she could not refrain from multiplying by three in a strange sense of loyalty.

Then she spoke of her own income and her small annuity. From their current income they had saved one hundred pounds and of this, eighty had gone to Mr Homer for the premium. William nodded. That seemed settled.

She then spoke of Annie's career and her father's wishes that she should go to a school in Holland like Cousin Polly. Annie's eyes shone at the prospect.

She longed to go abroad. But first they must all be economical and Annie must finish her pupil-teaching training.

It was done. Now fond rapture took over and she said: "Oh my bonnie, bonnie children, you William, a chemist, you Annie, a teacher. What will you be Edith?"

Edith did not know. The suggestion that she be a teacher like Annie did not appeal. She only thought of the lessons for the morrow.

Annie saw Marianne's face looking so young in the red glow of the stove, but she recognised the inner glow as she foresaw success for her children. William said goodnight and went upstairs. This reminded them that it was well past Edith's bedtime.

When Marianne and Annie were alone the question was asked. "Do you think William is happy with us?"

"Not very" replied Annie. "I think he gets tired of women all the time."

"Goodness, I can understand that" said Marianne, with her knowledge of the prison. But she did not.

William climbed up to his room full of foreboding. The die seemed to be cast. When later his mother looked in he pretended to be asleep. So he never saw the look of puzzled affection with which she regarded him. If he had he might have opened his heart to her.

Monday morning is the usual day for new ventures in work and it was no exception in William's case. As Annie was on holiday, she walked part of the way with her brother to Mr Homer's shop.

It was going to be a sunny day, awnings were coming down, and blinds were going up. Grocers and their assistants were setting out their goods on the pavements outside the shops and in their starched white jackets and long white fringed aprons they looked like wooden Mr Noahs from the Ark, straight and tubular.

Butcher boys in their blue and white carried shallow wooden trays on their shoulders carrying meat to wealthy householders who were able to afford another joint immediately after Sunday.

Many of these people knew Annie, she went through the town every school morning, they looked at the tall girl and recognised immediately that the taller young fellow with her was her brother.

Annie was happy, she was escorting William to his work. It would keep him at home, she wanted all the family to be together and it would also lighten their mother's financial load. Half-way down the street, William stopped and Annie looked at him very puzzled.

"Look, Annie, you can hop it now. I don't want them to think that my big sister had to bring me."

The brightness of Annie's day departed, she was hurt by his rough statement. She was hurt, too, because she saw the truth in it and it had never crossed her mind. She was only there because she loved him and in expressions of love she was always to be short-sighted in the interpretations other might give.

"Yes, you are right. Good luck," she squeezed his hand.

William walked on unhurriedly, he arrived three minutes late. So that Mr Homer's first words on that day were, "You're late. Remember, young man, that time is money and that time waits for no man. Quick now and make up for it. Go though the dispensary and Mr Bastable will show you what to do."

So William was met and dismissed by his employer and Mr Bastable, a lugubrious man with soft blue eyes and an air of defeat, gave a further stricture on the virtues of punctuality.

Willy's first task was washing medicine bottles, carrying carboys and Winchester jars. He hated it and watched the clock hands moving slowly dividing up the disliked day. The only bright event was meeting Lorimer, another apprentice - he showed William where to eat his sandwiches and also smoke - this seemed a great bond to William.

His day did not end with the closing of the shop. Grandma was ceaseless in her questioning about the work. William gave answers of irritating vagueness and they were totally unrevealing. Finally, Marianne laughed and said,

"You must stop, Grandma. He will tell us in his own good time. He's just like Annie. Won't be drawn and very stubborn."

What William thought of Homer's establishment was long repressed.

Annie returned to school, like all pupil-teachers, a few days before term began. The headmaster assembled them and gave them general instructions, then they filed out and began looking for books and making piles of the same texts together.

While busy with this, the headmistress darted towards Annie and asked her - when she had finished - to come to her room. Annie wondered what she had done that was wrong. In the tiny high ceilinged room Mrs Harper looked larger than ever and her firm round face sterner. She picked up a paper form her desk and smiled.

"Yes, I think you will do very nicely. West Anston wants a teacher for the infants until half-term, would you like to go?"

Annie's eyes shone. It was an adventure, it was acknowledgement of her success. She agreed immediately. The sternness of Mrs Harper returned immediately. "You cannot accept until you have consulted you mother and brought a letter showing her consent."

Annie looked at her and for a moment was not quelled, she replied, "But, of course."

The afternoon seemed long before she was freed. The preparations for classes she would not take suddenly had no interest. She ran all the way home and was immediately bilked in her excitement because her mother was still on duty.

Both Grandma and Edith knew that she was bubbling with news, but she refused to tell them until her mother knew first. At last Marianne came in, she looked tired, but the news revived her, she sounded the authentic note of approval in her congratulations. Annie was more than satisfied. After tea Marianne wrote the letter of consent.

A few days later, she set off from the house with her lunch in a basket an hour earlier than hitherto, she walked the short way up to the station where she caught the train to Anston.

Then began a long walk through a straggling mining village. She had seen the school from afar - after the church it was the largest building on the low hillside. The houses all around were grimy, there were terraces running uphill, their roofs not stepped but one long pitch of slate shooting up obliquely.

Annie felt afraid, it was all so dirty, all so ugly and mean. The school had a high gate and a sloping yard, and it comprised two high rooms divided by a partition. Even through her glove Annie had felt the grit on the gate, the door handle, she saw it in the grooves of the door mouldings.

It was dust that seemed to blow perpetually from the slag heaps. But inside, everything gleamed, the floor boards, the desks, the panelling of pitch-pine round the walls. There were flowers in jars on all the window sills.

The headmistress looked up from her desk. Though she gave one glance, it seemed to include two. She got up stepped down from the platform with a stride and shook Annie's hands with a firm and vigorous shake.

"My name is Hodge. You must be Miss Taylor?"

Annie replied "Yes," very softly. She was taking in the figure before her. It was a square face set on square shoulders, it was formed of rectangles, even her eyes seemed square beneath such straight black brows.

The wide mouth was full and long but squared at the ends. Annie wondered very much whether she would like her.

"So they've sent you from Wakefield. Was there no one older?"
"I am 15."
"You don't look it."

Annie took off her coat and hat and hung them up carefully and turned round. Miss Hodge dressed so severely, looked at the braided silk front of Annie's bodice and even more at the red rose that nestled under the white frill ruff round her neck.

"Goodness, the half-timers won't half rag this little doll." She resolved to complain, it was not fair to the girl, or to her, she thought.

She led Annie off to her class, Annie had never seen such children before. An effort to make them clean had been made by their mothers but they remained uniformly grey. They were quiet, subdued and keeping order was no problem at all, in fact Annie longed for more response. Yet at play-time they roared out in the yard.

At dinner time the children disappeared, Miss Hodge put a chair by the stove for Annie and with great strides marched to the door that led into her house which adjoined. Annie was puzzled, Miss Hodge was very kind but she was not a lady.

Pondering on this she sat very erect in her chair, but eventually relaxed and looked about the room. Again she remarked on the spotlessness of it and the brightness of the flowers and the pictures.

There were though, cracks in the wall, and she knew enough about mining districts to be aware of subsidence. Then she noticed the long gaps between the floor and the skirting boards and as she looked, she became aware that she too was being watched.

She froze, for by the edge of the hearth sat a very large, very old grey rat. He was suspicious and showed a yellow set of teeth and Annie drew up her feet and clutched her skirt around her. Miss Hodge entered carrying a bowl of soup. She laughed, "Oh, I can see you've met old Harry."

"Do you mean the rat?"

"Yes, he's been here longer than me. Give him a crust. He'll be very grateful and your friend forever."

Within a few minutes he reappeared, and because she had been introduced, her fear was less. She threw him a crust which he took and to her surprise nibbled very fastidiously. So began a friendship.

Ten minutes before school recommenced, Miss Hodge rang a warning bell. When the long bell rang she handed the rope over to Annie. When the children returned many of the older ones were missing and others had taken their place.

These strangers were greyer, some still begrimed. So Annie learnt of the half-timer system, children over a certain age were allowed to work half the day. One week they went to school in the morning, the following in the afternoon.

The school was still quieter in the afternoon for they were tired and Annie noticed that Miss Hodge was more patient, even gentle, with her afternoon class. After the break Miss Hodge said: "I'll take your class and you read to mine. We've just finished one book so you can choose the next."

Annie looked at the shelf of books and the new red binding of *Uncle Tom's Cabin* attracted her. Miss Hodge approved and Annie read it with such verve and pathos that the class was spell-bound. She was aware of the magic she had cast and rejoiced in it: she was also aware that she was showing the children that there were some who were poorer than themselves.

At the end of the day Miss Hodge said: "I'll take you to the station."

Annie was surprised and said: "But I know the way."

"No, it's just that I want to give my dog a walk anyway."

When she joined Annie a young hound bounded out. "I am walking him."

Annie did not know what that meant, but she was informed that people interested in the hunt exercised young puppies until they joined the pack. Annie did not see the irony of this teacher working amongst miners also supporting the way of life of the squirearchy.

As they went through the village past the terraces Miss Hodge said: "You'd better not look in through the open doors, or you will see more than you bargained for."

Instantly Annie looked through a door and there in a bath was a naked man having his back scrubbed vigorously by his wife. She turned very pink. She looked again at the headmistress, the square jaw, the straight brow and the hair drawn back and she realised that this was no ordinary teacher. She seemed at home in this grubby village, but she was also out of place.

"Do you come from these parts?"

"Good Lord, no. I am from Helmsley."

"That is in the North Riding isn't it?"

"Yes, the best Riding. Did you know that every person in the North Riding could have an acre of land. In the East Riding half an acre and in this, God forsaken Riding only a quarter?"

Annie did not. She was to remember this information the rest of her life.

"See you tomorrow. Thanks for coming. I say, you had better run for it."

Annie was delighted by this matter of fact praise, but she did not run, she merely quickened her pace. It was part of her dictum of life that ladies did not run.

At tea, everyone was eager to hear how Annie had got on and for once she was eager to prattle on about Anston the rat and Mrs Hodge. She told the story with a few exaggerations which Grandma detected every time. It was the mother, though, that noted William's silence and she asked him what he had done.

"Nothing much really, just lugging great bottles about, and being bossed around by everyone. It is all right for Annie, she can boss the children around."

"But I am sure that she does not," added Marianne quickly.

"Take no notice, Mother, William does not mean it and he knows that I don't."

Then William remembered that he did have some interesting information.

"I say, did you know that Mr Homer's predecessor was a Mr Gissing. He has a son, a writer fellow in London. He married a tart."

"That is quite enough William. You don't know what you are talking about, and I don't like it."

"I just wanted to tell you something interesting."

"Well, there are other things than nasty gossip."

"But it is true."

"As may be, but it does not make it kind."

Three or four times a year, tension would rise in the Homer establishment. It emanated from the house above the shop, seeped down the stairs and up the steps into the office.

The assistants learnt to walk with excessive care, but never learnt that this very care caused irritation and then rage would burst. The assistants who lived in, two of them, and who sat at table with the Homers never escaped, they lived as well as worked with the menace, so it became complex and intense. During one of these exigencies William had been crushing bismuth in a mortar.

His attention had been diverted by Lorimer who had been imitating an elderly and shy customer who wished to buy senna-pods. William took a double quantity when compounding the mixture - it wasted not merely the drug but his time, for it would not mix.

Mr Bastable, in order to divert wrath from himself, gleefully reported this minor lapse of William. There was a summons to the office.

"Taylor, I have bad reports of you. I have observed you, too. Don't you like it here?"

"Yes, sir," lied William.

The thought of the unhappiness it would cause his mother if he was dismissed overcame him.

"Then, if you like it, why don't you work better? This is no mere trade, you know, it is an honourable profession. It is an exact science. In our hands often hangs life and death."

He paused at the gravity of his words.

He often felt hurt that his calling was tinged with trade... he felt the stings of it frequently, words took flight, and he was consoled by his oratory. "I hear that you made a wrong measurement – that is an error – a very grave error and such will not be tolerated here."

His voice lowered "Or indeed, anywhere in the noble realms of our calling." Then temper once more took over and crashing his fist upon his desk he shouted, "I will not have it, understand, I will not have it."

His voice boomed through the glass partition into the shop, the assistants looked up, the customers looked uncomfortable and hurried away. William was sent into the cellars to sort out carboys. He sat on a packing case and put his head in his hands and for the first time for a number of years, he cried and longed for a father.

At the prison Mr Alderson was on his way to Marianne's office. His tall physique topped by a large severe face encircled by white hair endowed him with a very magisterial air allied with some divinity.

It was, though, a very English divinity in which notions of aristocracy were plentifully mixed. He rarely smiled, yet he was not disliked, he was respected and he was what most of the convicts and warders called "a proper parson".

Marianne shared this respect with them, she felt gratitude

towards him, he had been helpful, but there was a chilliness that repelled the Celt in her. She did not love him, as she loved Father Eyre, yet she had no leanings to Rome.

Chaplain Alderson, after discussing a prisoner, crossed his legs and smiled and asked if he might ask a personal question.

"I have a young man, in for stealing silver, he's been a footman. He says that he knew you?"

"What is his name?"

"Cheadle, William Cheadle."

"William, William." She could only think of her own William. Her mind went back to Hampstead, then to Derry Ormond and Mrs Somerset's plans for her marriage. She dimly remembered a page-boy. She stiffened.

She recalled the house, Mrs Somerset's pride in the fulfilment of her plans. There was a drift towards marriage with what she considered a highly desirable match. Then, the very next day she had met Benton.

The past flowed around her, upon her and in the flood she was shifted from a position she thought permanent. She had made herself happy and taught herself not to look to the past, she never asked "What might have been?"

"Yes, I remember the place. It was very beautiful."

"He tells me that it might have been yours."

"It could have been, but love and life move differently to aims and dreams." Mr Alderson went away well pleased. There had been to his mind a mystery about Mrs Taylor and he had uncovered it. The revelation in no way surprised him. He was only sorry that her dignity impressed convicts, warders and wardresses and not a large tenantry.

He left Marianne unnerved. So much so that when she returned home she claimed a headache and went up to her bed.

There she stared unsleeping at the white ceiling and she remembered the painted dome of Derry. She saw that she was surrounded by the small and the commonplace. She did not often acknowledge the shabby gentility of her life for her pride was great. But the struggle seemed hard and uneven. She did not weep, she did not cry for anyone.

Before very long, Annie came creeping into the room carrying a tray with a pot of tea. She looked at her in the dim light, she was like Benton... she screwed up her eyes and looked harder.

"Pull up the blind, dear, I cannot see what you have done to your hair." The blind shot up, the acorn bounced against the glass. Marianne was aghast, Annie had cut off her hair. The child proffered a brown paper bag full of something soft that shifted. She looked in and saw the long switch of reddish brown hair.

As she was about to remonstrate she looked at her child, her head was covered in curls and especially over her forehead, it was very pretty. To her amazement she heard herself say, "I like it. I like it very much. Why, you look like the Princess of Wales."

So Annie was the first girl in Wakefield to wear the Alexandra fringe and it had all been done by the barber in Anston on the way to the train.

Grandma did not approve. She thought and she said: "It makes you look what you are, flighty."

Annie was delighted with herself. It was not merely vanity, though there was much of that, it was also an assertion of independence. At tea everyone, even William, caught her gaiety and they all laughed and repartee crackled like shot around the table.

In the evening, Marianne and the three children walked in the Governor's garden. Years were forgotten, notions of dignified conduct were put aside by Annie as she and Edith chased William round the paths.

Marianne, as she watched them condemned herself for her foolish depression. These were her gift, her handsome healthy children. They were worth more than much rank and security. Yet still she sighed and though of Benton's sigh when he, too, quoted to her and himself Carlyle's great stricture: "Manhood begins when we have in any way made Truce with Necessity; begins even when we have surrendered to Necessity as the most part only do; but begins joyfully and hopefully only when we have reconciled ourselves to Necessity; and thus, in reality, triumphed over it, and felt that in Necessity we are free."

Her heart lifted a little. But a little wistfully she said to herself. "But I am not a man."

Miss Hodge liked Annie's way of teaching so much that she asked for her to stay the rest of the term and after that for another year. When winter came Annie often brought with her a pie which was heated slowly in the oven while lessons were going on.

Annie loved visiting the house, it was unlike any other house she knew. Like Miss Hodge it was unique for it was a continuation of herself.

At every turn the countrywoman was evident, there was a fox's mask hanging in the hall and hunting prints in the tiny sitting room.

During cold weather the plants which usually stood on the sills of the house and the school were gathered here on tables and stools. During these dinner hours Annie learnt much about Miss Hodge, of her father's farm and his dislike of industry.

He, like Grandma, cursed the mills. The difference was that Miss Hodge remained true to her background but had gone far out of her way to help those captured by industry.

Annie compared her with her mother.

Her mother was so elegant and so feminine, Miss Hodge cared nothing for her appearance, yet both shared an idealism of kindness and duty to others.

They had come to practise it in different was, Miss Hodge had made a choice, she wanted to teach "those poor little beggars". Marianne had come to her work among women convicted by force of circumstance. Both of them worked lovingly and progressively for their charges. She found it endlessly interesting to ponder upon. She admired both, but in totally different ways.

As she sat in the train going to Anston thinking of these careers she also thought about the contrast in the happiness of herself and the frustration of William. She was joyful and like a young swallow learning its powers on the wing, William was crippled by indifference.

Their attitudes were strangely symbolised in their secret games alone in their dinner hours. William went to the end of a long neglected garden between the houses behind the shop.

There was an old and broken outhouse. Among a phalanx of nettles he found old bottles - he set them up in rows and threw bricks at them. Annie's game was more dangerous, though she never realised it.

The centre of the schoolroom was a lantern skylight and its windows were opened by a long looped cord which was hooked to the wall. On the few sultry days it was Annie's job to tug at the rope and shift the grudging window.

She had to pull so hard she learnt of its strength - eventually it would creak open, flakes of dried up paint would flutter down and she would loop up the now lengthened cord on the hook. One day, alone, she conceived the idea of putting her foot on the loop and swinging across the room.

It worked well. She then, shortened the rope and swung across the desks sedately. She became more daring and learnt to push herself off and encircle the room. She was thrilled.

She was flying and she had always wanted to fly. She brushed past the chestnut-buds and the hyacinths in their glass bottles, her skirt flapped against the teacher's high desk.

She always felt exhilarated by this exercise. Miss Hodge sometimes wondered why Annie looked so flushed and bright eyed. She was never discovered, William was caught in the act and not only did he have to listen to a homily, but his wages were docked.

A Saturday, long planned by Annie, at last arrived when Miss Hodge came to have tea with them in Wakefield. As Annie had surmised, Miss Hodge and Marianne after a moment's appraisal and longer assessment understood one another and found much to admire and interest in one another.

Edith sat on the rug before the fire and listened to her sister's praises being sung and the proud but depreciating acceptance of it by her mother. She heard for the first time of the plan that Annie was to go to Holland to complete her education.

This met with mixed approval from Miss Hodge, she liked the idea. She, too, would have loved to travel - she had, however, conceived ideas that Annie should go to a college and train to be a teacher.

Naturally, Miss Hodge asked Marianne about prison life. She heard of the chapel, the library, the workrooms and the schoolroom. It was a guarded glimpse of another world. When she recollected it all in the quietness of her Sunday in Anston, she was surprised that what she remembered most was the descriptions of the prison.

She was a woman who seemed to have experienced the sorrows of the world, but come out of the furnace with humour and an undiminished supply of love.

She remembered the long white hands in repose on her black silk lap, or in intricate action at the piano. Thinking of her, she understood Annie much better, she saw where her gifts came from.

There was, though, a surprise in her admiration, for she wondered how so sensitive a woman could be so wholly unaware of the unhappiness of her son.

There had been more than just ordinary gruff awkwardness over the introduction and her own masculinity had felt a fierce kinship with the youth who felt chained and imprisoned. She felt it all the keener because she usually had such envy for men who had freedom. Usually so open in her speech, she, this time, withheld any comment to Annie on the subject.

On Sunday week, William and Annie came to tea with Miss Hodge. They were bidden early so that they could walk. Miss Hodge met them at the station with a fur hat securely tied beneath her chin and stout boots.

They walked up the valley and then scrambled up to the moor where the heather seemed to stretch endlessly and at the crest a great blast of different wind almost threw them off their feet. Miss Hodge strode along the sheep tracks breathing the air deep into her lungs, flinging out her arms.

Annie thought it exaggerated and slightly ridiculous, she did not want William to form a poor opinion of her, then she saw that William was imitating her. He too made comments on the purity of the air. They stopped, they faced the wind and seemed in their sniffings to be almost tasting it.

"Smell that, William?"

He sniffed the air like a terrier. "I think I can taste salt. Yes, it's the sea."

"Full marks. One sometimes gets a whiff of it up here. Do you like the sea?"

"I love it... that is what I've seen of it. I've been on a steamer from Greenwich to Margate. And that is hardly sea, is it?"

"Well, you've been on a ship. That is more than I have. What sort was it?"

Annie listened nonplussed. He knew the name of the steamer, he knew that it had been built in Sunderland. She heard technical terms, pistons, shafts, blades and Dorman Long all rapidly ensue. She had no idea that William knew so much about boats.

"William, I think you ought to be a sailor, not a pharmacist."

"That's what I would like to be."

"Then, why don't you?"

"Oh, things." The cloud, so often about him these days, descended again. At tea, Miss Hodge rallied William and he began to laugh and joke. Miss Hodge told stories of her father. William was put in the best chair by the fire and Annie hardly believed her ears when she heard her say, "If you want to smoke, do, my father always has a pipe after a meal."

As Annie folded up the tablecloth William took some cigarettes from his pocket. She froze with disapproval.

In the kitchen she dried up in great silence whilst Miss Hodge bent over the sink. Suddenly Annie could not contain her displeasure any longer.

"I don't think you should encourage William in his bad habits."

It was said. Miss Hodge paused, a saucer in her hand. She looked at Annie kindly, but there was a threat of storm behind it all.

"I think it is high time that you realized that William is a man. You all live in a very feminine little world and William does not fit into it."

Annie was not to be turned. She felt a loyalty to Miss Hodge, but a far greater one to her mother.

"Mother does not like smoking, but she lets him. Our Father never smoked, so why should William?"

"Because your brother is quite another person... and of quite another generation. Do you wear a stupid crinoline? Your mother did at your age. Fashions change in habits as well as clothes, my dear. And let me just add, your brother is a very unhappy and unfulfilled young man."

Annie went very silent, she recognised a truth, but she was not going to be convinced by anyone at that moment.

Miss Hodge did not have long to wait for her wish to come true and it was Mr Homer himself who executed the first step. He called on Marianne. It was Annie who answered the door and when she saw him her heart sank. As she announced him to her mother she saw that she, too, went pale.

She was aware of an uneasiness in William and she had suspicions which she named to nobody. As she went into the parlour untying her apron on the way, she even prayed that no money was missing, immediately she dismissed the idea, she just did not know what to expect.

Mr Homer sat in an easy chair, but he looked most

uncomfortable and turned his hat in his hand. He rose and resumed his seat when Marianne took hers and then almost fiercely said,

"There's no need to disguise things, Mrs Taylor, your son will never make a pharmacist, not in a hundred years. He just doesn't seem to be interested. I'm sure I don't know what these young men are thinking of these days. It wasn't like this when I was young. We took a pride in our work."

Marianne sat very upright, she was pained to the very heart, yet it was difficult to perceive for she sat in her habitual pose with her head on her right hand. She sighed involuntarily;

"Do you wish him to leave, Mr Homer?"

"Well, there is no point in wasting his, or my time, is there?"

She tried to gather strength by looking at all her treasures in the room, as if they would keep evil at bay, this little shrine to her family. She was given courage,

"There is the question of his premium, Mr Homer. I trust you will be able to return, at least, a part of it?"

To haggle over money when her son had, quite plainly, not done his duty pained Marianne even more. She was so inured to the misdemeanours of others in the prison she expected everything to be smooth and honest at home.

Mr Homer was not an insensitive man and rapidly he agreed to the return of two thirds of the premium. After this, there was little to be said beyond expressions of regret.

When she closed the door on Mr Homer she went slowly up to her room. She did not want to make excuses to Grandma and explanations to Annie and Edith.

She wanted to be alone and she wanted the help of her husband more that she had ever wanted it. She did not know what to do. Out loud in her bedroom she said, "It only, oh, if only, he were more like Annie."

The outburst shocked her for she strove desperately to show no favouritism even within herself. Her plans were crumbling, she could not see the future, she was afraid. She lay on her bed.

Later she went down. Grandma was darning socks and Annie looked up from her books at the table.

"What did he want, Mother?"

"It was about William, dear."

Grandma looked up sharply. "What's he been up to?"

Before Marianne replied, Annie said, "Does he want him to leave?"

Marianne was surprised and it was another blow to her pride. It was evident that Annie knew far more about him than she did. She felt that she was groping with only a shadow of knowledge about her son. A defence fell and she hissed, "Yes, that is the sharp concern of it all."

She sat down and picked up her needlework. Silence brooded over the three of them, the clock ticked, it seemed, loudly. Minutes passed and Marianne saw that Annie's pen had not moved, a page had not been turned.

At first, Marianne thought that she was shocked, then as she saw that her head was cocked towards the curtained windows, she realised that she was listening.

"Where did William go this evening, Annie?"

"To choir practice." The answer came out too quickly.

"I see, now that lasts about an hour. He must have left church two hours ago. Do you know where he was going afterwards?"

"No, Mother." It was done, the very thing she thought that she would never do. It was impossible. She had lied to her mother. Instantly within herself she blamed William, she blamed Miss Hodge, who had said William should be given more freedom.

"I think, Annie, you are not telling the truth."

Annie looked at her books. "I've told you. I don't know."

"Yes you do, Annie. I know you do."

"Yes, I do." Amazing rebellion swept over her and she allied herself with William. "We ought to give him more freedom. He's a man. If you really want to know where he is, he's with the Rullen boys and they've gone to the new billiard hall."

Marianne might have been lashed with a whip, she winced so. The billiard hall. It seemed to her not merely evil and low, but vulgar and degraded. She had seen the place where vulgar and idle men hung around the door.

"Your father would never have gone to one."

Annie did not reply to this remark. She was suddenly veering towards her mother's side, as she saw how hurt she was.

"Really, Mother, there's no harm. Why Miss Senior has a billiards table. That's where William learnt to play."

"Has he been to the Hall often?"

"Only a few times." Again she repeated, "But there's no harm."

"No harm. Wasting time. No harm. Wasting our money, hard earned. No harm. An evening in low company. It is no wonder Mr Homer wishes him to go."

Annie saw the deep chasm of a wound that her mother had sustained. She got up and put an arm around her.

"Don't worry, Mother. Everything will be all right. It will. We just have to let William go to sea."

"To sea, who says he wants to go to sea?" This was an hour of revelations for her.

"That is what he wants."

"Never." She remembered the months of loneliness her mother had endured shot with desperate anxieties. She did not want that for herself, or for any woman.

There was a low whistle. Annie let go of her mother and slipped into the kitchen. They heard the backdoor open and the key of the yard door turn. Marianne and Grandma looked at one another in silence.

It was evident that this was not the first time Annie had slipped out into the yard to open the door. They heard a murmur of voices. William was being warned. As he came into the light, his happiness was evident over which a cloud of anxiety was slipping.

Grandma pushed up her spectacles on to her hair. "Oh you wicked boy, worrying your poor mother like this. You should be ashamed."

"Well" was all he said and he folded his arms to await a familiar ticking off.

"Where have you been, William?"

"To the billiards with some chaps."

"Don't you think you should have told me?"

"You wouldn't have liked it if I had for, I expect, Father did not play billiards. So it would be wrong."

Marianne was cut once more. She refrained from any retort.

"What you do not know, William, is that Mr Homer has been here. He is thinking of terminating your apprenticeship. What do you think of that?"

He shrugged his shoulders. "Anything is better than that stuffy shop and dispensary lugging bottles about and giving pills to fat old women."

"Oh William. How could you behave so badly?" It came out as an agonised moan. "I spend my life surrounded by criminals and the last place I expect to find deceit is in my children. I am not going to say anything more."

She whisked from the room.

The remark broke Annie, who put her face in her arms and wept above the outspread books. "Oh William, you shouldn't, you really shouldn't."

Grandma rose looking grim and, for once, speechless. She left the room.

"The Prodigal Son got a better welcome than this. But then it was his father that took him in." Annie looked up at the youth. He looked as unhappy as her mother. Through her tears she managed to say, "Mother knows you want to go to sea. So you had better be truthful about it tomorrow."

It was like a dawn on a grey morning, sun breaking though clouds.

"You told her, Annie? Wonderful."

Annie was at last left alone in the room. Again she wept, for she felt entangled with love, loyalty and reason. She was torn between her mother and William and Miss Hodge, as reason, loomed behind.

She heard the door open but did not lift her head, it would only be William, then she felt her mother's hand running though the short curls at the back of her neck.

"There, there, my darling. Don't be upset any more." Annie's crying redoubled for here was sympathy and here was love. Marianne detected a bit of hysteria and more emphatically she said, "Stop that. I want to talk to you."

She sat by the dying fire and spoke of her family and how they had all been seamen. "The sea is in William's blood, he cannot help it. And I have put it there. We must send him to sea. I could not afford the Navy, so he'll have to be a merchantman. To set him up will cost money, if we don't indent him he'll only be a deck-hand. It will mean delaying your going to Holland, my dear. Can you bear that?"

"Yes, yes." She gladly embraced the sacrifice, partly for William, much more for her mother. It seemed to expiate the lie. But most of all it was because, though she wished to escape from Wakefield and this life, she desired much more to stay with her mother.

"I knew you would do that, my dear. Say nothing. William must tell me himself and he must make up his own mind. Now you must go to bed. You are not my bonnie lassie. You look a fright. But I love you, nonetheless."

She looked into her daughter's china blue eyes and she knew that if she had not been there her life would have been almost completely unendurable. Together they climbed up, arm in arm, the narrow stairs.

Mr Homer never mentioned his visit, but each was aware of its significance and an air of unease hung over their encounters.

For William, though, there was a gleam of light in the future and work in the shop had never seemed so pleasant before. Yet he dared not rejoice for he was suspicious, too, of his mother. He thought that she would prevent his going to sea. He was not even sure of Annie's opinions. But there was more light than before.

Marianne bowed her head to the order of the daily round, but she was paler than usual and it was noticed that details slipped her usually observant eye and vigilant memory.

When left alone she had an ache in her heart, she felt that she had failed as a mother to her only son. Looking back she knew that she should not have sent him so far away to school and with such short holidays. It had removed him from family affection. Yet she reasoned, he had wanted to go, the opportunity had seemed too golden to miss. Now he wanted to go still further away, but what could she do.

She understood the force of his hereditary passion and passion, she knew, breaks though most barriers and becomes united to its desire. She even remembered herself when she first met Benton and been swept along.

She knew that she must not impede William. But she did ask herself if his passion was restlessness in disguise. Only time would tell.

At Anston Annie was preoccupied, as well, and it did not escape Miss Hodge's eye. Soon Annie was telling her of the previous evening's scene.

"So what happens, now?"

"I suppose he will go to sea..."

"Can your mother afford it?"

Annie hesitated, "Not really. I shall have to postpone going to Holland that is all."

"I see," and the angles of Miss Hodge's face strengthened. She did not wish Annie to delay, she must go while she was still malleable. She was equally certain that if William did not go to sea, then he would go to the devil.

"So it will be your share of the money that equips him, eh?"

"Yes, I suppose so. But it doesn't matter."

"How like a woman. Men accept all our sacrifices. But you are right."

"I was very certain it was right last night. I am not quite so sure now."

"You are, Annie, you are. The immediate concern is William. You'll always come out all right. I see it in your nature."

Miss Hodge was suddenly seized with even more vigour than usual. "Do what you have to do, Annie, and you will save your brother's soul alive."

Annie smiled at the drama, but she saw that Miss Hodge had uttered it without a grain of humour. Then, recalling the intensity of feeling in that backroom the previous night, she agreed that it was true. It was very important.

"Yes, I will."

"That's a good girl. We all need freedom, but, I must admit, men need it more. Your William feels that he might as well be in prison as living beside it. You won't regret it. I know."

At the same time Miss Hodge wondered how she could help Annie and her mother, she was short of cash because she had just bought a small house at Hutton-le-Hole. Near, but not too near, her family.

School over, Annie went out into the bitter cold. Miss Hodge no longer escorted her, three young half-timers always waited for her and formed a tiny troop that took her to the station each night.

Miss Hodge watched it amused. It was one of the reasons she was not worried about Annie. In the train Annie was suddenly very happy as she anticipated the evening and the offer of release to William.

At supper, William was subdued and Annie wondered why her mother did not cheer him with the offer of a brighter future. As the two of them washed up, Marianne raised the question of the money and asked if Annie was still willing to forfeit her share for the time being.

Annie rushed in with a decisive Yes. Marianne was overcome by her fervency and looked down into the wooden bowl in the sink. She was touched and she prayed swiftly and fervently that all would be well for Annie, she deserved it.

She called back into the dining room to William telling him to stay downstairs as she wanted to talk to him. William sitting before the fire sighed as he contemplated another lecture. He joined his mother, Annie and Edie as they sat round the table for a council of decision. Grandma sat by knitting.

"Well, William, we have some news for you."

"Oh yes. Another job?"

"In a way. First of all, do you really want to go to sea and so badly nothing else will do?"

"Of course. You know I do."

Marianne flinched slightly at the aggrieved tone. "William do keep calm, we are not against you. As you know, we haven't much money, but Annie is willing to delay going to Holland in order to equip you."

"What, sis?" A deep flush came over his feature, for a moment they thought he would cry.

"When can I start, Mother?"

"First of all, you have to tell Mr Homer what you propose and explain everything to him. You must be completely above board."

"Oh, I can leave there right away."

"No, you cannot, William my dear. That would not be fair."

"But I don't do any good there."

"You must stay here until you have a good ship of a good line and all the equipment."

"But there are hundreds of ships going every week from Liverpool."

"We shall have to contact companies, my dear, it is not quite so simple. I shall begin by writing to some of my father's old contacts in Cardiff."

It was as if a dam on William's feelings was breached, they could not stop him talking, the sea, the distant islands, different ports. He told them all about his trips to the London Docks.

It was all an eye-opener for Marianne. The boy was miraculously alive, they had not seen him like this, not even Annie. He was so excited they became so interested that no letters were written that evening and at bed-time William kissed his mother with a spontaneity she had not known since he was a small boy.

The weeks that followed had a pent up excitement that gripped them all. Everyday there was an eager anticipation of the post and, according to the letters, so the sprits rose or fell. At last William was called for an interview in Cardiff. He went alone, in his best clothes and spent the night in the station hotel.

When he returned he seemed a man. He had been accepted and pronounced very fit by the doctor. He boasted that his knowledge of seamanship had amazed them. Now he had to equip himself and await a ship.

They all enjoyed the amassing of his kit – indeed, it was all theirs – for each one had made a contribution by foregoing some article of clothing. The pile grew in the parlour where it was heaped on the sofa.

During the last week of William's time at home they went to Leeds. This was an event to which Annie and Edie counted the hours. They shopped, they went to the new Art Gallery which entranced Marianne so much she was unaware for a time of her children's philistinism.

They went to a restaurant for lunch. Annie and Edie walked behind their mother and brother and noted the admiring glances which were given the handsome pair. William wore his brass buttoned jacket and a tie with an anchor pin and in the street wore his jaunty corded cap.

The greater distinction belonged to Marianne who, for once, lay aside her black and wearing grey silk with black ruching moved like a small Duchess leaning on her son's arm. Annie had trimmed her mother's hat with two pink doves which nestled against her dark hair. They were all proud of their mother.

After the lunch they went to the theatre and saw the D'Oyly Carte Company in Gilbert and Sullivan's *Patience*. Marianne was intoxicated by her children's delight and joy. It was also, for her, a glimpse of her old world.

She watched Annie particularly who sat upright and absorbed straining forward anxious to miss not one word. The world was opening up for them.

Chapter 11

Leaving Party

While the younger members of the family had been gallivanting, as Grandma described it, she had been baking. When the family returned they found every space in the larder filled with pies, tarts, cakes and none of them were for their consumption. Only then did Marianne tell them that there was to be a party before William's departure.

During the next day many relations came over from Armitage Bridge and Crosland Moor amongst them, the much loved Uncle Alan and the Donckersleys who, now, lived in their old home.

They were outnumbered though, by the Wakefield acquaintances and friends, the Chaplain came, so too did Farther Eyre.

When the party was well under way the Governor came and he gave William a long leather case containing his telescope. He had used it in India during the Mutiny.

As he presented it he made a speech about the duty of the young to be ambassadors of England as they built up the Empire. Annie was deeply impressed. The table amassed presents and both Annie and Edie were filled with love and pride for their tall, fair-haired brother whom everyone loved so much.

Annie was overcome with emotion and went into the kitchen and had a cry into her handkerchief. Grandma had noticed her disappearance with her sharp eyes, she followed her.

"What's amiss with you, lassie?"

"I'm so glad and proud that everyone thinks so well of William."

The grave old face darkened, she took Annie's hand,

"It's not William they love so much, my dear. It's your mother."

Annie was affronted on her brother's behalf, but saw clearly that her mother was loved and admired. Nevertheless she rushed to William's defence.

"How can you be so unkind? Poor William, going away so far and looking so handsome."

"Handsome is as handsome does", replied the old lady.

"Sometimes, Grandma, I think you are horrid and especially to William."

She flung out of the room. Her usually mild but observant eyes were flashing and the first person she saw was John Squires, a great friend of William, lean and dark with sloe-black eyes.

He smiled at Annie in a way that made her both hot and cold, which she both liked and disliked. As he unbuttoned his gloves he said, "And where is the conquering hero, your brother?"

Annie led him into the parlour towards her mother. When she turned to introduce him she discovered that he had not followed her, instead he was talking to some friends. Marianne had seen this and she disliked the rudeness, and she thought, "It is a good thing William is leaving such associates."

Soon Captain Armitage, after wishing William well, departed. Farther Eyre gave William the name of a friend in Sydney. This pleased Marianne, she feared bad company more than anything else and it seemed justified as she looked across at young Squires. But Marianne was enjoying herself as she moved among her guests and her family and Chaplain Alderson watched her benignly and pondered on his secret of what Marianne's life might have been.

Miss Hodge stood at the table looking at the presents, the telescope, the log book, the silver watch, the compass and a hip-flask. "Aren't they fine?" said Annie.

"I know of a better present that is not among them."

"What do you mean?"

"The means by which he can go as an apprentice at all."

Annie caught the drift of her meaning and was embarrassed.

"It's a great credit to you, my dear, but I am sure he will do you credit and it means I shall have you a bit longer."

A little later Annie saw William talking to Squires who looked at her and then her mother. They laughed with the corners of their mouths turned down. Annie had noticed that in men and she did not like it. In the hall she handed Squires his hat and gloves.

"Thank you, my dear. Your brother tells me that I must take good care of you. I hope you will allow me."

Annie was shy, feeling herself retreat into herself, and then she heard herself say, "That is very kind of him. I have looked after myself for a long time. You need not take William's place. He is not a great protector."

"Perhaps you did not need protecting as much then, as you do now."

He left and Annie thought him most objectionable.

Early next morning Marianne and William were off. There was a nip in the air when the cab arrived and the seaman's chest was heaved on top. William was excited but pale. Grandma bade him "Be a good lad, now."

Annie flung her arms round his neck and through her tears gasped,

"Oh, William, we shall miss you. Write often. Don't stay away long."

Tears came into William's eyes and he pressed a small envelope into her hand and into Edie's. Marianne called, quite sharply from the cab.

"Be quick. We should be off and at the Kirkgate already."

The hooves clattered, William leant out waving, but Annie was blinded by tears. Grandma put an arm around her, "Have a good cry, my dear, then you'll feel better."

They sat at the table and tried to eat breakfast. Annie opened her envelope and gasped. It was a photograph of William in his uniform looking straight into the camera as he leaned over a balustrade. She nearly exclaimed on his looking so handsome, but restrained herself.

"Look, Grandma – isn't it wonderful to have a brother who looks like that.

Grandma pulled down her spectacles from her forehead and peered piercingly,

"Yes, he's a fine looking lad." Then with a sigh, she added, "Let's hope we can all be proud of him."

"Oh, but we are already," replied Annie with an edge to her voice.

At the station William gave orders to the porter about his sea chest and Marianne looked on with pride. He bought the tickets, one return and one single. He behaved with the gallantry he had shown in Leeds and Marianne enjoyed it and covertly noted the admiring glances on the platform.

Yet she could not forget that she was seeing him off to sea and she hated the sea.

The journey was long and Marianne slept in snatches, she was very tired. It had been a busy week. In Cardiff they went straight to their hotel and then down to the docks. The gateman, seeing William's uniform let them in. Among the ships they sought the Cordillera.

It was a clipper. Her masts rose tall and slender and immensely high, the long deck was slim and narrow. Marianne admired it but feared it, it seemed so frail. She always had in her mind the vastness of the sea and the smallness of a boat.

But William was enthralled and rushed up and down its length on the quayside as excited as a puppy, the dignity of his uniform forgotten. Some of his pleasure infected Marianne.

As they had their dinner they talked of the party the previous night and Marianne asked who Squires was.

"Oh, he's a pleasant cove. I think he's rather stunned by Annie." Marianne stiffened, she did wish that William used less slang, but she retrained from reproof.

"And what is he, dear?"

"He works at a tailor's. Rydales, I think it is."

"Really", she said no more.

That night Marianne had a dream, one she had not had since girlhood after her father was drowned. She floated in a still and beautiful sky and looking down saw a stormy sea. There was a ship and the wind tore her, lightning ran along the rigging. There were men on board. Suddenly the sea formed a mouth, the ship was crunched, broken and swallowed. She awoke whimpering, she lay for what seemed an age and her heard beat fast and hard.

She groped for the matches and lit the candle. She looked at the clock. It was past midnight and she thought, "It is today that I say goodbye to William." Sleep and the dawn seemed to come together.

After breakfast they went down to the docks and to the office of Myers. It seemed familiar to Marianne, though, she could not recollect having been there. Mr Thomas, a partner, received them cordially. He remembered Marianne's father and thought he saw traces of him in William.

He told them that Captain Sparks was a first rate seaman and that William was fortunate to be serving under him. He added that he lived up to his name, but that he was a very just man.

He took them down to the ship himself, but the captain had

been called ashore. Marianne was sorry, she had wanted to see her son's chief officer. William was relieved, he had not wanted his mother around when he met the captain. They decided to go to the station and that Marianne would return home.

In the cab she held his hand very tightly, she dreaded the journey's end. She begged him to be good and to obey his officers in all things. She took from a bag her present. It was a Bible bound in green leather.

He took it between his hands and gazed at it and, then looked at his mother. "I'll do everything that is right. Don't worry. Soon I will be home and by then I may have sailed around the world."

At the station he stood to attention and saluted as the train drew out. His erect figure, his obvious joy filled Marianne with trust in the future. The picture of him, the green Bible in his hand... they were engraved in her mind.

Five hours later, William set sail from Britain.

Life in Wakefield without William was dull; it fell into its old industrious routine and was, once more utterly feminine. The weeks were punctuated by Sundays when all, except Grandma went to the parish church.

It always caused Marianne a pang to see another young man taking her son's place in the choir stalls. At Evensong they often went to the prison chapel where the prisoners roared out the hymns with a fervour expressing more than religious fervour. It was the joy of speech.

William soon became a hero. He was constantly enquired about, for any boy in a uniform and off to the Colonies was then an Empire Builder. His letters were eagerly awaited and in the kitchen a map of the world had been pinned up and a row of pins were ready to mark his ports of call.

The pins never moved for there were no letters, but none of them was concerned, letters from overseas were, they thought, prone to delay, often lost and, perhaps, he had no time to write. Even his mother displayed no great anxiety - she could recall when her mother often went the greater part of a year without news of her husband.

Each night, though, by her bedside, his photograph in a silver frame on the bed table, she prayed for him. Yet, when she lay down and rested her head, which seemed to grow wearier as the months passed, she had to admit that another day had passed which was easier because he was not present.

There were no rebellions in the household and nobody had to be reproved or constrained. It was an easy clan, the girls respected her instruction, whereas William had either resented it, or mocked it.

Yet there was one thing particularly which she missed his help in. William had not a trace of Yorkshire in his accent and day after day Marianne was trying to wipe out the idioms, more than accents which they picked up from school.

She did not want her girls to be hampered by their speech and she was ambitious for them, especially Annie. She dreamed of their marriages, happiness, wealth, success. The marriages were not to be like her own - yet she knew that if she could be given her time again she would marry Benton even if she knew the consequences of his early death. She still loved him and she saw him in Annie.

This first-born child was growing very tall, she had a charming figure, was slim but rounded with the necessary sloping shoulders and small waist of her day. Her face was round and was approximating beauty.

Her father's heritage was her complexion, she had a clear white skin finely grained and one thought of porcelain because her face was a mingling of creamy white and pink and the glaze was suggested by her round china blue eyes.

Her hair, like her father's was chestnut brown, but like her mother's waved and curls were rapidly coming into fashion. Nature had been kind to her and added to that she had her mother's sense of dressing with great care.

She was aware that men treated her with deference, whether they were the collier-boys squatting in the street of Anston, or Her Majesty's Inspectors.

Sometimes, though, when passing boys gathered at street corners, or lingering on bridges, Annie encountered glances that she did not fully comprehend, she only knew that instinct bade her be aware and somewhere in her heart she felt a strange fear.

She was still entirely ignorant of sex and lustful glances she equated with bad manners and bad manners she equated with violence. Her mother had instilled into her a knowledge that Wakefield, pleasant as it might be in parts, was a very small part of a far larger scene of life. Edith was less critical because the influence of her life was her grandmother.

The first danger to Marianne's hopes for Annie appeared in Squires. Quite suddenly, he always appeared in a pew close to them. Annie also met him on the way to the station. His attentions were both flattering and flustering and he was most persistent that she should go to the theatre with him one evening. At last, Annie grew frightened, for he stuck like a burr.

At last Annie told her mother, only to find that Marianne was not unaware. She discovered that her mother regarded him with abhorrence. She disliked him personally, she recalled his rude demeanour when he had been at William's farewell party, but even more he alerted her snobbery and she disliked his kind.

Unlike many mothers of her time, she could not watch over Annie constantly and she decided that when the time came to act she would do it quickly and ruthlessly. Her years of governing convicts had honed her assurance.

One summer evening they were all sitting in the small garden. The bell rang and Marianne rose,

"I'll go. I need some more silk anyway," she lay down her embroidery. As she went down the narrow hall she saw a male outline though the leaded panes of the door. It was Squires. For a moment she hesitated, then stiffened with resolve.

She opened the door and took stock of the young man. As she surveyed his clothes, her repulsion grew.

He was exquisitely dressed in a braided coat, his tie was a shade too large and the horseshoe pin sparkled in the knot too brightly. But most of all she disliked his sloe-black eyes.

Without asking he stepped into the hall and then asked if he might see Annie.

Marianne had to retreat and her hand held the newel post. She, too, felt a slight fear which sparked into a blaze of defence.

"Mr Squires, I believe?"

"Yes, madam."

"Have you come to see me, or my daughter?"

"Annie. I wondered if I might take her to the theatre?"

"Here in Wakefield?"

"Yes."

"Then you mean the music hall."

"Yes, madam." Again the madam had slipped out.

"Most certainly not."

"Might I then take her for a walk one evening?"

"What is your profession, Mr Squires?"

"I'm a tailor."

"Tailor. That happens to be our surname, as you are aware, but our dealings with your trade are restricted to the counter, young man. Your attentions are not wanted here. Good evening."

Every word had been heard in the garden, they had all sat immobile, also unbelieving. They found the words at ill odds with their mother, but the voice was hers. Marianne returned after a moment with a skein of silk in her hand, but very upright, pale and decisive. Annie looked up.

"Mother. How could you? How could you be so cruel? He was William's friend."

"Your brother had some very unsuitable friends", she said it as she looked at her work matching the threads.

"Well, I shan't forgive you. I think you've been beastly." She threw down her embroidery and rushed indoors. For a full minute Marianne held her breath fearing that she might hear the front door bang and the sound of footsteps hurrying up the street. But no... it was only the thud of feet running up the stairs and the slam of a bedroom door.

Marianne stitched away, her movements were staccato and over and over again she thought of the scene and the crumpling of the debonair and commonplace young man.

At first she was pleased that she had disposed of a menace to her plans, but her malevolence was dissipated and compassion took its place.

She was sorry that she had made a remark about the counter... that had been unkind. Yet when she thought of Annie she did not regret it, he was a vulgar young man and Annie worth much, much more.

Grandma said, "I hope you don't live to regret it."

Edith looked amazed and horrified.

"Some people can only be removed by brutal means. I have been hard. But as Captain Armytage says, "Soft surgeons make stinking wounds.""

That evening Annie remained in her room and for two days she was cool and reserved. She soon forgot Squires, he never crossed her path again, but the scene remained with her for a lifetime.

Squires was soon forgotten by Marianne. He was forgotten by Annie but not so easily. Marianne forgot, because her work engaged her attention constantly and at night, sitting by the fire, she would fall asleep.

It was a habit thought Annie and she did not worry and teased her mother that she was becoming an old woman. Often as her mother slept she would look up from her books and store in her memory the shape of the small neat head and the dark hair under the piled chignon. She admired the fine bones, finer than her own. She looked at her long slender hands and wished that they were her own.

One night as she regarded the sleeping mother she noticed something she had not seen before, the faint violet shading of her eyelids. It was delicate, pretty, fragile, but it was the beauty that holds sadness within it, it was like a petal and that spelt transience. Before Annie could consider this Marianne woke up and her bright smile dismissed gloom and she made them laugh with a funny story of a happening during the day.

Shortly before Christmas Marianne told the family that she had to go to Huddersfield on business. Annie wondered what it could be. It certainly could not be shopping for there had been rigid economies in the house since William's departure.

Marianne prepared for the visit with dread. When she arrived at Huddersfield station her spirits did not rise for the town was shrouded in fog, a thick greasy blanket smelling of wet wool.

She made her way up towards Marsh to the neat residential houses she once had hoped they might live in when Benton was alive. A trim maid answered the door and she was ushered in the waiting room.

When Dr Campion saw her, he recognised her, but found if difficult to reconcile the young wife he had known with this widow with such an air of authority although so gentle. He noticed instantly the tell-tale violet shadows, the finely drawn skin over the bones and her meagre flesh.

Very gently, very quietly he examined her and without hesitation her suspected tuberculosis. He noticed that her heart was straining, there was a probability of angina. She asked for the truth. He only confirmed her fears. He prescribed rest and, if possible, a move to a healthy air.

"That is impossible."

She thanked him, they spoke briefly of the children and she left and he went to the window to see her walk down the road before he called his next patient.

Grandma was let into the secret and Marianne ruefully said, "Doctors are not always right."

"That's true, but eh nay lass, give them credit, they usually are."

The old lady was broken in her heart, but filled also with resolve. She would nurse her daughter-in-law back to health. She had lost the battle with her son, this time she would know better. She searched out nourishing recipes to build Marianne up.

She bought dozens of eggs which she placed in a crock and filled with brandy, the shells dissolved and the mixture Marianne had to swallow.

The girls were kept in ignorance but the care and concern shown for their mother was obvious and they began to pamper her too. It was not very long before Annie saw a manifestation of sickness she had never seen before. Her mother suddenly stiffened, one hand clutched the arm of her chair, the other was raised to her breast, she kept abjectly still, except for a tiny whimper there was no vocal sign of the grinding agony within.

Annie saw her mother bodily shrink, her pale face turned a faint and ghastly green. The pain seemed so intense she hardly dare touch her for fear of aggravating it. Marianne's lips just moved, "Don't worry, it will pass."

In moments that seemed hours, it did, and half an hour later when Annie brought her a cup of tea she found her so recovered that she had taken up some knitting. Marianne made light of the attack, she was upset that Annie had witnessed it. These turns were infrequent and hitherto had always been endured in privacy.

On the train to Anston, Annie began to worry. The thought of death and her mother was banished from the forefront of her mind, but the shadow remained. She felt insecure and then insecurity at Anston became apparent.

Miss Hodge told her that the Managers had applied for another teacher and the request had been granted. Annie would have to return to the Lancaterian School and think of going to College.

Annie did not like the idea and with Miss Hodge she was able to talk it over.

The headmistress put down her knife and fork as they were having their dinner and looked at Annie,

"Annie, you are not just a teacher, you know. Your mother has seen to it that you are a lady. I'm not even certain you would like college. I think you should still go to Holland, but why don't you get a governess's post before then?"

Annie agreed, but she was dissimulating by silence, for she had other ideas. She was tired of teaching and schools.

At the station in Wakefield, instead of going downhill to the Prison, she turned up into the High Street. She went to Madame Cherie's the milliner.

Madame, in truth, Mrs Cherry, was shutting the shop, but she smiled when she saw Annie. Very frequently she had sold her ribbon and feathers.

"Can I help you, Mees Tayleur?"

"Yes, Madame, I wondered if you would have a place for an assistant?"

The smiling face changed to one of assessment, profit and loss. The accent slipped into a business woman's.

"As an apprentice?"

"No, as an assistant."

That bait of a premium vanished, but still the elegant girl stood there. She would be no loss and her trustworthiness seemed obvious.

"Well, perhaps, I could make room for you, but I could not pay very much while you are unskilled." She mentioned five shillings a week.

Annie was delighted. It was more than she got at school.

"I could start before Christmas. At the end of the term."

"That would be excellent. Your mother knows of this, of course?"

"No, not yet."

"You must get her approval. Then see me again. Goodnight, my dear."

Madame Cherie closed the door, pulled down the blind. She pursed her lips shook her head, gave a Gallic shrug to her Yorkshire shoulders and said aloud to herself.

"Pity. I could have done with a girl like that. But Mrs Taylor will never allow it."

Annie hurried home thrilled hugging her amazing surprise to herself. She imagined the startled surprise and gladness at the table. With the utmost difficulty she kept it back until the propitious moment, half-way though the meal. Her mother had sighed, she looked weary.

"I've got some wonderful news. I've been to see Madame Cherie and she will take me on as an assistant and pay me five shillings a week!"

It was Annie's turn to be startled. Her mother looked at her with fixed horror. She lowered her napkin and pushed her chair back from the table.

"Are you intent upon killing me? I am more horrified than I can possibly say. A shop assistant! A milliner! No daughter of mine will ever be a shop assistant and most certainly not to that bogus Frenchwoman. I cannot think what you were thinking of. I shall write to her immediately."

"But, Mother, I would love it. I would do it well, you know I would."

"No. There is no more to be said. I refuse to discuss it."

"But, Mother, what shall I be? A governess – a nobody, neither a servant, nor one of the family."

Marianne stretched out her hand. "That, my darling is how governesses are treated in England. Abroad it is quite different, especially with the right family."

"Think of 'Villette', Mother."

"Charlotte Bronte, my dear, was plain and a frump and not very charming. Don't take her as a pattern. You are a very different kettle of fish."

"How do you know, Mother?"

"Your father always told me so and I trust him and I ask you to trust me." As she said this she gripped her daughter's hand.

Annie bowed to her mother's word, as to the inevitable but it did not stop her dreaming of making hats of beauty and splendour.

Marianne was troubled and she was silent. She felt that time was short. She rejoiced that William was in his chosen career; her daughters, though, had yet to be launched. She wanted them away from Wakefield. She was nagged constantly by the lack of money to educate them abroad. Sometimes she felt at war with circumstance.

It was a dark week and the drab skies added to their depression, when suddenly, unannounced there came light. Marianne received a letter from a Mrs Pumphrey of Swale Hall asking her if Annie would consider undertaking the teaching of their younger son.

A week later Annie was on the train on her way to see the family. As the countryside flashed by, and she felt further from home, she thought of *Jane Eyre*. She identified herself still more when she was met at the station by a groom with a trap.

They drove a short distance to a long stone house, old beautiful but not imposing. No housekeeper met her, instead there was the mistress of the house a calm placid plump lady wearing a white cap. Annie's immediate thought was that Mrs Pumphrey was far from smartly dressed. She was led to the drawing room, a large low ceilinged room comfortable and again plain.

"How old art thou, Annie Taylor?"

"Seventeen, ma'am."

"Please do not call me ma'am. We are Friends, what you call Quakers, and as you are not one, you may call me Mrs. May I call you Annie?"

Annie, of course, assented and listened to the, to her, surprisingly objective description by the mother of her small son. A quarter of an hour passed and Jonathan came in. He was a flaxen haired child with a pale face. He had a very lively spirit in a frail form. Both he and Annie took to one another instantly. The mother smiled and Annie was engaged.

So Annie entered another world as different from grimy Anston as Heaven from Hell. With one she always recalled grime and ashy dust beneath the finger tips, with Swale spotless shining surfaces and the scent of flowers. She discovered that she had come there on the recommendation of Miss Hodge, who watched over Annie like another mother.

The year in Anston had taught her a great deal that she was never to forget and the children of poor homes were to be in her mind the rest of her life.

She learnt much, too, from the Pumphrey household, first and foremost that a simple life did not mean a haphazard or slovenly one and that if certain conventions were displaced other small ceremonies took their place. Mr Pumphrey might wander about the house wearing his hat, but his manners were impeccable. She feared a little their very gracious forthrightness when she offended. She realized, however, that she was always treated as an equal.

They continued to send the trap to meet her each morning, until Annie, who loved walking told them that they need not.

This independence pleased them more than she judged and on her arrival each day a silver tray with a silver mug with creamy milk and a plate with two biscuits was brought to her.

These unheralded courtesies impressed her. And Jonathan? The lively spirit became livelier, he was quick to learn, very eager to listen to her growing fund of stories and long rhymes and she took him on long walks on the moors nearby and his pale face took on some colour. It was a happy uneventful time.

Chapter 12

Swale Hall

Christmas without William was quiet, the festivities still took time and it was not until they were all over that the household sat down to write to the sailor of the family.

Marianne started off in good heart, she said how she wished that she was talking to him instead of writing. When the sentence was finished she tapped the pen against her teeth and wondered if it was quite correct?

Talking to William had often been an effort. She resumed writing and mentioned the plum cake which had lasted far longer because he was away! She told him how Captain Armytage had given them a goose.

She paused again and then related an evening when Mr Wilkinson the prison visitor had called. She told him of their suppressed laughter as he boringly talked of bishops and their relatives and how not one of them had dared to look at another for fear that their humour would burst its bounds.

Again she paused and wondered if William would be very bored with this account. She fiddled with her pen – it seemed to have failed her. Then she wondered if she had failed him, begrudgingly she admitted a truth that he was further away in spirit than in physical distance.

Almost aloud she said to herself, "But I love him." She went on with prison news, the main item being the the Governor was to leave in February. That, she knew, would interest him, for William had always respected him greatly.

Again she paused. Oh yes, the church. She told him of the choir, how they missed him and how Miss Scott's face was as red as ever, her voice still as loud. She told him of a party that was being given for the prison staff.

Once more she ceased to write. It all seemed so petty, so small. Her world, she thought, is small even claustrophobic.

Then as she realised she was dramatizing, she reminded herself of the cells, they were indeed small and the prospects for the inmates smaller and dimmer than hers. She folded up the letter and resolved to take it up next day.

The following evening she re-read her letter, there seemed such a void between what she wished to say and what she had written. What was she to tell him now? Of her intolerable weariness? The effort of the drag from day-to-day? Of her hopes for Annie and her happiness at Swale Hall?

Instead, she wrote of the parties, the chaffing from the officers about her age and dancing. But then questions broke through... was he taller? Were his superiors pleased with him? Suddenly her pen wrote not of everyday occupations, but moral ones.

He must do his duty to God, always be truthful, he must respect the officers. "Do not connive at anything mean, or underhand, but be open and above board."

She wondered if she should be saying this to her straying sheep now that he was independent and wandering so far away? She thought she could, for she loved him and she revealed it in, "You know you took more than your share of my love when you went, but I send you another budget for all that." She finished her letter, it carried her love and that was all that mattered.

In her years at Wakefield, Marianne had drawn strength from Captain Armytage. She did not merely admire this grave, just man, she had an awed love for him. He seemed the embodiment of justice, it was acknowledged even by the convicts, he was the law, but he was rare in that he could also be compassionate without weakness or sentimentality.

As the time drew near for his departure, Marianne was disturbed, a prop – though an unconscious one – was being removed. When his farewell came and she sat on the platform listening to the speeches, some trite, some fulsome, but in them all a vein of real regret, she remembered his friendship and protection.

An era of her life was ending. Captain Armytage spoke of the close of a chapter, but said that it was the unfolding, too, of a new one. There would be more ideas, more improvements... they lived in an age of progress.

She linked some of this with her family. They were unfolding, new ways lay before the next generation.

Easter was mild that year and Annie returned from Swale with a hamper of eggs, butter and many bunches of flowers. Together with Edith they helped decorate the church. Annie loved Wakefield church, she had been confirmed there and so, too, had Edith during Lent. That Marianne, Annie and Edith could all take Communion this year meant a great deal to them all, but most of all to Marianne.

They set off early in the morning though the blinkered streets, there was nip in the air, but there was promise of fine weather to come and the chimneys were still so the air was clear.

The interior of the church promised spring and to Marianne it promised more, there were texts on shields all proclaiming Resurrection and this she believed and loved to consider. Edith's attention was fixed to the prayer book, she was afraid of losing her place.

Annie's attention strayed to the flowers. Marianne listened intently and when she heard of Mary Magdalen in the garden going to anoint the body of the dead Christ and finding a Risen Lord, she though, as she always did, of her bathing the body of her husband shortly before he died.

So the past of long ago blended with a recent past and the unknown future stood like a mirage before them. It was only Marianne who was so preoccupied with the future, not her own, but her daughters'.

Tea that afternoon was a festival and Edith got out the white and gold tea service given by her father to Marianne at Annie's christening, it had a pattern of sea weed. Annie inspired by the use of silver at Swale rummaged beneath the stairs and brought out Grandma's Sheffield plate urn.

It was tall and slender and eloquent of Georgian grace, Annie loved it. She spent the morning cleaning it and she felt a stir in her heart as she saw the swags and garland of flowers emerge from the tarnish.

Even Grandma was pleased to see it again and said how once it had been used every day. She showed Annie how to lift the lip of the cylinder inside and draw out the iron bar which was then put between the pars of the fire on the range to get hot, "not red-hot mind you".

This then kept the boiling water in the vessel hot for a considerable time. Together the girls lay the table and cut bread and butter. They were just about to sit when there was a knock at the door.

"Oh dear, Annie, run along and see who it is."

From the hall there were cries of delight and Annie came back beaming: "It's Cousin Polly", the sighs of exasperation turned to exclamations of joy, a racing for more chairs, cups and plates. Polly, quiet, retiring but shrewd was a great favourite.

She was not alone. She was accompanied by a small dark lady in an unfashionable bonnet and brown silk dress that matched, too well her sallow complexion. Marianne regarded her for a moment and then stretched out her arms to seize her hands and say,

"Why, it's Miss Van Zuyl."

The happiness of the occasion was intensified by its unexpectedness and they all talked, often all at once. During the excitement the two dark-haired women covertly eyed one another in appraisal.

They were both 35 and they wished to compare what time had done to them. Their lives had been different, Marianne had met with widowhood, poverty and great anxiety but she had never lacked love.

Miss Van Zuyl had known constrained means but only of a genteel kind, her life of teaching had gone on placidly uneventfully. But the flame that freshens within had never been kindled and she seemed dry but not withered.

Her intellect prevented that and her large dark Jewish eyes were profound with wisdom.

So it was that Marianne saw the same woman she had met years ago, but older, and Miss Van Zuyl saw a woman who differed almost completely from the girl she had met in Whiteley Bottom.

She saw dignity and a great presence and she saw that Annie had inherited, or imbibed some of it although she looked extraordinarily young.

When they went into the parlour, the conversation never flagged and Miss Van Zuyl looking at the piano asked if Marianne still played Mozart. When she heard that she did she asked to hear some and Marianne replied.

"I will play for you alone while the others all go to church."

When they were alone Marianne grabbed her hand and said, "I am so very, very glad to see you. It is heaven sent. I still want Annie to go to Holland to finish her education, like Polly did, and because Benton was so insistent on it."

"Why don't you send her then?"

"Oh, many reasons." She was beginning to skate over the real reasons, but suddenly said to herself, "be above board." "I have no money. It has been spent on equipping and commissioning William."

"But, my dear, you do not need any for a girl like Annie."

"I, too, must be honest. I have been asked by some old friends, who keep a school in Leyden, to find them an English teacher. I have found her. Will you let me recommend her?"

Marianne closed her eyes and clasped her hands. It was an answer to spoken and unspoken prayers. She wished to say "Yes", but remembered, just in time, to say, "You must ask Annie that. She must decide for herself. But tell me of the school."

Marianne learnt that it was an exclusive establishment in a fine street in Leyden. It had a few tenuous links with the university. The principals were Mejuffrow Lange and Mejuffrouw Snoek. They were Protestant ladies of impeccable respectability.

When they all returned from church, the gaiety was even brighter for Edith gave an excellent imitation of a very pompous preacher that they had heard. Before supper Miss Van Zuyl had a word with Annie that brought a flush to her cheeks and made her eyes shine in anticipation. It was decided that she should return to Crosland Moor with Cousin Polly that night and talk it over with her new Dutch friend.

Marianne that night in bed thought that it was the happiest and most auspicious Easter that she had ever known. Annie's future was just beginning to look assured. But she ceased to think further when she contemplated the parting.

"It will be like losing a limb", she thought.

Chapter 13

Leiden

At dinner she found that Jan donned a tailed coat and served the dishes. It was the first time that Annie had been waited upon by a man. It pleased her because she knew that once her mother had always been waited upon by menservants.

During the meal, she was quite openly questioned and her interests were discovered. The Principals were pleased, but when they were alone said,

"Isn't it strange how English girls never know anything about paintings? I wonder why. We shall have to see that Miss Taylor attends the art classes."

Next day, Annie was taken for a walk and a rapid succession of images and impressions were made upon her mind. Annie was bewildered by so much and vowed that she would return alone to the Rapenburg.

After lunch she was given permission to wander at will throughout the school. She went from classroom to classroom. She first noticed that they smelt exactly like English school-rooms, chalk and polish. It was, perhaps, a little neater and barer than its English counterpart and most certainly it was lighter, she was getting used gradually to the larger windows of Holland.

The garden was walled. There was a broad walk, a covered area with rampant creepers where, it was quite evident, classes were often held.

As a garden it failed, it was strangely formless, there was no arrangement. There were flowers but they were in sudden rows which began and ended abruptly. Annie had a sudden longing for the gardens of the prison with their carnations.

In the evening, dinner was more formal for a guest had arrived, another maiden lady. She spoke faultless English. But it was the table that seized Annie's interest for, from her mother, she had inherited a great love for china.

She regarded the dinner service with undisguised admiration.. It was what she called Dresden, but the ladies pronounced to be

Saxische. It had country scenes painted upon it, animals and insects.

Each plate was different and some had hares, dogs, deer even hedgehogs on them. It was on these plates that her real initiation in the Dutch language began and over one meal she amassed a large vocabulary of animal nomenclature.

Annie wondered how often this china was used. She soon received the answer only on ceremonial and small occasions. When the meal was over Jan brought in a large wooden bowl which was placed before Miss Lange, who, without rising, produced a neatly folded apron which she tied over her shoulders and waist.

She turned back the lace cuffs of her sleeves to reveal strong wrists and she began to wash the dishes. Each lady present had been given a drying cloth and the plates were duly wiped, dried, and handed round for close inspection.

This was not a task, it was a diversion and the discussions it aroused was akin to passion. When they rose, it was to arrange the china in the great oak cupboard surmounted by blue and white vases.

When the doors of the cupboard had been opened Annie gasped at the treasures it revealed and she felt a great pang as she compared it with the austerity of her home in Wakefield.

They moved into the parlour, a room Annie had not visited. It had white painted panelling and the scrolled edges and mouldings were picked out in gold. It was unlike any panelling Annie had seen before. Here the ladies lapsed into Dutch. As she listened intently she became depressed for she understood nothing of what they said. A wave of homesickness swept over her like a cloud. Of homesickness she had been warned and her mother had given her an antidote,

"When you feel unhappy, do something immediately."

Annie asked if she might bring down her embroidery. The wish was gladly granted. When Annie reappeared with her work-basket, a present from Anston, the ladies were amazed at Annie's embroidery.

It was not the canvas Berlin wool work they were accustomed to, but silk upon linen. At first they watched her without comment and the conversation flowed on.

Strangely Annie found that because her entire mind was not

straining for meanings the recurrence of a sound became a word she could visualize.

Then there was a pause and she knew that they were all looking at her work. Annie showed them the different stitches, couching, stem stitch, long and short chain and broken chain. They saw that it was freer, more daring and imaginative than the old canvas work. They were impressed and soon came the question whether Annie would be prepared to teach the girls.

Annie felt the approbation rising as she consented. Had she known more of the language she would have known that they openly congratulated themselves on having acquired her services.

Next day, the Dutch lessons began in earnest with Miss Lange, who proved herself a patient but demanding teacher. Annie found herself hampered by her impatience, she longed to express herself and she missed greatly the ability to make a joke.

Life seemed so serious. In the afternoon she was left to her own devices and soon she tired of the garden and putting on her hat and her gloves she went out alone. She knew that she would find her way back easily for the street with its canal and trees was clearly identifiable.

She wandered through the alley-ways and furtively glanced over the stable doors into the houses. Around the Hooglandse Kerk, Annie noticed the houses and shops set into the very church walls. She became fascinated by the shops and the details of her walk. She came to the castle and went beneath the armorial gateway and climbed the steps to the battlements and there the whole city seemed arrayed before her.

The comparison with Wakefield was forefront in her mind. She thought of her home town as seen from Sandal Castle, there the hills were slight and gently undulating and the sky large and sweeping, here the land was flatter and the sky much greater and she noticed at once, considerably clearer.

The greyness that she had become so accustomed to was not here. She was aware that the paintwork of the doors and windows here gleamed, as they did only for an hour or two after scrubbing in Yorkshire. This was a different world and she rejoiced in every aspect of its strangeness.

She took her bearings, and leaving the Castle, made for the Rapenburg with its wider canal, its impressive houses, larger than the Hooigracht and its many bridges. She did not, yet, quite appreciate that she had not merely changed countries, but time as well, she had gone back.

She had left the bustling vigour of industrial Yorkshire for the, as yet, rural and mercantile economy of a small country. Even more she was comparing a workshop with a university town surrounded by fields. She walked on swiftly, but lingering, still, before the shops which where strange and enticing. Only when she began to retrace her steps did she realize that she was lost. Again and again she was confronted by the Town Hall with its double flight of steps. She was hesitant to ask directions, but she was beginning to be fearful for shops were beginning to close.

At last, she marched into a haberdasher's shop. The assistant spoke to her and Annie could only repeat the address of the school. She called the proprietor down from his stool at the cash desk, again Annie repeated the address. He smiled and then disappeared. Alone Annie found a piece of paper and she wrote the address down.

The owner returned with his wife who took up the paper beamed and again disappeared. She returned bonneted and shawled and smiling she ushered Annie out of the shop and down through side streets.

Very soon, they emerged through a gateway she had not seen before, into the familiar tree- lined street, which she saw, now, very clearly was much like many others. Annie knew her way, but the haberdasher's wife was not going to relinquish her charge easily. Annie, now, led the way to the door which Jan opened immediately.

A conversation followed between him and Annie's guide. While they talked the door of the study opened and a very anxious and perplexed Miss Snoek appeared.

"Where have you been, Miss Taylor?"

"I went for a walk and I got lost and this kind lady brought me back." Annie laughed. It rang very hollow in the hall and Miss Snoek ignored it.

"You had best go to your room and make yourself tidy for dinner."

This Annie did swiftly. She felt that her escapade had been an enormity and so it was in the Principals eyes. No young lady, she was assured, ever went out unaccompanied for this was a town full of male students and a constant and vigilant regard had to be maintained against their advances. This foolish experiment must never, never be repeated.

Annie apologised profusely, the ladies were mollified and regained their prim equanimity. Annie vowed that she would no longer go wandering, but that she would master the language and she set to that task that evening.

The following morning she had her lesson and she began to make progress. In the afternoon her interest flagged and instead of reading the alien page she watched a money spider run across again and again. At last she let it run on her hand and she carried it over to a clump of flowers where it could live undisturbed.

As she settled to her book again the maid, Mientje, came out and delivered a message of which Annie only distinctly heard the words Miss Lange and Miss Snoek. She rose and went indoors. With the Principals stood a tall dark haired young woman, Miss Anna Le Polle. She was a very neat young woman with large clear eyes and a wide and generous mouth. Annie liked her immediately.

Next day, Anna called for Annie and took her to her home on Witte Singel. There beyond a wide canal there were rows of new houses, each had a garden at the front and the windows were even larger than in the old houses.

It was into one of these that Annie was led and up to the "bel etage" where Mrs Le Polle sat in her drawing room. She was a stout lady who, once, had enjoyed the clear complexion of her daughter, but, now, it was no longer fresh.

The same generous impulses Annie had seen in the daughter were in the mother. The house was full of books, even on the stairs and Mrs Le Polle was eager to find some novels in English for Annie. Annie stopped her and said that she must learn Dutch and read nothing else.

After chatting a little while the older lady said: "Let us celebrate, let us have some wine." Annie was perturbed. Her provincial upbringing had taught her that wine was sinful and wine in the afternoon seemed still more sinful.

The glasses and decanter appeared and very soon she held in her hand a glass of port of the deepest red. It was so beautiful Annie thought it could not possibly be wicked. Men, she knew, always wished one another "good health," but what was she to do?

Sitting very upright, the glass in her gloved hand she bowed her head and smiled. It was a gesture they were never to forget for it was an extraordinary blend of childishness and regality. She, within herself, prepared to drink the wine as though it were medicine, but the port was smooth and gentle and beguiling.

"Heerlijk, very nice indeed."

She meant it and, as she drank, the friendliest of devils seemed to prance before her and she saw herself as wicked as William when he had first smoked a cigarette before her. The wine loosened her tongue and both English and a few new found Dutch words rolled from her tongue.

Too soon, Jan was announced as waiting below and ready when Miss Taylor was willing to go. She tied her bonnet ribbons and descended the stairs. Jan stood in the hall and he held her cape which he placed on her shoulders. It was Anna who saw that Annie did not wish to wear the cape. "Annie, you do not want to wear that do you?"

"No, I will carry it."

"It is expected that Jan will carry it for you."

Annie blushed, she had blundered. In the street she found that Jan walked a couple of paces behind her. She lifted her head proudly and liked to believe that the glances of passers-by were of awe at the sight of a young lady and her manservant.

She was walking in a waking dream, smiling a faint archaic smile. She was thrilled with life. She was brought to earth quite soon when she attempted to cross a road, Jan said very clearly, "Miss Taylor", she looked at him and he pointed to the opposite direction.

Humour and good manners open many doors and when allied with some beauty, they open still more. Annie was constantly asked out and every afternoon Jan was escorting her, or bringing her back from yet another house.

In the evenings, she got out her new writing case and in her best copperplate wrote to her mother. She related her triumphs and that Jan walked behind her carrying her parcels and she exaggerated the glories. In Wakefield her letters were eagerly read and laughed over; they recognised the embellishments and said, "How like Annie."

Marianne, however, in her reply said: "My word, lassie, you do get some invitations. I only hope that you will keep your head."

The mother also worried about her daughter's clothes and their suitability, she thought that a grey dress could be dyed.

"A dark crimson would be pretty, it would light up well and made to look quite gay with a little setting off in the way of frilling. By the by, lassie, how are you off for ribbon and frilling. Let me know in your next letter, my darling, and I will send you some. How are the gloves coming on, are they worn of an evening?"

When Annie received the letter she wept at the loving care of the content, but was disturbed by the lack of firmness in the writing. She wondered just how ill her mother was.

The days passed quickly and Annie's grasp of Dutch leapt daily. Each morning she worked with Miss Snoek on grammar, every meal and expedition was an essay into conversation. From Miss Snoek Annie learnt to teach even during hours of leisure.

It became a game that Annie loved and she gladly accompanied the Principal on shopping expeditions and gave orders at the shops. Not only was she gaining in knowledge of the language, she was growing in confidence.

On the last day of holiday, an outing was planned and Annie had instructions to wear her best silk dress and bonnet. She delightedly arrayed herself in her Sunday dress of blue silk with white ribbons: it was flounced and bustled and with it she wore a dark blue straw hat trimmed with cornflowers. She was well aware that she looked extremely pretty.

She waited in the hall and presently Miss Snoek came down the stairs in brown taffeta. Later, Miss Lange arrived in watered silk of black trimmed with jet. As they settled into the hired carriage, Annie wondered why they were so formally dressed for a day by the sea.

The Principals in their turn looked at Annie and noted how the blue of her dress matched her eyes and they wondered if they would have difficulty having so attractive a member on their staff.

Soon, Leyden was left behind and they were out in the meadows coming to small farms set along the canal, each with its own bridge with its high shaft and weight to make it into a drawbridge.

They came to small villages where the gables of the houses met neighbouring gable and looked like dancers linking arms facing their partners across the road. Then they came to the dunes, there were inclines and villages where prim houses regarded quietly but intently one another.

They seemed small worlds of gossip. She wondered if they might be calling on someone, but no, they walked the horses up a slope and at the crest they saw the sea and the pale golden sand and along the ridge they trotted.

On the beach there were great flat-bottomed boats squatting like hens. Around them, like chicks, were the fishermen and spread on the slopes were the nets with men and women moving slowly over them, some sitting and sewing together the rents.

Annie noted the black clad women with their white caps, this was, indeed, a different world. She was eager and alert and planning the letter she would write home that night. Eventually she was told to turn round and look ahead and obeying she saw in the distance tall houses crowned with turrets and a building with a dome.

It was all white and shimmered in the warmth, it seemed ghostly and unreal. Quite suddenly, a few feet below them, they saw the square of a barracks and lines of soldiers and lumbering up from it a cannon drawn by horses mounted by dragoons.

She had never seen soldiers before. They looked handsome and dashing, all that she had imagined. The outskirts of Scheveningen were reached and instantly they were in a highly fashionable town.

Seeing the people walking along the broad pavements, Annie knew why they were so correctly attired - here was wealth and fashion. The carriage turned down towards the promenade, there they dismounted and arranged to meet the carriage later that afternoon.

Annie was amazed, she had seen nothing like it in her life. The cafes spilled with tables and chairs across the wide boulevard and sitting at the tables were the most varied people she had ever seen.

Every nationality seemed gathered here… Germans, French, one race blond and large boned and the other dark and more neatly boned. But there were, too, dark coloured people dressed in silk and brocade, then men wearing twisted scarves of coloured material on their heads and, she noted, with large knives tucked into the broad sash about their waists.

They reminded her of the opera *The Mikado*. She had never expected to see such people in real life. Miss Snoek realised Annie's curiosity and she explained that these people were from Java, wealthy people, often princes. They sat at a table and an Eastern family was close at hand.

Annie watched fascinated, the women were so graceful and their movements so gentle, the children were quiet and well-behaved and the men, to her astonishment were mild, even secret, too. They drank from glasses and cups and used knives and forks.

Until that moment, Annie had used the word 'savage' to describe anyone with a coloured skin. It was a shock to her and she knew that her notions and prejudices would have to be modified.

Later, they walked and crossing the road they mingled with the people by the sea shore. It seemed so strange to her that such splendidly dressed people should be on the edge of the sand where others were bathing from machines and others sat in the wicker chairs like sentry boxes.

It was a bewildering mass of sophistication and simplicity and it was all very exciting. The two older ladies walked on either side of her, they talked a mixture of Dutch and English and they explained and pointed out to her the various nationalities.

Eventually they entered the Kurhaus and there they ordered food and listened to an orchestra.

By the window Annie could see the pavements and the road. There were carriages in a perpetual stream. The world seemed very large but not in the least frightening.

On the way home soon, almost too soon, the modish, the chic was left behind, Katwijk seem tame, yet also reassuring. They then came to the fields.

The moon rose and shone mysteriously on the cabbages making them seem like exotic plants from another world. As she gazed Miss Snoek confessed that she liked this sight more than the gaudy blaze of tulips in the spring.

Up in her room, Annie looked at her writing case. She vowed to write a long letter home next morning describing what seemed the most amazing day of her life.

The outing marked the holiday's end and during her Dutch lesson, Annie was aware that Miss Snoek's mind was wandering to her lists which she consulted now and again, even though she placed them face downwards to lessen their distraction.

In the afternoon she wrote her letter and as she did so she became aware of new voices and footsteps in the house.

Later that day there were teachers to meet at the evening meal which was taken not in the little dining room, but the large room overlooking the garden. There were seven teachers present, mostly middle-aged.

The most handsome was the French teacher. She was tall and fair with wavy hair that was loosely gathered into a knot at the nape of her neck. She had in her dressing an air, at once, informal and elegant. That evening she wore a black dress the bodice of which was enriched by a fall of fine black lace. Annie noted the softness and distinction if gave to an otherwise plain dress. She thought she would one day copy it.

The teachers all talked a great deal and there was, though Annie did not recognise it, an air of striving and competition in the conversation. They were attempting to out vie one another with their doings.

Annie began to feel insecure and her apprehension spread to her ability to control the pupils. She thought, too, of her anomalous position, part pupil and part teacher. She wondered if this would prove particularly difficult, for so often she had heard Grandma trenchantly declare someone as "neither fish, nor flesh, nor good red herring."

After the meal, she wandered in the garden and possibly her drooping shoulders caused Miss Lange to come out to her. Annie smiled, the smile was ignored and to Annie's surprise Miss Lange took her arm.

"I know how you feel. I remember thinking at my first school how remarkably clever the other staff were. They are not really. Teachers always show off when they are thrown together at first." She now smiled and added, "It is always the same."

Annie, who had been prepared to be guarded by smiles and charm, found herself saying, "But I also wonder about the girls. What will they be like?"

"They are a mixture, my dear, some intelligent, some even clever, but some are not. You should know, Miss Taylor, that I have no anxiety at all, you will soon gain their admiration and if you behave like a teacher, then, their respect."

Miss Lange led her back and introduced her to a small German lady, Fraulein Vogel. She was as dark as the Frenchwoman should have been.

She, too, talked of her holiday - she had been to Heidelburg.

It was that evening that Annie learnt the difference between living on an island and on the Continent. They all had been away to countries which seemed to her far distant.

Coffee was served in the salon and Miss Snoek immediately asked Fraulein Vogel to play. The small woman rose and without any hesitation went to the piano and raised the lid. She sat and Annie noted how her dress swept around her, but it was the calmness of her approach that struck her, there was no mock-modesty, no desire to be urged, as Annie was so used to in Wakefield.

The room was filled with the sound of Schubert and everyone was transfixed, books which had been taken up were laid aside, even Miss Snoek's lists were forgotten. The Lizt followed and the *Hungarian Rhapsody* made Annie's feet tap with exhilaration.

At last it came to an end and the little audience clapped and many compliments were paid. Annie remained quiet.

"Now, what would our newest and youngest member of staff like me to play?" For a moment Annie's mind was blank, then she remembered Mozart and her mother. "Some airs, please, from *The Marriage of Figaro*."

Miss Vogel beamed with pleasure. The music tinkled out precisely and seemed to fill the room with silver. Annie almost gasped when she heard *Fling Aside All Your Airs and Your Graces*. She also acknowledged that Miss Vogel played it far better than her mother. Annie blinked back some tears.

As Miss Lange and Miss Snoek talked by themselves, Miss Snoek said: "I see that Miss Taylor is not unmusical. She was moved by the music. Did you notice, Rosa?"

"Yes, I did. I think she knows more of music than art, but the tears, I think she was reminded of home. She is still very young."

In her room Annie lay awake. She thought of her mother, she thought of the pupils. These young women would be very different from the children of Anston. They would regard her possibly as an inferior, be demanding, pert and sly.

She knew that there would be none of the obstinacy and the dull weariness of tired little colliers to contend with. She became alarmed and panic stricken, but, at last, she fell asleep.

First thing in the morning she said to herself, "Term begins today." And immediately she crept beneath the bedclothes. All her anxieties crowded in upon her and she felt worse and worse. She then sat up, flung back her hair and said aloud her mother's words, "Do something."

Her eyes fell upon the hip bath, she got out of bed filled the bath with water from the cans, took off her nightdress and slowly lowered herself into the coldness that lapped about her.

Taking the sponge she filled it and with a gasp squeezed it over her shoulders. It was ice, it was fire and it leapt like flames down her spine. She gasped and laughed and the spell of depression broke and fell in splinters.

The house downstairs seemed different, there was an air of expectancy. The teachers were coming in to breakfast, the French teacher shocked Annie by appearing in a long negligee, she sat reading a letter and dipping a croissant in her coffee which Annie thought very slovenly, but she did not think of that for long; there was a letter for her.

Her mother wrote that young Dr Clark, who had replaced Dr Wood, had been to see her. He had given her sick leave and that very soon she was going to stay with Cousin Mary at Crosland Moor. The positive note of the plans reassured Annie, but she did wonder what could be the matter with her mother. There was little time for speculation. There were timetables to be discussed, classrooms to be allotted.

Miss Lange was like a queen, she presided, she interrupted, she decreed, the real arrangements were all made from the fluttering papers of Miss Snoek. Annie saw that they were an indivisible pair and that their charge was absolute.

As soon as they disappeared the staff grumbled. Annie found that all her mornings were devoted to teaching, that the French and German lessons were set in the afternoons so that she could attend.

Thought had been given to her wants. She was, though, disappointed that her teaching of needlework was regarded only as a pastime for the evenings.

The atmosphere of the house had changed. When the teachers arrived it became an institution and when the girls began to arrive it became a school. There was more liveliness and laughter and furtive talking that erupted into bursts of noise, wherever one went a girl would be encountered.

Most of the older girls were the same height as Annie, who in Yorkshire was considered tall and Annie thought that they all wore their clothes badly. They were much less subdued than English girls and they talked loudly.

Annie found straight away that her position was firmly that of a teacher in their estimation and that was largely achieved by her erect posture and grave deportment. Her movements became unhurried, her back was held straight constantly – and remained so for a lifetime – it was all that her grandmother could desire. Miss Lange noticed it and approved.

The first meal of the staff and pupils became a little feast with speeches of welcome to the school and dedication to learning. As the girls listened, more intently than in England, Annie had regarded them all.

She had expected plumpness, they were not. She had expected solid phlegm about their characters… instead she saw vigour and enthusiasm.

She became aware, too, that some had finer bones, flatter faces and darker skins, the Javanese blood revealing itself. She liked it that they were more openly mischievous than their British counterparts.

At dinner, wine had been served and very soon, one bold spirit had wetted her finger and run it round the rim of her glass. She was followed by others and soon there rang a shrill hum with an aimless piercing note.

Miss Lange rose to her feet, silence fell like a curtain, she remained standing and slowly surveyed the tables, taking in each pair of eyes as she raked them with her gaze, without words she condemned them.

A snigger broke out among the middle school, she turned towards it, the curtain turned to a blanket of silence. Then quite simple she said: "Thank you."

Annie stored the action in her memory. She admired the deliberation with which the action had been taken, no wasted effort, absolute economy.

When the girls went up to bed, Annie stayed below with the staff, when she went up she wondered if any tricks would have been played with her bed, but everything was in order. The shock came next morning when she looked into the dormitory through her window and saw the girls fully dressed and dipping a corner of their towels into the jugs and wiping it perfunctorily over their faces. Action was needed.

She opened her door and told them all to remove their dresses immediately, to pour water into the bowls and wash properly with soap and water. Grumblingly, they obeyed. They were good natured and expostulated that she did not understand them because the English all washed too much.

When they had their dresses on Annie inspected them, she looked behind their ears, the backs of their necks. She asked to see the finger nails and the palms of their hands. She pulled dresses, she straightened bows in hair and dresses, she asked that a button be done up. Within a week Annie's dormitory of girls was famed in the tiny world as the tidiest.

So one week became another and soon October was reached and life seemed settled in a disciplined regimen. Though in a school, Annie found that the world was wider than Wakefield. The backgrounds from which the staff and girls came were spread across the Continent and the Dutch East Indies.

A school remains a school though and little things were discussed, dwelt upon and magnified incessantly. Annie did not think that she wanted to be a teacher forever.

Gradually, all the people around her became definite entities and she found it hard sometimes to reconcile her first impressions with the reality she now knew. Of the staff Annie found Fraulein Vogel the truest friend, the one in whom she could confide.

Of the pupils, there was one girl round-faced, round-eyed and full mouthed with a snub nose who constantly drew attention to herself.

Frequently, her antics went too far and the jokes became insolence and she had to be punished. Subdued for a while she was irrepressible. Annie found her interesting - there was beneath the jollity a strain of melancholy which turned sometimes to cruelty.

She could tease with malicious intent and when she had hurt someone she seemed unsurprised but deeply sorry. Annie sometimes walked with her in the garden, or up and down the gracht beneath the trees and Margot would acknowledge her faults.

It was perplexing that with her periods of spitefulness there was an openness and a realisation of the cause of her unpopularity. She talked to Annie as though she was a mother figure, yet only a couple of years divided their ages.

When she discovered that Margot's father was a clergyman she wondered if, like some English clerical families, she felt isolated and removed from the common run of life.

It was as Annie sat thinking of her one evening that she was stricken with the thought that this little world was crowding out her family and it was with a deep pang she knew that she had not thought of her mother for an entire day.

She took out the letters. Grandma and Edith never mentioned illness, neither did her mother. But the letters spoke for themselves, the writing was increasingly spidery. That night she could not sleep for she kept asking herself, "How ill is my mother?"

All Annie's little experiences were described in letters home which were eagerly seized and read aloud and privately many times. The good news seemed to hasten Marianne's convalescence. Before long she was back at her desk in the prison.

She longed for news of William. She wished to be as proud of him as she was of Annie... still the weeks slipped by.

One morning there was a letter from Cardiff. Marianne was already at work. Grandma and Edith longed to open it, but they resisted the temptation and propped it on the mantelpiece awaiting her return.

At last she came in, she was tired and drawn. She spied the letter immediately slit open the envelope. She stood erect by the fire and the old lady and the young girl were to remember her expression the remainder of their lives.

They were aghast. She first turned pale and then grey, her mouth twisted with grief mixed with rage. She stood still and silent and then slowly crumpled on to a chair and covered her face.

"What is it, my dear, what is it?"

Marianne held out the letter, Edith took it and read out the name of the shippers and then:

"Dear Madam, it is with regret that we have to inform you that your son, William Henry Taylor, has deserted his ship, SS Corderilla in Sydney. We must warn you that should he be apprehended the appropriate legal action will be taken against him, yours etc. etc."

It was a terrible silence in the back room and it was Edith who broke it with the question,

"What does desert mean exactly?"

"It means run away from one's duty like a weakling and a coward" rapped out Marianne.

The older woman interposed, "Don't be bitter, my dear. We don't know the circumstances. Circumstances alter cases...."

"Yes, yes, I know, 'same as noses alter faces.' A wise saw for every occasion. But it does not help us. And I don't remember you pleading for him so often when he was with us. We are disgraced. As usual he has not given us one single thought."

It was like a bereavement without the dignity and trappings of mourning which always evoked respect. They all felt a sense of outrage and a deep sense of shame. They felt, too, that their sacrifices had all been in vain. The Prison, however, was a closely knit community, secrets could not be hidden long.

They found that beneath silence there was sympathy. The Prison staff were wary of judgement for they knew that human frailty was ubiquitous.

From that moment, Marianne withdrew in spirit. She became reserved and her mother-in-law regarded it with foreboding.

Marianne was tortured. She wished to forgive, but found herself unable, she counted the sacrifices that they all had made for William, especially she counted Annie's. She was forfeiting her maternal feelings towards her son, and such coldness was alien to her.

She thought that she had never understood him and now considered him far beyond the bounds of her comprehension. William's name fell from their conversation, if they were about to utter it they chopped it back. They decided not to tell Annie in any of their letters.

Annie's letters came twice a week. They visualised the Principals and the school, the pupils and the very rooms with their black and white marble floors. Annie wrote of everything.

During these days, Marianne's attacks of cramp in her chest increased in frequency and pain. Her breathlessness became obvious and she was forced to ask Grandma to call in Dr Clark.

He was a shy young man and Marianne had thought him unfeeling when he examined prisoners, she saw, now, that it was a cover for nervousness. He examined her with great gentleness and true deliberation. He ordered rest and quiet.

Downstairs he was graver. "Mrs Woodhouse, your daughter-in-law is grievously ill. There is little we can do. Are you prepared?"

"I have been prepared for a long time, doctor. My son died in just the same way."

"Shall I ask the chaplain to call?"

"Yes, to see my daughter-in-law, but not to see me." Her back stiffened and the young doctor could not resist a wry smile. He recognised a kindred spirit.

In the afternoon, while Grandma dozed in her chair, a railway van rumbled down the street, its huge hood cast a shadow in the room. The sudden darkness awoke the old lady and she was thoroughly wakened by the bell.

She went to the door, there, on the step in front of the driver, was William's sea chest. Unquestioningly she sought her purse, paid the man and signed the delivery note. Then she asked him to carry it in.

To her surprise he lifted it without effort and something loose fell and shifted inside. The door closed; the old lady was nonplussed for she did not know what to do with it, where could she hide it?

As she was pondering Marianne appeared on the landing and peered down. When she saw the chest with a sudden movement, betraying no illness, she swooped down. She untied the single cord around it and raised the lid and gave a piteous whimpering sound when she saw the green leather bible and a bundle of their letters.

She took them in her hands, sat on the bottom step and wept.

Mrs Woodhouse closed her eyes her mouth stretched in buried rage - had William been there she would have struck him and struck him again. Instead, she folded the suffering woman, more than a daughter to her, in her arms.

After an interval in which only heart-rending moans were heard, she led Marianne into the back room and placed her in a chair by the fire. It was, then, that Marianne spoke,

"To think that he took nothing, not one thing, to remind him of us. How could he?"

Then lifting her head, she pushed away all hard and unforgiving thoughts saying, "Of course, he had to leave with nothing, everything else was stolen. Oh my poor, poor misguided boy."

The candle flame of her life flickered... Dr Clark foretold death.

Canon Alderson said prayers, but Grandma remained calm, for she had seen so many deaths, always unpredictable and she refused to comment.

At first, Marianne worried about William, then she became aware of her own weakness more and she began to review her life and she longed for Annie, there was so much of her life that she had never told her.

She wanted to tell her of her own mother, of Mrs Somerset and the dream of Cleeve, the great house that could have been hers had she not met Benton. Thinking of Benton filled her with a new resolve. She must, must go back to Whiteley Bottom and the idea made her rally. She dressed, ate, but she remained weak and breathless. She confided in the doctor and surprisingly he agreed with her.

A week later, Grandma carefully shepherded Marianne to the station and on to Huddersfield. At Berry Brow a cab awaited them and they began the climb to Crosland Moor. It was the route Marianne had taken, it seemed an age ago, with Benton on her arrival in Yorkshire and then on their little wedding journey.

She thought it mysterious that the man for whom she had come north had been with her so short a time, while the woman by her side, of whom she had been afraid, was her greatest support and aid.

Sometimes life, like her son, was beyond her comprehension. As the thoughts passed in her mind, all unspoken, she patted the old lady's hand and she knew that even if she did not comprehend she did not regret.

Chapter 14

Marianne's Illness

Cousin Mary, tiny, sharp, whose gold spectacles glinted on her small round face, waited in her house listening for carriage wheels. Everything was ready. The house seemed to shine with its own light, brasses gleamed, wood glowed, floors reflected pools of radiance and each article, large or small, seemed to stand in its own cleanliness, casting its own precise shadow.

Everything was ready for Marianne, but it was also the state in which Mary perpetually dwelt. At last she heard a tired horse halt at her gate, she ran out and she was never to forget the sight in the gloom of the cab, Marianne almost fainting with exhaustion, pale beyond transparency and above all so thin, so wasted.

Marianne smiled and with it she banished some of Mary's immediate anxiety. There were no kisses, just the careful manoeuvre of the guest between the two women into the house.

For two days, Marianne remained in bed.

In that room she enjoyed peace and comfort and the view. She greedily rejoiced in the sweep of the sky and the width of the valley as it fell steeply to the narrowness of the river far below.

She realised that, like her prisoners, she had unknowingly longed for wider horizons. She lay in the bed and watched the clouds scudding, always it seemed, westwards and she wondered if Annie watched the same clouds in Holland.

Then she thought, she might see them, but she is far too busy to watch them, she reasoned. She rejoiced, too, in the room, its neatness, its highly polished furniture, its pictures.

One was of Garibaldi in his red shirt with his white horse, its head down as if to graze. There was another in an Oxford frame. It depicted a church tower by an inlet of water and a setting sun, but this was secondary to the text, "At Thy right hand there are pleasures for evermore." Psalm 16 v11.

She thought of Heaven. She knew it was not far removed from her, but life is an ingrained habit and she dreamed more of the village by the church with neighbours and of a cottage to be shared with Grandma and Annie and Edie coming for long holidays. William came as well, but never for long.

The quiet and cosseting in that room worked wonders. She got up and her first action was to write to Annie. Her italic hand sprawled, the pen seemed hard to control, but by an effort of will she continued.

She spoke of Cousin Mary and that her own health was mightily improving. She exclaimed with joy at Annie's letters and told her that Edie was nearby, staying in Whiteley. Of William she said nothing.

On the third page she looked at her letter objectively. The frailty of the writing alarmed her, she feared that it would frighten Annie still more. So hastily she wrote: "You must not be afraid at seeing this writing for it is poorly, like myself. But it will soon mend now. Well, my bonnie lassie, goodbye for the present and be sure to write soon."

Would she soon mend, she wondered at the lie to Annie, the person she loved most dearly in the world. She shrugged her thin shoulders gently. Life was incomprehensible.

She went downstairs for tea there John joined them from work. He had news for her of Whiteley, the mills and John Donckersley's progress. He had taken Benton's place and was forging ahead in his career.

Marianne felt a pang, for she wondered if Benton would have been offered a partnership. She dismissed the thought and listened and joined in the conversation. She became quite lively.

Over the days she did improve. The fresh air, the visitor, the excitement, but above all the love by which she was surrounded worked its own indefinable alchemy. The following Sunday she went to John's chapel both morning and evening.

The open zeal, the undisguised enthusiasm again fed her spirit. She returned from the ugly, bare little chapel humming one of the unfamiliar hymns. She felt so well that she proposed going down to Whiteley next day.

It was a true Yorkshire September morning with bright sun but with a sharp smell of autumn. The valley was in a mist and as they walked slowly downwards so they walked into increasing coldness, the sun was following them.

They passed many little gardens with bronze chrysanthemums

and Michaelmas daisies and all the leaves and every spider's web was beaded with dew.

Marianne saw that the area had gained in prosperity. She looked at the familiar steep hills and the viaduct which managed to be both ugly and beautiful at once. She saw more terrace houses and shops and already on this Monday morning the smell of wet wool hung in the air.

The grey stone house, still with white sills and window frames stood on the bank above them. At the window was glimpsed a figure moving. It was Cousin Lydia with her pretty face and fading red hair, but the door opened and bounding down the steps came the tall figure of Edith with her bright red hair flying behind her.

More than delight was written on her face, more than love, rapture that a miracle had occurred, that her mother was before her, restored. They clasped one another and went up the steps, into the house, where unthinkingly Marianne untied the strings of her bonnet and removed it.

Then she remembered that she was not in her own house and asked to be forgiven. It aroused laughter. Then trailing tired, almost dazed she went from room to room. She noticed changed in decorations, with gladness she hailed unchanged pieces, but she was seeking something less obvious, recollection and association and she smiled for she was remembering many things.

After lunch, she lay on John and Lydia's bed. She slept only fitfully, she thought much more, here she had borne three children, here Benton had died.

She was so full of the past that when she went to tidy her hair at the mirror she saw clearly, for the first time, her thin face, the prominent bones.

She was shocked and then thought that she had sought the face she had been used to seeing in the mirror years ago. She shuddered, she felt weak, she wished to be away. The house was full of ghosts and she felt foolish, it had been a mistake to return.

At the tea table Marianne expressed her resolve to go. Lydia demurred and spoke of her husband's disappointment, but Marianne remained adamant.

"No, my dear. I am sorry to miss John, but we have a long climb before us. Then they began the long walk back. Edith accompanied them, talking all the time. Half way Marianne sent her back, her breathing was more laboured and she did not want Edie to see.

After watching the happy girl run down the road, they too, tried to hurry - it only resulted in a fit of coughing.

Mary was alarmed and begged that she be allowed to find cab somewhere, but Marianne feared the delay.

They went on... she now began to clutch the railings to haul herself up and to steady her swaying steps.

They stopped frequently as she gasped for breath, and kindly housewives brought out chairs for her to sit on and gave her water. At last Marianne was too weak to object and Mary ran on up the hill to her home.

When she was in sight of her home she saw her husband standing at the gate. He ran to her and together they ran down to Marianne sitting on a chair at a garden gate.

Without asking, John picked her up - he was amazed at her lightness and with his burden he strode up the hill. With great steps he covered the ground, into the house, up the stairs and there he laid Marianne on the white counterpane.

Mary undressed her, washed her face and her hands and put her to bed. Marianne smiled and said: "I feel like Bunyan's Christian, I've climbed to Heaven."

Mary was afraid and Grandma was sent for.

Again the strong spirit rallied and within days they returned, as they had come, by train to Wakefield.

At home in Wakefield, Marianne went to bed and Mrs Woodhouse sent for the Prison doctor. The young man came instantly and he stayed long. There was nothing he could do, but having come so recently from Guy's Hospital he could talk of London, even Hampstead, to his patient.

He saw that it pleased her. After a few visits Marianne said to him: "How long have I to live?"

He hedged, "It is very difficult to tell."

"But is it days, or weeks?"

"A few weeks, I believe."

"Then I must send for my daughter in Holland. I must see her again, I must."

"Yes. I will see to that."

Downstairs, he talked with Mrs Woodhouse and with her he was more truthful and the weeks became days.

He told her of Marianne's desire to see Annie and the old lady said that she would write.

"I think that we had best send a telegram."

Edie was at school, so Dr Clarke armed with the address walked up to the Post Office and wrote out an urgent message for Annie's immediate return. It was early Friday afternoon.

That same evening an Englishman, studying medicine at the University of Leyden, called Taylor received the telegram. He read it, looked at the address and was on the point of going out to deliver it himself, when there was a tap at his door.

Opening it he saw a group of his friends who poured into the room. They had been drinking, they had some bottles with them and they were insistent that he drink with them.

The telegram was in his pocket but it was silent and the voices about him so commanding. Before long he was out with them continuing the celebration.

Next morning, with a hang-over, he dressed in a bad mood. He thrust his hand in his pocket and extracted the paper. He could not remember what it was, he looked at the address, he dizzily shook his head and, as if struck by lightning, he was sober and deeply conscience-stricken.

He seized his hat and walked around to the Hooigracht. He handed it to Jan with an explanation that it had been wrongfully delivered and quickly he strode away. His conscience lightened.

Within minutes, it was in Annie's hands and she rushed to the Principals. Miss Lange took the telegram, read it and handed it to Miss Snoek. They gave Annie immediate leave of absence and told her to pack clothes and they would discover the trains for her.

When she was out of the room Miss Lange said: "Did you notice the date? It should have arrived yesterday."

They called in Jan and he confirmed, what Miss Lange had suspected, that it had been misdirected and then delayed.

"We shall say nothing to Annie, she is too distressed. Shall you, or I take her to Flushing?"

It was Miss Snoek who saw Annie on board the boat. Annie's heart gladdened when the engines throbbed and she knew that she was on her way, but the boat moved too slowly, she could not wait to be with her mother.

In snatches she slept and, at last, she could bear her bunk no longer and dressing went up on the deck. There was England, soon, soon, she would be with her mother, but the ship slowed and idly nudged forward.

A sailor passed and she asked him why they went so slowly. "We have to wait for the tide."

An hour passed and Annie paced up and down the deck, willing without success, the ship to move and the tide to turn. Her handkerchief became a tight ball in her hand. Looking out at the sea, acute misery seized her and it seemed that a bar of iron, heavy, impervious to any amelioration, extended from the pit of her stomach to the bridge of her nose. Her features, she felt, were set forever.

At length, the boat berthed, then there was a wait for the train, her despair and frustration mounted. The train backed in to the platform and she was the first aboard it. With the movement came calm, but as they approached Wakefield again her unease claimed her. She jumped from the train as it slowed down, she ran past the ticket collector flinging her ticket at him and she ran.

She ran across the station yard, down the street, past the Unitarian chapel and along Love Lane. She thought she ought not to run, but still she did, she turned the corner and saw the house. She saw that though it was midday the blinds were drawn.

She never slackened, she flung open the gate pushed open the door and ran up the stairs. Edith emerged from the kitchen, tear-stained, Grandma behind her. Fiercely Annie demanded: "Where's Mother?"

Edith came round the banister and up the stairs, Annie was aware that she moved like a woman. Edith put her arm around her sister, and just managed to say,

"Mother died half and hour ago."

Annie went up the stairs and into the bedroom. Her mother lay still, a small mound beneath a white sheet. She stood by it. Edith stood in the doorway. Annie stretched out her hand to turn back the sheet... she hesitated.

Edith said: "Prepare yourself for a shock. Mother became very, very thin."

Annie jutted out her chin and turned the sheet. It was, indeed, a very thin woman that she saw, a familiar stranger. Then she burst out: "Oh Mother."

Grandma and Edith stood on either side, now. They let her gaze and weep. Then very gently they led her down the stairs. Annie wanted to know about the illness. They told her all except of William's desertion, that they decided to keep back.

"Did Mother ever ask for me?"

Edith looked at Grandma. She did not know what to answer. Grandma nodded. Edith replied with the truth.

"Her last words were, "Why doesn't Annie come?"

This released a floodgate of tears and they lay the weeping girl of the sofa. As always happens, the grief is overtaken by the organisation of a funeral and all three of them were involved.

Mrs Woodhouse cooked and planned still more... Annie and Edith wrote letters.

Then Annie looked at their clothes. The black they had she considered unsuitable and taking Edith out into the town they went to the draper who specialised in mourning.

The range was considerable and it was more than hinted that the depth of one's sorrow was measured by the amount spent. Numb though she was, Annie became alert and critical and she chose a dress and a coat for each of them.

Edith allowed her sister to decide. She was shocked at the price Annie paid, but was silenced quite easily by a quotation of their Mother, "Never buy cheap black."

To their amazement a letter came from Sunderland announcing that their mother's brother would come to stay and attend the funeral. They knew only of his existence, he had never helped his sister, they had communicated only at Christmas and perfunctorily. They awaited him with some apprehension.

When he arrived they were not reassured, he was unctuous and they distrusted him. He wished to take over the arrangements but Annie and Edith had together done it all. They disliked him and during the evening meal he began to rearrange their futures.

He offered a home to Edith explaining that his wife was an invalid. He considered that it would be unwise for Annie to return to Holland.

Annie looked first at her grandmother. She seemed to be crumpling, her usual straight back was bending and Annie knew the cause. She was being broken by the thought of parting from Edith.

"I am afraid, Mr Tayl..., I mean Uncle, that is quite impossible.

Grandma and Edith will be going to Crosland Moor and my school in Leyden is expecting me back."

Henry Taylor knew quite well that the slip of the tongue had been deliberate. He was annoyed. He then began evaluating the furniture and asking whose it was. He discovered that much belonged to Mrs Woodhouse. Later, he picked up the miniatures from the mantelpiece in the parlour and he said,

"If you don't mind I would like to have these, they are my mother and my grandparents."

It was now, Edith who was emboldened. "Of course, you may, but first we would like them to be photographed by Mr Owen, the prison photographer for us. They are our grandparents and great-grandparents, you know."

When the girls went to bed they grumbled about him and knew precisely why their mother had kept him at a distance. "At least", said Annie, "he is a very good counter irritant. Being angry is a change from being so miserable."

The day of the funeral was sunny and a breeze blew which made the flowers by the grave shudder on their stiff wires. Annie and Edith stood alone, apart, the only women present at the graveside.

The men of the family stood near and a small army of prison officers. They were watching the two tall girls, in stature so unlike their mother, but their calm they recognised as hers.

It was not until they were shaking hands with the Governor that they saw that Captain Armytage was by his side. They were glad to see him and he said quickly, "If you have any need. Let me know. I have a cottage if you need one."

They were touched and remembering his old kindnesses knew that his offer was genuine.

In the evening Uncle Henry began, once again, to look at the pictures and ornaments. His eye lighted on the walnut mirror with the gilded bird.

"Don't I remember that in the old home?"

Annie was aghast. She always linked this mirror with her mother.

She had always known it, but she was too shocked to speak. It was their grandmother who, without raising her face from her knitting, said: "It is quite likely you do. I remember Marianne hanging it up in her room before she was married. She loved it very much. So much I always wondered at her giving it to Annie on her birthday."

The girls listened amazed. They were relieved and their dislike of their uncle had redoubled. What really surprised them was that they had never heard their grandmother tell a lie on any occasion whatsoever.

The old lady went on imperturbably, "It is getting late. Perhaps you had better pack your traps ready for the morning. Don't forget the likenesses, will you?"

Neither girl looked at the other. They did not look at their uncle, the sarcasm was not lost. He left the room.

As the door closed Edith said: "I don't know how Mother came to have a brother like that." It was grandma who answered. "Families are the strangest things in creation." As she said it, she thought of William and she kept very silent.

It was when the uncle had departed that the little group planned in earnest. Crosland Moor, so lightly mooted, was indeed the choice of Edith and Grandma. She would be close to her sister and to Mary and Edith could transfer her pupil-teachership to the school at Golcar where Cousins Nina and Hannah taught.

Annie had intended seeing them settled into their new home, which was quickly found, but she saw that Edith was adult and capable. These two would manage together well. They were a unity.

Still Annie was ignorant about William. It was not that Annie said: "Had we not better get in touch with William's firm to let him know about Mother."

With great hesitation they began to tell her. She was angered that they had not told her, for a while she listened. The wave of desperate rage assailed her, she meant it for her brother, it fell on her grandmother and sister.

Again they all wept, this time each alone.

In her room Annie could not sleep. She got up, crossed the landing to her grandmother's room, asked her forgiveness... and the dark cloud of their sadness descended upon them again.

This last revelation seemed to numb Annie completely. She became marmoreal and viewed friends and relative with indifference. She believed that all her love had been for her mother, that there had never been any more to spare.

Next day, it rained and Annie looking into the brick lined street vowed never to return. While her mother had lived she had not disliked Wakefield but, now, it held her no longer.

She was bitter with rage at her brother - she could not comprehend his desertion at all. She knew that she would have done anything for her mother. William, whatever the hardships, had not endured a return journey, and an honourable leave-taking was beyond the most distant brush of her consciousness.

In the afternoon, while Grandma slept and Edith had returned to school, Annie walked out to the cemetery. She crossed the bridge with its chapel and looked towards Sandal. She looked closer at the modern meaner houses and, as she paused on the bridge, her fingers felt the shift of the grime beneath her fingers – even though her gloves. She felt great distaste.

Over the bridge she saw sitting by a house the harpist, his instrument covered with a canvas bag down to the wheels of the trolley. She smiled and went up to him. The bearded man looked up.

"Don't I know you?"

"You would remember my mother better. She never passed you."

"The little lady in black from the Prison?"

"That was my mother." Her face grew grave.

"She had died, I think."

"How did you know?"

"Your face, your clothes. When did it happen?"

"Last week. We buried her yesterday. I am going to her grave."

She hesitated, she wondered if it would be proper. Then she remembered her mother's joy in the harp and this very harp particularly.

"Could you come and play by her grave?"

Without another word he rose, grabbed the shafts of his trolley and trundled along the road by the side of Annie. They went up through the gates, up the long slope of the burial ground, past the chapel to yesterday's grave, there were already more.

As Annie looked at the flowers, he took off the cover and after drawing his hands over the strings making a flow of sound, "What shall I play?"

"Anything, anything... perhaps something Welsh."

The notes rippled like a stream around her, she could not help crying, but they were almost tears of joy. This was the real farewell. She was rapt and never noticed the advance of the Superintendent. The music faltered.

"We can have none of this."

Annie turned and looked. "He came at my request. He is playing for my mother."

She looked to young, so sad and at once so commanding the official relented.

"Only one more tune then." He walked a little distance away.

"Play 'Land of my Fathers.'"

As he played she watched the clouds and she was aware of other worlds, a portion of life was over, but only a portion and while she lived her mother lived. She felt closer to her mother than she had since she left some months before. She felt soothed and this moment meant more to her than the funeral.

He finished, she looked up, they both smiled and together they left. They looked a strange pair, the shabby man and the bereaved girl in elegant black. At the gate she gave the harpist half-a-crown.

"I wish it were more."

"It is kind. I do remember your mother. She never passed me by. I remember you and two others as well, you were always impatient to go, but your mother really listened."

Annie said goodbye and hurried home before he awakened more tears. The music had helped, being alone had helped, but it had not cured. After tea, she went up to her mother's room. She longed to feel something before she said goodbye.

She made a fierce effort to visualise her mother brushing the wave out of her hair, the vigorous strokes, the careful adjustment of clothes, the rituals at the washstand, all those things which had fascinated her by their meticulousness, memory only performed sluggishly, it was the edge of Schwarmerei, never of it.

Edith came up the stairs with a pile of folded clothes. She looked at her sister.

"Oh, Annie, I wish you were not like this. Mother would not like it, be your loving self."

"I wish that I could. I feel, I feel ... that I have no feeling left in me."

"We have on another. We have Grandma."

Annie smiled at the comforting girl and within herself agreed that she did have Edith, she did have Grandma. It was not enough. She had been found out. She had only really loved her mother.

The realisation shocked her and as she looked at her sister, the small face with the fine bones and the small mouth, for the first time in her life she saw her mother's neat small features.

Annie put out her arm and encircled Edith.

"You have Grandma. You, and quite rightly, were her favourite. You stay with her. Become a teacher and we shall both have a school in a nice town some day."

Next day, saying goodbye to Grandma was more difficult than either had foreseen. They both imagined that it was for the last time. It fact it was not.

At the station, Edith waved and waved and Annie leant out as long as possible watching her sister disappear from sight, then she sank back on her seat. Her face became set it gave nothing away, except to the young curate who looked at her mourning and the sort of protective armour of the features he had seen at many funerals. Correctly he surmised, "She has lost her mother."

Grimsby. It was, now, all so familiar, Annie hurried to the boat and she was shown to her cabin. She lay on the bunk and images of past events fell one after another on her mind. It was, she thought, like a kaleidoscope.

The images even seemed to click-clack as they shifted like the beads in the mahogany tube which they had held up to the light as children. At length the engines throbbed and the ship swayed, they were off. She swung her feet to the floor put a scarf over her head and went up to the deck.

There were lights on the quay, lights in the town, the sky was a dull biscuit chequered with dark clouds. It was sombre, it seemed to hold a threat. She looked at the water, it moved with a thick turbulence, waves and furrows streaking away heaving with a mysterious life of their own.

She watched transfixed, it was an image planted in her memory forever. In certain moods of sadness, reverie, these deep moving troughs, the broken V that lapped against the harbour walls haunted her, not with horror, not with pleasure, but with an acute reality. Did the waves represent the unseen forces of life? Did the absence of emotion reflect the state of shock in which she had been plunged? She did not know, she did not question, she just stared at the sea and the diminishing town. She stood so long that the head steward, who had watched her, came out touched her arm and said,

"I think you had better come in, Miss, you will get cold."

He led her into the saloon and without asking brought her tea. She was to remember him, too, the rest of her life.

That night, Annie slept soundly, she did not even dream. She woke to that terrible realisation that something dreadful had happened and then remembered what it was. This time she fought misery, she sat up, she looked out of the porthole, the long thin shadow of dune land was before her.

She went down to breakfast and the steward came to serve her. She ate porridge, bacon and egg, for she knew that she would not taste their like again for a long while.

She made her way towards the station platform. A man emerged from a group and came towards her. It was Jan, the school's manservant.

"Miss Lange's compliments, Miss, and she hopes that you had a good journey." Instantly the world, the civilised world of the school enclosed comfortably around Annie. She talked to Jan and kept him by her side, she was delighted to see him.

He guided her to the platform, to a carriage for Ladies Only and shut her in. He climbed up into a smoking compartment and found himself a cigar. Annie was surprised at the sudden relief and safety she felt.

That Jan had been sent seemed strangely significant. Life had changed... overnight she felt entirely adult.

Leyden was bright but windy and very welcoming. The clarity of the air was seen afresh, the place glinted as Wakefield never did. She crossed the streets, the little bridges and paused momentarily to look at Hoigracht. She felt a pang for Wakefield as she made her contrasts, but without her mother it meant very little.

In the school she was received instantly by the Principals, she was kindly questioned and as she made to leave. Miss Snoek said: "By the way, Miss Taylor, we have given you a room alone at the end of the corridor. We thought you might like more privacy."

She climbed the stairs, the steep beautiful stairs and went to her new room. It overlooked the garden at the end of a corridor. Her books, her pictures, her clothes, everything had been moved in.

Only that night, as she cried into her pillow, did she realize that this was why she had been given the room.

She was grateful, for months later she sometimes found herself waking in the middle of the night weeping.

Chapter 15

Sinterklaas

The school entwined itself into her whole being for the rest of her life; the marble floors, the baroque panelling, the vast windows with wonderful white lace curtains, the stoves with their horizontal pipes which were fitted into the fireplace chimneys in the winter, and always, the staircase with at its summit the marble basin set into a niche of the landing wall.

All these were to be instantly recalled at any moment over the next six decades. Even more it was the ethos of the school that remained, a formal manner, easily correct which covered an outlook amazingly liberal.

The Principals seemed to have the ability to gauge what was merely custom and what was true and right. It was all based upon a Protestant philosophy. Miss Lange and Miss Snoek had a perplexing role for they ran a school where a wide, lofty and generous outlook on life prevailed, but they were also expected by the parents to produce young ladies of impeccable manners and accomplishments without being burdened by ideas.

Added to this complication was another, the school was set in the midst of a thriving university town totally dominated by males. The principals needed the university, it gave their establishment kudos - they relied on the professors for guidance and help.

With it went the tacit understanding that both sides eschewed all contact with the students. It was a lay nunnery.

At this time Annie was well adapted for such a place, her home had become male-less, also her mother's outlook had been, very largely, Miss Lange's. The regimen of the place speeded Annie's recovery, there was work, lessons to prepare, exercises to mark and her own preparation for her lessons in French, German and Dutch.

She was busy and never free these months of the effort of learning to converse in another language all the time.

As winter gripped them, Annie discovered the subtle differences of cold on an island to cold on a land mass. Sometimes the chill was intense and it seemed more all pervading than in Yorkshire.

The letters from Grandma spoke of the cold, they also told of her preoccupation with Christmas and the making of puddings and a cake. Annie thought of the last Christmas wistfully, she thought of just Christmas in England, the stockings, the presents... the cards. But the thought of all that without her mother was so painful she was glad she was in a foreign land.

Very soon she was caught up in the Feast of Sinterklass. It came during term-time and the girls, in lieu of wooden shoes, put their slippers and shoes and boots around the stoves and fireplaces.

In the morning there were screams of delight and excitement as the girls found their shoes full of nuts, bon-bons and large capital letters made of chocolate, each girl having the initial of her Christian name.

There were no lessons and after a concert in the salon when Fraulein Vogel and several of her pupils played, hot chocolate was served from silver urns and spiced biscuits, speculaas, were eaten.

Annie found herself responding to the festive air and gladly went out in the afternoon with the entire school, all muffled and scarved to see the procession leading Sinterklaas on his white horse accompanied by his black page, Zwarte Piet.

The colour in the grey landscape of a grey day made the heart leap and Annie noticed that the stolid and reserved burghers suddenly were talkative and friendly, all barriers were broken.

This was the first time that Annie had seen so many peasant people. They had come in from the villages and she marvelled at the costumes of the women with their wide starched lace collars and caps.

She noted the heavy coral ear-rings and necklaces, all set in gold. She looked at the rounded faces, the pink cheeks, the glowing health. Here, indeed, was a different world to industrial Yorkshire, the people seemed better nourished and better dressed.

There were far fewer of the gaunt hollow cheeks she had grown so used to seeing in Wakefield. The dress along provided a brightness and gaiety that was often missing at home. But she had to concede that there were far fewer pretty women for they were less delicately boned. She stood wondering and watching, she did not see that she was also being observed.

After supper, stories were told around the stove and then the staff and the girls talked, with a freedom Annie thought unlikely to happen in England. It was Fraulein Vogel who asked Annie to give them a comment on the Dutch people now that she had reviewed them so thoroughly.

Annie blushed. Tactfully, she began by commenting on the people she had seen, the people from the land and the sea-farers, some from the farms, some from the dunes. She spoke of two Hollands, one, she thought, was heavy, patient with himself and others and most likely very stubborn.

Those from the coast were even more sunburnt, they were persevering but, possibly, quicker, more daring. They had to make decisions immediately… the sea would not wait as the soil usually did. But both fought the elements.

She ended by saying that they were all taller than most English people, which surprised them, and that English people were more varied in their looks.

Miss Snoek smiled, she had thought the question unfair and that Annie had answered it tactfully and thought that before she got into trouble she would say something.

"All you say is true, of the peasant people. We Dutch also vary a great deal from town to town. In Den Haag there are ladies and gentlemen, in Amsterdam there are the rich merchantmen, they are cosmopolitan. The Rotterdammers are like them only much more maritime. And we of Leyden, we are the academics. Like your Oxford."

It made Annie think how little she really knew of her own country.

Margo Haverschmidt was sitting by Annie, knitting with little zeal and still less accuracy. She pulled a face at her untidy efforts and said: "What are you doing over the holiday. Are you going home?"

"I shall stay here."

Margo pulled the corners of her mouth down in a grimace. In fact, Annie wanted Christmas to be like this, quiet, subdued and alone. She was anxious to explore more of Leyden, there was much she had not seen.

She thought, too, that now she was more experienced, she need not have Jan as her continual shadow, at least during the day. She was sure, too, that she would receive invitations.

A few days later Margo pushed a letter into Annie's hand with a laugh and ran away. Opening it she read, to her great surprise, that Mevrouw Haverschmidt and her husband would be very happy if Annie joined them over the Christmas holiday.

Annie had so reconciled herself to a quiet holiday, almost alone, she was troubled. She did not know what to do, so she resolved to put her problem to the principals.

"Of course, you must not refuse. The Haverschmidts are an interesting family. Margo's father is a clergyman, but he is even better known as a writer. He has written many stories. They are a nice family, you cannot do better. Yes, you must go."

Term ended, all was quickly tidied up, the pupils, and then the staff dispersed. Annie began her exploration of Leyden alone. She walked the length and breadth of the town, from flat meadow to flat meadow.

She found the markets and the blanket factories as well as the Botanical Gardens, the Laakenhall and the museums. She looked at the shops, the restaurants, the houses, she savoured it all.

She went painstakingly through the shops for she still loved clothes and she already detested the mourning she still wore and looked forward to the spring when she could modify it and relieve its inky blackness. She also knew that she had no money to buy anything else.

With leisure came time to grieve again. She had spent a happy evening with the Le Polles, a pleasant dinner, much talk and a game of whist and she had come away with a fistful of little parcels.

As she had emerged in to the east wind that cut, she had been cut by the knowledge that she had enjoyed herself and not once thought of her mother. She felt it was unfair that she should enjoy such company, the company her mother would have enjoyed.

She, thought Annie, should have lived among professors and learned people instead of the very provincial society of Wakefield. Then, again, she thought of her brother - she always linked her mother's death with his desertion. Her mouth set and her eyes hardened.

In the post next day, there was a letter from Edith. The move to Crosland Moor had been made and they were settled into the house and looking forward to Annie's visit in the summer. She then read that another letter was enclosed from their brother. Annie looked in the envelope, there was the letter.

She rather gingerly took it, as though she feared it. It was to their mother. It described the harsh life on the ship and how he, with two others, had left the ship, hidden in Sydney and then gone up country where they rounded up wild ponies.

It seemed to Annie that it was more a recounting of an adventure than a justification. She put the letter down and took up Edith's and finished it. Then she went to her desk, carefully wiped the nib of her pen, dipped it in the ink, and wrote to her brother.

Dear William

We have awaited your letter for a long time, I wish that I could say with pleasure. It is my very sad task to tell you that our Mother has died. She died in October at home in Love Lane. The last phase of her disease can be dated from the arrival of the news from Messrs Myers of your desertion. You do not seem to have realised in any way the sacrifice Mother made on your behalf in order to equip you and apprentice you.

You have caused us great distress.

Your sister, Annie.

She read it though she thought that she should have put shameful before desertion.

The bell for the midday meal rang. She put it down and joined the principals. She was unusually silent during the meal and they enquired whether the news from home was good. She replied that all was well.

Up in her room she re-read her letter. She added a postscript. "We are always glad to hear from you." Then she sealed it and just beginning to have second thoughts she walked swiftly to the Post Office and dropped it into the letter box.

When it plopped to the bottom she felt relaxed, the deed was done, she had struck the blow she had longed to strike ever since October. The image of her mother, gentle, small, determined and aristocratic was as clear before her as the great 17th century Town Hall with its steps.

The image of her brother was a tattered thing, out of focus and blowing away. She wished to think of other things so she went into a stationers shop and bought a box of grey writing paper for Miss Lange.

Then, she went to a haberdasher and bought some lace for Miss Snoek. She bought handkerchiefs for the maid and rather reluctantly she went into a tobacconist's shop and bought a box of cigars for Jan.

In the evening, after dinner, she gave her presents. As they opened them pleasure, she saw, was mingled with shock. They knew that they were presents well beyond her means. They were embarrassed. Annie had yet to learn that the Dutch, by nature generous, yet in occasional gifts were frugal.

A letter came from Schiedam, a long letter and not from Margo, or her mother but from Francois Haverschmidt himself. The warmth of his invitation surprised her. He looked forward to her visit but felt that he must warn her that his town lacked the beauty and cleanliness, which he had heard she liked so much, of Leyden.

It was he told her an industrial town and a great contrast to the scholarly realms of a university town. The letter amused her and puzzled her.

The journey was short and uneventful and Annie found herself anticipating blackened houses and dark smoky skies. The train passed some warehouses and distilleries and she saw many one-storied houses splaying out between the brick courts and roads.

It was very different indeed to Huddersfield and she wondered why she had been warned. At the station Margo ran along the platform in her usual enthusiastic way and seized Annie and then introduced her to her younger brother Frank. They all set off for the tram.

They left the shops and offices and came to the seemly and decorous houses of the professional classes. It seemed similar to much that she had known in Wakefield. They alighted and walked beneath trees to a tall house with a fanciful barge boarding alone in its small garden.

Even before she was inside she felt that it was familiar, it was akin to the Roberts home. Inside straightway Mrs Haverschmidt passed carrying a large bowl of fruit. To Annie's surprise, she smiled but did not stop, but bore it to the table placed it precisely and then returned and pumped Annie's had vigorously.

They gave her the tea, too long made, to which she was becoming accustomed. Mrs Haverschmidt was talkative and charming, but Annie could not forget the first impression of off-handedness which was in such ill accord with the courtliness of her husband's letter.

The room in which they sat was neither a conservatory nor a sitting room but both. Such a room Annie had never seen before. She particularly liked the elegance of the iron furniture which resembled the fine stems of rose bushes with bark and blunted thorns; they looked fragile but were extremely strong.

While Annie was assessing - or trying to - Mrs Haverschmidt, the hostess, was summing up her new guest. First of all she thought her far too pretty and she reckoned that she would not be a teacher for long. She wished that her own daughter had such a figure and sense of dress.

She had to admit that she seemed clever, she had gained a remarkable fluency in Dutch and only unusual words caused her to wrinkle her brow as she puzzled their meaning.

Annie saw a woman who had been handsome. She wondered if she was nervous and hid it beneath over busy domesticity.

She was certainly restless and unable to sit still for long.

At last the front door opened, whistling was heard and the sound of a stick rustling and finally banging among the others in a stand. The door opened to admit a tall square faced man powerfully built.

He moved to Annie with a strange mixture of gentleness and virility. He took her hand bowed over it and then brushed it with his lips. It made Annie feel like a queen. She smiled and inclined her head.

As he took his tea he talked of Leyden, the Leyden of his youth. It seemed a place of happy perfection. As he talked he became almost lyrical. He described characters who had lived there, it was like listening to Dickens in Dutch. She described it to her sister in a letter.

She noticed that Margo and her mother became restive and eventually Mrs Haverschmidt could bear it no longer and she interposed;

"Francois, do spare Miss Taylor. Not everyone sees Leyden as you do."

A shadow of a wince crossed his face. He put down his cup and leant forward. "Forgive me. I run on, I know."

"I love to hear you talk so. I, too, find Leyden very charming, but not, I must admit, quite so entertaining. Life in a Ladies' School is a little more restrictive." They all laughed. She added: "I would love to hear more."

He glanced at her to see if she meant it. He saw that she did. He then lifted his hands in a gesture almost feminine and at odds with his large frame and asked,

"But what of Schiedam. Does it not seem very dirty and ugly to you?"

"I was born in a valley in Yorkshire. It was grey, but yellow in the spring when the daffodils were out. I was brought up in a very black valley. My home is the workshop of the world and workshops are never clean."

"We must talk and walk tomorrow. We shall have time to please ourselves. Now you must excuse me."

As soon as he had gone Margo said: "You must not let Father be a nuisance. You need not walk with him if you do not wish."

Annie was surprised. There was an undercurrent. She merely replied: "But I do."

Chapter 16

Schiedam

Christmas was celebrated with great restraint. The quiet surprised Annie. In the morning, they went to the church and Francois Haverschmidt preached for an hour. To Annie it seemed much more like a Sunday than a festival.

At home, there was a Christmas tree and presents were given and received, but the rollicking spirit of England at this time was missing. Annie was not unhappy, she liked it that it was so different for it prevented her thinking too much of the previous year when her mother had presided.

Time passed quickly. She laughed with Margo, she listened to Frank and she tried to keep up with the heroic domestic duties of Mevrouw Haverschmidt. All the while she was trying to assess the household of disparate people, who, yet, shared so much.

In the children she saw traits of their father, especially in Frank, they were both gentle and had the grace and manners of a previous age. She saw, however, that both children sided with their mother.

There was a barrier of subdued irritability with their father, which every so often revealed itself. When the flow of language seized him they stopped listening.

Some time during the limbo of time that stretches between Christmas and the New Year, even in Holland, Heer Haverschmidt said: "Miss Taylor, I want to show you my poor Schiedammers. Would you like to take a walk?"

This was precisely what Annie had been waiting for, she wished to talk with him alone. Mevrouw Haverschmidt immediately said, "Oh, not one of your dreary walks. Take Miss Taylor somewhere pleasant." Annie hesitated and then said: "But I would love to see the heart of Schiedam. I am sure that it cannot be as bad as much of Yorkshire."

Margo and her mother looked surprised. They saw that she was in earnest. So without any more demurring and attempts at dissuasion, they watched Francois and Annie set off into the cold of a thaw. It was what the Dutch call "water-cold".

They left the leafy suburb and walked briskly towards the distilleries and the breweries by the side of the river. The buildings were familiar to Annie, large, imposing, large doors, huge gateways and large yards. Buildings with a purpose in mind and always surrounded by additional sheds and shacks to house expansion.

It was workaday, it was functional, it was dirty but the comparison with Huddersfield, or Leeds made it almost bright. The grime was not encrusted. Another skin with its own folds, coruscations and pits had, by no means, taken over.

Much looked dim, but the brick had been lashed with rain and scoured by wind. As the people were at work they saw little of the population. They walked down a narrow street. It was like some in Leyden, the familiar stable door, even on this day often open, gave her a glimpse into the stuffy crowded rooms.

Most of them seemed cheerful. Occasionally she was aroused to pity by a woman's face, the large mouth and eyes of a child which, she knew meant under-nourishment.

It was familiar, it did not, therefore, shock her, she accepted it and often to herself thought, "The poverty is less apparent than in Wakefield."

Francois watched and was surprised, for here was a pretty girl, whom he considered had led a very sheltered life, walking though one of the circles of Hell. He saw by the occasional look of sympathy that her feelings were not of indifference, but rather the acknowledgement of a statement of fact. At one point by the river, they could look towards Rotterdam, the wind blew across the waters and whipped colour into their cheeks and a dense cloud of smoke from a passing steamer made them hurry on.

Close by was a large glazed kiosk, inside were tables neatly laid with cloths. He ushered her in, he lifted his cane, a gesture which instantly brought a waiter. He ordered tea.

"You look sad. I am afraid that my walk has upset you."

"No, not your Schiedam. It was the ship."

"The ship?" He was puzzled.

"Yes, the ship. It reminded me of my brother. He is a sailor, or was. He deserted his ship in Australia. It broke my mothers' heart, she died. We had all made sacrifices for him to go."

"When was this?"

"Last October."

She looked at the strong but very sensitive face. She took courage.

"I have written to him blaming him for our mother's death. When I wrote it I was glad, but, now, I do not know."

He stretched out a hand to her,

"We do many things we regret in grief and anger. Why not write again?"

She looked at him with her large blue eyes and shook her head.

He knew all the signs of non-forgiveness.

"Write again. You do not know why he deserted. It may have been cruelty. It may have been evil that he fled from."

Annie looked and withdrew her hand. She had no wish to write. She still blamed him. But she could not deny that she regretted the loss of her brother.

"Yes, write. It will make you feel much better. You must not judge. You just do not know the reasons. Reconciliation is the duty of us Christians."

"I will write when I feel able, but not yet."

When they left they skirted by some sandy dunes. They reminded him of his first country parish and he spoke with nostalgia and humour. It was not, though, the wit of her Uncle Alan.

The river turned slightly. There was a slight rising formed by the flow of another small tributary joining the main confluence. They stopped, they turned. They noticed the thick turgid waters.

Francois grunted. Annie, to comfort him, assured him that the Calder was dirtier, fouled by mines, the mills and even coloured by the peat on the moorland at its beginning.

"Contamination is right neither here, nor there. Our people are sullied with filth. Industry is unnatural – evil."

Annie said no more, she had heard this strain before. It was a sign of frustration best met by silence. They made their way back along another path. Suddenly they saw a group of men some on shore, others on a boat with grappling irons and nets. There were two policemen. One approached them.

"Sir, please go back. Do not bring the young lady here."

François took her arm and retreated, but not before he had cast a sharp glance towards the boat.

"What is it?"

"One of the perpetual fruits of the river. A body."

Annie shuddered and made to hurry away. She was appalled, for in all her 10 years near the River Calder, she had never known of a body recovered.

"Does this happen often?"

"Too often, too often. Men in despair, girls in trouble, destitute men and women. It is horrible, horrible."

Francois groaned and a spasm of disgust and revolt swept over him. Annie's horror now became concern. Suddenly he looked so ill, so torn. He mouthed words without speaking. She was frightened.

"Heer Haverschmidt don't worry so. There is nothing we can do. It is too late."

She stretched out a hand to him and he grasped it and looked solemnly into her face.

"Yes, it is too late for her. But what of the others? Every death like that is our fault. We have failed. Christ is no longer with us. We are only institutions forever moralising. Man is in despair. We are doomed like birds with clipped wings chased by cats. It is awful."

Annie looked at the tortured face, her fear went, she smiled and found herself using her grandmother's phrase, "Don't take on so". In Dutch it sounded very odd and he looked at her in perplexity, but it broke the spell and he smiled.

But she knew that here was the real man, not the courtly man who said such pleasing things about one's dress, a brooch, one's hair. This was not even the man she had heard in the pulpit, this was a kind of poet moved and unconstrained.

He continued talking of the evils of poverty, the evils of wealth, the race for gain and the weakest falling in the struggle. It was a revelation to her. When they had been so poor she had never heard a word uttered against the system of life, one just bore the pain. Her prosperous friends, too, did not question it either.

This moment in the dunes were not only with a man beside himself, but opened her eyes to the fact that the way of life was capable of change. He still talked and she replied. His anger, for that was what it was and doubled by frustration subsided.

He seemed to forget about her and began to whistle softly and then with gathering strength. They re-entered the streets he whistled still, but less piercingly. At the gate he remembered to open the gate for her, but he flung it back with an unnecessary clang. He repeated this at the front door. Annie stopped, looked at him, smiled and said,

"In spite of all we saw, thank you for taking me."

He was compelled to look at her and like the sun coming from a dark cloud he, too, smiled. But it was not the man she had set out with. He saw it written on her face.

"Forgive me. I get upset. Sometimes the awfulness of life overcomes me and I long for Heaven. Often, for a Heaven on earth. Did I whistle?"

"Yes and sometimes very loud."

"I whistle because a dominee may not swear."

Annie was perplexed and ran up to her room to take off her outdoor clothes and think of the strangeness of the afternoon. She had encountered a man of greater depth, greater feeling than she had ever known.

She had been surprised by his vehemence, also the virility that had inspired it. She was so unused to male dominance, it was alien and she thought that a return to school would be a great relief.

Back in the family the talk was desultory until Francois went up to his study. Immediately, Mrs Haverschmidt and Margo began to question her with an openness that surprised her, there was no subtlety, no beating about the bush as there would have been in England.

Annie sensed not only concern, but an unhealthy anticipation. She mentioned the search for the body, that silenced the ladies, but not Frank, he took a young adolescent's ghoulish interest in it. His mother sharply reproved him saying that he would end up like his father, if he continued.

From that moment Annie became much more aware of the two sides of a camp within the household. It was a little like when William had been so rebellious at home - his mother and grandmother had lectured him too often. Now, as then, Annie found herself with a foot in each camp. She was sorry for both, but rather more for the dominee.

When she went to bed she was very tired, but she picked up her mother's photographs, one at 19, the other taken at 36. The eyes and the mouth in each suggested humour. It struck her with force that this was the very quality missing in this house.

They had so much more comfort that they had experienced in Wakefield, things were easier in so many ways, but they were not as happy. Money, one was told so frequently, did not bring happiness, but it had to be experienced to be believed.

It was more natural for her, though, to think of people than things and gradually the memory of her mother took central place.

It started with the memory, so stark, of the body that she had seen. Not really her mother at all. She saw her mother setting out each morning, most carefully dressed for the prison; her mother at the garden party looking so young and pretty in a coloured dress.

She remembered her mother in Milnsbridge, her father still alive, looking out across the mill-town across to Marsh where she longed to live. Annie recognised that had her father lived they would, indeed, have moved there.

Yes, her mother had deserved better things. She also clearly saw that, in spite of hardship, her life had always had laughter, and that, she, now, knew was worth much more.

The next morning was her last. Mrs Haverschmidt darted back and forth, ordering, managing and the bustle of her dress flicked back and forth adding to the air of business, even turbulence.

After lunch, Francois said: "Annie, you have not yet seen my study!"

Annie missed the glance that passed from mother to daughter. The study was forbidden territory, few were invited there.

"She does not want to see that dismal old hole. She has a train to catch."

"My dear, she will catch the train. I shall see to that. Anyway, you know very well there are many trains."

The study was at the top of the house. There was a door to the corridor at the top of the stairs, so that when shut in he was not only isolated from household noise, but even removed from them.

The room amazed her. All round were low shelves of books, that was expected, but above them were cages of birds, canaries, finches, waxwings, small parrots. They chirped and sang and whistled.

She looked in surprise and was fascinated by the hopping colourful birds. Mr Haverschmidt opened a door and a bird jumped on to his outstretched finger, then flew swooping to perch on his desk.

"They are lovely", she said.

"My wife hates them. She cannot bear birds. She even hates feathers on a hat."

"Yet still he has them," thought Annie. "Perhaps that is why he has them."

In the train Annie pondered on her visit. It had been a success. She had not outstayed her welcome and she looked forward to seeing Margo again very soon.

The household gave her much to think of. The divide was greater than she had realised and the birds... "Yes, those birds. Didn't he see that they were prisoners of his making, just as much as the people of Schiedam with whom he sympathised so much?"

Chapter 17

Skating

At the Hooigracht all looked as neat and clean as it always did. Jan opened the door and welcomed her with a large smile over his broad jaw. She took tea with the Principals who were anxious to hear her opinions on a Dutch home.

Later over dinner they spoke more specifically of Francois Haverschmidt. Annie discovered that he was renowned as a speaker telling his stories. She learnt too, of the distrust he aroused in his fellow clergy, his ideas were too liberal for them.

He voiced his doubts and his radical ideas made him unpopular with many of the business men of Schiedam. Her eyes were opened to many things and what had been suspicions on her part were founded facts.

She felt a greater understanding of him and also of his family. She saw, now, very clearly that they were wearied by his ideals and the limitations that they imposed upon them.

Good though it was to be back, it was with a big sigh that next morning she took down her Shakespeare and began to prepare her lessons on As You Like It for the following week.

Like so many students and teachers of her age she had never seen it played in a theatre. To her it was a comedy with long quotable passages and a silly story. The wit she thought flat and the humour she found very difficult to render into Dutch.

She sat in her room working dutifully, rather mechanically. She was also cold - the heating pipes had lost their warmth. She looked out at the roof-tops. They were white with frost and the sight made her pull a shawl about her shoulders.

She returned to her desk, the link in her concentration had been broken. She was bored. She got out her mirror and solemnly regarded her face with round blue eyes, her seriousness amused her and her face broke into a smile.

That, she thought was an improvement because the mask of her face dissolved, spirit was added to its being.

She balanced the mirror against her books and began rearranging her hair, she parted it in the middle and made a fringe with wisps of curls, it did not please her. She pushed the crop of curls up, got a comb and began to remake the existing coiffure.

She sighed that her hair was not raven black, that her features were composed of rounds and not classic chiselling. She heard a floorboard in the corridor creak. Swiftly she pushed the mirror beneath some exercise books and looked intently at Act III Scene 2. There was a knock. It was Miss Lange.

"May I have a moment?" Without awaiting a reply she lifted a chair placed it centrally and sat on it. "I have a letter from Miss Burger. Her mother is ill, not expected to live and therefore she cannot come back this term. Who is to teach the needlework? Immediately I thought of you. Could you do it?"

Annie looked at the Shakespeare. Needlework would be a great relief, though she knew that the sewing would be in addition. She looked at Miss Lange. The neat authoritative lady was asking her a favour.

To her surprise she heard herself reply with determination. "I will most certainly teach needlework, but it will have to be the modern style. I could not possibly teach canvas work. Anyway the girls hate it. I would have to send for supplies."

"But are you agreeable to doing it?"

"Oh yes."

"Then let us talk it over in some warmth. You freeze up here. Why don't you work in the library?"

That question was unanswerable. She felt unable to say that she was able to be herself in her room and even if cold, she could play with her hair, re-read letters from Crosland Moor, dream and, sometimes still, weep when she thought of her mother.

In the stuffy heat of their room the two principals began to talk of the sewing. That Annie had consented pleased them. Ever since they had seen her work they had wished her to take on the teaching.

The only serious demur came when Annie proposed sending to Belfast for linen and looking for the silks in Leyden, their fear of expense was open. Miss Snoek made references to her account books and she found that canvas had also been expensive and linen might, eventually, prove cheaper.

This realised their enthusiasm kindled. When she left them she went straight to the library and wrote to Belfast. In the afternoon she visited all the haberdashers she knew and discovered the silks would have to come from Wakefield.

As always there was a subdued air when the girls arrived, this rapidly changed to exuberance which was only dampened when lessons began. Annie awaited Margo and when she came she had to wait until after evening prayers for a moment to speak with her properly.

It was Annie who pressed Margo's hand lovingly and when Annie asked after her parents her friend looked troubled.

"Father was very melancholic when you had gone, more than usual. We wished you had been there, you know how to listen. You know what to say. We don't."

Annie learnt that the local clergy had ousted Mr Haverschmidt from a charitable board. They thought him too liberal in every way. For two days he had remained in his study, he had even taken his meals there.

Annie found it hard to believe that she was able to supply a need to the Haverschmidts. She still thought that their world was so superior to that of Wakefield that they must therefore have greater gifts.

She was not aware of the uniqueness of every being. That she had a quality denied others surprised her, but not those around her.

They saw a young woman, very pretty and very graceful, they thought her younger than her twenty years, yet at the same time, they recognised a dignity and calm older than twenty by far.

When the embroidery classes began Annie's popularity increased for the girls were keen. The release from canvas work was a real release and it was with eagerness they began learning the new stitches.

They worked, at first, too rapidly, hurrying to finish their tray cloths and runners, keen to begin a new piece. The weather even aided her for it grew colder and more time was spent huddled round the fires.

The cold grew more intense. Annie no longer lingered in her room. It was a still cold such as she had never known in Yorkshire. Then it remained cold but the sun broke though and Annie was bewildered when Miss Lange told the school at assembly that the day was officially free.

There was a cry and a shout in which even Miss Snoek joined.

It then seemed to Annie that there were secret cupboards in every Dutch house, even in this school, for instantly the marble floor of the hall was full of dusty greasy rags and newspaper as skates were taken from their year old wrappings. She watched bemused for a change had come over the entire school, enmities became friendships, dourness in an individual became gaiety.

There were skates for everyone except Annie. As soon as this was known Miss Snoek took Annie to an ironmonger where she bought skates for her. They were an elegant pair, long with a curled upward prow. Annie likened them to a Viking ship.

As they returned the scene in the Hooigracht was a transformation. The canal, usually broken only by the passage of a barge every so often, was now alive and bright with flowing nimble people.

There was colour for scarves fluttered. From the school door she saw girls spilling and tumbling across the road, ducks on land, but on the ice they all became swift swans.

They all moved with harmony. Jan bound her skates on with strong webbing round her ankles, he gave her a broom and very timorously she launched herself on the ice. It was alarming and humiliating and she became acutely self-conscious.

Then a lady, whom she did not know, offered her a kitchen chair and with this before her she began to move a little more steadily.

Quietly, slowly she went from one bridge to the other and back. Her envy at the others was almost painful to bear. She looked again, up from the chair where her gaze and thoughts seemed concentrated, and found that Miss Lange and the girls had sped far away... they were like a flock of birds.

Annie was left with the more sober neighbours of the Hooigracht. She was glad of this staid company - it did not contrast so glaringly with her lack of prowess. An elderly gentleman came over to her rapidly, Annie started, she thought they would collide, but he stopped suddenly and leant back on his heels.

He complimented her on her improvement and then pushing away the chair and taking her left arm in his right tucked firmly in her back propelled her down the canal. They moved together, his rhythm became hers. She was alarmed at the speed with which the chill air met them as much as the sight of the houses flying by.

He sped towards a stall and Annie was bound to accompany

him. She thought that they were selling coffee, but when it was in her hand she saw that the mug contained very thick and very hot pea soup.

She had always hated pea soup, but this seemed different and she quickly emptied the mug with the horn spoon. Then her new-found friend took her back as swiftly as they had come. She thanked him and climbed up to the street.

Her head was in a whirl of ecstasy at the fleet movement. She sat on a chair and began to unbind the tight strapping.

The pain was entirely unanticipated, the flow of blood to her feet was unendurable... it was only with an effort she stifled a cry. She limped across the road, Miss Snoek had seen and knew the symptoms and putting an arm round Annie helped her to the kitchen calling for a bowl of warm water.

She told Annie to take off her stockings, turning her back on the embarrassed girl as she pulled up her skirts to perform such an intimate undressing in such unfamiliar surroundings.

When she put her feet in the water and the blood flowed back the pain increased then as the kettle increased the heat so the torture ebbed away.

"You have nearly learned to skate, Miss Taylor. You have certainly learnt how difficult the binding is, if too tight you stop the circulation, if too loose you cannot skate. Also, my dear, a novice must never stay out too long."

At lunch the room was full of high spirits and a lot of laughter. The cheeks glowed and the eyes sparkled, there was health and happiness and excitement. There was to be a return to the canal in the afternoon, Annie was almost persuaded to join them but Miss Snoek intervened. "There is tomorrow."

Together Miss Snoek and Annie walked in the afternoon. The goodwill the unity was everywhere. Annie had only known such a feeling once before, when there had been an explosion at a colliery near Anston.

Then the entire population had seemed one in the face of death. She thought it so odd that as the land and water froze so the hearts of a circumspect people conversely thawed. She wondered what it would be like when it was over.

It did not end. Lessons were forgotten, so it was with a glow of pride that she saw on the second night of holiday many of the girls brought out their embroidery in the evening without being prompted.

Annie went to the canal again, she tied her skates with Jan's help carefully, tight, but, she hoped, not too tight. Armed with the broomstick she gingerly made her way and then in a glorious access of confidence she flung it aside.

As with the unknown man she began to glide down the gracht, she had always wanted to fly, and this was the nearest approach. It was better than sailing over the desks on the end of the skylight rope at Anston School.

She felt like a swallow, especially as she swooped, unnecessarily cautious beneath the bridge.

Then she felt that she must return, she slowed to turn, she began to wobble and at the very moment she was about to fall a man's voice called out: "Speed up and you'll be all right."

She obeyed and was going back when she was overtaken by her black-clad instructor of the previous day.

Without asking he took her arm and again they greatly increased the pace. She blushed with the greatest pleasure when he said, "You are a great credit to me. You can skate."

For the rest of the day, "You can skate" rang in her mind.

At the end of the week the general excitement began to dwindle, the skaters were fewer and mostly composed of children and the dedicated dyke racers who practised for the long runs from mill to mill and dorp to dorp claiming their medals.

On Saturday it was announced that school would be resumed on Monday and by most of them it was hailed. That evening by the fire it was Annie's turn to read aloud. She chose Wordsworth and she read the celebrated passage on skating;

"all shod with steel

We hissed along the polished ice"

And she told them that she had never really appreciated it until then and especially,

"The solitary cliffs

Wheeled by me, even as if the earth had roll'd

With visible motion her diurnal round;"

She read them more... they questioned her about the Lake District. She had never been there. So she described Armitage Bridge and the steepness of the valley, the curve of the river, the daffodils in the churchyard and she left out the dyeing mills.

Later she read them Tintern Abbey and she was again fascinated to see their delight in places. Every Dutchman, or woman, she discovered was a natural traveller with a restless curiosity, far more than the Englishman, who in spite of an Empire, is always an islander.

It was during this time she came to see how little of her country she knew. Her knowledge was confined to a corner of Yorkshire. She thought very little about Wakefield, but much of their home there.

She seized all the letters from Edith and Grandma and wondered a lot about Crosland Moor. When questioned there was much she discovered that she hid the near poverty, the desertion of her brother and the dirt of the West Riding.

She felt a kind of shame about the grime she had grown up in. When she picked flowers here in the garden which she deemed unworthy of the name, yet she compared the leaves with the sooty leaves that had always to be washed when taken indoors in Wakefield.

She remembered the vegetables she had seen at the prison held beneath a pump before being carted to the kitchen for further cleaning. In these memories came home-sickness and she was saddened by the knowledge that the home she knew was no more.

Home was her mother and her mother had gone. Her mother's image was very firmly fixed to the very being of her soul.

Holiday came. It was Easter and the empty school Annie linked with the empty tomb. The greyness of Dutch religion was most forcibly impressed upon her that Easter Day. She had been surprised to find that there were still no flowers in the church.

She had expected a longer sermon, but not quite of the length to which the congregation was subjected.

Her attention had wandered and she had thought of the daffodils at Armitage Bridge and the sunlight in the Dales. It was on this day that her friendship with Fraulein Vogel took root. The church had oppressed them both, they had not been uplifted and as they made their way back to the school they compared their own country's customs.

Fraulein Vogel spoke of the flowers there would be in her Lutheran church and Annie told her of the texts and emblems they would have made on felt banners for the church in Wakefield.

They repressed their criticism as they took lunch with the Principals, but resumed them as they walked in the afternoon along the Rapenburg towards the Botanical Garden. There they saw the bulbs appearing in the borders and along Witte Singel they saw more flowers appearing in the grass by the canal.

They were reassured and their hearts lifted and when they got home Fraulein Vogel played Schubert and Lizt and spring seemed really to have come.

During the next days, the trees put out their soft down of green, but Annie was not content. She longed for primroses, until then she had not known that they were her favourite flowers. She had an intense desire to pick bunches of them, but here she never saw any.

Term began again and on the third Sunday in April she discovered that spring came to Holland. Trams, carriages, barges and even trains carried garlands of tulips and the whole population, it seemed, went to Haarlem. The school hired two waggonettes for an outing.

The sight of the bright squares of yellows and reds, pinks and golds amazed Annie. They were harsh blocks of colour, totally unlike pale primroses, but they were lively, bright and gay.

They trotted decorously through the fields and some girls were sickened by the heavy scent of the hyacinth fields just past their prime.

As they approached Haarlem the pace grew slower, the town was en fete, it was Kermis and the roundabouts, booths and swingboats cluttered the streets. It was familiar to her, but as she looked at the back-drop of the gabled houses she felt that this was more authentic, more mediaeval than the fair in Wakefield.

As she was looking about her, two girls seized her arm and led her towards a gaily painted restaurant on wheels, saying that she knew nothing of Holland until she had eaten a "poffertje".

The girls led a not unwilling victim to a table covered with American cloth, divided from its neighbour by a trellis entwined with artificial flowers and fern leaves. Then Annie saw the cook, his fat face glistened in the heat as he stood before a stove with a long iron chimney that glowed red with the fierce smoke.

She watched him fascinated for in front of him was a large tray with many rounded indentations. Into these he dropped a twist of paste that spread and from another he would remove a puffed up crisp-edged poffertje.

He moved and swayed like a ballet dancer in perpetual motion.

When the plate was put before her she found a very sweet small pancake covered with running butter and sifted sugar. Between the three the heap diminished rapidly. Then the girls ordered waffles which she enjoyed even more, again they were spread with butter and sugar.

Annie listened to the chattering girls, there was a freedom a release apparent in them she had not seen before. She looked from them to the people around her they were all laughing and happy.

She found it hard to accept that these same people should for the greater part of their time be so preoccupied with a gloomy religion and the severest of morals.

There were, she thought, two faces to the Dutchman, one belonged to the painting of Jan Steen and the other to John Calvin. One face laughed loudly, the other frowned. There were two persons in every Dutchman and they were either one or the other, there was no compromise.

She looked at the women and decreed them dowdy, they did not spurn fashion, but they were slow to accept it and they interpreted it in a way that eschewed line and unfailingly made friends with convenience and ease.

It made her think of her neat and often chic little mother and she felt a sweet sadness heightened by the careless crowds. Perhaps it was recalling her mother that made her look up from the crowds, above the gables to the sky, it was growing dark.

She paid the bill and went with her charges to the meeting place for the waggonettes. There was the familiar uneasy lull while names were called and the wait began for the missing people.

After 10 minutes, Annie volunteered to return to seek Fraulein Vogel and three girls.

She went back into the streets. It had become yet another world. The atmosphere had changed it was charged with something she did not fully comprehend, it was more than Jan Steen's freedom and jollity, it was licence.

As she made her way a man grasped her hand very hard. She faced the man... he was drunk and leering. Annie was seized with fear as he pulled her towards him. Suddenly with her free right hand she slapped him. He was surprised and let go and rubbed his cheek, shook his head and then, with a growl began to raise his head.

Annie ran away pushing into the crowd. She was suddenly much more afraid, she felt alien and unsure. She had forgotten Fraulein Vogel and turned to run back to the waggonettes.

As she moved forward she saw before her Fraulein Vogel hurrying for what seemed an eternity. She could not reach her because of the people.

At last she put out her hand to the slim black silk sleeve of her friend. Fraulein Vogel turned and smiled. The honesty, the innocence of the expression shocked Annie, it made the leering Bacchus even more repulsive.

"Why, my dear, you are shivering."

Annie could only nod and walk beside her. The Fraulein patted her hand and said nothing. As they approached the rest there were cries of welcome and disapproval. On board Annie watched the now colourless bulb fields sliding by, she thought of the man and his evil intent.

But what that evil was she did not know. She knew that she was ignorant of something. It was something of sex, but that was a word she did not use, even know. She called it something of the conjunction of man and woman.

Her fear was great for she was uncertain. She suspected that had the man kissed her on the mouth she might have born a child. She shuddered, a quiver going through her being. Her friend noted it and as she looked at the cold set face of Annie she wondered how she could help. With great intuition she said, "Were you accosted by a man?"

Annie looked at her, her mouth ready to say "No", instead she nodded.

"Quite horrible isn't it. I expect he was drunk as well."

"How did you guess?"

"It happens to many of us. It always spoils a pleasant day. Forget it, my dear."

To Annie's surprise, she did. The memory faded as she laughed at the excited girls who, after being silent in the darkness, chattered like birds in the light of the school and all tried at the same time to recount the thrills of the day. Then, Miss Lange lifted up her hand and cried,

"No more, no more. There is tomorrow. To bed, to bed."

Only in her room did the image of the man flicker like an image on a Venetian blind as she picked up the photo of her father. She looked at the round features, like her own, he, she thought, could never, never have been like that dreadful Silenus?

She took up the picture of her mother, she smiled at the suppressed smile on the daguerreotype, she looked at the wedding dress, there was no fear in this photo. There was no horror.

She opened a drawer and took out her writing box, she lifted the lid of the slope and took out an envelope. There were the last letters of her mother and there were, with them, two photos taken in the prison.

One, Annie remembered, had annoyed her mother for her dress was crumpled. Mr Owen had pounced upon her suddenly and made her sit for him without any warning.

It was a true picture, there was stillness in spite of the hurry. Annie saw the smile that lurked behind the grave eyes and she admired, as she had always done, the shapely slim hand that supported her chin.

Yet as she looked at it, Annie acknowledged that in spite to her love for her mother, in spite of all the kindness that had always surrounded her at home, she would never have framed the questions she wished now to ask.

Here was a point of her life which had to remain untouched. It was a portion of life that hadn't been catered for. Even as she looked, though, the question faded, she remembered only the love she had and which she missed so much.

Marianne Taylor, née Arnold, 1843-1890

Benton Taylor, 1835 - 1870

Stanley Royd Hospital, Wakefield - 1818

Annie Matthews and Edith Taylor, circa 1907    *William Taylor, born 1868, went to sea 1885*

Aunt Hart's parents on their Golden Wedding Anniversary

Cliff and Terrace, Scarborough - 1850

Annie's children in 1906
Nancy (Annie Beatrice) b. 1900; Kit (Ada Catherine) b. 1896; Alan b. 1903

World War 1 - Annie in the centre of a group of soldiers - 1916

Bombardment by German warships on Scarborough, 16th December 1914

Double Wedding 22nd April 1922 - Kit Matthews & John Barlow on the right and Nancy Matthew & George Lockwood, the author's parents, to the left

Edward and Annie Matthews, Mayor and Mayoress of Scarborough in 1926

Annie Matthews in 1916

Grandchildren in Spring 1938
David Lockwood aged 14. Dawn Matthews aged 8. Valerie Barlow aged 4.

David Lockwood with his grandmother in Winchester, 1939

Whitham Close, Kingsgate Street, Winchester - Annie's home from 1945-48

> David my Dear. It is too
> to think that in a few d
> shall have you home ag
> I do hope you will be
> and have no more rec
> or misgivings. Be sure
> keep you all I can. I
> no news. We are having
> peaceful time. and I h

Extract of a letter from Annie Matthews to her grandson, David.

Chapter 18

Bulbs and Sea

The summer, as in England, stuttered and stammered into being. Annie was very aware of its sudden chills, she was still wearing mourning after seven months and she longed to change, but all her thicker clothes were black.

She had bought material in blues and mauves and made herself new dresses – and it seemed there would be no chance to wear them. She longed to wear colours again for she knew that they became her, they also lifted her spirits and mourning had no meaning for her, there was still bleakness, even despair, in her heart... it bore no relation to the black clothing.

Sometimes when she felt rebellious about it she recalled that her mother had worn black most of the time, but Annie would toss her head and say to herself, "I am another generation."

At last, in June with a great suddenness the sun blazed and there was heat. A school holiday was decreed and the waggonettes once again, stood outside the school. The sun shone and they trotted towards Katwijk for a day by the sea, the parasols went up as they went through Rijnsburg which Annie thought looked almost English with its small houses and gardens.

On the dunes which sloped steeply to the sea they all climbed down, the wind caught their hats, but so did skilled and quick hands. A tent was raised on the sands, well away from the fishing boats which lay like the fish they caught, stranded on shore.

Some of the more daring girls changed into swimming costumes of serge and with much giggling and pushing and laughter a party ran down to the waves, where the shrieks and splashing were renewed with double vigour.

Annie watched them as if mesmerised. No other member of the staff joined them and she wandered down to the water's edge. Margo saw her and Annie laughed at the sight of the round happy face beneath a large mob-cap. Margo cried, "Why don't you come?"

Others joined a chorus, "Come on. It's lovely."

Annie shook her head and said: "I haven't a costume."

A dripping figure came out of the water. Annie was almost shocked - the material, though it made strange creases and folds, yet outlined the girl's figure very markedly. She was excited, vigorous and masterful and within moments Annie found herself in a tent and a borrowed costume was being given to her.

She was ready but shy and mortified at her legs being so visible. She pushed her head though the tent flap and was seized by Margo and her friend who pulled her down to the sea. It was cold but their exhilaration was infectious and only warning them that she could not swim she let them lead her out.

It was unlike anything she had known, she felt so free, so enraptured with another element. She had, to her surprise, no fear.

At lunch time the cloths were spread on the grass of the inland side of the dune by the maids. There they ate their usual midday bread and cheese and herring. When it was all cleared the girls sprawled, hats were off, or awry.

They looked like an untidy flower bed against the marram grass.

Miss Lange, upright on a folding stool beneath a black umbrella, condoned the sloth for half-an-hour, but when that was gone, pronounced that the girls must sit up and either in groups make sketches, or play charades, or recite.

Slowly with bashfulness becoming confidence they recited, they sang and one group even performed a small play. Everyone had taken part.

Miss Lange beamed and looked around,

"But, Miss Taylor, you have not done anything."

Annie's mind went blank. The poetry she knew was either too childish, or too serious. She stood up and waveringly began to sing Over the Garden Wall. She began softly, then as she became more confident, and the words came without effort about the forbidden love with the boy next-door, so her emphases became more definite and she enacted some of the roguish and arch looks she had seen on the Music Hall.

The girls applauded and demanded it again, but Annie saw that Miss Lange's hands were very still on her lap and that she was not smiling. Annie felt this silent disapproval more than the applause, it was very evident.

On the way back she thought much more of the censure than of the glory of the bathe in the sea. The cloud of reproach hung over her and she was not surprised that she was requested to come to the Principals' room after dinner.

Annie listened to Miss Lange's shocked surprise at the low and vulgar tone. She reminded Annie of the school to which she belonged and its ideals, succouring young minds with visions of purity, beauty and intelligence and then she added.

"You, even more than Miss Snoek and I, belong to a generation which is that to the new woman, you have a responsibility and you must accept it with due seriousness."

Annie defended herself, but indifferently. She was angry that anyone should impute to her vulgarity. It hurt. She knew, too, that they had misinterpreted the song. Annie went back to her room bruised and chastened.

In the vault of her mind she chanted, "They think me ill-bred. They think me ill-bred." She suffered the pains that are peculiar to the insecure. She had encountered superiority greater in its self-esteem than her own, which was always formidable.

She even questioned whether she should remain there and with even more bitter resentment she realised that she had no choice, she was penniless and homeless. However, the urge to return to Edith and Grandma was great.

She went to her drawer and took out a box in which was a leather purse. She emptied the money on to the white counterpane. There was just sufficient to take her home and back, but it would mean no new clothes for the winter.

Her mind was resolved, home she would go.

Before term ended there were examinations and then the prize-giving. Annie had made her recommendations and one was for Margo Haverschmidt for her essays in English on Dickens and on *The Merchant of Venice*.

The occasion was held in the Lakenhall, one of Annie's favourite places in Leiden, the great gallery on the first floor had furniture and china on view as well as pictures. She knew, too, of its links with the Stuart Princess Elizabeth, the Winter Queen of Bohemia. When the programme was printed she found that she was to sit, not amongst the pupils, but on the platform with the staff.

She was faintly surprised. She always maintained that she was "neither fish, nor flesh, nor good red herring." Also she still felt that Miss Lange looked upon her with suspicion.

On the great day the hall filled with parents and friends and Annie stood at the back giving out the programmes. She could look down the staircase and it amused her to speculate who the parents were as they climbed the stairs, she looked for resemblances to the girls.

There was one pair, however, that she recognised immediately, the Haverschmidts. There was the tall bulk of Francois with his fresh complexion and the busy nervous movements of his wife.

They saw her and beamed with pleasure and Annie was surprised when she was embraced by them both.

Annie had grown used to a certain loneliness in her life and as the arms encircled her she felt all the pleasure that contact with another human being arouses. She went up to the platform suffused with happiness... she was not alone, she was not friendless.

The speeches began, the reports the congratulation. Annie blushed when her name was mentioned in the teaching of English. Then the pupils came up for their prizes and the monotonous clapping began which became towards the close even painful. After the last girl had returned to her seat she heard Miss Lange repeat her name again.

"It is not our custom to give our staff prizes – but, then, Miss Taylor is not entirely staff. Over this year she has proved herself not only a linguist, she speaks Dutch, as you know, almost faultlessly, but she has also made her girls fond of Shakespeare. Well some of them. But she most certainly has made them all seamstresses.

"Therefore Miss Snoek and I decided that for one moment she will, this afternoon, be entirely pupil. Will you please come forward, Miss Taylor. An oval, carved oak frame was placed in her hand and she saw that it contained a sepia portrait of the Bard of Stratford."

She was overcome with pleasure and a certain sense of irony, this great Englishman, whom she so little loved, was evidently linked with her. She smiled a little bashfully which endeared her to the parents and then made a curtsey to the Principal that aroused the admiration of all for it was so graceful.

As she walked home with the girls in their crocodile line she saw the limes lifting their leaves in the wind, she saw the gleaming doorsteps, windows that glinted and pavements swilled and washed, she felt a kinship with this land. She appreciated it and, now she loved it and it seemed that a whole prospect of new life lay unrolling before her.

Life was wonderful. At school all was commotion with carriages at the door, trunks being loaded, girls saying farewell in tears, younger ones eager to be away.

Parents were being entertained with tea and biscuits in the drawing room and there François Haverschmidt talked with Annie. He praised her teaching of Margo. He complimented Annie on her dress of blue with black ribbons, Annie's notion of half-mourning. He also praised her curtsey and learnt that her mother had taught her.

"You must come to Schiedam again and teach Margo."

The idea appealed and Annie felt that she had been to precipitant in deciding to return to England.

The next day Annie was the sole member of staff left at the school. It was like the beginning of her career here, only so different in that she could speak the language of Miss Lange and Miss Snoek.

She also knew them better, she knew what to avoid and since the prize-giving she had almost forgotten the severe snub given after her singing at Katwijk. As they were together after supper Miss Lange asked Annie to become a full member of staff. Annie was pleased, she felt it a just reward and she accepted it.

They were all pleased and Miss Snoek wondered if she would like a different room. Miss Lange with that open matter-of-fact approach so typical of the Dutch spoke of salary and Annie in a sudden excess of confidence asked if she might have an advance. She was taken aback for Miss Lange asked, "How much?"

Annie had no idea and Miss Lange in her usual definite way said, "I will decide then."

Next day, there was an envelope by her place at breakfast, it contained money, more than she had expected and a note informed her that this was not an advance but an honorarium for her past year's work. If an advance was still needed would she make a request in writing. There was no need.

To Annie, it was akin to the moment when she had received her first shillings as a pupil-teacher and she had rushed home to her mother. She went up to her room, picked up the photographs and was overcome by a confusion of delight and grief that she could not share her triumph with the one who would understand and share in it best.

Chapter 19

Yorkshire, Grandma & Edith

Grimsby, flat, sprawling faced Annie, she looked at it without love, she remembered her slow approach when she had longed for wings. It amused her that as she saw the flat plains go by in the train, she thought them hilly, she had become so used to a horizontal landscape.

At Wakefield she changed stations with time to waste. She walked down to Love Lane, passing the old Unitarian School which she always thought so elegant. She saw a familiar face, so she pulled down the veil over her face.

For a moment she stood outside their old home, there was someone else living in it now. For a moment she rested her hand on the gate, it felt exactly as it had always felt. She reasoned with herself that it was not strange, she had left it not quite a year ago, but it seemed another age.

She had a strong desire to see Mrs Senior but there was no time. Going back to the station she looked towards Sandal Castle and her heart stopped for in that direction lay the cemetery and she could not bring herself to think of her mother's grave.

As she left Wakefield, so she left the haze of the industrial air, they moved towards valleys and high hills, they crossed over viaducts and the houses became stone and Annie felt an affection.

This was home. Again though the haze grew thicker and greyness prevailed and she missed sharply the clarity of light to which she had grown accustomed in Leiden.

At Huddersfield she prepared to change trains once more and go on a local to Berry Brow. There was a group of people at the end of the platform, suddenly a tall thin girl disconnected herself from it and with out-stretched arms ran towards her.

For a moment Annie failed to recognise her, but she too ran to the sister whose face was aglow with delight. Annie clasped her, but Annie knew that there had on her part been a moment of hesitation.

They put their heads together and arm in arm followed the porter to another platform. Soon they were on their way to Berry

Brow looking down on the thickly wooded valley with its looping beck at Armitage Bridge.

They took a trap and nursed the cases on their knees, first they descended then began a long climb. The houses jumbled, perched on rocks with steep steps were familiar but had been forgotten.

What Annie did notice was the grime and she thought of Francois' Haverschmidt's anguish at the pollution of Schiedam. It was nothing compared with this.

Edith began giving instructions to the driver, they left the village and came to a road where houses were scattered, still they climbed, but presently there were two stone houses attached with long strips of garden, before one of these they stopped.

Annie standing momentarily in the trap looked down and she had the feeling that it was exactly as she had imagined, yet in particulars entirely different.

This time, Annie ran for she saw the door open and Grandma stand on the threshold with her hands up to shield her eyes from the sun.

"Welcome lassie, welcome. My, how you have grown! What a tall girl and straight, at last."

After clasping the old lady, Annie answered with tears, "Yes, you always did say that my nose came in advance five minutes before my body round a corner."

"Well, I cannot say it now, my dear. Come in, come in."

The door opened directly into the parlour and the immediate, almost electric encounter between such well known and well loved object, for a second stunned Annie, for everything reminded her of her mother.

She looked into the back parlour where the fire in the range glowed and everything reflected light, plates, woodwork and glass. Annie said to herself proudly Yorkshire people are every bit as clean as the Dutch, perhaps even more so.

They led her to her small room upstairs. It was her bed, her white counterpane, her chair and the table she had worked on night after night in the parlour. In the fireplace stood her oil stove, but what caught her eye was a photo that she had not seen before, an enlarged picture of her mother in her wedding dress. It hung over the fireplace.

Edith watched her and read the unformed question and

answered it. "Yes, Mr Owen, at the prison did that for us before we left. It hangs in my room, but I thought you would like it."

Annie turned and embraced this very loving and generous young sister. She was reminded once more of the station, the love Edith proffered was so much greater than that she gave in return. She felt a stab of guilt.

It was nearly one o'clock and a very English dinner was ready. First they ate the Yorkshire pudding and then the roast beef. It was a joy to Annie to eat English food again and she ate heartily. Grandma and Edith watched her, the bond between these two had increased. It was obvious that they were in unison.

Seeing the love Annie rejoiced for it lessened her feelings of self-reproach. These two had always loved one another, just as she and her mother had made the other pair. They would not allow her to help wash up, so picking up the cat she sat by the fire.

The large black pet began to purr. Annie looked about her dazed with happiness and at peace with the world.

Yet, she knew that she was a different being amongst these things, she was not who she had been. She had learnt so much in Holland, her vision had been widened, she had been accepted there and in a small world she had triumphed.

She belonged to two worlds, it was restful to be home with, and here she sighed, the remnants of her family... yet her foot was already firmly on a stair that would lead her away and she did not know where, but it had to be followed.

There were rounds of visits to be made and many callers came, Mary was the most frequent, she lived close by. With her Annie learnt every detail of the days her mother stayed there shortly before she died. Though it upset her Annie could not hear too much of those last weeks.

One fine day the sisters walked up towards Meltham. At the summit of the hill, mile upon mile of multiple horizon spread, it made their hearts stop as it had their mother's. It seemed empty, vast and wild.

Annie felt that it was her land and an added joy was most strangely included. She knew that the hidden valleys contained busy villages. It was a land of purpose and it was a part of the Empire growing all around.

For the first time William was mentioned. Edith raised it.

"Do you think that we shall ever hear from William? You did write didn't you?"

Annie looked far ahead, she faltered, "Yes, I did and I wish that I had not. I blamed him, Edith, for Mother's death. I was angry and hurt. I wrote what I felt at the time. I do not think we shall ever hear from him again."

Edith burst into tears.

"Why did you do that, oh why? It was not his fault. Mother would have died anyway, ask Grandma."

"I know that I should not, but I was angry, very angry."

She put an arm round the sobbing girl who shrugged her away.

"I lost a Mother, too, you know. She wasn't just yours. Now you have lost me a brother too."

A long silence dwelt between them and then Edith, fighting her pride said: "If he writes it will be to you. Tell him that I would like a letter as well. I am his sister."

The pathos of the remark struck Annie very forcibly. She saw that Edith was struggling with life and not finding it easy. Her life was too entwined with Grandma's. She had been offered a place at Manchester Training College, but she would not take it for it would mean leaving the old lady.

Annie admired her loyalty, but it was a pity. She had been pushed out by her mother, if she had not she would, like Edith, have stayed. Now she saw that the world was wide and to be seen.

They had come to Helme, where their parents had spent their honeymoon. Aunt Christiana was dead, the farm had gone to far distant relations they did not know, but they looked at the solid house with its stone buildings.

They turned back the girls entwined their arms and toiled up the hill then at the crest began to trot and then run. They were children again and they talked of the funny things that happened to them.

Any coolness was melted they giggled and remembered old things and for the first time they mentioned their mother naturally. The laughter continued when they reached home and found Grandma searching for her spectacles,

"They are pushed up on your head" they cried and laughed all over again.

That evening, Annie looked though a copy of The Quiver and

the fashion editor was very fulsome of the subject of the new toques made of flowers. There were pictures and certainly they looked not only chic but pretty. Annie's imagination stirred and she was determined to make one, she even dreamt of it before she fell asleep.

There was velvet in a drawer, but there were no artificial flowers in the trimming box and none could be obtained in Crosland Moor. When later they were in Huddersfield, Annie went from haberdasher to milliner and on to haberdasher again.

The flowers she wanted were in the forefront of fashion, a few were to be had, but their expense was great. Climbing up to their home from the station Annie was disappointed, but it did not last long for looking at the gardens she devised another plan, she would use real flowers. At the gate she looked and there were many.

So on Friday evening. she folded, crumpled and smoothed and arranged the toque to her liking until it was a handsome, delicate and very elegant little hat. She planned to wear it to Uncle John's chapel on Sunday.

Grandma and Edith both praised it and Grandma declared it as fine as anything Lady Armytage had ever worn. They were proud of her, too, for she was a tall young woman fast blossoming into beauty.

On Sunday morning, early, Annie slipped into the garden and picked blue and purple and white pansies. As the other two drank tea in bed, which she had taken them, she sewed the flowers very skilfully into the mossy folds of the velvet. When finished she hid it under her bed in the dark.

When later she appeared for chapel, the approval was tinged with awe and pride. Annie set out with a happy Edith by her side. The little hat was a bright mound of colour amid the dowdy serviceability which was the keynote of the sartorial outlook then. It excited attention.

Pagan pansies found the warmth and fervour of the chapel a friendless wilderness and slowly, then with gathering momentum, they crumpled their petals and stalks wilted. Not until the close did Edith notice... she looked away she was embarrassed for herself, she was upset for her sister.

After much handshaking they escaped. Annie walked proudly, erect and then pronounced very firmly, "Do you know, I really do not care for Methodism at all, it is so," she fumbled for a word, "plain and colourless. The congregations are blind to beauty. I cannot really worship in such a place."

To her surprise Edith began to laugh, Annie was annoyed.

"Oh, do stop that and grow up. One cannot hold a conversation with you. The clothes, now, of that congregation they speak only of worth, of charm nothing."

Edith giggled still more and then burst out, "I expect you were put out because nobody remarked on your wonderful hat."

"Oh no, I take a much loftier view of it all than that. I liken them to the Calvinists in Holland. Their churches are equally ugly and their women dress abominably. But why do you laugh so?"

"Well, your hat is a bit dowdy now. It isn't a bit beautiful."

"Why, what has happened?"

Edith doubled up with laughter and clutched her sides and at last she gasped out, "Flowers fade on flirts."

Then she laughed still more. Annie for a moment looked puzzled, then looking round to make certain that she was unobserved, she unpinned the disloyal headgear. She gasped, her chin quivered, always her prelude to tears. The hat looked a bedraggled heap of limp stalks and crumpled petals.

Tears of exasperation and humiliation stung her eyes, but Edith's merriment overcame her and she, too, began to laugh, she tossed the hat in the air, caught it and began to pull out the flowers.

At dinner the story was recounted and not surprisingly Grandma improved the occasion with the saw, "Pride goes before a fall."

"But they were absolutely fresh" expostulated Annie.

"May be, but you should have given them a good drink first."

"How do you know?"

"My sister and I wore flowers in our hats long before you were thought of."

"Just wait. One day I'll have more silk flowers than anyone. I'm not going to be poor forever." It was said with an unusual vehemence and both Edith and Grandma looked at Annie and one another.

"If wishes were horses, beggars would ride," said the old lady. Annie ignored it.

The girls worked together, visited together and played as well. It seemed that something of their childhood had returned, they also talked and planned. It came about that one day sitting in the heather that was just beginning to bloom, Annie spoke of the future.

She mentioned Grandma's death which distressed Edith, but Annie said, "I am just thinking of what will happen then, my dear. Would you like to join me in Holland?"

"You could be a governess, as, I expect, I shall be. And truly, governesses are not the nobodies in Holland that they are in England. I would never be a governess over here."

Edith nodded, but was not enthusiastic and she dreaded the thought of a life without the old lady of whom she was so deeply fond. Annie noticed the reticence and changed the conversation.

One the last Saturday of the holiday Grandma had arranged a great family gathering and all three of them had been busy baking for days beforehand. The cottage shone with a new gleam, superimposed, declared Annie, on the former shine. The white china with the seaweed pattern was used.

The first to arrive were the two sisters Nina and Hannah. Nina looked old, shrivelled and her neat small mouth was pursed as if to repress the kindness that wished so prodigally to escape.

Annie always thought her the complete schoolmistress, a mixture of severity and compassion. Hannah, the younger sister, who also taught, shocked Annie for she had her hair cut short.

It curled like mediaeval youths and made a solid fringe along her forehead. She also sported the new pince nez and a long fine chain fell across her cheek. Annie looked at her in some surprise for she knew that she looked at herself, the same large blue eyes, the snub nose and rounded features.

The resemblance was also in their spirit, it was easy and relaxed beneath the correct and upright postures of them all. It was Polly that Annie waited for, for she had been her mother's particular friend and again Annie was to be surprised.

She remembered Polly with her dark hair brushed back over a pad with a black petersham ribbon sitting firmly in the centre of her parting with a fall of the same material that spread over the great cushion of hair behind.

She, too, had changed her hairdressing, she wore it in a bun, she looked older and less elegant and Annie longed for the old.

When, however, Polly began to question Annie about her old Dutch friend Miss Van Zuyl, then she recognised the same gentle character and the old bond reasserted itself.

Only as they sat down to tea did the Donckersleys arrive and instantly John dominated the room. He spoke of politics and it was only Nina, her pince-nez flashing as she gesticulated that challenged his statements.

Annie felt a flurry and an urge to make peace, but she noticed that John did not mind, he enjoyed it, but it riled her that he was so tolerant because, she felt sure, he thought her opinions were worthless because she was a woman.

Yet in her heart she could not dislike him and she liked him still more when he pressed her to visit them at Whiteley Bottom next day after church and have dinner with them in her old home. Lydia, his wife, nodded in agreement across the table and then called for silence.

John rose to his feet. He welcomed Annie back to home, even if for a short time. He warmed to a theme of Yorkshire, the workshop of the world. He reminded Annie that she came not only from a great country, but a great county, England's influence was spreading and Annie was playing her part. Then he alluded to the Bombardment of Alexandria and said that all Britain was saying,

"Well done Condor."

It was the message of Sir Wolseley Garnett after the crushing of Arabi Pasha. To which John added, "Well done, Annie."

Lydia then rose and pressed into Annie's hand a velvet box. In it was a sovereign brooch. Two long gold bars that enclosed and framed a golden sovereign. It was like the Crown brooch she had had as a child and had so often spent. This she was charged was a reward and a reminder also of her country.

Annie thanked them and replied that she was proud to have the gift, but she was still prouder to belong to such a family. This was true, very true, for she had noticed a far greater pride of Empire among the people than when she had left. There was a change and it was one in which she did not wholly share.

She was to ponder all this much more next day and as she and Edith walked up the hill from their dinner they talked. Annie had been saddened by their visit to the old house. She found she had remembered so very much more of the old home than she had expected. She regretted that it had become more conventional, more ordinary.

She saw so clearly that her mother's elegant hand no longer nudged everything into refinement and distinction. She saw more clearly her mother's taste and it pained her that her life had been spent among so much grime.

She wondered too, what her mother would have thought of the talk of the Boers in South Africa. She had found it distasteful and she was very unsure of the rights and wrongs of the Empire. Edith, she found, had imbibed the Imperialism unquestioningly.

At the brow of the hill they had turned round and looked in to the valley,

"Is an Empire worth all this dirt?"

"It keeps a lot of people in work," came the immediate reply.

"That is true – but Holland has work and far less dirt. Then there is all this killing."

"The trouble with you Annie is that you are half-Dutch already and you always were a peacemaker."

The conversation ended, as such talk usually does between intimates. They have no need to discuss for they know each other's minds too well. Talk is unnecessary.

Edith dreaded Annie's departure, she had enjoyed young company. Though her life was inextricably linked with her grandmother's, yet the wise saws and platitudes often grew tiresome.

Annie did not seem to see that a heavy burden of responsibility had fallen on very young shoulders. Annie was part of a wider world and she longed to be back in it. She looked forward to being on the staff and not in an anomalous position any longer.

She found herself just looking forward to Holland.

Chapter 20

The Ball

As Annie left the station in Leiden the effect of the place was immediate, from the entrance on its little elevation she looked across at the windmill, to the left to the level-crossing and the dome and towers of the churches in the town. She felt utterly at home.

Even the wind was a familiar friend. She walked with her heart singing through the gateway of the old town, through the narrow streets of Hoogland and towards the Hooigracht.

She was recognised and given a "Good morning" as she passed the small houses where women were swilling the pavements. The school with its large windows in rows flanking the panelled and scrolled door looked inviting, she tried the door handle, it was open, she let herself in.

For a moment she looked at the black and white marble floor, the steep but graceful staircase. She thought for a moment, not it was not home but she was undoubtedly a part of it.

She was on the point of going upstairs to her room, but decided very suddenly to see her classroom. Her name was painted in black letters by the door. She was filled with pride.

The room opened into the garden, she envisaged readings in the summer outside. She looked at the tortoise stove and its long black chimney and the high wire guard around it. She opened the roomy cupboards and noted that there were already empty shelves for the sewing materials.

Another cupboard with glazed doors contained the English classics. The areas on the wall looked blank and she planned to find pictures, landscapes of England and townscapes of Holland.

Behind her desk she decided to hand her picture of Shakespeare. This was her little kingdom and she was determined to enjoy it, she could hardly wait for term to begin in two days time.

Her room held no surprises. She was suddenly tired and she lay on the white counterpane of her bed. She was too excited to sleep and she stared up at the high ceiling. In the sunlight she noticed how far fewer motes there were in the air.

She looked at her dressing chest, and as she gazed, she knew that as it had not been dusted for two days it would hardly be noticed. But in Wakefield it had been a different tale.

However, when she thought of the gleam on the furniture at Crosland Moor, she looked pityingly on the lack-lustre surface of her wardrobe and dressing chest.

The Dutch, she often thought, can wash and scrub but they cannot polish. When downstairs she looked at the bowed fronts of the bureaux and cupboards in the salon, they call for love and she vowed to teach the girls how to really "frame" when it came to some elementary housework which needed to be added to the syllabus.

When the girls arrived many hailed her with affection. They were the easy ones to deal with - there were the new girls, unhappy, shy, and these she regarded as her special care. She enjoyed drawing them out and making them talk of home and not just mourn over it silently.

At supper she looked at the girls. The tall fair girls with square shoulders, which she thought inelegant, were the Dutch. She recognised the shyer darker creatures with fine bones, these were the children of mixed marriages. "There, now," thought Annie, "the Dutch have their Empire, too."

She became aware of one pupil who seemed more mature, certainly more aloof, than the others. She seemed to repel any advances from those around her. Later, in the Common Room, Annie found her once more surrounded by isolation, she had a book on her lap but it was totally disregarded, she looked at Annie with defiance.

Annie spoke in Dutch and it was met with a mute stare. German elicited the same blank look. Then she tried French and instantly a flood of language flowed of which Annie understood very little, but a small and interested crowd of spectators gathered who translated for her.

She learnt that the girl was from Egypt, her home had been bombed and that her father was at the embassy in The Hague. Annie smiled, patted the girl's shoulder and noted that the girl jerked away, clearly resenting the contact.

When all the classes were assigned, Annie found this young Frenchwoman in her elementary English class. Annie's happiness in her place in the school, her own classroom was suddenly flawed. There was a dark, even if small, cloud in the hitherto unbroken blue sky.

The class began to be disrupted, Annette sat, often lounged, most insolently at her desk and very purposefully she used such colloquial French that Annie certainly did not understand. There were occasions of outright laughter at Annie's expense.

The unease became distress as Annette gained easy victories. Every lesson became a battle of wills and Annie was driven to sending the girl out of the class for only then did peace and order return.

So it was the Annette spent a period of each day standing in the corridor. It was Fraulein Vogel who spoke to Annie telling her, very kindly, that her inability to cope with the pupil was noticed.

Annie was utterly perplexed, she had always enforced order by gentleness and love – it had worked even with the roughest at Anston – now she found herself both frightened and mesmerised by the young Frenchwoman.

At night she even thought that she would have to terminate her position, worse that she might be dismissed.

Fraulein Vogel was surprised at Annie's attitude and when she wailed at the difficulty, she vehemently declared, "Annie, you must crush her at the next outbreak of insolence, if you cannot do it yourself, then, send her to Miss Lange. But the latter will not be to your credit. Master her yourself. You are a Yorkshirewoman."

It was with real dread that made her sick at heart and churned her stomach that the next English class began. At the very outset there was laughter in the middle of the room.

Annie rose and went to Annette swiftly, so quickly that Annette had no time to right her book, it was upside down.

Anger flamed and Annie raised her right hand as if to slap the girl. Annette cowered and the class were amazed.

Annie stayed herself and summoning her inadequate French hissed, "Vous étés une cochon sale et detestable." Annette sniggered, but also turned pale, and the spark in her eye did not die.

The lesson proceeded and went well, better than Annie had dared to hope, until the very moment that Annie began to relax and again subversive amusement broke out.

It was now Annie who was white with anger and she snapped out, "Annette, levez-vous."

The girl slowly rose to her feet. Annie resolved to speak in English, she believed the girl understood.

"I am very weary of attempting to teach you, Annette. You lead this petty and ridiculous impertinence. In England we have a punishment known as 'sending to Coventry'. I send you all to Coventry until I have an apology from you all and Annette in particular."

She, then, repeated it in Dutch adding that they would discover soon enough what Coventry meant.

It was Anna le Polle's turn to take the junior school for a walk. Annie asked if she might take them claiming that she needed fresh air. Anna gladly complied. The girls were waiting in the hall as Annie came down the stairs drawing on her gloves. They smiled… the smile was not returned. She brushed past them to the front door.

"Form in twos, today, we shall be an orderly English crocodile. She shall walk to the castle of Oegstgeest."

There was a murmur of excitement, it was not only a favourite walk, but one of the longest. Yet it had a greater charm, the little baroque building with its onion-domed roofs and turrets across a moat, all enclosed in a small wood which was a heronry, always drew forth Annie's greatest story-telling powers.

The door open the girls stepped out eagerly in to he street, they had forgotten Annie's edict, or thought themselves forgiven. From the back Annie rapped out in a manner they found totally alien, "Right", "Stop", "Slower","Quicker".

There were no halts, no story. At the entrance to the woods past the great gates they stopped and clamoured for the story to begin. Annie looked at none of them, only the distance. "Proceed", she called.

A dampness like the dankness of the decaying leaves fell upon them and they became subdued. Some of the smaller ones stole a smile with their eyes at Annie - she remained marmoreal.

They circled the moat, saw a carriage draw up and a man jump down, slam the door and run up the steps shouting something to the coachman.

Ordinarily this would have precipitated a stream of fantasy from their schoolmistress, but Annie seemed not to observe it at all.

Back at school the girls, their cheeks red with the exercise, drank their tea and ate their speculaas. Miss Lange came in. She smiled at Annie and the girls and instantly noted the atmosphere.

"You are all very silent after your walk."

They became even more subdued and shifted their feet and Annie replied.

"They are in disgrace, Miss Lange."

"I see. Then I will leave you."

Tea done, Annie dismissed them. She was not on duty that evening and she slowly dragged herself up to her room. In her room she flung herself on her bed. Her resolve was cracking and she pondered on what she was to do if Annette refused to apologise.

The idea angered her and she resolved not to compromise, she would return to England and be a mousy governess.

But she could not believe that she was wrong. The punishment was the one her mother had used, "being sent to Coventry". She remembered hot tears at the house in Whiteley Bottom. She shuddered as she recalled shouting at her father through the banisters as he stood in the hall below, "Don't care. Don't care." The words she realised, only now, were the very opposite of all she felt. But did Annette care, she wondered?

At dinner that evening the subdued air continued and at the end Miss Lange rose and said: "I notice your silence. Miss Taylor must be very angry with you. I do not know who, or what is involved, but you had best make your peace. Saint Paul said, 'Let not the sun go down upon your wrath'."

The time passed stiffly in the Common Room, the girls embroidered but there were murmurs. Annie remained aloof and when she was questioned she took the work in her hands and without a word showed them how to use their needle and achieve the right stitch.

The soft tick of the ormolu clock beneath its glass dome could be heard. Some were tired of the punishment and whiningly asked her to speak. They were like spaniels in disgrace. Annette was distant, too, and at last she brought her stitching to Annie.

It was deliberately untidy and taking out her scissors she carefully cut out the offending attempts at flowers, then, taking the coloured thread outlined the petals again. Annette took it, she was tense and every feature of her face was sharpened with resentment. Annie wondered even if there would be an outbreak of violence.

The class watched, the clock's tick again became audible. Annette moved, not back to her seat, but to the stove. She grasped the spring handle of the metal door and pushed her embroidery into the aperture.

The wooden frame stuck, she pushed harder and the frame snapped and she slammed the lid to. She looked for a moment triumphant as she swept the faces of the pupils with a glance. The girls were horrified.

"Get on with your work," was all that Annie said.

Annette returned to her seat, but Annie's heart thumped. What was she to do? She refused to break her silence, the longing though, was to run up to her room, hide herself. The girl was far harder than herself, what was she to do?

Her eye caught the print on the wall. It was of fishermen carrying a drowned man over the dunes, a huddled procession of widow, children. That, reasoned Annie was a tragedy, far greater than a schoolroom drama. But the other side of her replied, It is quite different, in the picture the only way to meet it was with fortitude.

Here was a battle of wills. Again she felt sick, she remained upright... her shoulders never touched the chair back. The bell rang, that meant prayers in five minutes time.

Annie rose and left very slowly. As the door closed behind her she sensed as well as heard movement within. She thought that the rebellion was on Annette's behalf.

With a calm entirely assumed she went to the drawing room. Only Fraulein Vogel sat there. Annie slumped beside her and she began to tell her the story, at the same time she wished to repress it. Fraulein Vogel said: "It is nearly over. Just wait."

Annie had a moment to disbelieve her before there was a knock at the door and a tear-stained and dishevelled Annette was propelled by hands and arms into the room. After a momentary continuance of the defiance, she stared down and said,

"Oh Mademoiselle, I am sorry, very sorry, I will do as you ask."

She did not look up, but she did not grovel and for that Annie felt a certain admiration.

"You speak English, I hear."

"Yes, Miss Taylor, I learnt it in Egypt, everyone spoke English."

"Then why did you pretend to be so ignorant?"

"It was the bombardment. I vowed never to speak English again. We were so afraid. You do not know what it is like to be shelled."

Annie rose, took the hanging head in her hands and looked at the blotched and swollen face, all the tenseness had gone, but as she did so she noticed a retraction, not from herself but something about her. Her hand instinctively moved to the focus of the glance. It was the golden sovereign brooch."

"You do not like this?"

The girl shook her head and said: "It reminds me."

"Then I shall not wear it," and there and then she unpinned it. "Now, quick, quick go upstairs, wash your face and come back to me here, quick."

Annie glowed, "I have won. I have won." She looked at the brooch, she wore it because it had been kindly meant as a gift, but she looked at it and agreed that it was not beautiful.

Annette returned Annie took her hand and led her into the big hall for prayers. Their late entry and together was noted, not least by Miss Lange whose theme for her address was obedience.

The school shook hands with the staff before they retired to their dormitories. When Annette stood before Annie there was a moment of understanding and Annie felt a desire to kiss the child.

Instead she said: "Sleep well, my dear and we will talk in the break tomorrow."

To her surprise, Annette gave her an elegant little curtsey such as she reserved for the Principal.

Annie went along to the common room her heart singing. To her surprise, all the symptoms of her crisis had been noticed and each one had a similar experience to recount.

It was one which each one of them had to win. This pleased Annie on one hand, she was not alone, but she had also thought that her own methods of dealing with children might be unique. She did not want to be like all the other teachers.

The Belgian teacher produced her familiar silver cigarette case and passed it around. Annie, when first she had seen it, had been shocked. Tonight most of the teachers took a cigarette, the box was before her, she hesitated, but a chorus of insistence made her take one too. Matches were produced and soon smoke rose in the air. Annie puffed gingerly, her stiff fingers held the paper tube at right angles and the rigidity seemed to spread from her hand to her whole figure.

But she smiled and said that she thought it a strange way to celebrate her little victory. In a deeper recess of her mind she thought of William and his smoking and that led her to think of her mother and although she took several more puffs, the memory compounded with the bitter taste made her press out the tiny fire and say to herself, "This is no occupation for a lady."

It made her look at her colleagues with a distance. In fact, the joy she had experienced was fast diminishing and up in her room she thought of the hands that had propelled Annette into the dining room.

She had unconsciously, but nonetheless deliberately refrained from identifying them. She saw those hands as the agents of the crowd, the mob and she had an instinctive dislike of the rabble which had been nurtured by her reading.

She had to acknowledge that the mob had been her allies and that was a bitter knowledge. As she fell asleep she acknowledged that she had changed sides and that the former enemy was to be her protégée.

In the garden at midday, Annette came to Annie who was sitting on the one seat the garden boasted. Again the child apologised. Annie shook her head saying, "We shall say no more about it. You disliked me because the English Navy bombarded you.

"I really had nothing to do with that, you know. We cannot judge a person because of their nation's politics. Tell me, was your father a Republican or a Bonapartist?"

"He was for the Emperor."

"So was I. Do you blame me for the death of the poor Prince Imperial?"

"No. Not now, but I might have done."

"Well, I must tell you that the whole of my class in Wakefield wore mourning for the Prince and that was in Yorkshire in England."

Annette brightened.

"Yes, we followed every detail in the papers and many of us went in spirit with our Queen to the unhappy Empress."

"My father says that the Empress is the most beautiful woman he had ever seen, or ever will see."

"By all accounts she is extraordinarily beautiful, but I admire her because what is even greater is that she is so brave. We all have to be courageous in bombardments, in school, in absolutely everything."

"The girls won't speak to me, now."

Annie looked at the anguished face. It was a different agony to the tenseness she had seen before. The bell, that controlled their lives, went, they went in together. Together they entered the class and Annette had no more trouble.

It was not until the end of the term that one of the girls asked Annie where her gold brooch was with the picture of the Queen of England.

"Somewhere in my jewel case. I realised it was not very attractive."

Annette sitting nearby looked at Annie and said.

"Miss Taylor, those pearls suit you very much better."

"Thank you."

At half-term, the Haverschmidts repeated their invitation and Annie went once more to Schiedam. The pastor seemed tired, but his innate courtliness was aroused by Annie. Mrs Haverschmidt noted the change of his mood - she had seen it all before, a new person, a new interest.

The eyes which had looked inward suddenly looked out again. The agony was replaced by alertness which became gaiety. He was, however, regarding Annie sharply, critically. When she had gone to her room and he was alone with Margo he asked if anything had happened to Annie.

"Why, Father, what do you mean?"

"Has she been ill? Has something upset her?"

"Nothing, as far as I am aware. She went home in the summer."

"That would not account for it. People usually become younger by going home; they revert to childhood, I know I always did. No, she is much, much more a woman that when I saw her receiving her prize."

"You are seeing things, as you always do, Father. You seek meanings where there are no meanings."

She laughed and he laughed as well, but he knew that he was

right. At dinner he watched her and again asked what is so different. As he watched her take the vegetables from the maid he knew what the difference was. There was a complete, an absolute absence of hurry in her, though her movements were fluid, everything had become deliberate.

There was a certainty about her that had not been there before.

On Sunday, the service over, with the long sermon preached, there was a sense of relaxation throughout the household. On the way back, Annie had mused on the fact that she found it difficult to understand why so clever a man as Francois Haverschmidt lay bare his soul so often and made it so open for misinterpretation.

She admired him, she loved his courage to be so sincere, but she knew that his wife and his children paid a price. They suffered because of the veil that was missing in him. This she only partially knew was the hallmark of the saint, the martyr's contempt for defences. It was something only the very strong, who appear so weak, can practise.

With Francois, too, there was the self-engrossment of the artist. His mind was the duelling ground between his profession and his art. Yet she found him easy to talk to and he found her easier than most.

It was on a walk that she rather haltingly confided in him the little affair of the schoolroom. She deprecated it all, even described it as trivial, but admitted that it had affected her deeply.

"Why has it affected you so much?"

"That is what puzzles me. I have taught rougher children far more easily and without revolt."

He changed his question, the story teller in him was not content with generalisations, he wanted something specific.

"What thing upset you most?"

Without any hesitation she mentioned the hands that had propelled Annette adding,

"I despised them so. They were beasts, a pack of dogs and I was equally tainted for they were fawning to me an Authority."

He smiled, "You did not like your allies?"

He turned and looked at her, her round open face looked hurt.

"No, I did not like my allies. I did not like what was happening. I did not like what I was doing. I had to do it. I had to break the girl's will and gain mastery over my class."

"And you have done it. Now you can sit back and enjoy them. I expect, too, that this will never happen again."

"I do not know. I have found something savage in life I had not bargained for and certainly not in the civilised ranks of society."

"Aha, I see you suffer from the English delusion that rank and goodness go together. They do not. The lust for power is in every rank of life. You, my dear, have found your power, you have won it. Keep it and use it wisely and kindly. God has given it to you."

He had lifted a load. Yes a power had been given her. She suddenly appreciated that her mother had far more power in the Prison and she had never spoken of it.

Annie knew, as well, that the power had been acceded to her as much from the convicts as from her position. If her mother could use her power with love, then she could most certainly as a schoolmistress.

When Francois returned to his old topic of dirt and pollution Annie laughed outright. She plucked a privet leaf, peeled off her glove and rubbed it... her finger remained white. "I could not do that in the West Riding."

She told him more vehemently than before of the absence of sun when the mills were working. How flowers had to be wiped before they could be arranged. How washing became spotted with smuts as it hung on the line.

"Then," he said, "I have a greater duty to prevent things getting as bad."

"Yes, that is true."

She could not change him. She did not wish to, she loved him as he was.

Back at school the year rolled on and as Kerstmis approached so Annie was determined that this year the girls should know something of an English Christmas. In class she read A Christmas Carol, for the school she planned an English evening and to have mince pies became essential.

She decided first to make a cake. She took over the kitchen and the entire school had a turn at stirring it.

Sinterklaas took second place as they looked to Miss Taylor's Christmas. Paper chains were made, paper lanterns constructed. Fraulein Vogel practised English Carols unknown to Annie. On the evening there were readings from the Bible, poems and as a carol was sung, Mientje, the head maid, carried in a huge dish of mince pies.

As these were being eaten there was sudden clapping for Jan appeared in his best livery. He bore on his head a dish on which rose the largest iced cake most had ever seen. The white sugar gleamed and Annie was embarrassed by the lavish praise given to her rough loops and garlands that surrounded the cake.

All she could think was, "What would Grandma have said of it?"

At the close the entire school sang Good King Wenceslas. It took Annie by surprise and brought such memories of home mingled with the joy of the moment that tears ran down her cheeks and her chin quivered.

The evening was a success and Miss Lange asked Annie if she had noticed that English had been spoken thought the evening without any enforcement. It had escaped Annie's observation.

There was skating again, the thaw of the Dutch formality and its immediate resumption as the ice disappeared was noted again by Annie. During the freeze, she had seen in Dennerweg a box of Seville oranges and she had longed for some marmalade.

On an impulse she bought some and wrote instantly to her grandmother for the recipe. With some of her class she cut up the fruit and put the pieces to soak in a pail, Miss Lange was interested.

Then, as occurs in a small world, a tiny incident gained a great prominence. The first making was a success and Miss Snoek, impressed by the economy, sent out for more oranges. Now the entire class spent an afternoon cutting, putting the pips into muslin bags.

The following day the boiling became almost a ceremony with a procession of girls though the kitchen watching the proceeding. At the end the jars were labelled and Annie decided that it should be served at breakfast along with the cheese, but in place of the jam.

There was a sudden rage to be English. Annie had a great burst of popularity. She was teased in the Common Room, especially when the older pupils began to copy her hair style.

One day Miss Lange said, as they drank their coffee, "Well, Miss Taylor, what would you like to Anglicise next?"

For a moment, Annie was silent, was it a test question. Then she remembered Miss Lange's lack of irony and to her surprise answered truthfully, "I would love to make the garden into an English garden."

Miss Snoek, who had a collection of pretty watercolours of still prettier English cottage gardens in her room, stirred with excitement. Miss Lange thought the idea good but no one knew how to set about it for there was not a gardener amongst them.

"Then you, Annie, will have to see to it. All the English can garden."

Annie was alarmed, she thought of the prison, the wallflowers, the carnations, colour and scent leapt like a flame in her mind. She had a sudden spurt of confidence.

"We shall have to begin with a lawn."

"Yes, yes, that is correct, English lawns are famous. I have seen them in Cambridge colleges," murmured Miss Snoek, enthusiastically.

"Then, Miss Snoek, I leave it all in your hands and Miss Taylor's."

Entrusted with the Principal's authority Annie with Miss Snoek were to be seen next day in their felt hats and capes pacing and measuring the garden. Annie had already a sketch. The gravel walks and the square beds, planted always with lines of annuals were to go.

The pupils were sent out in the afternoons to pull up the glazed tiles that sharply, but brokenly, defined the beds.

A jobbing gardener was engaged and an area that had, at least, been neat became a dark patch of dug earth. Annie was aghast. She was regarded as the director and her knowledge was minimal, but she kept quiet and remembered the vision of the garden she would like to have.

In the spring, a seedsman came to sow the grass. The soil was raked and raked again, it became a smooth plain and Annie marvelled at the meticulous way the pebbles and stones were all gathered to one end.

Then she took her class out, when, one windless day, the nurseryman with an instrument, like a fiddle with a bow, went up and down broadcasting the seed. Within a week the brown acquired a soft green haze. Luck seemed to be on Annie's side, nothing seemed to fail.

All this activity made the term speed by and one evening alone with Fraulein Vogel did she become aware that she had not been sad for many weeks, she had a new content. The two women sat looking out of the window, there were hints of colour and the grass had thickened.

But Erna sighed as she looked at it. Her dark face was brooding, it really only lightened when moved by music or laughter, Annie made her laugh, that was the basis of their friendship.

"Your grass is growing."

She turned from the window and looked at Annie, the curly hair massed in an Alexandra fringe on her forehead, but its tidy turmoil made the face beneath stiller and the skin smoother. She looked again at the large blue eyes and bowed mouth. She thought, "The girl is undeniably pretty."

"Yes, your grass is growing and you are growing, too. You are almost beautiful."

Annie laughed.

"No, I mean it and your life lies before you like a garden to walk in. We do not know what will happen to you, but we know, very well, what will happen to me."

This did not beg, it demanded a question and Annie obliged, so that with Teutonic truth and Teutonic earnestness that shocked Annie, Erna Vogel said;

"I will teach here until I am tired and old. I will return to my home to my older sister and my very old mother. I shall nurse my mother, then my sister. I will have a few pupils who will provide me with some extra money for concerts and the opera – but the prospect is very dull.

"But what can a plain woman with little money do? We are unwanted by men because we are not pretty and because we are women we are badly paid. This place pays us as fairly as anywhere else, but it is badly.

"They cannot pay more because they cannot charge more, parents do not pay for the education of their girls, only the boys. We are trapped."

It was spoken calmly, flatly and it made Annie's spirits sink for she recognised its truth. The future looked bleak, she never looked to it, she lived in the moment and made it happy, but she saw that there was a trap.

But she accepted the forecast for Erna, but she also thought,

"Something nice may yet happen for her, as she was sure it would for herself. Then everything will change."

She was young, middle age did not even begin to oppress her, and she did know that she was attractive. But she also knew that once you were poor it was very difficult to be anything else and trebly so if you were a woman.

It was significant that she did not say "the misfortune to be a woman". Annie would have hated to be a man.

She smiled and the serenity of her face, the almost curious calm, broke like a pond flurried by a breeze on a summer's day, it glittered. She stretched out her hand and patted a chair.

"Come, sit down, have your tea. Too much work, that is the trouble, you need a holiday. We all need a holiday."

"Holiday? I have to return to Essen, there is nowhere else. I live, Annie, in the shadow of factories. Krupps, have you heard of them?"

Annie shook her head.

"I live in a grey and ugly world. You, with your English gardens, could not understand." She took her cup.

Annie hesitated. She had discovered that if people thought you lived in a dream, which is far superior to the reality, there was little reason to disabuse them. But this time she did.

"Erna, I spent my childhood living on the side of a hill that looked into a valley where the mill belched black smoke all week. That was grey and sooty. It was not pretty, but I often thought that without the chimneys of the mills and the mean houses it would have been very beautiful.

"My father died when I was eight and we have been very poor, once we were even hungry. But God looked after us, we did not starve and most of the time we were very happy." She said it without vehemence.

Erna replied: "Exactly. We live in a world managed by men. Have you thought that it your mother had died instead of your father, you would not have been so poor. Your father would have married again. Men always do."

Annie was doubly stung.

"Erna, Erna. May be he would have married again but we would never have been so happy. Life without my father was only just bearable, without my mother it would have been unthinkable."

"I am sorry. I have hurt you. But, oh I do wish that I had been a man."

"Have you thought of all the things you would have to do that you wouldn't want to. Think of those dull and dreary clothes."

The Fraulein laughed. "Annie, the trouble with you is that you are so fundamentally frivolous."

The mood had passed, Erna was happier. She even said a few pleasant things about her home. The talk became the gossip of school which always bored Annie. So she began to think of the world and was it a man's world. Were women oppressed?

She had always thought of life as an inevitable flow. She had never questioned things. She could only think of the edifice of life in terms of her mother's life and then she did grieve.

Meanwhile, the lawn grew and Annie in the summer term allowed select groups to walk across it. Then Fraulein Vogel wanted to organise a game of rounders. Annie relented and allowed it.

To her dismay she became involved having no eye for the ball and running awkwardly she proved very bad indeed.

After one game she vowed never to play again and she did not. She was dumbfounded when she was congratulated on making a games pitch, just what the girls needed. It took a quiet Englishwoman to achieve that.

It was another dream of misunderstanding that Annie allowed to drift, though to accept praise did seem to her a little Machiavellian. Her motive had been beauty – and she had done it. The garden was transformed and she herself was both pleased and surprised.

One evening, as she walked with Miss Snoek she was asked, "Why is it, Miss Taylor, these roses look so much better than they did? They are the same old bushes?"

"Because they rise, now, from grass walks not the gravel."

While Miss Snoek nodded ponderingly, Annie wondered where she had derived such information. She did not think it was observation. Was it from Uncle Alan, Captain Armytage, or possibly the Pumphreys?

Miss Snoek liked to walk after the evening meal with Annie practising her English and this time she picked two roses, the first she tucked into Annie's bodice, the other in her own. During a momentary tussle between a thorn and her lace jabot, she volunteered a remark.

"Is it true that every Englishman wears a rose in his bottom-hole?"

Annie first turned bright pink and as her imagination romped uncontrollable giggles seized her. Miss Snoek looked questioningly and disapprovingly.

"Have I said something strange?"

Annie with a deep breath took control. "You have said something, Miss Snoek, that you must never say again. It is button-hole not ...." Once more laughter seized her.

Miss Snoek lifted her chin, the particular mixture of shyness and dignity that was herself, reasserted itself.

"That will be enough English for tonight, I think."

Though Annie laughed it made her wonder and the question she asked was whether she would have to spend the rest of her life with old maids until she was one of them? Whatever it was, she had no desire to be a man especially at that moment for she was contriving the most becoming hat she had ever made.

But again up in her room she imagined pink Englishmen with roses in their posteriors. She blushed, but still she laughed until she told herself that Erna was right, "I am fundamentally frivolous."

At the end of term, examinations over, the school relaxed, but the Principals were thrown into a state of great perturbation by an invitation to a Ball given by the Studenten Corps. Twelve young ladies were invited together with twelve chaperones.

The gulf between the university and the school was great and deep, yet at the same time links with the great institution were cherished, it gave the school a distinction denied other establishments of its kind.

To ignore the invitation would be churlish and offensive, even to decline it would be ungracious, but to accept it would be to court infinite difficulties. Yet it was an acknowledgement of their existence, almost an extending hand of equality.

Miss Lange calmly weighed these ponderables while Miss Snoek worried and fluttered about dresses, behaviour and even envisaged elopements. The keynote they agreed must be vigilance.

When the staff gathered after the evening meal Miss Lange asked if any of them could dance. Fraulein Vogel volunteered immediately that she loved playing for dances and it was only Annie who could dance.

"Then, Miss Taylor, you will have to give lessons to the older girls."

Next day there was considerable shock for the Principals. It was discovered that if the staff could not dance, the pupils could. Miss Lange took note that the worthy burghers of Holland were changing, when she had been young the peasants danced, the aristocracy danced, but the stolid enduring middle classes did not.

It was deemed frivolous, by many sinful. However, the lessons went on, the Common Room carpet was rolled up and the waltz, the polka and the Cotillion and the Lancers were practised. There was enthusiasm and great fervour. Only on Sundays, despite pleadings from the girls, was dancing forbidden.

The day of the ball approached and still Annie did not know whether she was included in the party. The silence was the result of the Principals indecision, Miss Lange and Miss Snoek discussed it at great length.

Their wish was that Annie should accompany them, her looks and her bearing would be a credit to the school, but they were also apprehensive that her prettiness might prove disquieting to the young men.

Three days before the assembly they sent for her and told her that she was to be one of the chaperones. Annie thanked them, but out of sight she wept tears of anger for the notice was so short and what could she wear? Her limited wardrobe had no ball gown at all – indeed, she had never owned one.

That afternoon she took a class out for a walk ostensibly for English conversation. They went to a haberdasher and there together they found a pattern for the perfect dress. Then they walked to a draper and bought many yards of white lawn printed with small blue flowers.

The girls were eager to help pin the pattern to the material and make the cutting. Annie had to restrain them. When, at last, the cutting was done Annie's heart failed her, there was yard upon yard to be stitched and she wondered if it could ever be done in time. That night she sewed until two in the morning, next day at every interval she flew up to her room and put in a few more stitches.

It came to the fitting of the bodice, this was difficult, it had to be creaseless... every fold had to be exact to outline her figure. She could not do it alone, so she enlisted the help of Mientje, the maid, but her attitude was inexact and she thought attention to detail inessential.

Annie despaired until she sat by Annette at lunch and confided her anxieties. Annette leapt at the notion of helping and as a Frenchwoman showed her thorough appreciation of absolute precision.

She knew, as if by instinct, exactly where a dart had to be made to achieve the perfect fit. Mientje, who was still hemming was awestruck by their zealous almost consecrated attitude.

On the last evening before the ball Annie sat sewing from eight o'clock until three, then she climbed into bed, so tired sleep would not come. Again and again she sewed, or she anticipated the ball.

After lessons in the morning, Annie with Annette as assistant had a last fitting. Together they were enchanted but also thought it made Annie look too young. Annette solved the problem, she decreed that Annie must wear a black ribbon around her neck, black bows must nestle in the folds of the sleeves and a larger black bow must be placed on the bustle.

There was excitement as the two hurried out to buy the velvet and with amazing swiftness they fashioned the trimmings and were pleased with the result. It was Mientje who had the task of ironing the skirt.

While the chosen girls went off to their dormitories to change, Annie bathed in cold water. Her firm young body glowed pink as she arose from the tub. After drying herself she slowly and carefully arranged her hair... this was always done with painstaking attention, but on this occasion with intensity.

At last every curl was in place. When ready to put on the dress she sent for both Mientje and Annette. It was with bright rapture that Annette buttoned the tight bodice down the back, then the skirt had to be attached and every hook and eye and tape done, patted and smoothed.

Finally, it was the jewels, her mother's engagement ring with its rubies and last of all the black velvet ribbon round her neck with its row of pearls above and below. As Annette surveyed her teacher she sniffed, tears of delight came to her eyes, and all she could murmur was, "Si charmante, si charmante",

She helped Annie into a dark Paisley shawl, also from her mother, it was like the moon going behind a cloud, Annette said so and Annie surprised herself by saying very calmly,

"It is only a temporary eclipse."

She went downstairs more confident and more certain than she had ever been before. In the hall she started adjusting the girls' attire with a tug, a touch and a pull where appropriate and each case making a world of difference.

Miss Lange appeared in black silk with fine black lace on her head instead of her usual white cap. Annie thought that indeed they were "a goodlie companie."

The covered waggonnette trundled to the entrance and they climbed up the step and door at the back and sat on the seats facing one another. The girls were suddenly subdued, the adventure was now in earnest and they wondered each whether they would enjoy it.

Annie watched them, she was equally anticipatory, she wondered, like every young woman, what encounters this would bring.

She reminded herself severely that she was a chaperone and, perhaps, she would not be asked to dance at all.

At the Minerva the cloaks and shawls were laid aside and it was then that Miss Lange saw Annie's dress. She took a deep breath, and she, who had admitted Annie's prettiness, now had to acknowledge that she was a beauty.

Her first reaction was that she must hide her, such looks, she had always known, were dangerous. Then she noticed the unhurried movement and how Annie was again marshalling the girls and once again putting final touches to their hair and clothes.

The little party sallied out of the robing room and along the corridor.

They queued to be received by the Rector Magnificus and his wife. Miss Lange led the way, Miss Snoek and Miss le Polle half way and then after three more girls, came Annie. The curtsies of them all were exemplary. They entered the ballroom, their charm in the corridor was suddenly dimmed for nearly all present were young and had that charm that only youth can bring.

Miss Lange led her troop to a row of gilt chairs. The girls were ranged decorously and decoratively round the room, the students stood in groups, tall creatures in black and white, they were surveying and assuming a nonchalance they did not entirely feel.

The Rector approached a fair young man, the group split up and with eyes that really looked they made their way to the girls and their older ladies, producing as they did so, small programmes with tasselled pencils.

A young man approached Miss Lange, bowed and after seeking permission approached two girls and initialled their programmes and his own. More came and Annie felt a little flurry of envy, she had not been asked. Then she saw the tall young man again and he requested a dance.

She received an encouraging nod from Miss Lange and she consented. She saw his programme and his wisdom impressed her, by each initial he put the colour of the dress of his chosen partner.

Annie watched the scene, it was all as she had imagined and it tied up with the memories her mother had recounted of life in London before her marriage. The orchestra struck a lengthy chord and as if choreographed the young men sprang into a flurry of action claiming their partners.

Annie's feet tapped to the music, being a chaperone was very dull, she longed to dance, she moved to sit by the Principal. At the same time a partner stood before her requesting the pleasure, Annie looked at Miss Lange who nodded and smiled.

The young man did not dance well, but at least they were moving and as they danced so the yardage of lawn in the skirt gained a velocity that moved, it seemed, both of them, the black ribbons with their long trailing loops fluttered and they were noted and Annie was dubbed "the lovely magpie".

More dances, more sitting put. All the girls were happy, no one had been overlooked, there were no 'wallflowers'.

At supper, the charges were shepherded and a lean moustached young man came to assist Miss Lange and Miss Snoek and, then, Annie. He escorted them to the last unoccupied table. He chattered easily and they soon discovered that he was reading law.

He paid the utmost courtesy to Miss Lange and she glowed beneath his attention, but she was shrewd enough to guess a reason and when he produced his programme and casually noted that two dances were not yet initialled knew that the invitation was not to her. When he asked Annie, she looked momentarily, she was glad of that, at Miss Lange who smiled and nodded.

The young man could dance and again Annie's flounces lifted

and they whirled round the room. This man can really dance, she said to herself, and he was handsome and he made the politest of compliments.

Annie was in a state of bliss. This is what a ball should be, she again said to herself. He suggested that they should meet next day but Annie pretended not to hear. The dance ended and he took her back to her place.

Partners were claimed and Annie moved along the empty chairs to sit by Miss Lange.

The older woman surveyed the scene, she was growing tired, the glow had faded.

"Do you know who that young man is?"

"No. All I know is that he dances very well."

"So he should he's been well brought up. He is the son of Baron Bentinck. His father is the King's Chamberlain."

Annie knew that the information was passed not only with triumph that he had supped with them, but also repressively, there was the implication that an impoverished young teacher must, of necessity, repel any advances from the aristocracy.

The message went home, but unwillingly. He was unattainable, but she comforted herself that it did not matter for she was not in love with him.

The dance became more vigorous, no girls were left unclaimed by the walls. Annie found that dancing with others lacked the élan she had felt dancing with the Jonkheer. But that was soon remedied for twice more he requested the pleasure and each time Miss Lange nodded with approval.

Again he asked to meet and Annie could not deny hearing, but she was smilingly evasively.

Back in her seat she thought how timid she had been to refuse a meeting. An opportunity was lost that would never recur. She was angry with herself. Helping the chattering girls into their cloaks and coats her heart felt heavy.

She blamed herself for a careful prim fool. However, her heart beat very fast when she saw him standing at the foot of the stairs, bowing to departing guests. He took Miss Lange's hand and kissed it.

He then took Annie's, he did not kiss it but as he stooped over it, his bright blue eyes looked very firmly into hers, and she caught the words, "The Botanical Gardens tomorrow afternoon."

The Sociable trundled over the cobbles and the girls could not stop talking Miss Lange reproved them and for the first time Annie noticed her authority failed. The Principal was tired and a little bored, also a little jealous of youth... she thought of what might have been.

Annie climbed up to her bed, her weariness was suddenly compounded, the sorcery of the evening with its alluring promises and the previous night of little sleep when she had sewn and sewn.

Her last thought before sleep enfolded her was that sewing had rarely been put to better use.

Next day, formal lessons were foregone and instead Annie chose to pass the time reading *She Stoops to Conquer* out in the garden. As they progressed, Annie became aware of the sniggering and she realized that those who had been at the dance were casting her into Kate Hardcastle and young Bentinck as Marlowe.

Annie froze and the humour of the play lost its warmth and became merely wit. She sat straight backed correcting pronunciation and explaining situations and so dismissed furtive laughter.

She felt happy under the blue sky and she wondered if she would walk that afternoon in the Botanical Garden.

They heard the door-bell ring very peremptorily and Jan across the lawn. He looked a little perturbed, anxious for Annie, whom he summoned to the hall. Annie followed him. She had no thought of disturbance or difficulty. She passed from the passage into the hall, instantly she was aware that it was darker than usual, as if crowded.

She did not expect to see a donkey and a cart with a towering array of flowers and an uneasy stallholder holding the reins of the donkey, enduring the indignation of Miss Lange and Miss Snoek.

The seller thrust a letter into Annie's hand. She tore it open. All it said was, "Please accept these flowers."

"Well?" demanded the outraged Principals. Annie could not forbear a smile. It was awful, but also a lovely moment of wonderful extravagance and it must not be wasted. She stepped up to the cart, looked at the flowers and took a bunch of roses. She went to the front door, Jan followed her - they opened the two leaves.

Annie spoke: "Please go as quickly as possible. The flowers are all yours."

The dealer, quick to see an excellent bargain and eager to leave the wrath of the Principals turned the donkey and with Jan's help they manoeuvred the cart up the steps into the street.

It was not an easy procedure and they called out when the cart sheered close to the staircase, or threatened to graze the doors. Annie studiously calm did glance at the marble floor and she was amazed that the iron rim had not damaged it.

At last, the cart was in the street and Jan closed the door shutting out the main evidence of the offence. But Annie knew that the storm would only now break about her head.

"Miss Taylor please come in", the Principals went into the study. Miss Lange as always the spokeswoman, said, "This is an outrage. You have brought shame upon our establishment. This had never happened before. How do you explain it?"

Annie looked down. She hated, hated being reproved, but as she did so she became aware again of the flowers in her hand. They were a tribute to her. She wished to answer, "Perhaps you have never had anyone as pretty as I teaching here before."

But in fact she remained silent for a moment, then with almost a smile as she looked again at the roses.

"I am very sorry if this has embarrassed you, but truly I am not responsible."

Miss Snoek now rushed in,

"Miss Taylor, you must have led this young man on."

Annie was stung and she replied fast,

"I have never led anyone on. I only danced with the permission of Miss Lange. Is that not so?"

"That is true."

But Miss Snoek was aroused, "I consider the entire episode a disgrace."

"Extravagant, silly, but not of my making, Miss Snoek. I think you must reprimand someone else, not me."

Annie felt most strangely calm and it flashed across her mind that if this were a stage this was the moment for her to sweep off. She was an employee and she waited.

Miss Lange was now very calm.

"The incident is closed. I see that it is not your fault. But, Miss Taylor, your triumph last night, you must remember is 'but an evening gone.' We have longer and harder work to do."

Annie bowed and said: "With your permission I will return to my class."

"Leave those flowers behind."

She was never to know if they meant in that room, or merely not before the class. They were suddenly very, very dear to her.

"Of course not, I shall put them in water first."

She looked at them again. Poor plain Miss Snoek, she saw flames of jealousy still leaping in her eyes.

Up in her room she put the roses in her water jug and she thought, "And these were only a fraction of the whole." With glee she danced across the room and then with a demure face tripped modestly and demurely down the stairs and across the lawn to the giggling girls.

She Stoops to Conquer was taken up again. Its liveliness was hampered by the need to explain, especially Miss Hardcastle's malapropisms. Annie felt there was a divide as deep as the sea between English and Dutch humour.

At lunch she was asked to accompany a child to the dentist. She regarded it as an indication of fate. She could not go to the Botanical Garden. But Jan Bentinck did. But of that she was not to know for a long time.

Term ended and the silence descended on the school. As always it ceased to be a school. Annie passed the time by sewing and reading. She was reading *Anna Karenina* in German. She became one with Anna.

She felt for her intensely, but she could not comprehend how she could relinquish her son for Vronsky, however unsatisfactory her marriage might be.

Fall in love, yes, but desert her child, no. She equated her mother with Anna. She remembered her struggles. She remembered how she had been sent to the Nashes, but she blamed circumstance completely and recalled far more vividly her mother collecting her for her return.

The meals with the Principals were easy within their formality, but Annie never felt entirely the same with Miss Snoek, the kinship had gone... she knew there was a resentment behind the small eyes she had not seen before.

The starkness of her unloved state had blazed too bright that one moment. Annie, who liked to admire, could admire no more.

But time with them was limited. She was off to the Haverschmidts at their cottage by the Zuider Zee.

The stations that Annie changed at, like the trains themselves, decreased in size and importance as she journeyed northwards. The last train was like a tram, it ran along the shore line, sometimes through water.

At last her station appeared, a mere platform built of railway sleepers. She got out expecting to see Margo and Frank, but waiting eagerly was Heer Haverschmidt. His courtly anxiety for her needs, his beaming smile, his faint shyness made her heart beat faster and unconsciously her eyelashes fluttered.

He was, without doubt, the most attractive man she knew. He tucked her arm beneath his own and they set off along the sandy track towards the village: her small trunk was being wheeled by a boy behind them.

The high street comprised the town and at each end there was a church, each boasted a tower, one surmounted by a cock on a weather vane which was the Protestant church. The other was surmounted by a cross... this was the Roman Catholic.

Each laid the claim to direct contact with Heaven, each laid claims by its doctrines to lead the inhabitants there. It was, thought Annie, typical that the Protestants had a weather vane - their religion always held hands with usefulness and industry.

Both churches where built of fine weathered brick, the majority of the houses between were of wood. The paint glinted in the sunlight, the paths were swept and the cleanliness and order was thrust forward so prominently as to be almost ungracious.

Yet she noticed that the people were friendly, the men paused momentarily and removed their pipes to mutter a greeting, the women smiled from the starched fences of their caps and collars. They obviously knew Francois and respected him.

He led the way to a small house of green painted boards with white window and red and white quartered shutters. The small garden was enclosed by white palings. It contained patches of colour and a few apple trees and remarked Annie to herself, "No plan."

But she reminded herself that she was on holiday and there was no need to rearrange anything.

The door opened and out bounded Frank who seized her hand.

Margo followed at a more sedate pace, Mevrouw Haverschmidt hovered behind.

Instantly, there was easy peace and the days passed languorously but very quickly. The days were spent walking the dunes and every warm day was spent swimming. For bathing the two men erected a tent in which to change, the men using it first, they braved the water while the ladies changed into their serge costumes with collars, puffed sleeves and pantaloons.

It was here that Annie learnt to swim a cautious and demure breast-stroke. In spite of changing immediately afterwards into their dresses and wearing large hats and using parasols their faces and forearms became tanned which distressed them.

Frequently before supper Francois would take Annie for a walk to the dunes, or the length of the village.

She listened to his reminiscence, his early lonely days in a country parish amidst a hard peasantry. She heard of his quarrels and misunderstandings with elders who questioned his beliefs. This interested her there was a human element she could understand.

When he talked lengthily of his theories of the Resurrection and his doubts of Virgin Birth, she was often bored, but she listened. She understood well why the family refused to, they had lived so long with his scepticism about the gospels. It had made their place in an orthodox society difficult, they, like him, were regarded with some suspicion. She listened because she loved him, it was a daughterly affection and when she had enough, or even more when she thought he had dwelt sufficiently long on the subject for his own good she would divert his attention.

She had learnt that to point out flowers was useless, even the landscape eluded his attention, but people and houses invariable magnetised his attention.

One evening after supper, Annie wandered alone on the beach. It had been a hot day and there was an almost phosphorescent sparkle in the sea.

It was to her a miracle. Then, she mused, the whole of life is a miracle, a huge enigma. Abstractions were not the highest point of her sagacity and her thoughts wandered to Love, of God, of Man and it led her very quickly to think about her mother. There was her example... she had to look no further.

Her hardships far outpassed her friend's but she had believed much more. She had lived in the present and planned for the future as best she could. Haverschmidt looked back, to the golden youth of his student days, the days of promise and nothing seemed to fulfil the dream of that time.

His belief was teased again and again by the scalpel of his intellect, he cut and pared and cut again, never seeing that he left his faith not just diminished but scarred with strange tissue.

Suddenly she laughed for she saw his kind as a Dutch garden, either too formal and regimented, or without design. "Just another enigma" she said to herself and gave herself up to the soft warm luxury of the evening.

Indoors, Francois talked with his wife and Margo and Annie. They had seen the almost abrupt assumption of maturity and, now they saw, beneath the surface sweetness, a hint, not just of authority, but of power.

It was latent, but they all agreed that it was there. It was Mevrouw Haverschmidt who guessed that his veiled potency had been aroused by a man. She felt a slight jealousy on behalf of her daughter at present it was lacking.

As this idyll by the sea was closing Annie found herself confiding thoughts she had barely entertained by herself. She talked of the heavy list towards masculinity in the arrangement of the world's order.

She said she had discovered that women were exploited and seeing the past anew, she cited her mother's case and, now, her own. Women had so little choice and too often no education.

These new ideas were received heartily and they warmed Haverschmidt's heart and her expounded further upon them. Feminine rights was another of his revolutionary steeds, but he ended very abruptly by saying, "Women, though, have always the upper hand, never forget it. Emotionally you are superior to men. So, in truth, we are your slaves."

"That is all very well if one belongs to a certain class and have security, but it is not true the moment a woman is poor."

Her unusual vehemence made him look at her. The tall girl glowed as he had never seen her before. It was not like her, he stretched out his hand,

"Don't spoil a happy, happy holiday with anger and passion."

She loved the touch of his hand, but she relinquished it

immediately and laughed, "There, you've proved my point. Men won't let women be themselves... always their picture of them."

"But it is so beautiful a picture."

The last meal was eaten under the big oil lamp. Mevrouw Haverschmidt was virtually back in Schiedam, household duties and prospects there already claimed her.

Frank was dreading school and Margo did not want to leave this quiet haven.

Francois was beginning to brace himself for another winter of turmoil. But he also knew that it would be punctuated by the praise and acclamation he received at his readings which were so popular and the source of his greatest happiness.

While they talked Francois, sitting on the sofa, put his arms about Margo. As she saw Margo nestle against her father's shoulder Annie felt a javelin of desire pierce her. The pain was dowsed as the wound was made and no one would ever have known the emotion that had thundered and roared behind the calm face bent over some embroidery.

Many decades later she said, I never knew what it was that I wanted, I think it was the affection of a father, the touch that I lost so early in my life. At the time she never asked any questions, she was of her age and some things were never asked.

School again and it seemed to Annie that she was wool in a weaving frame, flip, flop went the loom, the correct thing was done at the correct time and gradually the pattern emerged.

She was, now experienced... the preparation no longer took so long, the dread of appearing before a class had disappeared.

Life was easier and because it was easier it no longer flew by so quickly, even though every moment was occupied.

Often in her room she found herself thinking much more of her sister Edith and Grandma. She even wondered what was happening to William in Australia. She wrote more letters and gladly, even greedily, sought out and devoured those to her. She loved news of Crosland Moor, even though Edith hardly mentioned the school.

This she knew was because Edith did not like it. She loved neither her subjects nor her pupils sufficiently, so it was a long toil. Annie found it difficult to understand for Edith never had any trouble at keeping order. She had a caustic tongue which she never hesitated to use.

Annie wanted to rescue her, bring her to Holland, see more of the world, but she knew that Edith would never leave her grandmother. Therefore all plans had to be delayed.

In Edith's letters she read much more of bread-making and pickling ham. She heard of the cousins and their meetings. She knew how heavy the shopping baskets were when they toiled up the hill from the weekly foray for provisions.

Sometimes, the humour of the West Riding came though and Holland seemed suddenly very staid and predictable as it was flat. Yet as she looked up from her letter she remembered the murky obscure light of Yorkshire, the weeks when the sun was rarely seen and when it appeared it was filtered by smoke.

Here in her white room she had no need to look further to appreciate the difference in the quality of light, it fell with such clarity one almost expected a clatter. In Milnsbridge there was a muffled quality.

Annie did not appreciate painters, but she did love light and she loved cleanliness, she still rejoiced that lace curtains stayed white and crisp so long. In Wakefield the curtains acquired too swiftly a dirty stiffness that scratched the hand and always had a sooty smell.

As so often happens, when she was bemoaning the predictability of life, she found a letter not from England, but from Leiden and it had a crest on the envelope. For a moment she was mystified, but as she opened it remembered the Jonkheer.

The letter made her blush. It was a declaration of love. He wished to see her. She was flattered and the thought of the dance made her smile, and though the notion of resuming his acquaintance was very attractive, she wished that it could be untrammelled by love. At moments she dreamed of being his wife, the position, the wealth, the security had great lustre for her, but she knew that she did not love him.

There were two portraits in her mind... one was of a handsome young man, fair, tall and excitable. He had an easy confidence. The other was the mature figure of Francois Haverschmidt. The broad brow, the square face and often troubled eyes made Annie's heart beat faster.

She wrote a letter declining a meeting. She had not reckoned on his persistence, another letter came, its ardour embarrassed her but she replied. The letters ceased. This was a relief, but so inconsistent is human nature that she did not rejoice but became resentful.

It was, so she argued, for the lady to end a correspondence and he owed her a letter. At the same time she thought that she was aware of a change in attitude of Miss Lange and Miss Snoek.

They had been undisguised in their welcome, but now there was a wariness even a certain vigilance. For a fortnight she felt under surveillance and she could not think what it was. Her lessons were going well, the sewing even better.

One evening as she came down the stairs, the salon door opened and Miss Snoek stood there watching. Annie smiled and the return was frosty, she seemed to be looking at Annie's hand.

"Miss Taylor, would you please come in."

Annie felt alarm. Something must be amiss. Though in one respect she would be glad to have the dread revealed, yet there was a desire to ignore such things, whatever it might be. As soon as she entered the room she saw the lamp on the table and within the halo of its light a small pile of letter.

The envelopes were of pale thick grey paper, Jan's paper. Miss Lange sat in her chair, she indicated another to Annie. As she took it she remembered her mother's works, "He who fires first has the advantage."

But what was she to say, then she pointed to the envelopes, "So that is why I have had no reply to my letter."

Miss Lange was taken aback, but replied: "Precisely."

Annie was suddenly very angered, "I see that you have opened them. I have found Holland a very honest country, I am surprised. In England to tamper with the post is a very great offence."

Miss Snoek fussed forward. "We had to do it for the sake of the respectability of our school ... and for you."

Annie noted the afterthought. Miss Lange looked with her grave, grey eyes at Annie, Annie's estimate, in spite of her anger, grew, for without agitation, or emotion she said,

"I opened them. I did not like doing it, but duties make strange demands. May I say that I hold you entirely blameless, even though I have not seen your side of the correspondence."

The remembrance of the fortnight of suspicion made the young face imperiously blank, her snub nose rose and she clenched her fist she said,

"I am above suspicion, Miss Lange, in the whole of this affair.

You knew what happened from the very first and now, having read the letter you know more than I. I wish," she hesitated, but decided to say it, "that you had consulted me. I resent my letters being opened."

Miss Lange took them up and very gently placed them in Annie's hand,

"I am sorry, very sorry, they are yours."

"No," replied Annie, "they are public property. They have been opened and read. They are no longer mine. I will not have them."

She pushed them back into the pool of light.

Miss Snoek came forward. "But, Miss Taylor, you must have encouraged this attachment."

Annie ignored the remark and turned back to Miss Lange.

"I was glad that the correspondence had ceased. Now, I find that it had not. I am at a loss what to do. You have made me seem cruel and indifferent. What have you done and what will you do? We all seem cruel."

Annie's resolution was breaking and her chin began to quiver. Her she was diverted from emotion by admiration for Miss Lange.

"I see that I have made a most terrible mistake. I must see the Jonkheer myself."

"Yes, we must," said Miss Snoek," it is all very unfortunate. How can a young man of his position have come to regard you?"

Annie was stung and deeply. "Kings have been known to marry beggar maids and I am no beggar, Miss Snoek."

"Quite, quite, Miss Taylor. That has nothing to do with the case." Miss Lange frowned at her partner.

"But, my dear, we now have to clear this sorry matter up. Would you like us to see the Jonkheer – after all – we are in loco parentis?"

Had she used the singular pronoun Annie would have agreed, but she would not countenance Miss Snoek having anything to do with this personal matter. She felt a sense of relief that the blame had been implied at the beginning was, now, removed, even in their camp.

But she did not know what next to do. Only one factor stood out, she did not want Jan Bentinck to be hurt any longer."

"Give me until tomorrow."

Again Miss Snoek interfered,

"But we must act quickly. Delay will be unkind."

"You, Miss Snoek, have caused the delay. One night will make no difference."

She rose. Miss Lange again tendered the letters. Now all was calmer, the temptation of drama beckoned Annie and she followed.

"They have been tampered with. I make no claim on them." She left the room.

She ran upstairs leapt on her bed and cried and longed for her mother. She stayed late in her room and Fraulein Vogel brought her some tea. Annie kept her counsel and feigned a headache.

Annie was surprised that in this tiny world a secret could be hidden, everything usually seemed so open... rumours were rife over much smaller trifles. Surprisingly, Annie slept very well, but she awoke, like a person bereaved with the lull in emotions rudely shattered by the knowledge of an evil to be borne.

She was glad that the suspicion was over, but that Miss Snoek had suggested her unfit to marry above her rank still annoyed her. The interview had two results that were to be with Annie the rest of her life, a distrust of fussy spinsters and anger if ever a letter addressed to her was opened, even if inadvertently.

She washed, dressed and brushed her hair before the mirror and as she did so she knew who was to see Jan, it was not Miss Lange, certainly not Miss Snoek, it was to be Margo's father.

During the break mid-morning, Annie wandered into the garden. She was the only one that did this, it was accounted as a peculiar English whim, a desire like cold baths, for fresh air. It was solitude Annie wanted most.

The garden was beginning to show autumn and it hinted sadness rather than proclaimed it. It suited her mood. She was not sad, she was deeply perturbed and her unease was linked with The Merchant of Venice which she was reading with her class.

It had suddenly struck her that Portia was only able to show her ability and intellect when she masqueraded as a man. Why should that be? She usually loved her womanhood, but now she felt trapped by it. She considered herself well able to conduct an interview with Jan, but she was treated as if she were in a convent.

She resented, as she had not before, her lack of freedom. She was still very angered that her letters had been intercepted. This made her feel unsafe. In her innermost heart she did not wish Heer

Haverschmidt to intervene, but she knew it was a good compromise for she did not wish to Principals to do it.

Also she wished very much to see Heer Haverschmidt. But her thoughts reverted to the monstrous way women were treated, even by women. Aloud to the Michaelmas daisies she said,

"We are not foolish creatures at the mercy of ourselves and others."

After lunch she went in to see the Principals. The letters were out on the table again. Miss Lange looked up and smiled but it was obvious that she was troubled. This predicament had never occurred before.

She had to prevent girls becoming entangled with scheming men, especially if they were wealthy, but a member of her staff had never been involved before. The trouble was that Miss Taylor was too pretty was the opinion she held, but as Annie entered, she changed the adjective and replaced it with noble.

Annie had entered with her back straight, she had hesitated only momentarily before seating herself, and then after a small pause had said: "I have decided that Heer Haverschmidt must be consulted and that after we have seen him that he approaches the Johkheer."

"Ought we to trouble the dominie, he is a very busy man," interposed Miss Snoek immediately.

"Then I shall have to do it myself."

Miss Lange after a moment's thought said,

"That is an excellent solution which we should have thought of before. I will write to him immediately."

"You need not. I have already done so," and from the book she carried Annie produced a letter which Miss Lange's shrewd eyes saw was already sealed.

Next day, Heer Haverschmidt was with them. He brought into the school the outside world with him. When Annie came into the salon he stood up, caught her in his arms, lifted her off her feet and kissed her. Only then did tears start into her eyes.

He laughed and said: "What's all this you are up to? Undermining the aristocracy of Holland? We haven't as many to play about with as you in England."

The Principals looked shocked not only at the sentiments expressed, but at his easy intimacy. Then he asked in a most courtly manner that he might see Annie alone. The ladies departed.

Annie was surprised at how very glad she was to see him and took his hand. The whole affair tumbled out when she began to speak and it all seemed to regain its rightful proportions in his presence.

"You never told me about this when we were by the sea."

"No, it did not seem very important then. It only began when I received the letter. He says that he is in love with me. I replied cautiously. I am not in love with him, but I did not want to hurt him.

"I thought it was all over, then I discovered that Miss Lange and Miss Snoek had opened them. There they are." She pointed to the envelopes on the table.

He looked at them. "Have you read them?"

"No, and as they have been read I do not wish to. I think that they have been very dishonourable. I have not forgiven them yet."

Francois looked at her defiant face, it was a mask and he though, what a pity it all was, for she would make a good aristocrat.

"May I read them?"

"Certainly."

He waited for her to hand them to him. She remained motionless. This interested him.

"Will you hand them to me?"

"No. I will not touch them."

He thought that either she was in love with him, or these spinsterly women had deeply affronted her. The prurience of those whose chastity was forced upon them by their lack of charm was well known to him, but it still never ceased to surprise him.

He got up and began to read. Annie rose and looked out into "her" garden. Seriousness and sadness had seized her again, but she turned when he began to laugh.

"Well, my dear, you certainly turned his head, but it still does not make him turn a very good phrase. He's really not very bright."

Annie smiled and agreed. She again had the two pictures, the charming and handsome young man who danced so well and the man before her. She wanted someone like Heer Haverschmidt, a mixture of good looks, great intelligence and feeling. Again he laughed. When he had finished he said,

"What a storm in a glass of cold water."

Annie smiled, "We say a storm in a tea-cup, and I think that is more appropriate where these old ladies are concerned."

He was glad to see her smile and the mask rippled and fled from the lake of her soft features which reflected the sun, the clouds of her moods.

"You are quite certain you do not wish to read these letters?"

"Quite sure. If they amuse you, they would amuse me. I don't want to laugh at the poor young man. But much more I am angered that my letters have been read. Do they think me a ...," she hesitated for the word, "a strumpet."

"No, no, my dear. It is just that girls' schools have to be like Caesar's wife, above suspicion."

"I know. I know. But I feel affronted."

He was now convinced that the emotion was hurt and not love that motivated her and he thought diversion was needed.

"Let's go out for lunch. Fetch Margo, she must chaperone us or there will be another scandal." He thought it very funny. Annie thought it too near the truth.

"Do you think we ought?"

"I am sure we ought."

As Annie went to find Margo she thought how easy life was for a man. He is life's natural master – the inheritor of the earth.

The Principals were recalled, in minutes they were both mollified and relieved. Haverschmidt promised to deal with the young man, even the outing was approved and Annie and Margo appeared at the door in hats and capes.

They walked down Brestraat, the street forbidden to the girls, either individually or in groups - the Student Club was there. Annie was a little disconcerted, fearing that they might encounter Jan Bentinck.

Heer Haverschmidt with a girl on each arm was oblivious of this, he was elated. This was, for him the city of dreams still, it held all the glory of his youth, it held still hopes, some achieved, some unfulfilled, but nonetheless hopes.

It revived memories and he expatiated on them. They turned into the Rapenburg with its wide canal and 17th century houses.

"Where are you taking us, Father?"

"To the Doelen, my dear."

"Oh, how extravagant."

"It is not everyday that I am in Leiden and even rarer when I have two pretty girls with me."

They came to the chaste, yet baroque, building with its small double flight of steps. He ushered them in to a hushed atmosphere of luxury. Not only the staff but the very rooms seemed to bend with compliance to execute their needs.

A porter assisted the ladies and took their capes to a closet. Before a mirror discreetly hidden by the stairs, they arranged their hair.

They went into a panelled room with small tables where the silver gleamed in the light reflecting from the white starched linen. There were candlesticks on each table and what Annie had never seen before, pink shades to each candle.

The place glowed with the well being of a spoilt Persian cat, soft, warm and certain of itself, its purpose purely sensual. Annie unfurled like a rose in warmth. Their meal was less heavy than an English one, but less sprightly than a French one.

Annie noted everything. It was a welcome change to the bare boarded floor of the dining hall, the water jugs and dull cutlery.

Haverschmidt noted the unfolding of spirit and he decided that Annie had been long enough in an academic establishment. She needed a wider and a more elegant world. But where was that to be found for a poor young woman?

A respectable woman had no choice but to teach, but he saw her suddenly as the governess in a large household, that would be an improvement. The alternative was continuance at the Hooigracht until her youth had gone.

As he smoked his cigar he listened to the girls' chatter, it was innocent, for that he rejoiced, but it was also confined, their knowledge was so constricted. At last it was time to go and he escorted the girls back to the school and then with swift determination strode back to the Breestraat where he found the lodgings of young Bentinck.

He found the Jonkjeer jacketless with a heap of books by his chair, they looked unread. After an introduction he said that he was Annie's guardian. He was perturbed by the letters, as indeed she was herself, he explained.

The young man was instantly apologetic and Haverschmidt judged him as generous, impulsive and very immature. He appealed to the young man's chivalry, he explained her embarrassment and he even called his reckless gift of the flowers as irresponsible.

"We have made a world where we must protect women. Their virtues and reputations are of infinite value and we must value them. Besides, Miss Taylor is of that unfortunate rank that must earn her living, so she deserves our even greater respect and regard."

Jan, thoroughly uneasy, saw Heer Haverschmidt down the stairs and out into the street. He went back to his room and acting entirely according to his nature wrote a letter to Annie apologizing, but declaring his love and another to the Principals claiming all blame and announcing the cessation of the correspondence.

It was Haverschmidt who thought more, as he travelled back on the train. He thought of Annie, even more he thought of women and their strange predicament. He saw talents trapped and lives that could, so easily, be wasted.

There was no sphere for them beyond marriage and domestic duties and even that was governed largely by money. He sighed for he saw that it was like so much else in the structure of life at that moment which was monstrously unfair.

It needed a campaign and he was unwilling to undertake any more. He was already in the midst of challenges and crusades some of which he was winning, some losing. His nature made him consider the losses more than the gains.

In the evening, he talked of it with his wife. He sighed and predicted a bleak future for Annie. Mevrouw Haverschmidt looked up, "You underestimate women, my dear, and you particularly underestimate Annie. We must do something... that is true. We must find her a place as governess with a really happy family where she will be one of them and meet others. Don't despair. I would never, never despair for Annie."

The load seemed lifted from his shoulders, it was no longer his responsibility. There were many more perplexities in the labyrinth of Schiedam's politics – some of his own making. For he was burdened with a zeal for reform and what made it more difficult was his keen sensibility.

Loved by many, yet he was suspected by others, even feared as a disseminator of dangerous dissensions in matters of faith. Often misunderstood, more frequently misquoted, his life was full of hazards.

Chapter 21

The Theatre Visit

When the east wind blew over the Lowlands and the ice was forming, then thawing and growing again, so everyone complained as wrapped and hunched they hurried about their business, to shops, to lecture halls, to schools.

Leiden seemed to catch the wind that blew across the meadows and then divert it into new channels. Every street became a tunnel and the alleyways became funnels for cold, corners became places of gusty fury where winds met.

The herons lost some of their timidity and close to human traffic picked greyly on the shallow dykes between the houses, lifting their long legs in an elegant and spinsterly fashion searching for food... they gained a temporary trust and rarely rose to flight with that torpid effortless movement.

All Holland, man, beast, bird seemed to be sheltering from the wind that swept the open sky and shrivelled all in its path below.

Annie looked into her garden, it was grey, brown grey, green grey, a drabness covered all. She felt forced to find colour and a prophecy of spring. Out in the garden by the wall she searched among the rounded leaves for at least one violet - she found three almost stepping on them.

She even found three stunted snowdrops and covered them with some dead fern leaves. She pulled her shawl closer about her and though of the wind high up on Crosland Moor. There it would not scream at sharp corners and ooze down roadways as it did in this "water-cold" as they called it, but it would buffet and shake.

She had a vivid feeling for her grandmother. She thought of her hunching her shoulders, much against her will, pulling her shawl around her shoulders as she pattered to the larder busily making food to keep out the cold.

Back in her room, Annie put the three violets in a small inkwell. She thought of Edith, she was glad that she was there with Grandma. She thought of the relationship between the two, it was so much greater than her had been.

She knew that it had been "all mother with me."

All day long her grandmother kept coming to her mind. She remembered her sharp and shrewd aphorisms and wise saws that had so annoyed her as she was growing up. She looked at her hands and saw that they were her grandmothers, practical hands, not slim and long like her mother's.

At night before she slept she thought of the bravery of the old lady, it had always impressed her. She remembered her stoicism when their son had died and she loved her because she had so loved her daughter-in-law. Only this night did Annie realise that it was the old lady's presence that had enabled the family to stay together.

Momentarily, she thought of her adoption by the Nashes, but quickly shut it away. She thought how strange it was that only now, did she begin to appreciate her grandmother's valour. It had carried her though as she upheld her daughter-in-law as she had flagged beneath sickness at the prison and eventually died. She must, Annie thought, have been weary, but she never let it be seen. She began to marvel at her fortitude.

Two days later she found in her pigeon hole an English letter with a thick black border and Edith's handwriting. Instantly she knew. She ran up to her room with the letter, still she did not open it, but looked at the postmark and date, her chin quivered. At last she slit the envelope and read that Grandma had caught a cold. It seemed no worse than any other, but she had gone to bed, which was unusual. Next day, she had told Edith that she would stay there, but there we no need for her to remain at home.

Cousin Polly had taken her meals and Edith had taken her tea. That night she had kissed Edith as she always did but clung to her hand and said,

"My little Edith, you're a good, good lassie." She had fallen asleep and never woken.

Annie's feelings gushed forth for Grandma and still more for her sister who had borne it all alone. She thought of the funeral, she must get leave to return, but she read on.

"Cousin Polly and I have delayed letting you know to save you the cost of a sad journey, the funeral was this afternoon at Armitage Bridge. Grandma is buried there with Grandpa. Now, Annie, think of me as I know you always do."

Annie, when she told the Principals her news, was excused

classes the rest of the day and she kept to her room. After the first shock she found that her grief reverted to her mother and then her tears fell faster.

It was Fraulein Vogel who broke the unhappy spell and who made her talk of her grandmother. Soon Annie was telling her of the tall old lady with a ramrod back who proffered criticism without hesitation. Annie laughed when she recalled returned from school when she was about fifteen tired and drooping and was greeted with,

"Well, young woman. Your nose came round the corner five minutes before the rest. Have you no shoulders?"

Next day, she went into class wearing the statutory black which she hated. She wore white lace cuffs and a collar and as she had dressed it reminded her of Grandma's clothes. She felt that the mantle of another generation had fallen upon her, characteristics overlapping the generations like tiles on a roof.

It was Mientje, the maid, who first broke the news upon the school of Gooie Mie. A poor woman, she had lived not far away. She had a reputation for charity to those poorer than herself.

She had been arrested and bodies had been found in shallow graves. That a murder had been committed, and so close, sent a frisson of fear and fascination down all their backs. The whole basis of school with its lessons seemed suddenly flimsy, insubstantial.

The girls could talk of nothing else. Mientje became overnight a personality. She had spoken to the murderess. She had known one of the victims who had disappeared. She relished her position and in spite of reprimands was often to be seen talking to the girls.

Even in the Common Room it became an obsession and Annie and Fraulein Vogel resolved to dispel it from their minds. They decided to put on an entertainment. It was to be a play-reading of *Macbeth* with musical interludes.

They considered that this was suitable while murder was so much in their minds. But it was be exalted by poetry. The offers to be witches came from half the school. Annie chose Annette for Lady Macbeth and from her reading Annie had a vision of a cold and deadly woman that was never supplanted from her mind.

The need of a man for Macbeth and Banquo was evident from the start and Miss Lange had a couple of suitably histrionic students of theology imported. The rehearsals took every moment that was free in their days and the staff were glad to see the enthusiasm for the ghoulish murders of another street were greatly diminished.

Leiden as a whole continued to relish the macabre affair. Annie was too busy to think of the real bloody deeds, but she was also aware that having lived by a prison so long, she never regarded criminals as anything other than humans like herself. They might do monstrous things but they were not monsters.

At last the night of the reading was there. The room had been carefully prepared, the actors were ranged round a table, it was one step above the level of the room. Two oil lamps on the standards shone down on the little company, the rest of the room was dimness.

At the last moment Annie had frantically desired a Scottish atmosphere. She draped her tartan rug over the table and she had replaced a Dutch picture of a street scene with one of Highland cattle. She discovered that no one noticed her handiwork, but it pleased her. Annie introduced the play - she outlined it so that the young ones might understand something. She spoke of the morality, the temptation of power... and power often meant money. The unspoken allusion to Gooie Mie was not missed.

The play had been cut, but from the beginning a spell fell upon the school. The players gained a momentum, the work of rehearsals had been absorbed and the intensity and the feeling grew. There was not a cough, not a movement.

The Divinity student spoke with a new majesty and warmed and then glowed in his part. Annette reached new peaks in her portrayal and all disbelief in the girls playing men's parts was suspended. When Lady Macbeth walked in her sleep there was an intake of breath. The last scene secured all the honours for Macbeth, a good man poisoned by ambition, whose valour never failed him.

When the play ended there was a long pause. For a second Annie thought it had been a failure, then the clapping began. It ended when Miss Lange rose to make a speech. A wise woman, she said that she had intended pointing the principle of the story, but there was no need.

"Macbeth may have murdered sleep for himself, but he has not for you girls."

It had murdered sleep for Annie though, words, phrases slipped into her mind, sometimes strung themselves into sentences. The magic of the rhythm held her. She was almost dazed as she took part in the little party the Principals gave the actors.

Next day was the funeral of Gooie Mie's 16 victims. It seemed that Holland had converged upon Leiden. Miss Lange and Miss Snoek had been deeply perplexed as to how far they could allow the girls to take part in this spectacle.

The decision had, to an extent, been removed from their hands when the Burgomaster invited the school to watch the procession from the Stadhuis.

This would, at least remove them from contact with the sightseers gathered in the streets. The school marched in an orderly file to the processional route. They were all astounded to see the hundreds of people gathered and Miss Lange was anxious to see that none of the girls bought the crudely produced broadsheets which were being hawked.

At last they climbed the steps and into the great black and white marble flagged hall. Armour hung on the wall and a large picture of the Burgomaster appealing vigorously and dramatically to the women when they implored him to break the siege during the Spanish Rule.

Annie still full of *Macbeth* and always highly romantic thought, that is real history, not like this miserable Gooie Mie passing across life's stage, soon to be forgotten. She was not correct.

They were all led up a staircase to another committee room where three long windows looked down into the street. The children were, at first, hushed as they waited. Gradually the awe and novelty wore off, they looked at the portraits made fun of them and then began to speculate whether Gooie Mie would be present at this mass funeral.

Miss Lange and Miss Snoek began to despair of the whole venture when a small girl asked if the murderess would be in a cage. Miss Lange looked very distressed but moved swiftly to the large chair at the head of the table and standing by it commanded their attention.

She told them that this was a solemn occasion… they were in a privileged position. They were not like the common people in the streets witnessing a spectacle. As they came they must have seen that some were drunk, they were to remember the people poorer than themselves, people who sought work in the cities, like the victims they were about to see. An apparently good woman had poisoned them.

It was all a story of the sadness of evil in human nature and, as they had seen last night, it appeared in all classes. They were there to learn the importance of true moral values, the necessity of thrift... the need of people, like themselves to help others who were in need. Goodness had to shine in the work. If it did not, then civilization would die.

Annie listened and slowly her elation still present from the surging majesty of Shakespeare's language dissipated and she felt that she had come to earth. She had listened because she felt that it had been her mother speaking and she admired Miss Lange more than ever before.

She realised that she knew more of life than she had given her credit for, also she had high ideals.

The procession came, first there were mounted police and a great stillness fell upon the crowd, the sight of the nodding plumes on the horses and corners of the hearses struck everyone with a sharp poignancy.

It was a curious, ghastly show of pomp... it was a celebration of death. Each hearse seemed a drum beat and sent an echo into every soul. At last, the final hearse rumbled by and there was no movement from the crowd.

Then they moved quietly and quickly. When the girls congregated in the hall below and thanks and curtsies were made to the Burgomaster, they were all surprised to find the streets, so packed minutes before, nearly deserted.

All one saw were black clad people disappearing into door ways down side streets. The school walked back hushed and to Annie's surprise it lasted until bedtime. When she, herself, was in bed she thought of the strange day and she came to the conclusion that it had been mournful without being majestic and she found the poetry of Macbeth coming into her mind and utterly obliterating the recent real murders. She was not sorry.

Weeks later, when a late spring was trying to reveal itself, Annie saw a billposter proclaiming that an English company was performing six plays at the Schouwbourg in Den Haag.

The idea of seeing an English play thrilled her - the notion of taking the upper school pleased her even more.

When Annie mentioned the scheme to Miss Lange, it had instant approval. Annie pondered on the difference between English and Dutch Puritanism. She could think easily of Wakefield families who disapproved of the theatre and would not allow their children near such "a sink of iniquity". But here no one demurred. It was decided that they should see *Romeo and Juliet*.

The day of the outing came. Party dresses were worn and they looked gay and slightly incongruous beneath their warm coats as they set out for the train. It was not Annie's first visit to the Residency, it was the first where the beauty of the streets, the Bos really impressed her. She noted the elegance of the buildings around the Binnenhof and she, now, knew enough history for the place to leap alive for her.

She thought Lange Voorhout the loveliest square she had ever seen. The classical houses, the trees in the square and at one end the little palace. She loved it instantly. It was exactly as she had imagined it would be and to her joy the men and women were correctly and smartly dressed who strolled beneath the trees.

The theatre was on the edge of the wood, it was a chaste self-confident building. It had none of the slight vulgarity of Wakefield's theatre. Annie saw why theatres were more acceptable.

Inside the hats, coats, capes were all discarded and taken in at the garde robe. Here there were mirrors for everyone to adjust their dresses and Annie, removing her hat, lifted her curls with the hat pin as did the others.

When they were all ready they went out into the foyer. Here Annie's eyes were almost assaulted by the quiet splendour of the dresses and the flash of jewels – she had forgotten that she was in the land of diamonds.

They took their seats and Annie thought how different it was to the bundling of one coat beneath the seat as one did in Wakefield and even Leeds.

When the curtain rose upon Verona then her excitement ceased. The scenery sometimes flapped, the costumes were worn and Romeo and his Juliet were elderly. Annie repressed a smile when Romeo running in the market place showed a distinct bulge and wobble beneath his doublet.

When he spoke she forgot his fifty hectic years, he was able to sound young. There was a gasp, though, when Juliet caught the lace of the sleeve on the carving of a chair, the solid medievalism of the furniture remained firm, the worn lace ripped and then fell to dangle in a graceless bundle. Juliet's rouged pout was momentary but apparent.

All illusion was, for Annie, lost, still more when the plump little lady running from her nurse tripped over the carpet, regained balance physically but never again artistically. The girls sat mute, containing their laughter, often looking down for everything that now happened added to their mirth.

Annie was impressed by the stolidity of the audience, they had come to be improved and informed and their determination was not to be deflected. This was not true of the school and two little girls became almost hysterical in their laughter, so much so that Annie rose and led the two offenders out.

The manager in the foyer looked furious and was about to speak, but Annie spoke first, and in English. She apologised and then said with a large smile, "We, in England, never care for mutton dressed as lamb."

The little girls were still awaiting a reprimand, they still giggled but after apprehensive silences. They crossed the road into the wood and sat on the first seat they came to, then Annie laughed, pent up humour poured out and she laughed until she held her sides and the little girls rolled in the grass.

They were all abandoned in an ecstasy of relief and when the paroxysms died Annie told them to tidy themselves and they would go into the town.

They went from shop to shop, Annie had never seen such jewellers and furriers, it was a world of luxury making Leiden seen very tame. They went into the Passage, an arcade, where the girls found a toy and souvenir shop much more to their taste. Annie lingered by the large fashionable shop, La Bonneterie. She looked very carefully at the latest modes from Paris. There was still time, so she led them to a café where a quartet played and there they drank tea and ate moerkops. While they sat there Annie said: "It will, now, be your turn to act. When we go back to the others I shall be very serious and you must look extremely subdued." They agreed with great gratitude.

When the audience came out the Principals hurried over to

Annie, scolded the girls and sympathised with Annie for her sacrifice. Annie demurred a little. She said nothing of the play, for it was obvious that the actors had finally convinced them all.

Her own reactions were that she had enjoyed The Hague much more, its cosmopolitanism had impressed her. This was heightened when suddenly there was a clatter, a large carriage with four horses rolled by with two outriders, hats had been raised and a furtive cheer, Annie had seen a real King and Queen for the first time.

This glimpse eclipsed the play in the minds of all the loyal little Netherlanders. Annie was aware of the romance of someone exalted and remote passing at such close quarters, and the receding jingle enhanced the thought.

In Leiden books, learning, lessons enmeshed them all again. One night Annie decided to read Romeo and Juliet. She read and the actors from the English company never interposed themselves between her and the written word.

She was swept on. Very late, she finished and with a sigh she put down the book. Then aloud she said: "I would like to be in love."

From the moment of her recognition of this desire, the idea of love would without warning sweep over her. It was something new, yet even as she longed to be in love, she was aware that she stood before an abyss of ignorance, here was a mystery and a frightening one.

Love had a physical side as well and what that was she a little more than half-suspected, but did not know. There was no one she could ask. "If only Mother was still living", she said to herself. However, she hesitated there and asked another question of herself, "Could I have raised the subject with her?"

She did not know the answer. She did know that her parents had been in love, as a child she had sensed it and her mother in widowhood had spoken of it.

The term went on, "the daily round the common task". She did not agree with the next line of the hymn, "Will furnish all we need to ask." There was much more in life that Annie wanted, much more to see that she had not seen. Life was full of the unknown.

When term ended with exams the results in English were very gratifying. The Principals were pleased and considered another rise in Annie's salary. It was mooted but like many rewards never put into effect. Had it been Annie's life might have been different.

The summer holiday was spent again with the Haverschmidts by the Zuyder Zee. The same easy routine enfolded them, but Annie was tiring of the familiar. Each morning Francois wrote more stories and often after supper, he read them.

They were happy sentimental recollections of the past, evocations of his childhood. Annie listened and found so much of this Dutch life remembered was the life she understood in Yorkshire, the same but also wholly different. In the afternoons, they walked, when it was warm, they swam.

Annie listened. She listened to Francois' perplexities in the parish, he talked of the committees and how he was baulked frequently. The worst hurt was that his lectures had been boycotted by most of his colleagues. However, as the details of his professional life were disgorged, so the stings faded. He talked, then, on matters of faith. He questioned the miracles, he questioned the Resurrection of Christ. One day Annie was bored, like his wife and Margo, but sarcasm was a weapon she never used.

She looked at him, she looked at the sun sparkling on the sea and her eyes sparkled to match, "All of life is a miracle." He shook his head.

Annie continued: "There are so many wonders. I can easily accept a few more from Jesus quite easily. Why don't you forget those stuffy German theologians for a while and see 'the sermons in stones'".

"Oh, you English, you never take anything too seriously. That is why you always compromise and end up with the best of everything."

"That's why we are perfidious Albion," she laughed.

She remembered Annette saying it and the hurt had been very great. Saying it herself was quite another thing.

As they climbed the dune the deep loose sand shifted with every step and a long skirt became a dangerous encumbrance. Francois gave her a hand. As he pulled and she extracted one foot from the deep hole only to feel the other sink deeper, so she felt the warmth of his hand.

It was not a hot palm alone it was the communication of feeling. Quite suddenly as he hauled her Annie was half afraid, would he kiss her?

He felt her alarm, he respected it, and at the top of the dyke he loosed her arm and they walked in silence, then he began to whistle.

Each knew the small whirlpool of emotion they had been in, both removed themselves to ground they considered firmer surer: neither mentioned it to the other. The whistling continued and as they approached the little resort Annie was at pains to make him cease. Particularly she did not wish Mevrouw Haverschmidt to hear because it was a sure sign of distress and it might arouse suspicions which were unnecessary.

There were a few shops selling sweets, tobacco, souvenirs. Annie claimed a need for writing paper, she went in and Francois ceased to whistle. Inside were shelves with ornaments, windmills, paper knives, boxes and spill-holders.

Annie saw a miniature pair of wooden shoes, beautifully carved, with sharp pointed toes and a firmly chiselled design of a garland of flowers. Francois followed her glance saw the little shoes and whilst she bought her paper, he picked them up.

"You would like these wouldn't you?"

The tiny shoes looked smaller in his large hands, "Oh yes." It was uttered with such girlish enthusiasm that Francois was enraptured.

They walked back in silence, but the whistling had ceased. At tea Annie produced them, their significance had become great to her, they represented the moment on the dunes. She had wondered whether to show them. Mevrouw Haverschmidt handled the soft willow wood, she caressed the curves and the carving with her forefinger... praised them.

"You never gave me any like this, Francois."

Annie caught her breath, but smiled when she saw the sly humour of the remark. She looked across at Francois, his wide smile on his wide Dutch mouth made them all happy, it was all guileless and certainly guiltless.

At the end of the time there Annie was put on the train bound for Amsterdam. The city thrilled her, she felt the multiplicity of life there, the interlinking of nationalities and cultures, the wealth, the poverty, the arts and the artisans. She loved to walk in the grachts which she was shown as a visitor, the Prinsen gracht, the Heerengracht impressed her. The charm of Dutch 17th century architecture was never to leave her. She contrasted it with Leeds – the only other city she knew – there was little to compare.

Amsterdam wore its commercialism with a difference, one was monochrome, the other, as behoved its artists, was a masterpiece in dazzling oils.

Here there was a university, art schools, hospitals of renown, merchants and always the sea which came to the very houses, bringing mystery, variety, dirt and cleanliness. She stayed in a new flat near Vondel Park, the front door was reached by the steepest flight of steps.

Rachel Ananas, a Jewess, had been one of Annie's first pupils. She had married a doctor with a practice in the capital. Of the Jewishness of the household she was visiting Annie had given little thought, so when seen it struck her forcibly. The house, unlike most young homes, was most lavishly furnished.

It was fuller than any house Annie had yet seen. She liked it for its luxury, it was a sensual delight compared with the conventional rigors of the Hooigracht. After two days her critical faculty took note of a button too many in the upholstery, a fold too many in the draperies at the window.

A picture on an easel did not, in her eyes, need a shawl hung with artful casualness across one corner. Yet she had to admit that the house had splendour, it was not just pretension, it had beauty. She wondered and wondered then knew where the fault was, it lacked subtlety, it was a display.

Rachel's husband was charmed, or so it seemed by Annie's arrival, Annie failed to understand it, he beamed upon her with dark eyes through pince-nez. His first impression was an urbane jollity, but she learnt that those same eyes could grow darker and deeper with trouble, of his bright intelligence there was no doubt. His practice was good, and growing. It had been bought for him by his father, a diamond merchant.

Every day, immediately after breakfast, the doctor left and the maid from Volendam cleared away. The two women were left with little to do. Letters were written, invitations accepted, or declined. Linen was sorted and the cook interviewed. Annie watched with surprise. She felt no envy, Rachel's life seemed empty. It was Rachel, who was always quick to interpret a look a gesture, who said,

"Annie, I do believe you think that I am wasting my time."

"No, no," said Annie, a little too hurriedly, "but I do compare it with your wonderful essays at school. It seems that your talent is wasted."

"It will, all quite soon, be different. I am going to have a baby."

Rachel talked of the confinement, the plans and Annie was surprised that she had harboured no suspicion of the event and Rachel informed her that these were the good weeks. She had ceased feeling sick and she was not yet heavy. She spoke of it all with great frankness.

Annie looked at the contented girl. She looked beyond at the marble statue of a Greek girl about to step into her bath. She contrasted them, about one there was the almost furtive emotion belonging to the knowledge of something hidden and the statue was cold and still and beautiful.

Annie for a moment preferred the latter, but then while her heart pounded, made the first move to reveal her ignorance.

"Rachel, I do not know fully how babies are created, will you tell me?"

She instantly cast her eyes down on to her embroidery, her heart pounded and she felt oddly humiliated. But it was done. At the same time she wondered if she had been so indelicate she might be asked to leave. Instead, laughter pealed out.

"Oh, Annie, you don't know? And you, always attracting so much attention."

Annie thought that Rachel would not stop laughing, at first perplexed, then she joined in too.

"Well, Annie, shall I tell you?" She pondered a moment, said: "No, I don't think I will. If Nathaniel is in the right mood we will tell you together."

"Oh, but a man."

"My dear, it is something that involves both a man and a woman. I think it best that way. Didn't your mother ever say anything?"

"No. I think she died too soon."

That evening as the women stitched away, the dark young doctor and his pretty wife enlightened Annie. Nathaniel was used to lecturing, he talked dispassionately, delicately and he even made them both laugh.

Annie's thoughts at times panicked and she found looking at the statue restored her to calm. At first it disturbed her that her parents must have done this, it upset her ideal of them. But gradually as the doctor talked her fear flew and she began to feel relief.

Her mind nurtured on Christian symbolism, baptism, confirmation and marriage, felt that this talk was a kind of initiation to life itself. She was amazed that she had lived 23 years knowing portions of all this, but never the whole.

The memory of the statue of the Greek girl with her towel and jar of perfume was to remain with her for a lifetime and she was amazed that it was to stand for purity. When first she had seen it she had thought it immodest.

The days that followed were brighter, gayer and the two young women walked through Amsterdam carefree and very happy. The Markets lured them and the slightly muted colour of them she was to contrast with all other markets she would see, some seemed garish and some dirty.

On the train home to Leiden a young man sitting opposite looked at her, he saw the close moulding of the dark bodice over her bosom and sloping shoulders. She was a mass of gentle curves, the curl of her hair, the roundness of her large eyes, the small but full mouth, she was demurely baroque.

She happened to be the image of the beautiful woman of the day, pink, pretty. Had he read Meredith he might have said, "A rogue in porcelain." He would never have guessed that she was a schoolmistress for there was an absence of angularity.

When she spoke it was very quietly and in faultless Dutch. Her accent was untraceable beyond being that of the upper classes of Holland. Yet when he heard her, her very softness made him wonder if, perhaps, she was French. He thought, too, that her taste in dress and her carriage was Parisian.

Annie never even noticed him. She was thinking of Rachel, the momentous holiday and the baby that was to be born.

It was, though a great surprise when, later in the year she was invited to be present at the baby's circumcision. She was the only Gentile present and the older women were well aware of it, only Rachel and Nathaniel seemed oblivious of it.

Privately Annie thought the custom barbaric and when she questioned Rachel her arguments did not convince her and she did not like to mention it to Nathaniel. She saw that the friendship with Rachel would fade, even with one child she saw that her interest would become entirely absorbed in her family, like so many of her race. It was, however, a little insight that she gained into another section of society which was to last her a lifetime and the Jewish people were always to have her sympathy.

Annie was in her last year at the Hooigracht. She was tired of a school regimen and she had arranged for Edith to take her place.

Chapter 22

Perzik Hof

Everything was ready. All Annie's belongings were piled in the hall. They had been corded by Jan and the carriage had clattered to the door. The three ladies sitting in the salon knew that this was the end of a long and fruitful period of the school's and Annie's life.

The Principals were sorry, even a little sad to see Annie go. They contented themselves that in due time Miss Taylor's sister would be arriving. It was a little joke already that there would be no change of name for the school to get used to.

Miss Snoek was impressed by the Van Harencaspel equipage at the door and seeing it delayed as the boxes were put up on the roof gratified her. The moment of farewell came and Annie dropped a small curtsey and pecked each lady on the cheek.

It was a gesture that put her more firmly than ever in their hearts, it summed up the years spent together, a combination of respect and affection. Annie turned away tearfully, goodbyes always affected her - the sight, however, of Jan and Mientje waiting in the hall upset her even more.

She had a box of fine lace for Mientje and for Jan she had taken her silver crown out of its brooch, had a loop fixed, so that she could hang it from his watch chain. She had a little speech for him about having always a little bit to England about him.

The lace Annie hoped would enliven the caps Mientje wore in the evening. The words came out falteringly. From them she received a bow and a curtsey and the Principals watched more moved than they had expected.

In the carriage Annie sat back, the familiar streets of Leiden were going by and like thousands of students, she knew that it had made her and that a part of it she was taking away in her heart forever.

She knew that she would not be far away, but that she would always be a visitor. She knew that these years had been formative, she had grown up.

The town was soon left behind, two horses made light of the

carriage and after rumbling over bridges they came to high roads across flat fields.

The parting had taken so much of her thoughts that the future had not fully been anticipated: in fact planning ahead was never to be a great quality in her life. This was partly the result of her confidence which, as with so many of her contemporaries, was hidden beneath a sweetness of manner. She had such surety in the classroom that it had spread into much else of her life. She was sanguine.

As they approached Wassenaar, the great beeches rose imposingly and Annie looked out eagerly. She knew the house from her interview, it was large, stately. They turned in at the gates and she saw again the white gazebo, high white and with long sash windows gazing haughtily on to the road.

She had missed seeing it before. They bowled through the shrubberies, these were grounds, not gardens, she saw the house and the parkland stretching behind. As they drew up at the door the children bounded out, the boys led the way, one very lively.

Annie was sure that he would be mischievous. His older brother looked a little surly, the two girls were shy.

They all offered help with bags and parcels and led her into the large marbled hall. The first things that Annie noticed with surprise were two large trunks. Mevrouw Van Harencarspel came down the stairs saying that she was sorry that she was late and that everything was in rather a muddle, at the foot of the stairs she cried,

"Welcome, welcome Miss Taylor," with an effusiveness Annie knew she would never have encountered in England from a new employer.

She was led up to her room, all the children accompanying her. It was a guest room. Annie was relieved, she had wondered if it would be some poky place in a limbo of its own, neither quite family, nor as austere as a servant's. Her two trunks were brought in by the footmen.

When everyone had gone she opened the lids to relieve the pressure on the clothes inside. She began hanging up her garments in the large cupboard, virtually a little room with a small window. After tidying her hair, washing her face she went downstairs. She noticed that a coat and a parasol had been flung over the trunks. Was someone going away, she wondered?

She knocked and entered the drawing room, the Colonel was sitting in a chair overlooking the garden, he rose and shook her hand. He was all that Annie expected a military man to be, tall, well groomed with broad shoulders.

His gaze was very direct. Mevrouw Van Harencarspel poured out some coffee... they talked of the children and the lessons she was to give. The Colonel leant forward,

"Your first consideration must be Lykle. He is to go to a prep school - that is what I believe you call it, in England in the autumn. You must improve his English."

"That means in six weeks' time. I will do what I can. I see that he knows some already."

"Oh, yes. He is quite good," said his mother.

"Not nearly good enough," said his father very emphatically.

Only then did Annie hear that they were both going to Baden-Baden that evening. This did surprise her. A bunch of keys was pushed across the table to her. As they were pushed, she saw a mark appear on the satinwood, as she took them up she exclaimed, "What a pity."

"We are a careless household," said the Colonel.

Annie noticed that it was said with a mixture of annoyance and defeat.

At lunch, Annie watched everything with the keenest observation. She saw how everything was done, how the butler served, what the footmen did. She thought that the silver needed cleaning.

She remembered, "We are a careless household." The food, however, a plain Dutch midday meal, was excellent.

After lunch, Annie was taken to the schoolroom, like most English nurseries it was on the top floor. She saw that the English books were few and would hold no interest for them. She went downstairs immediately and found the Colonel in the hall.

"Colonel, there are no books suitable for Lykle. May I buy some?"

"Of course. Go to a shop you know in Leiden and have them charged to me." Then after a moment's thought, he said,

"Here, you had better have some money."

He opened his wallet and gave her more money than she had ever held in her life.

He saw her surprise and misinterpreted it.

"We shall be away only a fortnight. But I will give you a note for the bank."

He returned later and gave her a letter addressed to his bank in Den Haag. Annie thanked him, but knew that it would never be needed whilst she held such riches in her hand.

The carriage came and Mevrouw Van Harencarspel, flustered to the last climbed aboard and to the waving children who pursued them down the drive she blew kisses. Annie stood on the steps her ears ringing with the Colonel's last words said loudly in the presence of the menservants,

"Now, Miss Taylor, you are in sole charge - report to me if you need anything, or if anything goes wrong. You can telegraph me."

When the children returned Annie asked them to take her on a tour of the house. They insisted on her seeing everything, but she refused to enter their parents' bedroom. It was the most luxurious house she had ever been in, but it was untidy and dusty in corners. "We are a careless household" seemed true.

In the hall she asked to be taken to the kitchen.

"The Keechen?" enquired Lykle.

"Yes, the kitchen, la cuisine."

He responded buoyantly and led the way through the door by the stairs. The servants' quarters, instantly Annie saw that it was better than in most English houses, to begin with it was light, there was no gloomy passage.

In the kitchen the Cook and the maids were preparing the evening meal. Katje, the youngest child, introduced the cook. Annie praised the lunch and she saw that it pleased. The kitchen she found tidier and cleaner than she had expected, the scullery was spotless. The copper pans gleamed... the scrubbed wood had a luminous dull glow.

From there they went naturally out into the yard, to the stables and to the gardens. There was a large walled kitchen garden. The children took her to the greenhouses, then along the trim walks around the beds. They showed her the peaches, hot and soft hanging by the sun-baked wall.

Gerard showed her how to pick a ripe one, cup your hand beneath, give the branch a small shake and if it fell into your hand it was ripe. There were many trees all stretched like captives on the rack on these walls. Only then did the name of the house come to Annie's mind, "Perzik Hof". It was well named.

In the evening, the gong sounded in the hall and Annie looked at the children who had changed into more formal clothes. She straightened bows and sashes, brushed stray hair back from brows. Then a completely new task, she turned out pocket flaps, nudged ties into the centre of collars.

"Why bother, Miss Taylor, it's only us?"

Annie looked proudly down her small nose.

"Why only us? Everyone is worthy of the best."

She shooed the children before her. In the dining room she made them stand behind their chairs and say in English,

"For what we are about to receive, may the Lord make us truly thankful."

They fumbled and smudged the English, so as they unfurled their napkins, she taught it to them again. The tureen was placed before her. She noted the bare hands, they had been gloved at lunch-time.

Her heart beat very fast indeed, she was not absolutely certain of the conventions, but she took a leap and prayed that it was the right one. Carefully addressing the butler as Mijnheer she said: "Please take this soup out and bring it back with your gloves on."

The butler looked angry for a moment, Annie willed herself to gaze at him without flinching. The tureen was lifted taken away, it seemed that they waited minutes, during which time Annie's heart beat very hard again. Then the tureen reappeared and in white gloved hands.

"Dank je wel, mijnheer."

It impressed the children, it impressed the staff, but most of all it impressed Annie who had felt sick with fear at so addressing a man.

At the end of the meal Annie rose and the children chanted the grace that she had taught them but with the tense changed into the past. Annie noticed that the butler joined in the "Amen" who looked at the footman who strode with some alacrity to move her chair, whilst the other opened the door. But Annie paused.

"Now, we have thanked God for a good dinner. Who do we thank next?"

They looked at one another, they had no idea.

"What about the cook? So, now, you say to Mijnheer Bouwerman, Please give my compliments to the cook. Now say that."

With shyness they said it to the butler. Annie, to make certain it was understood, repeated it in Dutch.

Until 11 the next day Annie gave them formal lessons then she walked Lykle alone round the grounds talking to him in English. They went to the gates and then along the high wall. It was an overgrown piece of the grounds, but it led to the high gazebo that Annie had seen.

Strangely none of the children had been there. Together they climbed the steps and found the door locked. Annie produced her bunch of keys and to the delight of Lykle almost the last they fitted into the lock turned and with pressure from them both the rusty and unused hinges creaked and growled open.

Inside they stood still, amazed and enchanted. Long sash windows looked onto the garden on two sides and on to the road and down it on the other. In the corner was a stone fireplace with a series of steps into the corner above the flue.

"We must have this as our summer schoolroom."

Lykle agreed heartily, partly because cleaning it up would delay real lessons. In fact it postponed them just one day, for all the children became infected with enthusiasm and they carried buckets of water down and scrubbed the floors.

In the afternoon the staff were curious to see what had been done and they too joined in restoring the elegant room to some of its grandeur. Annie was regarded by them all as a discoverer and interesting innovator.

It was next day while giving Lykle his lesson in the new room that they heard a long wail. It was Gerard. They left their books and ran down the steps, across the lawn through the drawing room windows into the hall where staggered Gerard with blood streaming from his head.

In a moment Annie and the butler had him in their arms and into the kitchen where they put him on the table. Cook ran water into a bowl and produced a clean cloth. Together they washed the matted hair.

Like many head wounds it looked far worse than it was, the wound was quite small. Lint and a bandage were found, they were always ready in the kitchen for burns. Gerard soon recovered and when Annie brought in some chocolate he was sitting up.

Then Annie questioned them and to her horror she leant that they had been throwing stones at one another in a mock war. All the adults looked very grave and Mr Bouwerman, Cook and Annie spoke solemnly. The children dismissed to their rooms Annie suddenly felt faint, it was the blood and the thought of what might have been and her great responsibility.

"What would you like, Miss Taylor?"

A bottle of brandy was produced, Annie shook her head,

"No, just a cup of tea. English tea."

The kettle was placed on the stove, the tea-pot brought out. Annie saw the kettle go off the boil, the pot unwarmed and she knew insufficient tea would be used. With a rather wan smile she said,

"Let me show you how we do it in England."

She poured water in the pot, swirled it round, put in the tea and then taking the pot to the kettle said, "The pot to the kettle. Never, never, the kettle to the pot."

She let it brew, as she explained, then poured it out. They all sat down.

They had become a little family. Her fears of insolence she knew were unjustified. She asked about the children and found out that they hardly ever went out.

"Then they are bored. We must have a day out."

Annie then asked the butler if any of the footmen swam. He looked perplexed then answered a little reprovingly.

"Every Dutchman swims. Doesn't every Englishman?"

Annie had to answer, "No."

It was then explained to her that with so many canals, every child was taught how to swim. He or she needed to, for at some time in childhood you fell in. Then Annie revealed her plan a day by the sea,

"But I cannot go unless I have a strong swimmer, in case, any of the children get into difficulties." She was assured that both Kees and Jaap swam like fish.

At teatime, Annie put the plan to the children and bathing drawers for the boys and costumes for the girls were found.

Next day, the sun was willed into place by the children.

The boys in sailor suits, the girls in a similar version but skirted waited for the carriage. It arrived, Kees already on the box, a hamper under the seat with whoops of delight they climbed aboard and set off for the sea.

There was not one of them not brimful of happiness and Annie watched the raising of the little tent for changing with great satisfaction. Only fleetingly did she remember that Edith was arriving in Holland this very day.

At Flushing, Edith watched a lady in a brown silk costume climb the gangway. She looked at Edith then away. She went down the companionway a few minutes later she re-appeared and with disbelief approached her and asked if she were Miss Edith Taylor.

"I am, are you Miss Snoek?"

"You are not at all like your sister."

"Everyone says that. We are quite different in every way."

"I thought you would have descended from the boat. I might easily have missed you."

"Oh well, all's well that ends well."

Maybe, thought Miss Snoek, but it is only just beginning.

In the train, Edith was much more talkative than her sister had been. She spent more time talking than observing, considered Miss Snoek.

In the Hooigracht she was given the room that Annie had vacated. That too, was a mistake. Annie had felt that she had earned the room and was grateful for it. Edith accepted it as a right.

The two Principals had grown very used to the great harmony that resided in Annie, they had relied upon it. Edith, they discovered at the first meal was much more free in declaring her mind.

When they were alone they agreed that Edith was almost certainly not less intelligent, but her gifts were quite different to her sister's. They were upset when they, only now, discovered that she was not willing to teach sewing. "I hate sewing," she had said.

Very soon it became noticeable that because Edith liked talking she found learning Dutch much more difficult. She was not patient to learn to express herself.

The sharp remarks she enjoyed making sprang to her lips but then were halted. She found learning Dutch very laborious.

Three days later, all working well at "Perzik Hof" Annie caught the tram to Leiden. She thought it exceedingly strange that when she saw the little city across the fields her heart rose.

She realised that like Francois Haverschmidt the place had a hold on her heart. It was not just the locality it was something metaphysical because there a change had been wrought in one – it embodied the change from girl to woman.

Annie reproved herself for, it seemed that she was more eager to see Leiden than her sister. As she crossed the bridge over the Gracht, she saw the door of the school open and Edith running towards her, legs and arms flying.

Annie watched and blushed, this would not do. Not do at all. They clasped one another in an embrace and arm in arm walked up to the school.

"How did you see me so soon?"

"I was watching and saw you in the little mirror outside the window."

"Ah, yes, I had forgotten, the traitors. That's what they call them. They reveal other people's secrets. But watch out, they reveal your own."

Edith wanted to take Annie straight up to her room. Annie shook her head, knocked on the door of the Salon and paid her respects to the Principals.

Later, when they went upstairs, she said, "Always consider them first and you will have no trouble."

Annie was touched to see that Edith had hung the enlarged photograph of their mother where she had hung her precious mirror. Edith talked eagerly of the cousins and Crosland Moor.

She also mentioned people Annie did not know. Annie saw very clearly that she had moved on, Holland was her home. She contented herself with the thought that Edith would soon do the same.

At lunch, Annie found herself talking quickly, too quickly, in Dutch, she checked herself and talked more slowly.

Miss Lange laughed and told Annie that Edith had been warned not to lose herself as she had done. There was no fear of that - Edith was more independent and self-reliant.

She battled with Dutch grammar which she was slow to grasp and she found that constantly she was disappointing because she failed to live up to the expectations that Annie had raised.

Annie saw all this and she arranged for Edith to come twice a week to "Perzik Hof" and have lessons at the same time as Lykle. It worked quite well... he learnt more English and Edith picked up some Dutch.

Annie was very happy as she watched their progress in the gazebo. She loved this room, her little empire. Edith loved the trees and the park, but she could not share Annie's enchantment in the house, even less the gazebo.

Annie felt so content in the elegant room beneath the ceiling painted with a god and a goddess and many cherubs. She indulged her fantasies. They induced none in Edith who thought it weird and old fashioned.

One late afternoon, after Annie had seen Edith on to the tram taking her back to Leiden, she did not go back to the house but towards the gazebo. She wondered at the difference between herself and her sister, there was a divide in temperament but a tie of blood.

She felt that she was her mother's creation and Edith was, perhaps, her grandmother's. She walked slowly through the trees and looked up as she approached the tall brick double cube, one above the other of what she, now, called her little house. She wondered why she loved it so?

The answer came very quick... "Because it is so beautiful." Then, only then, did she remember her mother telling her of holidays she spent as a girl in Gloucestershire, near the Severn where there had been a summerhouse elegant and old built over the road were tea was taken and a watch kept on the carriages and drays passing. It was an inherited predilection.

She mused again and it was probably the Celt in her that had become diluted by the time Edith was born. Yes, yes, Edith is a Yorkshirewoman and I am – she laughed aloud, she said aloud, "I'm a chameleon, a bit Welsh, a bit Yorkshire and now, it seems, partly Dutch."

When the Colonel and Mevrouw Van Harencaspel returned they were surprised and delighted, the house gleamed with a new shine to greet them. There were flowers in the rooms and in the hearth of the hall something they had never seen before, great fans of beech leaves. The children were content and they were very pleased at Lykle's progress in English.

School terms were drawing close for Lykle and Annie was often consulted about what he would need at an English preparatory school. She used her imagination and it did not play her false.

The term in the Hooigracht had begun and Annie was alarmed for Edith. She foresaw revolts and feline activity undermining her sister's authority.

She felt that everything was unjust, here was she looking after four children with ease, Edith was confronted by a school and a very insecure knowledge of the language. She reasoned with herself that she had earned the privilege to teach the children of the rich, but remained troubled that Edith might never gain this privilege.

At the time that Lykle's letters came from Seaford telling them all about his school life there, Annie received Edith, a disheartened and beaten Edith in her little house.

Edith seemed even more wan in face but angry in spirit as she drank tea, accepted comfort and advice beneath the gaze of the helmeted god and scantily dressed goddess on the ceiling.

At half-term Annie asked for free time to stay in Leiden. She refused to go back to the school whilst the girls were there, she went in the break. She saw instantly Edith even greater unhappiness in the school, it was lessened even out in the street. The school itself seemed to cast a cloud.

It was a perpetual reminder of her inadequacy and of her hurt pride. Annie talked with the Principals and she reproved them when they complained that Edith was not like her. They suggested methods of teaching that Edith might use, they found it difficult to tell her themselves. It was a most miserable tangle.

All four became unhappier and shied from the obvious solution of dismissal. The word was never used.

It was Edith, herself, who after a walk out to Oegstgeest alone who told them all very definitely that she must return to England.

Her resignation was accepted, a certain peace came and, indeed, the remainder of the term was comparatively happy.

Annie's even tenor of life continued and sometimes in the carriage with Mevrouw Van Harencaspel she contrasted the luxury around her, which she enjoyed, with the unknown struggle before Edith. Again, Edith provided the answer, she was to return to Cousin Lydia and from there she would seek and easily gain a place as companion to an elderly lady.

"I hate teaching," she said very defiantly.

Annie's heart rose and sank over the proposition. It looked bleak to her. She did not often make plans for the future, but this experiment had failed completely. The two young women walked beneath the trees, Edith kicking up the leaves, Annie more demurely pressed them beneath her foot, but both left an untidy swath where their skirts trailed.

Edith surprised her at the vehemence of her ardour to return to England. Edith seemed to miss her country with something bordering on despair. Her patriotism almost shocked Annie, for Annie failed to realise that everyone in England had become intensely aware of the Empire. Edith was infected by it. Annie did not understand.

In December, the sisters said goodbye. Edith was to go to Alderley Edge, Cousin Lydia had found her a place. The two wept on Leiden station - they were not sad because of the termination of a career, but the parting.

In the core of each was a gladness by one to return, in the other an acknowledgement that it must be so.

Winter always meant hard work for Annie. She believed in filling the days of her children and with Sinterklaas and Christmas coming, she set them all making a sewing presents. She was also teaching them long narrative poems to recite at the entertainments for the household.

When she was quite alone she was working at a new dress for Christmas day. It was of heavy dull red silk. It was a difficult pattern, for dresses in 1883 were plain and encasing. The bodice with revers had to be wrinkle-less and it had to fit over the bust like a snakeskin.

Often, often she was dissatisfied, but in the end it fitted. When the day came for wearing it she was disappointed, she had thought the red rich enough in itself, but it needed lightening, but it was too late.

She reasoned with herself, why go to all this bother, there was no man here to ravish. She did not even wish to catch one, there was, on her part, no hurry for the bridal bed. Yet that did not stop her speculating where life would lead, whom she would eventually marry.

On Christmas Day, her dress brought a sparkle to the Colonel's eye and Annie was not slow to notice that the butler and the footmen were silently admiring. It made her content, pleased, but she still thought the dress lacking.

In the afternoon, the presents were taken from beneath the tree. Annie watched carefully for the reactions to the children's presents, it was the Colonel who responded most and declared a pen-wiper a great improvement on the usual cigars.

Annie laughed and called him a hypocrite. What Annie was not prepared for was the lavish presents they gave her. From the family came a sable muff.

"This is particularly from Lykle, my dear," explained his mother, "without you he would not have done so well at his English school."

It was what she had long, long wanted. But that was not the end.

"These are an after-thought. They are not new. I do not wear them any more. But they are just what your dress needs."

Annie opened the box and found a short string of pearls that precisely encircled her neck. There were seed pearls, too.

"They will all add light to your dress."

Annie looked in the mirror. She saw a round fair face that glowed with happiness and security. At the same time she wondered how Edith was spending this day.

The New Year was to be spent in Schiedam. To return to the Haverschmidts was, in effect, to return home. The easy relationship held. There was, though, an undercurrent, Francois looked older, more troubled and his wife and Margo showed their irritation more openly and often with sarcasm.

Again Annie went out visiting with him walking and listening. She recognised the same perplexities, the same social injustices, the same suspicions about his beliefs. He was still hurt. One day at the café on the dunes, while he drank a Genever and Annie had tea, he lamented the past. Annie was surprised,

"But you have done so much and so well. Some criticise but others love you. You must not forget your own Dutch proverb, 'Tall trees catch the wind.'"

He looked and smiled, he thought how her eyes beguiled with such sympathy.

"Ah, Annie, you can say that, the world lies still before you. More than half of mine has gone."

Annie's face suddenly went marmoreal, yet remained very fragile,

"The world before me? What world? Living in other people's houses; bringing up other people's children. What is to become of me? I am a woman and I have no money."

"You will marry, my dear, a good decent man and have your own children."

"Are you so sure? Men like money, too, you know."

She was angry with herself that she accepted the flattery of his certainty.

"I think for marriage you will have to return to England. In some ways things are easier there."

"How do you mean?"

He did not answer he only said, "There's plenty of time."

They hurried back home for the cold was intensifying an icy wind blew over grey still water. Annie looked at the man by her side and she hoped that she would find someone like him – clever, courteous, observant of the needs of others and, perhaps, troubled. It was, she thought, a pleasing thing to be needed.

She thought she could do Mevrouw Haverschmidt's work better than she did, she was often impatient. She, also, did not want a life like Mevrouw Van Harencaspel, the Colonel was altogether too self-sufficient. She had nothing to do, the house ran itself. That would not suit her.

In the evening as the women sewed Francois read aloud, not one of his own stories, but Our Mutual Friend. They were coming to the last chapters. When he finished he gave a great sigh of contentment and of envy.

"I wish, oh I wish I could write like that."

Annie said nothing but echoed his desire. If only he could, but she found in his stories a thread of sentimentality always knotted and tangled in the web of the fabric. Francois was unable to depict real evil.

He wrote like Dickens in *The Old Curiosity Shop*, never as in *Great Expectations*. He was also more intellectual... ideas mattered more than the story quite often.

Suddenly, as if unconcerned, he said: "Tomorrow is the Theological Society. Does anyone want to come with me?"

There was a distinct silence. He laughed and they all laughed and Annie said, "I will come if you like."

With relief the two other women exclaimed how good it was of her. Haverschmidt was glad that someone from the house was going. His wife and daughter glad that it did not have to be them. Each had a reason for pleasure, but no one admitted the true reason.

The debate was on the Resurrection. The assembly room was three-quarters full and Annie was interested to see how representative of the city the audience was. There were ladies in furs, their prosperous looking husbands.

There were trades people and a goodly proportion of pious women in drab clothes, who Annie irreverently called, "the dowdy population of Heaven" a phrase she had picked up in a book. She regarded them all - they all seemed thoughtful people, evidently interested and she thought of herself, she was there only for politeness' sake.

The motions for and against were proposed. Haverschmidt tore the flimsy evidence... he put his case forcefully and well. These were the things she often heard quietly, meditatively on a walk but here in public they seemed so different, they were hard, shocking.

She felt some waves of horror flow from those around her. What amazed her was that this sensitive man seemed unable to feel it. She found herself clutching her hands until they hurt, she was willing him to stop, even recant.

When the debate became general, the chairman had to call for order as some of the criticism became abuse. Haverschmidt seemed undismayed, he smiled at Annie, he surveyed his outstretched boots. His motion was, of course, defeated.

The theologians met together, they slapped one another's backs, they might disagree but they understood. But the less educated stood and watched and none of them spoke to Annie, they considered him, Annie heard the word, 'an infidel'.

She felt cut and hurt and not for Francois, but for his wife and children. She understood more clearly the cause of the sarcasm. They, poor things, were so weary of all this.

Suddenly he was by her side. "Ready to go?"

On the way home she saw that he was depressed and she talked many trivialities. She checked herself and with a thudding heart said, "Why do you do this? It serves no purpose, it undermines belief, hurts some, angers others. I... I... think it... most unwise."

"But, Annie, I want to make people think. Too many are like parrots, repeating creeds they know only by rote."

"I know. I know many are like that. But they have no time and no ability to be otherwise. They are not students, but people who need a faith to help them in difficult and busy lives. That, I am sure, is what my father would have thought."

"So you think I should stop?"

"Yes. But not for the people here... because of those at home. It is very hard for your wife and Margo. They suffer criticism but in a more cruel feline way at the Bible classes and the Missionary Guild. Women can be very unkind to one another, you know."

"Perhaps you are right. I see it only as an intellectual crusade against unthinking acceptance."

They walked on in silence.

"Couldn't you put some of these thoughts and theories in your stories instead?" She did not think he could, but thought it a tactful way of softening a blow.

"I have to do what I think is right, my dear. I have heard these arguments before."

At breakfast, next day, Francois announced that he was going to clean his bird-cages. Mevrouw Haverschmidt compressed her lips. It was clearly understood that she would have nothing to do with the birds.

She disliked them, she feared them. Margo usually helped her father reluctantly, she felt a sort of disloyalty in aiding him. Annie knew this so she volunteered.

The study was at the top of the house with a very large window with a view that swept over the houses to the river. It was a large room and one wall was hung with bird-cages. Finches, canaries, wax-bills, even some wild birds hopped from perch to swing to see d bowl in neurotic movement.

Annie, a woman of her time loved their song, enjoyed their bright colours and with the exception of a thrush, felt no compunction at their captivity. As she submitted each day to the encasing of her body in a tight corset so she accepted many constrictions in life, social, traditional, even these birds.

They took down the cages, washed the glass panels, dusted the bars, gave them fresh seed and sifted clean sand on the trays. But

Annie did wonder why he had so many. Were they to spite his wife whose antipathy to them he was well aware of? Or were they a defence to keep his wife out of this room?

As he handled the fluttering occupants so tenderly she thought it was pure love of the creatures themselves. However, it remained strange and she remembered many talks with her mother on people's motives, they were often so complex.

The conversation between the two at work reverted to their discussion of the previous night. Francois admitted that he would miss quite desperately the vigour and aggression of debate. He feared its loss. Annie defended her stand stressing and the unhappiness it brought to his womenfolk.

"You ask me to be untrue to myself."

"No, just quiet."

"Annie, you speak Dutch like one of us, but your mind is entirely English. You live entirely empirically. No wonder the British have such an Empire!"

The pun amused him.

Annie pointed out that the Dutch had an Empire too. Then more gently he asked her what she was going to do in the future. She did not know.

"Go to another family, I suppose. That is the life of a governess."

"Don't you want to marry and have children of your own?"

"Yes, one day, but I have not met the man I should like to marry yet."

"No idea at all?"

Annie blushed, looked at the little green finch hopping excitedly in its cage.

"He must look like young Bentinck, but have your mind and that is not possible." She laughed.

"Why my mind?"

"Because you do not bore me. Many people do, you know." She thought of her sister and dismissed the thought instantly.

"I think you should go abroad. You have not seen Italy, even Germany for that matter."

The vision of Italy, warm beneath the sun appealed on that cold day.

"You are quite right. I do let things happen. But I do not think you know how difficult it is for a woman to do otherwise."

The holiday came to an end. They all escorted Annie to the station and there were kisses, smiles and even a gulp as she left. The love between them all was mutual. It had an effect. Francois did temper his radicalism, but the reputation of being a rebel remained fixed in most people's minds.

Alas, Mevrouw Haverschmidt could not change, her humour was sarcastic and the delight in verbal score would not be denied in her. Margo curbed her tongue... she saw the hurt the barbs caused.

Thinking of the family she had just left so intricate in its feelings, the family she was returning to so commonplace beneath its grandeur, she thought it intriguing. It was in German, but she realised that she had read the sentence with complete comprehension. She bought it and so her life was nudged into another stream as surely as a rock diverts a stream.

Annie's time at Persichof did not end abruptly. Another summer was sauntered through, almost literally beneath the beech trees. Lykle returned for holidays, each time more of an Englishman.

He was Annie's favourite, Gerard she never completely understood, Bella and Nettie were good, but unexciting girls. The influence was Tolstoy, but not in the way he would have expected, she read more and more German.

She amassed a little library in the gazebo. In all this she was abetted by Fraulein Vogel who, like the Haverschmidts thought Annie needed a change even if she should miss her homely splendour in Wassenaar.

When the matter of change was discussed Annie procrastinated, at times she even prevaricated. There was a thread of passivity beneath her liveliness and charm which perplexed some of her friends.

So the loyal Fraulein took the matter into her own hands and one day a letter came that frightened and delighted Annie. It was from Herr Clausen. This surprised Annie, why had his wife not written.

It was business paper, too. The heading showed a large factory with smoking chimneys and small carts entering great gates where picture frames were made.

The letter was very correct and in spite of the stiffness of expression it was kind. In the last paragraph, the writer apologised that his wife could not write as she was unwell temporarily.

"Why did he not wait until she had recovered," she asked.

The Haverschmidts, to whom she took her problem, made excuses. Margo sat staring into the glowing stove and said,

"You will go. I know. You will not be happy there."

"Then all she had to do is return to us," said Mevrouw Haverschmidt.

Those were the words Annie had not hoped for but gave her her answer. Yes, she would go. She might not be happy. Nobody was happy all the time anyway. That happiness does not sting if one knows that one had a place of refuge, she knew that she had that here in Schiedam. She wrote to Herr Clausen, she accepted.

The last summer at Persichof was an idyll. Annie wondered why on earth she was leaving. There were picnics with all the family. There were trips to the sea with two tents now, one for the women and the other for the men.

The day of departure came. All was packed, Annie got up early and she went down the garden to the gazebo. She had the key in her hand. She stood at the bottom of the steps, but she never went up. She loved that lovely room too much. The girls cried, as the carriage took her to the station, but Annie knew they would soon forget. What she was certain of was that the house would become shabby for nobody would praise the servants' work.

Chapter 23

Cologne

It was a very hot day when Annie left Holland. The journey seemed long and once over the border, it seemed to grow more oppressively hot and the people more excited. There were flags everywhere, shouting and singing.

Annie grew very apprehensive. At long last she was beneath the great roof of Cologne station, a porter collected her trunks from the luggage van and then she anxiously awaited recognition.

The crowd of happy boisterous people thinned, everyone seemed to have an objective, or, at least someone to meet them. It was only now that she was aware that a tall fair man with a beard was looking at a photograph. He approached her and introduced himself, Herr Albrecht Clausen.

He apologised that his wife was not present. She was much preoccupied with a party they were giving that night. Annie had forebodings. He led the way to a smart carriage drawn by two horses, the luggage was stowed behind and they swept off into the stream of traffic.

The immensity of everything, from the station to the Cathedral to the tall houses impressed Annie, everything was on a larger scale than Holland, but she added less beautiful.

This great city reminded her of Leeds, but, once again, much larger. They drove out of the city, the edge of town was less prosperous, then came suburbs with tree-lined avenues with villas set in grounds. This had a similarity to Wassenaar, but it was newer and the houses had battlements, gothic porches, turrets.

Annie thought it rather vulgar and she looked discreetly at Herr Clausen and her alarms were largely allayed, he seemed gentle in spite of his size and he had been most courteous and pointed out the sights of the city as they approached them.

He, looking at Annie, a little more openly was surprised. She was neither his idea of a governess, nor an Englishwoman. She was tall and she was impeccably well-dressed. Something he had not found common on his business trips to London.

He thought her acute. She had asked very sensible questions in poor German... the German of a Dutchwoman. He wondered what his wife would make of her, he thought that she would be as surprised as he was.

The carriage slowed and turned into a drive leading to a tall brick house with a large doorway and tower above. Instantly the door opened and Frau Clausen cam out, she was effusive in her welcome and her looks matched her manners, a pile of fair hair curled in great profusion and there were stray pieces, like convolvulus tendrils which hung down and which she constantly brushed up with the back of her hand.

She ignored her husband completely and bundled Annie to her room on the second floor. It was large and suitably furnished and a door led into the schoolroom which was larger and well appointed. Annie's reaction was, "I could be happy here."

Frau Clausen whisked away chattering as she went down the stairs, leaving Annie to unpack and ponder on her impressions. She wondered what the boys would be like. She had not long to wait, they presented themselves, very correctly, at the schoolroom door, extended a hand and bowed. They did not enter until she asked them.

Hans-Peter was very like his father in feature, the spirit flickering behind his eyes was less perplexed however. He did not seem to have to use so much patience to make his life bearable. Ludwig was livelier and eager to please, he stole a hand into Annie's almost straight away. They showed her the room, the books, the cupboards where paper, pencils, pen and ink were kept.

With pride they explained the great porcelain stove with its swags of musical instruments and trophies of war painted in the baroque panels. In time that stove came to mean a lot to Annie.

At the moment she was happy that there would be no trouble with charges. They seemed equally pleased with their new English Miss.

They went downstairs and the epicentre of all movement, agitation was Frau Clausen. She wandered swiftly from room to room flinging out orders which were often countermanded. She roved with immense vases of flowers seeking a place for them. Annie casting an eye over the crowded rooms could not see space for anything more.

"There is nowhere," wailed the mistress of the house and trailed away. The boys led her from the drawing to the dining room it was gargantuan and all of it carved. It was oak, and the sideboard had bronze panels depicting the glories of the chase.

The long table was heaped with silver, porcelain and more bronze and where possible flowers. Annie found the contrast with Holland very surprising, everything was on a much larger scale, she saw similarities but the differences were more obvious.

Like all islanders she found this surprising, she had assumed that national characteristics were always marked by the crossing of water. Ludwig pointed out where she was to sit. This she had not expected on her first evening and immediately she was wondering what she would wear.

There was only one suitable evening dress, it was blue silk and had been re-made from one of Mevrouw Van Harencaspels gowns. It needed ironing. This meant a return to the turmoil below.

With her dress over her arm she began the descent, but heard voices raised in argument. She thought it would be better to appear creased at the party than arrive at an inopportune moment as the mistress quarrelled with one of the servants. Back in the schoolroom she felt very raw, new and disquieted.

What had she come to? Why had she left the safety of Holland. She did not know what to do. She was in a limbo of indecision, therefore extremely unhappy. To fear going downstairs she argued was cowardly, but another part of her considered it wisdom. Suddenly she saw that there was a kettle on the hearth and beneath it a gas ring.

She filled the kettle, lit the gas and brought out her dress and holding it before the steam almost miraculously the folds and ridges of the creasing disappeared. As she saw it rise and improve before her eyes so her spirits rose. The dress was ready. She went downstairs again to offer help.

Frau Clausen bustled through and brushed aside Annie's offer. Annie was sorry she had made it, the rebuff had been very ungracious. She went off in search of the boys. She went into the drawing room, a second viewing made it even more overwhelming, every article was immense.

The vases were bulbous and cancerous with decoration. Annie was amazed at the china figure, half life size of a boy, perched on a shelf, his legs dangled nonchalantly in the air. His tricorn hat was tucked under his arm. She had not seen its like before.

She looked to the shelves on the other side of the room and there was an aproned girl also sitting, a basket of flowers by her side, her ankles crossed above her red shoes. She noticed that the curtains were caught and looped up on hooks like dragons heads and claws.

Out in the garden she was assailed by hydrocephalic dahlias, staked and primly pinioned below but nothing could control the exuberance of their petals.

"I am in the land of the large," she said to herself, adding "Red is synonymous with beauty in Russia, I believe, size must be all here."

Just as she was beginning to be anxious about the boys, they materialised, to her surprise still tidy. That was unlike boys in Holland or England in a garden. They took her on a voyage of discovery that interested them far more than the details of the schoolroom.

She was led to greenhouses, a walled garden, and to her delight a small orchard where brown hens pecked and scratched. They were the same size as hens in England. The boys began to correct her German.

"All right. You teach me today, but tomorrow will be my turn and you will speak English!"

They played tig on the lawn and they were both surprised to find that Miss could run.

Back in the house the boys' supper was served in the schoolroom. Annie told them a story and they went to bed.

Annie would have liked to rest, it had been a strange and eventful day, she wished to take stock of everything, she was suddenly tired, but she had to dress for dinner. When she sat before her mirror which she had hung between the windows, she was reassured, she did not look as tired as she felt and she became excited as she manoeuvred herself into her dress.

She went down, lingering on the landing watching the guest arrive. She noted instantly that everyone was more elaborately dressed than any she had seen before, and like the furniture, size was a keynote, the bustles were large, even a bow florid.

Her own dress became diminished and her bust and her bustle

seemed to diminish. She took a breath and went down, for a moment Frau Clausen looked as her without recognition behind her eyes but with a bright smile.

"Miss Taylor" murmured her husband as he took her hand. Annie curtsied, it was advice she had learned from *Alice in Wonderland*, "curtsey while you're thinking." She had found it worked wonders, it gave a grace note of time, a moment for people to reflect, also she knew that she did it beautifully.

"My dear, you look so rested and charming in the sweet dress I almost did not recognise you."

Frau Clausen took her into the drawing room and introduced her to a large and firmly seated lady. She asked after Annie's journey and then talked of Hans-Peter and Ludwig. She was their great-aunt and they were obviously favourites.

It was an easy entry into German life. She soon discovered the gemutlich that lay just beneath the surface. The Germanic proportions began to fall into perspective. Contact was changing all. She even laughed at a joke, that pleased her she was beginning to comprehend them properly.

At dinner she sat by the family lawyer. He was very correct and spoke slowly, Annie thought that his deliberation was habitual and not only on her behalf. From him she learnt that the flags, the crowds, the very dinner they ate, were all in honour of Sedantag. Annie felt a shudder of surprise and antipathy.

The battle of Sedan was one of the first political events she could remember and, then, all the sympathy had been for the French and the plight of the Empress Eugenie had been the current topic of conversation.

She found herself surrounded by patriots, she felt very alien. She remembered that she had felt a little like this when she had discovered how her family had all become passionately imperialistic.

It made her recall her father's death, the horrors of her adoption. She also remembered that the year had ended happily when she had been re-united with her mother. She remembered the death of the Emperor at Chilehurst.

She kept her counsel, but felt that she was on "the other side."

Later in the drawing room, Herr Clausen came over to her. He asked if she liked her room and the schoolroom. He added that he thought she would find Hans-Peter and Ludwig fairly easy to handle. He then smiled and surveyed the room.

"It would seem that tonight they are all Prussians, a very military people. But, Miss Taylor, not all Germans are champions of Mars."

"Do not worry. I met with this kind of thing when I was last in England. But it is not the same in Holland."

"Patriotism can be very dangerous, I think. I worry sometimes."

He led her to a lady with a long narrow face. Annie, at once, thought her an artist. There was sensitivity as well as intelligence written on her face and in her gestures. Annie asked her if she painted.

"No, I play the piano. Soon I expect, I shall be asked to play."

She was and as the notes of Schumann hung dreamily in the air Annie noticed the change in atmosphere. The patriotic heartiness was replaced by a warm, sweet reverie. Annie had experienced nothing like this in England, or in Holland, there the effect of music worked slowly, a lulling gradually of the turbulent emotions, here it was as if a thick curtain fell that blocked out all that had gone before, she found it amazing.

She looked around to see if Frau Clausen was equally moved. Yes, she too, was in another world. She lay back against the cushions of the sofa, the tension gone, she was in another world.

Annie watched her, it was, she admitted, a handsome head, but her expression was marred by the fierce desire to succeed. She looked ambitious. There was a glint in her eyes that looked over the high bridge of her nose that saw, only the moment.

As Liszt's *Hungarian Rhapsody* was thundering, so there was a rattle of tea cups and Annie was surprised to see that large creamy cakes were also proffered and taken. She wondered where, after so ample a dinner, they found room for these pastries.

She was tired, so tired that she lapsed into Dutch. Then with relief, she saw that some guests were departing. She rose and asked Frau Clausen if there was anything she could do. For a moment the older woman paused. She was seeking a task, none came to mind, so she said, "No, my dear, you have had a long day. Go to bed." Then more kindly, she added, "Tomorrow is a holiday. Come down only when you wake. Sleep well."

Annie soon took off her clothes and climbed into the high bed, feathers beneath her and a feather quilt above.

It had been a long day. She was in a new and exciting world.

She slept so soundly that next morning when she woke she looked at the ceiling, it was totally unfamiliar. But she felt no fear... and only gradually emerging from unconsciousness did she remember that she was in Cologne.

When she went downstairs she was amazed to find how late it was, but comforted when she realised that Frau Clausen was still not about. Not until lunch did she appear and then in a negligee and with her abundant hair in a plait down her back.

Life in Wakefield, still less life in a young ladies' school in Leiden had prepared her for such informality. She found it all very interesting.

Germany she had so often been warned was quite different to Holland. She thought that she had understood it, but experience is the only teacher. She only truly knew the extent of the difference the following day, her third full day in the land, when she received a long form from the Taxation Office to be filled in immediately.

Her earnings were so small she thought it a ludicrous joke. She filled in the form she posted it back. The response was a request that she visit the office. This did alarm her, she hoped that Frau Clausen might accompany her, but hints were ignored.

She learnt only slowly that hints swift to be taken in Britain, even by Yorkshiremen were only slowly interpreted in Holland and never in Germany. So alone she went to the office.

She was not kept waiting. The official a slim young man treated her with formal good manners and asked questions, all of which had been answered on the form. At the time it did not strike her as odd, merely a waste of time.

The interview over, the official rose and opened the door, then, to her great surprise escorted her down the large staircase out on to the steps. He bowed over her hand. There was a man sweeping the street.

Herr Clausen, when she recounted her adventures at dinner, laughed. Like all good working citizens he thought civil servants only too eager to waste time and grasp every pfennig.

Later in the evening, as he smoked his usual cigar, he asked a question that surprised her. "Have you ever met the Crown Princess Frederick?"

"No, I have not."

He said no more and Annie was unwilling to pursue the topic of the lonely Englishwoman in Potsdam. The rumours concerning the Crown Prince's health, the calling in of an English throat specialist, Dr Morell Mackenzie were too well known. However Herr Clausen, a man not given to dogmatic statement said.

"Your Princess, Miss Taylor, is a clever woman, far too clever for Prussians who suspect any woman who shows any signs of intellect. Worse than that, she is tactless. She had made many enemies, Bismarck and her own son. That was not wise at all."

"But I am sure that she means no harm."

"That's not enough. People are quick to condemn the stranger within their gates, as I am sure you are aware. In fact, I think she could well have learnt some lessons from you. You seem above suspicion."

He laughed and taking up his newspaper did not see that the last remark had not pleased his wife.

As always, the least of Annie's causes for anxiety were her charges. She had learnt, possibly, from her mother, and a succession of good teachers how to be firm, sometimes inflexible, but always understanding.

Children responded to her willingly and easily. So the boys learnt quickly and they were more conscientious than any children she had known. But there were other worries. Frau Clausen was unreliable and unpredictable. Her servants either left, or were dismissed.

There were storms and often raised voices and Annie quickly saw that suspicion must never be raised, for once roused it never died until she had proved herself, to her own satisfaction, correct.

It was a household that pivoted on the mistress's moods and it affected them all, the boys in particular, for the moment they made a friendship with a servant it ended abruptly with that servant's departure.

Annie wondered that they accepted her so readily, she was the third in her line, she accepted their trust very gladly and it was not surprising that she ascribed all their gentle and quiet qualities as a bequest from their father.

There was one feature in the monthly programme that Annie came to dread, this was the large dinner party. It was always conceived in grandiose and pretentious terms, simplicity's shadow never hovered. Not only were new clothes required, but new table linen, china and glass.

The extravagance appalled her. She had become used to the economic ways of Holland. The week before such a gathering was always a time of complication. Herr Clausen became silent and occasionally burst into rage and his wife, who never openly attacked in any way her husband, turned her fury on all around.

One day, in the taut and tense hours before a party, a note was delivered saying that the hairdresser was ill and unable to come.

"My God, my God, this is the last straw."

Annie feared what the next move of this capricious woman would be - the servants were already edgy and nervous.

"Let me do your hair. Only I think I should begin right now."

To her surprise Frau Clausen consented. The need to begin at that moment was unnecessary, but it would remove the mistress from the scene of activity and her constant disturbance. One maid looked at Annie with gratitude. Annie and Frau Clausen went upstairs.

In the bedroom the thick fair hair fell densely around its owner. She was proud of her hair and sat there docile and purring. Very slowly Annie brushed and parted and plaited and unplaited, considering, revising and beginning all over again.

This hair was a shining symbol of all Frau Clausen, it was as golden and ostentatious as her house, but it owed everything to nature. Annie wondered whether it was really such an asset, it was heavy and often, however skilfully pinned would fall beneath its own weight. As the toiling went on so Annie heard confidences.

She did not like this... she usually took measures to avoid them. She thought that if she knew too much, then when a rupture took place it would only compound the enmity.

Frau Clausen was excited because her brother was coming from Berlin.

"Oh you will like him, Miss Taylor, he always has so much gossip to tell. He comes from a different world. We are only commercials here."

Annie looked forward to that... it might bring more brightness and elegance to the party.

"He will have all the latest news of the Court."

Annie looked forward to that.

Although the major did not wear uniform, the upright figure, the impeccable dress clothes made all the other men seem shapeless and dowdy. Annie was impressed. Gradually, the table fell silent over dessert as they listened to him.

He was talking of the aged Kaiser, the splendid young patriot the country had in Prince Wilhelm. He praised the tutelage of Bismarck and his apt pupil... "without Bismarck we should not be an Empire."

There were nods and grunts of agreement. Then he went on describing the sick Crown Prince at San Remo. The silence became greater as they listened for here was drama and again and again, the Crown Princess was given the role of the ambitious villainess.

Annie discovered that they called her, Die Englanderin. Annie began by feeling uncomfortable, then uneasy in her silence which she deemed disloyal. She prayed that Frau Clausen would look round at the ladies and rise, but she was spell-bound by her brother. Then she heard him say,

"Of course, it is well known that she only wishes to be as powerful as her mother."

"Excuse me," she heard herself saying and her heart thumped, "but you really do not understand the British Constitution. The power of the Government lies in the Houses of Parliament, not the Queen. May be that is what the Crown Princess would like to see in Germany."

The major looked at her. He saw a pair of very large blue and troubled eyes in an agitated face. But he also saw the prettiness.

"My dear Fraulein, I had not realised that we had an English lady present, forgive me. But we do have our reasons for thinking as we do. Is it not strange that with all our great medical doctors the only one to be accepted is a Scotsman recommended by your Queen? Was not the whole scheme set up at your Queen's Jubilee? We know the Crown Prince to be a man ruled by a woman. That is never wise."

He laughed. They all laughed and Annie noticed that the women did, too.

"Dr Morell Mackenzie is a very clever man."

"So is Professor van Bergmann, my dear lady. No, believe me, there are politics in all this and some of them are English. A Kaiser with cancer. A Kaiser who cannot speak."

"Perhaps his wife will do it for him!"

This caused another outburst of laughter and the servility in the higher pitched laughter made Annie very cold inside.

It was a moment of awakening for Annie. She began to see that the suspicion and jealousy, the lavish displays of this household were all part of a greater malaise. She realised that since she had left England seven years before, it had changed, she recalled herself how the Empire had come to mean so much more to the general public.

The almost casual amassment of territory was now a potent and important part of the nation's trade. She realised that the Germans were envious. She realised, too, that the dowdy Queen, the Widow of Windsor, even Mrs Brown, had become the potent symbol of all this growth and prosperity.

At that first dinner party on the Eve of Sedantag she thought how she had first thought of Napoleon III, then the Empress and later the Prince Imperial. She, now, saw that they were only pawns in a political game played by Germany.

She became afraid, for she feared Bismarck, she feared Prince Wilhelm… and she was beginning to fear Germany.

She found sleep difficult, the world was not the place she desired, or had thought it to be. She began imagining scenes, threats and she felt horribly alone. At last she reached for the matches, struck a light and lit the candle.

The light dispelled shadows, not only in the room but in her innermost self, for she had been saying in the darkness, "Where shall I go? Where shall I go?" The answer came with the light, it was obvious, "I will go to the Haverschmidts."

The following day lessons went well - Frau Clausen kept to her room. That was her practice after a party. The major had gone, everything seemed to be working normally, even serenely.

Annie made fun of her midnight fears. In the afternoon she walked with the boys. They climbed a hill and looked out over the city. This grey day it reminded her of Wakefield, she laughed at herself and said: "You're comparing a pinhead with a pumpkin."

The great cathedral rose with its spires and Annie thought how puny Wakefield's parish church would look in comparison. Cologne was grey, Wakefield was black. They stood and pointed out landmarks to each other.

There was a man close behind, an ordinary respectable looking man, he seemed familiar, she thought no more.

The newspapers speculated more and more on the health of the old Kaiser and even more of the Crown Prince who remained, even as Christmas approached, at San Remo. She could not help thinking that the Crown Princess must have often been extremely tactless and unwise, if the words attributed to her were true. They were now formidable weapons against her.

Shortly before Christmas, she went with her letters to the Post Office in the city. She bought stamps, she went to a vacant table and began licking the stamps and fixing them on her letters and parcels.

She became aware that she was being watched. She turned and looked into the face of a respectable man. He moved away. Had he remained still she would never have recognised him.

He was the man who had been near them on the hill, but even more sinister, by his walk she knew him to be the man who had swept the street as she left the Tax Office.

She felt a long flickering line of fear up her spine like a grass fire, leaping, dying, smoking. She left the office, walked down the street, as always and began looking in the shops. She was not being followed.

But was her parcel being opened? She smiled all they would find were a pair of gloves bought for Edith. Her letters, though? She tried to remember what she had said.

She wondered if she had commented on the Crown Princess. She continued walking along by the shops, but the windows held no delight for her. She only wished to return to Holland. She found herself near the cathedral, climbed the steps and went inside.

Even in winter there was a smell of the earth here. It was reassuring, something old and everlasting. She wondered if it was caused by the market women and shoppers who piled their wares and purchases inside the door as they went to pray.

Annie followed them. She sat before a clothed figure of the Virgin Mary and her Child. She heard the mumble of prayers and saw the brown puckered lips moving. She felt unable to pray to this statue, but she folded her hands in her lap, at first she just envied the uncomplicated and uneducated women.

She said the Lord's Prayer to herself in English. Then she thought of her mother and very slowly, like a jigsaw puzzle, she assembled the Lord's Prayer in Welsh. From this action came peace, but not happiness.

Christmas came and with it letters from Holland and England and a few little parcels which Annie was certain had been opened. On Christmas Day they all stood round the tree, and though there was movement... the candles flamed steadily, serenely.

A peace came to them all and everyone kissed. Even Frau Clausen seemed open and friendly, but Annie remained reserved in her judgements. She had known these friendly moods before, they vanished without cause and at a given moment, it was strange.

Yet as the feeling of Christmas dissolved, Annie felt that her only real friend was Caspar, the Great Dane.

He had been kept at the factory, but been brought to the house by his master when he developed an abscess on his paw. He soon recovered - the children loved him and never returned to his duties as a guard. Instead he accompanied the children and Annie.

He walked beside her always and sometimes growled at strangers. The minute, however, Herr Clausen returned, he was never far from his master.

The winter grew colder and the east winds were particularly fierce. In February came news from San Remo that a tracheotomy had been performed on the Crown Prince. There were dramatic accounts of the fitting of the silver canula into the Prince's windpipe. There were stories of the Crown Princess having slapped a surgeon when she saw her husband flinch.

Feeling, once again, focused on and against her. Sometimes, when Frau Clausen was bad tempered, the children unruly and a servant slow to obey, she wondered if she was suspected in some English conspiracy. But her nature was optimistic and soon she would be laughing with the boys.

February came and with it Lent and a great party arranged for Shrove Tuesday. It was not a happy time, the wind cut, the papers depressed, everyone seemed uneasy. A few days before the party Frau Clausen came down the stairs waving a letter, "Conrad is coming. He is shooting near Bonn. He comes to us tomorrow."

"He will be here for the party, then" said her husband, "that is good. It will be good to see him." He wiped his moustache in the ample napkin.

Annie wondered how sincere the remark was. She felt oddly

about his coming she would enjoy, she knew, seeing "such a fine figure of a man," as her mother would have teasingly called him.

But he had a power, an authority that she feared. He, also, represented to her the regime, the philosophy, all that she most disliked in a new word being used, Teutonism. She had a horror for the blind insensitivity of militarism, something inherited from her father.

She started confiding in Caspar and he seemed to listen and look with wonderful sympathy in his doleful eyes that seemed to comprehend all.

The table, at first sight, seemed a glimpse of summer. There were poppies, corn, cornflowers and larkspur. The plates matched. It was gay and very festive and Annie was enchanted.

To her surprise she found she was seated in a place of honour, by the major. His fair moustache, fair hair and shining clear skin made her heart beat a little faster, and as always happened, made her eyelids flutter.

He looked after her throughout the meal almost obsequiously. When they drank sweet wine and cracked nuts, she took an almond from the dish he proffered. He took the nut to open it for her, the pitted shell cracked, and carefully he extracted not one but two kernels. There was a general cry of "Ah" in an arch and knowing way. Annie looked puzzled.

Herr Clausen leant forward. "It means, Miss Taylor, that my brother-in-law must give you a present."

"Yes, indeed, Miss Taylor, what would you like?"

She was nonplussed, there were so many things she would like, even needed, but could not request.

"Some chocolate," she suggested.

"Why not a nice pair of gloves?" beamed Frau Clausen, who thought that more useful and suitable.

"I will leave it to the major."

The party ended with music and the particular dreamy warmth that Annie had come to expect. She went to bed happy and very relieved that not once had anyone mentioned the Imperial Family.

At lunch, next day, the major was a little late and he carried a parcel, a long slim flat box. He placed it on Annie's side plate. She opened it with a curious flutter of her heart, a warring of emotions whenever she encountered him.

Inside the wrapping was a box covered in brown striped silk, its lid was hinged and opening it she found a pair of the finest kid gloves, she lifted them to her nose, they smelt beautiful.

Frau Clausen looked pleased that her advice had been taken. Herr Clausen was pleased, too.

"Try them on." She lifted the right glove and began to smooth it on her hand, the progress was impeded, something hard and metallic prevented her middle finger entering the stall.

She withdrew her hand perplexed as she took out her hand so a ring slipped into her palm. The luxury of the gloves had surprised her... the extravagance of the ring perplexed her. It was gold and it formed a shamrock enclosing two emeralds and a ruby. Her first reaction was that she could not accept it. Herr Clausen looked still happier.

"Miss Taylor, a ring is the correct thing for a gentleman to give to his partner in a double almond. Well done, Conrad."

Frau Clausen took the ring and looked at it carefully, saying: "How very, very nice, you foolish spendthrift boy."

Annie felt this was a rebuke for them both. She retrieved her ring embarrassed. She liked it but wondered whether it were a bribe, what was expected of her from it? She slipped it on her little finger, it looked very fine and from his pocket the major produced a small leather case. He handed it to her - it was warm from contact with his body. She quickly put it on the table.

"I hardly know how to thank you. It is very kind." The first sentence was true.

Up in her room Annie held her hand up before her, it was a very pretty ring indeed, but it still made her uneasy. Because of this feeling she could not enjoy it whole-heartedly.

That night there came news that the Kaiser was ill and that superseded all else in conversation. Again, the Crown Princess came in for a great deal of criticism and the major and his sister both said that the nation required Prince Wilhelm at the helm.

Herr Clausen hoped that Wilhelm would be delayed long enough his accession to the throne for him to learn to temper his speeches with some peace and some wisdom. "He does not represent the Germany of Goethe and Schiller."

To this both brother and sister united, saying that the times were different, we were now an Empire and that his brother-in-law spoke like a true Rhinelander, provincial and without ambition for his country.

Herr Clausen smoked his pipe quietly and agreed that the adjectives suited him. Annie admired his imperturbability. She recognised in him a very wise man. Ever afterwards when her goodwill towards the Germans was tested she remembered him.

The major was returning to his regiment the following day, he was looking ahead, however, and planning with his sister a holiday for the whole family at St Goar. They would be able to make trips up the Rhine and the Moselle from there.

The idea appealed to Annie - she wished to see Coblenz. Bingen, and the castles and the vineyards. The major became even keener when he discovered that Annie was not returning to England for her holiday.

On March 9th while Annie was walking with the boys on the hill looking across the city, they were suddenly stirred, even awed, by the sound of the great bell of the cathedral tolling. Slowly, regularly like a drum beat the air seemed to hold the ringing sound. It frightened Annie, for each stroke seemed to say, "Tod, Tod".

"Listen, listen," She said, "you may not hear that again for a very long time. The great bell is being tolled in the cathedral for the Kaiser."

They hurried home for they felt they should not be out unless they wore some sign of mourning. Yet as she had said to the boys that they might not hear it again, she wondered if that was true, it did seem that the new Kaiser Frederick was very sick. Annie knew little of cancer, but she knew that it was to be feared.

The weather turned colder, the east winds blew, but the new Kaiser returned from the Italian Riviera to his cold and suspicious capital. The papers, overnight, became more circumspect and speculated rather more on his health than his sickness.

Annie felt that she was witnessing history, her nationality she shared with the Kaiserin and very remotely she felt involved. This feeling was endorsed when she found that the man she called "The Spy" was even more in evidence.

Every walk she took was witnessed by him and the Clausens noticed his loitering outside the gates. Neither of them liked it and even considered sending Annie back to Holland.

The talk was perpetually of the handsome Wagnerian tragic

Emperor dying on his long-awaited throne. Every fraction of Court gossip was reiterated and embroidered.

There were stories that the Empress had ascended the steps to the throne with a bound, that she had been quick to receive the correct deference, even in the sickroom.

Annie thought that she was hated because she had spoken of her political desires and she had allowed her feelings to be seen. Annie ruefully thought that a spell as a governess in a foreign country, in another person's house, would be an admirable training for a queen in an alien country.

It would undoubtedly teach a woman to keep quiet. She thought of Wilhelm, too, there were no remarks about his waiting and waiting to leap up the steps to the throne, but they were obvious. But, added Annie to herself, the difference is that he is a man.

Every day brought fresh news of weakness, of rallying, but always of the wrangling of the German doctors with Morell Mackenzie. The quarrels manifested themselves in clumsy fumblings around a half dead throat.

People read with a morbid fascination even though it sickened them. Annie walked with the boys, the Spy at a distance, she kept her counsel. She longed, though, to talk to someone and one day as she stood in the poultry yard with the chickens pecking around her, she found herself unburdening herself to them.

"You are happy, you chase after food. You lucky, lucky creatures, you are not oppressed by all the things we are oppressed by." She talked of the Emperor, the cancer and as she went on, half confession, half reverie, half unspoken agitation, she found herself talking of the Major.

She described his fair handsome face, his erect carriage. The birds came closer and she squatted down to their level. Their strangely shrewd eyes looked at her obliquely. She felt such relief that she wished to stroke one of them, she put out a hand and destroyed their confidence.

They had seemed to comprehend and she gratefully flung out to them the last grains in the dipper. She walked swiftly back to the house, dread had gone and she said aloud as she went though the shrubbery,

"I can always go back to the Haverschmidts."

She was alone with Caspar on a sunny morning when she felt

rather than heard the great bell of the Cathedral toll again. Being alone, having no one to explain the phenomenon to, she felt this death more deeply. He had been too young to die.

She felt for his widow, but she thought that she must already know well what loneliness was. She knew that Bismarck was now in full power again. She felt that there was a danger in the world.

She turned back to the house. There was the Spy, moving towards her, her change of direction had disconcerted him. All her Englishness rose rapidly within her, she was tired of him, she resented him and "I can always go to the Haverschmidts" rang like the bell in her head. When level with him, she said,

"Good morning. You, now, have a new Emperor. I hope he will be as good as his father."

She did not await a reply.

The funeral was a muffled event, it was surpassed by the glory of the proclamations, especially that to the Army. This Annie read with a shudder.

"Thus we belong to each other, I and the Army, we were born for each other, whether it be the will of God to send us calm, or storm. You will soon swear fealty and submission to me, and I promise ever to bear in mind that from the world above the eyes of my forefathers who look down upon me, that I shall have one day to stand accountable to them for the glory and honour of the Army."

As she read it she heard the great bell again. She felt afraid for the world.

She read, too, of Friedrichskroon, where the Emperor had died. It had been sealed off to prevent papers being smuggled out to England. The widowed Empress was a prisoner. She thought it strange, a fantasy, but a week later she noticed that she was no longer being followed. The Spy had gone. A new regime was in command, she was no longer suspect.

The house had been rented at St Goar. The family boarded the steamer in Cologne and sailed slowly up the Rhine. They were all excited, Annie kept losing the boys and even their mother said, "Don't worry. They'll be in the engine room."

There Annie found them, they were watching spell-bound as they gazed at the great crank-shaft rising and falling, noisy but fluid in its angular rigidity. She understood none of these things, but she was interested that the boys were so soon engrossed in mechanical things.

She led them to the deck and there they leant out and watched the paddles as they went round, this she found different, the charm of water, the excitement of the ordered turbulence, the wake streaming behind.

This she could link with the scenery which she was determined to enjoy. Determination she found necessary, the country she found flat and only rolling, she had expected more magnificence, more grandeur. At lunch Herr Clausen understood her feelings and assured her,

"Just wait, Miss Taylor, until we have passed Bonn, then it grows more exciting."

Sure enough, the further inland they steamed, the narrower the valley became and the higher the hills. In time, she saw the castles that she had expected.

Some were on islands, others perched on cliffs surveying the great river. She was thrilled and the memories were to last a lifetime.

Even more than the castles she loved the little vineyards, tiny terraces where a false move on the tiller's part could plunge him to death. She loved the timber buildings – the first she had ever seen.

She wondered what life would be like in a village composed of one street facing the river and she asked herself, "Does life flow by and nothing happen?" Some looked so somnolent she thought it possible.

It was only on this voyage that she appreciated that this river was the central artery of Europe. She wondered about the lives of the bargees and their families. She saw children scramble over cargo and their mother knit and hold the tiller at the same time.

What language did they talk was another question she asked. What education did they have? At the broad confluence of the rivers at Coblenz, they watched the arrivals and departures. It was a large town and they all wished to get off and explore it. Herr Clausen promised them that they would return.

The boat continued up the Rhine, smaller boats went up the Moselle. The cliffs began to enclose and the power of legend seized Herr Clausen and he related the stories with zest. Annie felt that with the boys she was feeding here on some spiritual source, something ancient almost inexplicable in its power.

It was the magnetic pull of the past combined with landscape. The next stopping place was Boppard and then came St Goar.

The sun still shone, the sky was a pale blue, the houses were sandstone or half-timber and the streets narrow. It was enchantment and Annie's eyes grew rounder and brighter. They climbed into an open cab, the luggage piled around them and the boys hailed familiar sights like the sweet shop and the chandler's where fishing tackle could be bought. Annie gazed around and Frau Clausen said laughing,

"I do believe Miss Taylor will be a bigger handful than the boys, she is so excited."

The strain that pervaded the air of the house in Ehrenfeld seemed to have been left behind. The cab climbed up, stopped at a level crossing, and after the train had gone by, climbed on. Soon they turned left from the road and in at a gateway to a castellated house. It was almost as large as the house in Cologne - Annie had expected a more modest residence.

An old servant welcomed them, remarked on the growth of the boys and went back to her kitchen. All around the hall were antlers and large oleographs of Teutonic gods and goddesses. Frau Clausen now amazed Annie by summoning the servant and ordering her to make tea for "die schonste Englanderin."

Up in her room, Annie sank into a chair by the window that overlooked the roofs below, the railway, the bend of the river and Goarhausen on the other side which also rose steeply up to a cliff on which perched another castle. To Annie's delight she saw a light suddenly gleam in one of the deep embrasures.

"This is fairyland." Yet as she said it, it all became oddly familiar, it was not unlike Armitage Bridge even Milnsbridge, but with all the dirt and utilitarianism removed and replaced by romance. This she thought very strange.

Each evening, Herr Clausen read legends of the Rhine to the family. His calm face shone in the light reflected from the pages. There was great peace and Annie wished that it could last.

As it grew dark, so the lamp was lit and then the moths flew in and fluttered hovered and sometimes caught fire around the funnel of the lamp glass, then there would be a rustle in the shrubs as the evening wind blew.

Annie wondered how this family differed to a Dutch one - there was more fantasy, more imagination. It had to be added that there was more striving, too, and tempers were more easily lost. The stolid quality of Holland was missing.

It was noticeable that without neighbours and her husband's colleagues in the business world Frau Clausen was gentler, much more content and more understanding existed between husband and wife.

The quiet days passed and Annie often went up the paths through the little vineyards alone. At close quarters they did not seem as precipitous as they did from the boat and the Rhine from this high vantage point looked like a twisting snake.

On her walks she picked honeysuckle and foxgloves which she arranged and put all over the house, these, too, seemed to contribute to the dreamlike atmosphere that enveloped them all.

She wished that it could last forever... she hated the quarrels with the servants and the general tension.

Once on a walk she came upon a pair of lovers. They walked arm in arm, very close. They were so rapt in one another they never saw her until she was quite close. Then they smiled and said "Good afternoon", but they spoke from another world.

Annie felt a pang and asked herself why it was she did not fall in love. She missed touch. Nobody in Germany slipped an arm in hers, no one, like Mevrouw Haverschmidt would casually stroke her hair as she passed by while Annie read.

It was, she thought, a fair world, at the present, a little castle, even if new, with flowers, peace and legends, but it lacked any intimate meaning for her.

Back at the house, when she changed for the evening she looked in the mirror, she saw a tall young woman with a straight, proud carriage, a very small neat waist and a bosom neither too large nor too small.

She bent closer to look at her face, roundly oval and a complexion of white and pink and what she knew to be her glory, two large round Delft blue eyes and all beneath a fashionable pile of curly hair.

She wondered if, perhaps, she was too upright. Was she prim? That, she reckoned, was the pitfall for most governesses, those repositories of correct grammar and demeanour.

She sighed and went downstairs.

During dinner it was decided that next day Herr Clausen, the boys and Annie should sail up the river to Bingen. Frau Clausen said that she wanted to stay at home and write letters and sit in the garden.

"But you all go," She said very amiably.

They were to pass the Lorelei, so Herr Clausen read the story of the deceiving maidens. When he finished he shut the book with a snap and said to his sons: "Now, there's a warning. Never trust a woman."

There was a gust of laughter and both his wife and Annie rushed to the defence of their sex. It became horseplay and cushions were thrown around and order was only restored when one of Annie's vases of flowers fell over.

Early next morning the little group stood on the pier awaiting the arrival of the boat. Precise to the hour it arrived. They found four seats, waiters came and they drank coffee. The waiter mistook her for Herr Clausen's wife. This amused the boys who had noticed it immediately.

"Well, it is a compliment to an old man like me," said Herr Clausen.

Annie demurred, but not vigorously, she thought it a joke that would fade, but the boys kept it up calling her Mama.

At Bingen there was a festival, garlands hung across the streets, there was dancing. It was heady boisterous fun. They went to a fair and Herr Clausen won a rosette which he handed to Annie. She had been surprised at his skill with a gun. He was pleased with himself and tucking Annie's arm in his own, said to the boys, "Now find Mama and Papa somewhere to eat."

The boys wandered down the busy street looking at the inns, they were, as Frau Clausen had said, mostly vulgar places. Hans-Peter would call out, "Will this do?" Always Herr Clausen would shake his head. He knew, Annie discovered, precisely where they were going.

They left the town and started to climb the hill which led towards an imposing hotel with a long terrace overlooking the river. Annie was impressed, the position was magnificent, the great house sat like a saddle on the back of a vast animal.

Beneath a canopy they ate Wiener schnitzel and young and

tender cabbage that had been cooked in champagne. While the adults drank their coffee and Herr Clausen smoked a cigar, a sense of peace and well-being slipped over them.

"Well, Mama Annie, what are we to do with you?"

Annie was surprised at the use of her Christian name. She rather liked it.

"What to you mean?"

"Well, you cannot be a governess all your life. Have you no young man in love with you?"

"No. There is no one."

He doubted it and critically said: "Not anyone in Holland or England?"

"No."

"I am very surprised. What about marrying a German then?"

Annie was suddenly afraid... she wondered what he was meaning. Was he obliquely offering her himself? She parried it with a laugh and said, "I shall have to fall in love first of all."

"What about my brother-in-law? He needs a wife."

"The major?"

"Yes."

"I don't think he would marry me. He will want a Berliner gnadige fraulein, not an English governess."

"I think you under-rate yourself. He likes you very much. He gave you that ring."

Annie looked at the ring, she had never liked it. She had always known there would be a catch in it. Herr Clausen continued to watch her - he saw some of her thoughts, but by no means all.

"You could carry the palm off any Prussian lady. I can see you as a Colonel's lady." He smoked on happily and pleasurably complacent.

Annie sat very still behind a stiller face, she was far from complacent and all the innocent happiness of the day had vanished. She wondered if it had ever been innocent. The world expected her to marry and, as yet, she had not fallen in love.

Now it was expected that she should marry the major. The thought agitated her. She found that she did not so dislike the man so much as all that he represented. She had not forgotten his dismissal of the lately dead Emperor, his belief in the new and his deep suspicions of the Empress, 'Die Englanderin'.

Surely, surely he would not countenance an English woman as his wife? What surprised her was that they considered her suitable. It would not have been so in England, or so she thought. She did not realise that beauty and charm unlock most doors and strangely especially those that appear most guarded.

Annie was left alone at the table and in spite of her recent disquiet. She could not but admire the hotel. It was elegant, even a trifle opulent, but she admired the way the waiters came and without being officious seemed to anticipate their customers' wishes.

It was all so quiet, restrained and seemed to run on well oiled wheels. There was, she thought, much training that made a place like this.

On the way down to cheerful, hearty Bingen, where the boys had a ride on the swing boats which Annie was certain would make them sick, her fears subsided. She even began to laugh at the fantasy of Herr Clausen and herself marrying the major.

As the boat went swiftly down the river as effortlessly as a swan in pride with the wind behind its raised wings, Annie marvelled only at the scenery. Almost too soon they were at St Goar and climbing, rather wearily, the steep streets up to their holiday schloss.

Frau Clausen welcomed them all with wide smiles and bade them all hurry for dinner was nearly ready and she had a great surprise for them all which could not be told until they were all around the table.

As they ate the boys chattered noisily, they revealed everything, even that Annie had been mistaken for their mother. Their mother echoed her husband,

"That is a compliment for me."

Truly, thought Annie, this place had wrought a miracle. It all seemed too good to be true.

At last, their adventures recounted, Ludwig asked,

"What was the surprise?"

"A telegram. Your uncle is in Darmstadt and coming here tomorrow."

Annie looked swiftly at Herr Clausen. She wondered if his remarks had been preparing her for this. She wondered if there was a conspiracy. But he seemed as surprised as his boys and his delight was not unmixed with other feelings.

It was the batman who changed the atmosphere. He brought a certain formality to the household for he waited at table. He also made trouble in the kitchen, so that strain was re-introduced and the practice of diplomacy needed.

Annie noticed that Herr Clausen seemed to slip unobtrusively into the shadows when his brother-in-law was present. The major and his sister stepped forward. The legends were no longer read.

One evening, however, Ludwig begged for one and again his father read. But it was not the same. The major fidgeted with his cigarettes and his sister did not sew quietly but played Patience and made little noises of irritation when it did not work out properly. Their manoeuvres were subtle, half-unconscious and wholly successful.

When the tale ended, it became a text for a homily on the future greatness of a united Germany – a greatness to exceed that of any other empire. Annie kept quiet but, for the first time, thought with pride of the immensity of the territory that was shaded pink on the atlases.

Her mind flitted from Africa, to India, to Australia and Canada. She thought too of Yorkshire, "the workshop of the world".

The major, well launched on a favourite theme, spoke of the navy they were building. Here he specifically mentioned Britain. Annie was stung, she also thought these were strange words to hear from a man, whom others thought, wished to marry her.

She listened and as the glories of an up-to-date navy, unlike others it was implied, the demon of mischief crept into her quietude. With a wide smile she said, "But, Major, what is the use of a huge navy when you have hardly any coastline?

"Remember, we are quite different, we are an island and so need our navy to protect ourselves on all sides."

As soon as she had said it she regretted it. Her remark was considered typically English, true arrogance masked by humour. Their anger bordered on hysteria. It revealed to her the gulf between the two countries and the great envy the Germans had.

She was frightened at their vehemence, but she comforted herself that her ill-considered remark, if nothing else, would turn him from any designs of pursuit.

In the hall, on her way to bed, she met Herr Clausen. He looked grave.

"Keep off politics, Miss Taylor, please."

She needed no prompting.

Life overnight became more active and far less spontaneous: outings were arranged like campaigns with trains, walks, a carriage awaiting them at a specific spot in a forest to be met with at a precise hour.

When it rained and they slipped in mud Annie thought how much better it would have been to spend the fine day on a sudden expedition, even if less ambitious. But she held her peace and sitting bedraggled in the train was surprised to hear the major praise her stamina. He even called her an "old campaigner."

At dinner there was a pause in the conversation, they were all tired by the rigours of the day, outings were no longer just pleasures. Annie had put on the ring as a compliment to him, he remarked upon it and that the form was a shamrock.

"Do you have Irish blood, Miss Taylor?"

"No, none at all, but I do have Welsh blood in my veins."

This opened up an enquiry on Annie's antecedents and the origins of the Welsh and the fundamentals of their character. Having listened he then propounded a pre-destined conclusion that the Celtic and Prussian temperaments were much akin. Annie did not argue - it was ludicrous.

It was from that evening that he sought her out when ever she might be alone and the only place of safety was her room, which she liked anyway, looking out over the roofs to the castle on the other side.

He became more persistent and when he found the boys with her he would curtly dismiss them, even when she remonstrated. Her dislike deepened and unfortunately, to disguise her fear, she smiled too often and when she was agitated she fluttered her eyelids too prettily.

Her knowledge of men was, she was well aware, limited. She wished dearly that her father had lived longer. It was her misfortune to live in an age when the disparity of the masculine and feminine sexes was exaggerated because it was being eroded very gradually.

She had been brought up in Britain where, with her mother being the bread-winner especially, the role of the subservient woman was in question. She had absorbed unformed ideas about independence.

Then in Leiden she had lived in a school where men had played a negative part. Now she was in a land of male dominance. For her the holiday was being turned from a dream to a nightmare.

On the walks the major was ever by her side and he had an ally, his sister. That she expected but one day as they packed up the basket after a picnic in a shady avenue and they had set forth, the basket was taken from her hand, it was the major's hand.

Annie did not look at him but turned and to her dismay found Herr Clausen smiling at her as though to say "You have him."

She felt that she was in a web of misconceptions and deceit and for the first time she acknowledged that her very femininity had been an essential part of it.

Annie knew the very smell of the man, the tobacco, the leather, his sweat at the end of a walk and some smell she could never identify.

Once beneath the trees in the garden as she poured out tea, while they sat on the grass, he leant over the table cloth. The bright sunshine, the white blouse, the small brim of the hat that cast a shadow over her eyes so aroused him that he kissed her.

She sat back and put her hand to her mouth. Rather lamely she said: "You should not have done that."

"But I had to, you are so pretty."

She sat rather more upright and though she looked grave, her bust was raised into a more alluring posture. Again she kept quiet, but her heart was pounding. She did not appreciate that his was beating just as feverishly.

She did not love him, she feared him and her analysis went no further. She stood up and fled indoors. He was perplexed and angry... he had misread all the signs. Other conquests had been far easier.

Annie did not know what to do. She was unable to send him away, she felt herself the centre of a conspiracy and the three adults just waited for her capitulation, not with evil intent, but with that imperturbable and genteel prurience that surrounds so much of engagement and marriage.

Next day, there was a letter from the Haverschmidts. They were holidaying in Heidelberg and asked her to join them if possible. To Annie it seemed heaven-sent and the very touch of it was like a life-belt for a drowning sailor.

Her confidence returned. She sought leave and it was granted with great alacrity. Frau Clausen believed that the Haverschmidts would give Annie good advice.

Although Annie tried to avoid the major, he out plotted her stratagems and caught her alone in the drawing room. To her amazement the bombast crumbled beneath tears. Annie found this even more difficult to bear, it aroused her pity... it made her guilty.

Yet there were two layers to her consciousness, the surface wept in unison, but the bedrock beneath was contemptuous of his and her own tears. He caught her hand and begged her to call him Conrad and he proposed marriage. To say 'No' at that moment seemed like striking him while low. She begged for time.

"We must not rush into this. There are many obstructions. How will your colonel like an English wife for one of his officers?"

"When you marry me, you will become a German."

"Perhaps with as much difficulty as the Empress Frederick? We are a stubborn people, you know."

"You are totally different. Anyway, what have we to fear, the English and the Germans are cousins. There will never be trouble between our nations."

Again she begged for time.

She crossed the lawn to the house, slowly, rather forlornly climbed the steps to the house. Conrad watched her closely and reaching for his cigarette case took out a cigarette, tapped it and lit it.

He inhaled deeply, it brought no satisfaction. He was violently in love, he was possessed. His sister came out, he shook his head. Her eyes narrowed, she was angered and bruised for her brother's sake and asked what right had that English Miss to play such bashfulness to a proposal from her brother.

The magic of St Goar bade her keep silent, something Cologne never did.

Looking from her window Annie saw the siblings talking to one another. She looked at the navy jacketed man, tall, well-built. She wished for a moment she could love him. But behind the square cut face and the large blue eyes was something unpredictable.

"No," said Annie, "Something predictable, arbitrary and despotic."

She knew that he could give her security, a position, but at what cost? Her intuition over-rode every other consideration. She knew that there could be no gain. But she did not know what to do. She fell asleep.

She awoke feeling refreshed but the fear, like bereavement crept into her soul. She heartened herself by saying that there was only the evening to get through, then she would be with the Haverschmidts. It was a very trying evening for them all.

Awaiting Annie at Heidelberg station was the entire Haverschmidt family. They welcomed her with an enthusiasm which was very un-English and very un-Germanic, it was openly and uninhibitedly Dutch. It was precisely what she needed and she felt all the pent up emotions stream away.

Margo and Frank took an arm on either side of her and began excitedly to talk, both at once. A voice called out.

"Give Annie time to see the town. She's come to see Heidelberg not just listen to you two."

They all laughed, but it had been a reminder to Annie that she must look about her. Had she not seen the Rhineland, grown used to St Goar, Heidelberg would have been a revelation.

She had, though, grown accustomed to half-timbered houses, narrow, climbing streets and the narrowness of a valley. This town, however, had more, it had the air that only a university town can have and it was so old.

Annie caught her breath when from the statued bridge they saw the long pink sandstone castle. It shimmered in the heat and looked like a mirage, perched half-way up the steep bank: it was incredibly romantic.

Francois promised them a visit next day. They went into a tea-garden. The river flowed by on one side fast and exciting and on the other was the long slower drift of the endless procession of people.

Annie felt that she was with her own family, "No" she corrected herself, "better." There were some things she could never tell Edith, she could tell the Haverschmidts anything. She listened to all the little things.

Who was in charge of the birds? How was the new maid shaping? What the dining room looked like now it had been re-decorated... it was the unstudied talk of intimate people.

It was not until after dinner, whilst Francois smoked his cigar, something that young Frank now did, but not with the tranquillity of his father, that Annie began to tell them of the Clausen family.

Frank was restless. He wanted to return to the river, so his mother and sister rose to go with him. Mevrouw Haverschmidt knew that there was something Annie wished to tell and it was better that she left her husband to listen.

She knew that she would hear later from him. For both mother and daughter had noticed that there was a certain perplexity about Annie that they had not seen before.

Alone Francois opened a small floodgate, Annie's feelings, thoughts gushed out and her fear of the Major.

Francois glanced at her frequently, but mostly watched the orchestra. He listened, he saw Annie's plight, but he set it against the larger backcloth of women, like her, unprovided, sometimes unprotected in a world arranged and ordered by men. He saw the monstrous injustice.

Very tactfully, she mentioned the new German militarism, she was conscious of ears around her that would not agree with her sentiments. As he listened, Francois noted the pride with which two students nearby wore their fencing scars.

There was, he thought, a violence here which was greatly at odds with the gentle, even vulnerable face across the table.

At last she asked him. "Ought I to marry him?"

There was enough of the practical Hollander in him to see the advantages of such a match.

"I can only say that I have known very happy marriages where the love to begin with was all on one side. But I would advise you to obey your instincts. If you were more certain, you would not be asking me. The heart is a better guide than the head in these matters."

"That is exactly what I wished to hear you say. I thought that I was being foolish."

"You must not marry him if you fear him. That would be very wrong. Obey your instincts."

When the little family returned, Mevrouw Haverschmidt saw instantly that Annie looked happier and that her husband had the look, she knew well, of a man carrying someone else's burdens. She rallied them both to come and watch the dancing.

The following day they walked around the town. They explored the castle, they chattered unendingly, and all too soon they were having dinner and the last evening was upon them. It had been a happy, happy interlude.

At the station while they put Annie into an empty carriage, Frank ran off and returned with a nosegay, a tight bunch of young pine branches, some tight rose buds and the scarlet glint of cock's combs in the green.

It smelt of the forest, it represented all that Annie loved in the Germans. The train drew out and Francois promised Annie a good long uninterrupted read. She could not read, she did not even look at the scenery - she reviewed in her mind the Haverschmidts.

They were good, they were guileless and understanding. She thought how, like Frau Clausen, they were nicer away from their responsibilities. They were not worried. She only wished that when they were in Rotterdam that this understanding would continue.

The train went many miles before it stopped at a small junction. Annie looked out, it seemed deserted, she heard a door open and slam and then to her horror, the Major stood before her door.

He opened it, leapt in flung his case on the rack and his hat along the seat. He beamed a triumphant smile. Annie's heart beat alarmingly. For a second she likened herself to a rabbit confronted by a stoat. She banished the thought immediately.

"You followed me. You got on the train in Heidelberg."

"Yes. My plans went very well and my luck has held."

She looked at the smooth well cared for face and body and it aroused in her nothing but distaste. The air about him was of hardened discipline, but allied with something almost overpoweringly physical. It was that she feared. There was about him a sensuality that repelled.

"Aren't you pleased to see me?"

"No. I am very surprised. I thought you understood my feelings."

"Don't be afraid. I want you for my wife."

"I cannot. I cannot. I do not love you."

He moved towards her. She retreated further into the corner sitting bolt upright. Her heart banged again and she felt herself gasp for breath. She felt that she might faint, but feared unconsciousness.

She knew his strength and feared he might overpower her. There seemed a throbbing terrifying heat in the air. She was never more afraid... for he was aroused.

There was a sign of relaxation... he took out his cigarette case and the almost violent feelings subsided. He sighed as he blew out smoke and he began to paint a picture of their life in Berlin. They would have a house, there would be regimental balls, receptions and dinners,

"And you will grace them all." Annie almost feared this insidious persuasion more.

"Please do not speak of it. I cannot marry you. I do not love you."

He shouted: "Why, why?"

His amour-propre was piqued. He had never been rejected before so firmly. He started towards her again and desire glinted in his eye and again Annie started up and groped towards the communication cord. Seeing this attempt cooled him, but angered him as well.

"You little fool. Do you think they will believe your word against mine?" An iciness entered Annie's heart. She knew the truth of that remark. She would not be believed.

He did not cease talking and Annie, now, noticed that he was not entirely reasonable in his talk. He was possessed. He smoked constantly and he never stopped talking. Only fear kept her alert and awake for she was exhausted.

It was now that the longest hour of her life began, another hour before they reached Darmstadt. She knew that her vigilance was needed and that never must she in a moment of weakness give her consent to marriage. It would be used against her.

At Darmstadt she took down her case. He sat and watched.

"I shall catch the next train. Please delay. Give me time."

When her train came in she carefully chose a carriage already occupied. She did not know what to do. Should she go straight on to Holland. The idea tempted her, but then she thought of her clothes. She could not arrive in Holland with nothing and the Haverschmidts did not return until next day.

The ideas ran round and round her head and, at last, worn out, she fell asleep mesmerised by the constant repetition of the same puzzles in her mind.

She woke with a start and looked instantly for Conrad, she saw the staid people her agitation quietened. She decided to go back.

It was possible that they knew nothing of Conrad's schemes.

It seemed very strange to her that she re-entered the house as if nothing had happened. The only remark was at supper when her pallor was remarked upon. It was attributed to the long journey.

A telegram came from Darmstadt informing them that Conrad had been recalled to his regiment.

"What a pity," said Frau Clausen, "Just when you were getting to know him." She had re-entered the world of legends again, that evening it was difficult for her to concentrate, her own problems were closer and there was no magic to solve them. The boys did not seem to listen so avidly.

Next day, she understood why, they had dug an earthwork in the unused kitchen garden. There were deep holes cut into the ground, she did not call them trenches, there was a larger square with piled earth round it.

This she called a redoubt. Here the boys played mock battles. The major had infected the place. Dreams were being dismissed. As Annie walked away and looked out at the town below and Goarhousen beyond, she muttered, "There is something in the Germans I do not understand."

The truth was she understood too well the spreading militarism. The Germany of Goethe was being overtaken by the spirit of Frederick the Great. She had seen it. She had experienced it, something very close to madness.

That day she was very, very tired, too tired to be anxious, but the immediate past haunted her and she knew that she would have to make changes very soon in the future. The family went for a walk in the vineyards but Annie stayed behind and slept.

In the evening, she noticed that Frau Clausen kept looking at her.

"Is everything all right, Miss Taylor - are you well?"

Annie made a non-committal reply. Then she noticed that both of her employers were looking at her. This time she asked,

"Is something wrong?"

"Not really," and Herr Clausen laughed, "It is your eye. You've got a twitch, but it does not seem to worry you, so it cannot be important." Nevertheless, the Clausens looked at one another with concern.

Up in her room, Annie looked in the dressing-table mirror.

She could see nothing when she stared. She grew tired of facing herself and started to arrange her hair. Then she saw that indeed her right eye almost shut itself with an involuntary movement.

She remembered having seen that happen to her mother when she was distraught. Having linked it with her she felt reassured and felt that it would go.

The journey back to Cologne was on a rainy day. A gloom settled over the family, the boys were sad to leave the freedom of St Goar. Their mother began to fuss and consult her diary of engagements and suggested dinner parties during the winter and, as nothing could be planned, her appeals to her husband only brought out grunts.

Annie, too, was rapt in her thoughts, the dream, the nightmare. When they reached Bonn the sun came out and at Cologne the cathedral spires stood silhouetted against a red sunset. Annie was glad to see it she had grown fond of it.

The clutter of the house oppressed her, even though it all shone and gleamed from all the work the staff had put in before the family's return.

There was an interval of near tranquillity. Hans-Peter went to the Gymnasium, so that Annie had only Ludwig to teach. He was an eager little boy and willing to please. A bond of affection had sprung up, between the two and it saddened Annie that shortly it would be broken.

She had already written to Mevrouw Haverschmidt saying that she might have to come to them sooner than she had thought.

Frau Clausen's temper became shorter and sharper. There were glum periods when the couple did not speak at dinner and Annie found herself making conversation. For two days there was an atmosphere of suspicion and one evening Frau Clausen could keep her troubles and resentments to herself no longer.

Annie learnt that Conrad had been transferred from his crack regiment to a lesser one and then despatched to the Polish border. His career was in disarray. His explanations were brief and inadequate and Annie prayed that they would remain so.

Frau Clausen was determined to find out the cause. There then came news through another military acquaintance that the Major had been absent without leave. It became known that he had stayed too long in Darmstadt. Then another letter came and she discovered that her brother had also been to Heidelberg.

Instantly, she summoned Annie and asked her if she had seen her brother there. Annie's first impulse was to deny it. For a moment she argued that it was true that she had not seen him there. Instead she said, "Yes. He was on the same train going to Darmstadt."

"Why did you not tell me?"

"I wished to forget the whole episode. Anyway you would not believe me."

"Did he propose to you again?"

"Yes."

"And you refused! Good God, the pride of you British."

"If you wish to know more I think you had better question your brother."

The rage of Frau Clausen resembled her brother in the train and again Annie felt a terrible menace.

"You insolent English - From Empresses to governesses you are the same. You are all arrogant, all scheming."

Annie gripped the back of the chair and forced herself to say calmly,

"I think, Frau Clausen, I had better terminate my employment with you immediately. I can no longer stay under this roof."

"I think that my foolish brother has had a lucky escape. But you, you," she struggled for a word that would not come, "have cost him his career."

Annie left. She went up to the schoolroom, heard Ludwig read and when he had finished he said: "I don't think you were listening."

"No, I wasn't. The truth is, Ludwig, I am going to leave you and straightaway."

The small boy's face crumpled and he began to cry. Annie pulled him on to her lap and putting her arms around him cried too. It was a great relief, for she had wanted to cry for many days and had not.

She cried because she did not know where her future lay. She felt totally insecure and vulnerable. She was experiencing almost precisely the same emotions as the small boy upon her knee, that of being at the mercy of others.

"I think, Ludwig, you had better help me pack."

He scurried around bringing her books and writing materials from the schoolroom and she laid them out on the bed.

Lunch was eaten with a very heavy heart by the two of them. As they finished, they heard a heavy tread upon the stairs and Herr Clausen entered. He looked upset. He told Ludwig to go into the garden.

"Is it true, Miss Taylor, that you have given in your notice?"

"Yes. I cannot say any longer. I am blamed for her brother's misfortunes. All I did was say that I could not marry him."

"I know, I know. But some people cannot bear to be denied anything."

Annie was not unaware of the unspoken in that remark.

"Where will you go?"

She told him. He questioned her further. He sat down and very carefully made a note of the Haverschmidt's address. He asked further.

"If you want a reference, write to me at the office. Is there anything else I can do?"

"Yes, I am afraid there is. I have not been paid this quarter."

"I will see to that. When you are ready Ludwig and I will take you to the station."

Annie hurriedly packed her clothes and when it was done it was carried down for her. She followed it. She thought that this was the nadir of her life, but no sooner was that thought acknowledged than she raised her head and said aloud to herself, "It is not nearly as bad as when Mother died, Annie my girl."

Suddenly her spirit returned and she even managed to smile at Ludwig and his father who stood in the hall. She went towards the front door.

"No. I want you to see my wife. We are civilised people. We say goodbye."

He moved towards the drawing room, Annie faltering followed.

"Miss Taylor is here my dear, she has come to say goodbye."

Frau Clausen seemed absorbed ruffling letters before her. Annie noticed, with surprise that she wore gloves. Annie stretched out her hand, also gloved, their fingers touched and quickly retracted. Annie saw the hardness in Frau Clausen's eye and knew too well that it was identical to the Major's.

In the carriage there was silence. Herr Clausen still looked troubled. Annie wondered if there had been a scene when he had told her he would take her to the station. She felt sorry for him, she felt sorry for Ludwig, but knew that he would soon forget.

But her relief to leave was immense. She remembered that it was Herr Clausen who had met her and brought her to Ehrenfeldt, now the same journey was traversed in reverse. In the city they came to a halt, they looked out, there was a troop of soldiers marching by headed by a brass band.

The cymbals clashed and the drums banged, it all seemed so crashingly obtuse and fitting that this jangle should mark her going. She hated it and thought of a phrase she had read and did not know where,

"All the delusive seduction of martial music..." It was true. Herr Clausen mistook her dislike for hatred.

"Do not think too hard of the Germans, Miss Taylor. We are not all Prussians. We are Goethe, we are Heine too, Mozart as well."

"I do know. Yes, I do."

At the station he bade her stay by her luggage whilst he bought her a ticket. As he handed it to her he pressed into her hand a chamois leather purse, she knew well, it was heavy.

"Your ticket and our thanks. We will miss you, won't we Ludwig?"

She wished him to go, but he insisted on putting her on the train. As they walked along the carriages she said,

"A ladies' carriage if you please."

Installed she would not let them stay.

Only as the train pulled out she looked at the mirror set into the panelling above the seat opposite her.

"My mirror. Mother's mirror. I've left it on the wall." She had left, too, her father's common-place book. Hans-Peter had been copying out an English poem the previous night.

She could never bring herself to write to ask for their return.

Chapter 24

Holland

The train carried her away, away and for her it could not go fast enough. At last they came to the border and they stopped, then very soon after at the first station in Holland. She thought herself silly, but there was an urge to step out on to the platform.

When she did, she was glad, for, indeed, relief flooded through her, she was safe and back to where she belonged.

To her surprise, she heard familiar voices and there on the tiny station were Francois and Haverschmidt. Annie ran to the outstretched arms and sank within them. Francois managed to encircle them both.

They all boarded the train and went to Schiedam. Annie found that an operation involving the whole family had been arranged, the parents had gone to the border, Frank had been meeting trains at Rotterdam and Margo had waited at home.

When Annie heard of all this she cried… for this was love.

It was not until Annie had gone to bed that Francois asked his wife whether Annie had told her what had gone wrong.

"No. I think we shall have to wait. She may tell you first."

"I don't know. I am forever detecting changes in Annie. I have seen her develop. When she went to Germany she was self-possessed and dignified. Her dignity deserted her on the railway station. I was surprised."

"It will return."

The quiet dignity came back very soon, Francois knew, though, that it was wrapping around a real hurt. Five days went by until Mevrouw Haverschmidt and Annie were sorting through a basket of mending. Without looking up Annie said, "You must wonder why I am here?"

"Yes, we wonder, but you can tell us in your own good time."

She felt flattered that Annie was confiding in her, she had wondered whether all Annie's affection was reserved for her husband.

"Major von Barintz fell in love with me. He was Frau Clausen's brother. He is a Prussian. He even proposed. I was flattered but I never loved him. I thought I had made it clear but evidently I had not. His sister said that I encouraged him.

"He got on the same train as me in Heidelberg. He got into my empty carriage. At first he was quite pleasant, though I was afraid, but..." her voice trailed away. She looked out of the window and her right eye gave a sudden uncontrollable wink.

She took Mevrouw Haverschmidt's hand. She held it very tight. She sat more upright, still looked out of the window.

"He tried to seduce me."

She burst into tears. The women put their arms around each other.

"I was very, very afraid. He was beside himself with lust. If he had tried to overpower me, he could have. He was mad with lust. It was horrible."

The older woman clucked her tongue and said nothing.

"I made for the communication cord. He said they would never believe my word against his. That was what was so awful. I would never be believed."

"You are safe now, my dear. We are different in Holland."

"Yes, you are. I am so glad to be back."

"You managed to keep him at bay did you?"

"Oh yes. He managed to remember, just, that he was a gentleman. It seems silly, but though I was so frightened, the part that really hurt was that I would not be believed. Or worse, blamed for something I never intended should happen."

"Germans do not like the British at the moment. They are jealous of the Empire. Then there was all the trouble about the Emperor Frederick and Dr Morrell Mackenzie. That was tactless."

"I think that the Empress was driven to it all. Germany is a strange hard place."

Even as she said it she remembered the kindness of Herr Clausen and managed to say, "But not all of them."

Mevrouw Haverschmidt returned to the central topic,

"But you say that he did nothing to you in fact. All is well?"

Annie's head rose, she stared ahead,

"Yes, all is well. I am not a German's strumpet, even unwillingly."

Mevrouw Haverschmidt was shocked by the vehemence, but

glad to see some of the old spirit returning. She felt that she did know all. She told her husband. She told him most things even when he exasperated her with his melancholy.

It was when Annie was out on a walk with Francois that he said that he was glad that all was well with her. She knew instantly what he meant. For a moment she thought, then replied,

"But all is not well, mijnheer, I feel defiled. I disliked the man and I feel ashamed that I aroused such passions in him."

"It happens to us all in life, my dear. Don't you think that I do not know that there are foolish women who listen to me not for my beliefs, what I have to offer, but because they love me from afar?"

"I suppose that is true."

"It happens to us all. We must not take it too seriously, especially you, Annie, an Englishwoman. You English never take anything too seriously. You sometimes shock us. I think the trouble is that you have not been in love yourself, yet, but that will come, as sure as night follows the day."

Annie looked at him. He was in one of his happier moods when his charm was most apparent. She reflected that she was not in love with him. She was not one of his foolish women. But she knew that she admired him. She would like such a man for herself.

It happened that the Haverschmidts were to visit Leiden. Annie accompanied them and whilst they attended to their business Annie called on Miss Lange and Miss Snoek. The moment was opportune, the English teacher was ill, so Annie found herself once more back at her old post, even her old room. She was profoundly thankful.

The old life quickly enfolded her but she found the small rules irksome. She had been in a wider world and she wanted to return.

In the New Year she was once more in Schidam. One day there was no wind, the sun shone and over breakfast an outing was planned. They decided to walk by the sea at Scheveningen and eat at the Kurhaus. François, eager and happy, decreed that he would not go unless Annie wore her red velvet toque.

It was one she had made in imitation of Lily Langtry and its dark vivid colour emphasised the blueness of her eyes. The softness of the fabric matched up with her skin. She looked very lovely as they set forth and she was not unaware of the glances that were made towards her.

In Scheveningen there were not so many people, but enough to make it interesting as they paraded up and down taking the air and assessing the clothes of those around them.

They walked in the foyers of the Kurhaus but decided they wanted to walk still more before lunch, so they set out towards the Seinpost.

There the vast room with its huge windows looking out to the sea on one side, over the dunes on the other looked welcoming.

The waiters hustled silently to and fro attending to the wants of the clients and Annie watched and was reminded of the hotel in Bingen. Already it all seemed so far away – though the episode lay like a rock beneath the apparently unruffled water.

As the wind can disturb the lake and reveal hidden objects in the waves, so a thought would suddenly reveal to Annie the wound of the German experience. But she was blessed in that she never brooded, she had the happy knack of shrugging off the unpleasant and this day she remembered much more clearly Herr Clausen and their calm enjoyment of a well-nigh perfect day. It led to other memories but she carefully shut them away.

Margo leant across the table and said: "Annie, your hat is being noticed here just as much as in Schiedam. There's a young woman behind you who is often looking. Why it is Nelleke Bloem. Do you remember her?"

Annie could not turn and stare, she vaguely remembered a quiet girl, good at English in her first year.

"I think I remember her. She hated embroidery."

Margo bowed and smiled, the recognition had been mutual.

The menu was pondered, Heer Haverschmidt ordered. Annie looked out the sea, it was grey flecked with white and blue. In the distance great patches of light moved where shafts from the sun shone.

Her eye moved from the horizon inwards to the shore, the flecks, waves rising and running in. She noticed a man and his horse and cart. He was shovelling sand. He and the horse worked in complete unison, a thrust of the spade, a lift and throw into the cart, a word, it seemed, and the horse moved a pace, another bit of sand, another move forward.

They worked as one. At first Annie admired the horse, then the man. In spite of the cold he wore a thin cotton jacket that flapped around his hips beneath the broad belt and buckle.

She found herself appraising his wonderful posture, so straight a back, such square shoulders at right angles to his spine. She found herself further wondering what his wife and home and children were like.

His very movements seemed so certain that it indicated he knew precisely where his duties lay. She contrasted herself, like most women she did not know where she was going, they lived from day to day, making the most of the hour, yet it all hinged upon a man and whether he proposed marriage, or not.

She felt that it was unfair. She saw no solution to the quandary. She wondered if he enjoyed shovelling sand as much as she enjoyed teaching. Yet her occupation was a stop-gap until marriage came, if it ever did. She then remembered that she had been told not to be too serious, she was an Englishwoman. She smiled to herself.

The excellent meal over, Margo led Annie over to Nelleke. Of course she remembered Nelleke, but she was very much a woman, now, she wore soft furs, yet not so rich as those of the tall lady beside her, her mother, whom Annie described to herself as "of an uncertain age." A lady to be reckoned with, there was hauteur in her glance, everything, one felt, was open to the appraisal of her rules and notions which she considered absolute. Annie was introduced, the lady was a Baroness. Annie noticed the rectitude, the assurance as she took her hand.

She saw, though, also a basic humanity, that very quality she had found lacking in so many German aristocrats.

Nelleke expressed surprise that Annie was still at the school in Hooigracht. Annie explained that it was a temporary return until she found the right post as a governess once more. They said little more. They left and went out into a freshening breeze.

The women were pleased to have found acquaintance in a larger world. Francois laughed at them as they described minutely the diamonds they had seen and the worth of the sable furs.

He mocked them and Annie remembered The Vicar of Wakefield. Francois was well versed in womankind and privately he wondered what the ladies at the Seinpost were saying.

He felt sure they were discussing too. Had he known he would have heard, the Baroness say, "My dear, that Englishwoman... you must get hold of her for Kitty. She looks kind and clever, just the kind you want. And did you notice how she moved? She will teach Kitty good deportment."

Nelleke remembered Annie. She thought of the classes in the garden, recalled laughter.

"Yes Mother, you are quite right."

Back at the school she found a letter awaiting her, it was from Nelleke. It was formal and asked if Annie would be interested in undertaking the education of her daughter Kitty aged eight. Annie seized the opportunity and within a week was on her way to Den Haag for an interview.

She found the house easily near the Palace of Noordeinde. It was stucco faced with a flight of steps to the front door. She was surprised by the spaciousness inside. The furniture was mostly 17th century Dutch, great chests, oak tables with carpet coverings and solid cupboards and pictures all of that period.

Immediately she realized that she was in the house of people of great taste and modern in their taste for the old. Nelleke Van Prehn rose from a sofa where she was reading. She stretched out both hands to Annie who very properly called her Mevrouw Van Prehn.

Annie took in the tall young woman expensively clothed. She had charm but no beauty. The new leg of mutton sleeves emphasised the shortness of her neck. Annie never ceased to wonder that women in pursuit of fashion so often overlooked what in fact suited them. She thought how different the woman was from her mother, there was not the same assurance... there was a far greater sweetness.

If she was so different to her mother, what, she wondered, would her daughter be like. She decided that if she did not care for the child she would not take the post. There must be affinity of temperament between a governess and pupil or nothing is achieved.

In a class, differing opinions were stimulating, but with one pupil mutual sympathy was all important. She told herself that she was not so old that she must accept any post, nor so young that she must take a post to gain experience. Kitty entered with her nurse.

"Shake hands with Miss Taylor dear."

Dutifully the little girl did so. Annie found herself looking at a very fair little girl with hair like Alice in Wonderland. The child looked enquiringly then stretched out a hand and stroked her sleeve. Annie was conquered. She answered some questions about reading. Annie found that the child's learning had been neglected. Here she thought was a small mind to be enlarged and moulded. It was a task she would enjoy.

Over tea, everything was decided. Annie would finish the summer term in Leiden and after a holiday in England come to Noordeinde.

When Annie left her step was more buoyant, her carriage more erect. Her immediate future for some years was certain. She lingered by the windows of the Jeweller, the chocolate maker, the china shop and, of course, La Bonneterie.

The delight of living amongst such luxury appealed. As she went down the Lange Voorhout, a small military procession went by. Annie stopped to watch, again a smile played about her lips, it was so unlike a German band: they marched in step, but it seemed by mutual consent not command.

She looked up the avenue. There was movement at the doors of the royal palace. She felt glad that she was to come to Den Haag, it was correct, but it was not rigid, it was Dutch.

In the evening the Principals were glad to talk to Annie of her success. They enjoyed discussing the little Princess Wilhelmina and the much loved Queen Emma.

When Annie went up to her room it was to write to Edith. It was only, now, that she began to tell her a little of her German experience. She dwelt more on the prospect of a visit to England in the summer. The letter done, she got into bed. The future looked secure, the past slipped away, she soon fell asleep.

Chapter 25

Prestatyn

Grimsby remained soaked in the memory of her mother's death, it surprised Annie. She gazed on it with an unforgiving eye. In the ticket office she was nonplussed because the clerk failed to understand her when she asked for a ticked to Prest-a-tyne. He raised his voice and reiterated, "There's no such place."

"But there must be, I correspond with my sister regularly who lives there."

He looked again at his book in which all stations in the British Isles were listed and a little truculently he returned. "No place of that name."

"But I know that there is. Let me write it down for you."

She reached for her handbag, when a man standing several places behind her came forward. He raised his hat and said,

"Young man, this lady is a foreigner. You really ought to be able to understand her. She wants to go to Prestatyn in North Wales."

"Oh Prestatyn. That's quite different." Annie thanked the man with some embarrassment and took care not to disclose her nationality.

England certainly felt strange after these years - even in Lincolnshire she was aware of the rise of the land, almost hills. As she crossed England she was aware of the dirt and grime of her country, it surprised her. It was very ugly. She longed to stop in Chester, she looked at the pink sandstone of the walls and the cathedral in amazement, she had only seen its like in Heidelberg.

From the train she saw so much, but provocatively not enough, she vowed to return, the flat lands were a surprise, she had expected hills and mountains the moment she came to Wales. It was late afternoon when she arrived.

The sisters' hearts leapt at the sight of one another. Both missed kith and kin, Edith rather more than Annie. Annie saw that Edith had matured, but, alas, she thought, she had not learnt how to dress.

The younger sister led the way Annie was at once struck by the ugliness of the red-brick and the lack of harmony in the architecture. They came to a street composed of large villas each set in its own large garden.

It was an ugly garden, the beds were ablaze with yellow calceolarias and red geraniums and large laurel bushes. It was a place without a secret... it spoke only of a certain purse-proud respectability.

Inside, Annie was assailed by the heaviness of English respectability, it sagged with each heavy curtain, it was proclaimed by the weight of each bronze and piece of black marble. Solidity was displayed in the family albums on the draped tables.

Annie had forgotten it and she felt overwhelmed. Edith quite evidently thought herself fortunate, so Annie said nothing. She was led up the stairs to the owner's room. This room showed more personality and Mrs Cassidy sat plump and possessive in the centre of the room looking out of the window.

She was dressed in black and her dark eyes glinted with the same unyielding shallow light as the jet beads on the bodice of her dress. She looked swiftly and rather disapprovingly at the slim lithe figure. Her thoughts were, "She has no right to be so pretty," and "She is not at all like Edith."

Introductions were made, the journey enquired after then the two young women went downstairs for a cold supper. After it there was tea, as she drank it Annie stretched and luxuriated. She had forgotten just how good an English cup of tea was.

After the meal, Edith went to help the old lady to bed and Annie after unpacking looked about her. She knew nothing of the Cassidy family but that they were from commerce was obvious and Annie realized that she had absorbed other ideas and ideals living in Holland.

Edith was so warm and loving and Annie was glad to see her sister, but as she looked at her neat face beneath the heavy pile of red hair she thought it so strange that Edith could so resemble their mother and yet avoid entirely her beauty.

Annie resolved to go through Edith's wardrobe next day and make certain that she wore her clothes better. Her skirt hung badly, the frill of her blouse from beneath the tight belt was gathered in one place and blank and flapping in another. Her shoes were scuffed.

True, next day she did investigate her sister's clothes and the main fault she decided was they were put on carelessly. Within hours she did not see Edith's clothes at all, she just enjoyed her sharp wit.

The house, too, that had almost awed in its non-conformist conventionality and lack of originality was accepted and Annie had to admit that it was warm, comfortable and hospitable.

She sat quite often with Mrs Cassidy and came to appreciate her. She had no children, she had worked with her husband in the cotton trade. Together they had amassed a pleasing competency.

They had retired to North Wales but Mr Cassidy had very soon been called "to Abraham's bosom." The use this euphemism gave Annie the giggles, she had never heard it used in speech.

The widow presided benevolently over the fortune, she was a very generous benefactor of the congregational Church and it figured very largely in her conversation. Annie, listened and thought that this was akin to much talk in Holland and yet entirely different.

She knew that she would not be able to bear it, she would feel stifled.

It was not only narrow and constraining, it was also rooted in the past, Annie liked the future - that was why she liked children, with them one looked ahead. She found herself looking forward to teaching and moulding Kitty Von Prehn.

It was still a disappointment to her that Edith had disliked both teaching and Holland but she accepted that she had been out of her element.

The sisters came closer together on that holiday than ever before. As they walked past the hotels Annie discovered that Edith had every intention of going to London to a large hotel to learn to be a housekeeper and then manage a hotel of her own.

Annie's immediate reaction was, "what would Mother think." She wondered if it was quite correct. It was, indeed, strange that Annie whose world had widened, whilst her perceptions remained those of her mother, it made her a little prim.

Edith thought of her mother far less, she had loved her dearly, but as an influence she had come after her grandmother. They were very different, and although Edith appeared more spinsterly, she was, in fact, more daring.

Annie beneath her elegance was a little timid except when

roused. She was content to keep to prescribed paths, as long as they led upward, her sense of the proper was very acute but very private.

She said nothing, but she dismissed Prestatyn... it was, to her, ugly and provincial. Even the backcloth of mountains did not redeem it. It was Prestatyn that made her more pliant in approving Edith's desire to go to London.

She agreed because she knew the plight of Edith, it was the plight of all women unsheltered by a family. She felt on a large scale which, surprisingly Edith did not.

One morning Annie woke early and was wide awake, she sat up in bed and as she admired the view she began planning Kitty's education. She took a pencil and began to make notes of books, schemes, one step leading to another.

She became enthusiastic. When she went downstairs there was a letter from Holland - it was from Mevrouw Von Prehn. It was agitated and its lack of punctuation and dashes betrayed the writer's anxiety.

Kitty was very ill with scarlet fever and her life hung in the balance. Annie was alarmed - she felt that she already knew the small girl. She did not know what to do. She went into the town and there she saw a beautiful doll in a pink and blue dress. She bought it, had it wrapped and wrote a note to go with it in the shop.

She posted it straightaway. That made her feel happier about Kitty, but a dull apprehension now came as she thought of her own future. It was during this time that Edith asked Annie if she thought either of them would ever marry.

"I think so. I worry about who it might be."

"I don't think we shall at all. Do you realise that mother had had three children by your age?"

"No, I had not." She felt a chill wind blow through her mind.

"Oh, but, you will marry. You are so pretty. Have you never been in love?"

"Not really. Two men behaved rather stupidly and one of them very badly. No. I do not think we shall marry. Men like money and we have not got any. It is as simple as that."

Edith was shocked by this cynicism. She believed in love even if she thought it might pass her by. She loved novels, almost any kind. She read Dickens and Scott but lapped up Marie Corelli with equal voracity.

"Mother and Father had no money. They married for love."

"Times are different, now. Religion meant more then. They were both attached to the church. Their life was to be a mission. But as far as I can see religion in England is all muddled up with patriotism now."

"Do you really think so?"

"England has changed whilst I've been away. But is does not change the outlook for you and me. You go to London and learn all you can in a hotel and we'll run a boarding house when we are old ladies."

"Well, I think that would be better than a school."

Annie remained silent. Everything was insecure, she was uneasy. Two days later there was a letter from Holland. Kitty had turned the corner, when the parcel had arrived she had been in a deep, deep sleep, her mother had put the parcel by her side so that when she awoke she would see a present.

Although weak she had opened the box and rapturously hailed the doll. From that moment she had started on the road to recovery. The present and the recovery coming together secured Annie's place in their affections.

With this news Annie felt much happier and she looked forward even more to Den Haag.

On her last full day, Annie again went shopping. She bought a cut glass vase for Mrs Cassidy. It would, she thought, bring light and lightness into the ponderous household. For Edith she bought a leather handbag and a pair of silk stockings.

In the afternoon the two sisters went down to the beach. There they sat looking out to sea. Without any warning Edith grasped her sister's hand and burst into tears. Through her sobs she said, "Annie, why do you have to go back to Holland? Can't you stay here?"

Annie's chin quivered in sympathy and she drew her sister to her, she felt once more the elder, she patted her and said: "Have a good cry, my dear, no one can see."

The sobs lessened and Annie felt guilty to the very core of her being. It was true. Edith was alone with this one self-centred old woman. The immediate outlook was spare and bleak. She contrasted it with her own future. She was so looking forward to life in Den Haag.

She compromised, "I promise you that my next post will be in England."

This pleased Edith and Annie continued.

"You go to London. Learn to be a housekeeper and then move to a nice town. You won't come back here will you?"

"No, I won't. I'll go back to Yorkshire."

"I have to return to Holland. I have promised. What is more important is little Kitty is a very nice child. I can do something for her. But unlike you, I do like Holland."

"I wish we heard from William," said Edith sadly as they walked back to the house.

"I don't think we ever shall. I feel he had gone from our lives."

She did not add that she rarely thought about him, she always jettisoned unhappy memories.

After dinner Annie produced her present for Mrs Cassidy. She unpacked it carefully, it glinted and shone in her hand. The sharp dark eyes approved, but were as profuse in reproving extravagance as thanks which Annie thought ungracious.

Annie's heart sank as she saw the crystal carefully wrapped up again and put back into its box. It was, she knew, going to be put away in safe keeping.

"You sister is just as bad as you. You will neither be wealthy at this rate," was the final pronouncement.

Annie thought, "Well, Edith will never be cheese-paring. She may never be moneyed, but she will be happier than you."

She was surprised at her own inner ingratitude. She had never warmed to this dark keen woman. She realised that she had summed her up at the first meal they took together. Mrs Cassidy had masticated her food so thoroughly.

She ground and teased every morsel in her mouth, shifting it from side to side as thought intent on extracting every ounce of goodness in earnest concentration before she consigned it to the oblivion of her gullet.

Annie was even shocked at her next thought for she wondered it Mrs Cassidy was constipated, for her costive look made it seem she would part hardly with anything.

On the way to the station the sisters held hands. They were silent, they both disliked partings. There was again guilt in Annie, Edith stayed with a mean woman and she went off to a sweet child.

She squeezed her sister's hand.

"Don't worry, it may not be for long. We must march on with hope. Mother always did."

"Yes, she did. So did Grandma."

Chapter 26

Noordeinde

Back with the Haverschmidts, Annie felt much more at ease. She even felt it easier to chat in Dutch than in English. There was no need to pause to search for the right word which had made her self-conscious in England.

She also felt a greater bond with Margo than with her own sister, a fact which made her feel guilty. But Francois was not happy; his moods were unpredictable and, as ever, his wife and daughter were impatient.

Annie asked no questions. She just waited and on a walk he poured out his resentments and grievances. Annie wished that his family could have heard, none of the bitterness was against them, it was largely a disruption within the church and he was angered and even more hurt by it.

She looked at his round face, his wide trusting eyes. At first glance, it was a calm face, even assured, but in moments of repose they were shadowed with sadness. They had always had a certain dreaminess, allied with humour, but now they stared as much inwards as outwards and the lid no longer made a partial eclipse of the pupil.

After he had unburdened himself he began, because of his natural courtesy, to talk of her new task in Den Haag and Annie confided in him how much she was looking forward to living in the Residency.

"Don't get too grand for us will you?"

She laughed but it was true, she did feel that she was going up in the world.

At that moment, however, she was wondering what she would do if she were his wife. She thought that she would urge him to retire and devote himself to writing. She saw that he was forced into a position of leadership which he did not enjoy.

She thought, too, that religion was bad for him. He was forced to think about it constantly and there was a strand of cynicism in his nature that made it very difficult for him. Religion, which he was so able at proffering to others as a solace, was to him no solace at all, it made him introspective.

She thought he ought to be writing stories not these long, long sermons. Suddenly, she decided to put the idea before him. His answer was a strenuous 'no'.

"I must provide for my family."

"But you would with your writing."

"But it is uncertain. What if my ideas for stories ceased?"

"They won't. One story will lead to another. I know."

"I dare not. I would fear for the family."

"Then, you are no freer than I am. That is a strange comfort to me."

"No one is free where there is love. We are all bound, captured."

Annie thought a while. Her thoughts reverted immediately to her mother. She said: "That is true. It is very true."

"I think you are very fortunate. You are going to help form a little girl whom you already like. Half your battle is done when you love your pupil."

That was the thought that Annie carried with her as she sat in the cab driving from the station in Den Haag to Noordeinde.

As she alighted she saw the lace curtain flump down into place. Someone had been waiting her arrival and someone who did not disguise the fact. The front door opened and a manservant came down to carry her luggage and Kitty stood at the top of the steps. At a glance Annie saw how pale she was and how thin.

"Go inside, Kitty, go inside. You will get wet," were her first words to her charge and smilingly the child retreated inside. There she hopped from one foot to the other in excitement. Her cheeks might be colourless but her energy was very evident. She tried to grab Annie's hand but Annie said,

"Wait, wait. I have to pay the cabman."

"That is done, Miss," said the manservant. This act filled Annie with hope for the future, it was an act of understanding that the rich do not always have to the poor.

So Annie was dragged by Kitty's hand up the stairs. The little girl would have pulled her yet another flight up, but Mevrouw Van Prehn intercepted.

"Kitty, Kitty... that will do. Give Miss Taylor some time."

Then, turning to Annie, she said: "She had been so excited at your coming. Do forgive her."

"Let her have her own way. I shall be having mine with her all too soon."

The child hauled her up to the schoolroom and to Annie's room and she chattered all the time as she commented on the excellences there.

"The china jug and basin came from the best guest room. This armchair was in the dining room before and the carpet is new. Isn't it pretty?"

All this evident preparation filled Annie with a happy glow. Everything augured well. Probably because she had been thinking of her mother she suddenly contrasted this leaping lively child with the tired little creatures of Anston.

That seemed so long ago, the afternoon children, who came to school worn out by a morning's work. She had lived a long while in another world.

That afternoon she unpacked, she carefully hung up her few dresses and unfolded and folded again her underclothes as she lay them in the drawers. She took out her photographs, the miniature and, at once, the room became her own - all it lacked was her walnut mirror.

That had gone forever. Letters had gone unanswered. Annie pushed aside the shining white lace curtains, the elegant houses of Den Haag met her eye. Over the houses she saw the trees of Haagse Bos, the country came into this pretty prim regal little town. Again the contrast with Wakefield sprang to her mind.

With Kitty she began putting her seal upon the schoolroom. Together they shifted the furniture, placing the table nearer the light by the window. Annie did nothing without Kitty's consent - her idea was to make the room a place of joy, not merely work and duty.

Annie changed for dinner and went downstairs. She was surprised to find that Kitty was in the same dress, her mother was in a dinner gown. Annie suggested a dress for Kitty.

"Yes, why not? I never thought of it. Of course Kitty must change."

Annie led a remonstrating child upstairs. Annie took no notice but chatted about the merits of various garments and eventually a dress was chosen and put on without enthusiasm.

Annie brushed Kitty's hair. Again there were sulks. It was quite evident nobody was in the habit of brushing her hair regularly. As Kitty saw the change take place in the mirror she began to be interested and with her hand in Annie's she went downstairs in a completely different spirit.

At the drawing-room door Annie surveyed her again and gave the bow in her hair a tweak. They entered.

"What a transformation," cried the mother, "why didn't we think of this before?"

Annie looked at the very tall, well-built man who had risen from his chair and put aside his newspaper.

Mevrouw Van Prehn was so busy looking at her daughter, he smiled and introduced himself. Annie instantly compared him with Herr Clausen. He was younger, possibly, she thought, not so kind.

His face had the severe marks of a man who was intent upon his own way. There was a fold, a line, running from his eye to his lower jaw, which gave an architectural quality to his face. It made it perpendicular, but like most Dutch faces it was squared by horizontal eyebrows and a right-angled jaw bone.

At dinner they all talked and he drew from Annie a recital of her life to that point. Only later did she think how forceful he was beneath a very well-mannered charm. It was an English skill she realised that he had used to gain all the answers he required without any open questions.

This was not usual in Dutch, they questioned openly. Here, she thought, is a subtle man and one most certainly not to be underestimated. He also made Annie talk of the studies she hoped to embark upon and being a banker he was glad that she had not forgotten arithmetic in her syllabus.

It was his wife who ended their discussion with, "We've had quite enough of school and lessons, enough to put Kitty off forever.

"I intend taking you both out many afternoons, especially when my Mother calls." Annie noticed a momentary tightening of the line on his face. There was unspoken irritation.

When they were going to bed Van Prehn looked at his wife and he said: "Miss Taylor is very chic to be a governess."

"Yes, isn't she? I think she will be such a good influence in every way on Kitty."

Annie found that she was included to dinner every night even when they gave parties, which was very frequently.

She found herself on the edge of another sphere of Dutch life. It was where banking and commerce met with the aristocracy.

She listened a great deal, she observed still more, when she spoke she often made others laugh and she enjoyed that. Because of her quietness she was endowed with a profundity she did not possess.

The little capital talked very frequently of the tiny Royal Family. The health of the King was failing... he had reigned a long time. His life had been beset with misfortunes, his marriage with his first wife had not been happy, then he had lost his heir.

The Prince of Orange had been an unoccupied young man who fell, rather naturally, into dissolute habits. He died in Paris under mysterious circumstances. Annie was very frequently told that he had been led into evil ways by Edward, Prince of Wales.

It was when the prince died that the widower-king had sought a bride. To his subjects' amazement and great concern his choice had alighted on Emma, a princess of Waldeck-Pyrmont, who was more than 40 years his junior.

The round-cheeked, plump princess entered Holland on a flood of sympathy which turned almost immediately to admiration and affection. The marriage may have been arranged but she had a love affair with her adopted people for the rest of her life.

In December 1890 at the palace of Noordeinde the old king died. The Van Prehns lived but a few doors away. They felt it as not just the death of a monarch but of a neighbour. Annie and Kitty enjoyed being in the centre of so much activity. They were able to revel in all the ceremonial and trappings of royal death without any of the grief allied with such occasions. They walked in the streets observing the mourning, the tributes in the shop windows. They were able to watch the funeral procession from a balcony on the route to the burial place in Delft.

When the cortege had passed everyone relaxed, the crowds quietly dispersed and there was a subtle change of mood. In the house, wine and biscuits where served and whereas until that moment the conversation had been of the past, it now switched to the future.

The ability of Queen Emma as a Regent was never questioned - they hoped that the young Queen would not be too spoilt. It was the first time that Annie had appreciated the fickleness of public opinion. She was surprised and never trusted it again.

Kitty's grandmother was, now, not merely the lady-in-waiting to the Consort, but to the virtual sovereign and her own importance was strangely apparent. She was accorded more deference and her innate imperiousness increased, especially towards her daughter.

Sometimes, as she saw mother and daughter together, she was reminded of her own relationship with her mother, but there was a difference. Her own mother had not been so demanding and she did not think she had been so compliant.

The Baroness had always been demanding, she became more so. She never hesitated in asking Kitty to cancel an engagement if she desired her presence elsewhere. This meant that Kitty's friends and acquaintance found her unreliable. They were more chary with their invitations.

But most of all, Mijnheer Van Prehn was incensed by the capricious demands of his mother-in-law. His wife seemed strangely blind to his resentment. It meant that Van Prehn, Kitty and Anne frequently dined alone.

In the winter he would read aloud to them. They discussed the books and life in general, they all enjoyed one another's company. When summer came and he returned to discover that his wife was out, he would order dinner earlier and the meal over, they would catch a tram and walk by the sea at Scheveningen.

Then they would sit and drink coffee and watch the shifting crowds of people. They were very content and Annie was long to remember the curious combination of the splendour of the setting sun over the sea glorious, filling one with a feeling of religious awe, and the worldly charm of glittering fashionable people around her.

Still the nationalities of the world paraded there, the spectrum of the world it seemed, yet a tramway's distance was the prim, impeccable little world of Holland's highest society. The serenity she felt settled on her face and figure. She grew a little plumper filling the curves of her bodice a trifle more fully.

It was, though, her face which changed most subtly, it remained rounded, oval and it enclosed round eyes and a small but fully formed mouth that echoed her cheek's contours. Her nose remained snub.

It was a face that men - and women – looked at a second time, because besides the charm of prettiness, there was an uncalculated dignity in her movement. It was almost awe-inspiring. But fear was cancelled by the quick sympathy like a light across her features. It was an odd and fascinating combination and Van Prehn was glad to see it being reflected by his daughter.

One evening at the Kurhaus, the waiter referred to Annie as Kitty's mother. This amused Kitty, less so her father and deeply disturbed Annie. She recalled when it had happened in Germany, this time it hurt because, though she did not acknowledge it herself, she would, indeed, have liked to be married to Kitty's father. She was silent as they returned in the tram. This was something that lay way beyond all the tenets of her beliefs and rules.

She was a product of her times. She accepted a series of codes and constraints. She even saw part of the education of Kitty as an inculcating of those rules, to be absorbed early and easily, so that they were adhered to without conscious effort, just as much as one spoke a language purely and without grammatical errors.

The fright passed. When next a trip to Scheveningen was suggested, she found an excuse. She need not have worried for Van Prehn had no intention of the mistake being repeated.

After the long hard winter, the Court still in mourning. The Baroness called one morning and requested not for her daughter but for Kitty and Annie. She did not say where she was taking them, but she told them to dress carefully, no straying hair, no darned gloves.

Annie responded to the summons like a clarion call.

She brushed and arranged Kitty's hair after it had been done by her nurse and worried over her own dress. The three mounted the carriage and drove towards the Haagse Bos. It was Kitty who asked where they were going.

With subdued triumph the Baroness replied, "To meet two Queens."

Instantly, Annie looked more closely at their clothing and she wished that she was wearing a black and not a violet dress. They drove to Huis ten Bos, the House in the Woods. The carriage, slowed by the sentries, was recognised and went on.

A large semi-circular flight of steps led up to the main door of the Palace. Annie, like most of the Haagenaars, knew well the gilded crown on its cushion which glinted on the top of the dome above the trees, and most hard winters the public skated on the Lake hard by, a privilege denied that winter by the King's death.

Still Annie thought it unlikely that she would actually meet the Queen - she was prepared to be left in an ante-room. They were led swiftly to the central hall beneath the dome. Allegorical paintings swirled over the walls with great energy up from the floor to the clouds supporting thrones and chariots where gods and goddesses romped decorously.

The yellows, the russets, the gold and the red impressed both Annie and Kitty. The Baroness moved towards the double doors which were opened and she entered and they followed. She curtseyed low. Annie and Kitty repeated the courtly gesture.

They were in a Chinese drawing room. Figures from an ancient dynasty in Peking were on the walls, on brackets stood large Chinese vases. The Baroness took the hand of a very plump but pleasing looking young widow and curtsied again... she did so again to the serious looking fair haired girl.

The child smiled but not as broadly as her mother, her mouth shut and composed. She only permitted herself a hint of feeling when she was confronted by Kitty, one of her own age.

This, thought Annie, is all as it should be. The distance of majesty was being maintained. They stood a group of very darkly clad, very European women in the midst of an oriental room. They stood there conversing for fully five minutes.

Later, though she had been at such close quarters to the Queen Regent, Annie found she was unable to describe her any more accurately than from the many photographs she had seen. The two royal ladies were like their photos, yet unalike, and she was surprised by their animation once real contact was made.

She became aware, just as the nation was, of the genuine kindliness behind the prescribed graciousness of the Regent, but she was well aware that she was being appraised. Kitty talked with the young Queen and suddenly from the prim chrysalis of this personage emerged the girl.

"Please may I take Mejuffrouw Van Prehn to my room, Mamma?"

The queen relaxed into a mother busy in a conversation. Though she smiled indulgently, she gave her agreement almost unheedingly. Annie saw though the depth of feeling between these two, mother and daughter.

"Now let us sit down."

"So you are English, Miss Taylor. You sound entirely Dutch to me. Have you been here long?"

The Baroness interposed. "But, Ma'am, your Dutch is excellent, too."

Annie found herself saying, "And so do I, Ma'am."

Instantly, she smiled at herself and thought: "Here you are practising the language of courts."

As they talked, Annie wondered who it was that the Queen Regent reminded her of. She wondered if it was her own mother, no she could not see her slender supple mother in this tightly corseted lady with rosy cheeks and glinting spectacles. The only similarity with her mother was authority.

Then she remembered the Quaker household and Mrs Pumphrey. Both were very courteous and moved by a faith, there lay the similarity.

"You must meet my daughter's governess. She, too, is English, Miss Winter. You will have much in common, I expect."

The door burst open and in ran two girls, who felt the hand of restraint forcefully and slowed up and approached the very proper little group.

"Can, Kitty come again, Mamma?"

"I think that a very good idea for I want you to talk English to Miss Taylor. It will be good for you all."

So began another dimension in Annie's life when she accompanied Kitty to Noordeinde on foot, or in a carriage sent for them to take them to Huis ten Bos. Annie's meeting with Miss Winter was one of very guarded pleasure. They discovered little common ground - even the portions of England where they had lived were totally unknown to the other.

Annie found her very English and she called her starchy. What distressed her was that she thought her repressive in her influence on the young Queen.

As she walked in the royal gardens, she found much of the sorcery of royalty fade. What had been a fascination from afar, on contact was very commonplace, although expensive. One day as they waited for a few minutes in the hall of Noordeinde Annie admired the rich colouring of the marble pillars.

She touched it, rapped it, took of her glove, she expected a colder surface – it was painted wood. She smiled and she felt in an odd way comforted, it made them even more human in their desire to impress. There were frauds even in palaces.

It was on her return from the Palace that afternoon that she found a letter with an Australian stamp. She knew the hand immediately and her heart beat very fast. She went swiftly up to her room and felt great guilt for she had not thought of her brother for many months.

She sat on the edge of her bed and still turned the envelope and took a deep breath before opening it. She felt certain that he was about to heap resentment on her head. With a pair of scissors she slit it open.

It began, "My dear sister", the poignant reminder of their relationship was powerful, far more emotive than if he had merely caller her by her name, it brought tears to her eyes. There were no recriminations but a long chronicle of the events in his life and a justification for his desertion.

He said that his apprenticeship had been a waste of money, that he derived no benefit from it and had had less liberty than an ordinary seaman. It brought back her mother's sacrifice to her mind and still she felt annoyance. She clenched her fist and said aloud,

"He still does not realise what he has done."

She read on, how he had slipped ship at Sydney, gone up country and worked in a brickyard, then rounding up horses and breaking them in. It offended her, even though she was so glad to have word of him... she disliked his doing such menial work.

She read on that he had returned to ships, working on a coastal vessel, but he had to leave when one of the firm's ships came into port and he feared recognition. She remembered the threat of arrest and shuddered.

Before she put down the letter she read that he worked for a nursery and seed firm, he had been with them some years and had a position of trust and authority. That pleased her, yet at the same time, she wondered if it was true.

Willy had always had a good imagination, except she said to herself, when it came to understanding others.

Then he began to explain once again and ended, "However, I don't suppose you were as hard on me as I deserved and I guess I was growing too ungrateful."

The tears really ran, but again she agreed that he had been ungrateful. He asked where their mother's grave was, so that if he returned he might visit it. He asked after Edith and Grandma.

He then mentioned two friends from Wakefield who had gone out to Australia and were settling down well and then came the shock. He asked her to come out and join him. He assured her that she would like it.

When she had re-read the letter she put it back in the envelope almost reverently, but she had not forgiven him. She blamed him for her mother's death. She would never, never join him.

She no longer trusted him. Besides, he had offended her when he described Holland as a "God-forsaken land." It indicated very clearly the gulf between them, he was an Englishman with contempt for all other nationalities.

Only the ignorant and the prejudiced could say such things. She got up, went to the window, and looked down on the froth of green, like rosettes gathering on the twigs of the lime trees, so pale and tender a green and not thick enough to obscure the outlines of the trunk and branches.

"I think that I may never leave Holland."

At dinner, Mijnheer Van Prehn was in the highest of spirits. Not only had it been a good day on the Exchange, but he had a surprise for them all. A secret he tried to make them guess. Not until the pudding was on the table did he ask, "Have you all got your spring hats?" In unison they replied: "No."

"Then you will have to get them quick. We are all going to Brussels after Easter. I've decided that we'll all go. Last time we went away, Nelleke, you sat up all night so that your hair, so carefully arranged by Annie, did not have to be undone.

"But if Annie comes, she can do all our hair! We can show Annie Waterloo, we'll go the dinner and the ball en masse."

"But Kitty is too young," demurred her mother.

"Too young for the ball - but not for the outing. It will do everyone good."

Annie was delighted and already arranging her meagre wardrobe. Yet, she thought how strange it was that all this depended on the whim of a man. He decides, we all agree. It was exciting.

It was even sometimes a relief to have decisions made for one, she was always making minor decisions for herself, being alone. But was it right that the dominant male should make all decisions? She knew that women could rule their own lives, but when a man was present they always surrendered the right.

It was settled, it was decreed and Mevrouw Van Prehn began buying clothes for herself and Kitty. Annie began to refurbish her old ones. She accompanied them on shopping expeditions and when Annie lighted upon some silk jersey material Mevrouw Van Prehn bought it for her.

She was glad that she would have one new dress to wear in Belgium. These forays into the world of fashion were thoroughly enjoyed by Annie. She kept he eyes open and saw how various new developments were achieved.

On the journey from Den Haag across the flat country, level fields and bridges, the three women were excited. At Brussels they were thrilled, especially Kitty. The hotel was large and sumptuous and they all revelled in the luxury.

To Annie it was completely new, she had never stayed in a hotel before, but she admired the way in which all their requirements and wishes seemed forestalled as if their thoughts were read.

It was while they were dressing for dinner that Annie gave up the struggle to do up the buttons which stretched from her neck to her waist. She managed two at the top and three at the bottom.

She rang the bell for the maid, there was a knock and she called "Entrez". She was very surprised when she saw not a young woman but a young man, the valet de chambre. For a moment she faltered then explained her predicament.

Without a flicker of amusement, or disdain, he did up the elusive buttons. Then casting an eye over her, what she was sure he should not have, he said,

"Très gentille, mademoiselle, très gentille."

She thanked him for his help and, perhaps, even more for his compliment. She looked again in the mirror. She agreed with him. There was another knock and with a full expectation of the unexpected she replied. The door opened - it was Kitty with her bow.

The four met on the landing and mijnheer Van Prehn surveyed his womenfolk with some pride. Below there was already a crowd of well-dressed people. At once, Annie noticed how much more lavish and extravagant they looked than the Dutch, where wealth she had found was often difficult to assess from outward appearances.

It was as cosmopolitan as Scheveningen at the height of the season. But because they were in evening dress, more intimate, at the same time more revealing in every way. Van Prehn led the way through the throng to a smaller reception room, where other bankers were gathered.

He made his tall way to the host of the occasion, Baron Rothschild, and presented his family. Annie made a little dip over his proffered hand and she met a pair of very shrewd, but kindly, brown eyes.

They moved on to a group who hailed Van Prehn. Annie followed Kitty's mother in acknowledging the circle, tilted her head and with a quiet, a slightly shy smile whispered: "Enchante, enchante."

Van Prehn watched her with admiration. It was both a joy and a pain. The little party was afloat on a sea of sensual pleasure… food wine and a constantly shifting array of gowns. There was more shopping by the women while the men were in congress.

One day, Annie had a morning alone. She went in search of Charlotte Bronte's Pensionnat Heger. She found it - it was a closed almost furtive building casting a blank face on the street.

It was a glaring contrast to the many windowed open visage of her school in Leiden. She walked past it slowly, then back again. She thought of the two sisters there, both Yorkshirewomen, like herself, she thought of Emily's deep unhappiness, so unlike her own content.

She understood it better, however, and thanked God that she had been so much more fortunate. She was glad to leave the street though and hurry back to the opulence and comfort.

During lunch, she learnt that there were to be waggonettes to carry them out the field of Waterloo. As they drove out so they came to small valleys and hills, it seemed almost English. As they looked at farmhouses and barns and roads they all found it difficult to imagine killing there and the vast struggling movement of battle.

They climbed the huge mound with the lion presiding over it all. At once, Annie was transported back to Uncle Alan's house and the huge etching in the parlour the older Wellington surveying this very scene with his horse, Copenhagen, at his side.

She had so often, as a child gazed at the picture. She had never thought that she would visit the scene herself. Later in the panorama, Annie was horrified by the realism of the models, she shuddered at the violence and she watched the peaceable Dutch take so great an interest, forgetting that they too had been involved.

Later beneath beech trees in their new milky green leaf they had tea in a garden. The waitresses whisked in and out bearing trays and more interestingly wooden buckets bound with brass with a brass lining which was filled with charcoal and on this settled, like a broody hen, a brass kettle with a steaming spout.

Annie was happy, very happy and it showed in the glow of her eyes, her skin. When they drove back they were glad of their capes as the much cooler air blew on them. Kitty was chattering and Annie dreaming, only half listened... then she heard Kitty's lament that she had not bought a replica of the Waterloo lion. She had seen it in a kiosk and failed to buy it. This omission was about to eclipse, forever, the joys of her first trip abroad. Annie made soothing noises and promised that when they were in Brussels they would look for another.

At the hotel everyone descended with laughter down the little ladders, the men assisting the ladies in their long skirts. As soon as Kitty was down she pleaded that they set off at once to find another lion. Promising not to be long while the parents changed, Annie and Kitty set off.

Kitty was rapidly becoming tearful, but they hurried on to an arcade, where, Annie was sure, they would find another lion. The shop was just closing, but they let them in and there amidst the piles of bric-a-brac was a Waterloo lion, resplendent and on a small marble plinth.

They enquired the price and to Kitty's delight it was cheaper and better than the one she had seen at the battlefield.

Back in the hotel, the salons were empty, the corridors quiet. There was an air of pre-occupation and concentration. Behind each door was a woman struggling with buttons, pins, laces. Bells were being rung for maids, there were not enough of them to attend to every lady's wants.

The men, too, were losing patience and cursing as studs spun out of their fingers as they fought with stiff shirt fronts and collars.

Mrs Van Prehn was in despair. She was becoming petulant and blaming Annie for disappearing with Kitty to find a stupid lion. The door burst open and in rushed Kitty rapturously waving her parcel.

"I've got him. Miss Taylor knew exactly where he would be and he's better than the one at Waterloo!"

Mevrouw Van Prehn was glad to see her child happy, she was glad to see Annie back. She called to the dressing room,

"Are you decently clad, Kees? Can Miss Taylor come in? I want her to help me with my hair."

Van Prehn came in he was in his shirt sleeves, his tie was tied, his gold cufflinks glittered. Annie had never seen him without a jacket, or waistcoat. She felt a sudden intake of breath, she had not known, until that moment, how beautifully formed he was. She used the cliché of her day, deep within herself, 'a fine figure of a man.'

She looked down crossed the large room and saw his wife patting ineffectually at her hair. She was trying to make do with the arrangement as it held. Annie swiftly pulled out all the pins, the hair showered down.

Then brushing it she carefully, took strands, combed them, lifted them pinned them up and with the upper loose end, quickly with her forefingers rolled it into a little sausage that was then pinned and fluffed out.

She did this with a sure hand neither quick nor slow. Van Prehn took a chair and watched. He saw his wife being transformed. An ordinary head of hair began to look magnificent, a structure, a work of adroit artistry crowning a sweet face. Kitty, who was supposed to be washing and dressing cried in delight.

"Now", said Annie, "the worst moment of all. Where to pin the aigrette?"

She lifted the jewelled tortoiseshell sheath with its tuft of thin hairy feathers. Mevrouw Van Prehn wanted it in the centre pile at the back of her head.

Annie looked resolved and said, "No, no, no, that will make you look like a circus pony." They all laughed. It was placed a little to one side, a small straight sentinel over the baroque exuberance of the curls. They all agreed that it looked charming.

"Now the dress."

Husband, daughter and Annie all lifted the heavy brocade skirt from the bed. Mevrouw untied her peignoir to reveal, the brocade bodice already around her upper body, outlining and pressing up her breasts.

The three made a rough circle on the floor of the heavy material, Van Prehn's wife stepped into it and the three raised it up and began to tie the tapes and put the hooks in the eyes of the bodice, so that the two pieced gown became one whole.

"Doesn't Mother look beautiful," gasped Kitty.

"She does indeed." But Van Prehn looked for a moment not at his wife, but at Annie, their hands had touched and a sudden quiver of affection moving into ardour seemed to communicate itself from one to the other. Annie was too glad to feel guilt or shame.

Mevrouw Van Prehn gazed in the mirror and beamed at them all. She was pleased without vanity. She felt that her appearance was an operation that they had all combined it. She kissed them all.

"But Annie, Kitty. You must both cut and run. We shall all be late. I'll come and help you both when I've put on my shoes and jewellery."

In her room Annie took out her blue silk dress with its white lace trimmings all ruched round the shoulders and bust. She contrasted it despondently with the splendour of the brocade in the next room.

She did her hair, the same dexterity and purpose, calm and unhurried prevailed. She struggled into her tight bodice... managed some of the buttons. She formed a ring of the silken skirt and she stepped into it. Stooping down she raised it around her. She was glad to hear Kitty at the door.

"Oh, Miss Taylor, you look just as beautiful as Mother."

Annie kissed the child and she asked her to fix the hooks whilst she took out her only piece of jewellery, her mother's seed pearls which she had had made into a choker. They toned with the nacreous quality of her skin beautifully.

She looked in the glass, she was pleased, but thought it all very plain with the sumptuousness she knew she would meet with downstairs.

There was Kitty's bow to be done. Another knock and in came Mevrouw Van Prehn with a jewel case.

"Now what can we put on you, my dear."

A diamond and sapphire bracelet was clasped round her wrist

and ear rings to match. Annie looked again. The Puritan look had gone and she was glad, she did not feel like a Puritan at all, she did not analyse the reason.

The little party assembled on the landing and descended and the dresses plopped at every step where the trains fell behind them. It was a sound Annie was to love for a lifetime.

They were a little late and they crossed the dining room where most of the tables were occupied. Every eye of every woman was on the dress of another, the eye of every man was on the jewels those women wore. They were, after all, a company of bankers.

Van Prehn walked with pride, he was proud of his wife and his daughter, they were second to none in this company and he also thought of Annie, she looked so lovely. When they sat around the table he looked at Annie anew, he had not realised what a lovely long neck she had - the choker seemed to emphasise its grace rather than obscure it.

The dinner was a feast. It would seem that the kitchen had reserved its finest talents until the final meal. Annie teasingly said: "I am bound to say, I am afraid, that the Belgians are much better cooks than the Dutch."

Quickly the Van Prehns responded to the badinage and Van Prehn pronounced: "That's because the chefs here are all French."

Annie in her mood was not to be outdone.

"Then why doesn't Holland import some?"

The speeches were made between the courses. They were the first Annie had ever heard so she assumed that this was customary the world over. Kitty tired, though she denied it. Several children left with their mothers or older sisters. Annie led Kitty upstairs. The child was too weary to speak - the meal and excitement had exhausted her so that she was soon asleep.

Annie went to her own room. On the corridor she heard the music of the orchestra, in her room she picked up a novel. She put it down she could not concentrate. She went out and leant over the banisters, she heard not only waltzes but the swish of the skirts.

She did not know whether to return. She wondered whether she was wanted. As she was in this quandary Van Prehn came up the stairs, seeing her he stopped.

"Annie, aren't you coming down?"

It was the first time he had used her Christian name.

She ran down. She slipped her hand through his arm and they went swiftly down and straight on to the floor.

He found that the often prim little governess could dance. He was surprised and, yet, another part of his mind was not in the least surprised. She followed him easily, lightly and what was more important even, with charm.

The whole air of the ballroom had changed, the good food, the wine had broken the barriers of formality and in its place was gaiety verging on jollity.

At the end of the waltz he led her back to his wife. While she danced, another man approached and requested the pleasure. Annie rose and found that this time she danced with the son of a banker.

He discovered that she was English and a governess and he requested another dance. This piqued Mijnheer Van Prehn who asked who he was. Annie replied from Strasbourg.

"That means he has no nationality, he's neither French, nor German."

Annie was amused at the annoyance he showed.

It had been a few days of delight bordering on sorcery for them all, but Den Haag was their home and they hailed it with joy. Annie and Kitty, at once, asked that instead of returning in the carriage, they might walk and get some fresh air.

Teacher and pupil briskly made their way along the low neat houses of the workers and the small shops, everything growing larger and grander as they reached the heart of the largest village in the world.

To Annie it all seemed not only much cleaner than Brussels, but much more staid, a Protestant purity mixed with gentility pervaded the air. They felt the assurance of home.

As so often happens a different attitude dates from an event when something intangible had changed the whole temperature of the atmosphere. Annie was not longer the governess, she was a member of the family. Often, before, when conversation between husband and wife had become confidential Annie had quietly risen and left the room. Now her moves were foreseen and cries of "Don't go" were made. Thus Annie became more deeply involved in the family and circle of their friends. She became an equal in the eyes of all, except herself, for the others never seemed to realise how poor she was, the constant invitations meant that she had to spend much more on her wardrobe than she should.

At times, with growing frequency, she longed for a home of her own.

Van Prehn seemed to have forgotten the tremor that had passed between them as they had touched and Annie was careful to keep aloof. She even thought it had been her imagination.

A few weeks after their return, as Van Prehn was reading aloud to them, he kept making mistakes, misreading words. He rubbed his eyes and complained of soreness. At first they thought he was merely tired.

A visit to an optician did little good, he recommended stronger reading spectacles. Eventually, he went to an eye specialist and some drops were prescribed. He was a healthy man, unused to pain, the irritation annoyed him and the putting in of the drops became a thrice daily drama.

Mevrouw Van Prehn became nervous. She dropped the bottle, squeezed the dropper too soon, one day poked his eye... and he cursed her. Annie was shocked and Mevrouw Van Prehn in anger swept from the room saying, "You do it, Annie. I won't be spoken to like that."

Annie picked up the bottle, told him to put back his head and very slowly, very calmly put in the drops saying, "What a fuss about nothing."

It became her task and he submitted to it unflinching and without a murmur. Yet Annie both loathed and longed for these moments. After three weeks the inflammation went and Annie was hailed as the curer. Her reward was a week's holiday, she went to Schiedam.

The house was tense with emotion and Annie found that Francois Haverschmidt was more strained than ever. It was a week in which he had many committees and from each one he returned whistling shrilly down the street, a sound that made the women nervous, it boded no good.

One evening, Annie asked Margo why she was so sarcastic. To ask the question had taken her time and courage - it took more time and more bravery on her part no to run away from the bitterness and rancour that she heard.

Margo was coming to regard her father as an ogre of selfishness. She blamed him for all her mother's ills. She was acid about his chivalry and courtliness towards women. Annie found herself gazing into a deep well of domestic unhappiness.

She was also looking into Margo who seemed to hold a basin of the acrid waters of spinsterhood. She hated their poverty, which Annie considered a great exaggeration. She deplored their social life, the cramped contacts of a clergyman's circle, again Annie thought this over-stated.

What amazed her was that Annie found herself an object of envy.

"Oh Margo, you overestimate my life. You really do. I live in other people's houses, I eat other people's food and, I think, I am so tactful I have no opinions of my own."

Margo laughed. "Yes Annie, but that is your nature. When you do disapprove, you are silent and your silences are more disapproving than most people's words. I envy you that, as well."

Time always went very quickly there and Annie only partially knew that she brought peace and laughter to the household because she was not serious. On the last morning she helped Francois with his birds and then they sorted out books.

She questioned him about the heavy tomes of theology. She was amazed that so much could be said about so little.

"You either believe, or you don't. I believe, but I really don't want to read these books about Redemption and Atonement."

He laughed. "Annie, you are sometimes very heathen."

She made him talk, it was easy, of himself. She wished that Margo could open this door into his past. He in turn questioned her… he wanted to know if there had been any other men in her life since the frightening episode in Cologne. She shook her head and kept quiet, but was careful not to be utterly silent, remembering Margo's words.

"What a pity. You will make someone a good wife."

Annie wondered if he had ever made that remark to his daughter, or whether both he and his wife had fallen into the common notion of expecting her to remain at home to look after their needs.

She did not know the answer, all she knew was that there was a despondency wreathed around them.

When it came time to say goodbye, she thought of the agonies she had felt when going back to Cologne, or even to Wassenaar, but to return to merry little Kitty and the Van Prehns did, indeed, seem like going back home, and she did love Den Haag.

She loved its refinement, its exclusive shops, its galleries, the rounds of calls at the embassies. She thought that back in England Bath and Cheltenham must be like this, but added, here was the centre of government, the Binnenhof, the ministries and at the core of all the Court of the Queen Regent.

She was so used to listening to the men talk of politics, which ranged across Europe, she loved to talk of the two Queens. The opinion, and Annie from knowledge agreed, was that little Queen Wilhelmina was too indulged and too protected.

They thought, too, that Queen Emma should be less plump, but they all agreed that she made up for everything with her almost magical charm.

Kitty was now 14. Annie thought that she might stay for two more years. Her pupil was a credit to her, she spoke English very well, her German was good and her French far better than Annie's.

She had mastered all the mathematics she would need and she was surprisingly well-read, but like her governess she did incline to the sentimental. Their combined tears at a performance, in English of East Lynne at the Kurhous had embarrassed Kitty's parents.

In many ways Kitty was another Annie and she had her gift of wearing the simplest clothes with distinction. Their relationship was much like that of a much older and a younger sister.

It was well, for still the Baroness would demand her daughter's attendance in her crowded social life, with out Annie, Kitty would have been a lonely child.

More and more the running of the household fell into Annie's hands and she found herself replacing linen, making choice of a new dinner service, which on reflection years later, she found odd, but had accepted it at the time.

She became used to spending large amounts of money, she enjoyed it and her expenditure was never questioned.

She had the schoolroom redecorated making it into a sitting room for them both. It was such a success that sometimes rather than use the drawing room they all went upstairs to drink their tea there after dinner.

From the decoration of this room to others was but a step. Van Prehn had been to an exhibition in Paris of the painter Whistler. He had been impressed by his open spaces and the influence of the

Japanese lack of clutter. As he talked of it, Annie, Kitty became enthusiastic and they planned to made the drawing room Japanese. True, they chose delicate wallpaper with panels of mountains and pine trees.

They rearranged all the porcelain from the house, seeking out the oriental. They bought fans which they arranged on the walls, but it remained a compromise, for the solid Dutch chests, the marquetry bureau gave another taste, another nationality.

However, the combination of sumptuous and heavy curve and forms threw the lightness of the Japanese introductions into higher relief. It was, though, something neither Whistler, nor Van Prehn had envisaged. Annie loved that room dearly.

One grey wet day, Annie and Kitty returned from a blustery and dreary walk exercising their new possession "Quick" a small Dutch barge dog.

They found Kitty's mother and the Baroness returned from an embassy luncheon and they were bubbling with spirits and conferring in a very conspiratorial manner. They were busting to impart information, it came out immediately.

"Annie, we had news for you. You are to go out to dine tonight at Noordeinde."

Annie looked puzzled, where in Noordeinde?

"The Palace of course."

"But I've nothing to wear. Who is going with me?"

Annie was horrified and the older women had thought it would only arouse excitement.

"Don't worry about that, my dear, we will all see to it. The fact is the Queen had asked my mother to find a young lady for the dinner – a small party. I cannot go, I am married. Mademoiselle Kosteris cannot go, so we decided on you. Would you like it?"

The idea of dining at the Palace, sitting at table with a queen appealed, even if she were only a stop-gap, but she would have liked more time to consider and savour the occasion. There was a faint resentment at the irony of it all, she was considered good enough to dine with royalty, but as a woman and a governess she had not been consulted.

The lack of independence galled her. She was, however, first and foremost a peacemaker, she smothered resentment and thought that, perhaps, she had become so spoilt recently her character was becoming wilful. The Baroness left stating when she would return.

Up in her room Annie took out her blue silk dress with the deep ruching of White lace. It looked very ordinary, totally unsuitable, as she laid it on the bed had heart sank.

She felt that she did not want to go, she argued that it would be difficult and that she would be a fraud. As she was churning over these nullifying thoughts there was a knock at the door and in came Mevrouw Van Prehn and Kitty.

They were laughing and excited and amongst the cardboard boxes, cretonne covered boxes and small leather cases they also carried delight and it was infectious.

Within minutes they had Annie in her dress and Annie had to admit that once on it looked quite different. Mevrouw Van Prehn's wardrobe was at her disposal, but they all knew that this was best. It was the basis for the decoration, gloves, a small white silk cape, and then jewels.

They put the diamond and sapphire domed discs that Annie always admired in her ears, two brooches, one for the corsage and a larger one for the bodice. For her hair they wanted a long white veil but Annie vetoed it as ostentatious, anyway it disarranged her hair. She was arrayed in blue and white.

All was taken off and the dress taken away to be ironed.

The thrill seemed to pervade the household and everyone became involved in Annie's royal visit. The maids scurried, carrying water, the footman burnished her shoes and Kitty and her mother fussed and cajoled to such an extent that when it came to doing her hair she excluded them from the room.

Alone she took out the pins, shook it down and slowly and carefully put it up again. All the jewels were in place, she opened the door and went down the stairs, the light sparkled on the dress and the jewels and her eyes.

She carried a tweed cape over her arm. There were cries and sighs as they all looked at her interrupted by Mevrouw Van Prehn saying,

"But you can't take that cape, even only for the carriage."

She ran upstairs and came down with a pale grey cloth cape with scrolls of jet beads, "That's better."

"But what about the feather?" asked Kitty.

"I thought it might not stay in place."

"Let me do it then," and it was Kitty's turn to run upstairs and bring down the soft white feathers.

Sitting before the long gilt mirror in the drawing room Kitty deftly fixed the feathers in Annie's hair.

"Now you are really finished."

"Stand up and turn round," commanded Mijnheer Van Prehn, Annie did so very slowly. He was astonished. He had always admired her, first as a teacher. She had the gift of imparting her gifts to others. He'd noted that Kitty had placed the feather exactly as Annie would have done.

He'd seen Annie place it in his wife's hair. He admired her calm, a calm that became a harmony through her whole being, in her walk, her speech soft and rather slow and in her dress and, then, he remembered her exquisite handwriting.

All this went through his mind swiftly, but as she stood before him he was reminded most vividly of a painting of a girl he had seen by Renoir in Paris, round faced, snub nosed, the same calm and a glow of health, youth and something of the soul.

His heart beat fast and he strode past her to the hall to open the door before the butler, he had heard the jingle of the harness of his mother-in-law's carriage. The butler escorted Annie down the steps holding an umbrella, the Baroness leant forward, she wore jewels in her hair, she looked splendidly formidable and her dark eyes glinted with pleasure.

She was not condescending but she informed Annie of the form of events about to take place. The guests lining up in a drawing room, nobody sat, the Queen would enter by another door with her suite, there was a general bow and curtsey and then as she met her guest s each woman curtsied.

She had hardly finished as they clattered past the statue of William the Silent. Suddenly Annie felt alarm… even the protection of the Baroness did not wholly allay her feelings.

They entered a long somewhat sparsely lit room, it had a cold formality and Annie immediately likened it to a railway waiting room, its occupants were always passers by who were anticipating and never living in the moment. There were others ahead of them.

Eventually, they came to the drawing room where a little more than a dozen people waited. The Baroness was the sparkling catalyst who brought life to a subdued group, she knew many of them. Annie discovered that she was to be partnered by a young Englishman from Oxford.

He was doing research on the Dutch and English royal families in the seventeenth century. He was shy, he was very scholarly and from Devon. Annie cursed it that whenever she met someone from England she never knew their county and none of her English acquaintance seemed to have travelled north.

The Queen's arrival was announced, a line formed as if by magic. The Queen was in black thick silk with folds of black lace about the bodice, she wore pearls and a long black veil sparkling with black sequins.

Annie was so thankful she had not allowed Kitty, or her mother, to dress her in a veil, no other woman wore one. She spoke with animation to each of the guests. When she was before Annie she hailed her as a friend and recalled the meeting in Huis ten Bos.

Annie was impressed that this stiffly dressed, stiffly corseted lady could have such charm, her smooth skin was impeccable, almost like a wax-work, there were no lines on her brow or around her deeply set eyes.

Annie noted the lovely veiling again, it was ethereal, so light and it imparted a fairy quality to this very solid lady. It was, she thought, allied to the light humorous side of the Queen. When the Baroness curtsied a formal welcome was given, but the underlying friendship was evident.

Dinner was announced and Mr Anstruther took Annie's arm and led her to the dining room. They all stood while a clergyman said a lengthy grace. The Baroness whispered, "He's always so long-winded the food is cold."

The food was warm, but not hot and it was not as exciting as the fare they had had in Brussels. Annie's social antennae were at work, this was not as opulent an occasion as the dinner in Belgium, but it was much more certain, much more secure.

There the thought that someone might behave badly was not entirely absent, here the very thought was impossible. The most likely visitor she thought would be dullness. George Anstruther was, she discovered interested only in his research, an enthusiast, but likeable. It was only later in the great saloon that Annie found a real companion... the Clergyman of the interminable grace. Quickly she discovered that he knew the Haverschmidts.

"A most laudable man, but full of mad ideas theologically, and branded also as a socialist."

Annie detected in him the conventional man, kindly but quick to shrug off the unacceptable and with a good-natured laugh. Such people she thought can often be dangerous.

He did know Haverschmidt's stories and together they talked of them. Just when they were really interested and finding a topic that truly interested them, a lady-in-waiting approached and told her that the Queen would like a word with her.

Annie rose and together they crossed the room to the fireplace and watched for the present occupant of the space by the Queen on the royal sofa to rise. Annie was slightly amused as she listened to the practised chatter of the lady-in-waiting.

The gentleman by the Queen rose and the plump hand patted the vacated space and looked and smiled at Annie. To Annie's surprise the Queen began to talk of Annie's childhood, she even knew that her mother had been Matron at Wakefield Prison.

As she talked she saw some of the same motherliness in her that was her own mother's. What was it, affection, or understanding, or both? A visit to England was proposed and they hoped to visit Windsor, again Annie could tell her nothing of it. A smile, a wish to see her again and Annie found herself gently dismissed.

The Queen rose, everyone rose, a silken subsiding of ladies into their skirts, royalty had gone. They waited in the hall. The guests were all very talkative and there was no longer the awed hush that had controlled them before.

Back at the house Annie was eagerly awaited. The Baroness drove on after patting Annie's hand saying, "You did very well, my dear, not a foot wrong. I'm proud of you."

Strange, thought Annie, it had not been difficult.

"What was it like?" asked Kitty.

"The food was not as good as in Brussels. We were all very well behaved. The Queen looked very nice indeed."

"How was your dress?" asked Mevrouw Van Prehn.

Annie smiled. She had rehearsed her little phrase, but nearly forgot it,

"I was, how shall I say it… exceptional in a delightfully unexceptional way."

Van Prehn asked the next question which was more difficult to answer, "Did you enjoy yourself?"

She looked at them. She looked very young, far younger than her years and with that triumph that only the young can, at times, achieve.

"Yes, I did enjoy it," she looked around, as if to find the words to express a very difficult thought, she smiled, "It was a very prim and proper excitement."

While she stood there she reached her hands up to her ears and removed the diamond and sapphire jewellery. Holding them by their hooks she shook them, light flew out from them. Mevrouw Van Prehn sighed,

"What a pity to take them off, they looked so pretty."

Van Prehn just looked, he said nothing. He was more impressed and shaken than he dared to show.

He was appalled at the emotion that had opened like a great hole in the path of his existence. He felt that he could only fall in. He hardly dared look at the girl, he was glad the jewels were removed, that, at least divested her of some of the attraction, but glancing again he saw that the glow remained.

Annie was oblivious, she was isolated on the little pinnacle of her achievement and she loved the entire family.

Sleep fell upon her like a curtain at the end of a play, but before she truly slept she laughed, life was a great comedy.

Van Prehn shuddered, a fear crossed his soul and he was angry that his wife was so unaware. As she undressed she talked of Annie and her charm. Quite often she talked of the very thing he wished to avoid, sometimes quite dogmatically he stopped her prattle, but on this occasion he dare not in case it aroused suspicion.

"Kees, you are very silent?"

"Yes, I am very tired."

In bed, the vision of the girl climbing the stairs, her skirt bunched up behind her pleased, amused and almost taunted him. As the memory came, so the eroticism magnified.

"I thought that you were tired," said his wife a little wearily.

Exhausted he flung back on the pillow, so much and so little, satisfaction of the moment, but no fulfilment. He lay awake, his thoughts rampaged and he heard movements in the street he had never heard before.

Next morning he rose early, he breakfasted alone and on plea of business left soon. He walked swiftly and energetically in the Bos, those seeing him approach moved out of his way.

He seemed unaware of them. He looked overbearing, hard, yet his only thought was that life was the very devil. How was he not to hurt, not to hurt and that included his entire family of daughter, wife and governess.

Meanwhile, the three women took a lingering breakfast, Kitty was eager to hear of the previous evening, her mother, too, did not tire of hearing of it. Then they planned the minutiae of their day.

Fortunately, there was a fluctuation, enough to cause concern, in the stock market, it engrossed Van Prehn's attention, he was glad of it. There was a new anxiety in South Africa, the future there no longer looked so secure.

The day ended, the offices closed, clerks went home. Van Prehn Lingered. He tried to read, but the office bored him, he was by nature a domestic man and home was the very place he most feared.

Again and again he muttered, "It's the devil, it's the devil." He did not mean it theologically, his thoughts did not stray that way. If he had been an Englishman he would have packed his rods and gone up to Scotland, but being a Dutchman, a man of the city, he could only walk, sit in a café, watch the world and never really forget.

"What is the matter, Kitty?" The girl lagged behind on their walk back from the dunes. There she had kicked up sand, not from joy, but because her lethargy made her unwilling to lift her feet.

"Come along, dear, we shall be late."

The child smiled half-heartedly and then Annie noticed that though her cheeks were pink, she looked pinched about the nose, even faintly green. Annie turned back,

"Are you all right?"

Listlessly Kitty smiled, "Just tired, that's all."

Annie slackened her pace and they walked slowly along the streets. They walked arm in arm, Annie realised that the child was ill. At last they came to the house, went up the steps, into the hall and there Kitty half swooned on to a chair thrusting her feet out, she looked like an ill-managed puppet.

Together they struggled with buttons and removed her coat and hat, Annie saw that she was more than limp she was nearly unconscious and she kept lifting her hand to her throat.

She was guided back to the chair. Annie called out,
"Come, come. Hilke, Hilke. Mevrouw Van Prehn."

The mistress and the manservant appeared and Hilke picked up Kitty and carried her up to her room. As the mother and governess undressed the child they felt how hot she was, burning to their touch.

Hilke was sent to fetch the doctor. They forgot lunch and both sat by the bed of the obviously sick child.

"Just a sudden fever," they said to one another. "There's a lot about at the moment."

It allayed none of their fears. They recognised it as something worse. The doctor arrived, and as soon as he entered the room, he sniffed the air. Rapidly he moved to the bed, he opened her mouth and placing an ivory spatula on her tongue peered into her mouth and throat.

He really had not need to see the mucous forming. He recognised the look and the smell of diphtheria – there were many afflicted in Den Haag.

He looked impassive, he removed his pince-nez, tapped them on his left thumb. He was not giving himself time.

"I expect you have both realized that little Kitty has diphtheria. Keep her covered, but cool her face and make certain, though she objects, that she drinks as much as possible. Fortunately it seems, at the moment, a mild case. Do not leave her. Do not let her get out of bed. I will send round a nurse."

With the nurse Mevrouw Van Prehn and Annie took turns, even if mild to the doctor, it frightened them. For five days they watched until the fever began to subside and then Kitty began to swallow a little more uncomplainingly.

Often Annie had found herself praying for Kitty: she had always loved her, but the prospect of losing her had mightily endeared her. It was a prospect she had never considered. Kitty lapsed into her childish ways and begged for stories, Annie read, but the tales Kitty wanted to hear were those she invented.

They were sometimes fairy stories, more often tales of two little girls Annie and Elizabeth who lived in England. These were tales of Annie's own childhood.

Quite quickly, Kitty recovered and only a day intervened between sitting on a chair in the schoolroom to skipping about it in her dressing gown, vigorous bouts of energy followed by sleep, sometimes tears.

The fear over, the Baroness began once more to claim her daughter's time. It was Annie who now felt tired, even unlike her, irritable, she longed for peace and to be left alone. One day Annie reprimanded Kitty very sharply and Kitty complained to her mother. Annie was very fortunate for the mother immediately took her side.

It was that same evening that Annie found it difficult to dress for dinner, the simplest action like adjusting the shoulders and sleeves of her dress were arduous tasks. At the meal she failed to respond when spoken to, all her attention seemed taken up in the task of swallowing.

With alarm she knew that she, too, had diphtheria. She rose and asked to be excused, for she wished to go to bed. The next moment she was in Van Prehn's arms being carried up the stairs.

In the strange half world of reality and dream she was grateful, she was going upstairs, they were not putting her in the light swaying ambulance she feared so much. As he laid her on her bed she tried to smile.

Once again the doctor was summoned. After his examination his face was not impassive but grave. He asked if they wished to send her to the infirmary and in unison the Van Prehns refused.

"Then, I must warn you, this is a much more serious case than Kitty's. Fist of all she is a grown woman and her vitality has been lowered. I always worry much more about mothers who catch diphtheria than the children who give the disease, for the mother is usually worn out. I will send a nurse."

They asked for the same one who had tended Kitty.

The prognoses were all correct, Annie grew worse and in her delirium called again and again for her mother. The nurse watched by night, Mevrouw Van Prehn by day, Kitty was sent to her grandmother.

She seemed to gain consciousness but relapsed and it seemed that a tracheotomy must be performed. Mijnheer Van Prehn objected strongly saying,

"That will surely scar her throat?"

"Yes, a scar, the choice is that... or no life at all. But I can wait a few hours more."

Van Prehn walked up and down. The nurse sat crocheting by the shaded light. She watched the anxious pair, she wondered for a quarter of an hour, then, taking her courage in her hands, said, "You could get some of the powder from the East."

"What powder?"

"Haven't you seen advertisements in the paper? It is a powder made from a plant." She was deliberately vague. She continued, "Doctors won't prescribe it but I've seen it work wonders. But you must not mention me."

She told them to place an advertisement in the paper immediately.

Van Prehn rushed down the stairs into his study. He roughed out an urgent plea and then, grabbing a coat, ran out in to the night. He ran all the way to the offices of the Haagse Courant and demanded the editor. Van Kleek was a member of his club.

He explained what he wanted. The editor said that the paper had just been set up.

"But a life depends on this. Van Kleek I'm not a begging man, but I do beg this of you."

The editor looked, he knew these pleas. He also knew Van Prehn to be a controlled man, he had never seen him so agitated. He rang a bell. The paper was handed to a clerk and told that it was imperative that this be inserted at once.

The door closed, Van Kleek went to a cupboard and took out a bottle of brandy. He poured out a glass and handed it to Van Prehn.

"Put that down you, quick. You look as if you need it."

It was downed immediately.

"I'm off home, now, anyway. So I will walk you home."

The two men walked thought the dark streets. Like a good journalist Van Kleek listened and he thought this is not the usual reaction to a governess's illness. He wondered but being a good Haagenaar, he kept his counsel.

Van Prehn found his wife waiting, the doctor had been, her throat seemed no worse, but they were to send for him immediately if her breathing became impaired any further. They waited and waited.

The grey dawn brought the paper, the advertisement was in and within an hour a lady called with the powder. Van Prehn paid handsomely and rushed up the stairs. Annie lay on her back, her mouth open and the bubbling sound uglier, more obscene, "God don't let her die looking like that."

"How do we give it to her, nurse?"

The nurse rose, took the packet and asked for writing paper. She folded it with a crease and a narrow valley, she placed a little of the powder in the little V. "We blow that down her throat."

"I'll do it."

Van Prehn took the paper, the nurse on one side, Mevrouw Van Prehn on the other, they raised Annie. Her head fell forward, her breathing stopped for a moment, they all felt alarm. They lifted her head, the rasping sound of breathing resumed.

The two women propped her head and opened her mouth, Van Prehn carefully inserted the paper as far as it would go and he blew. It was done with the skill often given a beginner, the powder flurried direct to the fulminating throat. The patient coughed, gasped sank back.

Van Prehn could bear it no longer he strode from the room. As he went down the stairs he found himself crying and praying. He, also, acknowledged that what he had done he could have done for no other living creature.

An hour later, his wife came into his study.

"It has worked, Kees. She is breathing better, her pulse is slower."

"Thank God. Thank God."

They both clasped one another in their arms. Their relief was mutual, but one was riddled with guilt.

Later, the doctor came, he mounted the stairs swiftly, unannounced, he was not sniffing, he was listening. He did not hear the noise he expected. He examined Annie.

"She is very much better."

They agreed.

"Has she been given anything?"

"Yes, doctor," said, Mevrouw Van Prehn, "some powder I heard about."

"I thought so. Well, you've probably saved her life and I could not have given it to her."

When he came down Van Prehn stood at the bottom of the stairs.

"Will she be all right?"

"Much better, very much better. I ask nothing, but you acted wisely."

It was the beginning of a slow return to life.

It was a deliberately long convalescence. A prolonged period in bed, then a week within her room when visitors were allowed. The first were the Haverschmidts who were shocked to see the wan and thin face and wasted hand. Francois brought violets which Annie buried her nose in with rapture. She held hard on Margo's hand,

"I am lucky, so lucky to be alive."

"God and your good friends have preserved you," said Mevrouw Haverschmidt swiftly, believingly and confidently. Her husband more thoughtfully agreed but hedged his agreement with wonderings.

"Yes, you have been preserved. God must have a great task for you. I wonder what it can be?"

Annie smiled, "I don't know. I am not very good at looking too far ahead."

When they had gone she looked at her violets, she carefully untied the raffia and arranged them in a silver bowl, their scent wafted up and she thought of the garden of the Pumphreys outside Wakefield.

One evening, Van Prehn saw her turning the violets head down in the water.

"Why do you do that?"

"Violets live on dew and drink through their heads." It seemed to work and ever after he kept her bowl replenished with these flowers. A week later as he sat by her bed, he reached out his hand to hers, she left it there for a minute then patted it and removed hers, she looked both troubled and pleased.

She knew that he loved her... she hoped he was not aware of how her heart beat.

Downstairs, the evening meal went by with its usual dignity and occasionally the clock added his repetitive sounds to the conversation. Van Prehn and his wife were tired, they had been though a strain.

Their need for change made them plan for Kitty and Annie. They wanted to take them to the sea. The First suggestion was Knokke, but it was dismissed as too near, an insufficient change.

Then Mentone was considered, but dismissed as too far for

invalids. Next day Van Prehn heard of a boat going from Rotterdam to St Malo, on to Spain and then back. Instantly he booked passages for them all.

When the trip was announced, Kitty was thrilled and she found Annie hard to rouse. Annie feared the journey on the boat. She was apprehensive of the entire venture for she was still very weak.

Kitty and Mevrouw Van Prehn packed for her and the decisions she had to make as they brought clothes for her inspection tired her. Still she had not left her room, still she had not been downstairs.

The day arrived and, as usual, she had her breakfast in her room. Her small trunk was taken downstairs, then she put on her outdoor coat and arranged her bonnet, already she felt weary and unable to cope with the journey. The door opened and Van Prehn entered,

"You're looking fine, my dear."

He put his arm around her and swung her up and carried her down the stairs. The very movement made her giddy, she shut her eyes and she only flickered them as she felt cold air on her cheeks and then the outstretched arms of Kitty and her mother as she was fitted into the corner of the carriage. Van Prehn climbed in and they were off. At the station, once more, he carried her and he placed her in a corner seat with her feet up on the cushions.

Annie closed her eyes when the train moved out for she felt a strange and alarming vertigo. Fortunately the journey was not long and when the train stopped she was again hoisted up and carried on to the ship, down to the cabin where the two women helped undress her and placed her in her bunk.

At first, Annie felt another sense of cold fear, her imagination romped, what would she do if the ship foundered, she had no strength to save herself. Her weakness saved her from panic for, worn out, she fell into a sound sleep.

She never heard the ship leave the harbour, she never noticed the pitch of the waves, she slept through lunch-time, she slept through tea and only awoke in the evening wondering where on earth she was.

She tried to think what room in Noordeinde had such an array of odd decorations along the ceilings and walls. Then she dimly saw that they were pipes, then the shudder of the engine was noticed. "We are at sea," she said to herself.

As she pushed herself up in the bunk, the door opened quietly and there was the eager face of Kitty. "Why you are awake, you've slept nearly all the way."

Annie was never to forget that she awoke on the ship feeling well. It was as if the sea had placed a distance between her illness and herself. She got up and went slowly up the stairs to the deck with Kitty. St Malo was almost in sight, the large houses, small modern chateaux stood on little promontories of the jagged rocks on either side.

The ship turned and the walled city was visible on a smooth flat plain. She felt a thrill, akin to that when she had first come to Holland. As the ship drew nearer the harbour they saw the ramparts and then the blue smocked men in sabots at the quayside.

When the boat tied up and almost before the gang-plank was in position the blue men were scrambling up, elbowing each other aside. They looked large, fierce and they gabbled, the two of them shook their heads and then ran down to their cabin.

Mijnheer Van Prehn appeared, he organised his women-folk and even subdued the porters, the luggage was lifted and they were swift to follow. Van Prehn was surprised at Annie's sudden strength to climb the stairs and down the gangplank to the quay.

A carriage was hailed and the luggage put in a hand-cart. They set off towards the walled town.

They went in through a great gateway into narrow cobbled streets. It was shadowed and mysterious and to Annie the Revolution did not seem far away. She was surprised when they stopped not before a large and imposing hotel but a small inn with a courtyard abutting on to a narrow street.

It was called La Relais, it had catered for coaches before the railway came. A gallery ran round the courtyard and the bedrooms opened from it. They were led to their rooms, the porter from the harbour soon arrived with their luggage and they were shown to their rooms.

Each one was inspected by the family and when a small back room was found to have been allotted to Annie, Van Prehn said that they would leave immediately. Annie tried to pacify him, but was told peremptorily to be quiet.

Mevrouw Van Prehn shook her head at her and frowned. The threat of departure revealed the sudden discovery that there had been a cancellation and Annie was led, accompanied by the family to a fine room on the corner of the building with two long sash windows set in the thick granite walls looking into two different streets. Annie was delighted.

The dining room was a plain room a step down from the courtyard. The women wondered at the clean but austere surroundings. Van Prehn smiled and assured them that the fare would make them forget the almost monastic surroundings.

It was true. They sat a long time at the table, darkness fell and when the Van Prehns went for a stroll, Annie climbed up to her room tired, in spite of her long sleep on the ship.

Over their croissants and bowls of coffee next day they planned a tour of the town. A hat shop seen on their walk was promised as one of the delights for Annie. They walked the ramparts, they peered in the church and the evident Catholicism shocked the Hollanders, but Annie did not mind.

In the afternoon they sat on the beach and all except Annie paddled. Annie crocheting laughed to herself at the comic undignified sight of the bunched up skirts and the rolled up trousers of people who above the knees seemed eminently respectable.

They widened their excursions, went to Dinard and even went into the casino and watched with proper Dutch horror the spectacle of men, and women, gambling and losing large sums of money.

Their hotel that evening seemed even plainer compared with the garish establishments they had seen. They boarded a train, one day, and travelled to Mont Saint Michel. Annie had, by now, recovered some of her vigour and she walked along the causeway to the small town growing like an encrustation of limpets on the rock and rising up to the spire of the abbey.

Van Prehn had been there as a young man, he enjoyed showing them all that he had so enjoyed before and he would not let them leave until they had eaten an omelette. Though they were safe on the causeway they hurried when they heard the warning bell announcing that the tide was on the turn and would come back at the rate of a galloping horse.

The days passed quickly and the last day arrived. Annie went out alone to buy presents. She bought boxes of sweets for the servants and a silver milk urn for Mevrouw Van Prehn and a small work box with a picture of the ramparts on its lid for Kitty.

Then she wondered what to buy for Van Prehn and she thought that men were so difficult when it came to presents. Suddenly he hailed her in the street and walked along beside her.

She saw approaching them what at first appeared to be a dog, then at closer quarters she saw that it was a man with wheels strapped to his hip - he was legless from the thighs and he propelled himself by walking along on his hands which were protected by pads of leather.

She gave a swift intake of breath, it was audible horror and involuntarily she seized Van Prehn's arm. He was also appalled, but with less emotion. Quickly he placed his other hand over hers and commanded her to look away.

She looked at the stone gables of the houses, for a moment they seemed to rise and might fall upon her. She could not forebear a backward glance. This both reassured her and further horrified her.

He had padded to a boulangerie and giving a little push backward and a small swivel had thrown himself upright between the wheels. He was smiling and speaking to the baker. At once he proclaimed himself to be a human being, but he also looked to Annie, exactly like Quick, their dog, sitting up and begging. Her grip tightened.

"How can such a horrible thing have happened?"

"War, perhaps. We are not used to things like that in Holland. He could have been a young man in the war with Prussia."

It was to both of them an almost cataclysmic revelation of the horrors of war, the intolerable mutilations. It eclipsed forever in Annie's mind any of the glory to be seen in pictures of cavalry charges so popular in Britain. Together they talked of it.

It had evaporated any appetite for shopping. They climbed the steps to the ramparts and continued to talk of France's love for la gloire miliaire and for England's still growing Empire.

Holland's colonies were overlooked with the ease a true Hollander possesses. Anyone seeing the couple, well dressed looking out to sea, would never have guessed the depth of the disturbance they had both received.

It was a double disturbance, the terror of war and the equal insecurity of their relationship.

Annie had betrayed all her feelings by seizing his arm and he had accepted it.

The personal feelings were, now, uppermost, but neither spoke of them, they stared out to sea. Annie stood up and looked at him. He was the man she loved in all the world, but she forced herself away.

"I will go back. You come later. Do not follow me."

He half rose, Annie hurried away. Her mind was whirling and as she resolutely made her way she forgot to give any thanks that she could make her way without fear of fatigue, that her strength had returned. All she was aware of was that her heart was pounding and the question was raging in her head,

"What do we do, now?"

She was surprised that she had said to herself we and not I. That was a bad sign.

She returned to the hotel by the ramparts, passing the statue of Chateaubriand, the plunging horse, the swirling romantic attitude matched her feelings, but in hers there was no sense of triumph, only anguish and torture.

She looked down into the street below to a courtyard were men and women were drinking. They were peasants and burst into sporadic and unfinished song. Annie watched them and thought that their lives were physically harder than her own, but they were happier.

They were uncomplicated, almost, she thought uncivilised, but she with her gentility, hampered always by a lack of money, had in many ways less freedom, less choice. They were happier than she.

Back in the hotel she lay down on her bed, her heart still ached. When she emerged nobody could have known of the tension she concealed.

During the meal, Van Prehn corrected Kitty who was eating clumsily, "Why on earth, Kitty, can you not eat neatly like Miss Taylor?"

Kitty put down her knife and fork, "Must I do everything like Miss Taylor? Must I eat, drink, cross my ankles and not my knees like Miss Taylor? You'll make me hate Miss Taylor."

"Stop it, both of you," said Mevrouw Van Prehn. "Kitty is quite right, Kees, nothing is more boring and off-putting than being compared with someone who appears to be perfection."

Annie looked at Kitty's mother, was that irony intentional?

"Yes, you are quite right. I remember in Wakefield a teacher holding up another pupil as an example. I hated her."

Annie's suspicions died and she reproved herself for thinking there was any sarcasm in the remark.

Later, in the evening, one of the guests sang. Her clear soprano filled the room, every word was clear, and every word was of love. Tears came into Annie's eyes. She was glad when the lovely voice was stilled and they went upstairs to pack.

She put her clothes in slowly, reluctantly, she did not want to stay, she did not want to go. She did not know what she wanted beyond the love of the man she loved.

On the ship in a mercifully calm sea, Annie became much calmer and, she thought, duller. They went northward, never far from the coast and everything steadily became more level, until at last, Belgium and Holland seemed to just float on the water itself.

There was bustle at Rotterdam, there was bustle at Den Haag… and the welcome back to the house. Life fell into a familiar pattern and the crisis seemed over. Van Prehn took care never to be left alone with Annie.

He did, however, become moody and critical of his wife, what she said and what she wore were so often wrong. Annie's heart stopped at times for she expected a comparison with herself that would betray all.

Then the conjunctivitis returned and his eyes became agonizingly tender. Once again drops had to be administered, again his wife became agitated and the task was assigned to Annie. The day came, as it must, when Mevrouw Van Prehn was out with her mother and Annie was alone.

In his study Van Prehn sat in the large chair facing the light, Annie pulled his eyelid, dropped in the liquid. It was done. Van Prehn put his arms about her and kissed her on her mouth. There was the dual mixture of horror and delight, joy and terror. She pulled herself away.

"Kees, Kees, you must not. No more, or I shall have to go."

His pleasure turned instantly to remorse,

"You are right. But what are we to do?"

She with a medicine bottle in her hand, he with tear blotched eyes, reddish rimmed. Annie burst out laughing,

"We do not look very romantic."

For a moment, he looked angry, then joined in a rather rueful smile. A week passed, the fever was over.

A great peace came when another conference of bankers was called, this time, in Paris. It was mooted that all of them should go. Annie hesitated and then, making some exams of Kitty's the excuse, ensured that she and her pupil should stay behind.

Left behind, with the demanding grandmother frequently descending, they lived very quietly and serenely. Their outings were to Huis ten Bos where they took tea with the Queens and spoke in English. Once while the girls were away in the wood, the plump Queen walked with Annie.

"It seems to me, Miss Taylor, that you have become as Dutch as I have. Tell me, do you miss your country?"

"Sometimes, not often. My life here is so full. My parents are dead; I have one sister. There is not much to link me with England, now. I think of Holland as my home."

"Yes, Holland is my home, my family. I have more reason to be attached than you. I even think that the Dutch have forgotten that I am a German."

"Yes, of course they do. I think the Dutch are more quick to accept strangers than the English. The Dutch are not islanders."

"That is true. I do not think that my dear sister, though she is loved, will ever be considered English. I find that unfair. The Hanovers are after all hardly English either."

Annie wondered whether she would ask how long she intended staying in Holland. She did not know the answer. She knew, however, that tact was Queen Emma's great gift. She never asked awkward questions.

It was one of the reasons for her acceptance together with her natural charm. But Annie, who so rarely thought of the future, did wonder just how long she would stay. In that garden the future opened like a gulf, it was open but it was unseen.

She knew that it was foolish, even evil to stay so close to the unattainable, but she lacked the will to go.

She looked at the neatly raked gravel path... her life was not so neat. She looked back at the house where the gilt crown gleamed on the dome. Above that a blue, blue sky. She saw immensity, it gave her hope because she saw at once the littleness of her life, her emotions.

"I shall have to return one day. Perhaps not so far away."

"I expect you will, my dear. You will be missed."

The little words of royalty weigh more heavily than those of lesser folk. Annie began to find strange meanings in them.

There was great excitement when the Van Prehns returned. The house had been cleaned and polished and polished again. Flowers had been arranged and furniture rearranged anticipating the summer.

They had been bidden to remain at home and not meet them at the station, but they listened for the carriage and, on the very hour, they arrived as anticipated. Mevrouw Van Prehn looked happier than Annie had ever seen her... she glowed with a new life.

She wore a hat from the rue de Rivoli. Cases were carried upstairs but beautifully wrapped packages came into the drawing room, Van Prehn excitedly arranged them.

The trip had been a great success in every way and it reflected in the bounty he was about to dispense. There were presents for everyone, the housemaid, the Cook, the man of all work.

When the servants left the largest package was unwrapped. It was Mevrouw Van Prehn's. A large canvas box was revealed, printed with squirrels, beavers, and seals. It was opened and from it was lifted very tenderly, a coat of black sealskin.

It shone with a living life. She slipped it on - it fell in deep folds to the ground. Sable formed a collar and cape. The sleeves were puffed, then gathered at the elbow and neatly at the wrist.

Kitty and Annie were speechless. It was the most beautiful garment they ever had seen. They went up to feel its texture but were unable to resist an embrace for it made her seem the embodiment of all motherliness, beautiful, soft, loving and wonderfully attainable.

Next came a smaller, but similar box for Kitty. From it came an ermine muff and hat, both were trimmed with black tipped tails. It was put on and declared perfection. Then there was a box for Annie.

Opening it, she found a tippet, gleaming black seal edged with sable with a collar that stood like an Elizabethan ruff. She arranged it on her shoulders,

"Why you look like Mary Queen of Scots", said Kitty admiringly.

They all trailed up the stairs on this hot spring day delighting in their presents which would have to be put away for months.

Before the mirror in her room Annie looked at the tippet. It was extremely beautiful, but it made its own demands, a new toque, a new dress even. It was odd, she thought, to live like this, one foot in luxury and the other in circumstances to warrant the adjective, straitened.

Edith's life in Prestatyn had been dull and with each day of Mrs Cassidy's tight cling to an outworn life had become harder and duller. Her days by the bedside of the old lady had become longer and her freedom non-existent. Often Mrs Cassidy had looked into Edith's face with fondness and gratitude and said,

"You are a good girl. I shall not forget you."

The days came when she never left her bed, Edith had to wash and attend to her perpetually. She, too, became pale and waxen and it was Mrs Evers, the cook, who insisted that Edith went out each day for some exercise and to gain an appetite.

"It you don't, you will be ill as well and where will Mrs Cassidy be then?"

As the end slowly approached Mrs Cassidy became querulous and Edith's temper frayed under the strain and it was Mrs Evers who bore the brunt of Edith's sharp criticisms. The cook bore it silently, she shrugged her shoulders, and mused that it was the way of the world, "Lesser bugs have lesser bugs to bite them."

Life was made up of a thousand little pyramids of degrees of rank and dependence. Mrs Evers, anyway, could practise forbearance with some ease, she was shortly to marry and have a real married title, not just the courtesy one of a cook. Edith, too, had her dream. She was still determined to go to London and learn about hotels.

This dream sustained her for she was very bored. Her life in Prestatyn had always been cramped and living in the house of an elderly non-conformist had confined her world still further.

The greatest excitement had been the visit of the minister and his wife to dinner on Sunday. She had learnt, though, to look at the mountains, often when sad at heart she had climbed up to the upper landing and looked out toward the rising hills and there, on a day of clear vision she had found compensation.

A love of hills and moors had always been hers, and possibly their absence had accounted for her finding Holland so alien.

Edith was tall, slim but life had put a droop upon her shoulders and her bright eyes were obscured by pince-nez, so that one saw too obviously the small mouth that appeared crabbed but was, in fact, kind.

She did, however, have a tendency to look back to the past with pique. She felt that life had been unfair. She posed the answerless question about her father's death, her mother's subsequent struggle.

She remembered her mother with a tempered love, the person she could not help but love, but she ever remembered the greater portion was returned not to her but her sister. She did, though, balance it by knowing that she had been her grandmother's favourite.

There was cause for discontent and with a system that ensured that once you were out of fortune's favour it was very difficult to regain it. Luckily, she was blessed with humour more than her sister.

She had a quick mind and great vigour. It was, though a repressed life for a young woman and the ethos of her day accepted her unthinkingly as a sacrifice silently saying, "What can a penniless young woman do?"

Eventually one morning as the dawn came up over the mountain Mrs Cassidy ceased breathing, she had ceased to live, weeks before. The maid, Mrs Evers and Edith all wept, but it was also relief and apprehension for the future, they thought it for the old lady alone.

The funeral was large and because of the flowers, brighter than her life had been. Several relations materialised of whom Edith had never heard. She had been warned that this was the usual occurrence at a death where there was money to be gained.

She sat dry-eyed in the chapel and heard praise sung which sounded hollow. She thought there was an echoing timbre in the minister as well. As she left the graveside on the hill cemetery she thought of the Will, she was far from alone in this.

As she was driven back with relatives to whom she made small talk, pointing out features of the town, she said to herself, "I don't think I shall be mentioned in the will at all."

When it was read a great chill settled over the family, they had not been remembered, the minister, too, was aggrieved, for the bulk of the money went to her former chapel in Manchester.

Edith received £10, Mrs Evers five. In the atmosphere of injury Edith was glad that it was no more. The relatives did not delay their return. Edith and the cook had been appointed to keep charge until the old lady's possessions were dispersed.

It was then alone together in the house they began to grumble and recall the niggardliness of the deceased.

Edith put her plan into action. She wrote to several London hotels offering her services as a housekeeper. To her surprise, she was accepted on her testimonials by the Imperial Hotel in Russell Square. It was Mrs Evers who went first, though, to a place in Chester, where she would remain a few months until her wedding.

When Mrs Cassidy had died, Edith had been surprised at how good a cook she was and how on the slenderest means she provided interesting food.

"Mrs Evers, if I have the hotel I want and you need work. I will engage you as my cook. I mean that."

The last night she spent there entirely alone. She wandered from room to room in the denuded house. She thought it very strange indeed that in its empty state it had as much character as it had when Mrs Cassidy had truly lived there.

The old lady had gone leaving so little trace of herself. Edith thought it was because she had not known how to give and as on the staircase she looked up to the mountains that had a bluish tinge in the sunlight mixed with the pink of the sunset she vowed that she would never, never be mean.

Next morning, after turning every key in every lock she took her Gladstone bag, went through the front door, closed it and very firmly locked it and tested it. She felt that she was shutting very securely a sterile portion of her life.

She walked swiftly through the streets to the solicitor's office. She went in and was about to hand the key to a clerk, when he stopped her and asked her to wait a moment.

"But I have a train to catch."

"It is important but will not take long."

Mr Evans came out and smiled, but Edith was not beguiled, she was apprehensive… she wondered what misdemeanour she had committed. She felt like a child summoned to the headmaster.

He led her into his office, asked her to sit down and sat behind his desk. He put his hands together solemnly.

"Miss Taylor, I wish to say as an outsider how impressed I have been by you loyalty to Mrs Cassidy. I am sorry that you were so poorly provided in the Will for all your attention.

"My hands were tied, but I do know that my client was grateful. She feared her relatives and she left a little money, many months ago, in my care for bequests which would not be made public. I have this for you."

He handed her a very thick envelope. It was unsealed. Looking inside a little reluctantly, she was embarrassed, she saw the thinnest of tissue paper… there were five £10 notes. She had never seen notes of such value before.

"That, I think, you richly deserve."

Edith's heart fluttered, she felt guilty as she recalled how she and Mrs Evers had mocked her parsimonious ways. Then she remembered her vow looking at the mountain and she extracted two notes.

"Would you please send these to Mrs Evers. I think you have her new address."

Mr Evans smiled more approvingly at her.

"Put them away, Miss Taylor. I have sent precisely that amount to her in Chester."

Edith thanked him. She walked to the station with a lighter heart and with less criticism for the place than she had ever before.

She did not even hurry and thought that if she missed the train there would be another. She did not miss it and as her second train took her thought the Pennines she looked again at the envelope in her handbag and sighed with satisfaction mingled with surprise.

At Huddersfield she felt so wealthy she took a cab and drove the entire way up to Marsh where Cousin Lydia had, now, moved. Edith had not been there before. The cab stopped in a quiet road with young trees and flowered gardens.

It was neat, prim, solid. As Edith regarded it she felt a pang. The Donckersleys were rising in the world. Mr Dockersley had taken her father's place in the mill. Her mother had always wanted to live in Marsh.

It was not quite fair. The instant, however, she saw the face of her cousin, a face that so matched the neat, demure and prim little garden and house that she forgot her carping.

Lydia was surprised at her bold plan to go to London. To her it seemed far away and, indeed, another world.

Edith reminded her that her mother had come from there and

managed to cope very adequately with Yorkshire.

Lydia wondered whether her mother would have approved for as she said, "Your mother was always such a lady."

The return of Henry Donckersley was not anticipated by Edith with any joy. She felt sure that he, too, would add disapproval to his wife's fears. Soon the dog barked, she heard a deep voice in the hall and she knew that he had returned.

She went down, he kissed her and told her that she was a real Taylor with her auburn hair.

At supper, Lydia rather timidly raised the subject of Edith's future. He listened intently. He knew the hotel. He often travelled to London on business. He thought it a grand idea but added, "When you know enough, come back to Yorkshire. Work here and then, perhaps set up your own place. I am sure there are good openings in Scarborough. It's a champion place and very popular.

"You mark my words, go there and you will never look back." Edith had never been to Scarborough. She hoped that it was brighter than Prestatyn.

Edith's letter from Marsh brought a pang of homesickness to Annie which she was about to indulge, but there was another letter from Margo. She opened it slowly anticipating its contents and was shocked to find that it was a passionate appeal that she should try to visit them immediately, as her father was so deeply melancholy.

An appeal to Mevrouw Van Prehn brought instant understanding. Later that morning, Annie was in the train for Schiedam. She tried to read her book but looked up at her suitcase and the wonderful box from the furrier in Paris. She knew that she was on a sick visit and thought her new present would prove a diversion.

As she went through the gate she seemed to feel the tension. The curtains, untidily looped, were an indication of something wrong. When Clara answered the door the atmosphere was even more apparent.

While Annie spoke with the maid, Margo's voice called, "Is that you, Annie?"

Margo appeared, her plump good-natured face troubled and almost angular, her full mouth pursed and anxious.

"Oh, I'm so glad you've come. It is awful."

Annie went into the room. Mevrouw Haverschmidt rose, took

Annie into her arms and wept straight away. Looking about Annie realised that all routine had gone. She guessed that they had not eaten properly.

Before she even began to listen she asked if she might have a cup of tea because she was so thirsty. When it came she poured out for them all while they told their tales. The black moods of her husband had been worse and a meeting had upset him, he had become suspicious.

Then she described how he had written a letter. As she was leaving the house she offered to post it.

"I put it in the box at the end of the road and went my walk. When I returned he questioned me and when he learnt that I had not taken it to the Post Office, he swore at me. He never asked me to go to the Post Office. If he had asked I would have done."

She burst out weeping, then in muffled sounds said: "It is all nothing, really. But, oh, he had never sworn at me before."

Annie thought of the violent whistling she had so often heard and his remark, "A Pastor may not curse."

"Where is he, now?"

"He stormed up to his room two days ago and has never left it."

They told her how they had pleaded with him and there had been no reply. Furthermore, to make certain they would not enter the room he had let all the birds out of their cages.

"You can hear them flying about." The memory of the whirr of their wings made Mevrouw Haverschmidt shudder.

Margo interposed. "We sent for the doctor. Father refused to open the door, but he did speak. He told him to go away and mind his own business."

Margo began to cry. "The doctor said he might have to send for a man who would take him away to a hospital. A private one," she gulped.

Annie also shuddered. She had never thought that it would come to this.

"I have a plan. He loves Hutspot. It smells so good. Let us make some and leave the kitchen door open, so that the smell goes up the stairs to tempt him. He must be hungry."

The ruse made both mother and daughter smile and Mevrouw Haverschmidt said: "I always thought it was the Dutch who are practical. The English, we are always told, are pedantic."

Alone, Annie admitted to herself more fear. Like her mother, she had a great fear of insanity. She left her room and went up the remaining stairs. At the top she sat on the step and called out very softly and strangely self-conscious,

"Mijnheer Haverschmidt. Mijnheer Haverschmidt."

There was no reply, but she knew, somehow, that he had heard, because the stillness was greater. She sat there for half an hour calling his name, then she kept silent. She heard a movement and a low hesitant voice,

"Is that really you, Annie?"

"Yes, it is. I would like to see you."

Yet as she said it she feared... for what if he was mad?

Then she said: "I am getting very stiff sitting here. I am going to get a cushion."

She groaned as she got up and laughingly said: "I must be getting old."

As she went downstairs she smelt the stewing onions in the hutspot, it made her hungry... she hoped the ruse would work, she told them to leave the kitchen door open. She went back upstairs with a cushion and a book.

Her reading she discovered was automatic, she covered a whole page and the sense had not registered at all. She was listening, she discovered, so intently. As last, she heard what she wished to hear,

"Annie, Annie - are you still there?"

"Yes, I'm still here. Why don't you let me in?"

"I cannot, I cannot."

"Then let me just see you. Open the door."

"Is there anyone else with you?"

"No. I am quite alone."

"You will think me mad."

"I don't think so. I expect you to be unshaven and dirty."

"Go downstairs. I am coming out, but no one, no one must see me."

"I promise."

It dawned on Annie that he must have a slop pail with him. He had been there three days. She suddenly felt hot and cold with a fierce sense of shame. It was as if all the hidden aspects of life were revealed. She ran down the stairs, afraid. She entered the kitchen, where all three women were.

"We will keep the door shut for a while."

They looked at her. "Is he coming out? I must go to him."

"Please don't"

"But I am his wife."

"I think he wished to be alone just a little longer."

"I don't understand. I simply don't understand."

Again Annie found herself listening, she heard a furtive tread. She heard the flush of the lavatory, so did Mevrouw Haverschmidt.

"He needs me."

"Wait, please wait."

Mevrouw Haverschmidt looked determined. Annie wondered how to prevent her.

"All the birds are free."

That decided the issue for the moment and Annie went back up the stairs.

It was becoming oddly macabre within such domestic limits. She felt it was a bad dream. At the top of the house the door was closed, she guessed it was locked.

"Mijnheer Haverschmidt?"

"Yes, what now?"

"Are you coming down? Do you want hot water to shave with?"

She did not know whether she had gone too far in suggesting this, but he said: "Yes, yes."

Again she ran down the stairs and from the tank in the range a jug of hot water was filled. She went up again.

"The water is in your bedroom."

He opened the door. Annie was shocked to see his dishevelled appearance. He looked wild. His eyes had both sunken in and yet appeared prominent for they flashed with suspicion. She felt a stab of fear but kept saying,

"He is only ill, ill."

She heard the birds and she smelt the stale air. The window had not been opened and the place stank of tobacco.

"While you shave and wash, I will catch the birds."

"How will you do that?"

"My old aunt always threw a duster over her canary when it got out."

"Quite right. I have a large silk one." He even smiled.

He held the door open, she entered. There were so many birds, she had not realised how many.

"I think we had better do this together."

The frightened creatures fluttered pitifully. They crashed against the books in their fear and when caught seemed relieved to hop, once again, within the narrow confines of their cages.

The last one captured, she flung open the window and a gust of fresh air blew in. It seemed to have a miraculous effect on Francois. The activity of catching the birds had brought colour to his cheeks.

"Annie, I am glad to see you." She smiled, then the schoolmistress, so rarely evident in her rose, and said: "I too am pleased to see you. But I shall be better pleased when you are shaven, clean and tidy."

For a moment he hovered on the threshold of the door, but the smell of food reached him and bracing his shoulders he went down to his bedroom. She watched from above, pity wrung her heart. She looked on a man burdened with too great a sensibility.

When eventually he came down, he kissed his wife and Margo, and sat down at the table. They all pretended that nothing had happened. But something had happened, something more significant than just a mood and they were all very well aware.

During the meal Francois suddenly said: "What is the day?"

"It is only Wednesday, my dear, plenty of time for sermons yet."

He seemed relieved and Annie noticed a new tenderness in his wife's voice.

The depression passed and next day he went out walking with Annie, he was in a nostalgic mood and talked of his childhood and then the terrible loneliness of his first parish in the country with no one to talk to. It had been a considerable shock after the talk, talk, talk of Leiden.

On Friday, he seemed his old self, and on Saturday, silence prevailed as he wrote his long sermon for the next day. Next day he preached, the church was full. In the pulpit he looked firm and commanding... it seemed that his faith, in spite of his questionings, was firm and strong.

His text was "Beloved, let us love one another: for love is of God and everyone that loveth is born of God, and knoweth God."

"If only, if only," Annie thought, "he could remember that." Only the three in the pew really knew of his dark moods.

She hoped that Margo would be more patient and Mevrouw

Haverschmidt less disappointed. She knew that she was, in fact, worn out by his demanding temperament. Annie realised that she, unrelated, to an extent uninvolved, was able more easily to see the need for rallying and humour, which they, so woven into his emotions were unable to do.

Next day she was to return to Den Haag. There she would be entangled in another set of emotions. She was content to let the next day look after itself.

In the train Annie kept thinking of the strong, firm face she had seen in the pulpit and contrasted it with the haggard and haunted look she had seen when he opened the door of his study.

It had been a shock. She thought of Mevrouw Haverschmidt and Margo, outwardly such capable and imperturbable people, the very persons who dealt with situations competently, but none of it was so.

Life was, she thought, largely illusion, one believed in a conventional framework to give one assurance. She looked at her fellow passengers and thought that she had no knowledge whatsoever of their secret thoughts, each man, every woman was a mystery.

Gradually the thoughts led round to herself and her predicament.

What did others see? A pleasant young woman of good upbringing and virtue was what she hoped they saw, but she was beginning to doubt the validity of such an impression. She was, she knew, a young woman in love with a married man and she lacked the will to move away from the source of this love.

She was, she knew, in danger, but what was she to do? The answer was obvious but she was unable to bring herself to do it.

Noordeinde welcomed her home and at dinner she felt that she was at the very fount of love, their delight to have her back was obvious, Kitty idolised her, Mevrouw Van Prehn loved her like a sister and Van Prehn just loved her.

Annie looked at him as he ate so heartily and she felt a flutter in her heart and a sharp stab of her conscience. All went quietly, smoothly and all glided smoothly and without revelation.

A few evenings later, the Baroness whisked her daughter and granddaughter away to a conversazione at the Palace. Van Prehn and Annie were left to dine alone. It was the very situation that

Annie wished to avoid, but against which she took no precautions. She failed to admit that it was inevitable.

While they were served, they talked generalities. Both the food and the wine were good, and when he talked of his day at the office, he made her laugh. There was, though, something in the air that Annie refused to recognise, partly by wish, partly through ignorance.

She left him to his port and cigar and went to the drawing room. There she picked up her embroidery, she put it down to look around the room, it pleased her. It was, in fact, her room, she had chosen, or caused to be chosen, the wallpaper, the Chinese vases, the silk screen with glistening cranes flying across grey silk, had been found by her.

Very softly she said: "This is my room", but even as she said it, she knew that it was not.

Van Prehn came in, still smoking his cigar. She poured out his coffee. He smiled. She picked up her needlework, but that did not stop her heart thumping and her breath almost betraying her.

"Annie, Annie you do know, don't you, that I love you?"

She never looked up. At the same time she was exalted to hear it. She was in love, it was undoubted. The only other man she knew well was Haverschmidt, Van Prehn was so different... here was a man uncomplicated by codes of belief, doubt and despair.

Yet, she did not analyse it, there was an element of pity in her love for him as there was for the much older man and who so obviously needed sympathy. She grieved that he was left alone so much, was ignored by his mother-in-law whose philosophy, if such it could be called, included a contempt, not at all Dutch, of trade and the banking she considered close to it.

What she did not comprehend was that her contempt was returned. Her son-in-law thought monarchy an outmoded system of government and the tattle of Court, in which Annie often joined, bored him with its pettiness and lack of reality.

The blind-sided view of politics and statecraft he thought foolish and sometimes dangerous, for he admitted that palaces still held power, but greater power was in the world of economics.

His mother-in-law was, by her unthinking demands, undermining their marriage and because Annie was so attractive he did not care. For some time he had sought other sexual excitement

- he had found it easily, he was much alive and urgent in his desires.

He was, however, discreet and endeavoured always to protect is wife and Kitty from any knowledge of this kind. He was totally successful. But now, in his own home he was confronted by something far greater than mere appetite. It was pure love. Its purity he had only plumbed when she had so nearly died.

He awaited an answer. Annie sitting bolt upright staring at her needle burst into silent tears. He got up, sat beside her and put an arm around her. Annie intended rising and leaving, but she stayed... she even relaxed and sank against his arm.

He pressed her to him, he kissed her and she never resisted. All she was aware of was that she loved him. They sat like this some time, saying nothing, savouring the closeness, but, also, vigilant for the sound of his wife and Kitty's return, the knock of a servant.

Then, with that strange formality that pervaded all their lives, they parted. He moved back to his chair and he chose a smaller cigar. Then he suggested that he should read to her. Annie picked up her embroidery, gave a swift look at her hair in the mirror and resumed her work. She barely heard a word of his reading.

Beneath her outward and very correct composure her emotions raged. Her love for this man was so close to her in every sense... against everything she had been brought up to regard as true and good. Thinking of good she remembered her mother and an unseen shudder crossed her unseen soul.

When Kitty and her mother returned, Kitty leapt and spun and the skirt of her dress stood out. It was both excitement and relief. In retrospect it had been a grand occasion and hallowed in her memory, in the event it had frightened her into silence.

Mevrouw Van Prehn had been bored and as she came in said: "You lucky things, having a nice quiet evening at home. My knees are stiff with standing, the Queen never sat down, so none of us could. She's not usually so thoughtless. Besides, I never talked to anyone interesting."

"Did you expect that you would there?" enquired her husband.

"Oh, sour grapes, my dear."

"We have been having some *Sherlock Holmes, The Speckled Band.*

"Did you get very far?"

"No, we'll go back."

Annie felt very guilty, she had not been listening whilst he read, but she had given every indication that she had. This, she said to herself, was the beginning of real deception.

Once again The Speckled Band was begun. Silence fell, 'Court knees' were rested and Annie, this time, took it in. In fact the story became etched and she could repeat it almost perfectly to her children and grandchildren. When she went to bed she wondered how she would ever sleep. Every time she thought of Van Prehn her heart seemed to leap, but she was also so adept at closing doors on reality, like most women of her class and generation, that she wondered if she was really in love.

She did sleep. Van Prehn by his wife's side was much more restless. He knew well that spiritually he had committed adultery. It pained him far more than many of his more serious infidelities. He kept repeating to himself "Annie must go… must go." But every time an anguished cry of "No, no." came. At last he fell asleep.

The following day unrolled equably and mid-morning, as they drank coffee, Annie said to Kitty and her mother without warning, even to herself, "You know, you do not need me any more. I have taught all I know. I must go."

The cries of "Nonsense" and "We cannot do without you," were reassuring, flattering, but Annie was determined to ignore them. But not just yet…

In the following weeks nothing occurred, but then, the too frequent criticisms of Mevrouw Van Prehn's clothes began. On one occasion, Annie came forward too vehemently to protest… it was then that Mevrouw Van Prehn had her first and sharpest suspicion.

The thought fell on sterile soil, she loved her husband and loved and trusted Annie. She did not distrust her husband, but, like Annie, she thought men another species, not comprehensible to women. They were driven by urges and desires which ladies did not possess. Ladies did not enquire too deeply.

Yet Annie was in love. She watched Van Prehn, she found that she loved his features, his movements and his talk. Sometimes, the chatter and gossip not only bored her but annoyed her.

Sometimes, when she saw him fondle Kitty, she longed to feel his arms about her once again. It was then that she knew her position to be perilous. She busied herself in the small duties of the moment and took care that it seemed that she was serene. She even, at times, deluded her own self, so time slipped by.

It was on a spring afternoon that Kitty felt unwell and Annie instead of taking her for a walk, put her to bed. She read, but the young woman soon was sound asleep, Annie looked at the sunshine and decided that she would take advantage of it.

She went out down Denne Vecht, past the Palace, past the shops, thought the Binnenhof and out towards the Haagse Bos. All the people were relaxed in the sudden warmth, there was a feeling of ease even amongst the most the most proper of the Haagenaars, winter seemed over and all the effort of keeping warm and alive appeared to be over. Annie felt her being bend and respond to the sunshine.

She was intent on seeing the deer in the park. She came to the wooden palings that enclosed them, she revelled, as she always did, in the softness of their dark eyes, the slim elegance of their shape, their muted colouring, their spotted flanks. She loved the way they moved... even when afraid they moved with grace.

She heard her name. She had no need to turn her head to know the owner of the voice. Like the deer she was afraid, but she did not move away. Van Prehn took her arm and they walked, he took his hand away, the likelihood of being seen in this small city was only too likely.

They walked away from home, towards the lake by Huis ten Bosch, and there sat on a seat watching the ducks.

"Annie, if you love me, allow me to get a divorce."

A look of great shock rippled across her usually placid face. He saw it and continued,

"I have thought of this constantly. It is the only answer. We cannot go on like this, pretending that nothing has happened."

Annie's eyes opened wide. This was what she wished to hear, but the word divorce was spelled out in her mind in capital letters and then her own name followed as the cause.

"Oh, how horrible."

He looked hurt and surprised. It was evident to him that though Annie's love was undoubted she had never considered the next step.

She trembled and put her gloved hand in his. Reading his thought she said: "I do love you. I love you very much, but... "

"But what?"

"Think of your wife. Think of Kitty."

"Do you love them more than me?"

She took in a deep breath and looked into his eyes with her round blue ones, a blue that denied all coldness.

"I love them as much, yet in an entirely different way. You must give me time. A lot of time."

"Why? We have lived beneath the same roof for four years for God's sake." She flushed at his naming God.

"You know my worst faults. I know some of yours." This he added with a smile.

"You have not thought of all the consequences."

"Me? I most certainly have. Not to think of them and the future is one of your faults not mine. You never think of the future." Then with unusual spite he added,

"And least of all your own. You will be an old maid still teaching children before so very long."

That angered her. "And you have not thought how hurt your wife and Kitty will be. You have not thought of your position, still less mine. I should always be remembered as the governess who wrecked a marriage. The circle of your friends would never forget. Ours would be a very lonely life. Think of that."

"It is lonely already. God damn my mother-in-law."

"Don't say that, curses always come home to roost."

Annie rose. "We must return separately. Give me time."

She went home very slowly - the brightness seemed to have gone from the day. She went back to the place she had grown accustomed to call home.

As soon as she was in the hall, Mevrouw Van Prehn called out, "Come, Annie, come and see what I have bought." Annie went into the conservatory at the back of the house, half-room, half-green house and there was a suite of chairs and a table.

They seemed to be made of slender boughs and twigs, Annie touched them - they were iron. Even in her perplexity, Annie said how charming she thought them and did not add that she thought the ground on which they stood was very insubstantial.

Upstairs she threw herself on the bed. She wanted to cry but could not. She knew that she could no longer live this lie. She remembered how often people had said,

"I can read you like a book."

She had always resented it. Now, it seemed that she was able to conceal the most momentous issue of her life from those most closely involved.

Dinner that night was strangely easy and in the evening they listened to Sherlock Holmes again, this time, The Colourman.

It was as though Annie was sleep-walking through life. She seemed to have lost her will. She wept, now, when alone for she no longer felt perplexed she felt guilty. She vowed that she would not go to the lake, as he had asked, but on waking the first thought was that she was to meet him there.

Late in the morning she made an excuse about some shopping, she was not explicit and, for the very first time Mevrouw Van Prehn thought that Annie had lied to her.

At the meeting, Van Prehn was angry. He accused Annie of playing with his affections, of being a coward and afraid of public opinion. She was cut by the first remark and acknowledged some truth in the second.

There was, though, a vein of true virtue in her that he found to be immoveable. He sized her and kissed her passionately on the mouth, she let him, but within herself she seemed to watch somewhat alarmed.

When he released her she stood up. He was so torn with emotion that he looked at her with amazement. She looked so neat, so trim, so tranquil... then, he saw the strange flutter about her right eyelid which she tried unconsciously to blink away.

He had noticed it before when she was deeply agitated. He put out his hand to her. She pretended not to see and hurried away. It seemed that the further she was away from him the greater her passion cried, until it screamed.

Had anyone been near they might have heard a faint moan as she walked briskly but meanderingly along the path beneath the oaks. Her mind was both blank and at the same time alive with images, she walked straight to Noordeinde.

She entered the house and went instantly into the drawing room. Mevrouw Van Prehn was alone. She looked up.

"Your shopping done?"

"There was no shopping. That was, I am afraid, a lie. Oh, oh, something so terrible has happened."

Mevrouw Van Prehn leapt up and came to Annie with outstretched arms, "Annie, my dear."

Together they sank on to a sofa. "You must, must know. Kees and I have fallen in love. I must leave immediately."

Annie awaited, she even thought there might be a slap, certainly a revulsion. There was not even a removal of the sisterly arm - it tightened.

"I knew, Annie, I knew in my heart."

Then they both wept and Annie as she cried mourned not just the man she had lost but the love of this whole family. Everything was slip, slip, slipping away... nothing in this household could be the same again. The intrusion of a different love violently dislodged all other affections, or so it seemed.

Something was ending precipitately that had grown slowly. Each of them like plants in a border had thrived each in its own way, yet all in the same conditions. That could be no more.

Worn out with weeping, they made plans. Annie was to go to friends immediately. The Haverschmidts were contacted and she was to go there. Van Prehn, then took himself off on business to Milan and Annie returned to pack.

Everything in the house reminded her of him. She packed listlessly and put many things aside for the servants. Mevrouw Van Prehn took note and saw that many of these things were replaced for Annie was not looking to the future.

They gave her an extra trunk. Annie accepted it all in her desperate unhappiness. She failed to contrast it with the suspicions, the drama and unkindness in Cologne.

The last evening came and when she went downstairs there was a well kept secret. Van Prehn was there. Her heart leapt, he smiled, but was tense and a pulse throbbed in his jaw. They all talked of her immediate plans.

Kitty gave Annie a tray cloth she had embroidered. Then it was Van Prehn's turn. He took from the mantelpiece a small leather case.

"Annie, you must accept these with the love of us all. There is nobody else like you. We are going to miss you terribly."

He only looked at her glancingly as he spoke. Annie opened the case, a pair of diamond and sapphire ear-rings, identical to Mevrouw Van Prehn's.

A sharp joy stabbed her, this was his present, and she knew, knew full well that he had first felt the stir of love when she had returned from the dinner party at the Palace wearing his wife's jewels.

She started to say thank you, but her chin quivered, her eyes filled with tears and no more was said.

When it came time for her to go, Mevrouw Van Prehn rose and said: "Kitty and I will take you to the station. Come, Kitty, let's put our coats on." They left leaving Kees and Annie alone.

"Annie, will you be all right?"

"I think so. I shall be with the Haverschmidts. I shall find another place. I may even go back to England. I don't know. Ten days ago I still thought of Holland as my home."

"Will you promise faithfully that you will let me know if you are in any difficulty?"

She felt strong enough to stretch out her hand to him.

"Yes, I will, if that will help you."

"Oh, Annie…"

It was time to go. He turned his face downwards to the fire, he could not bear her to see his face in the mirror over the mantel. He could not bear to see her go. Annie hurried out, pulling her veil down over her face.

She forgot all manners and hurried out to the carriage before the others. Sitting side by side the two women held hands. There was no speech necessary.

At the station the train drew in at the platform, fortunately, there was no time for constrained talk. All three clasped one another briefly but closely. Annie sat in the train looking down on to her hands.

A clergyman noted her, he saw her distress. She was not in mourning. He assumed that she was in the first hours of bereavement. He was absolutely correct.

Chapter 27

Doorn

So often the visits of Annie to Schiedam had become missions of ministering to the minister. But now it was Francois who had to rally Annie on their walks, she fell into silence easily.

When something, and he never knew what the trigger was, fired her to speak it was to listen, to his surprise, her questioning whether she had done the right thing. She could paint an idyllic picture of life with Kees very swiftly.

Francois listened long - he learnt a lot of woman's psychology which he had not fathomed before.

Being, however, a Dutch dominie at the end of a long period of listening, he would deliver a little homily. To this Annie listened… sometimes she was convinced, at others very sceptical indeed. He promised that there would be a reward for her noble action. This she doubted deeply.

One day she sighed very loudly and unconsciously, Margo looked at her friend. "You should be glad, Annie, that, at least, you have been loved. I…" Her sentence was never finished.

"I know, I know, 'It is better to have loved and lost, than never to have loved at all'. But, I doubt that very much indeed."

She felt for the first time the impotence forced upon women. She felt no resentment to Kees, but she felt that both he and she had conformed to a man's notion of the world.

They had behaved correctly, as was expected in a society dominated by male values. Yet, she also knew that she could not have behaved in any other manner, she was entirely of her time. Any bitterness was outweighed by sadness. The love of her life had passed her by.

She had lived so long in other people's houses that she knew instinctively how to fit into another tiny community. She was alertly aware of others. With the Haverschmidts it was easier than most places for she seemed a member of the family, but she was keen to find herself another place and assert, at least, a measure of independence.

She advertised discreetly and had a number of applications. She met a small girl of eight, a bright and happy child, but Annie had loved Kitty too much to change to another charge. She feared that she might contrast the child unfavourably. At last she accepted a post as companion to an invalid in Doorn.

Before she went, she confided that it would be a dull job, it would lead nowhere, but in her state of numbness she did not mind. There was within her a pool of despair.

At Doorn, Annie expected to hire a cab for herself and her trunk. To her surprise her charge's elderly husband was waiting for her with a very smart waggonette.

To her greater surprise the driver was her employer himself. He welcomed her, her trunk was placed behind with some cases, the groom gave her a hand up to the seat beside the driver and put a rug across her knees, then he got in behind.

Annie had never sat up so high behind the horses and she found herself gripping the iron rail at the end of the seat very tightly. She was soon to discover that these black Flemish horses with their sleek coats that glistened as if polished and with long tails almost to the ground, were Heer Van Houten's ruling passion.

The stables were as spacious as the house and slightly better kept. When she arrived she was led upstairs to see Mevrouw Van Houten. The room was darkened with blinds, the pale woman half lay on a long seated armchair. With a wan smile she stretched out her hand. She was dressed, a phenomenon that Annie did not realise was exceptional. She spoke slowly and quietly. She aroused great sympathy, even in her husband, although his inability to comprehend it was plain to see.

Annie's duties were, first of all, to nurse her charge, to make complaints to the housekeeper, soak handkerchiefs in eau-de-Cologne and place them on the sufferers brow and tend the many plants in the room upstairs. Annie foresaw much boredom.

The house was large and built at the beginning of the century and she learnt from the servants that it was called the "sugar mansion", for in it had lived a succession of merchants from the Antilles and the Dutch East Indies.

Van Houten was the latest in succession. The gardens were open, neat and dull. There were no secret corners, no hidden borders. After one afternoon, Annie had fathomed their interest.

The only place of activity was the stable... there something was always happening, a mare foaling, the visit of the blacksmith.

To Annie it had some interest, but compared with The Hague and its cosy cosmopolitanism, it was dull indeed.

It was while she tended Mevrouw Van Houten that Annie, for the first time, ceased to regret her mother's life. Until that time she had regarded that much loved life with pity, it had been so hard, so unfortunate, but when she compared it with this rich invalid's, she saw it as full of purpose and love unbounded.

She had been a woman with ideals. Her work in the prison had become a vocation and the upbringing of her children a mission. This protected woman, who did nothing she did not wish to do was aimless, her days unoccupied.

As she watered the plants under the wistful eyes and slightly querulous voice, Annie compared these orchids with the wallflowers and auriculas at Crosland and the cottage garden teemed with a much more vivid life.

On her walks she found herself thinking less of the Van Prehns and much more of William in Australia. She wondered what he was doing. Then, with a tinge of envy, she thought of Edith in London counting sheets and supervising staff.

Her life, she thought, cannot be as dull as mine. It was at the end of one of these walks that she found a letter from Edith announcing that she was leaving Russell Square and returning to Yorkshire; to Scarborough where she had a post as housekeeper in a large hotel.

A wave of nostalgia overcame Annie. She looked out at the well-shorn lawns, the tidy statues on their scrubbed stone plinth, she thought not of Wakefield, or Crosland on the edge of the moor, but of Armitage Bridge embosomed in its sycamores. But where was Scarborough?

She went down to the room that called itself a library. The section on farriery and stable management was excellent, but the rest sparse. It did, however, have several good atlases. She looked up England. She looked for Scarborough - it was further north than she had imagined, she saw that it was close to moorland, that the coastline was broken.

Would it, she wondered be like Prestatyn? She remembered that with distaste, she placed no reliance on Edith's discernment.

At dinner Annie shifted the conversation from a recent drenching of a horse to Indonesia. Mijnheer Van Houten liked to reminisce and his ramblings opened a new world to Annie. She imagined the ports and palm trees and the colourful people, but she listened detached, for it was a world she had no desire to explore. As she was thinking how boring it would be to have summer frocks only and no furs at all, Van Houten said: "Why don't you let me get you some introductions out there? You would be married in a month."

Annie smiled and thought not just of the lack of furs, but of the idle and gossiping life of the East. She shuddered as the thought came to her that she might return like Mevrouw Van Houten, a prey to imaginary diseases.

After settling her patient, for so she now regarded her, for the night Annie embroidered but she began to worry the bone of her future. She was 30, yet she knew that she looked 10 years younger.

Her face, her figure beguiled any assessor of her age, but the listener could gauge her years more accurately. She frequently made pronouncements and they were the definite judgements of the older woman.

Awaking one morning to the sun coming in sharply round the edges of the blind, Annie heard the clacketty-clack of the lawn mower. She listened to the familiar noise of the well-oiled machine.

She got up and looking out saw the donkey, in his little leather shoes being led up and down, up and down the grass. Her heart did not stir, she felt that her life was identical to the donkey's.

She would sponge Mevrouw Van Houten's brow, she would read to her, she would be soothing and reassuring, but she would not cure her, any more than the donkey would stop the grass growing.

Later in the day, the clacketty-clack still went on and Annie made it say 'Ever the same, Ever the same'. At lunch, Mijnheer Van Houten suggested that he take her out for a drive. She accepted the invitation gladly.

She climbed up on the waggonnette nimbly and confidently, she was used to its height now. They trotted through the minute town, past the great house then along the straight beneath the trees.

They came to a heath and as the horses cantered the vehicle rumbled smoothly. It was exhilarating and the warm air rushed on their faces. Annie felt jerked out of her despondency.

"I think we must give the horses a drink... ourselves as well."

The horses were pulled up at a long low inn. Van Houten called imperiously to the groom and in the same abrupt tone to the innkeeper, who had come out wiping his hands on his apron as he heard the unusual noise on a sleepy afternoon. For himself and the groom Van Houten demanded beer.

"And, I suppose tea for you?"

"That would be nice."

"Damn you, girl, that is no answer. It is, for me, not even true. Tea is not nice. Do you want some or not?"

"I do want some tea and I do not wish to be spoken to like that."

"That's better. Show a bit of spirit."

Inwardly, Annie seethed and she knew that this life could not go on forever. The excitement of the gallop dissipated like a mist in the sun and her old perplexed question returned... how was she to spend the rest of her life?

She listened with only half an ear to the conversation with the innkeeper of horses. She poured herself a second cup of tea and there was no slackening in their interest, so she rose and wandered into the other room.

She knew very little of inns either in Holland, or England. This was plain, clean and dull... whitewashed walls, tables with kitchen chairs around them, and a sanded floor. There was a small counter, the bar. Another door opened into a kitchen and here Annie stopped for at the table sat the innkeeper's wife.

She wore the white cap of the province, a blue bodice and a black skirt that hung in folds. She was cradling a baby with her sturdy left arm and with her right hand she fed the baby with a spoon.

The baby kicked and waved with contentment and made cooing noises. There was an atmosphere of unquestioning happiness in the air. The mother looked up and smiled. Annie stepped forward, the woman spoke,

"Have you any children?"

"No. I am not married," then, as if ashamed of her maiden state, she added, "yet."

"Ah, you will be and you will have a baby as bold as this one."

Annie looked at the waggling child, now looking over his

mother's shoulder with unfocused eyes, he was preoccupied with wind. Annie knew that she would love a child of her very own.

"May I hold him for a minute?"

The tiny boy settled very quietly in her arms. She had not held a baby for years. She carried him to the window, he was not beautiful, she thought, but he was capable of evoking all the tenderness of womanhood by his very need.

"Miss Taylor, Miss Taylor, we must go." Annie slowly re-crossed the room and handed back the baby,

"You are very lucky to have so fine a child."

Outside she was surprised when Mijnheer Van Houten said: "You're going to have your first driving lesson."

Afraid, but excited she climbed up to the driver's seat. The groom placed a rug around her knees. Van Houten climbed up on her left side and then very carefully without any of his usual brusqueness he arranged the reins in her hands.

The horses knew there was someone else holding the reins. They walked sedately forwards for longer than usual, then gently broke into a trot. It all seemed beguilingly easy, beneath the avenue of trees they gathered speed and the pace quickened when the heath appeared.

Annie was afraid and at that moment the reins were very skilfully and deftly taken from her. She felt a great relief, the horses, too, recognised their master's hands and slackened instantly until bidden to gallop.

Over the next few weeks Annie had a lesson each day. She was pleased to see that she was becoming more adept. She felt the invigorating throb of power, but, strangely, she did not enjoy it.

She went with carrots to the stables where she fed and stroked the splendid beasts, but she kept some for the donkey who still regularly pulled the machine with a clacketty-clack up and down, up and down.

The letters from Edith about her new job were, at once reassuring and disturbing. Scarborough was evidently a beautiful place, the people interesting. The work, now that the season had begun, was hard and concentrated.

Annie still did not approve of her sister being a housekeeper, it smacked to her too much of domestic service.

She told herself that no one in her family had ever been in

service and Annie had a very definite sense of rank.

In Holland a governess was, always, a member of the family, of equal rank. In England, too often, the place was in a limbo between the servants' hall and the dining room. Nobody was quite clear. This knowledge kept her in Holland, yet, she knew that she could not stay forever.

The weeks became months and the little boy at the inn which they visited regularly on their drives began to stagger on his feet. He tottered with triumph in his eyes and determination on his square Dutch mouth.

Annie watched him with a warm interest. He had meaning for her. He seemed to awaken an instinct long suppressed.

There had been no letter from Edith for six weeks. Annie was not surprised, for she assumed that she was busy. When she did hear she heard of the dismissal of staff and that Edith had been retained.

Again a snobbish disapproval coloured Annie's thought, she did not like to imagine her sister in the market of labour. The donkey had ceased to cut the grass. He was put into the orchard where he restricted its growth in more natural way. Annie fed him still.

"You are waiting, old fellow, for your work next summer. I am just waiting." Annie felt depressed, an unusual occurrence.

At this time came a letter from Edith, it was not her week for writing, Annie wondered what could be wrong. It spoke of her loneliness, her longing for her sister and most remarkable of all, the prospect of a post with an old lady, she was not an invalid, but who needed a companion.

Edith had enclosed the address and after a morning of daydreaming a bright future in an unknown town, she sat down and wrote to Mrs Matthews.

In Scarborough the dark haired lady took the envelope. She did not think she had ever seen such exquisite handwriting, a pure copperplate that flowed with its own harmony. Before she even read the contents she was impressed. She put the letter at the very bottom of her reticule. That evening at table with her son, Edward, she questioned him about Edith.

"She's a nice girl. Well brought up. She's very capable but inclined to be sharp."

"Do you mean she is bad-tempered?" Mrs Matthews hated rows.

"No, just too quick at times. After all, she does have red hair."

A few days later Edith came to tea. Mrs Matthews encountered a tall young woman with, as her son had said, red hair. She noticed that her dress hung upon her badly, but this was soon forgotten when the bright girl began to talk.

Mrs Matthews remembered much more the kind eyes which were also, she thought, very observant. She heard great praise from Edith of her older sister and, quite openly she said that it would be lovely for her to have her sister in Scarborough.

Alone, Mrs Matthews argued that the only fault, which she had not seen, was that Edith could be sharp and bad-tempered. But when she looked at the flowing handwriting on the letter from Holland, she surmised, and correctly, that no one with so serene and balanced a hand could possibly be irritable.

So having considered it for a day, she sat down and wrote a letter, with more care than the first one, and offered her the post of companion. She had not consulted her children, she rarely did, unless they were involved directly.

They knew nothing of her dealings in property of late. They did know that she had a weakness for diamonds, but they also knew that her taste in jewellery was good. She had been widowed long, but had learnt to fend alone long before the death of her husband.

He had been impetuous and improvident and a gambler and she had very early in her marriage learnt that she must handle the quite large sums he would give her after months of penury with great care.

While he sought gold in California and in Australia she had brought up her family by herself in Liverpool. He had always returned, never empty handed, but never with the riches that had seemed to him, so certain in his unsubstantial enterprises.

Living alone she had become secretive and she had her own reasons for knowing that she had need of a companion.

When Annie read the letter she felt very discouraged. The world seemed grey, the future uninviting. She might be changing one boring post as companion for another. She was almost tempted to stay, but then thought of Edith her only close relative.

However she wrote and accepted the offer and proposed coming to England in December, after Sinterklaas, she would like to spend the festival with the Haverschmidts.

When she told Mevrouw Van Houten that her sister needed her, the poor woman moaned and whimpered... and for a few minutes, Annie wavered in her resolution. Then she argued that another sympathetic woman would quite easily be found to minister, perhaps more willingly, to her needs.

Over the next weeks boredom once more enclosed her, and when October came there was not even a donkey cutting the grass to compare herself with. She even began to look forward to the future.

The leave-taking was kindly, courteous but it lacked depth, no great roots had been thrust down. For the last time, on the way to the station, she took the reins of the black horses, this, she thought, she might miss.

From Schiedam Annie made sorties to her friends. Miss Lange, Miss Snoek, they both seemed exactly the same, they made her feel very, very different, for she was not the inexperienced girl who had come to them.

Her heart, her being had been frightened... and had loved.

She recognised in them something that had never been stirred. It was with much hesitation that she wrote to Mevrouw Van Prehn, but she did wish to see Kitty before she left. She was invited to lunch.

When she arrived at the station she found Kitty, fast growing up awaiting her. They both wept at seeing one another and together arm in arm they walked through the streets to Noordeinde.

The reception into the house was almost emotional, they were all so pleased to see her and she had to go to the kitchen and see everyone. She was missed because she had never been replaced.

To her great surprise and even alarm she learnt that Cornelis Van Prehn was returning as well.

When he appeared he looked flushed, he took her hand and kissed her on the cheeks, as they did so her heart beat violently and so did his.

But they relaxed and they all talked as if no cloud had ever passed over the four of them casting such ominous shadows. When Kees had to go back, they kissed once more, their pulses seemed slower, but as they waved to him from the upper window Annie knew that the tall, upright man, the man whom she had loved so dearly was hurrying, hurrying out of her life.

It was on the train returning to Schiedam that she cried a little, a quiver of her chin and then two tears, just two... then her pretty face became a blank.

On her last evening, Francois made a speech at dinner. He described her career in Holland, a little triumph he called it. Annie blushed as he recalled her early days in Leiden she found she had forgotten her happiness. She had not forgotten Cologne... there an acid had etched deep into her memory plate, bitter, black.

The evening was made memorable by Margo. The plump, jolly Margo stared into the flame of one of the candles on the table, she was foretelling the future. Suddenly, the game became serious, it seemed that a spirit came into the room and it spoke through the girl. "Mrs Matthews has a son. You will marry him, Annie."

Annie was startled, but laughed, it seemed beyond possibility, Kees was still very, very close.

Next day she left in rain.

Holland had been her home for 12 years. It was home to her, she did not know to what she was returning. As she stood on the deck and saw the deep curved furrow behind the boat, a draught of dark water, thick viscous, between the quay and herself she felt a moment of panic.

She was leaving safety, sobriety. Holland was a land of good sense, a link was snapping. Holland had been so much more to her than a school, a home. It had been a matrix that had nourished her. It had made a large part of her character. She might have mused longer, but, as always, when at sea, she felt violently ill.

Chapter 28

Scarborough 1893

Grimsby again. Annie looked at it from her porthole in the cold light of this December morning. She saw as much as she wished, she felt no desire to go up on deck to hail England. She thought of Grimsby only as the port whose tide deprived her of a last sight of her living mother. She hated it.

Ashore she found that there was a long delay before her train, she went into the hotel and ordered tea and bacon and eggs. The excellence of the tea was lost upon her, she had grown so used to Dutch tea, but the succulence of English bacon and eggs with a generous supply of what she called "Yorkshire dip" raised her spirits.

She felt happier when she returned to the station. A young commercial traveller, very neatly and smartly dressed, helped her with her attaché case, lifting it on the rack for her.

The young man, sitting in his corner glanced appreciatively at her beauty, but he was checked by her complete stillness. She betrayed no emotion, her face never moved… she stared out of the window.

Annie did not know where she was going. She was on a journey she did not wish to make. She felt defeated, a pawn in the grip of a faceless and anonymous power. She was not afraid, but she was bemused, almost indifferent.

It was only when on the outskirts of York, near some allotments, when she saw some donkeys on waste ground that she smiled for the first time. She smiled because she loved the patient furry beasts.

They aroused her pity, their lives seemed unrelieved drudgery. She also smiled, though, because she thought of the donkey in Doorn, she thought of herself, "Well, here's a donkey that has escaped."

Instantly, thought, she said to herself, "Escaped to what?"

She pondered on the strangeness of this homecoming, it was devoid of joy, because there was no home to return to and Holland had become her homeland.

At York she changed trains. The vast arc of the station impressed her - it was even larger than Cologne. Half-way between York and Scarborough the hills ceased to be mere rises and became real hills. Her heart rose.

On the outskirts of Scarborough, she saw a lake and another high rising hill covered with trees. Suddenly they were enclosed by gas works, houses and the terminus. Looking out of the window she saw her sister's eager pointed face and pince-nez beneath an unbecoming hat, her first thought was, "I'm needed here, I must change that instantly."

Edith clung to her sister and Annie felt the strong bond of family. All was going to be well. The luggage was entrusted to an out-porter and the two sisters, arm in arm, left the station and crossed into the town.

Annie looked about her. She was impressed... the stone built station, the large hotel opposite. Edith led her into a broad high street and up into a tea room. The main sale here was pop-corn and Annie looked in amazement about her at the gilded cupids holding up ropes and wreaths of pink, white and pale green pop-corn.

It was sumptuous rather than pretty. Upstairs, trim waitresses in black with starched aprons and with caps with long white streamers moved between the tables.

Annie was surprised by the elegance, she thought that she had said farewell to it in Den Haag. Scarborough was, quite evidently, not in the least like Wakefield, or even Prestatyn.

"I hope you will like the family, Annie. They are quite nice. Perhaps, they are not quite grand enough for you. Old Mrs Matthews is not a happy woman. She lost her eldest daughter and her grandchild within a week. She has never got over it. I'll say no more. You will hear about it."

"Poor woman."

"She also has a daughter and a son living with her. The daughter is married and they are planning to have a hotel. I rather like the son."

Edith blushed as she mentioned the son.

"What does he do?"

"He has a shop and he mends clocks and watches."

Annie's face went blank. She had noticed the blush and she did not want her sister to marry anyone in trade.

"I see," was her only response.

The elegance around Annie suddenly looked rather tawdry. She was aware that she was moving into a very different society. She felt the cold wind of insecurity and it made her speak her mind.

"Never mind. A year or two and we shall have our school, or even boarding house. I must get used to things. How do you like housekeeping?"

"I love it. Much, much more than teaching."

"Yes, I thought you would. Well, don't worry. I will teach and you can run the house."

She looked at her watch and hurriedly pulled on her gloves and added,

"I think I must go and meet Mrs Matthews without any more delay."

She had recovered from her gloom and was, now, alert to everything about her. She was very surprised at the number and size of the shops and their grandeur and evident wealth in the place. It struck her that money was more obviously seen here than in Holland, but she wondered if it was as great or as secure.

They turned down a somewhat narrower street, Huntriss Row. They passed bakers, a chocolate shop, an art gallery and a large and empty dairy. Vast porcelain storks stood on either side of the window and much smaller figures between of cows and milkmaids.

She saw all these with the special eyes one gives to the new, which in time becomes the familiar. The first encounter is always so different to the habitual, like and unalike. At the end of the street they came upon a broad three sided square, on the one side was the gigantic and monumental Grand Hotel with its caryatids and towers like kilns.

On the opposite side were 18th century houses with bow-fronted windows and fanlights and steps. Annie, though, did not see these but the foaming grey sea riding in the glinting in the cold sunlight and beyond the slopes of green grass and bare trees and beyond, yet again, the cliffs.

"Why, this is beautiful."

Her perfunctory imaginings of the place had been mightily surpassed. She then noted the cannon and the anchor in the central garden. Suddenly Edith said: "Here we are."

They were outside another 18th century house. Edith went up

the steps and rang the bell. After a minute the door was opened by a maid who smiled in recognition at Edith and cast a swift glance of appraisal at Annie.

They entered the hall and were led upstairs. In the drawing room sat Mrs Matthews, beneath her white cap was strong dark hair and equally dark brown eyes were set in a wide brow above a jutting but sensitive nose, her mouth seemed insufficiently modelled. She hesitated, then, rose to greet them. Annie was startled to see a faint, instinctive recoil from her as she was introduced, but this was overcome by a cry of welcome. Annie wondered what that would mean.

They all sat and talked of Annie's journey, her sea-sickness. Mrs Matthews confessed to never having been abroad. She did, however, decree that Annie must rest immediately.

When Edith left she pressed Annie's hand and said,

"Everything is going to be all right."

The older woman took Annie up another flight of stairs and let her to a room at the back. She had her hand on the door, thought a moment and said,

"No, not that one."

They went back along a corridor to the front. The window looked on to the central garden, the immensity and floridity of the Grand Hotel and then down to the sea.

Mrs Matthews turned back the counterpane and patted the pillows.

"Now you must sleep and come down when you wake. Time does not matter. Sleep till supper time if you want."

Annie lay down very thankfully, she felt assured. She was meeting with kindness. Life was, she knew, going to be very different but before she slept she knew that she would cope. She heard the roar of the sea, then, she heard no more.

When she woke, hours later, it was dark, for a moment she did not know where she was and even said aloud, "Waar ben ik?" Then recollection rushed in, she rose hastily, fumbled for matches, lit the candle by her bed and then the gas mantle.

She drew the curtains, but not before reassuring herself of the scene below, the cannon, the anchor could be made out in the flickering light of the street lamps. The sea was not visible but clearly audible. She changed into a blue merino dress trimmed with white lace and a little nervously went down.

In the sitting room with Mrs Matthews were two younger men, both tall. One with a high complexion and a determined face, ambitious, Annie thought. That was Frank White, the son-in-law of Mrs Matthews.

The other young man was taller. It seemed very much taller, because he was very thin. His fair hair curled he had very blue eyes and a very straight nose. He appeared tired and a little hesitant in marked contrast to his brother-in-law who was alert and eager to impress.

Mr White immediately made conversation with Annie with ingratiating charm. Mr Matthews watched, he seemed to be thinking and then he spoke a sentence of the most execrable Dutch that Annie had ever heard.

She did not recognise the language at all with her mind, but by instinct she asked him in Dutch to repeat it. Slowly he enunciated the sentence. Grammatically it was unsound and the accent was vile, but she understood him.

He had asked her if she had had pleasant dreams. She then asked him how he had learnt Dutch. She thought it must have been from a fishing vessel calling at the harbour. He told her that he had been for some considerable time in the Cape Colony.

As they all talked, Annie realised that she no longer thought in English, she was translating everything before she spoke. She listened very intently and they were all very considerate.

She wondered when they sat down to the evening meal where Mrs White was. She was told that she was unwell, in her room and that her baby was expected hourly.

For the first time in her life, and ironically while she was no longer a governess, she felt like Jane Eyre. There were things happening silently, distantly in this bourgeois house of which she was unaware.

The conversation was sporadic and a little constrained. At the close of the meal the two men excused themselves. Frank White went up to his wife and Edward Matthews went out.

Back in the sitting room a pause came in their conversation, Annie suggested that she should read, Mrs Matthews demurred, but said that she would much enjoy a game of Bezique. So Annie was initiated into the mysteries of the game.

She was intrigued by the little clocks that recorded the scores. She enjoyed it. She was to discover that playing cards was the great English pastime, very much more than in Holland.

Annie slept soundly that night, she never heard any of the goings and comings of doctors and nurses as a baby girl was born. Mrs Matthews could talk of nothing else and at mid-day Annie was taken up to see Mrs White.

Annie saw a young woman, thin, like her brother with high cheek bones and an aristocratic nose. She looked very well-bred, Annie felt that she should like her, but she did not warm to her. She was full of complaints and her mother sympathised profusely and patted her hand repeatedly.

She took little note of her reservations for she thought it unfair to judge any woman so soon after the agonies of childbirth. As she followed Mrs Matthews down the stairs she thought that certainly she was in another sphere of life and encountering the fundamentals of life.

This, she thought, is not a world of the mind. Yet she knew that all would be well. She was unafraid.

Mrs Matthews decreed that they should go shopping, Annie was not in the least averse, so hatted and caped they set out after lunch. They went up the Cliff and this time, instead of turning left they went to the right, past a fine red brick house that reminded Annie of Holland with its Dutch gables and into another street.

Annie instantly likened it to Brussels. There were jewellers, tailors and a shop that almost equalled the Bonneterie in Den Haag. It was called Marshall and Snelgrove. Annie was delighted and surprised - this seemed another country to the 'Wakefield by the sea' that she had feared.

Mrs Matthews made many purchases, nearly all for her daughter, a night-dress and matching peignoir, which though Annie admired it she would never have bought. She was aghast at the price.

She realised that the mother wished to compensate her daughter for the dangers of childbirth, but she thought the purchases of Eau-de-Cologne and scented soap and lace edged face flannels rather frivolous.

She was to become used to this constant expenditure and later she learned a reason.

Christmas came and went very swiftly. The happiest part of the day was when Edith joined her and they walked on the Spa, looking over the bay to the harbour and the Castle.

The town intrigued Annie. It was made up of so many different communities, the fishing folk, the trades people, the professionals, but she saw very clearly that it all depended on its continuance as a thriving and fashionable resort.

She had never been anywhere like it before and it was, she kept saying to herself, so beautiful. She still looked on hills and cliffs with an excited surprise.

She could not say what it was that so thrilled her, she was not good at analysis. The reason, probably, was that she was in the midst of so much variety, all her previous experience had taken her to monotone places, beautiful, interesting, except for Wakefield which, rather unfairly, she had dismissed from her life.

Back at the house on the Cliff, she sat with Mrs Matthews. Annie discovered that Mrs Matthews preferred talking to being read to. She talked of her husband, of the family in Liverpool, Annie found it very interesting.

While they were talking Frank White came in - he looked almost wild, certainly disturbed.

"I don't know what to do. I can't stand it any longer, someone must take over Tranby. The baby keeps us awake all night."

Mrs Matthews looked up from her game of patience.

"Well, Frank, you cannot expect me at my age to take on a toddler. You will have to engage someone."

Annie felt a wave of sympathy for this usually genial, imperturbable man. She felt, too, that she was largely unoccupied.

"I don't know very much about small children, but let me have him."

There and then Tranby's cot was moved into Annie's room. Removed from a tense parent and a minute sister whom he seemed to resent, he quietened immediately. Annie found him very easy.

In the often warm winter sunshine, Annie took the small child out in his wicker-work perambulator. She walked in the shelter of the cliffs and houses, climbed up to the great castle that dominated the landscape, and walked miles past the fishermen's cottages at Sandside and up Paradise Walk.

She explored the long terraces of respectable little houses near the cemetery and she began to fall in love with the town itself. One day, listening to the fisher girls as they gutted the herrings and threw them into barrels, she found herself unable to comprehend anything they said.

She felt a shiver of distaste for they never spoke, they only shouted and it offended her. She swiftly left the harbour and climbed up to St Mary's church. It was a cold bright day, the bay sparkled and the town encircled the bay.

The red roofs below her were wreathed with smoke, then there was the vast silhouette of the Grand Hotel beyond the white stucco of the elegant houses of the South Cliff beneath.

Down by the sea was the French inspired building of the Spa. She left the graveyard and went up higher to look northwards and the other bay.

The stuccoed houses stopped suddenly on the cliff's spur, the valley below was rough and wild. The open land rising from the shore looked even savage, primitive. Beyond there lay Durham, Northumberland and Scotland. The thought excited her.

As Annie settled into a new way of life, enjoying the town, loving the renewal of contact with her sister Edith, so she mused on the family with whom she lived. There was much she did not comprehend.

They were not at all like her family. They were reserved and at times she thought unsure. They sometimes deferred to her opinion, little things, mostly matters of taste and politeness of form. She was surprised.

One Sunday, there was a sudden influx of visitors, they were busy. Annie offered to go to Evensong instead of the morning service.

"Do you go to church every Sunday?" Mrs White enquired.

"If possible I do."

She noted the covered surprise. In fact the return to England brought to her the great benefit of the Church of England. She rejoiced in the liturgy and the unfolding of the familiar phrasing which was almost new to her again.

It was a link, too, with her mother. She hardly thought of Wakefield at all, but when she did it was the church that she recalled.

"But, then, of course, your father was in the church, wasn't he?"

Annie had forgotten that phrase used to describe a clergyman. She remembered her father's churchwarden's duties in Milnsbridge.

"Yes, we all went."

The baby cried and Mrs White whisked away. Annie thought no more of it. It was next day that she understood the family far better. Mrs Matthews came in from a shopping expedition in the rain.

She stumbled against the wall as she came in. Annie hurried forward, "Mrs Matthews, you are ill."

The elderly lady looked at her for a moment with suspicion that was dropped instantly as a tear ran down her cheek.

"You have overtired yourself walking. Look at your dress."

It was spattered for six inches with mud - she had not lifted it in the street. Annie steered the old lady to a chair and untied her bonnet strings. She seemed better, so she ran and called to Kate to bring a pot of tea.

When the maid brought the tray in, she looked at Mrs Matthews, raised her eyebrows and looked at Annie with a smirk that Annie ignored, she considered it impertinent. She wondered if she should call the doctor, but decided that the walk had just proved too much.

When a cup of tea had been drunk, Annie listened yet again to the story of the death of her eldest daughter Ada and then her granddaughter.

"My two darlings in one week."

"How awful," soothed Annie, "What a terrible shock for her poor husband."

She thought that to spread the misery of the bereavement might help.

"Poor John Barnes!" spat out the old lady. "Why was John Barnes so scared for his fair skin, he left when Ethel was ill. He used to call across the road to discover how she was."

She then lowered her voice, "And he was so afraid of catching diphtheria he never even followed the coffins." Annie had not heard this addition to the story before. There was much, she thought, hidden in this family.

She wondered if it was an English trait she had failed to recognise before, being too young to have encountered it.

Mrs Matthews fell asleep and Annie thought it best to leave her there. She picked up the bonnet and the jet embroidered cape. It was exceptionally heavy, she wondered if this was, perhaps, the cause of the exhaustion.

When she opened the wardrobe door there was a loud clink as the cape brushed against the wooden panel. Annie thought that strange and she looked inside the cape. A bottle protruded from a capacious pocket. She uncorked it. It was whisky - the same smell she had faintly noticed in the drawing room.

She was very dismayed. Many things were now clear, most of all, why Mrs Matthews needed a companion. But why had nobody warned her? She answered it herself, had she known earlier she might not have stayed.

Even now the idea of seeking another post was in her mind. She moved to the window, she saw the sea, murky and grey horses rode rather tardily in to the shore, she knew that she did not wish to leave this town. First of all she told herself, she must get Mrs Matthews to bed.

Downstairs the old lady was snoring in her chair.

"Come, Mrs Matthews, you are very tired and you will be more comfortable in bed." An eye fluttered, she blinked and rather blankly followed Annie. Her gait was steady. Upstairs Annie assisted her in removing her dress and then left as she changed into her nightdress. Having given her plenty of time she returned and knocked.

Mrs Matthews was in bed. She looked perturbed. She looked at Annie with pleading eyes and with great difficulty asked,

"Did you find the bottle?"

"Yes, I did. I have taken it away."

"Oh, I am sorry, very sorry. I will not do it again. I really will not."

"Where did you get it from?"

"Carraways."

"Now go to sleep. We shall say no more."

"You won't tell Bea will you?"

Annie looked at the unhappy woman. She suddenly understood the reason for the expensive presents. The poor woman was afraid of her daughter.

"No, I will not tell."

Annie went up to her room. She was surprised at her calm as she stepped into this whirlpool with unblinded eyes. She got out her best costume, her sealskin cape and toque. She wished to look authoritative.

She went up the Cliff, found the grocer's shop. The rounded body and face of the owner were obvious as he stood with his long white fringed apron reaching to his boots.

"Mr Carraway?" He affirmed that. "I believe Mrs Matthews was here earlier this afternoon."

He looked a little uneasy and suggested that they went to his office. He led her to a small glass paned room which surveyed the shop.

"Is it the whisky?" he asked immediately.

"It is indeed the whisky, Mr Carraway. Would you be so good as to cease selling Mrs Matthews any alcohol in future? If she asks why, say that Miss Taylor has forbidden it."

"That is all very well, Miss."

"Miss Taylor, if you please."

The grocer blushed with anger but kept calm.

"That is all very well, Miss Taylor, but we have a living to make and she will remove her esteemed order."

"I give you my word, Mr Carraway, that that will not happen. But tell me. When Mrs Matthews was here was she..." Annie faltered for the right word. "Was she confused?"

"Yes, Miss Taylor, she usually is when she comes. Do you know where she had been before?"

Annie's mind was shocked that Mrs Matthews had probably been to a public house and if she had she did not think she could bring herself to go in to speak to the landlord.

Mr Carraway surprised her.

"I think if you go to the French pastry shop you will understand Mrs Matthews' condition."

"The pastry cook's!" said Annie with surprise.

"Yes, Miss Taylor, down the street."

Annie did not wish to ask for any further enlightenment. She rose from the chair and an over-zealous grocer fussed at the doors. Annie looked at him as she left and said,

"Now, remember, Miss Taylor forbids it."

As she went down the street she pondered on how anyone could become tipsy on Madeira cake, even brandy snaps.

The amusing side of the situation struck her and by the time she reached Le Tissier's Café she was smiling quite broadly. She looked through the window and saw well-dressed ladies eating cakes and drinking tea.

She looked about her and she became aware that towards the back of the shop were some soberly dressed widows. She looked again and she saw that their eyes shone brightly, too brightly, and that they were drinking from small glasses.

When her tea arrived she asked if she could have some cordial like the ladies.

"Exactly the same?"

"Yes, please."

The cheerful red liquid shone in the glass. Annie tasted it. It was cherry brandy. The mystery was solved. This was where Mrs Matthews got her drink. She wondered if she should keep the secret the old lady had besought her to keep. Again she smiled and said to herself, "To keep the secret that everyone knows that is being kept from me."

One her way back she passed a shop she had not noticed before, it was full of clocks and there was Edward Matthews. He looked up, recognised her and beckoned her in. He opened the door and very soon began showing his clocks. There were those encased in buhl, there was marble, there was ormolu.

He showed her one surmounted by a wily looking gentleman wearing a ruff, with a plumed hat lying importantly on the table that housed the clock. She recognised it immediately as Henri IV of France and Navarre.

She recalled his statue on Pont Neuf in Paris. She told him, she explained too, that the King always wore white ostrich feathers. He was interested in the information… he was interested in the informant.

With his back to her as he replaced another clock he said: "Are you happy with us, Miss Taylor?"

"Yes, I like it here. I am very fond of your mother but unfortunately I have not seen a great deal of her recently, rather more of your nephew."

He looked thoughtful and then asked, "Where is my mother now?"

Annie smiled and said,

"That reminds me of 'The thane of Fife had a wife.'"

They both laughed. Annie was glad that she understood for this family laughed a lot, especially at table when Edward and Frank White bantered one another with quick words and she usually missed the point.

Later, she realised that it was the fashionable humour of Oscar Wilde, a swift play on words which was not at all kin to Dutch humour.

"But the question - your mother is safe and asleep. I put her to bed."

After a slight hesitation he said,

"Has she been drinking again?"

"I am afraid so. This is the first time that I noticed it." She paused, "Why did nobody tell me about this? I only discovered because Kate smirked. I think I should have been warned."

The reply he made, she had already made to herself.

"But if you had known you would not have stayed. I am glad that you came. You must hand that baby back to my sister and be with my mother more."

"But that will mean telling your sister and your mother asked me not to."

"Yes, that is difficult. I'll have a word. Anyway, they will be going soon. My mother has given them a property on the Esplanade and they will set up their own hotel. Don't worry."

Annie left thinking him a very pleasant young man.

He in his shop watched the tall elegant figure go down the street. He wondered how so aristocratic a young woman came to be a companion.

When Annie went into the house she found a very flurried Mrs White who angrily asked, "Why did you let my mother go out alone this morning?"

"Because I was taking your little boy for a walk."

"Don't you realise you must watch my mother?"

Annie opened her large blue eyes wider and asked very innocently,

"Why?"

"Don't you know? My mother…" she hesitated and changed 'drinks' to the more acceptable, "is sometimes intemperate."

"So I discovered this morning. Why did nobody tell me?"

"It is not a nice thing to say about one's mother."

"It is not a nice thing to do to a stranger. It smacks of false pretence."

"I suppose you will leave us now and just when mother has got used to you."

"I did not say so. I have not considered it. I wish you had all been more open at the beginning."

With that she went up the stairs her heart pounding. She hated scenes. Yet she also knew that she was not unduly upset. Edward, she did not just feel she knew, would be a great ally.

It did not take Annie very long to discover that the Matthews family was extremely conventional. They were not secure in the way, she realised her mother had been in spite of all her troubles.

This family was perched rather than rooted in respectability. She found it irksome. She spoke of it to Edith who replied, "We cannot be too critical. Who are we?"

Annie felt stung by this and though she made no answer she thought, "We are Taylors, we are Bentons, we are Arnolds."

Annie stayed, partly because she liked Mrs Matthews, partly because she loved the town and felt her Yorkshire roots grow once again. The greater part, however, was that she recognised, now, that she had a purpose, like her mother her character demanded that she did good, she had been moulded by her upbringing.

She looked so feminine, and with a tulle bow beneath her chin, even kittenish, but she belonged, even slightly unaware, to the movement of the Women of the Nineties. She eschewed the stiff starched collar and blouse with a tie, the hard boater by which, some women, asserted their rights as emancipated being.

Her sympathies lay with them, but her war was fought with disguised and utterly female guile.

When the Whites moved to the new house the tension in the house disappeared instantly and Mrs Matthews was happier. Spring was approaching and with it came letters from former visitors wishing to book rooms.

As Annie watched Mrs Matthews' interest revive, she encouraged her to accept them, even if she was really retired.

It was Annie who wrote the letters and when the time came made up the bills. She enjoyed it.

She also watched how Mrs Matthews set about administering the house, counting linen, ordering food, discussing menus with the cook and engaging more staff. She found herself receiving the visitors, soothing differences, listening to complaints, which were few, and talking to the great variety of people who were washed up on the holiday tide of the seaside town.

She found it diverting, even exciting and often, often surprising. None of this escaped the very shrewd observation of Mrs Matthews. Annie was now very much more than a companion and it had happened so gradually she was almost unaware. Edward was also observant and he admired her more and more.

He suggested walks and they were much in each other's company. He had never seen a woman who remained beautiful and elegant all the time. They discovered that they had much in common.

Most of all, though, he was grateful that - at last - his mother seemed to be placing the tragedy of her daughter and granddaughter's death behind her. She had indulged in a very Victorian obsessive woe.

With Annie, too, he found he could talk of South Africa and, unlike, many girls, she knew exactly where it was and what were its problems. She knew much of Shakespeare and he told her of his experience when, at 16, he joined a company of players.

He travelled with them over Yorkshire, to Durham and Newcastle, to Carlisle and lastly to a triumph in Liverpool. As the reviews in the local papers hailed them, all seemed well, then the manager decamped leaving the actors and actresses unpaid. Edward had walked from Liverpool to Scarborough rather than seek out his relatives in the city. He had slept in barns, eked out his food and reached home.

A result of this episode was an undying love for David Copperfield. It cured his theatrical longings, to the relief of his mother, but not his love of the theatre. When the summer came he took Annie to see Henry Irving and Ellen Terry at the Opera House.

Annie learnt that these luminaries were not far distant on the stage but in the town: they even shopped, buying gloves and stockings at Marshall and Snelgrove like ordinary human beings.

Edward was asked to repair Sir Frank Benson's alarm clock when his Company came.

The two faces of Scarborough were revealed to her... both had a fascination, the winter town with its wildness, facing a stormy sea, but with great shafts of sunlight thrilled something deep within her, some elemental chord.

Then there was the summer countenance, pretty, fashionable and rather frivolous in a decorous way. She loved that too. What she did not see was that Edward was in love. When on a cliff path beneath the Castle he proposed one afternoon, after all the agonies and apprehensions young men underwent in those days, her reception was amazement.

Her thought flew back to Van Prehn, she looked at the bay the sea sparkling in the sunlight, and she said very firmly, "No. I am afraid I cannot." She did not love him and she could not marry him because of a place.

What she failed to see was that he was in love, the furtive love of a shy man. As they walked home there was silence and constraint and Annie found herself thinking of the Van Prehns again and again. She made a trite observation to break the mute air and he responded angrily.

Edward was hurt and for several days he avoided her, fortunately they were very busy with visitors and it was not at all difficult. Strangely, Annie did not think a great deal about it, the thought of leaving because he had proposed and she had refused never crossed her mind.

Mrs Matthews, however, was not so obtuse and she was wise enough to refrain from any comment.

Gradually, the contact and the walks were resumed and as they went along a cliff path towards Cornelian Bay, Annie in a pale blue dress and a small brimmed hat trimmed with cornflowers, they came upon a photographer with his tripod near a stile.

There were, now, very few visitors. He claimed them, arranged them, Edward sitting on the step and Annie leaning over the upper part of the stile. Edward treated it as a joke. Annie was more self-conscious and thought it would be silly and sentimental.

She was right and when they were having tea at a hut about the waterline in the bay, they laughed at the ridiculous pose in the picture which had been quickly exposed. It was made even more saccharine because the photo was pushed into a cardboard frame decorated with sprays of flowers.

"We certainly look very sentimental" said Annie rather sententiously.

"A couple of 'sawneys', I think" said Edward

Edward was again struck with fear, he looked at the round face beneath the blue hat, he did not see the hat, he saw the eyes which were the same blue neither light nor dark but changing. His happiness was linked with those eyes.

"Will you reconsider what I said six weeks ago?"

She looked at him, she saw the faint tremor in his hand as it stretched towards hers. She could not hurt him so she let him take her hand. When they touched she knew, she always wondered how, the depth of his love, but she knew, hers for him was nothing in comparison, but she liked him.

She smiled a prim little smile, with her mouth firmly closed. Her eyelids fluttered as they always did when she was unsure of herself.

"I will really think about it."

"You will?"

"Yes. And I will let you know."

As she said that she knew that she would say "Yes". It was the same when she bought something. She sometimes delayed, but she always bought it in the end, partly because she wanted it, but there was also a strain of sympathy for the seller, she never wanted to hurt their feelings.

When no one was looking he took her hand and kissed it.

As though she stood a long way off from herself she watched and heard herself say,

"I have thought about it. I will marry you. But Edward I bring you absolutely nothing. I have no money, no parents. It is just me alone you marry. Is that enough?"

"More than enough. Mother has a house, yes another one, she thinks I don't know and she will let us have it. We shall set up in business straight away. We'll do wonders."

It was the first time that Annie had heard of this, it did not surprise her, it was just another of the secrets of this family.

What did surprise her was that she liked the idea. The thought of a home of her own that was more than just a house, something to be created, made beautiful and managed appealed greatly.

She had loved the big houses she had lived in and though the prospect before her was a business not just a large house in the country, she loved it.

As they walked back along the Esplanade Annie saw something she had never noticed before, this tall young man by her side, her future husband, was a little like a photograph that she had seen of the young Francois Haverschmidt.

And then she remembered Margo's prophecy, "Mrs Matthews will have a son and you will marry him." Life was very strange indeed and this likeness to Margo's father stranger.

She wondered why she had never noticed it before. She knew, too, that the similarity of feature was matched by a similarity of moods, Edward's wit was quicker, still too quick for her very often, but there were the periods when he was withdrawn and sometimes morose.

Mrs Matthews was about to be cross, they had stayed out longer than intended and dinner was being served and she had to receive two visitors by herself. But as soon as she saw them she guessed their plans.

They went into her drawing room and they told her. For a moment Annie wondered whether she would be well received, the next moment the little lady's arms were around her in a sudden long embrace. Annie melted, it was like being in her mother's arms again and that was precisely, but unconsciously what Mrs Matthews intended.

That she had never been tight in Edward's arms, yet, never crossed her mind.

That evening she was occupied with the new guests. Later, she sat in the office and wrote letters and made up the books.

Strangely it did not strike her as very prosaic and mundane for a woman just engaged. She saw it as a foreshadowing of her life. Edward had gone out, but not before giving her a brush of a kiss and an extremely happy smile.

The books done Annie pushed the chair back from the desk and began to dream. She wondered whether she would have children. She would love, she thought, to have a daughter like Kitty. Holland was never far from her thoughts.

She looked out of the back window. The sky was not yet dark... she got up, put a shawl around her shoulders and went out. She crossed over to the seats above the zigzag down to the Foreshore and looked out to sea.

The tide was in, the lights of the Spa mirrored in the swell of the high tide around the battlemented sea wall.

Very faintly she heard a crescendo of music; the concert was ending at the band stand. She remained there looking at the view of which she never tired. Gradually, there were voices as men and women came over the Spa bridge, returning to their hotels and boarding houses.

There were men in opera hats, tailed coats and white scarves, women in evening dresses, many of them in high necked dinner dresses, like Annie's own. Annie watched them, butterflies, she thought, returning to their colonies until the dawn.

She looked at the dresses - they were brighter than those in Holland. Some were very ostentatious. Jewels gleamed beneath swathes of veiling and tulle. She watched contentedly, she liked to see this fashionable crowd. As she watched, she turned her back to the sea and looked up the Cliff.

The grey stucco of number 12 loomed. It was three times as large as Mrs Matthews' house... it was to be her home. She thought what an excellent hotel it would make.

"There are the people, there is the house in which our future is to be moulded and made," she said almost aloud to herself.

Annie was happy. She felt more secure than she had ever done in her life, her happiness almost surprised her. As she danced down the stairs she saw the post had arrived.

She picked it up, sorted out the visitors' letters, put them in alphabetical order on the table, then sorted through the rest.

Bills, bookings. She saw one for herself from Holland, from Margo Haverschmidt. She put it in her pocket to savour later. It was another busy morning and only before lunch did she have time to open the letter.

The agitated scrawl immediately warned Annie that something was wrong. It was a cry for help. Francois Haverschmidt had committed suicide. White and tense Annie read on, horror and guilt gripped her with kneading torturing fingers. The last words of the unhappy girl went straight to Annie's heart,

"If you had been here it might not have happened."

She read the death announcement enclosed and saw the time and date of the funeral. She must go.

Downstairs, Mrs Matthews looked into Annie's face and said with concern, "What is the matter, my dear?"

Annie related the news rather baldly and the old lady shuddered.

"I must go to them. Can you spare me for a week?"

When the visitors had eaten, Mrs Matthews, Edward and Annie lunched in an almost empty dining room. He, too, was instantly aware of Annie's distress and he went up to the station to find out the times of the trains and boats.

He found one that would get her to Flushing the following evening. It would mean a very early start.

Annie rose at five. She had slept only fitfully. Downstairs, she found Edward already up. He carried her case for her to the station and as she fumbled with her gloves and handbag in the ticket office he said: "It is all right. I have your ticket."

He produced it. Annie took it. She was confused.

"I must pay you for it."

"Why? We are almost married"

He put her in the train and just before the train pulled out he said,

"Annie, Annie, you will return, won't you?"

She put out her hands, seized his.

"Of course, of course."

Edward's face brightened, the gloom that had surrounded them fell away. The train jerked, they still had not kissed, she jumped up leant out and their first real kiss was broken by the moving train.

She hung out looking at his youthful figure and she saw what she had never noticed before so clearly that he was very like Haverschmidt. She sat back and knew that whatever happened she must return.

She looked at the ticket in her hand, it was a return ticket. She smiled and realised that he was making sure, as far as he could, that she would return. The tragedy of Francois receded as she thought of her happiness to come.

The door opened, "It's Mejuffrouw Taylor. It's Mejuffrouw Taylor!"

Other doors into the hall opened and there stood Margo and Frank. They all fell into one another's arms. As Annie looked at them she was struck that they were all familiar faces, but with a dreadful spiritual change – they were stricken.

Each one had a particular tale to unburden to Annie. Each had a personal feeling of failing, of guilt. Annie listened, she clasped them to herself and Annie began to blame herself for being so far away.

The funeral was large and very impressive, Schiedam mourned. The unity among churches for which Francois had longed and striven, seemed, in his death, to be accomplished, at least momentarily.

They all dreaded the orations and Annie feared the Dutch love of truth which so often insisted that a spade be called a spade. In each prayer, each address she waited for the dread word suicide to float forth in the air above them blatantly, yet spectrally.

Not one of the preachers did so. Driving back from the cemetery through the crowds, past the shuttered shops Annie thought that he was bidden farewell with a magnificence that somehow had evaded him in life. With the graveside harrowing, it seemed that resignation had come to the family.

Margo was the first to emerge from total sadness with a smile, now, asked Annie whether Mrs Matthews did, indeed, have a son.

"Yes," replied Annie, "and as you foretold, I shall marry him. And you are the first to know."

"I knew it. I knew it."

The fulfilment of her prophecy pleased her greatly and seemed to restore some of her confidence, which she seemed to spread to the remainder of her family. The days ticked slowly by and Annie knew that she must return.

She carefully refrained from contacting Den Haag, though she longed to see Kitty. Holland she saw was becoming a portion of her past, a rich and broadening part of her development. It became clear to her that she had compared Holland, even Europe, with a small portion of the West Riding of Yorkshire.

Her knowledge of England had been so limited, even, now, it was far from great, but England had become desirable and Edward, too. What she failed to notice was that England, Scarborough came first.

As she went about the house she thought how very much more comfortable Dutch houses were, they were warmer and they managed to combine comfort with some beauty. She still found English houses of the middle classes stiff and cold.

She hated the unused parlour, some as welcoming as station waiting rooms. She vowed that her home would be different and she had the ideal very firmly in her mind. It was with happy anticipation that she wrote to Edward and Mrs Matthews announcing the day of her return.

It was midday when she arrived back and she was very surprised to find Edward awaiting her on the station. She did not know how adept he was with a Bradshaw, he had ascertained two probable trains, he had met the first and she had been on it.

His pleasure was obvious even though he tried to restrain his pleasure. Annie felt a mounting love for this surprising man.

It was, as they walked down the narrow ugly tunnel behind the houses of the Crescent that they planned their marriage. It was to be at St Mary's and in December. Although it was so close to Christmas, Annie decreed that it should be on December 23rd, the first anniversary of the day of her arrival there.

The dying summer season engulfed them, the hardest part of the year when the staff were getting tired and the visitors were annoyed at the shortness of the days and the colder mornings and evenings.

The dahlias were out in St Nicholas Gardens, the sands were les peopled and in the middle of September the flood of visitors suddenly subsided, the town weary, relaxed and yawned and began to "side up" the summer things and prepared for the winter.

The donkeys went up to their fields on the side of Oliver's Mount, the chairs on the beach were trundled away in carts. With a new enthusiasm the shops began displaying winter clothes, furs were draped over costumes.

They were tempting not visitors but the native population. Annie saw the real Scarborough emerge and it was still stylish.

It was in the window of Marshall and Snelgrove that Annie saw her wedding garment. It was utterly unlike anything she had imagined for herself as a child and young woman. It was a double breasted grey costume of the finest worsted cloth.

Its cut was impeccable and it became remarkable when after numerous fittings it moulded her figure like a soft armature. Small brimmed hats were just coming into fashion, but Annie preferred a small toque-like bonnet trimmed with ribbon flecked with steel bead embroidery, it tied beneath her chin. She allowed nobody to see her clothes.

The week of the wedding was cold and foggy. Then a wind crept up which cleared the wreathing cloud. On the 22nd, the wind became fierce. During the night it howled, ever fiercer, ever louder.

Annie was woken from her sleep by the rattling of the window and as she wedged it there was a crash in the street and a shattering sound. She shuddered and jumped back into bed. That night every loose tile in Scarborough was torn from its moorings, every rickety gutter fell and there were many chimney pots, or their fragments in the streets.

When they rose, the storm still thundered. Annie momentarily wondered if it were an omen, but smiled at her silly fear.

When she was dressed there was a knock at the door, there stood Mrs Matthews with a large soft bundle in tissue paper in her outstretched arms. As she looked at Annie she gasped, the beauty of her form struck her anew… the costume was perfect.

"My dear, you look lovely. I don't know whether you need this, I think you might, to keep you warm."

She placed the parcel on the bed and lifted the white paper. It was a stole, thick, round, like a boa constrictor, of the finest Kolinsky sable. It was beautiful and wrapped around her neck and shoulders better than her tippet.

"My, dear it has never looked so nice."

The old lady looked hesitant then said: "I do hope you will be happy. I am quite sure you are the right wife for Edward. Strangely I shall not miss him, but I shall miss you."

"But we shall be almost next door."

"Yes, but it will not be the same."

No more was said for there was a bustle of noise from below, Frank and Edward had arrived and it was considered essential that neither Edward, nor Annie should see one another until they met in church. Mrs Matthews went downstairs and went in the cab to the church with her son and daughter.

Annie was alone, she went down and there stood Frank White looking out at the storm before he turned round he said,

"What a night," then seeing her said, "Annie what a sight, you look wonderful." Annie was surprised at these compliments, her marriage outfit was far from romantic, but she smiled and was pleased. As Frank gave her a kiss he noticed that she trembled. To divert her he said,

"Look at my gloves."

She looked at the white kid gloves, they were blackened.

He laughingly told her that, at times, the wind had been so fierce as he crossed the Spa Bridge had had to cling to the tall spiked railings, moving hand over hand. The maid said the cab was at the door. As they went down the steps Annie felt the lash of the wind on her face, she had to grasp Frank more tightly than she wished. She was worried about his gloves.

"We must stop at Greensmith and Thackray's on our way and buy you a new pair." And they did.

They went slowly through the streets, there were few people about and the pavements and street were strewn with broken pottery and fragments of brick. At times the cab shuddered as a fresh gust from another corner caught them.

There was too much excitement in the perilous journey for Annie to be nervous. But as they left the houses, a fresh buffeting hit them as the wind howled up from the sea and across the churchyard.

Frank carefully handed her out and taking her very firmly by the arm guided her into the teeth of the wind, round the howling corner and into the porch. Annie was profoundly thankful that she had decided on a bonnet with ribbons, a hat would have been torn away.

The great church looked even larger and emptier than she had ever seen it.

She expected to see Edith, to her surprise she was accompanied by two young women. But she hardly saw them. She looked at Edward tall and in the spasmodic brilliant light, very fair.

The ceremony was brief and in the vestry the entire congregation met, including the young women, two sisters, whom Annie had not met before. The two carriages drove carefully up to Belmont where the Whites had arranged the wedding breakfast. It was all most efficiently and elegantly done, Annie found it faultless.

Yet it was muted. Mrs Matthews tended to recall the marriage of her daughter Ada, Annie and Edith felt the lack of a family. The two young women, the two Misses Lancaster, were a great asset, the older with a shy quiet confidence made pleasing conversation and her younger sister Kate made them laugh with her quick wit.

Frank proposed a toast and welcomed Annie into the family.

There was no need for Annie to change, but she still went upstairs with Edith and there she grasped her sister's hand.

Fears and forebodings were invading her heart, but she could not speak of them.

She had no idea where they were going for their honeymoon, but it was not that which worried her. It was the thought of the wedding night for she knew that she was not impelled by love.

From York they went to Bradford. She looked at the grey houses and the mills with a shudder, it was bringing her past too close to her. She put out her hand and Edward held it tight and she felt relieved.

Suddenly, she understood that she was no longer alone, everything would be shared. She told Edward of her fears and he held her close to him and whispered that all would be well. It was then that she knew she would come to love him.

At Bradford they had to change. Her childhood raced in upon her and though they waited in a room by a blazing fire, Annie went out on to the platform. She knew the very spot where she had climbed on the train with her mother to go to Wakefield. She said to herself, "That was a journey to happiness and this will be too."

When she went back to Edward he was surprised to see a different woman, her fears had vanished. It was is first real intimation of how her mood could change so quickly and all beneath an exterior calm that beguiled most people into thinking her invariably serene.

Their destination was Ilkley. When they arrived it was dark. The hotel was filled by elderly and middle-aged people. Dinner was served in the constrained silence typical of many English hotels.

Annie was very anxious to present a air of a staid long married couple. Her age, 31, had loomed up at her as she had signed the register that morning. It was something she usually ignored.

Then she still thought there was something slightly indelicate about a honeymoon, she suspected smirks and hidden smiles. She also was impressed by the excellence of the dinner and thought that a really good meal was of the utmost importance to a newly arrived visitor. She stored a resolve in her head.

In the drawing room they read magazines, they made a little desultory conversation with others. The Royal Family, of course, featured in these tentative essays into acquaintance and Annie was, once more, surprised at the complete change in the public's attitude to the Queen.

When she had left she was still the unseen widow of Windsor and there were jokes about John Brown, now she seemed almost deified. To her she was still a hard and ugly old lady who should make way for her son. She said nothing.

When Annie went up to bed Edward moved closer to the fire and filled his pipe. A man watched and whispered to his wife, "They are on their honeymoon."

"Oh, no. A girl like that would have been married a long time ago."

"How old do you think they are?"

"He's about 27. She'll be about 24. But I'm, sure they've been married some time."

"I don't think so."

Edward finished his pipe, knocked it out on the grate and threaded his way through the chairs and sofas.

"Goodnight. Goodnight."

Annie was already in bed, her heart pounding, she knew the theory of sex, she also knew that there was a world of difference between theory and practice. She did not say anything, but she wondered if Edward was as apprehensive as she was.

After the odd embarrassment of a man undressing in her room, then getting into her bed, all seemed well, especially when the light was extinguished. Instinct and nature overtook intellect and after a moment of pain she relaxed.

When it was all over Edward fell asleep quickly, Annie stared up into the darkness. Her feeling was that it was a strangely overrated business and with that she, too, fell asleep.

Next morning, as she did her hair, she looked into her face with concern, it looked exactly the same, she was surprised to see no change, yet recalling the feeling of disappointment thought why should there be. Downstairs, at breakfast she was intent on imposing the illusion that they had been married for a long time. She ordered breakfast and questioned by the waiter about porridge answered, "My husband always has porridge."

Whereupon Edward lowered his paper and said, "I never touch the stuff."

The remark was heard and the middle-aged man looked at his wife and said: "I was right... so much for a woman's intuition."

They walked on the moors and Annie recaptured some of her

love for them and she thought of Armitage Bridge and Crosland Moor. She found Ted, as she called him, humorous, quick witted. His play on words still sometimes defeated her. But they were at one.

In the afternoon Annie went out alone to buy Christmas presents, for Ted, for the other couple, for the chambermaid and the waiter.

On Christmas Day, Annie wore for dinner what she called her wedding gown. It was blue merino with a long line of brown fur that rose from the hem to the right of her bodice, followed the yoke, encircled her neck and then descended the seam from her left shoulder to the edge of the little train.

With it she wore her sapphire and diamond ear-rings. Edward was for a moment speechless when she entered the drawing room and very proud when he saw that all eyes were on her.

The tables had all been put together for dinner. Constraint flew, there were crackers and afterwards they played party games. Edward became the leader and he decreed that they should now play charades.

He grabbed Annie's hand to lead her off in his group, very firmly Annie resisted and from that moment he knew an area of defeat. Annie never acted and she never dressed up. He found it strange, he never knew the reason, nor would successive generations.

It was only after Boxing Day that they began to eagerly anticipate the future. They began by criticizing the hotel, then planning No.12 on the Cliff at Scarborough and resolving that their hotel would be the finest possible.

Their aims were identical and the days ahead so exciting that the present was a nuisance. They longed to be home.

Chapter 29

12 The Cliff

On the first day of 1895, Edward and Annie entered 12 The Cliff. Strangely, it was Annie's first visit. As Edward pushed hard at the great front door which was jammed and swollen with disuse Annie felt a tremor of fear and she asked herself whether they had weighed the balance of the future correctly.

The door suddenly gave and swung back to reveal a hall which was wide enough and long enough, but dark. It was not welcoming. Edward strode in and flung open a door on the right, Annie entered.

It was a perfectly proportioned room with elaborate moulding round the ceiling. There was a high fireplace which Annie recognised to be Adam. At one end, opposite the bowed window, was an apse with an alcove and on the panel in high relief was a figure of a Grecian deity.

Annie was enraptured. "It is like Wedgwood china." In her mind she saw it furnished with Chippendale and Sheraton. Her delight was enhanced when Edward said,

"There's an almost secret cupboard here."

He opened the panelling at the side of the fireplace revealing a large space. Out in the hall again they remarked on the darkness and Edward said that he would lighten it with white paintwork.

He opened another door into a slightly smaller room with a cornice. There were round headed alcoves on each side of the chimney breast with a bracket for ornaments. Annie instantly saw this as the drawing room. Behind was a dark room looking into the garden.

It was fitted with cupboards and that they decided would be their office and private room in summer. They climbed the stairs, shallow treads with fine balusters. It had beauty and dignity, the rooms above echoed those below but the mouldings were simpler.

Annie felt even with the dusty bare boards that this was home. She imagined the rooms as they would be very easily.

Below, in the basement were many larders, a servants' hall and a very large kitchen with a long range and a stone flagged floor. Leading from that was a scullery with sinks, copper boiler and two pumps. It was here that Annie's heart sank because it was thick with old greasy grime.

As she stood there she realised that she would be the mistress of a large staff and she knew that meant anxiety, but she dismissed apprehensions, reminding herself that she was no longer alone.

They climbed up to the second, third and fourth floor. She noticed straightaway that the treads of the staircase leading to the topmost floor were higher than the rest. Edward told her that the floor had been added later.

She foresaw how visitors would be disheartened on a first visit to their rooms, disappointed that their rooms were so high, tired of the climb, they then encountered steeper steps. "A pity, a pity", she murmured half to herself.

As they descended to the refined details of the lower rooms Annie exclaimed, "Oh we shall have these rooms beautiful in no time at all."

Edward put his arm round her waist.

"Annie, do you dance?"

He had never asked before and it was something she had done only rarely since her days in Leiden. She nodded. He seized her and they waltzed around the empty room. They danced perfectly and they both knew that a new range of life was opening before them. They were in unity.

The long hard work of the winter began. Ted began painting and decorating the main rooms, and Annie, with helpers, began a thorough cleaning of the basements. She turned out unused larders, throwing away the sediment of a century.

The place began to smell differently and Annie was full of admiration for the women who cleaned, they skimped nothing. She had forgotten that Yorkshire women were every bit as good as the Dutch at scrubbing and better at polishing.

The house, even bare, seemed to breathe again, when they entered in the morning the clean smell of soap greeted them and Ted moved upstairs with his paint and paper. They worked too long and too hard.

One day, Annie offered to help Ted, he was papering. She put on an apron and under his direction began to paste the paper on the long trestle table. She was not adept, she used too much paste.

At first he was patient, but when after he had dealt with an awkward corner, finally got it right and then he could not flatten the paper because of a thick blob of paste, he cursed, Annie tut-tutted and he turned round and exasperatedly pointed,

"But look what you've done, you blasted woman!"

Annie had never been sworn at in her life. She was appalled, she was affronted, and she had decided some half hour before that she thoroughly disliked papering. She carefully scrapped the paste from the brush on the side of the bucket and looked up at her husband.

"Never speak to me like that again. I am not one of your little black boys in the Cape. I shall never help you decorate again."

She never did. She was never asked.

Annie discovered that Edward had a very sure eye for good furniture, he loved antiques, but he loved clocks more, so that soon the many mantelpieces of No 12 each had a timepiece.

Annie chose the fabrics and sewed, with a machine, yard upon yard of material for curtains. The windows were her great concern and having lived so long in a land that prided itself on the excellence of its lace curtains she was determined to emulate Holland.

She wrote to Nottingham manufacturers for catalogues and patterns and she pored over the full page illustrations of the designs, lace curtains looped and velvet, or brocade to shut out the darkness and wind.

The change overtaking the interior of the house was visible from the outside.

Their schemes had to wait. However, their notions of what was suitable was beyond their means and much had to be bought which they intended discarding later. This was a scheme that Annie found difficult to accept.

The big room with the apse and Adam fireplace had been transformed by white paint and a paper of floral garlands she considered 18th century, but she disliked most of the furniture.

She was, fortunately, slow to speak her mind, she had lived in other people's houses so long she kept her opinions to herself. Sometimes she had to remind herself that this might be a business but it was, also, her home.

One room on the first floor she had claimed as her own. It overlooked the sea and until Ted's relatives and friends teased her out of her pretensions she called it her boudoir. Mauve was the fashionable colour and it predominated in the chintz covers.

She asked Ted for a mirror to go over the fireplace and he returned, one day, to her dismay with a large unframed looking glass. Her dismay quickly turned to delight, she let him fix it to the wall and she bought yards of lilac silk which she looped and draped around the ugly edges. It became a startling but beautiful feature of the room.

It gave not only light but luxury to the room. She never ceased to be proud of this handiwork long, long after such swags and loops had been banished by more austere fashions.

They began to engage their staff, a cook, a kitchen maid, a porter and a parlour-maid who could supervise the chambermaids and the two waitresses. They were ready for their first visitors at Easter. The place sparkled with the comparative youth of Edward and Annie.

As summer approached, so their booking increased and Annie was upset when Edward rather than lose a booking put a bed and a wardrobe in her boudoir. She learnt that her extravagant ideas of life were to be confined to the winter months.

She consoled herself. She was too busy to sit there, anyway. The summer seemed bliss to her, she had chosen her staff well, and had no difficulty in running the house smoothly. She never feared giving orders, but she did it so gently they seemed like requests.

Her aptitude was noted by her sister-in-law who found it easier to do a job herself than ask one of the servants. Their temperaments were very different. Beatrice was hampered by a shyness that seemed to hobble most of her family.

Annie recognised it in Ted, though he hid it more successfully. He was not at ease with the visitors, his hard day of supervising done. When dinner was over, he liked to escape to the male companionship of his friends at the Club.

Annie enjoyed putting on an evening dress, dining, sometimes alone, and then trailing in her long gown round the rooms. She sat and talked with the guests who had not ventured out to a concert, or the theatre, she enjoyed their company.

When they went to bed, she would go to the office, put an apron over her gown and reply to the day's letters, entered the bookings and make up the bills.

Late in July she began to tire, from being tired she felt ill and, eventually, she went to the doctor who smiled as she related her symptoms. She even thought one of his questions highly indelicate. She was pregnant.

She hurried back to No 12, she was uncertain of Ted's reaction. He had seemed very pre-occupied by the business. His talk had been wholly of food and furniture lately, together with schemes of expansion. Nevertheless, she told him as soon as she returned.

He sprang up, seized her in his arms and congratulated her whereupon she very demurely, but considered herself very daring, replied that he, too should share in the felicitations.

When September came they both looked forward to the second week when the season ended, the visitors, or most of them, would depart and Scarborough would be itself.

Ted spent time with the books, Annie's takings at the office and his own expenditure on food and equipment.

To Annie's surprise he told her only that they could take a holiday and furnish the remaining empty top floor. When too tactfully, she endeavoured to find out the exact state of financial affairs he said dismissively, "Don't worry your pretty little head. I'll deal with that side. Go and buy yourself a new dress."

She was annoyed by his secrecy. She had encountered it in his mother, but there, she thought it was more just. She took him at his word, though, she went to Marshall and Snelgrove's and bought not only a blue serge costume trimmed with frogging, but an afternoon dress as well.

She loved the clothes, but the bill she hated, without a word she put it on his desk. If it alarmed him he said nothing and Annie assumed that they had done very well that year. There remained in her resentment that though their life was indeed a partnership and their work entirely joint, yet she was denied the final knowledge of their labours.

She had lived for 30 years and for nearly 15 of them earning some money. She had managed her affairs, modest though they might be... now she was treated as a silly little woman.

She was angry but her upbringing had so constrained her that she would never confront Edward and demand an outright answer.

She did not dwell on this grievance long, she never did, but she looked to the birth of her baby which would be in April, an awkward time just when the season was beginning.

Mrs Matthews and Beatrice came to help. Between the mother-in law and daughter-in-law a happy bond existed. With Beatrice Annie never felt sure, there seemed a mistrust - even jealousy.

The delivery was fairly swift and she was told that she had a baby girl and she took it with delight, but drugged with the fumes of chloroform and exhausted with the pain, she fell in and out of consciousness.

She held tight to Mrs Matthews hand for now the doctor was to bind her with broad bandages. She saw Beatrice and the doctor and then was surprised to hear her sister-in-law say,

"Bind her tight, doctor, don't let her lose her lovely waist."

Until that moment, she had never known whether she was accepted, or even liked.

The baby thrived and named by Mrs Matthews, Ada, in memory of her eldest daughter. Annie found in motherhood the role she had always wanted. She glowed in the feeding and washing and cherishing of her child.

She walked her for miles in the high wicker perambulator that Edward had bought. There was, though, a dark cloud looming on the horizon. The hotel was filling up, her duties to the business called and the day came when, with Ada she went out in a carriage to a moorland farm to be left with the farmer's wife, who already had the White children.

Annie wept on the way home and Beatrice consoled her with telling her that it was only for a matter of weeks and that the very highest in the land handed their children over to nannies.

It only partly assuaged Annie's suffering. Fortunately, she was so busy when she returned that she was unable to wallow in self-pity.

Many of the previous year's visitors returned and both Edward and Annie were pleased to show them a hotel greatly improved. Not only was the furnishing better, but all principal rooms had electric light.

This caused much comment even some excitement, especially when it wavered and threatened to fail.

Annie loved talking to the guests in the evening and soon some of them became friends. Life was full and life was interesting, they talked of many things, the likelihood of the Queen's abdication after her Jubilee cropped up frequently, still Annie hoped that she would.

True, most Yorkshire people distrusted the Prince of Wales, for the scandal of Tranby Croft had been in their county and very close. Annie argued that he led a fast life because he was unoccupied, but then she still lacked the peculiar reverence that most people had for this mother-figure at the head of an Empire.

But no sooner had the throng begun to thin out than Annie was out in the carriage again to collect her baby. She had seen her weekly, often more, so that when she took Ada in her arms the babe seemed to look back with her deep blue eyes and dark thickening shadow of curly hair.

The hotel became a home again even though they retained some residents for the winter, two bank clerks, a young solicitor and two elderly ladies and Mrs Matthews who came to live with them.

That winter Edward was initiated into the Freemasons and their life became more involved with the town. It became very much more social, there were dinners to attend and dances and two great balls, one in anticipation of the Jubilee, at the Grand Hotel. Annie loved these for she loved to dance and she loved to dress for the occasion.

She was not at all displeased when she read an accurate description of her dresses in the local paper. Yet the business people of Scarborough all regarded the Jubilee with apprehension, they were sure that all the money would be spent in London and there would be none to spare on a seaside holiday.

They were wrong. The summer was fine, the atmosphere of the country very relaxed, there was a feeling of great security and for the first time since her return, Annie felt a glow of patriotism.

Mid-season she knew that she was pregnant again and thankful that this time the birth would be before the tide of visitors came in.

The pregnancy was very calm. Annie knew what to expect, she had none of the fears that had tormented her before. In March, she had another little girl and as she looked at the child's violet blue eyes and dark hair, she named her before any other claims were made, Edith, after her sister and Marianne after her mother.

The baby had from birth a placid charm, she was eager to make contact, she smiled a real smile of pleasure before the stipulated time. Annie loved her intensely and worried far less about her than she had done with Ada. Everything connected with her was easier.

The visitors were upon them and Annie resisted sending Edith to join Ada at the Cartwright's farm, but the pressure became greater and Annie realised that she was unable to do justice to either Edith, or the guests.

So once again she made the journey up towards the moors. There she consoled herself with the sweetness of Mrs Cartwright and the scrupulous cleanliness of her kitchen, but as she drove home fierce rebellion leapt in her heart and mind.

She began to instance to herself wives who never made this sacrifice, and in an angry game of Happy Families, she named teachers, solicitors, chemists, grocers, clergymen, none of whose wives paid this awful penance of separation.

In the hotel she had to deal with the complaint of a couple who were dissatisfied with their room. With a great effort not just of patience, but of sweet guile she listened and soothed.

Then she made certain with the waitress that she serve them swiftly and assiduously at dinner.

That summer was to see Annie swim like a swan in pride into her task. It seemed easy, she had a tried system and timetable and though she sat up in the office late at night doing the books, she always gave the impression of being leisured with time for anyone who needed her.

Her staff were so reliable she was able to visit the little girls twice a week. She played with Ada and walked Edith up the lanes in the pram. At last, September was with them, and Annie instead of being wearied brightened visibly at the prospect of but a few days more and the children would be home again.

One Thursday, as she stood talking in the hall to some departing guests, she saw Mr Cartwright standing at the door. She always admired this sturdy and independent man, but there he seemed ill at ease and out of place, his breeches and rough tweed jacket contrasted with the blazers and smart flannel trousers and the lace and broderie anglaise of the ladies. He eyed the chattering groups. Annie went to him and she was alarmed.

"Mrs Matthews. My wife wants you to know that the baby is not well."

"What is the matter?"

"Vomiting and a looseness of the bowels."

Annie was instantly relieved, but said, "Have you called the doctor?"

"Not yet, we thought you should see her first."

Annie walked swiftly back to the office, she left orders and messages and getting her hat and coat and with a sudden percipience of danger, her nightdress and brush and comb; she joined Mr Cartwright in the trap.

He, his responsibility shifted, relaxed and talked of the harvest, then of the war in South Africa. Annie replied, but only with the surface of her mind. She kept saying to herself, soon, soon, the children will be safe at home.

At the farm she picked up Ada who had run out to greet them. Mrs Cartwright, wiping her hands on her apron hurried out.

"She's much quieter, less fretful."

The use of the word fretful with Edith shocked Annie, it was not in character. As she bent over the cot she was upset to see the damp dark curls in flat whorls over her head and she had a feverish flush that she had never seen on her before.

She called for lukewarm water and taking off her own jacket, picked up the beloved child, untied her long dress and began to sponge her.

She hugged her and instantly she became fretful, the proximity of another body's warmth upset her and resolutely, but very reluctantly, Annie lay her down again.

At noon the young doctor came. He looked very grave and said that she must be fed only spoonfuls of water and frequently. These only served to make the child sick and her nappies even wetter. Then, very ominously, they were stained with blood.

The doctor had dealt very gently with Annie, he asked the whereabouts of her husband and when he was back at his village he telegraphed him.

When Edward received the grave news, he silently fulfilled all his duties. He saw that dinner was served, he even, rather tersely, talked with the guests and as soon as he could he leapt on his bicycle and pedalled into the country.

Annie had gone down into the kitchen sick, sick at heart and very fearful, she had gone to the door to the yard and she heard footsteps coming up the long hill. She recognised them as Ted's and rushed down.

As soon as he saw her he flung the bicycle into the hedge and ran to her, she burst into tears and repeated again and again,

"Oh Ted, Ted. It is awful, awful. Come and see."

When he peered into the cot he was even more shocked than Annie for he saw a child on the verge of death. He shuddered and his shoulders shook and no noise came. His grief was more impressive by its silence.

"It's all my fault, my fault. You should have kept her. Damn, damn the hotel."

It was, now, Annie's turn to comfort him. They sat close together on the double bed overlooking the cot.

"I'll stay until midnight, I'll go back, see that the boots have been done and breakfast is on the way and come back. You go to sleep. I'll watch."

Worn out, Annie soon fell asleep only to awaken to the ghastly realization when Ted called her before he left.

"She is much quieter."

He cycled in deep misery back to a seemingly empty Scarborough. He coasted down Falsgrave, pedalled up the slope towards the station, then free-wheeled down Westborough and Huntriss Row.

A solitary policeman trying shop doors was the only sign of life. At home he found that Manners had locked up. He went in, switched on the electric light that usually gave him a pleasurable thrill.

He was struck at once by the evidence that Annie was not there, the cushions were squashed and crushed on chairs, newspapers were untidily dropped on the floor. Mechanically he fulfilled the task he had seen her do so often, he plumped up the cushions, he picked the newspapers and magazines, he gathered up a handful of flower petals.

He loved Annie more at that moment than ever, he loved the very person not the beauty. He knew that she contributed so much to their success. He longed with all his heart to repay her with the life of their child and he knew his wish was forlorn.

He looked in everywhere and down in the basement he found the night porter cleaning the shoes.

"How is it, sir?"

"Bad, bad."

Annie sat by her child, she seemed to shrink before her eyes. The quietness became unnatural, she picked her up and cradled her and sang very softly to her. Slowly her song became a series of little moans, as she rocked back and forth, back and forth.

She was the immemorial mother with a dead baby in her arms. She awoke to the fact, looked at the child kissed her and lay her on the small mattress, straightened her and covered her with a sheet.

Her feeling had changed, the real child was there no longer to love. The Cartwrights found her sitting cold, determined, shocked. They took her to the kitchen and gave her tea. After some time she said,

"What is the time?"

"Nearly seven, Mrs Matthews."

"What is the day?"

"Friday."

Then as if memory was a well she wound up the windlass to today and its date. Yesterday was another world, another life and the day before had been happiness.

She went into the garden, it was dawn, there was no colour, it was a world of grisaille. No colour, no feeling. Everything seemed distant, very distantly distant. She resolved to go and meet Edward. She went towards the gate, then remembered that she had not washed.

She went in and asked for water. Everything had been anticipated. The Cartwrights had vacated their room, they led Annie there and Mrs Cartwright poured the water into the bowl, adding cold from the jug.

"There, now, you wash yourself and you'll feel much better."

Annie washed. She felt no better. She turned down the sleeves of her blouse and put on her jacket. She looked at her hair. She carelessly thrust the comb in. She did not care. Annie did not care.

As she went through the kitchen she said, "I am going to meet my husband."

"Please stay here. He will soon be with you. You are more comfortable here."

"No, No."

She was like a wild bird entrapped in a room. She seemed to dive with a swoop for the door.

Out to the gate, she opened it and put one foot outside.

Her hand went up to her head, "But I have no hat."

Though pained, bewildered she knew that old shibboleths must be obeyed. No lady ever went out of doors without a hat.

She went back, up the stairs to the room where Edith lay. She hesitated, crossed to the chair, picked up her hat. She hurried, she felt that time had been lost, she hastened down the long hill. Fatigue came upon her, it jumped.

She questioned her hurry saying to herself, "Why hurry? There is nothing more to hurry for. Life has ended."

The sun was slow that morning, she walked for a mile into mist and Edward was nearly upon her when she saw him. Again he shoved his bicycle into the verge and ran and caught her. He led her to a grassy bank by a stone wall and there she wept in his arms. As she cried he cursed God that he had allowed such a thing to happen.

Back at the farm the doctor explained that Edith had suffered a common complaint of summer. No one was to blame, a fly, possibly, had alighted on a cup, left a germ. It could happen, and did, anywhere.

Mrs Cartwright sat tense, upright and ready to justify, or weep. The doctor made it easy for her and it was Annie who seeing another suffer stretched out her hand to the clenched fists and said, "There, there, Mrs Cartwright. I knew it was not your fault. It might have happened to me."

She wanted to add "Just as easily" but could not.

Mrs Cartwright wept and her husband led her away.

The undertaker. Decisions...

"We'll bury her here in the village," said Edward.

"No, no", said Annie very vehemently. "We will bury her in Scarborough. Then I can visit the grave."

So a plot was bought in the cemetery among the winding paths in the deep ravine behind the North Cliff.

It was fortunate that it was the end of the season for Annie fulfilled her role in the hotel like a puppet in marble. She received the visitors and bade them farewell with a numb dignity.

Her smile was distant, it had a strange quality like flowers on a tomb.

She recalled all names, guests and servants, she remembered the insignificant details of their lives, but it was an effort and lacked all spontaneity. Most recognised it for what it was and pitied her.

Weekly, sometimes more, she walked along Victoria Road, Aberdeen Walk to the cemetery. There she found a kind of peace, this shrubbed, leafy glade, a cleft in the landscape had a kind of beauty, it brought solace.

Annie had loved this child dearly. She thought of those dark violet eyes, she was never to forget them. She was also angry, she blamed the hotel, their life, that made them part with their children. She blamed Edward, but that was a thought she pushed away as unworthy, but she never reconciled it wholly.

She thought more of her child and gradually she came to recollect that her mother too had lost a child and it, too, had been named Marianne. It was a name to be avoided, but to Annie it was a sanctified name.

She thought of her mother and began slowly to see that her plight had been worse, at least Edward was not dying as her father had. Then she thought of her father, his gaiety, his intellectual tolerance and vision. All these things, at that moment, seemed lacking in Edward. Again she dismissed the thought.

It was not just Edward that distressed her, it was the family. Their attitude had been so conventional. Her refusal to wear mourning after a fortnight they regarded as lacking in feeling and they attributed it to her vanity.

Black for so young a life, so fresh, so pure seemed to her unfitting. It was only to her a trapping and contained nothing of the essence. She also believed fervently in another life.

She could not speak of this to Edward or his mother, they seemed afraid to discuss it. They feared it as morbid. So it was the Vicar, who remained unshocked by the lack of black bombazine, who listened and marvelled at the serenity that was emerging from the shadows of her grief. Of her feelings to her husband she never spoke to anyone.

Edward was by no means unaware, beneath his veneer of convention he was deeply sensitive and he was pained by this beautiful woman, whom he called his own, who had retreated and become oddly unattainable.

He wished to help her and spare her. He again talked with accountants and once more told her to buy whatever she needed but of profit and loss he never spoke. This hurt Annie even more for she saw any gain, this year, against the loss of Edith.

Yet she would not and was quite unable to confront him. Her subtle hints were ignored. She wondered if she loved him at all and that made her feel guilty.

In October, Edward decided to take Annie and Ada up to Northumberland to stay with a cousin, a land agent on a huge estate. The large and rambling house and the kindly cousins wrought a change.

Often Edward went out with Harold to see outlying farms and attend markets. He enjoyed the life. Annie walked and talked with Bridget in the garden, and often in the grounds of the great house. She responded to the moors, the stone walls and the sheep. It was home and she recognised that here the sheep were cleaner. Ada prattled and ran and delighted everyone.

One day, other cousins came and one, Geoffrey, a lad of sixteen attached himself to Edward. Annie saw that her husband had the gift of talking with boys about to be men. Geoffrey went walking sometimes with Edward, sometimes, less willingly with Annie, and sometimes with them both.

After lunch it was proposed that the three, plus Ada in her pushchair, should walk towards the Fells. The men adjusted their pace to the push-chair often giving Annie a hand up the steep, often rutted, road.

As they climbed and the views widened the infinity of hill revealed themselves and the hearts of them all soared. Even Annie climbed well beyond the self-imposed wall of her unhappiness.

Now and then a pheasant would rise, and stuttering his alarm, fly across the road. Edward began to pick up stones and threw them at the stuttering birds. One he seemed to wing and he ran ahead, leapt over a wall, Annie felt a spurt of admiration at his agility, as he dropped out of view.

Another pheasant slowly, lumberingly, rose up and gained the opposite wall. Geoffrey flung his stone, he missed the bird, but as it flew they saw Edward's head rise beyond the wall, the stone struck with a thud and there was a softer sound as he slumped into the bracken, then a terrible stillness.

Annie let go the pram, she flung herself over the wall, rushed through the long fern to the fallen figure. She saw the blood at the back of his head, she turned him over. "He's dead," was all she thought.

He had an opaque pallor, she loosened his tie and undid his starched collar, she chafed his hands. Her thoughts fluttered like bats disturbed, half of them were fears, half, she discovered, were love. Then to her intense relief he opened his eyes, he even smiled.

"I knew you'd come, Annie."

He fainted again. By this time Geoffrey climbed over, whiter faced than any of them.

"Is he all right?"

"I think so. But it was a mighty foolish thing to do Geoffrey Armstrong."

Edward's eyes fluttered again and his uncomprehending eyes fought for focus. He saw Annie, he saw Geoffrey.

"That was a bloody silly thing to do Geoffrey."

"What dreadful language, Edward. You'd better get up." Then thinking better of it said, "No, lie still."

Turning to Geoffrey she said: "Run and fetch a cart from the farm. I'll stay here."

"What about Ada?"

Annie realised that she had forgotten her child. She realised that she had let go the push-chair on a hillside. Another fear seized her, "Is she safe?"

"Yes, she is quite safe. I'll bring her to you."

Annie and Ada waited half-an-hour before they heard the jingle of harness and then the sound of the hoofs on the road. There was time for Annie to give thanks that Edward was alive and Ada, in spite of her own forgetfulness, safe. She ceased from that moment to question her love for Edward.

Edward was put to bed and the holiday was extended by a week. Edward thrived on the attention Annie gave him and the holiday became a muted honeymoon.

The depression returned when they were back in Scarborough and Edward became irritable, he suffered severe headaches. Gradually he got better and particularly after he began planning an extension over the garden at the back.

Together they entered into this scheme, Annie's only reservation was that she would lose the garden.

A large dining room was to be built there with a still-room and a great scullery beneath. Over the dining room was to be a rookery of rooms. When the architect's plans were before them Annie's enthusiasm leapt and she began, too soon, to think of details, before the footings had been laid, she had furnished and decorated them in her mind.

One day, going up Huntriss Row, Annie turned into the auctioneers' rooms. She wandered round the furniture, silk fronted pianos were abundant and unwanted, she noted.

Then she saw a Chippendale chair. Its strong straight lines reminded her of the chair they had in Milnsbridge, but this was Chinese Chippendale with a lattice of asymmetrical slates.

It enchanted her, she found the porter and left a bid. Then she saw a Chinese carpet and fell in love with that.

She saw quite suddenly that the drawing room with its Adam fireplace must be Chinese. When she went into the hotel she was struck by the prevailing darkness of the hall. She opened the door into the room she wished to change, it was full of light. She called Edward, "I've had a good idea."

"No more expense, I hope?"

"No a lot. Just imagine, Ted, a wall made of glass along here. The hall will be no longer dark. This room too will show to advantage when you enter."

"You're right."

When it was mooted to the architect, he agreed. He made a plan of the partition. They both disliked the dull squared panes. The architect knew their disappointment and said, "But what do you want?"

"I think my wife would like Chinese Chippendale. She wants an oriental room."

He led the way to the newly arrived chair.

"Exactly right. It will suit the room and the house."

Annie smiled and when Edward was called away, she said.

"Come and see my carpet. But don't tell my husband."

She led the way to the top floor and there rolled up by a bed was a carpet. Together they spread it out. It was a pale grey with a deep border of blue and there were boughs of cherry blossom and in the centre, floating, like islands, were flowers in stylised patterns.

"It is beautiful. Where did you get it?"

"At the same sale where I bought the chair. I've owned up to the chair but not the carpet yet."

Thus into a marriage where there was love, unison of aims and taste, discord grew. Edward was unable to discuss finance and he saw no reason why Annie should be involved.

Annie had no income, she put the bills before him, and like so many men of his time, he exploded and demanded explanations.

Annie dreaded scenes and the solution was placed before her, through her hands went all the bills, the flow of cash. It was corrupting. Sundries became an ever larger item in her accounts.

The extensions were opened. They were a success. Annie loved the dining room, equally she approved the large serving room with its lift. The spacious scullery below she was glad of, but she rejoiced that it was not her province.

All those greasy plates, the pans, the steam… she just could not take it. What she was unable to stomach was the hopelessness of the men who worked there, engaged by Edward, the seasonal kitchen porters.

They lived in doss houses, they drank and their weak and pitiful faces brought sadness to her heart. They reminded her of Wakefield Prison and outcasts of society.

The floor above was a different world and the combined taste of husband and wife made beautifully proportioned rooms magical. But it was a business. That was something Annie never quite understood, yet she adapted. She adapted more than she knew.

The little rooms above the dining room she disliked, she dubbed them the bachelor wing. They had no outlook, only into the well of the building. They were useful in the high season, but in her heart she was always ashamed of them.

Chapter 30

Bicycles and the Theatre

The great bicycling craze had reached Scarborough. Edward and Frank were among the first enthusiasts and together they pedalled round Forge Valley, even to Whitby and once made a long trip to the Dales - a trip that broke a friendship, for in their daily settling up of the accounts, Frank charged for the adhesive and the patch from his repair kit when Edward had a puncture.

It was a charge never to be forgiven and resulted in the return home being made in silence.

Annie enjoyed seeing her husband ride off in his Norfolk jacket and tweed cap and she thought of cycling as an entirely masculine domain, though she knew, of course that some women had taken to the wheeled saddle.

Therefore, it was a great surprise to her one day when she came down the stairs and was confronted by a shining black machine in the hall which Edward proudly held. Its curve had elegance and Annie thought it rather charming but she envisaged herself dusting and polishing it rather than riding it.

Ted enlarged on the picnics they would undertake, even nights away from home, the North Riding was in the compass of their wheels. Annie became alarmed at the prospect and she decreed that she would never wear those unbecoming "bloomers".

In the afternoon, the bicycle was wheeled out on to the Cliff and the flat road in front of Cliff Bridge Terrace was considered the ideal place to "get the hang" of cycling. Ted ran with one hand on the handle-bar, the other on the saddle, so encircling his wife, but it gave her no confidence.

He walked, he ran, up and down and up and down and he began to shout at Annie to pedal. As her nervousness increased so her propulsion faltered. It never was understood by her that the pedalling achieved the balance.

After an hour they were both tired and disappointed and they decided to rest. Ted leapt on the bicycle and showed her how it was done. She smiled and said: "I shall manage it tomorrow."

Next day the lessons were resumed, there was a slight improvement, but when for a moment Ted removed his hands, so Annie became rigid with doubt, if not fear, and she nearly fell off.

"Annie, you just are not trying!"

"I am, I am. You must be more patient."

Gradually, on the fourth day, the lesson seemed to be learnt that she had to press the pedal in order to remain upright. She understood the theory, at last, but as soon as Ted removed his arm she failed to put the idea into practice.

What amazed her husband was that the inner still calmness of her character in some strange way allowed her to remain stationary and upright for seconds longer than most people.

It was on the fifth day, when no progress seemed to be made and Ted became aware of smiling faces at the windows of the houses overlooking his practice ground, that he lost his temper.

"Annie, either I am a completely incompetent teacher, or you are a damn silly woman. I think it is the latter."

With an odd dignity she stepped down lay the machine down on the road, its wheels slowly turning and said, "Edward Henry don't you dare to speak to me like that."

"Well, I don't know what to do. Beatrice learnt quickly enough, why can't you?"

Annie heard the remark, but she was already walking away up to the Cliff angry because he was cross and angry because she was beaten. She was nearly in tears, but pronounced fiercely to herself that bicycles were for men and children, some women, but certainly not for ladies. But she knew that this was not true.

She went straight up to her room and after tea had been brought to her, she opened the wardrobe. There hung a costume in two shades of blue. She took it out, held it against herself and saw that the jacket with its double breast and leg o'mutton sleeves looked most becoming.

She held out the skirt, as advertised the panels at the side hung gracefully – all designed to look stunning on a bicycle.

"What a pity if all that is wasted."

The fact was that Annie had never in her life been taught by anyone to play a game.

When others had rounders in the Wakefield playground, she had extra lessons as a pupil-teacher.

She was totally without training between hand and eye, other than with needle and thread. She lacked a certain co-ordination. Yet she could dance and remembering this she thought that surely in time she would learn.

At tea she said: "I'm sorry that I am such a dunce, Ted. But it does seem so difficult. What can we do?"

Her act of palliation had come a little too soon.

"I don't know. But I am not going to try any more. You just don't seem to try. I can't understand it."

"Perhaps Frank could teach me."

"No he won't."

"Could we advertise for an instructor?"

"Now, that is a better idea, but I can improve on it. I'll write to the makers in Coventry to send up their instructor."

A week later, a man in a brown bowler hat, a yellow waistcoat and a brown suit that managed to be bright presented himself. He was Mr Truscott from the Black Country. Annie looked at him with both alarm and distaste.

"I believe you have come to teach me to ride the bicycle?"

"That's right, little lady."

This form of address was very inappropriate as Annie was a head taller than Mr Truscott even when he wore his bowler hat.

"The name is Mrs Matthews."

"We had a letter from your hubby."

This was an expression she had never heard before, but she immediately disliked it.

"Hubby? The hub of the wheel of my bicycle? I never realised it could write."

The barb, as sharp as the spoke on the wheel went home. He changed his stance and his manner.

"I will show you to your room."

There were few visitors, Annie led the way upstairs, she had intended giving him a front room, but her sense of social gradations was keen, she thought a back room, one of those she disliked was quite good enough. But then thought better of it and led him to a front room, but on the second floor.

She went down muttering, "Hubby. Little lady!"

Later, rather anxiously she asked him how long it took to teach someone to ride. She felt unable to bear him for long.

"It all depends, Ma'am. There was an old gentleman, it took me six weeks to learn him."

"Six weeks!"

"Yes. Nice old geyser he was... squire of his village in Lincolnshire."

"I think we had better begin straightaway."

They set out for the terrace with the machine. He surveyed it.

"No nearly long enough. You have to turn before you've got any idea of balance."

Mr Truscott looked at the slope behind the Museum. It was one of the steepest slopes he had ever seen and it led to a road with sharp inclines down into the valley and up out of it.

"What about that road?"

He pointed to the valley.

"Yes, that is long and straight."

"That's where we must go."

They went down to the main road, he assisted her on. Annie admitted to herself that he seemed very sure of what he was doing. Like Ted, he put one hand on the bar and the other in the small of her back.

"My husband put his hand on the saddle," she said reprovingly.

"No use at all, Ma'am. No offence meant, but if you want my hand off your back you must pedal."

Anne felt put in her place and she momentarily thought the man a monster, but she obeyed and put pressure on the pedals and she felt the hand removed from her back. She gave him full marks for running, he never became breathless although they went up the mile of the Valley four times and on the last journey down he removed his hands and he saw that she could balance, but he knew that he was in for a tough assignment.

"Well, ma'am, that's enough for today. You've done very well indeed. All we need, now, is practice."

Next morning they were in the Valley again. He made adjustments to the height of the saddle. He raised it, he lowered it. He put it in precisely the place it had always been, but Annie declared it made a world of difference and she set off pedalling alone.

He ran alongside, never left her and frequently he had to seize the handle-bars, but he never let her fall.

"Poor, Mr Truscott, you must be tired."

"I could do with a beer."

"Of course you could." And taking a sixpence from her purse she said, "Have a nice little walk by the sea and have a drink on me."

It came a little primly and oddly from her mouth, they both laughed and she blushed.

On the Foreshore, he found a pub and very soon some companions as well. When asked what he was doing, he replied, "The best job in the world. Teaching a very pretty lady to ride a bicycle and she hasn't a notion."

They all laughed at his good fortune.

But the notion was gradually forming and on the fourth day Annie discovered that she had to wheel her own bicycle down to the training ground because Mr Truscott was wheeling Edward's.

Annie was not certain that she approved of this for she thought of her instructor very much as a groom who should lead her horse.

After two runs beside her, he decided to risk it and mount the other cycle. They pedalled up, they free-wheeled down and for the first time Annie felt the excitement of the wind on her face and the whistle past her ears and the joy of knowing that she was in command.

This dominion was still wobbly for she still tended to put the front and only brake on too quickly which caused a jolt.

"One more day, Mrs Matthews, and you will be able to send me to Coventry."

She laughed at his little joke.

"I will never do that, Mr Truscott. I enjoy our talks."

It was true. She had learnt about his wife, his two boys, one of whom sang in the cathedral in Coventry. She had observed him and in spite of his vulgarity she saw that he adapted himself to the company.

She even repented that she had thought of consigning him to a back room, for after all he had taught her to cycle. His clothes still worried her.

On the last day, they rode up the valley and then down Falsgrave into Westborough and down Huntriss Row.

"Our best ride yet. You've done excellently."

"I am very grateful, Mr Truscott, you have really taught me."

"My pleasure. I don't often come to such nice places."

"Oh, but you will. You'll go all over England teaching people. I know you will, you are a born teacher."

She looked at his ill-made face. It reminded her of the faces of Wakefield, the product, the human product of the industrial world, pinched, cramped. It was, though, an honest face. She had perched in that world, she had escaped, she wanted others to escape as well. She produced her purse from her pocket and he said,

"No, no. I don't want a drink. I really don't. I'm not so sweaty when I don't have to run."

"It is not for a drink, Mr Truscott. It is for a nice suit. Go and buy yourself one and let me see it at lunch time."

To his surprise she put a sovereign in his hand. She looked at him. She paused, as if a sudden thought had struck her she said,

"Mr Truscott, gentlemen never wear brown suits, you know." She gave him a beaming smile.

At lunch he wore a dark grey suit and when he said good bye Annie saw that he had a black bowler hat as well. They parted well-pleased with one another. Annie had not made a gentleman of him and he had created a very imperfect cyclist… she never really learnt to steer!

The sun seemed to shine on Scarborough in spite of the Boer War and life was for Annie carefree, but always with the diminishing and still black hole of despair when she remembered her dead baby.

She was unable to speak of it to Edward, not because he was cold or indifferent, the opposite - he felt about it too much. Annie had learnt that, like many men, he masked his emotions. There were whole areas which she discovered she was unable to discuss. She wondered why the Matthews had this secretive streak, it was alien to her.

At this time Edward became a Freemason. Suddenly the social circle was wider. There were outings in the summer and in winter little dances as well as an annual ball. The hotel became the venue for the dances and the place echoed with laughter and tricks. It was the great age of elaborate jokes.

There was staying in the hotel a handsome youth who was learning banking. Annie in her conversations with him learnt that he had loved acting at school and often played female roles.

When the next dance was due, she dressed him in a long white nightdress, put a mob-cap on him and a shawl round his shoulders. As the guests arrived she told them that she did not wish to be a spoil-sport but they must be fairly quiet for she had an old aunt staying who was fiercely evangelical and disapproved of dancing. She was, though a sound sleeper and already in her room.

Just when the dance was really in swing, an irate, even hysterical old woman entered the dining room. She called them "Sinner", "Limbs of the Devil". An embarrassed hush fell over the proceedings and before Annie could disengage herself, Edward's mother had gone over to pacify the old woman.

"Mr dear, my dear, they are only young people enjoying themselves. There is no harm. Their pleasure is innocent."

The 'old lady' raised her arm and said that the place was a whitened sepulchre and their prancing would lead them straight to Hell. The piano and violin had ceased and awkwardness was bordering on indignation.

Annie ran across the room and with an outstretched arm pulled off the mob cap and the curls and Henry Green was revealed. The dance was resumed with even greater enthusiasm, but Annie had to pacify her mother-in-law who had been completely taken in.

It was a time when there was already a slackening of some of the rigid attitudes that had prevailed in the 70s and 80s in provincial Britain. It even affected the Queen who seemed more energetic and ready to see and be seen than ever before.

Annie often tired of the eulogies about the Queen that she heard so often. She still maintained that the Queen should have abdicated and given her son a proper role in life.

To most people, South Africa seemed a long way off, but not to Edward or Annie. Edward sided with the British and Annie felt sympathy for the Boers.

With war Edward's attitude became intransigent and his views harsh and dogmatic. When General Butler returned from his post in the Cape and was reprimanded for his criticisms of the British there, Edward rejoiced, but Annie felt certain that the General knew much more than he divulged.

Annie found him irritating and her annoyance with him was exacerbated because she was once again, as she termed it, "in the family way." She hoped that the baby would be a boy, it would please Edward and she did not want another little girl she could compare with the memory of Edith.

The baby was due in December. The event had been planned - never again would she part with a small baby to any other woman, this baby would be six months old before the summer season got underway. Annie also had another plan of which her husband was entirely unaware; secrecy was catching.

That summer was not the easiest. The gaiety seemed strained and the number of families in mourning cast a shadow over the summer crowds. The war was taking its toll. When winter came, Mrs Matthews joined them once more.

Annie enjoyed her company. It made her content when she compared the calm that she, now, displayed with the constant repining of a few years previous. The tragedy of Ada and Ethel's death was no longer harped upon. The death of Edith had taught her tact on the subject.

In September, Kruger took refuge in Lourenco Margues. It was thought to herald the end of the war and at the end of the month Pretoria was annexed. The Boers began the guerrilla warfare at which they were so adept.

A wave of anti-Dutch feeling swept the country and Edward went with it - the common cry was "Hang Kruger". In the evenings Edward read the papers aloud and he found much to upset Annie.

Annie was deeply disturbed and often to calm herself, she walked on the Spa and gazed out at the sea and thought constantly of peace. She found herself unable to reconcile her knowledge of the Dutch with the atrocities that were being trumpeted in the news.

It was, though, her husband's jingoism that really hurt. He made the war a personal matter. She dreaded to return to the sessions by the fireside and the wretched paper. One evening, as he read of the isolated outposts of the British being captured, Annie could stand it no longer.

"Stop it. Stop it. I cannot bear it any longer. I won't believe it."

But he did continue, relishing in the gruesome detail of the hanging of an officer. He lowered his paper and was struck in the face with the edge of the book she had been trying to read.

Annie was astounded and afraid at what she had done. She stood up, rushed to the door and as she saw him rise and the blood run down his forehead, she felt relief that she had not killed him or damaged his eyes.

Then her anger returned and with splendid grammatical rectitude she said: "You may read, but nothing shall make me listen."

It was Mrs Matthews who comforted and consoled her son, but she also reprimanded him and told him that if he taunted Annie in this way he would make their baby very bad-tempered. She applied the same threat to Annie next day.

Meanwhile, Annie fled to their room. She locked the door and late at night stiffened with alarm when she heard her husband try the door. She feared he might shout, or force it. He turned away. Next morning he was contrite and so was Annie when she saw the small gash on his forehead.

In December, three days before her own birthday, Annie gave easy birth to another daughter. The child so resembled Edith that Annie's heart turned and then rejoiced with a deeper feeling than she had known since leaving Den Haag.

At Christmas she was up and showing her baby with great enthusiasm to the callers. Edward wanted her called Annie after her mother and Annie asked her sister-in-law to be a godmother and inserted Beatrice into her name, but with a great lack of logic, they called the baby Nancy.

People began to speculate about the Queen's health. Bulletins were issued and Annie watched the spectacle of the nation in the grips of dread. Her feelings to the old lady had changed, true - at the Jubilee she had been unable to work up any fervour for someone so very ugly, but she had admired the old lady's courage and determination in the past two years.

She had visited hospitals constantly, had opened bazaars for the relief of the widows, it had been amazing in one so old. The general talk was as if the world was coming to an end.

At the close of January the Queen died. Instantly, the streets were filled with black coats and hats and there was a hushed air. It was on these black streets that Nancy had her first outings in the perambulator.

After the burial, people relaxed and freed themselves from their obsession and Annie was gladdened that people now began to admire her child. Annie proudly described Nancy as the "newest Edwardian".

The baby thrived and Annie had a great urge to take her two

daughters to Armitage Bridge and Crosland Moor. Something stirred deep within her to return with her offspring to the roots she had not dared to face.

Being a mother made her able to think of her own mother without the pain of loss that she had felt so deeply. So, in the lull between Easter and the summer season she returned.

The sight of the smoking chimneys of the mills as they approached Huddersfield horrified her - it was even dirtier than she had remembered. At Berry Brow she rejoiced because the young sycamores were in fresh leaf and the bend of the valley was at its most beautiful.

It was at high tea with her elderly cousins that she felt different. Her experience had been so much wider. However, she was clear-eyed enough to see that behind the parochialism was a kind of earnestness, an honesty that she found sometimes lacking in Scarborough.

She understood why Holland had seemed so congenial to her… the same seriousness of purpose underlay everything. She loved Scarborough but though she loved its frivolity, there was a corner in her mind that slightly, very slightly disapproved.

At this table the humour was trenchant. It was not as witty as Edward and Frank's easy badinage. Here she was surrounded by schoolteachers, engineers and dyers and their sight seemed set on higher things than the eager making of money.

In a strange way she felt convicted as they admired her dresses. Was there, an implied judgement? The memory of her mother brushed all aside. Her love of clothes in no way exceeded her mother's.

The two girls were made much of and especially by the beautiful dark-eyed Nelly and she claimed Ada as her bridesmaid in her marriage planned for the autumn.

One afternoon, Annie set out for Crosland Moor. As she pushed the pram up the steep hill she thought of her mother struggling up this hill shortly before her death. She felt a stab of pain.

When she reached the cottage set back from the road with its garden full of wallflowers Annie felt that she had strayed into a Paradise of Love.

When the door opened and she saw the tiny figure of Annie Hurst she gasped and became a child. Inside she seemed to step back home. She had forgotten that Aunt Annie had housed so much of her mother's furniture.

She noticed instantly the alabaster urn with the doves on the central table in the parlour, the Parian figure of Queen Victoria beneath a glass dome. These had been considered beautiful and rare in her childhood.

Ada went off with Aunt Annie to the kitchen and Annie sat at the primly laid table, white lace cloth over the thick chenille. Annie's heart thumped and gingerly she raised the cloth, she did it as hesitantly as if it had been a woman's skirt.

There were the splayed legs from a central pillar. It was the table she had sat at night after night doing her homework. Another memory was aroused and she felt for a rough hole on the underside... she found it.

Guilt made her blush. She had made that fortunately unseen disfigurement with William's pen-knife. She had borrowed it to sharpen her pencil, she had delayed talking in the kitchen and her mother had told her she really must go back to The Merchant of Venice. She had returned and being bored, with the knife in her hand, she had cut a little hole, the symbol of ennui.

The past was rushing in too quickly and she felt her chin quiver, always a prelude to tears. The door opened and in came her aunt with a plate of bread and butter in one hand a teapot in the other.

She looked at Annie. She knew everything, she offered no sympathy, but briskly poured out the tea and said: "You must be fair fashed pushing that great pram up the hill."

Annie looked at the shrewd face. She saw how Ada kept close to her side the old lady had a magnetism. She saw in her the solution to all her anxieties.

"Aunt, could you come to Scarborough in June and stay with the children until September?"

"Eeh, that's a long time – but I've never been to Scarborough and I'd graidly like to see the sea again."

"Edward and I would bring you back when we come to Nelly's wedding."

From that moment, this Yorkshire relic of her past became a pervasive influence in her life, the lives of her children and the whole families of the White's and the Matthews.

A few weeks later, Annie Hurst moved to Saint Nicholas.

Besides a very commodious domed trunk and several expanding hampers all strapped she brought a Chippendale chair which earlier in the century had been turned into a rocking chair.

In this, every night, she sat looking out to the sea knitting socks, or darning them, sipping very slowly a glass of stout and eating digestive biscuits. She was very content. She was ruffled in August when her room was required and with Ada and Nancy she was despatched to a farmhouse in Scalby for a month.

Thus began a scheme of things that was to last for many years.

The black clad figure with a white lace cap on her silver hair was to be the totem of the children. She was vigilant, often aggressive, and watched over the children fiercely. It was as if the maternal spirit pent up within her for 60 years and unexercised blazed in these her last years.

Each winter, she returned to Crosland Moor. But the time spent there diminished and diminished until eventually she gave up the cottage, moved her furniture to Saint Nicholas and in Crosland stayed with cousins on her annual visits.

Annie was once more pregnant. The baby was due in January. It was dark and very cold and the waiting became increasingly tedious and uncomfortable. Then a fear seized Annie… she dreaded that her child should be born on January 27th for that was the birthday of Kaiser Wilhelm and Annie hated him.

She found his treatment of his father and mother unforgivable and, once again, Annie found herself out of step with current opinion. But she was certain that one day most people would agree with her.

Annie remembered the bombastic speeches on January 27th which were reported in the Dutch papers, she feared for a child born the same day. She believed in the stars. The days ticked very slowly by and on 24th and 25th Annie was very nervous.

The 26th was windy and dry and Annie set off alone for a walk. She crossed the Spa bridge, toiled up to the Esplanade, walked down to the bandstand and up the steep paths on the cliff to Holbeck Gardens.

She retraced her steps and went along the Spa buildings past 'the monkey cage', long non-existent, up to the Broad Walk and towards home. To her delight, on the bridge she experienced the first twinge of pain. After lunch the contractions began.

Edward, who pooh-poohed all superstition, remembered that a sovereign assurance of the birth of a boy was to hang a top hat on the bed post. He crept into the room where Annie lay and telling her placed the hat on the brass knob.

Whether the walk hastened the delivery of not, whether her desire impeded or helped is unknown. To her own mind she had achieved all she, and Edward, wanted, a boy was born.

Edward was so delighted that he gave Annie sole choice on names. Dearly, very dearly she wanted to call her son, Benton. She had fears though, the names of her parents seemed short-lived names and she dare not repeat the sad agony of Edith Marianne.

So she chose the name Alan after her favourite uncle, the husband of Annie Hurst. Mrs Hurst hurried back to Scarborough and was greeted by Nancy as "Nana" and that became her name for the rest of her life and long after. She claimed Alan as her own and jealously watched over him.

The new Edwardian age that Annie so eagerly awaited seemed slow to come. The mourning of the old Queen lasted long and Annie listened almost incredulously to the stories of her saintliness.

But the official period of mourning ended and attention began to focus on the coronation. The hotel keepers were anxious and asked the question whether people would spend their money visiting London and foregoing their summer holiday by the sea.

Suddenly everything was thrown into disarray by the illness of the King. He developed appendicitis. The interest in King Edward doubled - his popularity was assured by his swift rallying and decision to go ahead with the coronation only weeks later.

The real joy of the country came, though, with the signing of the Treaty of Pretoria. There was no one who did not gladden that the interminable and non-winnable war of South Africa was over.

It was then, that a warm softer air seemed to blow across Britain and some of the rigidities of the former century relaxed. This new freedom was more apparent in a sea-side resort than in the great manufacturing towns, for after all pleasure was their peculiar avocation.

The theatres became more light-hearted and for a lady to be seen at an operetta was no longer considered indelicate.

With the Freemasons both Edward and Annie went to the light-hearted musicals, but they both preferred real drama.

They never failed to attend the seasons of Shakespeare given by Irving at the Opera House and both loved the enchanting Ellen Terry. Edward was so well versed in the plays as productions. Annie, product of her schooling, knew the plots sources, she recognised contexts still. Edward was a little in awe of Annie's knowledge, so it was with relish he seized upon a remark of hers as they came away from *Richard III*.

He was praising the performance of Sir Henry as they walked along St Nicholas Street and he asked for her agreement and she replied, "Yes, his voice is good, but, oh dear, he has such poor legs."

He loved teasing her and this opinion from his scholar was treasured and used often.

It was about this time that Annie was, one day, walking on the Spa with Ada who was arrayed in a white hat with a white ostrich feather and a dress of white broderie anglaise. Annie watched her child running ahead with great pride.

She stopped to talk to an extremely well-dressed lady of statuesque build. As Annie came closer she recognised the lady to be Lily Langtry who was appearing in a play at the Spa theatre

"What an enchanting little daughter you have", murmured Mrs Langtry.

Annie, the fond mother, could only agree and she thanked the elegant stranger. But Annie had a pocket of Puritanism in her, she did not approve of a woman who used her beauty and traded her favours.

She did not approve of a woman, who, it was alleged, had put an ice-cream down the neck of the King when Prince of Wales. So her thanks for this admiration were tempered and whenever she repeated the story she added, "Of course Mrs Langtry would admire Ada. Their colouring is identical." Both had dark hair and violet blue eyes.

The order of life did not change rapidly. The careful gradations of rank were considered and observed, but money became more important, it opened doors which previously had been tightly shut.

There was blitheness about, and life, especially on holiday, was carefree and full of gaiety.

Happy relationships were formed by visitors in the hotels. They took their holidays together, returning year after year, so that many hotels had the atmosphere of a country house party.

High spirits would break out. Charades, an impromptu dance, would be held without any anticipation. Over these occasions, Annie reigned benevolently, finding costumes and dresses, but she never, never took part. Her role was always a presiding one beautifully groomed and beautifully dressed.

The glowing lines of the Princess gowns suited her tall and still slender figure, suited her to perfection. It was, now, that she began to move, as she was the rest of her life, like a queen amid a little court.

The running of the hotel had fallen into a very successful division of labour. Edward organised, he bought the food, he supervised the menservants, he saw to the maintenance of the building. He made decisions and plans.

Annie ran the office, often working late into the night writing letters, adding accounts. But her chief contribution was in looking after the visitors and in cherishing her staff. She gathered to herself a group of wholly reliable and industrious workers.

This even extended to the purely seasonal workers, who always asked for a place at the next season as they took away their final autumn pay. There were three pivots to the staff. The first was Edward's chosen man, Harry, the head porter, who was truly the foreman of the working establishment. Of equal rank was Maria, the cook.

Annie regarded Maria as a plain middle-aged woman of very uncertain temper and a perfectionist to the point of neurosis. Quite slowly, Annie discovered more about her. The first thing she noted was a tendency to drink, but only when the season was over.

Annie sighed and thought that there was a price to be paid for everything and she was so excellent a cook she could not be dismissed because she drank.

She also learnt that when she was paid in the autumn it had to be in golden sovereigns. One year, she had given her money in notes and when investigating some unseemly noise in the kitchen had come upon Maria laughing hysterically and throwing one note after another into the fire.

One autumn, Annie paid her and she asked her about her holiday and her return in a few weeks to cook for the family and, of course, whether she would be with them in the summer next year.

"I don't know that I will be with you at Easter, ma'am."

Annie blanched, "Not be with us," she gasped.

"No. I shall be having a baby in April."

Annie could not believe her ears and Maria was very calmly stirring a pot on the stove.

"But, Maria, you are not married, are you?"

"No, but he's a good man. He'll stand by me."

"Oh, my poor, poor girl." Annie wished to put an arm around her, but was inhibited by a sense of rank. But she was so upset she did rest a hand on the print cottoned sleeve and said, once again, "My poor, poor girl. What will you do?"

To her astonishment, Maria laughed.

"Why what I always do. Hurry it on, have it and hand it over to my mother."

Annie moved a pace back.

"You have other children?"

"Three, but only two of the mites lived."

"This, then, will be your fourth?"

Maria nodded.

"But, Maria, you shouldn't. It isn't right."

Annie was stunned by shock.

"I know I shouldn't, ma'am, but I do."

"But where are your children?"

She was amazed that she had not heard of them. There were lives being lived beneath her roof of which she knew nothing at all, she felt a kind of guilt. She wondered if she had been sleep-walking through life.

She saw life as a paved street, stone flags beneath one most of the time, but every so often railed areas and manholes with another life going on beneath your very feet.

"Where are your children?"

"Why, with my mother in Falsgrave."

"But why, Maria, did you never tell me? You should see them more often."

"They are happy as they are. I'm happier here cooking, seeing the people."

'Seeing the people' thought Annie, she sighed. She knew what 'seeing the people' meant. She was amazed that Maria, who never left her kitchen, yet knew all the visitors, what rooms they occupied, and she recognised them all by their shoes, skirts and trousers as they passed by the basement kitchen window.

Annie extracted, without any difficulty, the address. She did have to give a promise, she easily gave. For the notion had never crossed her mind, not to send for the police.

As Annie went upstairs she felt the sudden burden of a secret. She did not like secrets they made life complicated, but she was going to keep this and for very good reasons.

The first was that she had no intention of losing the best cook in Scarborough. She was far too valuable an asset for that. Then, in a manner that proved her to be an Edwardian, she argued that Maria's tempers and weeping were of far greater annoyance than her morals, and she had learnt to tolerate those.

She knew that she would have to keep this knowledge from Edward for she was most uncertain what his reaction would be. Sometimes he was alarmingly conventional, then he became dogmatic and she found this difficult to counter.

There were even deeper reasons, beneath her calm beauty lay troubled reactions to all things sexual. She did not understand a great deal and feared that her own pleasure with her husband was shameful. Thus everything on the subject was shut firmly and absolutely away.

However, Maria and her children were not shut away and in the afternoon, without consulting Maria, Annie cycled up to Falsgrave. She found the mean little street, almost an alley.

Leaning her bicycle against a wall she went up the brick paved path past a great many children who, she was glad to see did not look ill-fed.

She found the house, the door was open and on her knock a voice shrieked from the back followed by its owner, a bent old woman wiping her hands on a grimy cloth. She wore a small black bonnet somewhat askew. Seeing Annie she bobbed a curtsey.

"You must be Maria Holliday's mother. I am Mrs Matthews."

The smile on the old woman's face turned to fear,

"Is anything wrong?"

"No. I just came to see that everything was right."

"Please to come in."

A chair was lifted, dusted and placed by the fire for her. Four chairs, a table and a rickety cupboard were the furnishings of the room. A sack before the range served as a rug. It was a picture of poverty and reminded her very forcibly of Wakefield, it was children from homes such as this that she had taught.

"The children are not yet back from school, I suppose?"

"That's right. Grand bairns they are."

"How do you manage on Maria's money?"

"Oh very well and especially with the food you send."

Annie was silent. At the same moment she noted a plate with the hotel crest upon it on the table. She asked more questions… where was a pump, or tap for the yard? Did they have sufficient coal and she would like to see where they slept.

She felt no compunctions whatsoever at asking these questions, the old woman saw no reason to withhold answers.

Annie felt a right to know. She was led up the stairs to sparsely, bleakly fitted rooms, two rooms each with a double bed. Fleetingly Annie wondered where Maria slept when not at the hotel, but the question was dismissed instantly. What she did note was that all was clean although very sparse.

Downstairs, the children clattered in and almost as a reflex, their grandmother cut each a slice of bread and smeared it with jam. Annie extracted shy answers and learnt their names. She found threepenny bits which she placed in each grubby hand. For the grandmother she had half a crown.

As she walked down the alley a tear glistened in her eye and her chin quivered. She was appalled, but she also admired the spirit of the household but the emotion came from the eruption of memories of Wakefield, her grandmother struggling, her mother working.

She was so upset that she was just mounting to the incline up towards the station when she realised that she had come there on the bicycle. She went back, mounted and began to pedal home.

The combination of sorrow for so many in the world and her own inefficiency at steering meant that she never saw the extended whip of the cabby.

She was only aware of the sudden collision with something, smooth, round and soft, the clatter of her machine and terrifying visions of horse legs and wheels.

Suddenly she was angry, she demanded why the driver had suddenly turned his animal. The cabby was not only a peaceable man, but he recognised her. He threw the reins to a bystander, assisted Annie into the cab and gave the bicycle to a lad to wheel alongside them.

Dishevelled and shocked, Annie kept her head down. She was humiliated and somehow the news of her accident had come before her and Edward and Ada were on the door step to see her arrive.

Ada was just relieved to see her mother alive, but Edward was furious and not with the driver.

"That, Annie, is the last time you ride that damned machine. You are incompetent, incompetent."

Annie burst into tears, recovered herself and said: "I quite agree. It's a hateful contraction and no means of travel for a lady."

Edward gave a sovereign to the cabby. Together they examined the horse and both gave thanks that the beast was old and docile.

Prosperity continued in Scarborough and the two hotels of the Matthews and the White families were an indication of this. The fortunes of the families increased in conjunction with the town.

Both Frank White and Edward became town councillors. This meant that more of the running of the hotel fell into Annie's hands, yet still she was kept in ignorance of the true financial state.

It irked and she refused to plead for enlightenment. Her reply was to become a suffragist. Edward smiled tolerantly comforting himself with the thought that, "It will come to nothing."

Annie was not alone and in the movement she found two of her dearest friends. One was Annie Chapman, a small vivacious woman with an extremely independent mind and unafraid of action which she could volubly justify, on occasions when Annie would remain silent.

The other friend was much more akin to Annie. She was Florence Tindall, the daughter of a Scarborough portrait painter who later became a photographer. The pictures of Mr Lancaster hung in every fashionable home in the town.

Florence was quiet, gentle forbearing. She was also subtle, the most subtle of the three, she never opposed her husband, a demanding man. His favourite and thoughtless tyranny was to expect his wife to wait up for him when he was out with his freemason friends enjoying a convivial evening.

Mrs Tindall waited up, she crocheted and made up the finest of lace cloths, she made many. She also read and, when her children were launched into the world and her husband died, leaving her well-provided, she surprised everyone by becoming a pillar of the Literary Society and opening a shop selling, among other things, her wondrous table-cloths.

Annie Chapman had no time for such silent rebellion. She caused shock by building a house in Stepney, a little suburb, without any reference to her husband whatsoever. The first he knew of an almost finished new home was when a friend at the Lodge asked him how he would like living in a brand new house!

Annie did not rebel because her marriage entailed working in a business, her life was busy and fulfilled. Her only sorrow was that in summer she saw so little of her children, but every Sunday she visited them.

Her worries for them were few for she knew that they were under the exceedingly vigilant eye of Mrs Hurst, now called Nana. Though they loved Nana, their mother was the star of their firmament and this star moved with a steady regularity into their orbit every Sabbath afternoon.

As soon as dinner was over, Nana dozing in her chair, Ada, Nancy and Alan walked along the road towards Scarborough to meet the cab. They climbed the bank and waited… sometimes it seemed an unconscionable long time.

But come she always did and the memory of it was of perpetual sunny afternoons, a smiling and loving mother beneath a flower-encrusted hat with a huge shallow basket of peaches, apples, grapes, pears and oranges on the seat before her.

These were supposedly the 'left-overs' from the Sunday dessert. In fact, they were the best, picked from the fruit before it was taken to the dining room. Nancy was to remember these afternoons the rest of her life and whenever she thought of them she saw her mother as Flora and the basket as a cornucopia, Edwardian abundance.

Seeing her children grow so healthily made Annie more aware of others far less fortunate placed in the lower tiers of the structure of social life. She thought of the West Riding, which she always equated with want, and she had an idea and she put it to Edward.

She wondered why she had not thought of it before. "Why don't we have a great tea-party for the Sunday School of Hannah and Mary?"

"I am quite willing, if you can persuade the staff to work on a

Saturday afternoon, which is always a busy day with the arrival of visitors."

To persuade her staff was easy, so three weeks later Annie and Edith walked down to the sands to pick out their elderly cousins and the children of Milnsbridge. To pick out the 150 children was not a difficult task.

To recognise that they were poor was not demanding either, large eyes and large mouths were set on pale faces where the skin always seemed stretched.

They seemed unaware of their deprivation and were enjoying their day. After greeting the cousins the two sisters led the way along the Foreshore and up the Zig-zag to The Cliff. It was in the hotel that silence fell on the chattering horde, they were over-awed.

For a moment, Annie thought they were not going to eat the huge high tea she had organised, but soon they fell on the food, a contented silence reigned followed by very high spirits.

Annie felt a flow of joy and sheer delight as she plied the children and talked with them. Edward watched, a little aloof; to see his wife besieged by them all made him proud. He was, though, aware of time and the arrival of the London train bringing another wave of visitors.

He also saw with a clearer eye than Annie the disturbing number of cripples in that dining room and he sent Harry, the porter out to get Mr Woodhead's waggonnettes to carry the entire party up to the Excursion station.

This was removed from the proper railway station because Edwardian Scarborough did not encourage day trippers in their elegant upper-class midst. For the first time he saw the evil in the system.

When it was time to go the waggonnettes were there and with shoving and squeezing the vast crowd were stowed in and driven away. It was a deed that Annie was never to forget and she loved her husband more for it.

This trip became a fixed event and, always, Edward had a surprise. One year he had the entire donkey population brought up and a little ragged cavalry rode up to the hotel, all the weakest, all the smallest.

Annie was very thankful her children were so healthy.

One morning as Annie was writing letters in the office, Beatrice came in. At once, it was evident that she was extremely agitated. Annie waited to hear some misdemeanour of Frank's, but it was her mother that was causing the grave anxiety.

Mrs Matthews lived in a flat in Vernon Place during the season, but for the rest of the year lived with one or other of her two children. Beatrice had been to the flat and found her mother muddled and then she had discovered the bottles.

Beatrice was an ardent teetotaller. She wept, was horrified, ashamed... she even felt mortified telling Annie of this.

When Beatrice had been comforted and her confidence restored, the two women went up to Vernon Place. The old broken lady sat in a chair by the window weeping. She cowered when her daughter came in. Annie kissed her and put an arm about her. Until that moment she had not known what to do, she knew, now.

"Grandma, you are coming to stay with us for a while. Bea and I will pack your things."

"But what about Sarah?"

"Sarah can come too. We will soon find work for her at St Nicholas."

So the old lady and her maid came to the hotel. She continued to weep at intervals and was easily disturbed. The children irritated her.

"Edward, your mother is, I am sure, ill."

"I think you are right. We'd better send for Dr Salter."

The young doctor came and in his examination found that Mrs Matthews was suffering from cancer. It was a secret that the old lady had tried to conceal for far too long. Patient and doctor knew the outcome, but the younger generation did not.

Downstairs he broke the news very gently, he made no promise of recovery, but he promised pain-killers. It was Edward's first close hand encounter with death and it marked him, his depressions became more marked.

It was the cause of constant friction between him and his sister for he smuggled into the bedroom small bottles of whisky for his mother to dull the pain of her body and the anguish of her mind.

Annie found herself the buffer between them, she sympathised with both, she tried to soften Beatrice's hard attitude. But she recognised that she had taken this stance impelled by a fierce revulsion which would never move.

As more visitors arrived, so Annie had less time to give to nursing, so a house was taken, by the two families at Ayton, a village a few miles inland, and there Mrs Matthews spent the last years of her life.

In the midst of this turmoil, Nancy developed a sore throat. At first it was treated as a childish ailment, but Dr Salter soon diagnosed, quite easily, scarlet fever. There were tears from Nana, tears from Annie and a horror beyond tears for the bewildered little girl.

It took Dr Salter to reassure her and under his supervision she was wrapped up in some outdoor clothes over her nightie, with socks and shoes on her feet.

He carried her down the stairs and out into his carriage. He showed her the fittings of the small dove grey padded interior. There were embroidered straps for raising and lowering the window, more straps to pull on when one rose to get out.

There was a small silver tube with a little trumpet at the end with a whistle attachment. This could summon the attention of the coachman and Dr Salter could give instructions. Best of all to her was a small ivory fan which folded out and notes and messages could be pencilled on it, then folded up it slipped into a neat little recess. She played with it for a long time.

At the isolation hospital Dr Salter carried her in, he carried her down the corridor and she was placed in a small room quite alone.

"This, my dear, will be your own little room for the next week. You see that window? Your mother will come and see you there, this afternoon." He was gone.

Strange nurses came in. They peeled off her outer clothes and shoes, they took off her nightdress and then put her into a plain white one that felt harsh and scratchy. She submitted in utter silence.

Fortunately, she felt too ill to care and fell sound asleep. When she awoke she did not know where she was, she lay rigid and frightened. Soon a nurse came in and she was coaxed to eat a little food.

She was told that when she next woke up her mother would be there. With that knowledge, Nancy fell fast asleep dreaming of the soft feel of her mother, the sweet smell of her mother and the sensation of complete security she gave.

She awoke to a little tapping and scratching sound and her first thought was of little mice. She liked mice. She opened her eyes, recognised the bleak little room with its strange smell and then saw her mother, round eyed, round faced at the window smiling, yet looking anxious and concerned.

Nancy found herself too weak to sit up, she tried to raise her arms, they did not respond. She could not hear her mother, she hoped that she smiled. It was a nightmare. The nurse came she spoke to her mother in a way she had never heard her mother addressed before, her mother disappeared. Nancy was very afraid.

"Your mother will be back tomorrow. Now, you just have to be a good girl and we shall have you better in no time."

Gradually, Nancy improved, her temperature no longer soared. She even sat up in bed and looked at the books which were sent to her. The evil was that as she got better, so she felt the situation more keenly, she longed for her mother to appear behind the glass pane… but it was also the very acme of frustration.

She did not need just the sight of her, she needed the comfort of her touch, she merely wept and tears ran down her mother's face too. The disease took its course and, at last, Nancy was allowed from her bed. She sat in a chair by the window and when her mother came, she could, at least hear her.

The nurse began to speak of return and a day came when she was permitted to sit in the garden with her mother, but with a little hedge between them. Annie told her of happenings at home, how Ada and Alan were, how Nana missed her.

Annie even got Nancy to read to her, but she, too, longed to clasp the poor thin little wraith that Nancy had become. But they both took comfort in the knowledge that soon she was to go home.

The night before her release she was taken to the bathroom and put in the big white bath with the shining brass taps. The nurse was called away. As she scraped herself very half-heartedly she noticed the pink rash again… it was round her wrists, her knees and a faint flush was on her chest.

She smothered it in more soap. The nurse returned, rinsed Nancy, lifted her from the bath. Nancy said nothing, she just prayed and prayed that she would not notice, but as she was dried the nurse lowered the towel and peered.

"How long have you had this?"

"I don't know. I've just seen it."

"I am afraid, my dear, it will mean your going back to bed."

Nancy went silent and pale. The pallor showed up the rash more vividly. Back in her room her temperature was taken, it was up again.

"There'll be no going back for you, I'm afraid, my dear."

Nancy howled and a smack was the only restorative to calm.

Next day, Dr Salter came. He was told how uncooperative she had been and he mildly reproved her. He examined her and listened very acutely to her heart with his stethoscope. He smiled and patted her cheek and said: "We'll have you home this afternoon."

He had diagnosed not another recurrence of scarlet fever, but a new fever, rheumatic.

When Dr Salter came to tell her Annie was horrified. It was the most stressful time she had ever known. The hotel was full, Mrs Matthews was slowly dying at Ayton and, now, Nancy was seriously ill.

"Oh Ted, what are we to do? Your mother, now this... and all these people, too."

He put his arm around her.

"Mother is the concern of Bea and me. We'll see to that. You must look after little Nancy."

As he uttered Nancy's name, a muscle in his jaw quivered and a tear came into his eye but did not fall.

"I'll get you a little house."

Annie packed a case with clothes for Nancy. It was to have been a joyous return but was sullied with apprehensions and fear. Annie sighed. She was afraid. She feared illness and she was filled with apprehensions for this, her favourite child.

She had little time for morbid thoughts. She had to organise everything for the coming week at the hotel. She had, also, to pack and provide food and linen for the cottage, a cottage that she did not know.

Life seemed strange, menacing and unreal. When Edward returned he had the key of a little house on the Scalby Road. In the afternoon he went out there with Annie, together they put up a bed in the small front room and later Dr Salter arrived with Nancy. She was carried straight to the bed.

The fever was a recurring one. Often her temperature remained normal, then it would shoot up. Annie devoted all her time to her and never let the child see how anxious she was.

Both Edward and Annie watched with alarm as the fluid in her chest moved slowly and inexorably towards her heart. Dr Salter came daily, sometimes twice and jokingly, cajolingly he applied blisters to the child's chest, these filled rapidly with fluid.

He made it a game and he drew patterns, sometimes animals on the thin little chest. Very carefully he avoided using the already tender patches when it was possible. Like the parents, he admired the patience of the quiet little girl who was so entirely trusting once she was within the boundary of her home.

During this time a special bond was forged between Nancy and her parents, they were never to forget that this was the child they had fought for with death. Slowly, very slowly, the fever withdrew, but she was kept in bed and only permitted to move extremely gradually.

She was carried from her bed to a chair. Later, when her bed was taken upstairs, her father every night carried her upstairs. This continued for a year. It became his unalienable right.

He also bought a donkey for her called 'Ginnie', so that when the family walked, Nancy could accompany them.

It was like its small mistress, much indulged. It used to trot ahead of them all, look round and if it was tired and the family seemed distant, would lie down with Nancy on its back. It made its own demands, especially in feeding. Annie discovered that it liked nothing better than rice pudding, so every other day a large pudding was made especially for the animal.

Winter came and they watched vigilantly over Nancy. Thin and pale she was, but her energy was great and constantly they had to stop her running. She learnt to sit quietly with her parents, or Nana, when Kit was playing with friends and she became adept, as her sister never was, at manipulating her father.

In time, she was to be the spokesman for her older sister and younger brother whenever they were in trouble, or wished to ask a favour. If Nancy interceded, or made a request it was always granted. Instead of causing friction between the siblings, it cemented their friendship for they were grateful to their diplomatic sister.

With the spring they saw Nancy gain a little flesh and much

more colour in her cheeks, they relaxed. Even Dr Salter ceased his gloomy prognostications. As they did so, Edward's mother became considerably more gravely ill. Her spasms of pain were agonising.

Like most patients with cancer at that time she was insufficiently drugged. Only whisky brought her a measure of oblivion. Edward brought small bottles of it to her and when too weak to hide the evidence Beatrice discovered the connivance between son and mother.

Beatrice had been afraid of her father's drunken rages and in her teens had been impressed by the work of the Temperance societies. She became a teetotaller with great fervour.

When her mother drank her horror was first to her offended principles, but, now, added to it was the fear that her respectability was threatened. She was too angry to confront her brother and she sent Frank to speak to him.

Edward listened with growing anger as Frank expressed his wife's and his own abhorrence and disapproval at his supplying his mother with alcohol. Annie stood by, afraid always of violence. She feared even more, violence within the family.

As Edward took a deep breath, he felt her hand upon his shoulder. While even at that moment he liked her touch, he shrugged his body away.

"Frank, you are talking of my mother, not your own. My mother is suffering and if my drink brings her relief, by God, she shall have it. You can tell Bea that. And I think it a fine piece of hypocrisy that you come and play the preacher when we all know you enjoy a drink, except in your own home."

Annie sensed that more would be said, she saw the angry flush on Frank's face. It had been implied that he was not master of his own household.

"Please, please stop. We all have to think of what is best for Grandma and everyone. I think you two men will have to run the businesses without us. Bea must be with her mother by day and I will come each night."

So began a difficult summer. Every evening at nine, as darkness began to fall, a cab came and took Annie to the station. At Ayton Annie walked up to the house. Always Beatrice was waiting by the window for her. She always had a tray of tea ready for her.

The two women became friends in this illness; it was a

friendship that Annie nurtured for she revered the ideal of the family.

After talking and hearing how the old lady had been, Annie went up to the bedroom. Each day she saw more decay but the decline was slow, so slow that they became almost impatient and ashamed of their feelings.

When the old lady slept, Annie opened her case and wrote letters accepting bookings, acknowledging cancellations, doing the books. Sometimes she would stop and look around the impersonal room which told no stories.

She wondered if it would, one day, recount how an old and unhappy lady died here, and that while she lay dying her daughter-in-law wrote mundane letters while the whole of the unknown stood waiting entrance. Annie dozed and in the morning she caught the train back to Scarborough.

The days became weeks, the weeks became months. Beatrice was worn, Annie exhausted. They felt a loyalty and supported one another. It was the husbands who became anxious, for Beatrice became thinner than ever and Annie seemed lost behind a placid mask.

They remained adamant that the poor woman should remain with them. They refused to countenance a nursing home.

Then one evening, as they turned their patient, Annie remembered an old wives' tale of her childhood, 'You can never die on a feather bed.' She wondered… could it be true?

Downstairs she mentioned it to Bea, and to her great surprise Bea was seized with a great will for action.

"We will change the mattress straightaway."

So the two women began the macabre task of stripping one bed and bringing the mattress into the sick room. Then they lifted the almost comatose woman into a chair. The act chilled Annie to the bone, it seemed brutal, insensitive.

The pained old eyes opened, the mouth writhed in an effort to speak, but no words came and her eye had the blank regard of a parrot's.

As quickly as possible they pulled away the down mattress, bundled it through the door to the landing and with more difficulty raised the firm rigid structure on to the bed frame.

They made the bed and then lifted the tragic lolling figure on to the new resting place. They felt guilt, as though they were hastening death, but the old woman sighed and sank into a deep sleep. The two women held hands and looked at the older generation depart as women had always done. The night passed, the old lady still breathed, their guilt receded.

Another day, another evening and Annie was, once more, in Ayton. At one o'clock when all was still and silent, Annie heard footsteps, then the faint clang as a bicycle was leant against a wall. She went down. She opened the door and the light of the lamp fell on Edward's anxious face.

"Are you all right?"

"Yes, why have you come?"

"I felt that I had to. How is mother?"

"No better, no worse. It cannot surely be long now?"

The door of a bedroom opened and Beatrice peered down with a candle in her hand.

"Oh, Ted. What is it?"

"I felt that I had to come. I'll sit up. You two go to bed."

They were both so fatigued they never questioned him but went into the spare room and together climbed on to the feather mattress. They fell deeply asleep.

At six Edward came to them.

"I think the end has come."

For some time Edward had listened to the laboured breathing. He had counted, sometimes to 80 and 100 between the gasps for breath. He awakened the women when it seemed the end must be.

The three stood round the bed. The old lady never opened her eyes, she did not sigh... she ceased to live. They waited, they counted. They dreaded another gasp, another intake of air, another grappling together within themselves of courage to acknowledge the truth. It was undoubted death.

Without a word, the two women removed the pillows, lay back the head paused for a moment looking at the face and then lifted the sheet over it. It was done as if they had rehearsed it many times.

Edward watched and then he said that he would find an undertaker. Beatrice had foreseen this and told him to go down into the village and tell a woman who laid out bodies.

Beatrice was already anxious about mourning.

She had black clothes with her, but she looked towards the

funeral. This shocked Annie and she wandered into the garden, down to the river and looked across to the meadows beyond.

It was all very tranquil, but Annie described it to herself as indifferent. She repeated to herself again and again, "It is all over, it is all over." For her mother-in-law she was glad, the pain, the suffering was over.

To this Annie also added that unhappiness is over. She had long known her mother-in-law's deep, unspoken unhappiness. It was an unhappiness her children could not bring themselves to acknowledge.

Annie looked at a clematis flower. It moved very softly in the faint stir of the air. It was purple, the colour of mourning, and Annie looked at it closely and knew that her feelings for this event were as nothing to her misery when Edith had died.

They were also nothing compared with her thankfulness when she finally knew that Nancy would live. She instantly resolved to return home and leave Edward with his sister.

"That is proper; that is right."

In Scarborough she walked past the hotel down to the bottom of the Cliff. She stood by the seats and looked out to sea. The mile of sand stretched before her, her heart lifted, she seemed to see eternity and the pressing tyranny of present time fled away. She walked resolutely up to the hotel.

In the hotel she was asked by the staff immediately about Mrs Matthews, she told them, they were quiet and then left her. She went through the rooms, puffed up cushions, moved ornaments an inch, half an inch, she gave a tug to curtains, she looped back lace curtains.

She was leaving her mark upon the rooms. She went into the kitchen and spoke to Maria. She went into the store and the maids came with their buckets to collect washing soda, soap, and hand in old scrubbing brushes for new ones.

Annie was heartened to see that all was going like clockwork along the tracks she had laid.

It was after his mother's death that Annie noticed a change in Edward. She knew that the funeral had brought him no comfort. He had been fussy about the strict observance of conventions.

Before the carriages had arrived he had objected to his wife's hat. He considered it too smart for the occasion and Annie had gone upstairs, without demur, and changed it. To him his mother was dead, he did not believe in an after-life, so he could find no solace there.

He became withdrawn, he had no time for the visitors and often, at the end of the day, he would put his head down and march through the hall where people were chattering happily, out into the open and up to his club.

Annie dreaded those moments and had learnt never to detain him to speak to a visitor... that often made it worse. He had lost all small talk. The staff, however, never ceased to revere him and his grudging praise was sought.

His standards, like his wife's, were high, but he attained them by different means, their systems were complementary and led to success.

In the winter, Edward was skating on the Mere and he fell. His whole weight met the ice on his forehead. He was unconscious for some minutes and then concussed. He was nursed at home, kept in darkness and when he emerged he was extremely sensitive to noise, high pitched noises caused him pain. The children had to be restrained often.

Annie, like Francois Haverschmidt, loved caged birds. She always had a canary, loved their song, adored their colour and rapid movement from perch to perch. Annie learnt to cover the cage when Edward entered the room.

One tea time he came in Annie and the children were around the fire. The children were happy, but Alan, still a small boy, would not fold his bread and butter into a small triangle.

Ada stirred her tea noisily. He saw all this slackness. Annie was too easy-going with them, but he held his peace, until the canary burst into high pitched song. He bore it, then, he could stand it no longer.

He picked up his napkin ring and flung it at the cage. It struck not the bars, but the glass panel which shattered and fell tinkling to the carpet. Annie was appalled at the violence, Ada was afraid and with Alan drew closer to her mother.

Nancy, looked up at him from her chair and said, very reprovingly, very decisively, "And now Daddy, look what you have done to Joey's windows."

It went straight to his heart.

"I am sorry Nancy, but I can't stand that racket."

There was silence. It was broken by the little girl.

"Well, you must show that you are sorry and buy him a new window straight-away."

Annie laughed, but she envied her child who was able to speak so openly to her father like that. She knew that she could not.

At a party, books and authors were being discussed and Edward said that he never ceased to enjoy Sir Walter Scott and Annie said tartly, "Yes, so much that Guy Mannering has been on your bed table for at least two years."

It had made everyone laugh, but it made Annie realise that Edward was no longer a reader, there was a blank in his life. Still, during the long winters he rolled up his sleeves and with Harry, the porter, decorated one room after another. He was always occupied, but his life, at its core, was not filled. He took up wood-carving, but to everyone's annoyance wished to practise it in the drawing room, where the family congregated.

Annie therefore encouraged him when, one day, he was asked to stand for the council and represent the ward where they lived. At a stroke his moods receded. He had a worth-while occupation beyond his home and he enjoyed it.

Annie was fulfilled by her family, but, by her mother, she had been made aware of a duty to others less fortunate. The visit to Maria's mother had reminded her of poverty. Then she had been made aware of the ignorance of many young mothers.

She had talked of it with Beatrice and together they engaged a midwife to give lectures in the church hall of Holy Trinity on the basic principles of baby care. They were taught how to bath their babies, their correct feeding and dress.

They were very successful and soon a committee was formed and the first clinic was thus established in Scarborough.

Annie was no spoil-sport. She loved dancing still, she loved the theatre, yet, often, she thought that Scarborough was dedicated to frivolity. She missed the underlying seriousness that she had known in Holland and which was apparent in the West Riding.

When Edward was on the council, Annie found that much more of the work of the hotel fell on her shoulders. She found increasingly, too, that they were beginning to lead separate lives.

The house was run by Annie, the food was still bought by

Edward. He took pains to know the butcher well and he visited the farmer who supplied milk and eggs.

He went out to the gardens of the smallholder who trundled his vegetables into the town on a truck. He went everyday down to the harbour to talk with the fishermen and buy their catch. He loved auction sales and bought well.

He had an eye for antique furniture and clocks, but as with so many hoteliers, there was always a leaning towards the opulent. Annie's taste was purer. It was she who bought the Hepplewhite chairs and the Sheraton sideboard. Annie had other extravagances.

The traveller from the Belfast Linen warehouse beguiled her with his expensive wares. He found that she unerringly chose the best. He returned every year, he congratulated himself on his astuteness, but Annie, interested in the Women's Movement, then noticed his patronising manner.

He began to refer to the 'fair sex' and he placed his rather plump hand on her sleeved arm. He went away aware that his hand had been firmly removed from her sleeve, yet the order still firmly booked. When he reached his head office, he found that the order had been countermanded and that Mrs Matthews was never at home when he later called.

The representative from the firm of Wedgwood was an entirely different matter. Well-dressed and impeccably mannered, he unpacked with fastidious long fingered hands his china from neat hampers lined with padded pale blue silk.

He brought out the blue jasper ware and Annie involuntarily gave a small gasp of pleasure. But she noted that the cups made a grating noise on the saucers that irritated her. The tea pots, jugs and basins could not be foregone, they were ordered, and many dozens of white and blue cups and plates of glazed china that blended.

Annie had a vision. The long low room overlooking the garden was to be a tea-room for the residents. While Edward was away she had it decorated by Harry, she made up blue curtains, bought table cloths of blue and white.

On the mantelpiece she placed the blue Delft clock, the present of the Van Prehns. The room was ready, the vision realised, she was thrilled. A few days later, the bill arrived from Wedgwood. She was so alarmed she took to her bed. She could not sleep.

She imagined again and again the terrible interview she would have with Edward. At last exhausted, she fell soundly asleep.

When she woke she only recalled the bill after a few minutes. Her fear had gone. She knew what to do - she must take Mr Borthwick into her confidence when he came to check the books that evening.

He advised her, he covered for her and he suggested that she saw the bank manager. They were all too eager to help a lady in distress and they made the way fatally easy for her. She was safe and in her new found safety crossed the road from the bank and gazed critically into the windows of Marshall and Snelgrove.

Annie's life was one of content. She was more fortunate that most of her friends in having work, which she shared with her husband. It was a task that enabled her to keep her family about her for most of the year, but if she had been asked to analyse her role she would have emphasized that of being a mother.

In fact, it was her maternal role that spilled over into the hotel with the staff, with the visitors.

With her daughters she had a special relationship and with Nancy it was particularly deep. What she did not realise was that she failed with her son, she repeated her own mother.

She wished to make her son into something he was not. She wished to dress him prettily, this he resented. She arrayed him, once, and only once, in a suit of bottle-green velvet with a collar and cuffs of lace. He was uncooperative when dressed in this Fauntleroy garment.

His mother and sisters declared that he looked sweet, his father merely growled. Alan wore it for the wedding they were attending and, like most people, forgot what he was wearing as things of greater interest and importance seized his attention.

When some time later he was asked to wear it again he resisted and he lost the battle, but a war does not consist of one skirmish. The road outside the hotel was being repaired, a huge tank of tar bubbled close to the front door... the thick glutinous liquid was being spread.

Hopping on the steps he happened to fall. He howled, the suit was ruined, his mother cross. The suit could never be worn again.

The three children remembered the entirety of their lives, the long stories, the equally long narrative poems their mother would retail to them. One poem was about a very boastful and impudent little pig. He never obeyed his mother, he annoyed everyone around him. On a walk a mastiff tore his ear, but still he persisted in his disobedience. By a well he wished to show his agility, he leapt, he fell and lamented in the water,

"Oh Mother, dear Mother", the drowning pig cried,

"I see all this comes of my folly and pride"

With that he sank and died,

While his mother and brothers wept round the well-side.

Ada and Nancy loved this story, but Alan was alarmed, he wept and was only comforted when his mother concocted an alternative ending in which the pig was saved and he began a new and better life.

Alan, the last of the children, found that he had to vie for his mother's affection. She listened to her daughters recounting of life at school, the injustices, the jealousies, the loves and the hatreds.

It was something she well understood. Alan had no such complications to relate, so, gifted with an imagination akin to his mother's, he told of his amazing encounters with lions which trotted down to the sea after eating two adults in the valley.

"Oh, Alan," exclaimed his sister Ada.

"It's true, it's true," he shouted.

"Yes, yes, I know, my dear, it all happened and then you woke up."

Then they all laughed, except Alan. Strangely Annie never seemed, until much, much later in her life, to remember her stories of daring and heroism when she had been so unhappy in Bradford.

There are varieties of blindness and Annie, for all her love, had blank patches.

The second Thursday of the month was Annie's day, the day she always half-dreaded, her 'At Home' day. First of all there was the food to supervise and as one never knew who was coming, one never knew how much to prepare.

The next anxiety was, "What if nobody comes?" The last apprehension never occurred. She did, however, enjoy dressing for the occasion and this Thursday she had a new gown of mauve silk and voile panels.

She was becoming a matronly figure and she did not mind unduly and everyone else thought it natural and fitting. When the last adjustment had been made she went downstairs, book in hand.

She sat by the fire in the drawing room and tried to read The Old Wives' Tale. She was enjoying it but at that moment could not concentrate. She rose up and moved a china ornament a couple of inches. She thought a picture was not quite straight and she re-arranged some gigantic poppy seed heads, painted, which were in a large oriental vase.

The first guest arrived. It was Beatrice - she seemed uneasy and though they kissed, as sisters-in-law do, there was restraint.

"What is it, Bea?"

"Have we offended you? Is everything all right?"

Annie was mystified, but not surprised. She had encountered this several times. Their husbands were rivals, but only Frank took this rivalry seriously. The two brothers-in-law plied the same trade, were both Freemasons, both were on the Town Council.

They mounted the steps of ambition together, were constantly compared. To Frank it all mattered, to Edward it was something which happened without undue effort. Frank took umbrage... Edward strangely managed to be both popular with his fellows and aloof at the same time.

It was, perhaps, the absence of striving that made him trusted. Honour, little honours, came his way with ease. Annie viewing her sister-in-law with some pity, said: "Has Edward walked past you again?"

With surprise, Bea answered, "Yes. He looked deliberately the other way. What have we done?"

"Oh, Bea, you should not take this to heart so. You know what he is like. He's done it before and, mark my works, he'll do it again. He was just thinking of something else."

As she said that she felt a pang and she wondered if he was pondering the cost of her new dress. He had not mentioned it, but that did not mean that he had not noticed it. And it was not yet paid for.

They were interrupted by the arrival of Mrs Tindall, Mrs Hopper and Miss Lancaster. Slowly the room began to fill and Annie moved serenely round the room, she was a swan, she knew it and she also knew that her pond was not her hotel alone, it was Scarborough now.

Everyone was talking and she looked through the Chinese Chippendale glass panelling and saw Ada and Nancy return from school. They looked at her, smiled, but went straight upstairs to change into party dresses.

They returned, Nana having brushed their hair, tied their sashes and straightened the lace of the deep yokes of their collars. They were beautiful children and Annie was proud of them. She watched them greeting people and talking. Ada was particularly good, Nancy a little slower and shyer. As she watched them ambition stirred, they must, they must go to a good school. By good Annie meant not only morally, academically good, but socially so. She would do something about it the next day.

The gathering surged, frothed and bubbled like the sea on the sands below the cliff, not so many yards away, and like the sea, the tide turned and ladies began to make their excuses, make their thanks and depart into the gathering dusk.

At her desk the following morning Annie wrote a letter to the principal of St Athelstan's school. She asked if she might see the school and arrange for her daughters to attend. She suggested a day in a fortnight's time when she might make the journey.

In the afternoon, she posted the letter with many others she had written and then she walked alone on the Spa. She was very calm and dreamt of the future and success of her children in luminous flashes, her thoughts kindled her face and her eyes shone and her lips curled into a smile at the visions she conjured for them.

She envisaged travel, society and a life of tamed adventure for them. The French Empire feel of the Spa helped the grandiose dreams. Though she herself felt secure, like most parents, she wanted a greater security for her children. It all seemed accessible.

Life was busy. The castles in the air disappeared, but were not forgotten. As she went through the letters in the office, she made neat piles, bookings, bills, estimates, Edward's world, and private correspondence.

There was one with a Skipton post mark. Eagerly she opened it, and as she had surmised, it was from the school. It thanked Mrs Matthews for her enquiry, hastening to say that its classes were full and, then, added that it did not think that the children of a tradesman would be happy at their particular establishment.

Annie winced and a tic quivered round her right eye. She left the office, almost as if it offended her. She crossed the hall and went into the deserted drawing-room. She saw nothing of its charm.

She went to the window, lifted back the lace curtain and gazed at the sea. It matched her mood... angry.

She saw life in the waves, all seemed set fair, a sudden wind and everything was in disarray. The physical sense of sickness subsided. Annie went out and to the dining room where Edward was slowly and deliberately spreading his toast with Oxford marmalade. He looked up and instantly said: "Is something the matter?"

"Yes, there is. I have been insulted. You have been insulted. Read this."

He took the letter. He, too, was angered.

"And that hoyden of the Forshaws goes there, doesn't she?"

"She does."

"Well, we found out in time didn't we? We don't want our girls to grow up to be snobs, do we?"

Annie looked at him, her non-church going husband, whom she thought, just now and then, not quite up to her standards, and she acknowledged that he was teaching her Christian philosophy. He was right - she had bolted with sudden ambitions. She bent down, and putting an arm round his shoulder, kissed his cheek.

"Thank you, Ted. I will write and tell them just that."

"Yes, you write it. You'll put it well. But don't post it until I have read it, will you?" Then he dropped his voice and added, "If you had asked me first I would have advised you not to write there anyway. Don't do that again, old girl."

"No, I won't, indeed, I won't."

She wrote a letter of great gentleness. It seemed meek, but it ended that the school's ethos and values did not entirely coincide with the Christian ideals of her husband and herself.

Annie shrugged off most things, but she had been stung.

It was only her dearest friend, Mrs Tindall, who noticed that Annie seemed not to concentrate on the needs of the person with whom she spoke as she usually did. It was unusual. Annie never forgot that lash to her pride.

After an unusually busy season, it was agreed that both girls should board at the school they were already attending in Scarborough. Ada questioned the necessity of this move, but, when, answered calmly accepted the decision and even enjoyed the camaraderie of the other pupils.

Nancy wept bitterly, she held very tightly to her mother's hand as they crossed the bridge to the South Cliff. Her deep unhappiness communicated itself easily to her mother, who began to feel that she was abandoning her offspring, unwisely she began to sympathise, but the fateful journey continued.

At the school's gates there was a burst of hysteria, but she was calmed. A teacher took charge, she ticked their names off a list. Then came the real goodbye. Ada had spied some friends and her apprehensions had departed - not so Nancy, she clung round her mother's neck, she felt the softness of her fur tie, it was a symbol of her mother's tenderness.

She was disengaged and a starched cuff scratched her hand as she was led to the dormitory. There she ran immediately to the window to watch the grey hat surmounted with wings below her being borne away a little irresolutely, but with gaining purpose. She howled.

The regime of the school took over completely, its rules, its notions, its so-called philosophy prevailed. But the gentle child had built an impenetrable fence. She would not be consoled and refused to be cajoled by her sister.

She ate very little, the staff tired of coaxing her. When they pointed out that the poor children of Leeds would love to have her food, she pushed the plate away from her and gladly offered it for them.

On the eighth day of her captivity she refused to get up. She would not speak and Miss Schofield, much annoyed, sent for the doctor.

Dr Jackson, a friend of her father, came. Nancy had never seen him before. He felt her pulse, he took her temperature, he tapped her chest and left the room. Out on the landing he said: "There's absolutely nothing wrong with that child. It is all in your hands. You will have to coax her."

Miss Schofield clicked her tongue against her teeth. It was all very troublesome and trying over one small spoilt girl.

They did succeed in getting her out of bed, she even began to eat, but was uncommunicative and plainly unhappy. The doctor came again and he asked to be left alone. Very patiently he questioned her and he received monosyllabic replies.

A short firm negative had come to the query about her happiness there. He stood up, began to put his stethoscope back in his

Gladstone bag. He looked at the pretty face... he had never seen such severe homesickness. To his astonishment, he heard a sentence flow from her mouth. He was astonished, too, at the sense,

"The trouble is you don't understand my case."

Without a smile he deferred to the nine-year-old.

"Don't you think so?"

She shook her head.

"What if I prescribe some medicine?"

"It won't do any good."

"You don't know what the medicine is. What if I say the best medicine is that you go home?"

She looked at him unbelieving, but could not dowse the leaping flame of hope.

"Then you do understand."

"I think I do."

In the hall he spoke to the headmistress.

"Miss Schofield, I think this child is still too bound to her home to be here."

"I quite agree. She had been spoilt. She is quite unlike her sister."

Miss Schofield regretted the loss of revenue Nancy, as a boarder, would bring. She was wise enough to see, however, that the unhappy child would be a poor advertisement. She also quite genuinely loved children.

Nancy was back in the classroom that afternoon. She learnt nothing, all her concentration was towards the close, when her mother would be there. It was with such joy she recognised the winged hat in the hall, but though Annie kissed her she was left to understand that she had been very naughty.

When Miss Schofield said, "Your mother has come to take you home. We have decided that you must be a day-girl after all", the sentence was unfinished and ended with the ominous words, "until you are a little older and more sensible."

Nancy looked appealingly at her mother, but Annie refused to give any sign of approval. Nancy knew that this was a battle she had won. She knew that she had a certain power and with a child's wisdom kept the knowledge to herself.

At home, she met with her father's hard stare, she set about beguiling him, she handed him his tea, without being asked, she folded her bread and butter as he wished. She made conversation with both her parents they had to join in. Within a half hour she was back in their good graces.

They were glad to have her home. Nancy discovered that she now had her parents to herself. Alan was still often with Nana in the nursery… she realised that she had a unique position and enjoyed it. She achieved a very special place in their affections.

The leisurely quadrille of Edwardian life continued its set of flirtation and dignity, a careful round abiding within certain rules. The women pretended that the life of their drawing rooms was real, but they knew that it was not.

The real world, one constructed and dominated by men, was outside their front doors. They opened the doors, they smelt the danger… they closed the door again. But there was a stirring of the consciences, a spirit at work that despairingly and overtly thrust a thin arm through the illusions with a demand. Annie and her friends were ready to meet the demand.

One day, as Annie sat in her office writing letters, a shabby woman came to the door. Harry, the porter, kept her on the step and brought Annie out to her. Annie sent Harry away, listened and then asked the woman in.

She was a widow with three children. Annie looked at the sharp, pinched but refined face, there was a similarity in situation to her mother - she was moved. She gave the woman tea as she recounted her woes, they were worse than Annie's mother had known.

She went into her office and took two sovereigns from the petty cash. The woman was deeply grateful.

Annie saw her out. She returned to the small table where the tea tray stood and noticed that all but two of the sugar lumps had gone from the basin. Her immediate reaction was indignation that the woman had stolen, but it was immediately expunged by sympathy for a woman whose need was so great.

The woman returned. She never stole again for she was confident of a piece of gold. She came regularly and Annie felt pestered and she then decided to investigate. She walked up to a court behind Queen Street. She found the house easily, she knocked… but there was no answer.

She turned the knob and entered. The floor covering was a sack before the range. By the low fire sat a Mongol child, who smiled…

Annie shuddered and called it an idiot to herself. The table was dirty. She began to tidy it up and found a cloth, then dusted the mantelpiece and the cupboard against the wall. Annie had never seen such penury.

Suddenly, the door burst open and two children rushed in opened a bag and poured on to the table a heap of crumbling cakes. Only then did they become aware of Annie.

"What are those?"

"Three pennorth of stale pastries."

As she watched the children joined by their deficient sister fell upon the food. The small unappetising heap soon disappeared and the two school children went out again. Annie took a chair and waited.

The minutes passed slowly by and shortly after two, as Annie had anticipated, when the pubs closed, Mrs Helme came in. Her face had the oily bonhomie of beer, but she was alert and immediately became fawning.

"Where was the dinner for your children?"

"They get it themselves when I am out."

"I have seen it. Stale pastries."

Within seconds, Mrs Midgley was being marched up the road to a butcher. There, three pennyworth of bones were bought. They were carried back. The fire was stirred, water was fetched from the pump and the bones put on to boil.

Annie only left when the soup was made, then rolling down her sleeves, picking up her jacket, she said, "I shall call again. I shall expect to find your children better fed, in clean clothes and you sober."

She put half a crown on the bare table.

"And I shall hope to find this table scrubbed."

Annie thought that her first duty was to get the Mongol child into a home and through Edward's contacts on the Council this was soon achieved. Annie kept an eye on the family, the house did become better kept, the children were better fed, but the lapses were many. She realised that the clinic she had started was very important.

Annie enjoyed this, she glowed when she saw babies being brought back better tended, better fed. But not for one moment did she think that her mortal clay was the same as theirs. As she often told her children "Noblesse oblige," and she very firmly meant it.

To be middle-aged, to belong to the upper classes and to be beautiful was to belong to a most privileged portion of Edwardian society. Men, moved by the same instinct as their king, revered a fine woman.

Annie occupied such a place and she had her admirers, one in particular, a close friend of her husband held an especial place. He came to see her frequently, he came to drink tea and gaze and to confess.

His relationship with Annie was une affaire blanche. But he had other passions which were not so white. He loved the theatre, he loved actresses. He was a chemist, they were often in need. He was able to supply their wants. Their demands upon his person and his purse alarmed his wife, who in turn was Annie's great friend.

Poor man, he thought himself in love, but really he worshipped from afar and turned his tea-drinking by Annie's fireside into acts of penitence in a confessional. Annie listened, she never showed shock and so, like so many of her protected class, learnt a great deal about the world from which they were parted.

All England was confined within the fences of respectability and conventions were paramount and in the middle classes they were stricter, more incisive. Some of the shibboleths of her husband's provincial respectability she deemed not only stupid and illogical, but hypocritical.

The profundity of her disapproval he discovered in the winter of 1912 when thick snow fell. It was this fine snow that drove Annie to confront her husband's unquestioned acceptance of his family's beliefs.

The snow fell and unusually in the salty air it lay. Annie with Kit, Nancy and Alan trudged through it to the service at Christ Church. They were all Sunday dressed and a little subdued.

The hearts of the children sank as the iron gate of the alley from Huntriss Row clanged behind them. They were missing sledging time. The hymns, the prayers, worst of all the Litany, dragged like a wounded snake before them.

Chapter 31

Town Councillor

At last the ordeal was over and Annie promised them, as they had been so good, that they could get out the sledge after dinner.

At dinner, Edward carved and Nancy, when asked what she wanted, replied demurely, but cunningly, "A long straight piece, please, Daddy, with no bones."

There was, this day, no need to chivvy the children into eating. They gobbled so much so that Edward chided, "Not so fast, no so fast. There's no hurry. You're not catching a train."

"No, but we are missing the snow. We must be off," said Nancy very firmly.

Edward looked up, over his forkful of food which he slowly lowered down to his plate.

"Sledging today, on a Sunday?"

"Yes, Mother says we can."

"You will do no such thing on a Sunday."

Annie looked up across the table.

"But I promised them, Ted. There's no harm."

"It is the Sabbath."

"That was yesterday, Ted, and we are not Jews."

"I will not hear of such a thing on a Sunday then."

Annie's wide blue eyes, nearly always mild, glinted.

"I shall not break my word to them, Edward. A promise is a promise. They have been to church." She could not resist it, "as we always do… which is somewhat more than you do. God won't mind if we go out in his snow."

"I forbid it then."

"But I don't until you give me one good reason why they shouldn't."

"What will people think?"

"That is what people always say who cannot think for themselves."

"I am shocked, Annie."

"Then shocked you must be for we all are going. The snow may have gone tomorrow."

Edward knew that he was beaten. He had not thought it out, he had only reacted. He grudgingly admired Annie... this firm side of her was rarely seen by him. She usually just circumvented him.

"Oh well, you go then. But you'll shock everyone."

The children had sat very quietly. They were totally unused to such argument. Nancy had begun to cry, she disliked the anger. Kit was the first to smile at Alan and Nancy, but it was Nancy with tears on her cheeks who said, "That's settled. You had better come too, Daddy."

"Well, I'll think about it. But oh, I really don't know."

He did and even more, he dragged the sledge up to the Mount and on the steep slope by Queen Margaret's School he piled the children on the sledge and shoved them off on the icy run that glistened where the other toboggans had been.

They slid quickly away and he ran quickly and agilely after them, catching them up mid- Ramshill Road where they slowed up to a halt. He grabbed the rope and ran and they glided along.

Near the Congregational church they gathered speed. Annie stood on the steps of the Cambridge Hotel with her sister and was aghast at the speed with which they all sped by. She was alarmed and without a word rushed after her family, fully expecting the sight of a crumpled broken mass of bones.

The sledge had gone down the steep road to the valley and the sea. She hurried along. Near the Aquarium she saw a crowd of people cheering the happy, excited sledgers. She saw from afar a tall man in a black coat thickly coated with snow rise up from behind a group of children. It was Edward.

"There won't be a button left on his coat."

She reached them all.

"Mummy, it was wonderful."

She beamed on them all... she saw them all as her offspring. Even as she smiled she thought how strange that her husband, the taboo once broken went so much further than she would ever have done.

Nothing, absolutely nothing would have induced her ride with them. She watched very happy, very secure, very pretty, very upright, holding her sable muff and aware of the soft touch of the matching fur at the nape of her neck.

She saw the Vicar join the bystanders, he was laughing, his children, too, were speeding down the hill. Kit, Nancy and Alan with glowing faces were looking up.

"My children, Canon."

He looked and stretching put his hand to the still snowy Edward said, "I did not know you had so big a boy."

Later, as they climbed the Zig-zag, all of them feeling triumphant, Annie said: "You see, Edward, we of the Church of England are not puritans like you dissenters."

He laughed. "I thought all chapels and churches were tarred with the same brush. Except you, you are always the exception."

That night as she read comfortably in bed, a fire in the grate sending leaping light and chasing shadows across the ceiling, she thought how fortunate she was. She loved Edward and she adored her children and she also loved helping run the hotel.

When thinking of her content, she thought of others. First there was her sister, Edith, running a larger hotel, but alone. That was not so easy. Then she thought of Mrs Midgley and the forlorn court near the Opera House... she vowed she would visit them next day.

The house was dirty once more, the fire had gone out. When Mrs Midgley returned, she immediately made excuses and Annie admitted that some were valid. But she asked, "Were you never in service?"

"No, ma'am, I was a waitress at Quigleys."

"So you never learnt to keep house."

That explained a lot. Working men whose wives had been in service in good homes invariably were better housekeepers and very often those women had higher aspirations for their offspring.

"You must find yourself a better place."

"How can I?"

There was justice in this question. Only a personal intercession on her behalf would find employment for this shabby, dejected and defeated woman.

"I will find you a place. I t will not be in a hotel."

Mrs Midgely became the twice weekly cleaner at the Vicarage in the Crescent.

More and more, Annie became the lynch-pin of her family and the hotel. The cry of the children as soon as they entered from school to one of the servants was, "Where is our mother?"

The immediate question of Edward when he returned from one of his many committees at the Town Hall was, "Where is your mistress?"

In these years Annie learnt to delegate and her place became just above the turmoil. Her calm affected the whole establishment and the dignity she had always possessed became more pronounced.

She never hurried and her expectation of deference meant that deference was nearly always given. Yet she never became hard, her regal bearing - and such it was - shimmered with quick sympathy.

Luckily, she possessed an equally quick sense of humour. It is interesting that her nephew, after 60 years in Australia, recalling her at this time, the close of King Edward's reign, described her as imperial.

Edward and Annie had, now, so good a union that they admitted their differences of taste. He enjoyed sport - he founded a Boys' Club and played golf. Annie did not care for physical activity, nor had she any desire after one attempt to accompany him to the golf courses of Jersey, or Scotland.

She had soon tired of the ladies' chit-chat in the club-house, or hotel. Neither, more strangely, had she any desire to visit France, so Edward went to Paris with one or other of his friend. It suited their purpose for one of them had to stay in the hotel. Therefore, it became the custom for Annie to take her holiday, after Easter, with her children.

Once they went to London, they stayed at the Strand Palace. They visited the Tower, the British Museum and many other sights. They attended a session briefly in the House of Commons and when leaving Annie took a short cut and they found themselves standing before the throne in the House of Lords.

There they were rescued and courteously escorted through the Great Hall to the outer world.

Yet, of all the things Nancy recalled most was how their mother paused in Whitehall in a cold wind, pointed out the window through which Charles I had emerged to be beheaded on the scaffold. The enormity of that deed was passed on to another generation. Annie was still a born teacher.

Annie noticed that Sarah Bernhardt was appearing at a theatre that very afternoon. The chance to see the legendary actress was too great, she argued within herself that it would help the children's French.

The last seats were at the front of the dress circle. The curtain rose and Annie entered another realm, she forgot her girls... she forgot her son. When the interval came, Annie to her astonishment, found three restive children.

However, tea came on a tray which diverted them. She handed her cakes over and was more than content with the thin bread and butter which she loved. Alan took out the cannon which she had bought him at Hamley's that morning.

He rolled it up and down the velvet covered parapet. Then he rolled some silver paper into a pellet and pushed it down the barrel. He shot it aimlessly into the air - it made a great arc and fell into the stalls.

Annie, thinking of the play, never heeded. Alan made another pellet. He inserted it and then took aim at the bald and perspiring head of the conductor who was trying frenetically to draw enthusiasm, feeling and subtlety from his orchestra.

He levered back the handle, released the spring and the missile sped with surprising accuracy. The bald head was struck and the enraged conductor turned and glared at the audience. There was a subdued titter. Annie was alerted and found her son's delighted face betrayed all.

"Alan, how could you. Poor, poor man. You are very naughty."

She grabbed the cannon and stuffed it back into its bag and glared at Kit and Nancy who were giggling.

"How could you? I am ashamed of you all."

Her back stiffened, her face looked troubled. They were quick to perceive her anger, which always manifested itself in grief at their behaviour. They were looking crest-fallen, when a military looking man in the seat behind took up a box of chocolates from his wife's lap, leant forward and said, "Here, young man, take these. You've given me the best moment in an awful afternoon."

The lights dimmed, the tigress tragedienne emoted, but for Annie the spell was broken. She was aware of her children's boredom and also that of others in the auditorium.

Alone that evening, Annie sat in the writing room, she was telling her sister of their adventures, but her pen ceased to move across the paper. She was still thrilled to have seen Bernhardt, but as she recounted it she was aware of how the real world had dragged her away from the world of imagination.

The world, she thought, always did that. Her whole life was doing it. She felt a shudder of sadness, but shrugged it off almost immediately.

Kit's trust in her mother was profound. She admired her mother's calm, so she was quick to see that her mother was becoming agitated when next day they were on a bus. The streets were becoming poorer, meaner, the people more ragged and bedraggled, they seemed to be in a different city altogether.

Annie's unease gathered strength when two policemen boarded. The sergeant remained on the platform, but the constable came down the gangway looking at the passengers.

He looked at them, then conferred with the sergeant who came forward while the constable kept watch. He asked Annie where she might be going.

"Quite the wrong direction, ma'am. You must leave at the next stop and we will see you back."

They alighted from the bus under escort. The evil of Limehouse affected Nancy who clung hard to her mother's hand. The sergeant talked humorously, but his jocularity was grim.

They walked, it seemed to Nancy, an unending street and at the corner stopped and the sergeant blew his whistle. An air of menace hung around. They waited, it was cold.

"I think we shall be all right, officer. We will find our way."

"We won't leave you unescorted for a moment, ma'am, so we need not discuss it."

From the gloom two policemen emerged. The sergeant handed his protégées over, saluted and turned away into the mist. One long street, followed another, and there was another wait until the next patrol took care of them.

Just as Annie began to despair in spite of their guardians, the busy maelstrom of a fashionable street glowed at right angles before them. The constable wished to put them on a bus, but Annie asked him to get her a cab.

He stepped into the road, stopped a hansom, and handed them in. The cabby spoke to them through a small trap-door, pulled a lever and the flaps, forming an apron closed in front of them.

They looked on the back to the gleaming horse, the reins fell in a curve before them, the horse led them into a current of cabs, carts, buses, motor cars and people.

Back at the hotel Annie ordered tea in their room. She had already said that it would be a good idea to return to Scarborough next day. As she drank tea, her courage returned, she no longer felt so tired.

"Perhaps one more day. We haven't been to Liberty's yet."

The event that pleased Annie most in the wider world was the introduction of the old age pension. It pleased her that Nana was able to feel a measure of independence. She had always displayed it, her sharp tongue had cut many pompous self-delusions to pieces, but she never forfeited the respect of any and strangely most especially those she had castigated.

Annie knew many others who were given a new view on life because of this pension. Yet in politics, she remained firmly Conservative.

King Edward died and his son George ascended the throne. The summer of 1910 was subdued in colour. Black, white and mauve prevailed in the fashions, but the happiness was not darkened, the spirit of the age remained.

It was at about this time that Mrs Pankhurst came to stay at the hotel. Annie was expecting someone more formidable and overbearing. She was surprised at the frailty and gentility of this great campaigner.

She attended the meeting in the Methodist Chapel. There were many people she had never seen before, many of course, were from afar drawn by the magnet of the famous name.

She realised that she was more elegantly dressed than most and, in a way, she felt rebuked. The other women were more earnest. She also felt that they had more reason to fight.

As the meeting progressed, she became even more impressed by the seriousness and as questioners stood, she discovered that she did indeed know many. The manageress of the gown department in Marshall and Snelgrove's made a very good point.

Annie had never thought of her other than as a fine appreciator and purveyor of delectable clothes. There were men, too, Mr Outhwaite, the solicitor, whose question became a speech.

She appreciated that he furthered the cause but he was always long-winded. Then she noticed the Vicar, their eyes met and they smiled. She was very surprised at his presence.

The arguments put forward seemed to Annie irrefutable.

Men were in charge, men did keep women down, even if they did it unthinkingly. She knew it from experience. She knew that her mother had been exploited, her sister was and she ruefully admitted that she was as well.

However, she had tougher thoughts when a young woman stood and enumerated the evils of men. Annie looked at her hat, her hair and her clothes and she said to herself, "What you say is true of your own experience because you have never tried charm."

It was then that she recognised that the meeting had been surprisingly lacking in humour.

As she left she encountered the Vicar again. "I did not know that you were a suffragette, Mrs Matthews?"

"Well, I am not quite certain that I am. Very nearly though."

"We shall have to talk about it one day. There are going to be many changes."

Back at the hotel, Annie made certain that there was tea and sandwiches for Mrs Pankhurst and her party when they retuned.

When she looked at the little woman so gentle, sipping tea by the fire. She found it difficult to link her with the woman on the platform with her rapid gestures. It was in the voice that she found the real link. There was a small strain of hysteria, or fanaticism. Annie feared it. She feared all violence.

The league that Annie joined was the suffragist. Its aims were the same, but it preached a more peaceful campaign and it had the backing of many prominent members of the Church of England.

Her loyalty increased as the Suffragette movement became more militant. She deplored the action of the suffragette who killed herself by hurling herself beneath the hooves of the king's racehorse at Ascot.

She was appalled at the violation of everyone's rights when letter boxes were set on fire. This upset her, she thought of important news between families being lost, hearts even broken. Letters had played such a part of her life, they still did.

Now as the owner of a hotel she wrote more letters than ever. She took great care over bookings, her letters were all written by hand. Her calligraphy remained as clear and as harmonious as ever, it always delighted recipients, for it summed her personality.

Yet she admitted that in writing courteous but formal epistles she lost the art of spontaneity. She thought her personal letters conventional and stiff.

In the late autumn of 1912 Edward was surprised to receive a letter from Berlin requesting a suite of rooms for one week in the name of a commander in the German Navy. Annie had some delight in replying to the letter in the same language as the request.

Within a fortnight the Commander arrived with his valet. He was handsome and debonair. His charm made Annie think she had misjudged the German people so long ago. She watched her visitor and was pleased when he kissed her hand and called her gnadige frau.

One evening, while everyone was at dinner she went into the drawing room for her usual inspection. When she made certain that the curtains were all hanging properly, that the cushions were plumped up and arranged, and the hearth cleanly swept, she found the Commander reading a newspaper.

He instantly rose and as the Dresden clock chimed, remarked upon the time and that he was late for dinner. He did not hurry away. Annie asked him what he had seen. It seemed remarkably little.

"Would you show me your town?" he asked.

It was arranged that they went out on a foray at 10 the next day.

He claimed that he had not been to the Castle. Annie thought this strange, for it was so obvious a landmark. She walked him there, explaining that it once had been a Roman signalling station.

He paced the green fields between the outer walls and the keep. With his binoculars he raked the harbour, the Spa and the North Bay.

As they walked down to the fishermen's quarter he asked her if she had enjoyed her time in Cologne. She was amazed, for she could not remember having told him that she had been there.

"How do you know?"

"Either you or Mr Matthews must have told me."

He asked her questions about the fishing fleet, the cargo boats and the steamer from London. She told him to ask her husband for he would know the answers better... he came to the harbourmaster most days. He seemed surprised that there was not even a token representation by the Royal Navy. Annie laughed but then thought how typical was that German reaction.

Next day, he went with his valet to Filey. He visited Bridlington and pleased Edward by comparing the elegance of Scarborough very favourably with the other resort.

When he left, both he and Annie thought that they could do with more visitors of his calibre. Only at dinner did Annie remember to ask him when he had told the commander she had been in Cologne.

He had not done so. She felt uneasy, Edward thought it odd, but they laughed at the thought of the Germans bothering to keep watch upon her all these years. Annie's suspicions were aroused but soon forgotten.

Life was busy, even in winter. Edward's duties to the borough became even greater when he was made a magistrate. He still found time, though, to decorate rooms during the off-season, Kit and Nancy and Alan were willing helpers and he never mocked their efforts. He never asked Annie, her portion was to choose the paper and the paint.

Edward was now 50. He was much mellower, given to periods of melancholy from which he could be rallied fairly easily. He remained a demanding father, Kit feared him. Nancy always intervened when there was trouble and invariably won.

With Alan he was both soft and hard... his inconsistency made it difficult. Annie's yea was her yea, and her husband's waywardness shocked her. She was known to have wept once when he formally beat his son.

She was more displeased when Alan had been sent to bed early for some misdemeanour by his father, who then discovered that there was a boxing match at the Boys' Club and he roused Alan to take him. Alan was triumphant but Annie's silent disapproval was manifest with them both.

When they had been small children, her greatest and most effective punishment had been to "Send them to Coventry." It always worked. Her silence could be eloquent and more powerful than words.

The servants knew this, too, and the absence of praise as noted. She used it even on her friends and quietened gossip by it. Regard was given to her gentle nature, her calm and sympathy was known.

She was very fortunate to live in an age that recognised this, for her age wished to conform… self-improvement came by adherence to it. Things were to change.

Chapter 32

The Great War

One morning mid-season, Nancy was helping her mother sort out dirty linen into laundry baskets. They were in the stone flagged basement behind the kitchen with the door open to the inner courtyard.

The two worked together counting the sheets and towels. When they were not counting they were talking of the family, friends and visitors. Nancy was much taken by a lady whose clothes each year were strikingly modish. This time she wore 'harem trousers', baggy masses of material gathered at the ankle.

When she stood still it looked like an exaggerated hobble skirt, when she moved the separate entities of the legs became apparent. This garment had caused great merriment amongst the guests and the owner, a cheerful extrovert, had gladly walked up and down the stairs and hall to show off the latest creation. Nancy's taste was much more modest, but she was nonetheless fascinated. Annie thought it most unbecoming and worse, ugly.

They heard the kitchen door to the area open, Maria pattered up the steps and then quickly down again, they went on counting. Then the door opened again and then running steps through the kitchen to their door which burst open without a knock.

"Ma'am, ma'am, come quickly, quickly."

Annie and Nancy looked at one another. They sighed inwardly, another catastrophe, another resignation, another flood of tears and all because something had curdled, or the meringues threaten to flatten.

"Come and see, quickly, everyone's coming off the sands, they are pouring up the Cliff."

They followed her, but Nancy ran ahead up the area steps. It was true, whole families with buckets, spades, chairs, towels and parasols were marching purposefully up from the shore and into the town. It was flight, it was decampment.

"How strange… what can it mean." Annie turned down the frilled cuff of her blouse sleeve, buttoned it. She was perplexed and a woman sensing her perplexity said, "It's war."

Annie, calling Nancy went in at the front door. She was quickly followed by a new family from Paisley, they looked flustered and the children were upset. Mr Ogilvie asked for his bill, adding, "We have to return immediately. I'm a territorial."

"Then we are at war with Germany?"

"I fear so."

"Go and pack and I will have your bill."

In the office she lowered the mahogany flap of the counter. As she held it, she seemed to feel the whole world tip and she was seized with a terrible aching and echoing fear that was physical as well.

It seemed in an instant that she foresaw all, a strange vision, remote beyond anything of her experience… it was darkness, death, terrible noise and a terrible immobility that seemed eternal. She pulled herself together, sat down and snapped at Nancy,

"Give me the bill forms."

Nancy picked them up, but was shocked at so peremptory an order from her mother. Annie saw it. "Sorry, my dear. I don't feel very well. I really want to cry, but we shall be too busy."

Other families came in with the same demand - she asked them all to pack. When the Ogilvies returned wearing travelling clothes, she felt that she was looking on him for the last time. She took his cheque and went with them to the door.

"We'll soon have this thing cleared up. We must make a good show at the start. Then we shall all return to your beautiful town. It's a pity, but there it is."

Annie's round eyes were like troubled seas, the blue seemed grey, but a smile came to cancel out her fears. To reassure was her constant habit.

"Of course you will. But tell me are you sure of the trains?"

"We will go to York by the first available and back to Scotland as fast as we can. Ordinary time-tables will be awry, anyway. Troop movements, you know."

Annie saw that he was already the officer.

"Of course, of course. Good luck. God be with…"

She turned into the hotel her chin quivering.

This was all so much more sudden than the Boer War which had crept up on them. There was no time to think, the office was besieged... almost everyone was going home. It was a calm panic, an instinct of them all to be on the patch of earth they called their own. That seemed to be where safety lay, or where the call to duty would be heard.

Again and again Annie wrote the date... August 4, 1914. As she wrote it she knew that she would never, never forget it.

The hotel was half empty. It was sad for the weather was splendid. At a stroke, Scarborough had assumed its winter character. It all seemed unreal such emptiness under a blue, blue sky.

The phrase that it would all be over by Christmas wore thin swiftly. Annie had always mistrusted such optimism, it was founded on ignorance. She had not forgotten the only just contained frenzy of patriotism she had seen in Cologne on Sedantag.

She remembered Germany's vast resources, and above all, its huge army and the militant streak in most people that she feared. She could not forget, either, the mysterious premonition in the office when the world seemed to tilt on the first day of war.

Her belief in her premonition was strengthened when she received a letter from Mrs Ogilvie telling her that her husband had been killed in the retreat from Mons.

Edward volunteered but was disqualified because of his age. He was told that his duties lay on the home front. He enrolled in the Special Constabulary and to his children's amusement was given a truncheon.

September and schools were open again and the absence of visitors was no longer noticed for they were not expected. In spite of the news from France, life began to resume a normal aspect.

Annie found herself, like Edward, dropping into the sale-rooms in Huntriss Row to see what was being offered. Their desire to beautify the hotel was back again. The news grew worse.

November and December came. With Nancy's birthday came the first gleam of light, at least for Nancy, when she awoke on her birthday. She turned in bed and for a moment felt fear, she had touched something like an animal.

Sleepily she put out her hand and, as she did so, knew what she was to encounter. It was a muff, the present she so desired. Her joy was so great she fell into a sleep of blissful contentment.

Three days later it was Annie's birthday, her 52nd. Alan, at Drax, remembered the day and sent a card of very gaudy roses with an edge both deckled and embossed. His mother thought of him choosing it in the village post-office.

From Kit she got a fern which she hoped she might keep alive and from Nancy a handkerchief sachet which she had made herself.

She dressed slowly, she always did, today as she brushed and combed her hair she looked into the mirror more critically. She saw a much plumper woman than had been reflected even five years before.

She still had a waist, but she was thicker in body and her face rounder. She sighed with relief when she peered nearer and looked at her skin, it was pink and white and almost without wrinkle. Her complexion was as finely grained as when she had been in Holland.

"I am lucky in this. After all there is little merit in being handsome at my age."

This she said to herself, but she did not believe it. Then she recalled a sermon she had lately heard of the body being the temple of the spirit. She agreed, temples were places of beauty and decorated for the Gods.

With this muddled justification she chose rings for her fingers and the pearls she always wore around her neck. She thought of the visits she would receive, first there would be Edith, then Beatrice and Annie Chapman, but her real anticipation was reserved for her dearest friend, Florence Tindall. The birthday went well.

On the morning of the 16th, before dawn there was a scream followed by a muffled crash. Edward woke first. "What was that?"

"The sweep is here, dear. Perhaps he has dislodged a brick in the chimney."

"That was no brick, no chimney sweep."

He leapt out of bed and as he did so there were more whistling screams and heavy thuds and the whole house shuddered. Edward rushed out. There was a rush of feet along the corridors, doors banged and a babble of voices.

Kit and Nancy burst in and ran to the bed. They were about to jump in, but their mother was getting up. There were more rushing noises, more violent rattles to the very foundations and the sound of window glass tinkling to the ground.

Fear spread like a dark stain throughout the little community, residents, staff all converged upon the bedroom all crying: "What shall we do? Where shall we go?"

Annie seemed to tower, she looked at them all.

"You will remember that you are Britons."

There was a little silence and then she continued, "You will go to your rooms, put on your warmest clothes and go down into the basement."

Without another word they vanished except for the two girls. Annie turned to them and said: "Get dressed, come back and keep your heads high. There are no cowards in this household."

As the girls dressed, the shells exploded outside and Kit was so frightened she jumped into the wardrobe. Nancy seized her and very firmly said, "Mother says we are to get dressed."

In the basement in the corridor, the kitchen to the left and the staff hall to the right, everyone assembled. Annie announced, "You will be perfectly safe here."

She called for a chair, climbed on it and counted the people.

"Where is Mr Brigg?"

"Who's Mr Brigg?"

"The chimney sweep."

Nobody had thought of him. Then Annie said: "Has my husband come back?"

Nancy without waiting ran up the stairs, she ran through the hall to the window of the drawing room, her heart leapt with pride and fear at the same moment.

She could see her father at the bottom of the Cliff looking out to sea with his telescope.

"Nancy, come away from that window this instant. Where is Mr Brigg? I thought he was in here."

She whisked around and crossed the hall and into the Chinese room. Bent before the fireplace, the chimney sweep was moving his brushes on their long rods.

"Mr Brigg, Mr Brigg, you must leave that immediately and come down."

"Not me, Ma'am. I shan't budge until I've done this job. Not for a few Germans."

"But I insist, Mr Brigg. This is my house and I shall not have you killed in it."

Neither of them saw that Nancy had run to the door. She had seen her father running up towards home. The door was of solid oak, nearly 200 years old, the same age as the house and it had swung perfectly all that time but its alignment had been changed in the last half-hour.

The shells burst more intensely followed by the splatter of metal on the pavement. To Nancy it was a nightmare, she tugged, she pulled at the large brass door knob. Her father pushed on the other side... it would not shift.

"Stand back, Nancy, I'll run at it with my shoulder."

With a scraping screech it shifted over the tiles, he leapt in. Together they closed it and then bolted every bolt and turned the key.

Down below, tea was being dispensed and everyone was eager to hear what Edward had to tell. He thought that there were three destroyers in the bay. The Grand Hotel had received the brunt of the bombardment.

He told them that in the lulls the ships turned to fire more broadsides. The screaming shells, the sound of falling masonry continued, then quietness came and gradually they all relaxed.

"I'll go out again to see what is happening," said Edward.

"No, please dear, wait a little longer." And everyone agreed and he waited another 10 minutes. The light grew stronger over the door, creeping in at the fanlight. Edward went to that door and up the area steps.

Courage returned, voices began to rise and toast as well as tea came round. Maria started cooking some bacon and the most fearful heart filled with daring.

Edward returned. "They are sailing away."

"Then I can get on with my chimneys."

"Do be careful, Mr Brigg."

"I'm as careful as I can be, you know, Mrs Matthews."

His professional pride had been hurt. Annie knew instantly,

"Goodness me, Mr Brigg, not about dust. I mean your life."

The remainder of the day was alive with rumours, the main one being that German soldiers had landed at Filey. The railway station was besieged.

Sixteen people were killed and some quite far inland. Innocent lives had been despatched to an eternal silence. Britain was shocked that its shores had been attacked - Whitby and West Hartlepool all suffered after Scarborough. The War Office, for the first time, realised Britain had a coast line and troops were sent to the seaside.

Annie voiced her disillusion to Edward and asked: "Where was our Navy?"

War for the Matthews had begun in earnest. Annie read between the lines the accounts of the battles. Her premonitions were being most dreadfully realised.

On New Year's Eve, Edward sat staring into the fire. "What is it, Ted?"

"I cannot go on like this, Annie, with nothing real to do. We cannot even afford it."

"But, my dear, the place is to be commandeered, we shall be paid."

"Very little. I don't expect it will cover the damage. I must go and find some employment. My old skill with clocks and having a steady hand should make me useful somewhere."

Annie suddenly knew that he was hiding something. She knew that she was on the edge of discovery, so let it take its course.

"Where would you be useful?"

"In munitions - setting bombing devices."

Annie was appalled, the colour drained from her face. She feared for him, even more she was repelled that he would be making instruments of death. Her horror came out in a jumbled and muddled fashion.

"But, if I don't make them, I shall be helping Krupps make still more. This is a terrible war, a very terrible war."

"I know, oh Ted, I do know that."

"Well, my dear, I have applied and I have been accepted and very soon I shall have to go to Leeds."

Annie rose, she held on to the mantelpiece.

"It is going to be so horrible a year for everyone, everyone. I don't wish to wait up for it."

"You are absolutely right, dear. I'm coming, too. At least I'm not like those poor devils in France."

"No, dear, no."

So 1915 came and in February, Edward was making instruments of the finest precision and fitting them to torpedoes. Every fortnight he came home for a weekend. It was usually Nancy who met him at the station and walked with him back home.

The girls were at a small private school, with their cousins, run by a retired public schoolmaster, Mr Latham. Their former school had evacuated itself to Ilkley after the bombardment.

Nancy learnt more in her short time at this school than ever before. She liked the old man and her regard was returned. He was unused to dealing with girls… they hoodwinked him more than boys had ever done. He trusted Nancy and one day he said to her mother, "Your daughter has the honour of a gentleman."

Annie remembered that the rest of her life. It made her proud and mostly because she knew that it was true.

Life was far from inactive at the hotel. It threatened to be full of soldiers, cavalry men. Annie had her much-reduced staff making up the beds. The Colonel came to inspect, looked quickly around, then turned to Annie and said: "I will send some men to do the job. All these carpets must come up."

Annie was surprised and when she took him up to the bedrooms, and he found beds neatly made up, he gasped.

"Mrs Matthews, most of my men don't know what a sheet is. They have never had one at home. I beg of you to strip these beds immediately."

Annie smiled. She neither assented, or dissented. She knew exactly what she was going to do, the sheets would be left exactly where they were, she would see that these men were received with hospitality.

She knew what lay ahead for them and wanted their time beneath her roof to be comfortable.

A week later, she had to admit that the Colonel had been right. The sheets were stained and ripped for some had gone to bed not just with their boots on, but had not bothered to remove their spurs! Annie never complained to the Colonel, she never admitted to Edward the expense and loss.

It seemed that Annie's family was suddenly expanded and every evening there were homesick soldiers sitting by her fire sharing their lives with her. She had removed the sheets, but she knew that the Colonel was wrong when he said that most of his men did not know what a sheet was.

Annie's knowledge of the lives of many widened almost beyond belief. When the men left they gave her pledges of themselves, buttons and badges, she put them in a basket. She looked at them and grew ashamed that she could not remember precisely who had given them to her.

Picking up a West Yorkshire Light Infantry badge, she recollected quite another man in its connection. She sighed and hoped that her prayers were answered. Some wrote to her. She was amused and disheartened by their phrases, "in the pink" was a very popular expression and they nearly all ended with, "hoping this reaches you as it leaves me at present."

She was deeply moved - that so many of her correspondents never wrote again was not lost upon her. She hated, hated the war. There was one manifestation left with her forever of this hatred, she could never tolerate loud bangs and explosions again. Fireworks were anathema to her.

Spring almost surprised her... she almost thought that the seasons would cease. No visitors, nowhere to put them, anyway. Annie began to feel insufficiently occupied. Edward was lonely... he was looking grey and tired.

Annie and Kit decided to join him in Leeds. Nancy was to remain at school, this plan she very soon reversed, she was not going to be left behind, even with the dearest of aunt's.

Edward was at the station to meet them. Annie noted, at once, the greyness of the sky, something she always associated with Leeds. They went by tram to Headingley where they approached a large Gothic house with a gloomy garden of laurels and rhododendrons whose leaves all wore a cerement of crusty soot.

The interior of the house was dark, solidly furnished. It seemed to gloat in its dull durability. Everything pronounced its worth and its respectability, even the aspidistras.

Kit, very quickly, found herself a job in a brick company, she was in the office filing letters. Annie by no means approved and before she had made up her mind, the same company had offered a post to Nancy on the telephone exchange board. She thought that all would be righted after the war.

Annie was left at home. She began by rearranging the furniture in their rooms. She put the stamp of her personality upon it. She spent what she had never done before, a long time cooking food for her workers when they returned.

Soon everything fell into a pattern and she had time on her hands. She walked for miles and miles investigating her surroundings, she wandered far from the prosperous suburbs, she came to the miles of mean streets. Her sense of justice was enraged when she talked with wounded men sitting on the steps of their poverty-stricken homes. Was it for this they had fought, she wondered?

She was upset and she thought she was upset because she was not fully occupied. Her sympathy was even a kind of indulgence. Twice a week she helped run a canteen for servicemen.

There she met another volunteer, a sweet but anxious woman with both a son and a husband at the Front. Annie discovered that she was also the owner, with her husband, of a munitions factory at Hunslet. To Annie, the makers of munitions were faceless evil people, but she was surprised.

She was even more surprised when Mrs Osselton asked her if she could take over the management of the canteen at the factory. Still greater was her surprise when she found herself approaching the place one morning to take over.

It was a grimy place of poor brick with one yard leading to yet another and large sheds sprawling over the waste scrubby land. It spelt despair to Annie and she felt herself shrink in stature.

She showed her card to the man at the gate and he cheerfully directed her. She followed signs to yet another low brick shed, it was the canteen. She opened the door and immediately came upon a woman wearing a man's cap slopping dirty water from a still filthier mop and pail.

"Good morning."

"G'morning."

"Are you a Yorkshirewoman?"

"Aye and where might you be from?"

Annie almost answered Scarborough, but quickly substituted Milnsbridge. "And there, might I say, we pride ourselves that in spite of a lot of muck we are very clean. Please change that water, at once. And before you ask who I am, I am Mrs Matthews, your new manageress."

The woman scuttled out of the door through which Annie had just entered. Annie surveyed a fleet at anchor of grey rather greasy tables. She looked with horror at the hand marks round the hatch behind a grime encrusted counter.

She wondered with real sickness what the kitchens would be like. She opened a door and saw women preparing vegetables, further on another woman was cutting up meat, she sighed with relief, the women and the place were clean.

She introduced herself and shook their hands and very carefully memorised their names. The senior woman led Annie to a tiny office with glass panels. It smelt fusty and airless with cigarette smoke. She propped open the door into the kitchen.

She took off her hat and carefully lifted her curls that had been flattened by her headgear with her hat-pin. From a bag she took out a capacious white apron, one of Maria's, and put it on.

In the kitchen she found the menu for the day, stew followed by rice pudding. She watched the knife being urged laboriously through the hunks of red flesh. "That will never be tender by lunchtime." She vowed that stew would be prepared the previous day. She found the women suspicious. She wondered what had happened to the previous holder of her place. It was as she came out of her office she heard, "Hoity-toity, I should think."

That she thought must be me.

"Perhaps I had better live up to it."

At noon, as she looked at the meagrely stocked larder, she was startled by the siren, followed by a human surge of women and girls pushing, elbowing and shouting at the counter.

Annie looked at them with amazement. They were as voracious as a pack of wolves, they were greedy. The money they had earned had made them bold. There was a sudden dispute about the amount of meat on a plate.

Annie moved forward to see that justice was at least attempted in the ladling. She gave thanks that she had once been a schoolteacher.

Very swiftly, like all meals, the result of much work was soon dismissed, and the place was empty.

The staff opened an oven and took out a smaller dish. The table in the kitchen had been laid with a white cloth, she saw a tray prepared… she knew that it was for herself. It was going to be brought to the stuffy little enclosure.

"I will join you at the table, if I may?"

At the table silence fell. Annie took no notice, she chatted, she found out where they lived and if they had children.

The ice was broken, as she knew it would be. They drank strong tea and a packet of cigarettes was produced. Annie unhesitatingly imposed her first rule.

"I am sorry, if you wish to smoke, you must go outside. I cannot possibly allow it in the kitchen."

There was a slight shrug but the packet was put away. In their place came photographs, pictures of children and of husbands. Three of these were in France and Annie's heart turned as she looked at the stiff pictures of men in uniform sitting in the clutter of photographers' studios.

"But I know this man," she exclaimed.

It was of a stocky man who had been billeted at Scarborough, he had sat one evening by their fireside.

"Are you the lady at the hotel who put sheets on their beds?"

"Yes."

"Well, my Herbert thought the world of you."

Annie felt both embarrassed and weak. But she was astute enough to see that those wretched sheets had won her an ally.

When they had cleared up, Annie found new places in cupboards for brooms and mops which had until then huddled in a corner. She pushed open windows – but the air that came in was not fresh, it held the tang of chemicals.

As the women left Annie stood by the door, as she would in school and wished them good-night. When they had gone she took real stock of her domain. The kitchen was clean, the dining room, as she ever persisted in calling it, was grimy and the larder sparse. She wondered about her priorities, her instinct was to clean the whole place up, brighten it. However, reason told her that she was running a canteen and first essential was food.

"Stock up your larder, as best you can. See your suppliers," she said to herself.

That night she took home with her a batch of invoices to note the names. Edward and the girls were amused by "Mother's job" and she felt affronted and when the teasing had gone far enough she replied.

"I don't understand any of you. Edward, ever since I married you I've had a job. Kit, do you think St Nicholas ran all by itself. You are a strange lot."

She was put out, but Nancy steered her to the fireside, brought her the attaché case of invoices and pencil and book. As the rest washed up Annie lost herself in the revelation of these papers.

As she had suspected, enough food had been coming in, it was in the kitchen it was "lost". She knew that she must keep a vigilant eye. She would continue to bid them all good night at the door, it would make it harder to smuggle out packets and parcels.

Yet she did not suspect the women, beyond the pettiest of pilfering. She thought it was her predecessor.

So began for Annie an unexpected period in her life and often she said to herself Nelson's words, 'a long pull and a strong pull.'

It was with amazement that Annie encountered quite open bribes from the representatives who came to see her and at a time of apparent shortage. Her manner usually became grander with her distaste. But she reserved it for the tradesmen.

Still, she sat with the women for dinner and it proved the most rewarding part of the day for them all. With their enlistment they spent two afternoons scrubbing every inch of the 'dinning hall', they all brought pictures for the walls.

It took a year for it to be re-decorated. Annie thought she noticed that there was less pushing, less raucous laughter.

This canteen had been she knew, from the start, a little battleground. She had won the first battle by her usual means of guile and manoeuvre. There was another battle, though. Beneath her beauty, her easy elegance lay not just a strange practicality, but a moral seriousness.

She was the product of her mother and those maiden lady teachers in Leyden - it had never been lost under the Edwardian gaiety. She still looked at the women claiming their food each day with some dismay and the snatches of conversation appalled her.

She never forgot that their work meant the deaths of many and she was logical enough to include herself. Perhaps because of that logic she was given drive to try to put it right. She was well aware that poverty and constriction had driven them to these factories.

She appreciated their delight in freedom and having money to spend. She deplored, though, their notion of finery, but it was their heedlessness that hurt her.

They seemed to ignore the war. She understood, but felt that their minds needed to be prised open. She was shocked to the very core when she overheard a girl say with a laugh, "as for me this war can last forever."

Annie pinned up a notice board in the 'dining room' with a map and little flags, she put up pictures of the front but this defeated its own object for she could not forbear showing the more heroic and compassionate elements of the conflict. She noticed that after initial and glancing interest it was as ignored as the other pictures on the wall.

The winter of 1917 was trying to everyone. War had tired everyone. Kit and Nancy were surprised when their mother snapped at them. It was out of character. Annie was worried about Nancy who looked, as she termed it, 'peaky'.

She needed to take them away and Beatrice invited them all to Scarborough for Easter. It was gladly accepted.

At York station when they crossed the bridge to another platform, Kit, Nancy and Annie all felt elated and a sense of elation came over them. The greyness of the West Riding was fast receding behind, the particular gris-noir of Hunslet way, way behind.

The girls saw their mother take a sudden lighter step and her eyes sparkled. She was free.

The White girls were all on the station awaiting their arrival. Ethel, the eldest, took her aunt's arm and they all walked up to Tranby House. Ethel thought her aunt looked tired and worn. Above the High School Annie stopped and looked across,

"Just look at the valley, Oliver's Mount", then she lowered her voice and with strange love said, "And the sea." Then some tears came in her eyes.

"What is it, Auntie?"

"I am just being silly. I began to think I should never see it again. I am just so happy to be home."

"You need a rest, I can see. After lunch it is straight to bed. You've been overdoing it."

Annie smiled, and squeezed the loving girl's arm in her own. It was wonderful to be cosseted.

At Tranby the sisters-in-law met, kissed one another and looked appraisingly at the other. Lunch was ready.

As a good meal was eaten, Annie felt glad to be with part of Edward's family again. She was, in fact, fonder of them than he. Bea was sweet but constrained, she was ever thus. There was a divide in temperament... there was the rivalry in business, the Council by their husbands.

There was in Bea a greater reserve than Annie ever appreciated, her own marriage was so much easier.

Annie never knew whether her sister-in-law was very wise, or a little stupid. She was wise, but, nonetheless, deeply hurt by her husband's infidelities. She reacted in a truly Victorian manner by pretending that none of these affairs had happened.

It preserved her marriage. Annie's life was not so complicated - the only stumbling block was finance.

The next day was Good Friday. Annie had equipped herself with black and the two families walked up to St Mary's for the three-hour Service. The black cross set high above the chancel arch in the shadows looked dark and murky.

Annie never liked it, but thought it appropriate for the day. The crucifixion was a dark and horrid business. The Vicar spoke of the cross dropped jerkily into the hole in the ground, making the wounds scream with pain beneath the sudden dragging weight.

Annie immediately thought of the men wounded in the trenches, dying where they were, or jolted on stretchers. It was all an intolerable nightmare. Her patriotism and her work upheld her, but her imagination was too vivid for her to be duped by the Daily Mail, though she loved it.

She welcomed Lloyd George's premiership, even though she did not trust him. He was younger and had more energy than Asquith.

A phrase from the pulpit summoned her straying thoughts. She looked at her watch - an hour and a half had gone by. She looked at her sister-in-law, they both nodded almost imperceptibly and then nodded to the girls. They knew that in the next hymn they could go. Outside, the girls opted to walk down Paradise Row to Sandside and then to walk back along the Foreshore and up to their home. As always, Nancy and Sybil linked arms.

"When you've left school and the war is over, what do you want to do, Billy?"

"I'd like to be a nurse."

"So would I."

Ethel and kit became involved in the conversation. Ethel kind and dutiful had not thought beyond running the house for her mother. It was Kit who surprised them all,

"I'm tired of offices and buildings. I hate Leeds. I want to be a landgirl and work on a farm and now, not later."

"Oh Kit, mother will have a fit. She wouldn't like you getting dirty."

"You'd talk like a yokel. All eehs and aahs," said Ethel.

"I wouldn't. Anyway it was you who shocked your mother by saying, after a summer on the farm, 'gie us a bit of baacon in me 'and.'"

They all peeled with laughter and ran along the sands, their skirts, two inches shorter than their mother's, giving them greater freedom.

Back in the church the two mothers sat together. They were each precise and very respectable, but each in her own way. Beatrice was tall, upright and thin with a frail dignity, Annie plump, matronly almost without wrinkle, a rather aristocratic little partridge.

Each of them was worried. Beatrice wondered about her husband in France working with the French Red Cross. Annie was anxious about Edward. He was working far too hard, especially as he was now an inspector for the Government, going from factory to factory. He should have been with them, but he would not stay at his brother-in-law's house.

Another dread of Annie's was that if the war lasted much longer, Alan would be called up.

The service over, the two tall women walked down the hill. They passed the Opera House and turned up Westborough. All the shops were shuttered and barred. Good Friday was like a national funeral and in 1917 more significant than ever. The sun was warm and Annie slipped off her fur and looked at the blue sky.

"It's going to be a lovely weekend for the visitors."

"But you are one," laughed Bea.

"So I am. I always feel sorry for the people from the West Riding. And, look, I am one."

The mothers caught up the girls before they reached the house.

"You must all be famished. Soon there'll be tea."

As they ate toast and hot cross buns the bell rang. It was Alan. Annie ran to him and clasped him. He was resentful.

"I thought you'd be at the station."

"But you know where we were, dear. You are a big lad. We've all been to church."

She led him into the drawing room. He rather perfunctorily kissed his aunt, then settled with his cousins. With them he seemed a different being. Annie noted it, not for the first time she wondered if she would ever quite understand her son.

She even wondered why she hadn't gone to the station. It just had not crossed her mind. She would have gone for either of the girls. She saw in him something of her brother... intractability.

"Oh well, early days," she said to herself, consolingly.

Easter Day, the sun shone. The bay sparkled in the light, making great paths that shimmered to the horizon. The houses shone, roofs glinted... there were yellow daffodils beneath the bare sycamores.

A smoky haze hung over the harbour, but even that Annie considered an entirely different smoke to that of Leeds.

There was much chatter as old friends were seen they all became excited and the war drew away from them all. Yet later in the day Annie noticed some very over-dressed visitors, a kind new to Scarborough. She recognised them as the profiteers.

She disapproved not only of their wealth but their taste. Some of the men looked just like the cartoons she saw in Punch... fat, a little greasy, with cigars and gold tie-pins a shade too large.

At lunch it was a bunch of white swallows around the table. Only Alan was different in his tweed suit and maleness. The rest wore white blouses and worsted skirts - it was a uniform. The two older women suddenly felt cold.

"Nancy, would you fetch me a cardigan from my room?"

Upstairs, Nancy herself felt cold. She got her own cardigan, then raided every room and went down with a bundle of woollens. The light seemed different, she looked up to the dome... it was opaque, no longer clear. She opened the dining room door and said: "Look at the snow."

It was falling fast. It was Annie who said, "I hope it's not falling on those poor fellows in France."

On Monday, Kit and Nancy accompanied their mother to St Nicholas. It looked like the day, cold bleak and grey. Paintwork was peeling, the curtainless windows looked blind and blank. Their hearts sank.

The door was answered by a private. Annie asked to see the officer-in-charge. A young subaltern came, removing a cigarette from his mouth. He saw Annie standing very upright at her own front door.

"I would like to see my private rooms."

There were muffled demurrals, Annie did not smile and the young man went away for the major. As they waited Annie's eye roved. She was relieved to see that not one pane of the glass had been broken in the Chinese Chippendale screen between the hall and the drawing room, now an office.

The floors, though, upset her, very scratched and grooved, hollowed by the door and very rough with hobnails and spurs. She looked to the staircase and almost gasped - the centre of each tread was hacked as if by a jagged saw. More work of the spurs.

The major arrived and he led Annie to the locked rooms. Entering her mauve sitting room at the back, she beamed to see her desks and tables. She opened a cupboard - her ornaments were exactly where she had placed them. She looked at the Major.

"Thank you, thank you. You have been a good steward."

The bedrooms were the same.

As they went down, the major leading, turned and said: "I am sorry about these staircases. But the War Office will compensate."

The girls were surprised at their mother's reply.

"The Tsar has lost his throne. Thousands have lost their homes. It is not in me to grumble about floor boards."

They found that Maria's kitchen was used only as a canteen for tea and cocoa. It looked empty, forlorn.

"Do you think there is any possibility of our returning now and again?"

"You were here when the first troops came. I think it might be possible. But you never know with red tape."

Annie suddenly turned to Kit. "Why don't both of you go and see if the bicycles are still in the snicket under the scullery."

As soon as they had gone, Annie said: "I am worried about my younger daughter. I want to take her away from the bad air. She is not well."

The girls returned. "Yes, they are all right, but they've got flat tyres."

The major laughed. "Leave them that way, they'll by safer."

Annie returned to Leeds, her intention to get back to Scarborough as soon as possible. But her task there was by no means done.

Edward was glad to see them. Annie's first thought on seeing him was that he looked drawn and tired, he was ageing. Youth had clung to his thin long frame a great while, but it had gone... the long hours, the deep concentration had taken their toll.

He listened patiently to their stories and not until Annie mentioned the stairs at St Nicholas did he really respond, "What a damned shame. Sir Richard Arkwright built and climbed those very stairs. It won't be the same when the treads are new."

Their work entangled them all and Annie was trapped in the routine of the canteen. Once again she wanted to widen the imaginations of the girls there, but how to do it? She seemed defeated.

The answer came through Kit and Nancy who with other friends visited a hospital at Temple Newsam every Saturday. At first, Annie in a fit of maternal protection had not wanted them to encounter gruesome sights.

They had been horrified by her objections and their father had backed them. Annie soon saw how ill this spasm of concern matched with her general attitudes, even her patriotism.

The girls had been upset, but they soon recovered and it was they who said, "Why don't we put on a big spread for the fellows somewhere and get them out of the hospital for a while?"

A hotel proved too expensive and then Annie thought that this was just what was needed at Hunslet.

"Let us entertain the lads at the canteen. I'll get the women interested."

A collecting box was sent round the tables on pay-day, enthusiasm kindled... and very soon, Annie had more volunteers than she needed.

One afternoon early in the summer, when the sun tried to pierce through the perpetual haze, the bus loads of wounded men in their 'hospital blue' lumbered into the yard and disgorged their bandaged, splinted and crutched men.

Annie watched with a thumping heart. It was worse than she had imagined, her chin quivered, she gulped back tears. First of all, they were taken round the shell sheds. They hobbled, but they joked, and Annie saw what she had wished to see... compassion rise in the hearts of the girls, it was revealed in their faces. The interest often became bold and Annie saw that the men enjoyed it.

Annie's greatest pride was for her own staff, the canteen had been decked with paper-chains, balloons and greenery and the food both cooked at the kitchen and brought from many homes astounded her.

There was a group photograph which appeared in the paper. It set a fashion and other factories and groups followed this lead. There were more visits to Hunslet and when winter came they organised a trip to the pantomime.

Annie was proud of her women and she told them so, it also affected the factory girls. However the real work always fell upon Annie, the toll of these months had been hard upon her.

Her prime consideration, however, was Nancy. She was always thin, but now she was pale and lacking in energy. Kit was altogether tougher but she tired of her dull and repetitive work. She still dreamed of working on farms.

Nancy was the first to escape. She returned to Scarborough to help her aunt at the Cambridge Hotel. It was the first time that Nancy had travelled alone and the entire family went to see her off.

This little group had grown closer more self-fulfilling in these last months. The war had driven them into a shell of independence. It was Edward, the most reserved who hugged Nancy and said that he would miss her.

"But you have Kit still, Daddy."

He realised his lack of diplomacy. "Of course I will. But let's hope we shall all be together soon and this dreadful war over."

Annie, the most easily moved of them all, stepped forward. She took one hand from her muff and put it on her daughter's shoulder. She pecked her cheek. To an onlooker, it was stately, distant, but never to the family deeply involved.

The guard's whistle blew. Annie moved forward again.

"Just one thing, dear, do kill those awful aspidistras." The train drew out with four people laughing.

This also amused the young soldier who sat opposite Nancy. At first, Nancy took no notice of him, but when she looked up from her book, The Amateur Gentleman, she found him looking at her.

She smiled a little shyly, her eyes shadowed by her wide brimmed felt hat. He leant forward and he talked. They parted at York and he helped her with her suitcase. It was an encounter Annie would never have countenanced... she would have sat still and unapproachable behind her spotted veil.

Another generation, with other attitudes, had arrived.

The Cambridge Hotel was a solid stuccoed building on the South Cliff close to the Valley Bridge with its toll.

Unlike many hotels in Scarborough, it had been built for its function. Inside its broad double doors was a long and wide corridor with marble-topped chiffonier backed by mirrors, or steel engravings. Above them were antlered deer heads.

The public rooms were spacious and great windows flooded them with light. The office also dispensed drinks, but the main sale of beer and spirits was in the Vault below.

Here Aunt Edith lived in semi-state. Like her sister she was surrounded by a loyal staff who stayed year upon year and growing as set in their ways as the stuffed animals in the hall. It was not, for Nancy, a return home, this was a much more Victorian establishment with an elderly clientele. It was solid, bourgeois and lacked elegance.

Even in war time, it was noted for the excellence of its table and there Nancy, as her mother intended, even more her aunt, put on a little weight and colour came into her cheeks.

Good food and fresh air did their work. One of Nancy's principal tasks was to exercise the Pekinese twice a day. Often, she crossed the bridge to spend an afternoon with her favourite cousin, Sybil. Together, the girls savoured manifestations of adulthood by smoking cigarettes in the summer house.

Nancy had left the grim war time dawning of a new life for women and returned to the role of the daughter of the house. She arranged the flowers and cared for the house plants. If there was any rebellion in her, only the aspidistras felt it.

These unyielding plants represented to her all the frustrations and pretensions of shabby gentility, non-conformity and deadening provincialisms.

She was ostentatious in her cherishing, she watered them constantly, she washed their leaves twice weekly with milk and water. After seven weeks of incessant blandishment one died and Nancy replaced it instantly with an azalea that glowed brilliantly in the drabness. Its colour was appreciated.

It took much longer for the others to succumb. Poor Aunt, she was mystified that with Nancy showing such care they should die. Aunt and niece got on well together. Nancy ignored the sharp reprimands and the insistence of always being right.

She thought it strange that her aunt, who had hated teaching, was still in her manner a schoolmistress, whereas her mother, who had enjoyed it, showed very little sign of her former avocation. Both shared a lively wit.

In Leeds, the long haul continued, Kit in her office, Edward making longer and longer journeys inspecting projectile factories, Annie to her canteen. The nation was tired, the war dragged like a lingering fever.

Its monotony and its hopelessness drained most people. Annie thought that she had won a battle with the munitions girls, but fighting and squabbling broke out among them as they queued for their food.

Annie's appearance had once quelled these little eruptions, but no longer so quickly. She noticed a new attitude. She found it in no way strange that the new impertinence towards rank occurred at the same time as the murder of the Tsar, the Tsarina and their children. This happening upset her deeply – before others grasped its import, she knew instinctively that it was the end of the world she had accepted as a norm.

Shortly after the report of the murders in Ekaterinburg, Annie was at the station awaiting her local train. As usual, there were many groups of girls waiting. Annie noticed a young man, smartly dressed in civilian clothing. He was a strange sight at that early hour. She thought no more.

When the train drew in there was a surge and Annie noticed the young man get in the carriage before hers. As she read her paper, she heard shrieks of uncontrolled laughter... it had a hard, evil note, an element of devilry.

She thought she saw an article of clothing fly past the window. She heard more taunting laughter and then to her amazement she saw a pair of men's trousers flap past with the braces flying like pennants.

The train stopped at a halt, the laughter increased and she saw on the platform the young man clad only in socks and shoes thrust out on the platform. Without thought of consequences Annie pulled the communication cord, fumblingly grappled with the door and stepped down.

The guard hurried up. The young man, white and cold and shocked, half crouched as if to hide his nakedness.

"Quick, give this man your jacket." She began to pull it from his shoulders. They wrapped the coat around the man and led him to the guard's van, the whistle was blown and the train proceeded. They gave the man a cup of tea from an enamel can.

At Hunslet, the train emptied and a great coat was found for the still shocked unfortunate man. Annie accompanied him to the small office but left considering this an affair for men. Of womanhood she felt most bitterly ashamed and, also, surprised.

As she walked to the factory she became pale with anger. These women, she thought, were like the Maenads of the French Revolution.

In the canteen the women were preparing the food. Annie looked at them with a wildness they had never seen before. She sat down, and for a moment put her face on to her outstretched arms.

Then taking a deep breath she told them what had happened on the train, adding, "Those who did it were some of those we feed each day."

She stood up. "I cannot agree to feeding savages. I thing they should be punished."

There was little love lost between the munitions workers and the canteen staff and they with energetic consent agreed with Annie.

They turned off the gas beneath the pans, they folded up cloths, they stowed away utensils, they left vegetables soaking in water. In their words, they 'sided up'. Meanwhile, on the large blackboard that served as a menu, Annie wrote: "Owing to a most regrettable incident on the train this morning, the canteen is closed. A E Matthews."

When all had been done she told the women to go home. They refused to go. They foresaw, which Annie did not, another incident.

"No, we stay until dinner-time is over."

They began to wait with increasing apprehension. The siren sounded and they heard the rush towards their building, they heard the steps slow, followed by a silence, then a murmuring. They awaited shouting and banging on the door.

For the first time, Annie really felt afraid. She wondered if she had done the right thing. There was a rap on the door, Annie asked Mrs Slocock to open it. There stood Gladys Forshaw, a forewoman, noted for her abusive rhetoric. She was angry, she was hungry. Annie rose from her chair slowly. She listened to a vituperative speech. There was a pause.

"I have listened. I know that the girls are hungry, we are hungry too, but we are also too sick at heart to eat. We shall not feed savages."

With a sneer Gladys Forshaw said: "Then you'll have to tell them."

"I will."

Annie went outside and instantly asked for a chair. She climbed on it and went so pale that her colour seemed tinged with green. Her staff stood behind and beside her. They noticed that she had a nervous tic, of which she seemed unaware, on the right side of her face which made her eye shut and blink.

Suddenly she felt justified and right in all that she had done. She spoke to them in grief, she was upset by their behaviour. There were cries that they could not hear from the back. The chief cook got another chair and in a loud harsh voice that echoed back from the far wall repeated Annie's words. Then she spoke in her own words,

"Mrs Matthews is shocked, so are we. She says you don't deserve food after what you've done, and so do we. She says we are fighting to save people from bullies and that is what some of you have been to a defenceless man. If you don't apologise, she will leave – and that goes for us as well."

Annie's colour returned, all her thoughts, all her sentiments had been uttered more plainly than she could ever do. She had always known that she was no orator.

They waited. Annie began to count slowly, she reached 14. Those on the edges drifted away, she descended from her chair and they went indoors. Inside they all smiled at one another like victorious conspirators.

It was not long before they heard scuffling... the mob had turned on the protagonists. This Annie had foreseen, but its swiftness surprised her, it took longer with children in a school.

There was a knock at the door and a dishevelled young woman was pushed in. Annie recognised her instantly. She was a coarse woman of low intelligence. She haltingly blurted out an apology.

"Do you know who that young man was?"

"No."

"Do you know what he was doing?"

"He weren't in uniform. He was a white feather."

"How do you know? I know that he is an engineer. He designs the very armaments you make. He, like us all, is in this war, what you did was evil and inhumane. It was not worthy of womanhood. I am ashamed to be of the same sex."

The girl began to cry.

"Stop crying. I have not finished, yet. You will write a letter this very moment. I will see that it reaches the unfortunate man through the police."

Fear did truly reach the girl and when paper and a pencil were produced, Annie dictated a letter which the girl wrote with very great difficulty. When it was done, Annie said: "As you have owned up, you may have some bread and cheese."

Then Annie saw that there was bread and cheese for them all. The girls came in slowly and an unusual hush hung over the usual rowdy room. It was all over.

As they washed up Annie was summoned to the Manager's office. Annie went off quite happily - to her the incident was closed with a letter of apology. As soon as she saw the grave face of Mr Mellors she knew that she was to be reprimanded.

"Mrs Matthews, is this true that you refused the girls food today?"

"It is, Mr Mellors and I hope that you know why."

"I do. It happened, though, outside the factory gates. It was a matter for the police, not private hands."

"But I happened to be on the train. I saw the entire incident. The girls were like savages. I do not feed brutes."

Mr Mellors was surprised. He had regarded Annie as a mild, maternal woman, possibly easily swayed, but very efficient in her usual task.

"Mrs Matthews, you must see that you are employed by us to see that the girls are fed. You went beyond your duties. You took the law into your own hands."

"You forget that I have run my own business for a long time. I have been a schoolmistress. I cannot, and I will not, made a distinction between moral rights and wrongs in or out of the factory.

"I saw a wicked deed done. I have tried to right it and I have brought home a lesson. I do not think that I should be reprimanded."

"But you must see it from our point of view. There are unions."

"Mr Mellors, do not give way to mob rule. Look at Russia."

"We are not here to discuss politics."

"No, but they always intrude. I see your point, but I think you are wrong. I had forgotten that I am an employee. I apologise. Shall I write to the Directors?"

"We will keep it to ourselves."

Annie took the pencilled note from the main culprit to the Stationmaster in Leeds. She was thanked.

That night she told Edward and Kit, but not until their meal was over. Kit glowed with pride, Edward replied, "You were right, but you were wrong, dear. That was how you run St Nicholas, but not big businesses. The world is changing."

Annie said no more. She knew that the world was changing. She had known it for some time.

The canteen continued. Britain was tired, Annie was tired. The rooms in the drear house became a prison. The unexpected, unwonted happened, Annie became ill. Nobody had known her stay in bed before.

Kit nursed her, she coughed and coughed and Annie wondered, when at a low ebb, if she had contracted her father's tuberculosis. It was no more than bronchitis, but it persisted until she went to stay with her sister in Scarborough.

There Alan joined them from school. He and Nancy were amused by her wheezing and Alan said, "It's very little different to the creaking of your corset."

This shocked Annie, but when everyone laughed she also joined in, and so a family saying was born… "Isn't it rude, but isn't it pleasant?"

Back at Hunslet the cough returned. The doctor advised her to leave. When the last day came Annie knew that there would be a present. She had turned a blind eye to whisperings in corners and seeing money change hands.

What she had not expected was a collection from the shell-shed as well as the canteen. She was presented with a silver cake basket, which Mr Mellors said he was certain she was capable of filling.

When she rose to thank them, she felt a real gratitude, not mere tears and Kit remembered her last sentence.

"I have loved you all and that was why, once, I was so very angry."

She walked away for the last time. She looked at the mean

houses, the women in mourning. She knew that she was lucky in having a son under age and a husband over age. Uppermost in her mind, though, as she looked at the area was pity and the words floated into her mind,

"The still, sad music of humanity."

Chapter 33

Post War

"When will it be over?" These words were repeated again and again by Annie as she moved from one damaged and forlorn room to another in the hotel vacated by the army. Even as she said it she knew that it was far from the whole of the truth, an armistice would not heal the man wounded only yesterday, make the dead of this very morning alive again.

It was, though, what everyone had been longing for. Annie was restless, she roved through the great house, she was not alarmed or dismayed by anything she saw. The damage was what she had expected and it was a small price to pay for the relief the whole nation felt.

It was while in the topmost bedroom, looking out towards the Crescent that a maroon suddenly crashed, it seemed, overhead. It was followed by another. They were fired, she knew, from the Lifeboat station. It was the 11th hour of the 11th day of the 11th month.

Annie moved to the front of the house and looked out on to the Cliff. How different it was, not a soul to be seen, from that day in August four years before when entire families had moved up from the beach.

She felt that she, indeed everyone, was different. How many of those feet hurrying home had survived, she questioned.

She went down to Maria in the kitchen.

"It's all over, Maria."

"Ah thought so wi' that commotion."

"One would think they could announce peace with something other than yet another explosion, wouldn't you?"

"Do you think they'll hang the Kaiser?"

"It's very unlikely, Maria, he has gone to Holland."

It was strange, when Queen Wilhelmina had given sanctuary to Paul Kruger at the close of the Boer War, she had been proud of the young queen's courage. But, now, she was far from sure. She thought that he should be made aware of his crimes.

Annie sat down and Maria pushed the kettle over the fire on its angle iron.

"We'll have some tea to celebrate."

Musingly Annie said, "We'll soon have the Master home and Miss Kit. Oh it will be good to see them."

"We'll have to think of the next season. Everyone will want a holiday next year. Goodness, the Master will have his work cut out redecorating the rooms, those rooms at the back."

Annie smiled. Maria was a worker. When not occupied she anticipated the next busy time. All Annie could do was feel the relief still flooding though her. It went like the warmth of the tea into every part of her being.

"I think I'll go out for a while. I shall be back for lunch."

A little later she emerged wearing a light grey coat, a felt hat trimmed with soft blue feathers. In her hand she carried a small black leather-bound prayer book. The Cliff was deserted, Huntriss Row was full of smiling and eager talking shopkeepers, and children were running their way though their elders, freed from school.

Beyond the newsagent, Annie turned into the alleyway that led to an ugly tarmaced yard encircling the church. She walked to the west end, went up the steps and very gently pushed open the green baize door. She tip-toed, for she did not wish to disturb anyone. She was entirely alone, still quietly she crept up the aisle looking at the names on the pews. When she saw her own she sidled in. Sitting, she peeled off her gloves, pushed the hassock into position, knelt and put her face in her hands.

She thought that she had come to give thanks. She found herself saying she was sorry that she was there alone. She felt pain for God. She also experienced a surge of one-ness with him, she seemed to slip from herself and into another life.

It was something she was never to encounter again, the memory of it was to remain with her the rest of her life and also be very clearly dated. At last she sat back. She looked at her wrist watch, then looked at it again.

It seemed that an hour had gone. In fact, barely 15 minutes had gone by. She began to think that she belonged to a very strange religion, so proud of its heritage, so dignified in its buildings and worship, but on a day like this empty.

She was quite certain that the cathedral in Cologne was

thronged with praying people, a constantly shifting pattern. She wondered, as she had many times over the last few years, about Konrad. He would be middle-aged, if he were alive.

She still sat awhile and, like Maria, began planning for the future. She wished that Edward was with her. She rose and went out. There were more people about and they were drifting towards the Town Hall. The street before the Dutch-gabled house was packed with a dense crowd up to its undistinguished steps.

The Mayor stood in the doorway, the beadle near him, a proclamation was to be read... a list of festivities was announced. The Vicar stepped forward and the crowd solemnly said the Lord's Prayer, and the National Anthem was sung.

Tears came to Annie's eyes, but she knew it to be emotion on the surface. The crowd thinned and she felt a hand slip under her arm. It was Jack Chapman.

"You should be inside, not here, Annie."

He led her through the dispersing crowd and into the Town Hall and into the Mayor's Parlour. A glass of champagne was put into her hand. To her surprise, her mind slipped back to Cologne again.

On very special occasions, the cabbage had been cooked in champagne. She saw Beatrice and the sisters-in-law kissed one another and together, because they were unaccompanied by their husbands, went up to congratulate the Mayor.

When Annie entered the hotel, the telephone rang loudly in the empty house. She stiffened and approached it almost fiercely. It was Nancy, a happy bubbling girl inviting her to a party, that very night, at the Cambridge.

"What shall I wear?"

"Your very, very best."

"I see. Tell me, does your aunt need some help?"

"No, we've plenty of staff."

Annie thanked her a little stiffly. The telephone was an instrument she was to live with another 30 years and never come to terms with. It made her frigidly formal.

Maria had laid the table in the back room for lunch. Annie looked at it, picked up a tray, put the cutlery on it, and carried it downstairs.

"Maria, today is a very special day. We cannot eat alone."

Annie thought it would be like having meals with the staff at the canteen. It wasn't Annie who had to make conversation all the time. Maria was embarrassed... it was a mistake.

There were no more meals for Maria to prepare that day, so Annie gave her the day off. She knew that Maria would want to celebrate. She knew that she would go to the Music Hall, she would get drunk, find her way back and spend the morrow weeping. This was the price she paid for keeping the best cook in Scarborough.

She went up the uncarpeted stairs and to her room. Opening her wardrobe she surveyed her clothes, things she had not seen for three years. She chose a grey net evening dress covered with silver beads and black bugles.

She had forgotten how heavy it was, four years ago it had been considered very chic. Carefully she tried it on, it fitted, it was even a little loose. She had lost weight in her illness. She found her work basket and took the dress down to the kitchen where the only fire burned.

She took in the dress and, as she did so, her spirits rose. When she had finished, she went up to the office, found her keys and opened the safe. Walking inside was walking into the past, here were things valuable in monetary terms, here were many sentimental things, to Annie, of incomparable worth.

At length, she came upon the leather jewel case of her mother-in-law. She turned another key and opened it, on the first tray were her old, old friends, the Van Prehn diamond and sapphire ear-rings, the diamond and sapphire brooch shaped like a crescent moon.

She took the case away, locking the safe and returned to the kitchen. Before a mirror she put on the ear-rings and shook her head... they still splintered with light and her eyes still matched the blue stones. She took out a choker of pearls. On another lid was the tortoise-shell band with its row of little diamonds.

"Yes, life will be fun again."

Yet as she lay out her clothes on the bed, arranged her jewels on the dressing table, the intolerable sadness of the loss, the maiming, the monster of the suffering and unhappiness of the last years overpowered her again.

She gave her head a little toss as if to throw away such thoughts and went down to the kitchen again to make a pot of tea. She hesitated whether to make a half of a full pot of tea. She reproved herself for such thoughts of economy on such a day.

As she did so, she heard the sound of a key in the door in the hall overhead. She heard it pushed open, it still stuck. Her thought was that it was Nancy and she ran upstairs, she turned the corner to the last four steps up into the hall, it was Edward.

They fell into each other's arms. The emotion, so long pent up in Annie, flooded out and she wept. Edward's eyes dimmed as well. Still they had not spoken. At last Annie said: "I've let Maria go. There is a pot of tea in the kitchen."

Had Annie been more introspective, she might have been surprised at the profundity of her joy that Edward was with them. Often she thought that having Kit, or Nancy was enough. Having Edward sitting before her made her realise how she had missed him these last months.

At first to be in Scarborough had been enough, having Nancy nearby had made it seem complete. She looked at him, he was older... he was tired. His clothes were shabby, he never did look after them, but he was handsome.

She told him of the party. They went up to the room and sought out his clothes. Annie was oblivious of his desires, but surrendered easily as they slipped into bed and all she said was, "Oh, Ted."

When they dressed, Edward looked taller and more remarkable in his dress suit, his gold-studded shirt. He looked at himself in the cheval mirror and gave a wry smile. He emphasised the concave curve of his spine and said: "If I go in here, then, I must come out here, mustn't I?"

Annie concentrated on arranging her hair, When it was finally as she wished, she inserted the tortoiseshell band. She despaired as it disrupted a pile of painstakingly arranged and engineered curls.

At last all was done. Then she took it off, removed the ear-rings and brooch. It was not yet a time for finery, she thought.

Edward went downstairs. He noted the damage. The treads to the stairs were the worst and he said: "Lift your dress, darling. You could easily tear it on these splinters."

She came down into the hall. From the penumbra of the shaded light, for a moment he saw a tall, beautiful young woman, the one he had married nearly 25 years before.

They walked over the Spa bridge then along Birdcage Walk, as always. Edward started with her - they were arm-in-arm. They talked of the children, the future and gradually she felt his hand lighten on her arm, it lifted and he was walking by her side.

She knew that he was away, away on a track of other thoughts, where she could never follow him. At the same time his stride lengthened and he was ahead of her. She smiled and said to herself, "Well, it was always like this."

The Cambridge Hotel blazed with light through the glazed front doors. There watching was Nancy, pretty, very slim dressed as Pierrette. She saw her parents, she gasped that it really was her father. A fraction later, she rushed down the marble steps and over the road and threw herself into her father's arms.

"Oh, Daddy, I didn't expect you. How lovely."

"And you, young lady, have put your hair up without my permission."

She squeezed his arm,

"But you don't mind, do you?"

"Nancy dear, run on in. You mustn't be out here in that thin dress. You'll catch cold."

Nancy clung to her father, then her mother and all three entered together, when Coniston, the head porter, opened the doors with a broad smile.

The party was underway and there were great cries of welcome when Edward was seen. Down the room, trident in hand bore Britannia wearing a gilded helmet and pince-nez. She flung an arm round Edward and kissed him. Annie watched,

"Is it fancy-dress, Edith?"

"Well, it is for me and any who wanted to. I did not bother to tell you for I knew that you wouldn't."

It was true, Annie never dressed up. Annie thought it comic and she always wondered if it revealed dissatisfaction within the person... they were not what they wished to be. For her to be perfectly dressed was a part of life and she wished to be no other.

With a sister's awful clarity she looked at her sibling and thought that she looked neither charming, nor patriotic, but rather ridiculous. Fortunately, none of this disdain was revealed and Annie was soon laughing at a joke and smiling contentedly at the happy crowd.

Everyone was there, she said to herself, correcting it to everyone that she knew.

There were games, charades and a supper more splendid than

had been see for a very long time. Many wondered how it had been managed. Edith had long planned this party, waiting and waiting for the day when peace should come.

She had been determined to celebrate. Annie was still troubled by the deaths, the maimings, the sufferings... it informed her as she rejoiced to look at the young men and knew that their future could be counted in years with some certainty.

She was glad that she had not put on her diamonds, she wore only pearls. She watched Nancy dancing, light, lively, a merry child.

She wondered at her use of the word child. She was a young woman and popular it seemed. She would have to be more vigilant. She wanted Nancy to marry the right man... that was very important.

On the way back to St Nicholas, Annie hung determinedly on to Edward's arm and she voiced her thoughts about Nancy. Edward agreed.

"We'll have her back as soon as the house is straight again. She'll be a great help to you."

The delays of compensation and the procrastination of builders were the pre-occupations of the first months of 1919. A portion of the hotel opened for Easter. It was the happiest Easter any of them had ever known and an air of relief mixed with the joy of being alive was alive in everyone. It was remarkable.

It was in April that Annie read in the Daily Mail of the conditions in which some Land Girls were living. It filled her with alarm, the article spoke of poor food, insufficient facilities of washing and drying and worst of all, damp bedding. Instantly Annie wrote to Kit.

The letter reached Kit in Essex after a long, arduous but delightful day. The farmer, a retired army officer, kept Shire horses. These were far more important to him than the crops he might grow. The work of the girls was magnified because he was adamant that his beloved animals should not be over exerted.

So the team was constantly being changed and the horses rested in their stables after a few hours. Kit had been looking after the horses. She rode the teams back and forth from the yard to the fields... she groomed and fed them in their stalls.

She was completely fulfilled. When she read her mother's letter she was a little annoyed, then she laughed. She was in a different world. She wrote back faintly mocking her mother and not answering the questions.

Annie read the letter at home and looked perturbed and she then announced that she was going down to Essex to see for herself. The next day she went to London, her fear of damp and rheumatism driving her steadfastly.

Kit was very surprised when a taxi arrived at the farm when the girls were eating their dinner and from it emerged her mother. She went out, half expecting to hear some dreadful news and discovered that it was a visit of inspection.

Kit, a little reluctantly, led her mother to the great kitchen where they all sat around a large table. The first thing that Annie's eyes noted was that there was no cloth, then she saw that some of the hands of the girls were not over-clean.

They spoke with accents and though, quite different, less harsh, she recognised the coarseness that made them kin with the munitions girls of Hunslet. She sat down and talked with them and not a suspicion was raised among them of the severe appraisal they were undergoing. The meal over, one girl said, "You stay with your mother. I'll do your turn at drying."

"That was very kind of your friend. Where do you sleep dear?"

Kit led her upstairs. Her room was above the kitchen and shared with two others. Annie felt the wall as she climbed the stairs, it felt damp. The ceiling sloped and two dormer windows pierced the roof. There was a damp patch over one bed. It was not Kit's.

When she was aware of her daughter's bed, she turned back the white counterpane which, she agreed, was spotlessly clean. She slid her hand between the sheets, she felt damp. With sudden alacrity she tossed back the clothes and pulled the top sheet off, went downstairs and held the sheet before the fire, then bundling it she walked to a mirror and pressed the warm material to the glass, she held it a moment then withdrew it. There were steam marks on the mirror.

"You are not to sleep in that bed another night, Kit. You are coming home with me."

"But, Mummy..."

The quiet resolve, the slightly lowered face and the eyes that looked at one only intermittently... all this showed the determination of her mother. It was the face that the staff sometimes saw, but rarely her children.

The bailiff was informed and he raised objections and mentioned the County Organiser. Annie immediately said that she would see her as well. So, it was that Kit was taken away from her first taste of freedom. Annie's fear of damp beds was great for she always had a spectre of tuberculosis.

She did not want her parents' disease to reappear in her children. Kit returned, the season was hectically busy, she was too busy to repine and Annie made sure that her girls enjoyed themselves. Scarborough was frenetically busy, much was going on and to be a pretty girl was to be sought after and pursued.

Edward was busier than ever with Council work which left Annie supreme at the hotel. There she reigned and it was now that the adjectives stately, regal and even imperial were used by observers of her.

The hotel bore the stamp of her personality unmistakably, yet still she groped in the dark about the true state of any of the finances. An unacceptable attitude, because it had gone unchallenged and so became accepted. Stubborn decisions had won an unjust victory.

Being a magistrate and on the Board of Guardians brought Edward into contact with hundreds of people. He worked unflaggingly for those who through illiteracy and lack of intelligence somehow missed their rights.

There was more visiting than he could cope with, so Annie took on some of this work, which she did with great ease. This work strained Edward and when he was tired he became uncommunicative, even morose, and the people he most wished to avoid were the visitors.

If he was in one of these moods, when evening came, he would lower his head and march to the door across the hall almost challenging anyone to impede him with small talk. It was evenings such as these that Annie and Kit and Nancy most enjoyed, beautifully dressed they, like their mother, wandered through the rooms and sat and talked with the families.

Kit was bold, adventurous and humorous. She made friends easily and in the winter visited them, she went hunting and attended point to points. Nancy was quiet, but her wit was even quicker than her sister's, but she was overshadowed by her mother, whom she adored. It was significant that Kit chose her own tweeds and tailor-made clothes. Nancy loved appropriating things from her mother's wardrobe and adapting them to modern fashion. Annie lost the tortoise shell bandeau which had often nestled in her hair. Nancy wore it across her brow.

Life seemed very assured, but life was changing, the old values were being questioned so the outward manifestations of life were changing. The first of the events in social life to be abandoned was the monthly At Home.

It was deemed boring, gossipy, extravagant, for one had to cater for an unknown number. The girls thought it constricting and Kit refused to play the piano any longer. Annie missed the dresses. She had loved tea-gowns which were warmer than evening dress and just as elaborate. It was now that she gave up dancing - she did not enjoy the fox-trot.

It was at this time that a Polish family came into contact with Edward. They were refugees, their plight was great for the parents were unable to read or write and English was quite unintelligible to them.

Their children picked it up quickly, so quickly that they forgot Polish. Edward decided to employ Anton, soon named Tony, as a porter and then Mary, his sister came to be a chamber-maid.

Tony stayed some years, then threw it up to become an unskilled labourer in the marine engineering works in Middlesbrough only months before the markets began to fall.

Mary stayed at the hotel. She was a strong boned, broad faced peasant girl, but endowed with intelligence and adaptability. She so proved her worth that when the staff were thinned in the autumn, she was retained as a housemaid.

She loved work. Even when talking with a member of the family she would produce a duster from a pocket and polish a piece of furniture as she talked. This endeared her to Annie, but the day came when Annie confiscated the duster and substituted a pencil and paper and made her sit down.

Every day that winter Annie gave her lessons and at the end of it she could read and write. She became Annie's personal maid and her great love was to care for her mistress's clothes, brushing them, washing them, laying them out in the evening.

This became a more and more important task, for both Edward

and Annie were involved in more public engagements. These they did extraordinarily well, Edward could always make an impromptu speech with seemingly little effort and Annie talked and moved and smiled with consummate charm.

The 25th anniversary of their wedding came in December 1919. It was a great gathering of friends and relations. As always, the Matthews far outnumbered the Taylors. The highlight of the evening was when the three children gave a sketch satirising the public life of their parents.

Alan imitated his father making a speech and Nancy opened a bazaar with great charm and generosity and total inaudibility. When the spring came they took a holiday but characteristically it was apart. Edward went to Jersey to play golf and Annie took her children to Edinburgh.

Annie had read her Stevenson, but somehow, it had not prepared her for the thrift, even, parsimony of Scotland. There were shortages, but she was shocked to find margarine served at the breakfast table of the Great Northern Hotel.

She wrote to her grocer in Scarborough and Mr Edwards sent a pound of butter by return. This was duly brought to their table. There were whispers all around and Kit was upset when she heard them described as war-profiteers, but Annie and Nancy thought it a joke.

All day long they walked the city and Annie, from her incessant reading, dwelt on the more romantic aspect of the life of Mary Queen of Scots.

The overwhelming impression made on Nancy was the poverty around the Royal Mile. She never forgot the tenements with washing strung out across the streets and the men and women lost in a personal nightmare of drunkenness.

In fact, it so shocked them that they were glad to journey on to the Trossachs where they stayed in a hotel with fairy tale towers capped with conical slate roofs like candle snuffers. It reminded Annie of the Rhine.

It was here she discovered the real joy of bridge-playing which she took back to Scarborough with her. Bridge now replaced the At Homes and the gossip of the gatherings was by no means lessened.

It would seem that no three women were so in tune with each other as Annie and her two girls. They shared the same interests largely, their humour coincided, yet in these post-war years Annie failed her daughters.

They were obviously of different generations, but the war had made a huge fissure in the beliefs and notions of the western world. No longer was everything so certain, so sure. Annie belonged to the secure generation, her daughters to a newer more questioning one.

Yet in their happiness they failed to recognise it. The love they bore one another was deep, but the discussion of things that mattered was superficial.

Scarborough still hosted young officers on leave, or stationed at the barracks. A lonely young man, often bored, with some money in his pocket beguiled the time with a pretty girl. Henry Howard was no exception. He met Nancy as she walked the Pekinese, Ching, on the Spa.

He was handsome and well-bred. It was a chance encounter and by his design it was repeated. To Nancy it was intriguing, flattering and when he asked her to accompany him to Tea Dansant in the ballroom there, she agreed.

So one afternoon, wearing a felt hat with a broad petersham ribbon and a Harris tweed costume she set off very casually for a walk.

"Aren't you taking Ching, dear?"

"No. I may be in too many shops for him."

Nancy blushed. She believed it was the first lie she had told her mother. She hurried out, the page smartly opening the door for her. Henry was leaning over a balustrade smoking, he looked up and smiled. He hurried forward, took her arm and they walked towards the ballroom.

Nancy felt that all eyes were upon her and most of them were envious. In the large room with its dotted tables over the strip of carpet that edged the room, Nancy saw that she was improperly dressed.

The women wore floral dresses of chiffon and hats with feathers. Henry Howard seemed not to notice and his evident pleasure of her company dismissed all her anxieties. In fact he thought her prettier and younger than any of the others and in her tweeds she reminded him of his cousin in Sussex.

He helped her off with the heavy jacket and he suggested that they should dance. Again he thought himself a lucky fellow for

Nancy danced so smoothly, sweetly, they fox-trotted elegantly round the floor.

"Do I look very hot, Henry?"

"No, just a pretty pink."

"Oh, is my nose shiny?"

"No, but your eyes are."

Over tea, he talked of being demobbed and going to the farm and Nancy very innocently said, "You should talk to my sister, she's the farmer of the family. She was a land girl until mother found out that the dormitories were damp. So she came home. I don't think Kit noticed the damp at all."

Without enthusiasm he replied that he would like to meet her. He asked her to dance again.

Twice a week they met and nearly always Nancy wore the heavy costume. It seemed such a good disguise for her intrigue.

"Now, Henry, you must come and have tea with us. Mother will be delighted to meet you. You'll love her, we all do."

That very evening as they sat by the fire, Annie put down her sewing and rose, saying, "I've just remembered I never finished the letters this morning."

Alone, Edward lowered his book and regarded Nancy. He could not believe her to be wanton. She had all her mother's innocence and better still without her mother's guile that was so difficult to detect.

"Nancy. Your uncle tells me that you have been seen dancing on the Spa, is that right? I told him it could not be."

Nancy blushed and looked hard at her knitting pattern... it was a moment that seemed eternal.

"Yes, I have been four times with Henry Howard."

"Does your mother know?"

"No."

"I am very surprised, Nancy. It is not like you to be dishonest."

"But, Father, Henry is a very nice young man. He is going to farm in Sussex."

"What he does, does not matter. The thing is you have done this behind our backs. I am shocked. You must let this young man know that your relationship is ended."

Nancy felt dumbfounded, she felt terrible guilt because she had been deceitful, but she also thought of Henry's fresh young face and she knew that she would never meet anyone so pleasing to her again.

She looked at the cracked tiles in the hearth where the shrapnel had fallen in the bombardment. Her father was still talking.

"Your mother has always thought so highly of your sense of honour."

Nancy cringed and wished Mr Latham her old schoolmaster had never made that flattering remark.

"But, Father, I have done nothing really wrong. All I have done is have tea with this very nice young man."

"Do you realise, my dear, what sort of women go to the dances in the afternoon on the Spa?"

"They look very ordinary to me."

"Well, I assure you that they are not. What if this young man thinks you are like them?"

She felt shame spreading like a stain across her person. She thought, also, of Henry and knew that he had only the kindest thoughts about her.

She was right, but Edward's profound sense of middle-class morality had asserted itself and by keeping the matter from his wife her more tolerant outlook never softened this issue with understanding.

His next remark had hard consequences.

"I have not told your mother. She would be too hurt."

Submissively she replied,

"Yes, Father."

She wrote a note to Henry, saying that she could not see him at the moment. He was surprised, but by the same post came news of his 'de-mobbing' and a larger future loomed before him.

These years were busy and Edward talked vaguely of turning No 12, The Cliff, which he had acquired, into a more continuous part of the hotel. Annie said nothing, she hoped by silence to delay any such undertaking.

She loved No 12 - she had made her drawing room there, the sea was more visible, but it was the look and feel of the rooms that truly charmed her. She loved the Adam fireplaces, the six panelled doors and their large brass locks with drop handles. They made her think of *Quality Street*, a play which she loved and saw many times with touring companies.

She hoped to leave it unchanged and would divert his thoughts to his plans for making a new park on the North Side. He had ideas of a lake and a glen. He considered the North of the town neglected.

At this time, with two daughters at home and a staff she could trust unquestioningly, Annie's task had a certain ease. Maria still dominated the kitchen, neurotically serving up Lucullan meals and tears concurrently.

There was large, fat, Martha who, now, presided in the stillroom serving from and constantly polishing the great copper hot water urns with their surging gas flames. She seemed content to be in the beams of her mistress's smiles and gratitude.

Her precipitate marriage to a steelman from Sheffield had foundered at the end of its first winter because she insisted on returning to St Nicholas for the season. It was considered a joke that she only visited her husband when there was a cheap day excursion from the town.

Harry, the head porter, was trusted implicitly but with less justification. He was, in many ways, the foreman of the staff and he exacted his dues from his underlings.

The office was in Annie's hands. Still she wrote all the letters by hand. Still she wielded a generous petty cash, but even this did not cover her generosity. The autumn was a nightmare to her. She loathed paying off the seasonal staff and sending them to Durham and Northumberland with so little money.

She topped up their wages with a bonus which appeared as 'sundries' in the accounts. She sometimes let Edward think she had spent the money on clothes. She disliked arguments when he would wave away airily her notions of charity.

He worked hard for organised charities, but the personal ones he dismissed. Annie knew better than he the houses, crowded cottages, to which they returned.

With the two girls acting as receptionists, the whole establishment ran smoothly and more than that joyously. Life was a constant shifting pattern of people moving in and out of their orbit.

The girls also fell in and out of love. Annie watched their affairs and kept remarkably distant. They talked with her, but never once, did she give them the slightest knowledge of sex.

Even their periods, the usual time for such explanations, had been glossed and glided over. Annie always intended to tell them, one day, but the thought embarrassed her and she shrugged it away.

Annie was a woman of her time. In many things she was better informed than her mother, possibly only because she had lived longer, but in some ways was more ignorant and even blind.

She was the product of mid-Victorian philosophy, tolerant in many, many ways, but bound by sexual taboos to avert her eyes from the carnal. She sent her girls into the world incomplete. Also, as was the way with women of her generation, she became possessive of one daughter.

That daughter was Nancy. Maybe because she had experienced illness she loved to nurse others. She wished to train at a London hospital. Her cousin Sybil was training to be a midwife, Nancy was very envious.

Nancy persisted in her desire but Annie evaded the issue and delayed. Edward was called in when Nancy persisted... he buttressed his wife's concern. They considered Nancy not strong enough. At last Nancy's wishes were placed before the doctor.

He, too, looked at a thin but very pretty girl, he thought of the hardness of hospital life and he judged also that within months she might be married.

Nancy's resentment was, at first, fierce, but of short duration. Her mother strewed her path with delights and charms, as she did for everyone. No one knew better than she the art of beguilement.

Chapter 34

Double Marriage

The summer of 1920 brought a family from Leeds to St Nicholas, a Mr and Mrs Lockwood, with their son and a daughter. The mother, a sweet woman in awe of her husband, aroused Annie's compassion.

The husband she did not like so never considered him, but the son she found charming and the daughter she found quite engaging. The son, they soon discovered, was a nervous young man, still suffering from the effects of life at the front in France. They were a very united family taking their pleasures together.

At that time, the Matthews owned a dog, Peter. He had been purchased more than a year previously together with a monumental pedigree. As he grew it became evident that his mother had indulged in other relationships.

He was mongrel, but of outstanding character and an intelligence that became legendary. The family were disturbed because Peter had fallen to the illness known as 'Sand Fever'. Many dogs transferred their allegiances to a family to the pack of dogs that roamed and scavenged on the sea shore.

It was a sickness feared by dog-owners, for once in the pack, the animals rarely returned for any length of time to their homes. They were lost and despaired of. Peter left home and he returned at only lengthening intervals.

He was petted into better behaviour and beaten. He invariably escaped and was found down on the shoreline. The lure of a wild life was irresistible.

They were even considering having him destroyed, rather than see him become wild and mangy, a vagrant of the canine world.

Peter had returned and Nancy was speaking to him severely at the front door. Jim was watching.

"Will you let me have him for a while?"

Nancy looked up at young Mr Lockwood. She had not noticed him sitting on the seat outside.

"Do you think you can do anything?"

"I can but try. I'm usually rather good with animals."

He asked to be left alone with Peter. They shut the two in their drawing room and heard every now and then the drone of Jim Lockwood's voice as he talked and talked to the dog.

It went on for two hours. At last the door opened and the young man came out. Nancy, looking in, saw Peter asleep on the rug before the fireplace. He did not move. They never did anything else to Peter and he never again recurred to his nomadic ways.

What had been done they never knew, but they were very impressed. His very quick wit did the rest.

Nancy, like the dog, was mesmerised. She went out with the family, who seemed delighted by her company and discreetly left Jim and Nancy together.

Later in the year, Nancy went to stay with the family on the outskirts of Leeds. She found that they lived in a solid house with a circular drive, pillars to the door and a yard with outhouses to one side. The interior she found reflected Mrs Lockwood, sweet, gentle and out of date.

The house was comfortable, even pleasing, to Nancy. However it contained an ethos she did not comprehend. It was a typical house of the West Ridings, respectable, endurable, displaying more worth than beauty. It managed to combine an uneasy alliance of non-conformity with, by the women, an unhappy tolerance of their menfolk's hard-drinking. For the first time Nancy noticed the division of the sexes.

Men tended to gather at one end of the room and women at the other. She found a kind of hardness in them all. When she mentioned this to her mother all she said was, "They are rather different, my dear."

She thought that Nancy's reactions were not of great importance for the friendship would not last.

Jim Lockwood was in love and he pursued Nancy with determination. He charmed her parents, he was amusing, was quick with repartee and he could play the piano with seductive ease. This was a valuable accomplishment in an age where the gramophone had not yet taken hold.

Once again, Nancy was invited to Bruncliffe. After Sunday lunch, the girls announced their intention of going out in the governess cart. It was brought round and Nancy stepped in with the two sisters. They soon left the dotted houses in their grounds and came to meadowed country. She discovered that they were driving to the prisoner-of-war camp which was set in the park of a mansion.

When they passed the lodge gates at the drive entrance, Nancy saw clearly and with distaste that to drive to this camp had become a Sabbath pastime. Cars and the occasional carriage passed down the narrow drive which was lined on each side by barbed wire fences, behind which stood row upon row of bored and dispirited German soldiers.

Freedom in the form of comfortable nouveaux riches flowed complacently down the road and grey stricken captives watched them with a feeble interest rather than resentment. Nancy had never experienced such utter hopelessness.

She spoke her thoughts and was aghast to hear, "They are not men they are animals. The sooner they are shipped back where they belong the better. I hope the ship sinks."

Nancy cried out, "Stop, stop."

Marnie surprised, reined in the pony to the verge. Nancy grappled with the small brass catch, opened it and jumped down. She hurried, then slowed with shyness as she approached the fence.

She suddenly wondered if her gesture might be misinterpreted. The men were not wary, they just watched. She opened her handbag, took out her cigarette case and going up to a sullen but handsome flaxen-haired Saxon, scooped up the cigarettes and pushed them with embarrassment into his hand.

He looked surprised, then a smile cracked the scowl of his face and he drew back his hand.

"Danke schon, danke schon, gnadige fraulein. Danke schon."

Tears started to Nancy's eyes and even more when he promptly shared them with those around him. They lit matches, drew on the cigarettes and the blue smoke drifted overhead vanishing into the branches of the trees. They smiled, waved and called out "Danke schon." Nancy smiled and went back to the trap. Marnie and Olive looked on stern and disapproving.

"Why on earth did you do that? Those men would have killed our brother." Nancy did not answer.

"Quite right, Marnie. It's a disgrace, giving them cigarettes. They are still our enemies."

The sudden rallying of subdued Olive stung Nancy as much as the venom of their thoughts.

"What did you do in the war?" she asked.

"We worked for our father in his office."

"I know, all of you making a nice lot of money by dyeing blankets for the Army. It's a strange kind of patriotism."

They were shocked by her vehemence. They had considered her a mouse until this afternoon, but one to be encouraged for she had a good influence on their brother. The rest of the journey was uncomfortable and silent.

At tea, sitting round the dining table, which Nancy thought very démodé, Marnie related with some flourish Nancy's doings. She expected a derisive laugh. Mrs Lockwood pouring out the tea, looked up and said: "That was very kind, my dear. But was it quite right?"

"Yes, I do. They looked so bored and miserable, like inquisitive cows peering thought a hedge."

"I said they were animals, didn't I?"

"Now, now, Marnie, not so hasty."

Jim had been watching and listening and a look of anguish crossed his already tense face.

"You women know nothing of war. Nothing. Yes, I would have killed them. They would have killed me. But if one of them had found me unarmed and wounded he would have helped me and I him. You, you can't understand. The Germans did not know why they were fighting any more than we did."

"Oh, but you did know why you were fighting, my dear," interposed his mother.

"The Germans, mother, thought that they were fighting for their freedom as much as we did. I am very glad Nancy gave her cigarettes to the prisoners. If I'd been a prisoner I hope some jolly German girl would have given me some."

He smiled his rather broad but still shy smile and looked at her.

"You'd better get used to Nancy. She's the only girl for me."

Nancy was pleased, she was flattered. But she did not really want to get involved. She diverted her thoughts from her emotions and considered how she approved his sentiments about her action.

This tolerance reminded her of her parents. Her mother often pronounced her hatred of the Kaiser, her deep distrust of the

Prussians, but of the rest, she said they were like the British... both good and bad.

Flora, the tall and gaunt and very ill-named maid, was off-duty on Sunday afternoons, so Nancy helped with the washing-up in the big scullery beyond the kitchen. She became aware of Jim popping his head in and out of the doorway.

At last she went into the kitchen and hung the tea-towel on the shining brass rail over the range, looked momentarily at the diamond patterned rag mat on the floor and the huge dresser where Olive hung the tea-cups.

She then went into the dark back hall and straightaway the door of the little, rarely used morning room opened and Jim emerged. He took her arm.

"Come in here, Nancy."

He looked agitated, almost confused. He drew her in and together they sat on a black horse-hair sofa, banished from a front room, Nancy would have said belatedly. Jim put his arm around her - she did not stop him, neither did she respond. She was a little afraid, rather more surprised, but when his mouth sought hers, she turned her head so that his kiss rested on her cheek.

"Will you marry me?"

"Marry him" the thought shuddered through her mind, bumping with amazement. Yet she was honest enough to admit that the thought had occurred to her. But the reality of a proposal was a shock and the prospect looked utterly different.

She knew that she was hedging and she gave an answer even more old-fashioned than the house she criticised.

"You will have to talk to my father."

"But would you like to marry me?"

He looked very young, very entreating, as though his life hung upon her decision. But though moved she said no more than, "I might."

"I'll take you back to Scarborough, then in the car, first thing tomorrow."

All night Nancy kept waking up and the chasm of an unknown, uncertain future opened up before her. She was afraid and of what she was afraid she did not really know.

Next day, when the Wolds were in view and the car began to chug up the steeper hills Nancy's heart contracted, then stirred.

Home was not far away and, it seemed, her future would be settled.

She panicked slightly at the thought that they would wholeheartedly approve. She was certain she would have them to herself. As they passed the Mere, then the gas works which stank and then entered Falsgrave, Nancy's hopes of a delay foundered. When they stopped outside the hotel Nancy rushed in.

"Where's my mother?"

"In her room, Miss Nancy, with Mrs White and Miss Sybil."

Nancy hurried in. They were having tea with small tables and a tiered cake stand. Seeing them all, and she loved them all dearly, she felt safe, her qualms evaporated like morning mist. She was in her own world once more. They all chattered.

The door opened and Edward and Jim came in. They both looked pleased and happy. Nancy felt a terrible pang of fear.

"Well, Nancy, this young feller-me-lad tells me that he wants to marry you. Is that right?"

Nancy looked around, her mother smiled uneasily, her chin quivered, always a prelude to tears. Sybil looked startled but glad for her cousin's sake.

It was Auntie Bea who sat very upright and pondering said, "Ted, you are rushing things. You must give Nancy time to think. There is no hurry."

Edward invariably disregarded any advice his sister might give and he turned to his daughter. "Well, my dear?"

Nancy wished, dearly wished to say, "I don't know." There was a look of expectation on every face, it would disappoint everyone. She thought that she was very lucky to be asked to marry, she knew many girls of her age would never have a chance.

She regarded her mother, who looked serene behind the surface tears. She thought that if her mother thought it was all right, then it must be. It was only her aunt who was reacting differently, she seemed like Justice weighing everything in a balance and refusing to be imposed upon.

She found herself respecting her aunt more than ever before, yet still she heard herself say, "Yes."

It was a word that seemed to have been said at the end of a very long gallery. The next moment she seemed to be in Jim's and then everybody's arms.

At breakfast Annie picked up a letter. She turned it backwards and forwards, the postmark was local, the handwriting unknown. It was childish, unformed but pretty copper-plate.

She slit open the envelope and as she read, turned pale. With a gesture of repugnance she thrust it to Edward. He glanced at it and said: "It is unsigned. I never read anonymous letters."

"You are quite right, Ted."

She took the letter and went with it towards the fire, but just before she put it in she looked at it again. Ted looked up.

"Annie, for goodness sake put it in the fire before it makes you suspicious – that is precisely what the writer wants. And if you are suspicious you always find something to justify it."

Annie nodded thoughtfully and dropped it in the flames. Nancy watched with curiosity and then asked, "What was it about?"

"It was about one of the servants and, I expect, from another."

It was first of a spate and Mary was always the target of the venomous writer. Edward had many things on his mind at the time and put the incident out of his head. The staff he considered his wife's realm, his world was increasingly outside on committees.

Annie did find herself watching Mary, she tried to curb it, but nonetheless she had a regard for her, she wanted the best for her. It was only, now, that Annie did see that Mary, always striking in her uniform, was equally handsome in her 'outdoor' clothes.

Tall, upright, she was becoming an impressive young woman. In fact, Annie coming upon her one day in the street thought immediately of Anna Karenina. Until, that moment she had thought of Anna as a small dark Frenchwoman very chic. She felt the image was corrected. Anna would have looked like Mary.

One afternoon looking out at the sea, she saw Mary emerge at the top of the area steps. She walked up the Cliff and a man came from Bar Street, slipped his hand under her arm and they walked towards St Nicholas Street. She deliberately suppressed any further thought, but hoped all was well for Mary's sake.

Suddenly Kit became engaged to John Barlow. Both Edward and Annie had some reservations about this marriage. John was tactless and interfering and played a little too much the officer that he was.

He was undeniably a dashing figure and they could well see his appeal to Kit. When they met his parents, they liked the father, but his mother they found sharp and dour, they did not like her and considered her a woman of very limited horizons.

This news meant that there would be two weddings and it was decided to make them one great occasion. Annie found herself making a thousand plans. She was still a vigorous healthy woman, well able to deal with the challenge.

Her heart was not in the task. She was uneasy about Kit and she thought Nancy too young. Possibly because she was uncertain and unsure she looked to her staff even more.

One day, she was in the stores giving out soap, scouring powder, new mops, cloths and brooms. Usually, the girls knew precisely what they needed. She had learnt not to ask for lists for many, and though they could read, had difficulty in writing.

This day Rebecca, a round faced, round red-cheeked girl – not from Middlesbrough, but nearby Scalby - pushed a list into Annie's hand. She read it absently, emptying soda in a jam jar, lifting up another floor cloth. As she returned the list she looked at the writing. It was familiar... it was that of the anonymous letter. She was aware that she hesitated, she knew that Rebecca noticed.

"What pretty handwriting. You are a credit to your teacher. Where did you learn such lovely copperplate?"

Rebecca, confused, frightened, returned in her mind to school.

"At Scalby School, Miss."

"Oh, I hope I am not a Miss any longer. That would be very awkward."

The maids all laughed. Rebecca laughed, relaxed, but stiffened as Annie said, "I've seen that pretty handwriting before somewhere. Who's next?"

Annie decided not to tell Edward, but she wondered how to deal with this odd little incipient drama. Annie noticed the small country child. Her dowdy clothes were rustic, the other girls, bred in towns, had learnt to be far smarter than their mothers had ever been.

Annie suddenly had a plan. She decided to take her under her wing - and more than that, under Mary's wing as well. So she had Rebecca dusting and cleaning in her private rooms and this led to Mary showing the little girl how to lay out Annie's clothes for the evening.

Weeks passed, Annie never spoke of her suspicions, yet each knew that the other knew of the anonymous letters.

Later, Annie began giving Rebecca clothes. She advised her and taught her how to dress. The little rustic began to resemble the town-girls. She even acquired a boyfriend and to Annie's relief he was from Scalby. Annie watched over all this with fond eyes and, as is so often the way, she failed to notice, or interpret, her dearest daughter's perplexities.

Nancy went quite frequently to Leeds. Jim was always at the station to meet her, and, as always, he charmed her. He took her to the dyeing works. The cleanliness of the vats, the scientific precision of the preparation of dyes impressed her, but the squalor of the buildings and the neighbourhood depressed her. It reminded her of the war.

She asked again and again how people could survive in such ugliness. With Mr Lockwood she went to lunch in a large public house nearby. They escorted her to a dining room upstairs. She thought this dreary and ugly when left alone as they went to the bar for drinks.

It was, then, that she noticed how briskly Jim's glass was emptied. She refused to count how many pints he had drunk. She noticed that he was more talkative than usual.

When, later in the afternoon, they reached Bruncliffe Lodge, Mrs Lockwood hurried to embrace Nancy. Of all the family she was the one she liked best, an opinion she never changed. To kiss this motherly woman was natural, to kiss his sisters she found difficult.

Next day, Mrs Lockwood and Nancy went up to the linen room at the top of the house. Together they sorted out old, not so old and fairly new sheets and pillow cases. The old lady talked and mostly of Jim. She was proud of her son's war record, but she thought the price he had paid had been too high.

"No, he was never shell-shocked, but he did have nightmares and some moods. They are passing, think goodness."

Then laying her hand on Nancy's arm she said: "I am very glad you are taking him over. You will, I know, be the making of him."

This remark filled Nancy with both pride and a certain amount of alarm. She had never considered herself capable of making anyone... that was the sort of role she left to her mother. Being young and romantic she recalled that room with its skylight for evermore and she interpreted it all as an omen rather than a warning.

Other weekends followed and Nancy noticed that there was a

relaxation - the Lockwoods were taking her for granted. Her Matthews pride did not know whether she approved of this, but she also enjoyed being jolly with them, though it was a rougher jollity than she had ever known in Scarborough.

On one Saturday night the father and his two sons went out, the women talked and knitted and Nancy became aware of a tension in the air. They were waiting. She thought that they had sometimes waited for her father to return from the Masonic Club, but nobody had been apprehensive.

They heard footsteps on the gravel, feet stumbling on the steps to the front door, a fumbling for the door knob and Mrs Lockwood looking up frightened, displeased and upset. The door opened slowly and there was Jim smiling vaguely and rather stupidly. It was Mrs Lockwood who moved over sharply to her husband and said, "How could you let this happen?"

Her husband looked back at her with a slowly comprehending look then replied, "Pretty Nancy. She's too good to see us like this I suppose. Well, she'll have to learn."

The ugly truculence frightened Nancy. The next moment, however, Jim was kneeling at her feet. Again she did not know what to do. He blurted out again and again, "I'm sorry, very sorry, sorry... won't do it again."

Even as he said it she did not believe him, but she raised him to his feet.

"It is all right, Jim. I understand."

As she said it she knew that it was a lie. She did not understand. He fell on his knees again and weeping put his head in her lap.

"I knew you'd understand."

He wept. This brought tears to her eyes. She had never seen a man weep. She was alarmed, but all she said was, "You must go to bed."

Jim's father and sister led him away, with alacrity and an expertise that bellowed warnings to her. She was, though, too confused to interpret these signals rationally. She was afraid and the future opened like a hideous chasm before her.

Instead of admitting anything she talked, small talk amid a stunned and shocked silence. They all awaited her reaction and she refused to show any. The sisters answered with a yes and a no.

Silence gathered again and the clock on the mantelpiece ticked audibly. Nancy remarked upon that. They were unsure of what to make of this strange calm girl.

The door opened and Mrs Lockwood came in. She went up to the sofa and sat beside Nancy and took her hand.

"Perhaps, my dear, it is as well that you saw that. Jim does drink. It is the war that has done it. The main trouble is that so much of his work, like his father's, is done over a drink in public houses."

"Can't he do other work?" asked Nancy a little coldly.

"He could. He's a clever boy, always was. But the business... it needs him. He has a place in it."

Then turning, appealing she urged, "I am quite sure you are his best hope. He loves you. He will do anything for you. If anyone can stop him drinking, it is you."

Nancy listened. She wanted to do the right thing. She also wanted to do the good thing. She was aware of her inexperience, even incapability. The two girls came and sat on the floor by her, they backed every word their mother said. Nancy just did not know what to do and she felt utterly alone.

Again the door opened. There stood Jim in his dressing gown. Once more he apologised, once more he promised not to drink and maudlin tears began to fall. Marnie went to him, took his arm and led him from the room saying, "Keep this till tomorrow. You'll feel better then."

Nancy started up and watched the puppet-like figure of the man she was to marry being coaxed up the stairs. The drama of the occasion seized her... it was like an act on the stage. Suddenly she found herself playing a part, clinging to the door and weeping and managing to speak eloquently.

A portion of her stood aside and watched with some admiration this performance. It brought an immediate response. All three women vowed continual help. They praised her and when she said that she would try they said that she would never, never regret her decision.

Going back in the train she pondered on it all and her heart beat fast. The more she thought, the calmer she became, the motion of the train soothed her, everything was flying by and her pains seemed to fly with them.

She began to imagine herself in a successful future, a house full of sunshine and a strong and happy Jim beside her. Yes, yes, she would take on the task. It magnified in her mind and became a mission to which God had destined her.

Once more, drama appealed to a young mind unacquainted with harsh reality. Far more seriously she decided that she would not tell either of her parents, or Kit.

No sooner was she across the threshold of home than she sensed that something was wrong. Her mother seemed older. It was the first time she had noticed that. Annie was more pleased than usual to see her daughter and clung momentarily longer when she embraced her.

But she kept her secret for many hours, until they were going to bed. Then she confided that Dr Salter had found a small lump in Edward's mouth. It was not serious, but it would require a small operation to have it removed.

Nancy did not need to be told more... she knew that her mother feared the dark hand of death, but neither confided openly so much. In bed Nancy cried.

"What a terrible, terrible weekend."

The operation went very smoothly and Edward was about and well so quickly that the shadows that had frightened moved far away and thoughts were centred on the wedding in the following April.

Houses were rented in Leeds and in West Hartlepool. Annie bought linen, towels and helped them make curtains. Edward found more excuses to attend auction sales, which he loved, and he stalked down antiques, buying them, as far as possible in pairs.

He gave to each a Buhl cabinet, to Kit a mahogany table and to Nancy a 17th century gate-leg table. The presents seemed equal, but it every case Nancy's possessions were slightly better, rarer, finer.

The households equipped, Annie then turned her attention to the trousseaux. Silk and crepe de Chine had pride of place. Nothing was forgotten, a room was set aside for each girl. Annie's purchases alone meant that the bed was piled, even before the presents began to arrive.

Annie enjoyed it immensely. It seemed that the planning, organising and giving was making up for all the inadequacies of her wedding day in the storm so long ago. The wedding was to be a great day for everyone.

The day, so long planned, in April was bright and fine, but the ermine stoles of the brides, given by their Aunt Beatrice, were needed. Annie, too, wore a similar stole and with her velvet pansy covered hat, erect stance, energetic step and stance she resembled her contemporary, Queen Mary, a similarity that would not have pleased her.

No one can escape the subtle marking each generation stamps upon its children. If Annie looked regal, her daughters looked less so. They were pretty and desirable in their virginal clothes, but there was something comic in the descent their veils and headdresses made upon their brows.

This was matched by the upward ascent of their skirts' hems towards their knees which revealed long white stockings on long white shapely legs ending in slim satin shoes with diamond buckles.

According to Annie, Scarborough held its breath for the occasion. Certainly the Town Hall emptied of its staff as the procession went down St Nicholas Street. If people did not actually line the street, many made it their business to be on the bridal route as it passed. It was a measure of the popularity of Edward.

Annie bowed to her many acquaintances, but inwardly she was deeply and suddenly disturbed. Nancy had spent the night and morning weeping rather hysterically. It was unlike her. Annie knew that something was wrong and much more wrong than she had ever divined.

She begged Nancy to tell her, she even told her that she did not have to marry, but as she hugged her child, she knew her child hugged a secret.

At St Mary's she was surprised to find Canon Cooper awaiting her and leading her to the porch where she was escorted up the aisle by the groomsmen. She looked at the flowers, listened to the organ played by Mr Keaton, and the buzz of subdued chatter.

Her first thought was that it was all very different to her own wedding in the same church, empty with swooping draughts from the gale outside. Yet she knew that her heart had been happier.

She looked at the grandeur and saw with dreadful clarity that all this was show. She had laboured on the trappings of the occasion and not searched out the reality beneath. She looked at the grooms divided by their best men.

Of John's dazzling good looks and soldierly bearing there was no doubt. She still did not like him, but Kit was in love. Jim, whose humour, gaiety and music had always beguiled her, looked, she saw for the first time, unfinished.

He was an unfinished mould. She could not bring herself to say weak. She was afraid… a dread for her most loved child seized her and her unhappiness was great.

The service began. The liturgy controlled the minds so the emotions and tears were only temporarily dammed.

But in the vestry they flowed and Dr Salter said: "Such emotional things weddings."

Nancy moved mechanically, doing everything she should at the correct and prescribed time. But she only became a real human when she was placed in the car with Jim when she noticed that he had neither his hat, nor his gloves… they were in the vestry. The first act of her married life was slight exasperation.

Chapter 35

Married Daughters

All went as planned, nobody misbehaved. Everyone congratulated everyone else on the splendour of this double event and Annie straight-backed, her head on one side smiled. But a more terrible emptiness opened before her than she had ever imagined and allied with it was fear and guilt.

Next morning, as Annie sat in the office writing letters, her sister arrived, as she did each day, a custom Annie considered very aggravating. Not unnaturally, she craved praise for the smoothness and excellence of the reception which she had arranged the previous day.

She wished only to prattle endlessly of the wedding, the flowers, the clothes, the people. Annie looked at her sister almost uncomprehendingly, she felt so desolate and until she had thrown herself into the pile of correspondence, she had been reliving the misery of her mother's death so long ago.

Her feeling then was the feeling she now had. Annie mentioned this, but Edith could only think of the glories of the day.

"It was a terrible day, Edith. I should never have allowed it. Whatever possessed me to lose both of my girls on the same day. I must have been mad."

Her despair seemed selfish, but it really was apprehension for Nancy. She knew, but could not declare it, that the marriage would go utterly wrong.

Edith, walking back over the Spa Bridge and along Birdcage Walk, pondered, as she so often did, on the unnaturalness of her sister, whom she failed to understand, yet blindly adored.

Life was full and busy. Edward returned, one morning, from the Town Hall to tell Annie that he had been made an Alderman. It had, of course, been mooted, but they had kept it secret, they were both very pleased, it seemed a just reward for his work on the Council. The season looked promising, the bookings were up and Annie had a new pupil.

With Edith, Annie had gone to Ravenscar. They had tea at the

Raven Hall Hotel and there Annie had seen a slim, pretty girl with a gurgling laugh and a pleasing crow to her voice... she seemed to epitomise gaiety.

"That, Edith is the very girl I want to take the place of Kit at St Nicholas."

Annie knew the managers of the hotel. She discovered that their receptionist, Tansy, was the daughter of an actor and actress in the West End of London. Annie asked her if she would like to work in Scarborough at the end of the season, Tansy was only too glad.

For Annie it was like having a daughter around again, but, perhaps, it was even better, for this daughter was also a pupil and a very apt one. Annie taught her the craft and wiles of hotel keeping as she had never taught her children.

She had no need to preach charm for that Tansy owned by nature, but the tricks, and the tricks of the building were important to impart,.

"When you are showing rooms at the top of the house, watch very carefully how your clients manage stairs, don't hurry them, pause, direct their gaze out of a window, talk to them. Most specially, if you are going to the top floor, remember that the last flight of stairs is steeper. Stop before you begin to climb and go slower, then they never notice."

When the full season started Annie confided her greatest guile of all.

"Some people, when they arrive, tired from their journey, are bound to be disappointed by their rooms if they are at the back. They will ask for me and complain. See that they are given tea and tell them that I am out and I will see them after dinner."

This Tansy did and she watched the ensuing little drama. Annie, dressed superbly with her diamonds and sapphires in her ears, pearls about her throat and a sapphire crescent brooch she inherited from her mother-in-law, would appear very serene and calm after the complaining couple had had a very good dinner.

She listened sympathetically, she would see what she could do and she sent them away more than mollified. Annie enjoyed it, it was better than Bridge. It was a vital part of the game of life. But she was tiring.

Three weeks after Edward was made an Alderman, another lump appeared in his mouth. Again it was removed, again it was pronounced benign. Dr Salter came frequently and he played his profession's stratagems.

If he had his doubts about the innocence of the disease, he hid them. He grew even fonder of his patients and as he saw Annie lose the bloom in her skin, which she had retained so long, he determined to advise her on the undesirability of dyeing her hair, a secret, she thought, was entirely between her hairdresser and herself.

How was this to be done tactfully? The day came when in the bright sunshine she came out on to the porch with him. He looked up at her with his usual admiration, another of his arts, well practised. He looked steadfastly at the hardness of the colour in the bouffant curls, he took a breath, then said, "What a pity, what a pity."

He got into his car and drove off swiftly. Annie was momentarily surprised and did not know what he was alluding to, then realised it must be her hair. She thought it out of place and sought a mirror. There was nothing disarranged, but for the first time she noticed the discrepancy between the apparently young hair and her ageing pearl-like skin. She ceased her visits to Madame Bazin.

She watched with some delight and growing self-congratulation on the silver quality of her hair which received far more praise than her coloured curls had ever done.

At the beginning of June there was a telephone call from Leeds. Nancy's baby was imminent, a month early. Annie had been preparing for the birth, the cot was bought, but the hangings unmade.

The nurse was booked for a month later. Annie was alarmed, but too occupied in contacting the nurse, and buying all the small necessities for an accouchement. Annie knew nothing of the events leading to this premature labour.

Jim, after a long period of abstinence, came home drunk. Nancy had been unable to sleep and had become worried. When she heard the feverish scrabblings of his key searching for the lock she knew his condition.

She ran downstairs to let him in. He had lurched in and fallen, then crawled to the foot of the stairs and sat with his head in his hands.

He was apologetic in sober spasms. Nancy helped him up the stairs.

He had leant heavily on her as she propelled his to the bed. He had fallen across the eiderdown and Nancy had eased off his boots, heaved him up and taken off his jacket and waistcoat. He had fallen asleep almost directly.

Nancy was distressed and disappointed, but she too fell asleep, only to awake early with pains she recognised easily as the first warnings. With great difficulty she had wakened Jim. He had been both sullen and guilty and Nancy had been imperative as to the action they had to take.

"Get your father's car, at once, and drive me to Mother."

His father had taken more persuasion than either of them had reckoned. Only when Jim threatened to hire a car at the firm's expense had the old man relented. Neither Mr Lockwood, nor his wife believed that Nancy was near her time, they considered it an excuse to go home.

Driving as fast as he dare, Jim went via York and Malton. He was cautious and Nancy urged him to drive faster. They never stopped and early in the afternoon, they arrived at the hotel.

The day was hot and close and Annie most unusually was flustered. She wondered why the baby was so soon, she never voiced her question, the nurse was already there and she sent immediately for Dr Salter.

Nancy' pains were urgent, incessant. Annie was so perturbed she was excluded from the room, she upset her daughter. Evening came and rolls of thunder roared overhead and as the storm died away, a very small son was born to Nancy and Jim. Nancy's first emotion was fear that she might break the frail little child.

He was placed in the unadorned cot and Annie was allowed in. She stood on one side holding Nancy's hand and Jim stood on the other – but not holding her hand.

Dr Salter beamed. "Well, you have a small but healthy little boy. What will you call him?"

"David," said Nancy.

"George," replied her husband.

"Well, you can decide that tomorrow. Now you must go to sleep."

"I think he should be called Nicholas," said Annie.

When Annie left the room she hurried straight to the room where her friend, Mrs Tindall was staying. She knocked.

"May I come in, Florence?"

The door opened. There was her oldest friend, still fully dressed but with her hair in a plait. She knew that a baby was on the way, she looked at Annie's shining eyes,

"It's a little boy. Come and see him."

Quickly, Mrs Tindall coiled up her hair, pinned it and followed Annie. Together they looked into the gaunt cot, the baby moved its hands, screwed up its face and slept on. The experienced old eyes took on a look of youth again.

"What will they call him?"

"Probably David George, or George David. It hasn't been settled yet."

"I think he looks more a David than a George, don't you?"

Annie pursed her lips. "Well, I prefer David to George, it reminds me of my Welsh mother. But I would like him to be called Nicholas, after the Cliff he was born on and the hotel."

The two women went downstairs to have a celebratory cup of tea. While they were having it Edward came in. He was instantly told the news and his immediate reaction was, "How is Nancy?"

Next day, Mrs Tindall bought material for the cradle, blue with yellow butterflies and when it had been cut, Nancy asked for a work-basket and began to sew the hems. There was alarm the following day when the baby turned yellow and matched the butterflies, but the doctor was reassuring.

The baby's progress was slow and worrying. It had for Nancy the blessing that she was advised to remain at home and not return to Leeds. This also suited Annie very well, the baby became her new toy and she walked with the pram with a swiftness not seen in her for many years.

She delightedly showed off her grandchild, she seemed oblivious of his fragility and, very strangely, she was blind to her daughter's slow recovery. She never sought a reason for the delays made to returning home.

Soon, everything changed, for she had to hurry up to Hartlepool to Kit who had a miscarriage. It was then that Nancy returned to Leeds and the smouldering discontent over the naming of the child.

Nancy did not like her father-in-law and his name was George.

She would not agree to David George, still less to George David. Her public reason for the dislike was that it sounded too like David Lloyd George.

She also wanted to call her son Nicholas, but the Lockwoods laughed at the name. So the christening took place in Scarborough and the babe named David and no more. Resentment smouldered in the Lockwood family, also in Nancy, but she confided in nobody except her cousin Sybil.

It was a lonely life that Nancy led. There were days when she had only her child to speak to, her neighbours thought her la-di-da, her speech distanced her from them instantly. She loved her house but not its position.

The antiques her father had given her made it a small jewel but Jim did not care for it. He was dutiful, he no longer drank - he had even, at Nancy's persuasion, signed the teetotal pledge. His family considered this ludicrous. The problem was not only drinking, it was lack of common ground of interest, a love of dogs was not enough. It did not even induce them to have an animal of their own for Nancy, revealingly, said, "We have Peter in Scarborough."

Now that Jim avoided pubs and all drink it became obvious to Edward and Annie that there had been more trouble there than they had believed. Edward was fond of Jim and he tended, very unfairly, to compare him favourably with his other son-in-law, John.

John was always so full of advice and persistent in outlining plans to improve the hotel. It was he who finally pushed Edward into the long discussed plan to make the two houses, one complete hotel. Annie, who had played a delaying tactic for so long could not bear to see the Georgian bow windows go. She went away.

It was a mistake, her vigilance over many features was needed, when she returned she found her much loved brass door locks had gone and worse, an Adam fireplace had been removed and a modern replacement in the 18th century style put in.

She lost heart. She had another greater fear, Edward's health... she knew that he had cancer. She was very afraid for him. Life was clouding over for many in Britain and the Matthews were not immune.

David was 18 months old. He was the usual inquisitive and mischievous child. He could be very quiet and deeply engrossed in his play.

Once he reached the sideboard and spent a happy half-hour mixing jam with mustard, salt with sugar and chutney with everything. Once, before a little dinner party, he locked the sideboard and would not, or could not, tell where he had put the key. His mother was, at times exasperated with him, but usually his flaxen hair, his deep set eyes and his vivid red mouth, "The only good thing he inherited from the Lockwoods" melted her anger.

She spent many lonely hours talking to him. Sometimes, when very depressed, she would put him in his pram and walk to Kirkstall Abbey and as they encircled the ruins they would consume together a bar of milk chocolate. She knew it was not good for him and rationalised it into a necessary solace for herself.

All this meant that a greater and deeper bond was developing between them and Nancy did not recognise that her husband, always vulnerable, was becoming jealous. When, at last, it became apparent, Nancy became over protective of her child.

One Saturday in winter, David had croup. Jim had gone out for an hour on business. The hour became four and there were no provisions in the house for Sunday. Nancy did not dare to take David out in the cold wind.

At last Jim returned... he was not sober. There was no alternative, she asked him to watch over their son while she went shopping. David was put in a play-pen close to the fire. There was a guard before the grate.

When Nancy returned, she heard screams of fear as she entered the small garden. She ran into the house, dropped the food and opened the sitting room door to find it full of smoke. Jim was fast asleep and David on a rug smouldering with fire. She snatched up her child, took him to the kitchen and calmed him, but not herself.

Sunday was silent, bitter with accusations and guilt. There was no conversation, each read a book, they did not read, they pondered on their own particular misery.

Next day Jim went to work. As soon as he had gone, Nancy packed a suitcase and wrote a note saying, quite inevitably, that she had gone back to her mother.

The hotel was still in turmoil when Annie returned from West Hartlepool. It was closed to visitors, furniture cluttered passages and there was dust everywhere.

There was another operation to face and again Edward walked

up to the nursing home unattended as he wished it.

It might have suited him best, but Annie already feeling helpless and full of dread, felt unwanted and unable to show her sympathy. It was her very sympathy that Edward feared.

Once again Dr Salter pronounced it a success, then, he began to explain that a portion of Edward's palate had been removed and they would have difficulty in understanding him at first.

The warning alerted Annie, but the whistling and the snuffling that slurred her husband's speech was far worse than she had anticipated. The surprise at missing his clear diction daunted her, she panicked and ceased to listen. She was on the verge of crying in both horror and embarrassment when she very sturdily spoke to herself.

"You used to be good at languages, turning noises into words, do the same now and remember it is your own speech." The concentration she had to bring banished feeling and very gradually the sounds assumed shapes and they became words, horribly distorted, but words.

It was not until she was out of the room and down the stairs than her tears overcame her. As soon as he was able to get up she had him home.

Edward was shocked. He knew that his days of public speaking were over. He lay back on his pillow and stared at the ceiling, broken. Annie was at a loss of what to do, as she held his hand she knew that far more than sympathy was needed.

She picked up the volume of Shakespeare that was always by his bed. She ruffled through the pages and, then, said, "Well, it's obvious why you never read this, Ted, the print is minute. It's only there for show."

They both laughed. He picked it up, he tried to read aloud. He lay it down and with a look that was at once forlorn and determined said, "Fetch me the green copies from the writing room."

Acting immediately on this Annie brought up the slim illustrated volumes, clearly printed and well spaced. He looked through, then he began to read one of Shylock's speeches. Annie recognised it and having that knowledge the words were easier to visualise.

When he stopped she told him what it was. He became excited, he sat up. Every time she knew a speech he was more gratified, a lustre came to his eye.

It was the beginning of his rehabilitation... it was a slow, slow climb.

He began to dress and shave and, then, for hours he would sit at Annie's dressing table reading aloud and watching his mouth enunciate in the mirror, he watched intently, analytically and above all he listened to himself.

Every afternoon Annie, after a rest, took out her embroidery and listened. It was repeated each evening. She wondered if it was merely familiarity with his voice that made her understand, or was his voice really improving?

She knew that at this time she had never loved her husband more, always he had shown his affection in a distant and teasing way. He had been self-sufficient and there had been little she could do for him, now he needed her.

As she left his room she was saddened by this thought for it had come so late. She foresaw the end of his career, all that he enjoyed, she thought his death imminent. Going down the stairs she saw the front door open and in ran David who went straight up to her.

She picked him up and gave him a hug, not just for him, but to reassure herself of love and life. She put him down when she saw Nancy, her best beloved child and hastening to her she enfolded her in her arms.

"Oh, Nancy, I'm so glad you have come. How did you know I needed you?"

All the storming emotions and confessions in Nancy's mind were sealed at a stroke.

"What is it? Is Father worse?"

"He can no longer speak properly. He won't see anybody except me. You can change that. But you look tired, dear, some tea first."

Over tea Annie explained her husband's ordeal, she warned Nancy that he was difficult to understand, she had become used to him. As they talked they failed to notice that the child had gone. They did not worry... he could come to no harm in the hotel.

They went upstairs. The bedroom door was open and they heard David and his grandfather talking. Nancy looked in amazement at her mother, her father was perfectly intelligible, a little hoarse and with the faintest of slurs.

In the room David was on the bed and Edward was beaming.

His grandson understood him, he had begun to think only Annie could comprehend. Nancy took over from her mother and with more jollity and less sympathy roused him from his fears.

She made him come downstairs. She even got him to talk to visitors, after a few days. Soon he was walking down to the harbour and around the Marine Drive.

One evening, after reading two speeches of Henry V to Nancy, Edward said: "Where's Jim?"

"Oh he's away on business for a couple for weeks, that's why we came."

"But you've been away two weeks already. Hadn't you better go back?"

"He'll come for us when he wants us."

Edward thought her off-hand way was a warning. He was perturbed but said nothing.

Nancy was more than content. She found it so restful to be back home and she loved looking after her father. It was so lovely she kept saying to herself to help someone who was helpable.

She admitted to herself that she was totally unable to help Jim any longer. She also found things to do in the hotel. There were flowers to do constantly. There was David to take out and Peter, the dog, to exercise.

She fell into her old routine of visiting Auntie Bea and her cousins. She began to think that her aunt looked at her a little searchingly and she felt guilty that she was a little devious. She did not know what to do.

She found that she regarded Billy with envy. She was training to be a midwife in Birmingham. At times she became depressed, but looking at her son bent over a rock pool she was content.

He would squat for long periods gazing into the depths, occasionally lifting a frond of sea-weed with a finicky left hand. She thought she was hiding everything very well and especially with her mother because her greatest happiness was being with her.

She had moments, however, of abstraction when her mouth drooped and her eyes saddened and Annie had noticed these. She had spoken to her husband and very wisely they waited. It was when the fortnight had become a month and Edward was once again attending committees that they really discussed it. "Something is wrong between Nancy and Jim. I am quite sure."

"It seems that Jim is away on business."
"You know, Annie, I don't believe it."
"I will write then."
"I think you had better telephone."

Annie recoiled at the thought... the telephone was still an agitating instrument to her.

"What if Jim should answer? It would be so embarrassing."
"Then I'll ring them up."

He did so immediately and shouted, as he always did, down the phone. When he returned he looked puzzled.

"I spoke to Mrs Lockwood. Nice little woman, always liked her. She seemed to think Nancy and David were recovering from colds, that's not so, is it?"

Annie's face clouded over. She loathed lies.

"What else did you say?"
"I said that Jim was very welcome. We'd be pleased to see him. But, you know, Annie. I don't think he's been away at all."
"What, oh what shall we do?"
"First of all, find out the trouble and then look for a cure. And, darling, don't let your imagination run away with you."

Dusk was falling and Nancy came in. David ran to his grandparents to show them the sweets Auntie Edith had given him and some brandy snaps. David pushed one of them into his grandfather's hand, a sticky act of generosity Annie resisted.

After dinner, David in bed, the three sat by the fire. Nancy looked at the Meissen candelabra and the clock. She smiled.

"Do you remember, Daddy, how that clock was covered in black paint and you and I chipped it all off bit by bit?"
"That was a tedious job. But look what was underneath the paint."

She looked again at the flower wreathed china with the delicate little white and gilt face. The cherub presided above and two goddesses flanked each side.

"Thinking of clocks and time how long are you going to stay, dear?"
"Tired of me, Daddy?"

It was said almost mischievously.

"No, thinking of Jim."
"Oh, he can look after himself. He doesn't need us."

Annie watched and seemed to feel the foundations of the earth move beneath her. She was full of apprehension. Several times she wished to interject, stop Edward probing, but she always retracted. Nancy noted it and stretched out her hand to her mother.

"It's all right, Mummy. It is better that it all comes out. No, I am not happy. I am very unhappy. Jim drinks far more than you think and I don't know what to do. Almost worse is that he's becoming jealous of David."

She, then, told them of the burning rug and David's screams.

Annie felt faint. It was all as bad as she had imagined in her wildest dreams.

Jim did not come, but Nancy went back. Annie was so upset she wept openly on the railway station.

A year passed, at its best it was lack-lustre, at its worst it was a nightmare. Nancy now encountered hostility from her sister-in-law and a certain reserve from Mrs Lockwood. Neither Jim, nor Nancy looked ahead. Like blinkered horses, they plodded from one day to the next.

At last Jim was laid aside from work by his father. Nancy thought that they might, now, begin to understand her plight, but they had forgotten how they had encouraged her to marry Jim to save him.

They sought a scapegoat and blamed her instead. They were concerned, though, and lent Jim their cottage at Monk Seaton in the Dales. Nancy loved the thick white walls and she arranged flowers and set them around the rooms.

She felt hopeful in this pretty setting. The first week was good, they went for walks, Jim played the piano and sang. Then he went to the pub, he got drunk and was raucous and rowdy. Nancy felt ashamed for everyone in the small community knew. She felt their pity and resented it.

It was followed by a day of remorse and a third day of violence. He seized the carving knife and brandished it, rejoicing in Nancy's fear. When he went into the scullery she rushed up the stairs, picked David from his bed and ran across the green to the farmers who sold milk.

Mrs Lightowler opened the door holding the lamp up high. She saw the terror in Nancy's eyes before she had said anything.

"Come in, come in."

Then with that particular blend of insight and concern given many Yorkshire people, she said, "Your husband at the drink again?"

Nancy could only nod. She was led into the large kitchen where the family sat before the fire burning in the range. With the same tone lacking all drama, she announced, "It's Mrs Lockwood and David come for the night."

It was Mr Lightowler who rose up and said, "Eeh, my poor lassie."

The fatherly concern broke Nancy, all her anger and resentment turned to tears, they gave her tea. Then the girls took David, still two thirds asleep and carried him upstairs.

Mr Lightowler and his eldest son went over to Monk's Cottage to see to Jim. They found him dead to the world on the sofa. He never woke while they took off his boots, put a rug over him, took away the paraffin lamp and left. When they returned and reported, the son grinned and Nancy was bound to smile, but at the same time she said, "What am I to do?"

"Go back home, my dear, your mother will be glad to have you. Then see."

"But I have no money. I must get back to the house in Leeds, there's money there."

"George is going in to the market tomorrow - he'll take you, first thing."

Very early next day, Nancy returned to the cottage with Mrs Lightowler. They packed a few things hurriedly and stealthily while Jim still slept. They climbed into the lorry. David was aware of a strange excitement as he sat on his mother's lap. They drove straight to the little house.

"I won't be long, George."

Nancy opened the door, picked up the post, put it in her handbag and ran up the stairs. She went to David's small room and opened the bottom drawer of his chest. There in a toffee tin were the sovereigns Edward had given him.

It was a store she never touched, there were 16 of them. Before she opened the lid she knew that it was empty. She knew that Jim had taken it. If she had had any reserves of strength she would have been angry, she just felt bottomless despair. She knelt by the drawer motionless. She was utterly humiliated, but also utterly resolved.

She went down, out of the door, locked it and went to the lorry.

"George, the money has gone. I've nothing. Can you lend me the fare?"

"Aye, when I've sold the cabbages," jerking his thumb towards the load behind the cab.

His crates were taken straight away and they drove to the station. It was there that David was surprised to see his mother put an arm round George, give him a kiss and tell him, "You're a man in a million."

Scarborough, for the first time in her life, seemed alien, almost hostile as she carried her case towards St Nicholas Cliff, changing the burden from left to right frequently.

It was Harry, out on the porch who saw her and sprinted up to her and took the case." Is my mother at home?"

"Yes, Miss. In the office."

Annie was writing letters, she knew from Nancy's look that all was ill.

"I'm home for good, Mummy."

It was not. Edward still believed in the good intentions of Jim and talking with both Nancy and his son-in-law he brought about a rapprochement. He understood Jim better than either Nancy, or Annie, also the force of convention pressed upon him far harder, than it did on these two of his womenfolk. Work was found for Jim in Scarborough and they took a flat in the Crescent.

These months of anxiety made inroads upon the youthfulness Annie had managed to retain, her skin retained its pink and white, but it was a petal without its bloom. Her elegance remained, veneering a maelstrom of thought and questioning.

Her husband was guided by a Christian ethos which was embedded in the society he moved in, without any of the beliefs of faith. Annie, now, found herself questioning the creed she had relied upon.

She felt guilt and she pondered all these things as she walked most evenings underneath the sycamores beneath the Esplanade watching the birds and rejoicing in the primroses. For the first time she wished that she had allowed Nancy to be a nurse.

She blamed herself for being too busy at the time of the marriage to really look deeply into the matter. She still blamed herself that Nancy had not confided in her.

Now, before her, stood the probability of divorce. She was a member of the Mothers' Union, she had drifted into it. She believed in yielding to certain circumstances, and Nancy's plight was one of them. Dogmatic rigours were not a part of her character and she found herself surprisingly rebellious.

As she considered everything, it all came down to the vision she had of her daughter's small, bewildered and unhappy face. Her thoughts turned often to the evening when Nancy had told them so much, and, as she added in her mind, by no means all.

She remembered how Edward, always so loving to Nancy, had said with that tone of exasperation he usually retained for Kit or Alan, "But why on earth didn't you tell us?"

The irritation of her husband had upset her, but the reply had stung her like a whiplash.

"It had all gone so far. I was afraid of what people would say, but most of all I did not think it was honourable."

The word honourable, honourable, honourable had echoed in her mind. She knew she had used the word frequently as she brought up her children. It had been the basis of her teaching and example. It had seemed so fine, so noble and aristocratic.

She remembered how pleased she had been when Mr Latham had said to her, "Your daughter has the honour of a gentleman."

It had taken the hideous madness of the war to show her how overworked the notion of honour had been. And yet, and yet she knew, she still believed it. She remembered an evening later, when more dispassionate the three had talked and honour, once again had been mentioned and Nancy had said,

"Daddy, quote me those lines of Shakespeare about the silliness of honour."

He had stared in the fire for a minute and then responded,

"Honour prickles me on,

Can honour set-to a leg? No. Or an arm?

That's old Falstaff for you."

Nancy had smiled and said, "But, you know, it's not true, Daddy."

"It is true and it is not true," said Annie, "I think of all those young men, who have sat by this very fire, who have died for a kind of honour. It was wonderful, admirable, but foolish and stupid as well. Oh, I don't know. I don't know."

Annie walking on the Spa, still, did not know. She became aware of the crows startled by her, the lonely walker, rising up from their nests and squawking crossly. She was aware that the world had changed, it made her feel older.

It had changed, she ruminated when skirts had risen from the ground, it had meant a huge step towards freedom and that freedom had been spiritual as well. Her vanity took over and she felt again her resentment that skirts had shortened, for her legs had never been as shapely and as pretty as the rest of her.

As she thought of it she looked at her right leg and said, almost aloud, "Too plump." Then she corrected herself severely,

"Annie, you were thinking seriously about marriage. You are being frivolous. Yes, yes. Things have changed. Better a bad marriage ended than enduring misery for everyone. No, God did not mean us to be unhappy."

It seemed her discussion had ended satisfactorily. She walked on. She was now down by the bandstand. The sea slapped the battlemented wall, a slopping noise that after all the years, still reminded her of Dutch housewives swilling pails of water outside their house and brushing with brooms vigorously.

Holland was far, far away and Scarborough was incontestably her home. She looked at the bay, towards the harbour and the truncated lighthouse, a tidied stump of the building the Germans had shelled in the bombardment.

Her eye followed up to the Castle, then slowly down to St Mary's to the roofs of the mass of the town, all those houses slipping, oh so slowly over the centuries into the sea. She loved it, she could not imagine ever leaving it.

Her gaze was blocked by the ponderous immensity of the Grand Hotel with its triple slate covered breasts. "Pity, pity," was all she said.

Back at the hotel she seemed needed by everyone. But everything had to wait, while she went from window to window on the ground floor adjusting the curtains which were not to her liking and that led to the plumping up of the cushions.

Up in her room Edward was dressing. She helped him with his tie. He smiled and she thought that he was better looking without a moustache. Then he said, "How would you like to be the Mayoress of Scarborough?"

She felt pride and delight and entirely for him. She kissed him and said, "Oh, Ted." Then she continued, "There's just one thing. The Council must give me a free hand to cleaning up the Town Hall, especially the chandeliers, they are really quite disgraceful."

"That should be easy."

Chapter 36

The Mayor

The mayoralty would be the crown of Edward's career, the reward for his constant work on the various committees of the Council. He was pleased, so Annie was pleased, but she feared for his health and she faltered before the added burden for herself.

She, also, thought that it was still some months off. She realised that she would have to find more help. Tansy was an excellent receptionist, quick, efficient and possessing great charm. Annie knew that she would not stay long for she collected proposals of marriage as churchwardens collect alms, she would accept one of them very soon.

Then Annie added an odd thought, she knew that she must find someone to help, in case Edward becomes really ill. The constant operations had become a pattern of life and they were all lulled into complacency. Dr Salter was invariably reassuring, so that Edward's visits of the Nursing Home were regarded as trips to the dentist. What Edward felt and thought no one ever knew.

One week Annie got behind with the accounts, Mr Bilston came to check them and found a muddle. "You know, Mrs Matthews, now that the hotel is so much bigger, this it too much for you. Can't you find a good book-keeper?"

Annie knew that he was right, she had been tired. She found it difficult to be welcoming and friendly with the visitors all the time, when she knew so much work awaited her in the office. She, also, knew that being a good hostess was the more important of the two. There would be even less time when she was to be Mayoress. Without consulting anyone she placed an advertisement in the Yorkshire Post.

A few days later, she received a few replies. Some were too old... some knew nothing of book-keeping. There was one application which had an urgent sound to Annie's ears. It spoke to her heart as well as her head. A girl, daughter of a miner, still in her teens wrote very carefully from Barnsley.

She was able to type, take shorthand and book-keeping was a

pleasure to her. There was a postscript in a very small round hand, "I have also attended the Art School and have a diploma."

From that Annie said to herself, "This child is not just ambitious financially but needs a more beautiful world than Barnsley can provide. She remembered Anston and the brightest of the children there. Without hesitation she sent a telegram.

"Come immediately. Bring a black dress."

Two days later Violet Presley arrived. Even Annie had a shock - the girl was small, dark with a sallow freckled face and her appearance was not enhanced by a black hat, black coat and black stockings. Out of sight both Tansy and Nancy laughed saying she looked like a scullery maid on her day off after a funeral.

Annie, when she heard of this was angry. She told them that they should be grateful for their own superior place in society, but never mock others.

Miss Presley, very soon to be Pressy, was there to stay. She was efficient and utterly reliable. She also watched Annie and Tansy and copied them. She was aware of what she lacked in social graces and was eager to remedy it.

The black stockings were banished forever on the second day when Annie gave her her first pair of silk stockings. Annie loved having her - she loved to have an apt pupil.

The mayor-making seemed a long way off, not merely because they were in the midst of the season, but Edward had to undergo yet another operation, Sir Ninian Simpson was coming from Leeds to perform it. He examined his patient, went back to his friends very thoughtful and after dinner walked to St Nicholas Hotel.

It was a still warm evening and when he entered he saw Annie trailing from groups of guests to talk to yet another, she was wearing the cloudiest of grey-blue chiffon. When he saw that his name was mentioned to her by the porter, he saw the grey film of her dress seemed to veil her face.

She came to him and took him to their sitting room. He watched her, she had a calm he hated to ruffle, but he was aware that she knew more than she showed. When Mary had brought in the coffee and gone, she looked at him with her large and trusting eyes. "Tell me the very worst, Mr Simpson. Is he going to pull through?"

"Yes."

The brightness of relief that shone through her face amazed him and he wondered where the light came from, the eyes, the mouth, facial muscles. It was a mystery.

"What I fear is that I may leave him with a worse impediment in his speech."

Annie closed her eyes. No, not that agony for everyone again, all she said was, "Oh, no."

"We may have to remove the palate. But it can be replaced by a good dentist. Very likely it will not be as bad as last time. Now, Mrs Matthews, when do we tell him?"

"Hint, don't tell. He's very good at reading between the lines. Can you get young Dr Ward to tell him? He's very fond of Dr Ward."

"As it happens he is going to assist me."

On the evening of the operation, Edward was alone. He had forbidden Annie to visit for her sympathy tended to make him sorry for himself. But in the very tidy, clean and impersonal room he felt the need of someone of his own. He remembered his niece, Vera... she was with her mother at Tranby House, next door. So he sent a message to her.

The strong tall girl came into his room. It was a rush of youthful vigour that came with all the future, which seemed to include him. She had flowers from the garden which she arranged and she talked all the while.

When she had gone he thought about her. He thought of his own children and Alan on his way from Australia to take over the business. Vera had brought a very positive spirit into the room and it still lingered.

Then the thought of his speech and all the impediments and frustration came upon him again. He had fully understood young Dr Ward, but he squared his shoulders against the pillow and told himself that he had conquered it once, he could do it again.

After the operation only Annie saw him. When he went home, once again he never left his room and Annie listened and listened as he read As You Like It again and again while she embroidered dragons on a runner to go on the ebony table in the Chinese drawing room.

She grew to loathe the dragons, they were evil, they became symbols to her of cancer, sinuously growing and corrupting all the time. She was appalled too, because in spite of the golden bridge that had been made for him his words were slurred, there was a constant whistle and, worst of all, the weight of the contraption tired him.

One evening, she could bear his pain no longer. She went downstairs and into the empty dining room. Tthere she walked up and down between the tables... the pacing calmed her, order was coming into the confusion of her emotions.

Suddenly there was a crash of plates and the tinkle of broken china from the Still-room. Annie hurried in and was confronted by the vast amplitude of Martha rising up with pieces of a plate in her hand. She smiled up at Annie, "Only one plate broken, Madam."

"That is good luck not good management."

Annie turned on her heel, retreated to the dining room went into the tea room and out into the broad strip of garden. She crossed the lawn to a rose bush, and looked at the unfurling yellow buds and never saw them.

Instead she saw the amazed and almost frightened face of Martha. She was ashamed of her snapping words, she had never spoken to Martha like that before. She went back. Martha was putting newspapers over the shining steel surface of the long hot plate. Martha looked up... she was surprised to see her mistress again so soon.

"I am sorry, Martha. I did not mean it. It must be because it's the end of the season."

Martha knew well it was more. "That's all right, Madam. It's the master really. By the way, did you know there's a new young dentist just below the Cambridge called Mr Tomlinson?"

Annie did not wait, she went straight to Edward. He was tired, disheartened, he did not wish to listen. In the night he lay awake, the world seemed black, hopeless. He argued that he could not leave his dentist for a younger man, it would be disloyal.

He decided to resign from the council next day. He would never speak well again. Then, for no apparent reason he thought of Vera, the loving, lively girl who had cheered him and he wondered what she would want him to do. He knew, march forward hopefully.

He slept late next morning and woke to see Annie in her bed cap, a strange affair of lace with lappets and a ribbon beneath the chin. It should have made a face pretty, it made Annie plain.

He reached out for the golden palate in the glass by his bed, with a slight wince he put it in.

"Morning Annie. What was the name of that young dentist? Make an appointment, will you?"

Mr Tomlinson came, he examined Edward's mouth, he looked at the golden bridge. He insisted that Edward visit him that evening at his surgery to make impressions. With new materials, new skills a lighter frame was made and wearing it Edward walked home.

He stood on the Spa bridge and looked at the harbour and the castle and said aloud, "Damned if I will resign. I will be mayor."

That night Annie finished the last stitches in the hateful dragons and she listened to *Macbeth*. She was getting a little tired of Shakespeare. Edward ended.

"You are back to normal, Ted"

"Yes, I know. I think you'd better go to Marshall and Snelgrove's and fit yourself up with some new clothes. We need a fashionable mayoress."

Weeks before the Mayor-making, Annie was busy preparing for the event. Her priority had been the Town Hall. She had enthused the staff in some miraculous way in the Spring-cleaning of all the main rooms.

Curtains were taken down, cornices dusted, carpets cleaned. Glass and mirrors were made to shine and the chandeliers that had so offended her with their accumulated fly dirt, sparkled.

When that had been achieved, there was the great dinner to arrange at the hotel. There were to be more than sixty guests, there were eight courses. Annie could now rest assured that the food would not be served with paroxysms of tears from the cook, for Maria had retired and her able, but not so imaginative successor, Elsie had taken over.

The first mishap had been Edward's insistence that Jim Lockwood should attend, although Nancy had left him. Edward still attempted to make peace, whereas Annie accepted the hopelessness of the situation.

There was a deeper anxiety in Annie, she worried about Edward and she never said again, "If Edward should be really ill." She knew that he was.

She watched him like a hawk endowed with compassion. She looked to the year with some foreboding. She accepted it because it gave Edward such pride and pleasure.

The dinner was, to her, the happiest of all the occasions for she looked out upon her family, the family into which she had married and her friends. She had a special smile for Mrs Tindall, who talked sweetly, almost timidly with those around her, captivating them with her shy charm and never, for an instant, allowing them to see that she was a woman of great character, even force.

She also regarded the dark beauty of Nelly Hurst, the only cousin to represent the family of Armitage Bridge, Milnsbridge and Huddersfield. Seeing the schools she had taught at, the Sunday schools she had visited all performed an elaborate drill in her memory.

She then wished and wished with all her being that her mother could have seen this day, which everyone declared to be a triumph. Quickly Annie made a calculation and realised that her young slim pretty mother, who belonged forever to the 1870s would now have been 83. She seemed far removed by time and, yet, ever closer.

As the guests departed Jim lingered in the hall. He looked appealingly at Annie.

"Where are you staying, Jim?"

"I don't know." He looked troubled, but slightly predatory, too, "The truth is, I've, left my money behind."

Annie was not surprised but she was horrified, to herself she said: "Has the man no pride?"

"Come into the office, we shall see what the petty cash can do."

She found the key, opened the drawer and from the well-worn tin took out five pounds. She gave it to him with the words,

"That will teach you to carry your cheque book with you in future."

It restored Jim's confidence, but not for one moment did it hoodwink Miss Presley. The truth of her suspicions was confirmed by the sigh Annie gave as she entered the amount and placed the book in the tin.

When Annie had gone, Pressy wondered how the debit had been described - she thought it would be under Annie's much favoured, 'sundries.' Instead she read, 'charity'.

Next day, Annie was at the Town Hall again supervising the flower arrangements and the general bestowal of the furniture. She thought the Mayoralty worthwhile for the change that had been achieved in the rooms. They were no longer dim, no longer dowdy.

Back at the hotel, there was much excitement. John Barlow was endeavouring to take charge, but the beadle arrived in time with the robes. The arrival of these impressed John, he always respected a uniform. They all walked over to the Council chambers.

The November afternoon darkened, the lights were raised, speeches were made and Annie's grandson became lost in a sea of friendly people who led him to the Parlour. He saw his grandmother, she stood beneath a chandelier, her piled up silver hair glinted… she wore an ash-grey dress that flickered with embroidered bugle beads. She smiled at him and held out a hand, he ran to her.

She held his left hand and greeted one person after another in so regal a manner that for two years David muddled this image of her with the pictures of Queen Mary that he saw in the papers. He knew they were different persons, but he was not quite sure.

It was a year of activity and expansive in every way. There were many official duties, there was the official separation of Jim and Nancy, the hotel embarked on a massive alteration, which, again, Annie deplored for her tea-room overlooking the garden went and a vast dining room took its place.

Alan and his wife, Dot, took over the management and Edward and Annie bought a house on Cliff Bridge Terrace to which to retire. The terrace was built in the reign of William IV and retained Georgian proportions.

It looked to the sea, both east and south, including the Spa Bridge, the Valley and the elegant Esplanade and the cliffs diminishing down to Flamborough Head.

Both Edward and Annie were thrilled with the purchase. Edward particularly, for there he could live unmolested by visitors. The renovations and decorations were performed in a grandiose and distant way.

They did not trail from shop to shop choosing papers, materials, lampshades, whole rolls of paper were delivered for their inspection, eager salesmen arrived with velvet and huge crates of glass lampshades were there for their acceptance or rejection.

They both entered into this with enthusiasm, something of their early days together in the hotel were recaptured. All the while, however, Annie was overcome by a feeling of dread.

She would look at Edward with his high colour, his flinches of pain and wonder just what the future held. What she really saw she censored even to herself.

The year was possibly busier than most and the apex came when the British Legion held a conference to which the Prince of Wales came. The chief guests of honour were Field Marshal Foch and Admiral Beattie.

Edward presided at the bestowing of the Freedom of the Borough on the honoured heroes of the war, there was a sumptuous luncheon at the Grand Hotel. Annie was charmed by the Marshal who paid her Gallic compliments.

She described him as "a little whipcord of a man." It pleased her that a national newspaper described her as his wife and commented upon her Parisian chic. She was proudest on this occasion of Edward and his speech. No one could possibly know the price of his diction, which was clear and incisive.

It was a year of triumph and a lot of humour, too. Embarrassments of the time became the jokes of the future. The occasion that amused the family, but still caused Annie a tinge of discomfort was when she was asked to open the Waterworks at Irton, a village outside Scarborough. She chose with her usual care a dress of Parma violet velvet to wear with her grey squirrel coat. The few steps from the car to the officials was without incident, the cutting of the ribbon to the new buildings occurred without a hitch. She was given a bouquet with large trails of asparagus fern.

"I thanked the pretty little girl for it… little realising that I was to be intensely grateful for the present."

Annie was asked if she would inspect the new plant. She walked from one building to another and became aware that as she walked so the dress rode up beneath her coat. She paused to look at tanks and small cascades of water, she questioned engineers who were surprised at the depth of interest.

While they halted and explained, so Annie surreptitiously tugged and pulled at her dress behind the vast camouflage of fern and chrysanthemums over which she smiled sweetly and listened intently.

Edward loved his year. Annie enjoyed it, but it never meant so much to her, she looked forward to laying the burden aside, to moving to Cliff Bridge Terrace, to watching over Edward and

Nancy and also having "a really good read."

The hotel was becoming alien to her, it was moving into another era, she saw it plainly and the difference was borne upon her astoundingly clearly when Alan was discussing the furnishing of the many new rooms over the dining room,

"You will have to go to some sales, like your father did. He always enjoyed them."

"We cannot do that, Mother, in a modern hotel, the furniture is coming straight from the factory."

She looked at the catalogues, fumed oak, all of the same pattern, lacking distinction, lacking personality and identity. She said nothing. Perhaps, that had always been her fault, she said nothing.

Whilst reading Sorrell and Son one evening, Edward came in. He looked flushed and happy. He sat in his chair still glowing. Annie had no need to ask, but she still did so, "Have you had a good meeting, dear?"

"Very good and very surprising."

"In what way?"

"They want us to be Mayor and Mayoress another year."

"Do you want to, dear?"

Again there had been no need to ask, this was the apogee of his career. But it stabbed Annie deeper than any knife. She thought it would kill him.

"Have you accepted?"

"I said that I would talk it over with you. But you do agree don't you?"

"It is a very great honour and you deserve it."

She burst into tears which Edward interpreted as grateful pride. It was fear.

It was Armistice Day. Again there was the service on the pier, the dropping of the wreath from the lifeboat and the firing of the maroons that Annie loathed. Wearing her sister's black sealskin coat, her hat pulled well down on her forehead, Annie was cold, her face went pale and her mouth was pinched.

She hated wind, she hated war, she hated bangs, but she argued within that dislike it all as she did, it was no use making a fuss and it would not last long. As the east wind drained her of colour, so it whipped up Edwards cheeks to brilliance.

He seemed heedless of it and his heavy coat was unbuttoned and in Annie's eyes looked "very untidy."

It was when they got home, Edward uncomplaining, cheerful, that he began to feel ill, just as Annie was reviving in the warmth. He had a headache and she saw that he went to bed with a hot water bottle.

Next day, he seemed no better, so Dr Ward was sent for. He suggested that they called in another opinion. It was then decided that Edward should go to the Radium Institute in London.

It aroused immediate emotions, Hope and Fear in equal quantities. Within a fortnight a room had been set aside for Edward. In early December Alan was to drive his father up to the capital.

Always Edward had gone to the nursing home alone. It was only after the operations he had needed his wife. On this occasion they both spontaneously said that they would go together. Annie would stay in Hampstead with Dot's relatives.

They set off in high spirits and in fine weather. Just before they set off Edward went down to Cliff Bridge Terrace to look once more at his future home. The sun shone on the sea, the Esplanade was bathed in bright sun.

He rejoiced in the view. He closed the door behind him looking forward to his return. All the way to London he talked of the house, he began to furnish the room with all his favourite pieces.

Annie felt reassured and joined in, but stopped him being dogmatic about colours, "They must never be decided away from the place they are to be used," she declared with unusual downrightness.

She had, in fact, made up her own mind, the bedroom was to be yellow and green. The drawing room was to be blue and cream. The rooms at the back, she had decided must be mainly white to overcome their darkness.

At last, they arrived in Hampstead and a warm welcome from the Hendricks. At dinner that night, they were a jolly party and Edward the most amusing. Annie was glad that she had married such a man. Next morning Alan drove him to the Institute for a series of X-rays and preparation for the operation.

Annie walked on the Heath alone. Her alarms were great and so absorbed was she that looking up suddenly she was surprised to see a still horizon. She had expected the sea with its continual variations and eternal restlessness. Instead she saw trees and beyond them houses and the myriad of the city way below. She was glad to be alone for Mrs Hendrick, sweet and gentle as she was, had a curious knack of bringing any topic of conversation round to illness.

Annie smiled. She had discovered that when healthy people were discussed the absence of ills was considered really remarkable.

At four o'clock, Alan drove her to the Institute. She went straight to Edward's room, brought flowers and an evening newspaper and some sweets. She smiled... for a fraction her smile froze and she caught back her horror and controlled it.

Traced in blue upon her husband's temples was a map of the extent of the cancerous growth, it was life, a river delta around his ears. It was the geography of disease.

"Well, here I am. You didn't expect me to be wearing woad, did you?"

"No, but I always knew that you were an Ancient Briton."

She unwrapped the anemones, glad to look at something else, but the red ones looked like Remembrance poppies. She turned quickly to the wash basin for water, but really because her hand shook, she did not want him to see. But he had.

"Are you frightened for me?"

Her only answer was the slow course of large silent tears running down her face. They held hands.

"Everything is going to be all right. The surgeon is a very clever man."

"Of course."

"The operation will be at 11 tomorrow morning. I know the ropes well, so I'm not worried, so don't you be."

There was a pause. The whole of their life seemed to be unrolling between them. It had been a long time, nearly 35 years.

"I say, Annie, do take that quite awful hat off."

"Don't you like it?"

"No, you wore much prettier hats before the war. These things clamped on you forehead don't suit you at all."

She got up and walked to the mirror over the wash-basin and pulled out the two pins. One she clenched in her teeth, looking like the most harmless pirate with a cutlass in his mouth ever to be encountered.

With the other she carefully and slowly pushed it into her hair and raised the flattened sausages of her curls. Her husband watched, it was a motion he had seen a thousand times, yet it always fascinated him, it was curious and ritualistic and made such a difference.

He did not entirely analyse it, but he knew it was part of Annie's continual quest for perfection in the appearance of everything around her. It was a search he had entirely understood.

She returned and they again held hands. She told him of her walk upon the Heath and how she had missed the sea. He agreed and said that he was looking forward to walking round the Marine Drive soon.

He looked at Annie. He saw the same widely set large blue eyes he had fallen in love with. He saw the plumpness that had expunged wrinkles, but caused her jaw line to sag. He felt the deep affection of years that came from her face, but his love was tinged with sadness.

He knew, had always known, that her love had never been a grand passion. That had been missed.

Annie looked at a stricken man. He who had shared her life, given her children, whom she loved and, she added, "A very great deal", which implied a certain limitation. She did not know what she would do without him, she thought of Nancy and that brought comfort.

They talked of her, their regrets for her and their deep, deep love for her. They talked of Scarborough.

It was time to go. Alan came in. He seemed a little too casual. He chaffed his father and reminded him of his visit to him in the fever hospital when he had typhoid before going to Australia. They left.

They were silent nearly all the way to Hampstead. Then Alan said: "He will be all right, Mum."

She looked at her son, driving so well. He was so like herself to look at, but it seemed to her not at all inside. She wanted to be strengthening, bold, confident, instead she said, "Do you think so?" then added, more consciously, "I am glad you think that."

Her first thought on waking was, "It's Nancy's birthday tomorrow," then a black cloud of dread hugged her like a vast bear and her next thought was "It is Ted's operation today." As she thought of him the map of the blue tracings on his temples came to her gain and a sharper fear ousted the vaguer dread.

Soon after breakfast, Kit arrived from Hampshire. Annie saw her get out of the taxi from the window of her room. She saw that Kit was pregnant again and she knew that she must keep her fears to herself.

"What shall we do, Mummie?"

"We have to be at the Institute at half-past two, so let us go to Westminster. I haven't seen the Abbey since you were children. Kit was surprised at her mother's calm, but not in the least surprised that she knew precisely what she wanted to do. She had always been like that.

Chapter 37

Cancer

The paled sun slanted in through the clerestory windows and after pausing at the grave of the Unknown Warrior they moved eastwards. The memorials oppressed Annie and she began to wonder if coming there had been a good idea.

They found that Holy Communion was being celebrated in the Confessor's chapel and Annie quickened her step. During the service her mind wandered constantly, she was surveying the life of Edward and herself.

She corrected herself, for she was continually putting it all in the past tense. The quiet flow of the liturgy had given her strength but no hope. When they left, Annie hurried... she did not wish to see the memorials, especially as the one that caught her eye had skulls on it.

Kit looked and smiled. "What, now?"

"Let's go across the park and see the Changing of the Guard."

She wanted occupation... she did not want to sit across a table facing Kit. She might then have seen her fear. So, as they walked closely arm in arm they talked and they even laughed.

Before the Palace they joined a small group and watched the formal stamping, correct lining, the sharp angled ritualistic movements. Annie thought the men looked cold, particularly those being relieved and she was glad they had their grey coats.

It reminded her that she, too, was cold. After a lunch which neither tasted, they went to the hospital.

They were taken to a waiting room where Alan, already waited, was smoking. Annie put down her flowers, the door opened and the doctor came in. Before he spoke Annie knew. She looked at him, the mild eye suddenly keen and to both Alan and Kit's amazement said: "He is dead, isn't he?"

"Yes, I am afraid he is."

"How did it happen?" growled Alan angrily, as the blood fled from his face.

"His heart stopped beating under the anaesthetic, we massaged his heart. We did everything possibly."

Annie stretched out her hand to the doctor. "I am sure you did."

Kit remained stiff and tense but began to crumple. Annie put out a hand to her and then Alan moved over and put an arm round his sister. The doctor continued, "I do want you to know had he lived the outlook was very bleak indeed. The growth would have taken hold and very possibly within weeks he would have gone blind."

Kit gave a little gasp and Annie saw that the doctor had more to say.

"Alan, I think Kit had better have some fresh air."

When the door closed on them the doctor went on. "After blindness and deafness, it would have crept up to his brain."

"Then he would have gone mad?"

"Possibly so. We only knew your husband for such a short time, but Mrs Matthews, he was an incredibly brave man."

That made Annie's chin quiver and tears started to her eyes.

"I know, oh I do know. Now, please may I see him?"

"I don't think that would help you at all. He is bandaged."

Annie had a vision of Lazarus from a book of her childhood, tightly bound, like a mummy. The tight bounds on her imagination were broken and she shuddered. This time the doctor stretched out his hand.

"I'll see that you are brought some tea."

"Just one moment - I do, do understand, doctor. I had no hope, you see, after I saw the blue tracings on his temple. I knew. Yes, I did know."

Alan, still tense, still white, drove slowly up to Hampstead Annie and Kit clasped one another in their arms. When they arrived there was no need to tell the Hendricks anything, the news was obvious and their kindness and understanding quiet and tactful. After more tea, Annie said,

"Alan, you are the head of the family, now. Ring up Tonks and get them to arrange your father's funeral. Kit, my dear, you must go to my bed."

There was no need. Mrs Hendrick had made another bed straightaway.

The journey back seemed unending. Annie and Kit sat in a carriage next to the one with the blinds down where the coffin stood. Neither of them went in. Annie had sensed her husband's death, but she had never envisaged what it would be like to travel home without him.

Never for one moment did she think of Edward being the contents of the box next door. She slowly began to see that life stretched ahead without him. She began to feel afraid, then she rallied remembering that she had her family.

In Scarborough, Frank White had been telephoned with the news of his brother-in-laws death and he had promised to break the news to Nancy on this, her birthday. As he crossed the Spa bridge he remembered hanging on to the railings in the gale as he walked to Edward and Annie's wedding.

He loved his niece, he broke the news very gently, was deeply troubled at her distress. He gave instructions to the staff to look after her, an unnecessary command. Then he walked straight up to the Vicarage and told the Vicar.

On his way home he was still troubled. He mentioned Nancy's need to his wife and she unhesitatingly said, "She needs the next generation."

She turned to her daughter, "Vee, dear, get out the car and go to the school and take David to his mother. That will be the best comfort for her."

David, when deposited at the hotel door was confronted by a tearful Mary, who, as she took off his coat, told him he had to be very, very kind to his mother. Still nobody had told him why he had been brought home.

His mother was curled up in the green wing armchair before the Adam fireplace, she was convulsed with sobs. She looked at him, almost furtively, she did not smile, but she held out her hand.

He held her hand, she pulled him to her kissed him and, then, was shaken by another storm of tears. He did not know what to do, he was very puzzled. He also began to cry.

Nancy began to tell him that Poppy, as he called his grandfather, was dead. He wept, but mainly because his mother did. Then he thought that his mother needed cheering up.

He got down from her lap, went to the wonderfully concealed cupboard in the wainscoting and got out his newest toy, a Jack-in-the-Box, which Aunt Edith had given him two days before.

He carried it to the green chair. He pulled back the little brass catch, like a capital 'L' in copperplate, but upside down. The nodding head sprang up bobbing on the end of its spring. His mother looked, but did not smile. He did not know what to do.

Help was at hand. Mary came in, took away the writing pad and inkwells and laid the table with a cloth and plates. She returned with a steaming pot.

"This is lovely Irish stew. You must eat as much as you can."

These were words usually addressed to David, not his mother. They were ineffectual. She wept again and seemed oblivious of David's existence.

Mary, once again, came to his rescue, and took him down to the Servant's Hall. There sitting on a bench at the table with its scrubbed top, David began to ask questions of Harry, Mary, Martha and Elsie.

"You say Poppy has gone to God. How did he get there?"

He looked at each in turn and none of them gave him an answer. Mentally, he shrugged his shoulders, it seemed they did not know. It was all very simple, he thought, Poppy went down to the harbour, borrowed a boat, rowed himself out to sea, and there God let down a rope from the sky and pulled Poppy up to Heaven.

This theory entirely satisfied him and keeping the mystery to himself he asked no more questions. He played snakes and ladders with Harry and Martha.

At the station a detachment of policemen shouldered the coffin. Annie, Alan, Kit and John, joined by the White family stood and watched it carried to a hearse. Annie felt a glow of warmth when she was on the platform. It was good to be home.

She found it strangely comforting that Edward was so revered. She did not seem to feel the East wind creeping in at every entrance and eddying around.

At last, up in her room where a fire burned, Mary stood ready to help her and pamper her. As she moved about she relaxed and as she did so she became aware of a pain in her chest. Nancy came in... she felt her hand, then her forehead.

"Mother, you have a temperature."

She did. She had pneumonia. It was the nursing of Nancy that pulled her through. It was, as though, the anxiety of the last six years about Edward suddenly took their toll. She was immeasurable tired and slept and slept.

Dr Salter looked very serious and was not his usual consoling self. When the sickness slowly departed, then Annie recovered quickly, she was left, though, with a perpetual reminder of these dark days… she developed a tic in her facial muscles which quivered upwards and almost closed her right eye.

She never attended the funeral and only distantly knew that it was taking place. Weeks later, Nancy described it and she was shown the newspapers with the reporting and the photographs. It struck Annie that she was looking at the death of a distant monarch. It was grief at a remove. She could not believe that this was her husband being honoured and recalled.

When she heard of the will she was neither pleased nor hurt. It was all consistent with Edward's method. She was used to his secrecy and had never been consulted in financial matters.

The business had been left to her children with the proviso that they always looked after their mother. So everything was as it had been, her bills would be paid.

At Christmas, only a whisper of a celebration, she was given an album of photographs of the Mayoral year, such as Edward receiving delegations of ex-soldiers and cyclists.

She gazed at him with fondness and herself with criticism. She looked older than she had thought. It was, she mused only a record of the thinnest layer of an outward shell. What was happening inside could not be photographed.

She saw it as the year when Nancy's marriage broke up, the misery of the court hearing over the separation, and always, always, the growth of the cancer. That was how she really saw the year, all of them caught in the tentacles of cancer. It was even truer than she believed.

On New Year's Eve she went to bed extremely early telling herself that it would be better to wake up in another year – as it was.

Chapter 38

7 Cliff Bridge Terrace

The house on Cliff Bridge Terrace was ready. Annie had the strange pleasure of going round the hotel selecting the furniture and the ornaments she wanted for her new home. She took the Hepplewhite chairs. She had bought them herself - she also took the Sheraton sideboard, for long a favourite of hers.

From the drawing room she took the satin-wood desk and the best of the Buhl cabinets. The Meissen candelabra and the clock that matched so well also went down to grace her mantelpiece.

She took a great deal, but Edward had amassed so much over the years that these pieces were not missed, except by the real connoisseurs among the visitors.

They all fitted well and easily into the new house with its great sash windows and elliptical staircase.

The house mirrored well Annie's personality. It had a foot in two centuries, but showed her interests in time long before her own span. Yet with the clutter of silver photograph frames and ornaments a homely Edwardian look took over. The house seemed almost aristocratic, except that it lacked any good pictures.

Annie went to No 7 as an invalid, taking with her Nancy and her grandson. She needed a daughter to guard, nurse and comfort her, in short to be a companion. It was a familiar 19th century pattern and echoed among many of her friends and relatives.

The life she lived was of a former century, too. It was a stern regimen of nothing. She breakfasted in bed each morning, she rose slowly and did exercises... in her mid-70s she found it simple to touch her toes.

Then she dressed. This was a deliberate ritual, the dressing table was the altar, the boxes, bowls, brushes and tray the holy vessels and the mirror was its image. The dressing of her hair took precisely 25 minutes, the final arranging of the dress six, then a few minutes pulling, straightening, adjusting.

She never dressed in under an hour. The result was always a precise perfection, correct and within its formality, beautiful, it was like 18th century poetry, it achieved a kind of rapture by sheer precision.

If, that morning, she was receiving visitors for coffee the task was done, but if she was going out, there were then the shoes, the gloves, the coat and particularly the hat to be considered.

If these were put on, then a stately progress was made to St Nicholas Street, pauses before the windows and then a saunter through Marshall and Snelgrove's. This was to wander through temptation, the latest fashions were displayed and Annie was tiring well, before Easter of the dullness of mourning.

The statutory black hat with a long veil had been dismissed after but one outing, not only uncomfortable, but unbecoming as well.

There was lunch at the hotel. This was followed by a rest and a 'good read' until tea time. But on many afternoons there was Bridge, either at home, or in her friends' houses. There were two foursomes, nicknamed by her daughter as, The Big Four and the Chatty Four.

She was a lady without a definite occupation. True, she had committees… there was a Home for Unmarried Mothers which had her interest and support financially for many years. There was also the Home for Convalescent Children which she visited regularly, sometimes taking her grandson. Scarborough was full of women like her and Annie was always slow to analyse her feelings. Instead, the time was filled with diversions, films, theatres, picnics and a constant flow of callers.

There was always an extra cup and saucer on the tea tray and almost invariably it was used. Most of her guests were the friends of a lifetime, or connections of Ted in the Council House. Others were members of the staff from the hotel and, always, her family.

The talk might be gossip, but increasingly it was of the barbaric darkness that was crossing Europe and there was the Depression nearer at hand. The radio brought Jarrow menacingly close and there were bazaars held for the unemployed which Annie patronised and very frequently opened.

But the Depression bit home more closely, holidays were being curtailed, even denied altogether and the bookings at the hotel were no longer a dense mass on the chart. Annie had always kept the bookings in her own hand, she knew the preferences of her clients - they were her friends.

She worried about many things in the hotel. She went there twice a day, for lunch and for dinner. Sometimes, she would go up the Cliff wrapped in a fur with a scarf over her hair.

The front door would be smartly flung open by the page, or porter, her coat would be taken and before she went in to dine, she would wander through the main rooms, as she had always done, plumping up cushions, straightening chair backs, adjusting table runners, fiddling with the curtains.

She would move china ornaments a few inches then send in the porter to sweep a hearth. The difference one of these 'trails', as the family called them, made was very perceptible.

Much more subversively, as she sat at dinner, visitors would come up to her. She always knew their names, their families and she talked charmingly and graciously. The favoured ones were invited down to No 7.

Too often, Annie and Nancy heard the "the hotel is not quite what it was." It could not be, it was moving into another age. Annie was too close to her life's work for her own happiness, or the welfare of her family. The situation was never really considered properly, it was certainly never discussed.

Once, or twice a year Annie went away, usually to her daughter, Kit, in Hampshire, or later, Jersey. The preparations for these visits were arduous. Harry was sent for to carry the great cabin trunk from the attic to her bedroom.

There up-ended, it opened forming a small wardrobe with hanging space on one side and a chest of drawers on the other. When it was packed, Harry and another porter were sent for to carry it downstairs.

At the stations, impoverished porters, anxious for a tip, struggled with it. At its destination, her son-in-law with the gardener had to manoeuvre it upstairs. It is no wonder that he never forgot that his mother-in-law considered it necessary to have 14 pairs of shoes for a three week holiday.

Annie was an Edwardian woman, in many things pampered, but across the social spectrum all of them were exploited. They had little financial independence. Fathers and husbands demanded not only details of expenditure, but also gratitude for having provided the money at all.

It was never seen that the women earned what their husbands

gave them. This was even truer of Annie, by her very happy exertions she had created the hotel, but she had never received a regular income from it. Bills will be paid, it was the system, but that implied inspection and approval and certainly no autonomy. It had been easier to face her husband than her son. It was all extraordinarily unwise and never, never open.

The depression of the 1930s affected everyone. Some tried to ignore it, but its mean and unhappy touch was felt everywhere. It brought to the staff of the St Nicholas a new brand of workers, the daughters of the professional classes, who needed more money than father had left in order to live.

A new housekeeper was engaged. Her father had died in the unequal struggle to keep his farm going. Miss Park brought with her a fox's mask and brush to adorn her bedroom. She was a cool, observant young lady with a keen sense of humour that appealed to the younger Matthews.

She was, like them, happiest at the point-to-point, out with the guns. She had mixed with the County, but she found herself awed by Mrs Matthews senior. She was well used to the rather shabbily dressed squire's wife, but not someone so stately and perfectly dressed as Annie.

Both looked at one another and both put up barriers. Miss Park recognised well that she had encountered a personage.

Later, when she took her place at the reception desk and saw Annie move from room to room, she knew that she had met a perfectionist. She was very aware of a kind of coolness when she was discussing the races with Alan and Mrs Matthews heard them.

Annie did not approve when she heard Miss Park, now Parkie call her son by his Christian name. Annie continued, a little pointedly to address her as Miss Park. Nancy too, was drawn into this friendship.

And to her Annie said: "I do think it very wrong, Nancy, to make favourites in the staff. Why befriend Miss Park and leave out Miss Presley who had been with us eight, or nine years?"

"But, Mummy, Parkie is one of us."

"You mean she is not the daughter of a miner? I know my children's snobbery. And I have mine."

Pressy had always been a source of approval for Annie. They had done things together. Annie had wanted new pelmets in the

Chinese drawing room. She remembered that Pressy had a diploma in art.

So Pressy had made designs, Harry had cut out plywood to the desired shape and Annie had embroidered the material now stretched on the wood. It had been a very successful little collaboration, but it had never meant familiarity between them.

Annie saw that Pressy was a relic of the old system of self-help... she approved of that. She was sad that her children were 'bright young things', resting on a security, which Annie knew, but would not acknowledge, was not there.

It was with her grandson that she became, perhaps, most confiding. She turned to him more and more and their real bond came when one Easter she discovered how backward he was at reading.

He had been taken from the excellent school in Falsgrave where he had been happy and attentive, to a socially superior school on the South Cliff where he was not particularly happy and where his teachers were boring.

To discover that her only grandchild was approaching seven and unable to read had shocked her. She began an intensive campaign to rectify this while they were on holiday. Each morning as she drank her tea in bed he had to spell very simple words of the cat and mat variety. Then the history of the names of the days of the week were discussed and spelt. The headlines of the newspaper at breakfast were carefully deciphered.

Progress on walks was fearsomely slow, for they stopped before every notice and every hoarding. The result of this course was that, at the end of a week, he could read. The first thing he read of his own accord was a programme announcing that a Laurel and Hardy film was being shown at the cinema the following week. As a reward he was taken there.

The disapproval she felt for her children's actions which she suppressed, to David were voiced. He also learnt of her very great sense of humour and together they were involved in an episode that, at one and the same time, coincided with her sense of humour and her moral values.

They were visiting John and Kit Barlow. They were met at King's Cross and instead of driving straight to Hampshire, John elected to visit his sister Mary. David noticed a stiffening of his grandmother's spine at the proposal, but nothing was said.

Mary lived, at that time, in a flat recently vacated by Tallulah Bankhead in Half Moon Street. Only much later, very much later, did David hear his grandmother muse, "I never did know who actually paid the rent of that flat."

John, Kit, Annie and David stood on the landing and door was opened by Mary. She was wearing cocktail pyjamas of crepe de chine. Annie looked at this fashion with deep appraisal, the little party were led into a room of men and women, such as David had never seen before.

His grandmother was introduced to a number of people and the well-known charm and grace was shown. But when she sat, upright by habit on a striped silk chaise longue with a glass of sherry in her hand and her grandson on the floor at her feet, it was obvious that they were the catalysts causing a spiritual chemical reaction.

One by one, the guests made their excuses and departed. Mary bravely, even gallantly showed them over the flat and David had a vivid remembrance of the scores of Staffordshire pot dogs in the kitchen which she regularly took to New York, thus financing her trips for, then, a very small outlay.

Driving over the Hog's Back, David noticed that his grandmother was suppressing her laughter. She was giggling like a schoolgirl, it was very unlike her.

"What is it, mother?" said Kit.

"I am afraid that John, David and I killed that party stone dead, didn't we?"

John replied a little evasively, Annie still laughed and then said: "I don't think I've ever been a memento mori before."

Scarborough was changing and Annie was far too alert not to be well aware. A new variety of visitor was coming to stay, no longer so many professional people – they were beginning to make forays abroad. It was the children, now grown up, who had come there with their Sunday Schools for a day's outing.

Annie bemoaned this and, one evening on the Esplanade, said to her grandson, as she looked at the hatless young women, young men with blazers and cravats, "It was not like this before the war. All the ladies wore a real toilette and the gentlemen, if he wished to smoke, had a cigar, not these cigarettes."

She did not like cigarettes, but never raised the subject with her daughter, who, true to her generation, loved them. She was not quite so tolerant with her sister who, she thought, "should have known better."

The hotel had been booked for a large party of cotton mill workers from Lancashire, arranged by a trades union. Annie was little shocked, but kept her snobbish reactions to herself. Nancy disapproved and made some sardonic remarks... she told her mother that the dining room was filled with "factory laughs". Annie remained silent.

The following evening Annie accompanied her daughter up to the hotel. As she entered the hall she was aghast to see flat cloth caps on, it seemed, every surface. She halted and gazed.

Nancy picked up a new tweed cap, twirled it on her finger and then said: "Look, Mummy, it has a sheet of cardboard in it to keep it flat. Isn't that killing? Can you imagine it?"

"I don't have to imagine it, dear, I see it very plainly. But you mustn't laugh, they are our guests and we are receiving their money very gladly."

Nancy was rarely reproved by her mother and she looked crestfallen. Alan joined them and was equally jocular.

"Both of you are very snobbish. I must have brought you up very badly. You cannot have it both ways, you know. You keep your hunter, Alan, these people pay for it. What I am bothered about is all these dreadful caps."

Then she had an idea. "Get Harry to bring the what-not from the armoury and put it here. They can put their headgear on the shelves and everyone will be happy."

It worked. Annie did realise that the place was changing as she left after dinner. She was perplexed that as she made her way through the hall she had to say, several times, "Excuse me". This was very unlike her usual, regal exits.

One evening in spring Annie, instead of going through the reception rooms, went up to the half landing. Her intention was to look for a book in the case there. She stopped in amazement - there were some dark maroon curtains that shut off a staircase leading to a wing only used at the height of the season.

For years and years, Annie had meant to replace them, or embroider them for they were extremely dreary. What caused her surprise was that someone had beaten her, a stencil had been cut and birds flew, or fluttered, or sat in branches, all in gold and silver, bright beauty on a dark mass.

She wondered who had done it, was it her daughter-in-law? Then she recognised the hand of Pressy. Before she sat down at the family table she went over to thank Pressy, who blushed with pleasure. Like every artist, praise was much appreciated.

As coffee was being taken, Parkie burst through the doors. "I say, excuse me, but I've tremendous news. Eric has won the gold plate at Wetherby."

Eric was her brother and a keen amateur jockey. Alan immediately called for drinks. The talk became very animated. The drinks arrived.

"Don't you think we ought to ask Miss Presley to join us?"

She was sent for. Alan proposed a toast, but just before the glasses reached their lips, Annie added, "And I would like to add 'To Miss Presley' who has made a dark corner bright. Something I've meant to do for at least five years." Glasses were raised.

Going down the Cliff the old lady said to her grandson, "My family is so terribly English. Don't you be like that. They think far more of horses than beauty. It's too late to do anything about them now."

So Annie, with her ideals and notions firmly set in the 19th century, had to come to grips with the changing attitudes around her. Possibly it was her sense of fashion that helped her to see the need of adaptation and that everything was in a state of change.

She was fortunate that she was well-educated, which her children were not, so she saw things differently and had a deeper well of faith and philosophy to draw upon.

There was, though, an emotional weakness in her, she never really comprehended men. She had a fear of them, one she shared with many women of her generation. It came, basically, from never having truly known her father. He had died too soon to influence her and help her. Then there had been the shock of her brother's desertion of his ship, to which she had reacted so traumatically. Then came her real love, which had been forbidden from the start.

Edward she had, sometimes, feared with cause, she had often been dishonest with money, because she could not bring herself to be open. She now had a fear of her son, she concealed bills and she borrowed money.

Alan considered his mother extravagant. There was truth, but they were all extravagant... living in an hotel gives one folies de grandeur and a constant temptation to live beyond one's means.

There was unhappiness in the family and it mirrored the world. Nazism was casting a crooked shadow and the world pretended it was not happening. At this very time, Alan won the local point-to-point on his expensive horse. The family rejoiced and Annie was extremely proud of her fearless son. The feat was written up in all the papers.

The following day, Alan received a strongly worded letter from his uncle informing him that he should spend his energies on his business and not the race course. Frank also sent a copy of this to his sister-in-law.

As a mother, she rose to her son's defence. The triumph of the race turned to ashes in her mouth. She was angry because she more than half agreed with Frank. She wrote a letter of reproach and followed it, next day, as long arranged, by having lunch with the Whites. She took her grandson with her.

He recalls the strained atmosphere, an avoided subject, was as obvious and central as the epergne on the table. All went well until Frank, unable to keep his indignation in any longer, made a critical remark about his nephew.

It seemed Annie was prepared for this and a stinging rejoinder from her, so utterly unlike her, stunned the entire table into silence. David remembered the sound of the knives and forks upon the plates and the munching of the mouths, suddenly broken by the harmonious but overpowering chimes of the bracket clock.

Frank disappeared to his study. Annie went to the drawing room with her sister-in-law and nieces. Beatrice shed a tear and Annie's chin quivered. As she left, Frank came from his study amid a drift of smoke and the smell of a Havana.

The two looked at one another, Annie reproachful... Frank loved and admired his sister-in-law. He made as if to kiss her, she took a half pace back and gave him her hand. It was magnificent, majestic, but a very bad move.

Leaving Christ Church after a service one Sunday morning, Annie, Nancy and her grandson went down the 'snicket' to Huntriss Row.

Standing in the street across the road was a group of men,

working men. It was easy to define them then, even easier when, with some self-consciousness, they wore their Sunday best.

In their midst was Harry, one time head porter, who Edward and Annie had trusted for half a lifetime. To them he had been a faithful servant, to Alan a constant source of friction. He had never accepted the young man's authority and ultimately, after pleas by Annie to both parties, he had to go.

Annie saw him and bowed. Harry, looking very uneasy, looked past her. He never raised his wide-brimmed trilby hat, but there was a shift in his over-padded shoulders. Annie was deeply surprised and very pained.

In this tiny incident, years of trust were shattered. Her prejudices, all obscured by her beliefs and practice, were suddenly revealed in a swift amazed condemnation.

"What on earth has happened to Harry. He looks like a bookie's runner."

It was a mixture of sadness and of scorn and, in fact, absolutely accurate. The remainder of the day she was quiet. Nancy too, was hurt. She had known Harry all her life. Both of them knew, also, that this was an omen, the news was about that the hotel was ruined, their position undermined. Allied with it was a sense of betrayal.

Had they been totally misled by Harry? Annie, after this, was never so sure of anything any more.

One Sunday morning in the early summer of 1938, David and his mother were in the balconied bedroom of Annie. She was ill - she had been confined to her bed some two months.

The worries over money and the hotel, all suppressed and hidden, took toll of her heart. She had a coronary from which she recovered but her heart beat remained very erratic. That morning they were not concerned about her health but were awaiting a strange visitation.

Annie propped on her pillows, gazed through the window southwards, towards Flamborough Head. The high sash window on the other side of her dressing table was raised high.

Suddenly, away in the south, grey specks could be seen. As they approached their noise made them more fearful. The grey became black and assumed shaped, wings, tails, fuselage and the almost invisible whirl of propellers.

The German Air Force, in a gesture of friendliness and the greatest of goodwill, were flying over the coast of Britain giving a display of their might. They were malevolent and their roar seemed to shake the houses. Fear, as no doubt intended, gripped the heart of many.

David, with his vivid imagination, foresaw such a squadron flying from Cornwall to Scotland in a line across Britain, ploughing with bombs and leaving furrows of complete destruction.

Annie paled. "How horrible". The thought of war became another of her already sufficient anxieties. Her optimism deserted her. Her physical condition plummeted. The cause evaded both Dr Ward and the consultant.

Suddenly there was a crisis, breathing difficulty and multiple pains. She nearly slipped loose of the family gathered round. The doctor, now, realised that she had an embolism, then called phlebitis.

The clot moved and caused her the most agonising pain as the clot coursed through her heart. The family gathered in her room and her son held her as she requested saying, "Hold me, Alan, hold me or I shall go."

He held on grimly. The doctor pronounced death to be imminent and leaving the patient and a sorrowing family he went away. Next morning, about eight o'clock, he returned. He left his car on the terrace and looked up at the house.

He was surprised to see that the blinds were not down, the curtains were drawn back. He felt the partially made out death certificate in his pocket. Then he recalled that Annie had strong views on mourning and had possibly forbidden darkened rooms.

The maid let him in. "How is your mistress?"

"Sleeping, doctor."

He looked at her, he knew her to be a simple woman. He had twice committed her to the Asylum in York. He wondered what she meant. He sprinted up the stairs and was met by Nancy coming out of the bedroom... she smiled. He knew his patient was alive.

He followed her into the room. The old body lay peacefully asleep with comfortingly variable breaths. Her eyelids fluttering and she whispered, "Oh, Elston, are you still here. I have been asleep a long time."

"No, I have just returned."

He got out his stethoscope and listened. He heard the erratic beat, "like peas rattling in a bucket" was his description.

As he went downstairs he pronounced that she would very possibly pull through but she would be an invalid for the remainder of her life.

"What we must do, as soon as she had recovered from this at least partially, is get her up and moving. There is, now, more risk in bed than out of it."

She recovered. Many visitors came, flowers arrived, champagne and, David remembers well, a beautiful small barrel of oysters, which she adored.

Many weeks later, a friend volunteered to take her out in his car, the family Rover, in the financial crisis, having been sold. The car arrived. Annie was installed carefully into the front seat, with David and Nancy behind.

The scene which immediately followed bewildered David for a long time. It was a most extraordinary mixture of reality and regal grandeur around an impotent throne. The car stopped at the steps of the hotel and one by one the staff came out to congratulate Annie upon her recovery.

The men bowed and many of the women gave little curtsies over her hand. All this when the deck of the ship was awash? It astounded him. It frightened him. Annie had a word for each of them and always the right name.

Some 30 to 40 people had come out. At last the door was shut and they drove away up towards the moors. She loved the wide sweep of the view... she loved the colours and the clouds, but very strictly from behind the windscreen of the car.

She never wished to live in the country - it was something to be delighted in for short bursts of time. It amused Nancy and her son that, as they returned through Scalby, the old lady said, "Why are you going so slowly?"

"There's a 30-mile speed limit."

"I see. But isn't it slow?"

That summer of 1938, fewer people than ever were taking holidays. The hotel was half empty, it spelt, quite clearly, ruin. The two top floors were closed. Yet Annie's main pre-occupation was, like the rest of thinking Britons, the likelihood of war.

She embroidered throughout the Munich Crisis. She was staying in the hotel, she was in the very room she had entertained so many soldiers when the place had been commandeered in the First World War.

She found that reality of the past, too painful to dwell upon. She thought greatly of the pity of war, but her patriotism was also deep, but she felt for the Jews. She hated Hitler. Her thoughts and emotions were in chaos and just how deeply soon became apparent to her grandson. He had found a multicoloured dandelion leaf.

Annie, devoted to the beautiful, the curious, took it in her hand, she twisted it and then said: "So much depends today on the meeting between Mr Chamberlain and Hitler. I can think of nothing else."

It was true, for David looked from the real leaf to the embroidery and he saw that the whole leaf had been most painstakingly sewn in blues. Her thoughts were entirely in Berchtesgarten.

That same night, a number of the town's inhabitants went up to the factory floor of Plaxtons. There, on long trestle tables were gas masks. People were fitted with these rubber contraptions which, to David's amusement, emitted the most anal of noises when he breathed out.

Names were ticked off long lists. There was a hesitation when it came to Annie Matthews. There was a consultation and the senior ARP officer said he would call next day and fit her mask.

He came. He was given tea, but was not permitted to fit the mask. "What, upset all my hair?"

Mr Chamberlain returned with Peace. David saw men with tears bless the Prime Minister. Within months he saw the same men curse him for procrastinating. But the family had more ills to contend with much closer at hand.

Creditors met and creditors made statements. The family panicked and by forming a family square like infantry in an old battle, made a terrible mistake.

Annie, Nancy and the two grandchildren were left to pack up a lifetime of possessions, the belongings of three generations.

Annie went through No 7 with an undeviating sense of purpose. She restored to the hotel many, things of great value and when her grandson demurred she said: "Some of these are not truly my own, but belong to the hotel."

"But, Granny, we might be glad of them."

"So might the creditors."

She was being honourable, but she was also entirely optimistic, she felt quite sure that given a month, or two, they would return. So very firmly, Meissen was placed in Buhl cabinets. Equally thoroughly, she went through the hotel and it was in the staff hall that she spied an oak rocking chair.

"So, that's where it's been. That is mine. All the Taylor family have been rocked in that."

Twice she went through every room looking for a chest of drawers, she never found it. It had belonged to Nana.

She stood in the empty hall.

"This was my Chinese drawing room, once. It was very beautiful."

She opened the door into the writing room. The Adam fireplace, the shallow apse at one end with the Flaxman relief on the central panel still gave, even on that hollow afternoon, pleasure by the rightness of their proportions.

David looked at his grandmother. Her back was straight, her head held high. But he saw the misery move about her mouth. Here was her home... here her children had been born. Here she had lived happily, peacefully, if not lyrically, with Edward.

Here he had set out on his civic triumphs. Here she had made a little palace of charm that had made visitors friends. This was the house of her history.

Nearly 50 years later Miss Parke was to write, "I always admired Mrs Matthews. Never more than when the crash came. I did not think anyone could be quite so brave - but even better than that, she never, never blamed anyone."

On December 23rd 1938, a taxi took her, her daughter and two grandchildren up Huntriss Row to the station. It was snowing. They passed a few shop keepers hurrying to pull up blinds, turn on heating.

Annie said: "It is very strange. I arrived in Scarborough on December 23, 1893. Do you realise that not a figure is different from today's date, just a rearrangement? There was no answer to such a statement.

On the platform the White family huddled like a group of cold sheep. Annie quickened her pace towards them.

"How nice of you to see us off." There were heartfelt kisses all around. The train ambled through a snow-bound England. The two women in their fur coats looked like, what indeed they were, once wealthy refugees.

Chapter 39

Winchester

The whole occasion struck David as Russian. It was indeed, they were about to enter the blackest year of their lives of unhappiness, impotence, a certain indolence that was utterly Chekhovian.

The opening of the melodrama was in swirling snow. At first it appeared to be no more than the beginning of a Christmas visit. When Annie went into dinner, she was suddenly struck by the solemnity and immensity of the step that had been taken.

Her son-in-law stood before a joint of beef, he was sharpening the knife. He smiled, a smile that always beguiled his wife, but which his nephew thought never tallied with the flickering of his almond shaped eyes.

Annie very quietly asked him to be still for a moment, she said a few hesitant words of gratitude to her family in whom she had immense trust. She felt unhappy when she looked at the past, but felt safe with them for the future.

It brought tears to her elder daughter's eyes, admiration from her younger. Her grandson watched and listened uneasily. He never trusted his unpredictable uncle, he saw the smile disappear and one cheek be bitten which was invariably a sign of inward debate.

"Thank you, mother, for your kind words. We are doing no more than our duty."

He picked up the carving knife and resumed serving. Annie felt relieved that she had made the little speech. Her grandson wondered. He thought it wrong.

He also knew, that not to have spoken would also have been misinterpreted, for her son-in-law had a mind susceptible to suspicion, he was moved swiftly into moods of jealousy. There had been in Annie's simple words an unintended condescension. It was a part of Annie's unconscious... by some divination David knew that his uncle regarded it as the gesture of an imperilled monarch claiming rightful sanctuary from a sovereign hitherto considered inferior. Everything had been wondrously unwise.

January and February were cold and dark. The news from creditors' meetings was depressing and tended to become rancorous. The family was beset by fear and lost confidence. There seemed to be no way to swim away from this foundering wreck.

There was, but they paralysed themselves by hanging together. Annie and David bore the brunt, the young and the old always suffer in wars and emergencies, and their plight was the same.

They were not wanted, their presence, understandably, was resented. Veiled sarcasms became open and Annie took to her room and claimed illness rather than listen to recriminations, for herself she bore them, but never for her husband, or son. For the first time in her life her spirit was broken.

The situation threw the grandmother and grandson together very much more. As spring came, they walked in the evenings through the Abbey Gateway to the water meadows north of the city.

Away from the house she revived and she never repined over the past, but neither did she foresee with any sanguinity the future. They would laugh and comment on all they saw. The ends of the walks were oppressive for the joy fell off as soon as they entered the house. It was the unhappiest year of their lives for they were captive and the misery ground on and on.

The working together of the brothers-in-law was doomed from the beginning. It should never have been undertaken and one day the suspicions, the arrogance, but most of all the misery burst, and David was sent to bring his other uncle to the house. He did not wish to do it, but his aunt said, "Go along, quick, like a good lad."

His looks must have warned his uncle for he ran ahead in anger, the two men met in the hall, the quarrel was not stated, but they reared like stallions, they shouted and threatened. Then Annie came down the stairs slowly, pale with horror, still wearing her coat and hat.

"Stop, stop, please. Do not quarrel."

It was like water drops on red hot iron, a sizzle and then nothing. The voices rose and at the turn of the stairs Annie suddenly dropped upon her knees. The action sent a quiver of astonishment that momentarily stilled the tempest.

"Alan, I beg of you, say that you are sorry."

"Never, Mother, never, never."

"Oh, John." The words of pleading were never finished for David and his aunt, appalled at seeing her on her knees, ran forward crying, "Not on your knees, not on your knees."

Alan flung out, he flung out of the tentacle grasp of the family and swam in a sea where he should have been long before. His mother, woman of her time, took to her room. Her meals were sent up on trays and she remained out of sight.

There followed weeks of despair. The unhappiness was so thick it seemed tangible. Yet, the immediate family crises could not dispel the apprehensions of the world as it awaited Hitler's next pounce.

Annie read the newspapers avidly and she grieved for the Jews, the Czechs. She dreaded war. In the evenings on their walks, Annie and David saw, for the first time, conscripts in the town. Those to be commissioned wore white discs of hard cellophane behind the badge on their forage caps. David remembers her pointing out a bookish young man in uniform, "There, look. You don't usually see his kind of uniform."

There were to be many more of his kind in the streets of Winchester as the years went by.

One very bright, sunny Sunday, Annie rose earlier and with her grandson set off for the cathedral. As they walked along the lie-abed street she saw her son-in-law walking well ahead with his small daughter.

Annie's steps slowed. She wondered whether to let them go there untroubled by relatives. As she slackened her pace, so Valerie spotted her grandmother and said: "Look, Daddy, there's Granny."

Instantly, her father turned, glared and walked back to the house. Annie walked on imperturbably, but she was deeply, deeply disturbed. The music of the choir, the vaulting, the reredos with its balconied saints, did nothing to calm her sadness.

On the way home she said: "Evidently the longest cathedral in Europe is still not big enough for your uncle and I to worship in." They lingered at shop windows as they wended their way home, anything to delay entry into the hated house. When at last they did, they were met by Kit, very upset, and Annie forestalled her.

"I don't feel well, darling, I shall go up and lie down and David is off to his mother straightaway."

When David arrived at the country house where his mother was housekeeper, he told her of the day's happenings. She turned pale and then wept saying, "Oh God, how awful it is to be so poor and powerless."

As gazelles and antelope graze beneath the gaze of lions and, possibly, in some dim recess of the mind give thanks for each day they are spared, so did Annie and David. Neither wanted war, but both knew that war would provide them with escape.

The day came, September 3rd when the entire family gathered to hear the Prime Minister announce that war had been declared on Germany. All differences were buried in the face of greater disaster.

Then excitement seized the family and even those, not commanded to, helped polish a Sam Brown belt, boots and pieces of brass. A khaki tunic was ironed. They were arraying, and two of them very gladly, a hero for the war. John was equally euphoric at the prospect of leaving his relations.

Each day a summons was expected from the War Office. Each day when David returned home he would ask gleefully, "Has it come yet?"

At first Annie was inclined to think it amusing that the War Office was not so eager for her son-in-law's services. She also knew that his pride was piqued and told her younger daughter, "He cannot imagine that Britain can wage a war without his advice."

If no letter came from on high, many letters were sent to them. At last, in a fury he drove to London and did not leave the War Office until his application had been accepted and his destination known. It was Bombay.

"As far away from the Minister of War as possible," was his mother-in-law's observation.

Then there were delays of departure, but they were of days, not weeks, and the raft of security shifted uneasily.

Eventually the day came when he left. There were kisses and handshakes at the gate and gratuitous advice given even as he closed the car door. Annie stood smiling, but not waving as the car slipped off towards London. As she went up the garden path she said: "Strange, he said goodbye as though he would never see me again. Well, I am sure that is what he really hopes. I expect I shall die before he returns."

"Probably he'll get killed," suggested her grandson.

Annie looked severely at him, then wryly smiled, they became conspirators, they laughed, but she still said, "You may think that, even hope that, but you must, never, never say it."

They went in and ate a very hearty lunch. A great peace had been brought to the house by war.

On November 5th, Kit said to her mother, "Well, Mother, you won't be bothered by any bangs and fireworks tonight." Annie looked up from her sewing to agree, when her daughter said, "Mother, you have lost your twitch."

The facial tic that had been so much a part of her had gone. Like the stopping of a clock, no one was accurately able to say when it had ceased. When her grandson said goodnight to her as she lay in bed, a candle burning by her side, she lowered her Louis Golding novel and said, "I got that twitch with the shock of your grandfather's death. I've been cured of it by the blessed shock of your uncle's departure. Don't tell your aunt, she thinks it is the war."

Within a few months only Annie and her grandson were left together.

These two, with 60 years dividing them, faced the war together. Together they faced death, air raids made them rise hurriedly in the night and sit beneath the stairs often. The bombs seemed imminent, but Winchester was only the penumbra of the raids, Southampton received the bombs, the empty planes flew over the ancient capital, but still the old buildings shook.

So in common with so many they faced death from the sky. But they, also, faced a closer dance with death. Quite frequently the old lady's heart went into spasm, so the two stared at each other, gripping hands in a resigned horror and outfaced death.

Death stalked and struck suddenly, twice in the cathedral and an occasion in the south transept is etched with a kind of weird beauty on David's mind. During a hymn they had left the choir, struggled down the steps and to a wooden bench.

There, David holding his fainting grandmother saw so vividly the tension of pain, the lack of breath, the dim, but glowing ember of life reviving, then, just daring to hope that the caverns that had opened and shut were behind them, she had said: "Is my hat on straight?"

"Yes."

"Then we will go."

Putting his arm around her they went towards the door, the

verger approached, she lifted her head, put back her shoulders, whispered thanks for his help and they went out into the warmer but fresher air. Very slowly, stopping for breath and rest they made their way to Ethelred Road.

These experiences tested the tempered steel of the link between them already forged by many similarities of character and much misfortune. The war was a key period in the lives of most, it was with David, but in the oddest and most unheroic way.

Ethelred Road was a long line of detached and semi-detached houses, built by an enterprising developer in the latter half of Queen Victoria's reign. They were made for the professional classes, retired canons, doctors and aged masters of Winchester College.

There was a definable air of Anglicanism about them, proper, staid and prim. The houses, like many of the people within them, were stiff, plain and un-engaging, living to a pattern rather than in life itself.

Annie flowed into this life with an air of reservation. She discovered people whose lives had been so sheltered they never realised the hardships many had to contend with. It was partly a question of North and South. It was to Annie's view profoundly narrow and horrifyingly dull.

Into such a house Annie and David had been pitchforked when Kit and Valerie had joined John in India. Annie being considered too ill to fend for herself in the house, which was let furnished. They were paying guests.

They found themselves in an exceedingly genteel establishment, run by a Mr and Mrs Spurling. The conversation around the heavy oak table which matched the chairs around it and the towering cliff of the sideboard was often so pitifully polite and inane that it vanished altogether.

After her initial surprise, Annie had a desire to shock. Something in the paper made Mr Spurling make a pronouncement upon divorce. With great innocence Annie asked if he disapproved of divorce.

Receiving a denunciation, Annie prodded the conversation into a near discussion on infidelity. Annie looked cherubic, her face pink and white beneath her silver piled hair and her pearl choker. She trapped Mr Spurling into expecting a much higher morality from a woman than a man.

"But surely, Mr Spurling, what is sauce for the goose is sauce for the gander?"

"Oh, Mrs Matthews, you cannot possibly believe that?"

Her round eye seemed to become even rounder as she chimed, "Oh, but I do. It is only fair."

Annie's disapproval of Mr Spurling was to become more pronounced and more mischievous within weeks. In these unlikely surroundings David learnt more of the roguishness of his grandmother than he had ever known.

The other guest was a thin wasted lady, clad always in black. Miss Marsden had been a governess - her small charges, at one stage, had been those of a Grand Duke in St Petersburg.

There were two barriers to intimacy with this lady. The first was that she was almost stone deaf and the second was that she lacked any sense of humour or irony. Temperamentally, she was very unlike Annie, she was extraordinarily methodical and each evening produced a small cash book into which she entered all the slim expenses of her day.

Annie understood Miss Marsden. She knew that such financial scruples were the outcome of years of penury after her barrister father had left them penniless at the beginning of the century.

Annie found the cheese-paring of Mr Spurling harder to accept. With it went a rejection of all that the Spurling's had not experienced themselves... and that was limited. There was an incident, very small, that hurt Annie. Soap was coming into short supply. Annie volunteered that, "We shall have to make our own."

"I've never heard of anyone making soap," exclaimed Mr Spurling.

"In the hotel, in the early days, we always made our own. Of course, you need a lot of waste fat for the ingredients."

"Well, I never heard of such a thing before."

The innocent, but dull subject was dropped. Only later, alone, did Annie confide with surprise and a degree of hurt, "You know, they did not believe me."

It was the spring of 1940 and the Blitzkrieg spread like a great stain enveloping Europe. Mr Spurling thought that surrender was the only solution. Annie's patriotism was firmer and harder. She believed implicitly that Britain could not be invaded, the British Navy was insurmountable.

When the Channel Isles fell her belief was sorely dented. It seemed that every time they descended the stairs past the prints of grouse, capercaillie, pheasants and ptarmigan and into the dining room they were greeted with the news of yet another collapse, Norway, Denmark, Holland, Belgium.

Then came the agony of Dunkirk. Annie went to the cathedral to pray and on her way home noticed, she could not avoid them, the weary soldiery. They were the shambles of an army, weaponless, wearing a rag-bag of uniform…. some Belgians wearing only pyjamas.

They wandered idly, aimlessly in the streets and every church hall served cups of tea and biscuits with some humour and a definite sense of desperation. More than food, most of them needed sleep.

The green Close was covered in khaki-clad forms prone and unconscious. People opened their garden gates, notices proclaimed them open and shattered men sat on deckchairs and stretched on prim lawns.

Annie was greatly moved and suggested to Mr Spurling that he open his garden gates. To her agonised disbelief she heard, "But we do not know who they are. They might be undesirable characters." Annie picked up her small knife and let the blade tap dully on the damask table cloth.

She took a deep breath and said, very quietly, "Those men, possibly undesirable characters, are dying for you and me, Mr Spurling."

Silence fell around the table.

"I am sorry, Mrs Spurling. I cannot eat anything."

She rose. Mr Spurling leapt to the door and held it open for her, she glided through without any acknowledgement. Next she was seen walking down the drive wearing a white hat and a gauze scarf trailing over her shoulder.

She had gone to her room defeated, angry and impotent and utterly aghast at the lack of imagination. What could she do? She had to do something. On her table lay an unfinished letter to her daughter.

She knew, suddenly, what to do. She walked straight to WH Smiths and bought envelopes and writing paper and pencils. She crossed to the Post Office and bought stamps, then marched toward the cathedral.

After a momentary pause, she walked amongst the prone men.
"Would anyone like some writing paper?"

There was an instant response and soon she was surrounded as she gave out her stamps, envelopes and paper. All had gone before she reached the Close. She returned to Smiths' and bought more. The third time she returned the Manager came to her.

"Are you the lady giving out paper?"

He gave her a bundle of paper, telling her to return when she needed more. She had an escort, who carried her load, when she went under the flying buttresses into the Close and there she was greeted with a cry.

If the men had not been so exhausted she might have been mobbed. It was here, that she encountered the pyjama-clad Belgians. She faltered momentarily, ladies did not speak to unknown men was an unwritten rule of her upbringing.

The notion that they might be in nightclothes, had never been envisaged. She spoke French, then catching the sound of Flemish she spoke Dutch and was led to a group of young large-boned and fair young men in the shade of a green tree.

They found a chair and after nearly 50 years she found herself speaking Dutch as if there had been no interval at all. She listened to their tales.

At five o'clock she returned to Ethelred Road. Her heart was beating furiously, her legs ached mercilessly. But she was satisfied, she had done something and she had no need to be told that it was appreciated.

Next day she had to stay in bed, but Mrs Spurling took her place distributing the paper. When she returned she told Annie that her example had been followed, and that all the gardens in the Close were open now.

The men were absorbed by their units and regiments and the Close became the tranquil empty place it long and been. Annie ever remembered those days and often, years later, crossing by the Deanery she would wonder what had happened to the men, where they were, were they still alive, did they see their families? These were the question she asked and received no answer.

It was shortly after this time that her grandson announced that he was a pacifist. She argued with him, two stubborn natures met, but she won because she very subtly let him see that she was ashamed of him. It had been her tactic with schoolchildren, her family, her staff and it had unfailingly worked.

They left Ethelred Road and moved into rooms. They were dingy but clean and there they enjoyed more privacy, there was no longer timid conversation to be pursued at the dinner-table and there was more to eat.

The heart beat remained erratic, her minor heart attacks were frequent, but it rarely prevented her doing something she had set her heart upon. One hot summer's day, she walked two miles to have tea with Mrs Savage, a widow, an exact contemporary.

She was, perhaps, the only woman Annie was really fond of in Winchester. She reminded her of her Scarborough friends, though she did not play Bridge and she was a dedicated gardener, which Annie never had been, except in starts.

These two had books in common, they shared time and experiences in bringing up a family. They both loved fine furniture and china. To miss a talk with this old lady in her garden was not to be missed.

She toiled home, she did not collapse, but she had to haul herself up the stairs and lie on the bed before she attempted to undress and she fell into so deep a sleep her grandson thought she was dying. She woke next morning and only said what a very pleasant day she had had.

It was at this time, the blackest days of the war, when we were in retreat before Rommel in North Africa, that they were all invited out to lunch at an hotel with her god-daughter and her husband, who was stationed in the city.

Annie, as she so often did, got out one of her many hats, removed its trimmings, got out a very large pink chintz covered box full of feathers, ribbons, flowers, buckles and veils. She found a black ostrich feather. This she carefully and skilfully twined around the brim.

The day came for this lunch and David went up to her room. She stood before the long mirror with a hand mirror in her hand. She surveyed herself from top to toe and was well-pleased.

Her grandson looked and the despair of the times seemed to contrast so glaringly with the aristocratic frivolity of the feather that he began to laugh. Her perplexity was great, which only increased his mirth until he was holding his sides.

His mother hearing the laughter joined and she, too, hooted with merriment. It was she who enlightened her mother by saying, "You cannot possibly wear that hat, Mother. It makes you look like Henry VIII."

The juxtaposition of this gentle, elegant Edwardian lady and the despotic monarch caused even more laughter. She took off the hat and chose something more suitably sober for the times.

Barton Cottage had a succession of tenants, mostly officers and their families. The most recent letting had been to a barrister from London. The bombing had slackened and he and his sisters decided to return.

There was a likelihood that the house might be commandeered, so acting upon an impulse, Annie and David moved back. It was a house that held for them such bitter memories concentrated into so short a time, but so great was their relief to be independent of landladies that these recollections never entered their heads.

They moved back on a Good Friday. The wind was bitter, people muttered that the Romans had well-named Winchester, Venta Belgarum, everything seemed grey and dry and dusty.

The people seemed grey, even dusty, as well. But the two entered the house in a daze of joy, like cats released from long close confinement they wandered from drawing room to study, to kitchen to scullery, they could not settle.

They chose their rooms upstairs, began to unpack their clothes into the empty drawers of the scrupulously clean house, even the fires had been laid by the departing family. Annie, usually so quiet gave squeals of delight as she discovered yet another item of her past before her eyes.

The great cupboard was unlocked and the treasures were revealed, also a cloud of moths. Annie and David were so happy they began, but never finished, many tasks. They were both in a state of bliss, so well remembered that never an Easter comes, but David goes back to that Good Friday and Easter Day as the summit of all Easters.

David went into the garden. It was a loved place, spoiled by the half-achieved ambitions of his uncle. The lilies of the valley were still in their claustrophobic crowd in an angle between the shed and the ancient flint wall.

The Conference pear tree still hung over the orchard, it should have been trained neatly against the barn belonging to the house next door. Then he spied, on the ground, beneath some apple trees an object of a softer greyer green than the grass, it was a perfect nest from the previous year made of moss, hair and feathers tightly woven.

It was so neat, so round and perfectly made and proportioned. Both his grandmother and mother exclaimed at its beauty, Annie sat down in the kitchen and stared at it. Her face in an expression of rapture, so still that her pearl ear-rings never moved on their little gold stems, she was in a state of contemplation at this small wonder that expressed exactly her beliefs, her hopes, her desires, a home, a family and beauty.

She picked up the nest and placed it in the centre of the dining table and laid the table. When they all sat down, the three, as if impelled by one mechanism, put out a hand and grasped another, the triangle was complete, each hand held two hands of these two they loved most. They were home. They were alone, no landladies, no other "guests". They could be themselves and themselves alone.

As they ate, Nancy planned the afternoon. "You, Mother, must go to bed and rest. No folding of clothes, no wandering, just sleep. David and I will go to the cathedral for the last part of the Three Hours."

The choir of the cathedral was full of black-coated and hatted women and greyly clad men. Each one seemed preoccupied by, not Christ's crucifixion, but the hazards, terrors and anxieties of brothers, sisters, sons and daughters, husbands and lovers. It was a torn congregation. Something akin to despair pressed upon them all and David, in his joy, felt alien.

He looked at the painted boxes of the Saxon kings on the screen. He claimed kinship with them, they were secure in heaven and he was experiencing a heaven on earth at that moment.

He knew that the bones and ashes in the boxes were mixed, but he hoped there was some dust that belonged to Alfred there, for the garden where he had stood, an hour before, had been a part of the Hyde Abbey were Alfred first had been buried.

At the close of the service, pinched, sad people left and David's mother sought out a friend whose son was missing. Light gleamed, he was alive... he was a prisoner-of-war.

When they got back to Barton Cottage the house was empty.

Annie's room was pedantically correct. Every photograph frame was in its usual place, the silver brushes and boxes and tray in neat array on the dressing table, but Mother had gone.

"Where can she be?"

"I expect she had gone round to Hyde church."

"But she would be back by now. She would not have had time to unpack and leave everything so spick and span and go to church." Nancy got tea.

In the drawing room, the fire burning Nancy shuddered and said, "I had forgotten how cold this room always was with windows at each end. We'll have to make the study into the sitting room, it warms up quicker. But I do wonder where mother is, it will be dark soon."

There was a sound at the front door and after a pause Annie entered, hatted, coated, gloved with a basket in her hand. Her 80 years were rarely apparent, that moment she looked like a girl, her face shone. "Look what I've found."

She held out the basket and in it were the first small half open primroses, enough to made a good bunch. She sank to a chair and thankfully took a cup of tea.

"But, my dears, this Hampshire's nothing like Yorkshire for primroses. These took a lot of finding... just imagine what Forge Valley looks like now."

She found a bowl for them that fitted exactly into the nest and arranged them. As she did so she said: "I'll never believe they were that old rogue Disraeli's favourite flower. I am sure he wanted something more exotic, like an orchid. Something inscrutable and subtle, don't you? I expect he only said they were his favourites to please Queen Victoria."

She carried the nest and put it on the Regency ebony table, her favourite piece of furniture. It was an allusive gesture. It was a tribute to the household gods.

The months that followed were happy and David discovered, to his surprise, that his grandmother, whom he had regarded as either a rather grand lady of leisure, or an invalid, was able, in fact, to cook, to wash up and perform all the tasks of a housewife.

It was also, though, very apparent that she tired easily, her legs would swell, but her determination and zest for living was unimpaired.

Embroidery, so much a apart of her life, had been put aside, her fingers were too stiff and threading a needle had become difficult for both hand and eye. She had learnt to knit and a constant supply of socks reached her son and unknown soldiers.

David has a memory of her always with either a book or needlework in her hand. This should be corrected by the four knitting needles and her fountain pen. These were the days of her correspondence.

There were monthly letters to the Whites, Miss Henderson and Mrs Tindall in the Scarborough. There were weekly letters to her son, daughter-in-law and granddaughter in Scotland, as well as weekly bulletins to Kit and John and Valerie in India.

Then, two more correspondents claimed her attention. Dr Ward, who had carried a death certificate in his pocket to her house in Scarborough, suddenly became not an intermittent writer, but a constant one.

He wrote from Cairo, the desert of North Africa, Sicily and Italy. Then an old friendship of the beginning of the century was aroused, Frank White's brother in Canada wrote and after a long, long silence, letters flowed between them.

So the sight of the old lady with a tray turned upside down upon her knee before the fire became a very familiar sight and every post brought some letters.

Annie was asked if she could provide a room for an ATS officer from the Intelligence Corps stationed at King Alfred's College. So Pat came into their lives. She was a wonderful cook and was never happier than when inventing some amazing dish from scanty ingredients on the Aga.

Her friends started dropping in to the house, a lively stream of men and women. Annie opened and responded to their conversation with a knowledge and repartee that surprised David... it enlivened him and chastened him, for he had long inhabited a world of books. Annie and Pat decided to give a full-scale dinner party.

A dinner party, at that time was a rarity. It was David's first and he remembered sitting very quiet listening to the flow of banter around the table. There was a fashion for Dr Johnson at the College and suddenly he, Boswell, Mrs Thrale and Fanny Burney all seemed there as well.

The things David knew from books were, now, happening around him, and with an irreverence that he found very amusing. His grandmother seemed to preside and she joined in and when she was ignorant she cheerfully admitted it.

It was the side of her that had been seen most of all in Leiden and The Hague, but buried in the family, where love had usually overcome intellect, so that David had not thoroughly perceived it before.

Later, in the drawing room a man, whom David knew to have returned from France very recently, took a small upright chair and placed it by his grandmother. They were talking earnestly and independently while general lively chatter went on.

David saw that the man had a strained, even haunted, look and he even felt a pang of jealousy as his grandmother wrinkled her brow, bit her lip and listened very intently with her head slightly to one side.

Presently, he evidently dispelled the concern and David saw them laugh. All through the summer he came, sitting in the garden talking with the old lady. She learnt of his wife, his daughters, his lectureship.

One day his goodbye seemed more lingering. She never heard from him again until a fellow-officer came and told Annie that he had died in France. Annie was upset, tearful for a day and angry with war the next. Only much later, while she stirred soup in a pan did she revert to him and say, "He told me that he might never return."

On a dark winter morning bombs fell on Winchester. With a tragic irony the largest fell on a small queue of people awaiting a bus in Hyde Street, demolishing the grocer's and greengrocer's shops.

The wounded and the dying were taken across the road to the house of a lady where soldiers and sailors went briefly but constantly. We all knew what it was and all pretended that we did not. The raid occupied the attention of the city, the ARP, the WVS.

The homeless were swiftly housed and the grocer's business was set up in a vacant shop, long disused, by order, so that he could sell his regular rations. Annie watched all this and she awaited some recognition of Mrs Smith's prompt and open-hearted hospitality... none was given.

She spoke to Mr Hillier, the local air raid warden.

He blushed and admitted that nothing had been done.

"Don't you think, Mr Hillier, something should be done?"

"Yes, yes, of course," he stammered, "but she is not quite. Well, you know."

He endeavoured to spare this sheltered and conventional lady and he was astounded to hear, "But, Mr Hillier, we all know what she does and that does not entitle us to be ungrateful, does it?"

Annie had seen such confusion before. She knew that the excuse was that the Mayor was so busy. Inwardly, she castigated men generally as being moral hypocrites and cowards.

Next day, dressing more carefully than ever, she went down the street, opened the gate to the garden of the too-hospitable house and rang the bell.

Mrs Smith answered swiftly... it was part of her avocation. She was surprised to find Mrs Matthews there, but immediately took her into the front room which in Annie's words, managed to combine awful respectability with the utmost bad taste.

Annie sat smiling. She peeled off her gloves, laid them across her lap and after a few niceties, expressed the thanks of the entire neighbourhood for her gallant action.

Mrs Smith was touched and never forgot this gesture. It had an amusing outcome. Mrs Smith's daughter was an usherette, among other things, at the local cinema. Whenever they went with Annie, whatever ticket we may have bought, we were shown into the dress circle.

"Well, doesn't that prove that good manners always oil the wheels of life. Nothing like them you know."

Some of Annie's resilience was knocked away and she felt the cold more keenly. She lacked the ability to move swiftly to beat the cold. She blamed Winchester and compared the damp invidious chill creeping up from the water meadows with the blustering winds of Scarborough which, she averred, bumped one into vigorous warmth.

In December, she went down with pneumonia, she talked of dying and she was surprised at her grandson's defiance at the prospect of her death.

"But I will have to die one day, you had better get used to the idea. I am old and you are young and you will have to look after your mother."

Only jerkily did David realise that in most respects she had become his mother. They had shared so much together, read the same books, listened to the same plays and music on the radio, shared the same fears in the dread of night.

A bond had been formed in the face of a common danger. It had also provided time to talk of the past. Many people, then, had taken up Jane Austen and Trollope and Tolstoy - it was an escape to a more ordered and gentler world.

Annie and David had joined with others, but the two had escaped also into her memories. While the menacing, rhythmic hum of German bombers had reverberated overhead, she had talked of other sounds, the jingle of harness in the woods of The Hague and the seemingly futile intricacies of making calls in Edwardian times.

The hum they recognised so well was replaced by the doodle-bug and this terrifying weapon hastened the push in Europe. In the dreariness of February 1945, General Montgomery, talking to the whole of Winchester college, foretold with an accuracy which seemed uncanny to the ignorant, the date of the end of the war in Europe.

The war was ending and Annie learnt of the imminent return of her daughter, granddaughter and son-in-law with intense eagerness. She felt that in war everyone had learnt so much that the world must be a better place. Her optimism about her son-in-law was misplaced.

The euphoria of welcome and joy of return lasted four days, then jealousy seized her son-in-law with amazing, even demonic, force. Annie retired to her room and fell, once again a victim to pneumonia.

Once again she skirted death, but not with the serene inevitability of the previous winter but with a fierce fire, for hatred had leapt up in her very peaceful soul. Her indignation was aroused on her daughter's behalf who was torn in an agony of loyalties.

John bullied his wife and his daughter and one day she watched the three at work in the garden below. John moved swiftly, impetuously with shears in his hands, shouting commands.

Annie regarded it all with a cold venom that her grandson had never seen in her before, her blue eyes turned grey and she spat out, "That man is disgustingly virile."

She feared for her daughter and Valerie who heaved and hauled at healthy apple trees which he had unnecessarily felled. No doubt he felt he had to kill something.

David regretted again and again that they had not heeded his wish to rent a house from the College which, momentarily, had been available, but fear, poverty and lack of foresight had made him be over-ruled.

He loathed seeing his grandmother dependent upon a human weathercock. Recent history was repeating itself, but Annie, now, had a determination to stay alive. She refused to be bundled to death by this man, who, when she was gasping for breath had demanded the four shillings and three pence for the medicine he had collected.

Spring came, peace came, and in July, term ended. Annie made her last act of bravery and defiance. Her patience with her family, who permitted this festering situation to linger on, snapped.

She dressed, one morning, as carefully as ever, but instead of placing her nightdress under her pillow, when she made the bed, she folded it together with her brush and comb and placed them in her handbag. She went down the stairs and out of the house.

Her heart beat fast at her temerity. Mr Long, the grocer, saw her walking down the street with determination, he thought she looked well. She smiled and bowed to him. She walked along Hyde Street, Jewry Street, Southgate Street to Saint Cross Road to the College house where her daughter, Nancy, was matron.

She found her room empty, but sat composedly on her own Chippendale chair awaiting her daughter's return. It was then to Nancy's consternation that she said with spirit and intention, "I will never return to Barton Cottage. I have left for ever. I would prefer the workhouse."

The family was thrown into alarm. Even Nancy was not totally sympathetic, the family was alarmed and only her grandson applauded her action. A room was found for her in the temporary lodgings of her daughter-in-law and they were all galvanised into the action that should have been taken months before of finding a home where they could live peaceable and above all independently.

Witham Close, a large mainly 18th century house on foundations, possibly far older, had a flat on its second storey. It had four bedrooms, a sitting room, kitchen and dining room. There one portion of the family reassembled. Annie, now in her 82nd year, climbed the stairs infrequently.

The bedroom and sitting room became her home, there were her Sheraton chairs, her great-grandmother's rocking chair, her much beloved Empire table of ebony and her photographs.

From a bank's vault came pieces of silver not seen for many years which she disposed with care about the rooms. She was happy. She knew the end was almost within sight and had picked up a phrase from an aged canon, a railway enthusiast, "I am slowing down as I approach the terminus."

One muggy evening, the Oxford Union Debating Society came down from Oxford, bearing with them Peggy Ashcroft to perform *Much Ado About Nothing* in the Meads before the Old Science building.

There was a natural stage before the arcading with its vaulting. It looked correct, but the acoustics were appalling, the voices floated into the recesses rather than forwards, the audience became restive, there was an even deadlier distraction for them, a plague of biting mosquitoes.

The players worked gallantly, the audience behaved courageously and a witty play ended wittily for the actors applauded the audience. Going through the war cloisters Annie was asked by a friend for her opinion.

She thought for a moment and then said: "I do congratulate Shakespeare on a singularly apt title."

The financial affairs in Scarborough were, at last, being resolved and after years of penury, Annie found herself with some spending money. Spend it she did, two smart dresses, one for Nancy, one for herself and an expensive fur hat Nancy had longed for. Then there were the jewels, the sapphires and the diamonds, bringing with them memories of her mother-in-law and her lost love in Den Haag. She looked at them, they flashed in the light… she snapped the cases to and handed the ring to Nancy.

"Your hands are the most beautiful in the family. They are exactly like my mother's. The ring is for you."

To Kit she gave the brooch very gladly. She loved both her daughters dearly. To her grandson she said: "That brooch more than repays any hospitality I have had from your uncle, I am glad to say."

The money permitted her to see an eye-specialist.

She looked forward to the meeting and was quite certain that drops and new spectacles would renew her sight and enable her to read. She was resigned to never sewing again.

She was taken by Nancy in the invalid chair. They set out in sunshine, they returned in gloom actual, metaphorical. The consultation was never mentioned.

Only when she had gone to her room did Nancy say, "He was extraordinarily tactful, he wrapped up a hopeless prognostication so well I thought Mother might miss his meaning. It really would be kinder if she was less acute."

The knowledge that nothing more could be done damaged her spirit and she began to surrender life.

Quite suddenly, Frank White, now a widower, wrote that he was coming to London and he wished to see his sister-in-law. So after five years, the old contemporaries met. Annie wore a long woollen dress that concealed her swollen ankles. She looked extremely pretty... her pearls gleamed like her face softly. It was touching to see them together.

Frank was the only person left who had known her before she was married. He took away a memory of someone very bright, still beautiful, but "she had become so small."

Her world was retracting quickly. She got her news more from the radio than the newspaper. Socialists still made her "blood boil" and Mr Attlee was "a traitor to his class."

It seemed, though, that she was being shriven of trivialities, for after a lifetime of delight in dress, she lost all interest. Her grandson tried to read her the Daily Telegraph's gushing article on Princess Elizabeth's wedding dress.

As he read the glowing description and the tortuous links between this dress and her grandmother's, David was astounded to hear, "What rot. There is no resemblance at all except that they are both white."

Then, even more surprising, "What is a dress, but a dress... a covering for a human body."

On Christmas Day, she dressed with Nancy's help. Slowly, very slowly, she dressed her hair, each white curl in its place upswept on her head. By the time she sat at the table she was exhausted.

She watched the carving of the turkey, she looked around the table and for the first time, it seemed, she realised that she was not them, nor they her, she had relinquished kinship with all except her daughter Nancy.

She was one soul and about to depart. She turned the sprig of holly from the pudding in her hand.

Late in January, she told some of her family of a strange experience she had had that morning. She had woken and was immediately aware of someone in the room, "But I was not afraid. I switched on the light and there was my mother.

"She was looking at me and smiling and her hand rested on the bed-rail, then, she disappeared. I was wide awake. Wasn't it strange, my young mother looking at me, her old daughter?"

At the time she made her last conscious witticism. She had an array of pills to take, all made up for her by Mr Luck, the chemist in Southgate Street. A visitor asked her how she remembered to take the right medicine.

Her reply was: "We trust to Luck."

The last six weeks of her life were spent in confusion. The censor of her mind ceased to function, she spoke shrewd, sometimes hard thoughts, there were expressions of opinion she would never have uttered before because they were not kind, or Christian.

She died not quite soon enough. She stood on the doorstep of Death, knocking, it would seem, but then rapidly walking away when the summons was answered. It wore her most faithful daughter out.

With great difficulty a night nurse was found, a pleasant round body, who indiscreetly told her that she must go to sleep.

"Do you know what you have said? Servants may never speak so."

It took all Nancy's tact and charm to restore the ruffled feathers of a democratic soul. It showed Annie's rigid sense of rank which she masked so skilfully with charm. Annie had outlived her ethos.

Her funeral was at Hyde Church. There were far more people at the service than the family had expected. Nimrod from Elgar's Enigma Variations was played and a number thought it fitted her exactly. In the warm spring air, as the liturgy unfolded, a butterfly awoke and danced around the flowers on the coffin... that seemed very apt as well.

Something very definite went from the family with Annie's death, it was not just the person... it was a sense of order and a certain attitude to life. Living had been formulated into a type of ritual.

Prim is the word that springs to mind of one of her granddaughters, but it is not accurate, for that implies a stiff censoriousness often springing from a fear of life.

She obeyed the conventions, but was always ready to dispense with them when they clashed with her sense of love and justice.

Fanny Burney uses the word prim as a verb, to "prim up one's face", to assume an expression which its owner deems proper. That was true of Annie, it applied to the whole of her, it went into deportment, but uprightness was invariably worn with elegance.

David misses, now, almost completely, for it lingered in the remnants of her slightly junior contemporaries, the almost hieratic motions when receiving, or being received by strangers.

There was a tilt to the head, a calm assurance to allay suspicions, all conducted as the visitor was bidden to sit, or when visiting, as the gloves were peeled off, finger laid to finger and laid neatly across the lap. It had some of the unhurried order of the Zen tea ceremony of Japan. Rituals bring assurance.

Her greatest virtue was kindness, this made her gentle. Her key words were "Judge not that ye be not judged". This is a good basis for life, but it is not quite enough.

She managed to imprint herself on people's memories in an amazing way. An old man, 40 years after her death, spoke suddenly and without any solicitation of her vividly. David felt that he was being looked through to another generation.

A lady who, in her 20s, had met Annie Matthews, described the dress and hat she wore in detail. David was able to verify it from photographs, so that he could supply the colour, the combinations, they were not commonplace.

Oddest of all, her eldest daughter at a Conference sat by an elderly lady. Scarborough was mentioned, then the hotel. The old lady looked at Kit,

"Then you must be Mrs Matthews' daughter. She was the most beautiful woman I ever saw in my life. I remember coming in once, your mother moved to a fire that was burning low.

"She knelt to poke it and was about to blow the coals when my husband took her hand and raised her saying, "That's no thing for you to do" and he got down on his knees.

"I remember, I felt a pang of jealousy, I wished he would do that for me. He always referred to her as 'The Princess'. Fancy you being her daughter... that must be all of 50 years ago."

Some members of the family repined that she died so poor. David has seen many die, the full spectrum of society. It is a journey made, in spite of families and friends, ultimately alone. The only richness worth having at the end is love and that she had abundantly.

Love, generosity, quick sympathy and bravery, those were her qualities and I leave the last comment upon her to Gladys Parke, the housekeeper whom she accepted so slowly.

"I always admired her, even before the barriers were down. I admired her even more when the crash came. I truly did not know anyone could be so brave and what was even greater was that she never blamed anyone."

Her handwriting told the observer everything about her. It was a formal copperplate, but made her very own. Formal yes... but prim, no. And like her, it was wholly, wholly harmonious.

Postscript

by Dr. Wilhelmina Lockwood

David went to the Welsh university of St. David's College, Lampeter in September 1948, graduating with a BA in 1952. He was ordained as an Anglican priest in 1953. In 1981 he graduated with an MA from Birmingham University.

We met in 1950 in Heidelburg and married in 1954. I had qualified from Leiden University as a medical doctor. We enjoyed parish life, the arrival of three daughters, Diana, Helena and Laura and a foster son Peter, and the medical practice, celebrating our golden wedding anniversary in 2004.

David's cousin Dawn Barber (née Matthews) married an engineer, has two daughters and three grandchildren, and celebrated her golden wedding anniversary in 2008. His other cousin Valerie Hillier has four married children and nine grandchildren, all of whom live around Sir Harold Hillier's Arboretum in Romsey.